PARACHUTE KIDS

C. TANG

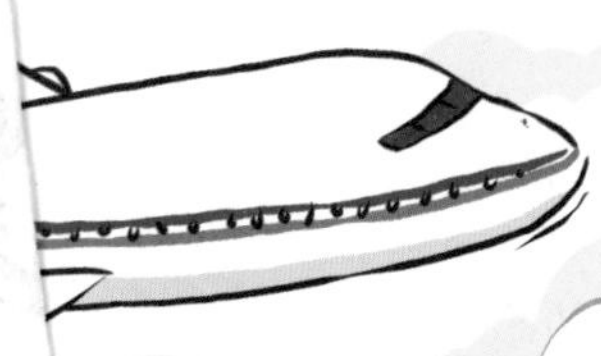

graphix
An imprint of
SCHOLASTIC

All rights reserved. Published by Graphix, an imprint of Scholastic Inc., *Publishers since 1920.*
SCHOLASTIC, GRAPHIX, and associated logos are trademarks and/or registered trademarks
of Scholastic Inc.

The publisher does not have any control over and does not assume any responsibility for author
or third-party websites or their content.

Library of Congress Cataloging-in-Publication Data: 2022004016
ISBN 978-1-338-83269-3 (hardcover) | ISBN 978-1-338-83268-6 (paperback)
10 9 8 7 6 5 4 3 2 1   23 24 25 26 27

Printed in China   62 | First edition, April 2023

Edited by Tracy Mack | Lettering by Betty C. Tang | Book design by Carina Taylor
Creative Director: Phil Falco | Publisher: David Saylor

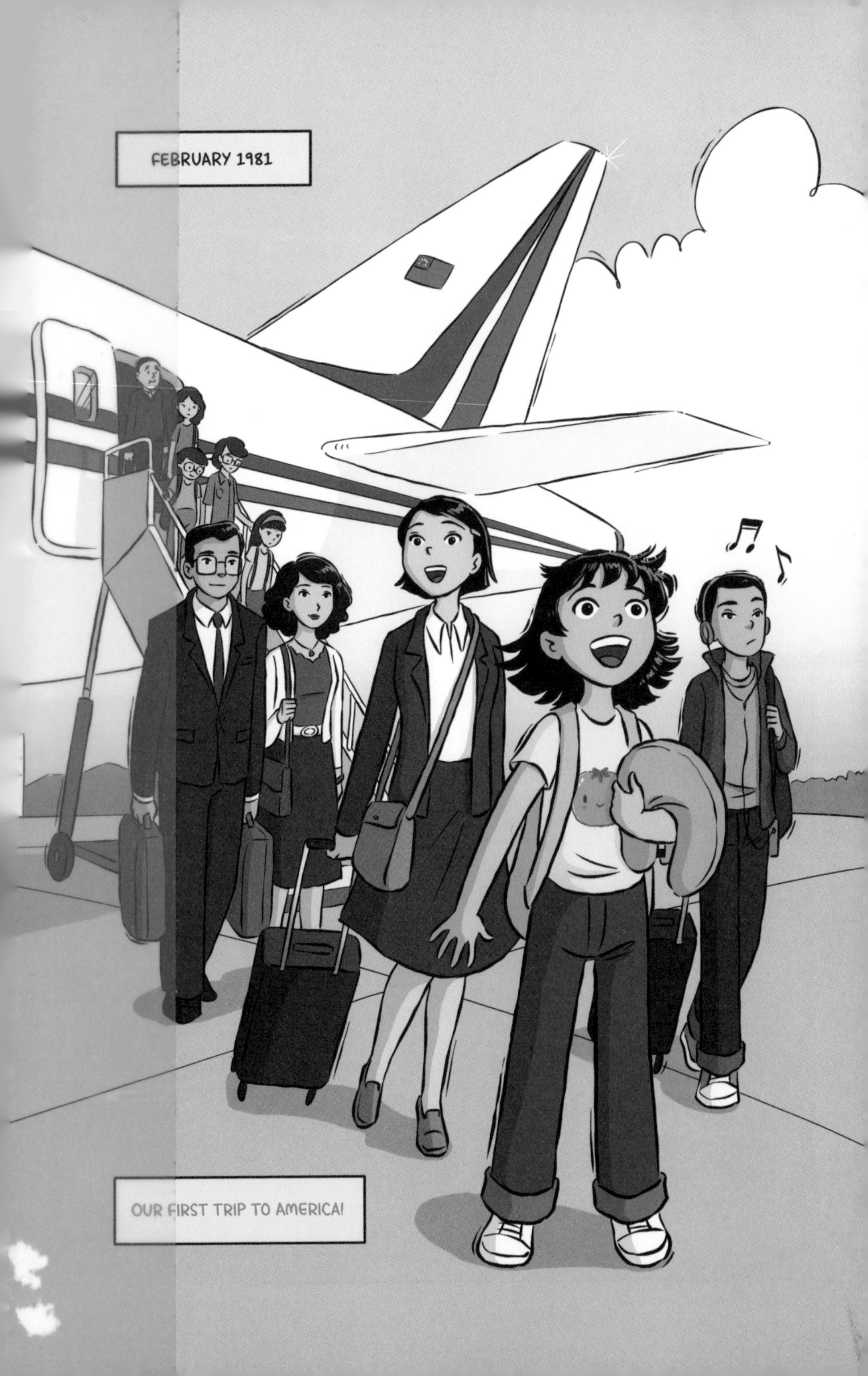
FEBRUARY 1981
OUR FIRST TRIP TO AMERICA!

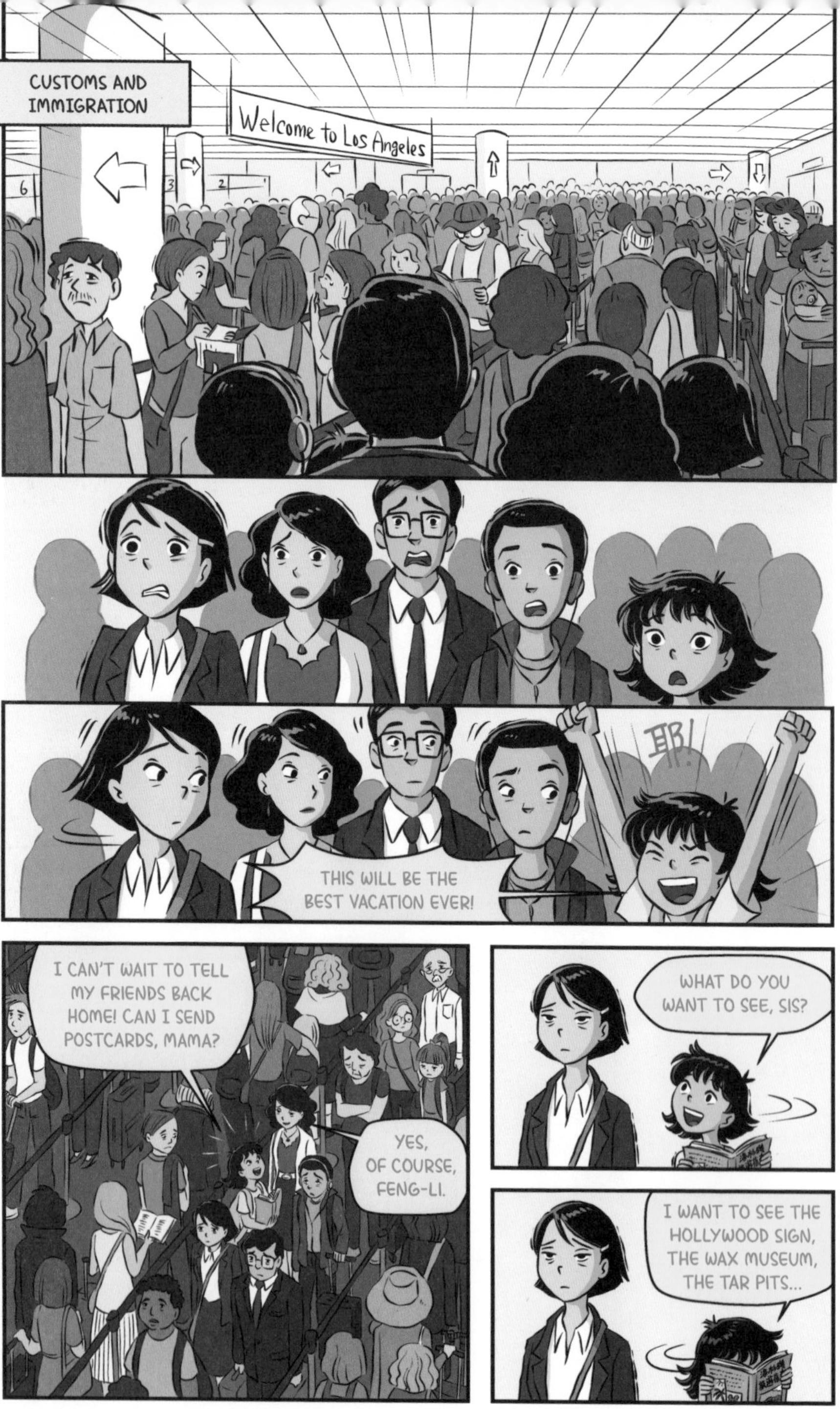
CUSTOMS AND IMMIGRATION
Welcome to Los Angeles
耶!
THIS WILL BE THE BEST VACATION EVER!
I CAN'T WAIT TO TELL MY FRIENDS BACK HOME! CAN I SEND POSTCARDS, MAMA?
YES, OF COURSE, FENG-LI.
WHAT DO YOU WANT TO SEE, SIS?
I WANT TO SEE THE HOLLYWOOD SIGN, THE WAX MUSEUM, THE TAR PITS...

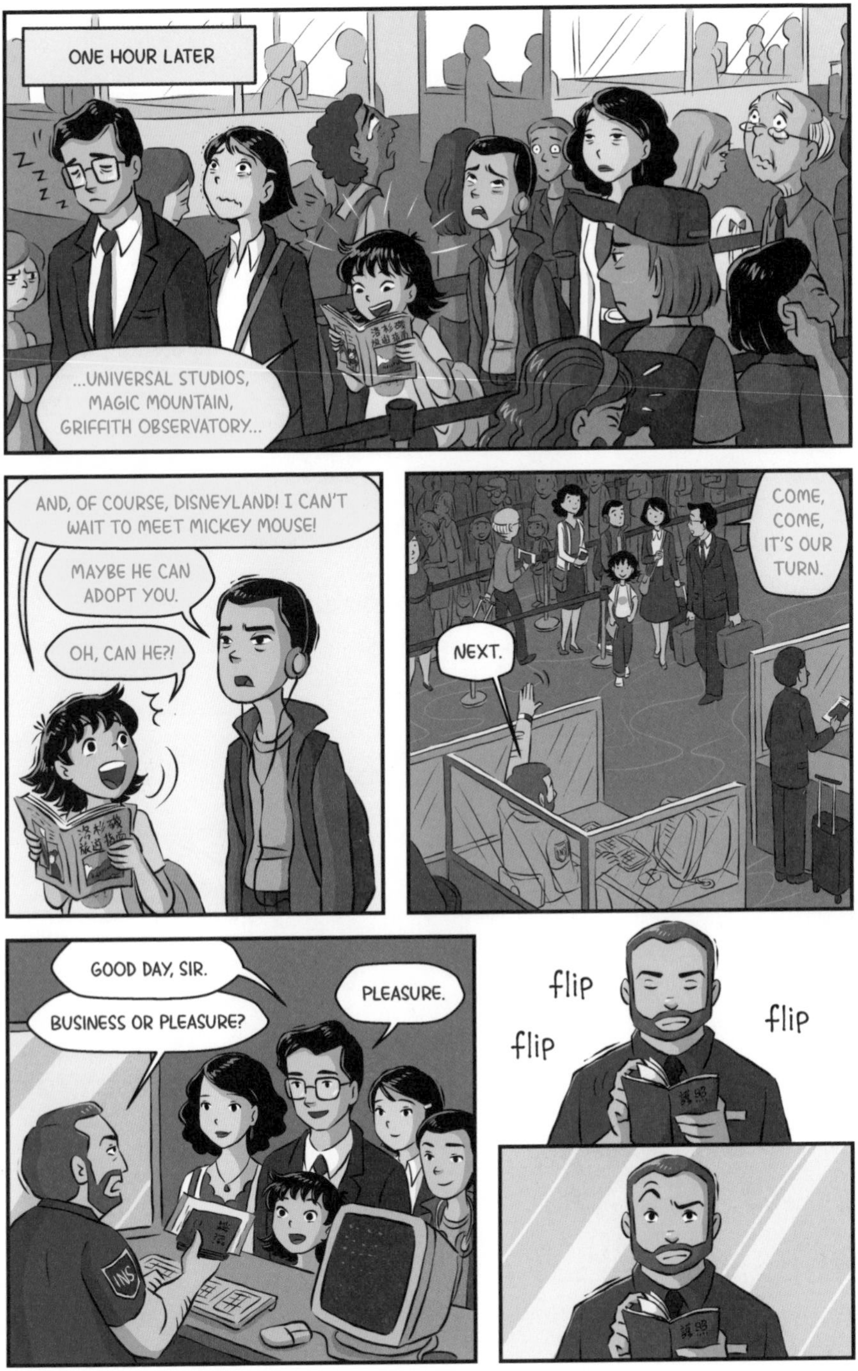
ONE HOUR LATER
...UNIVERSAL STUDIOS, MAGIC MOUNTAIN, GRIFFITH OBSERVATORY...
AND, OF COURSE, DISNEYLAND! I CAN'T WAIT TO MEET MICKEY MOUSE!
MAYBE HE CAN ADOPT YOU.
OH, CAN HE?!
COME, COME, IT'S OUR TURN.
NEXT.
GOOD DAY, SIR.
BUSINESS OR PLEASURE?
PLEASURE.
flip
flip
flip

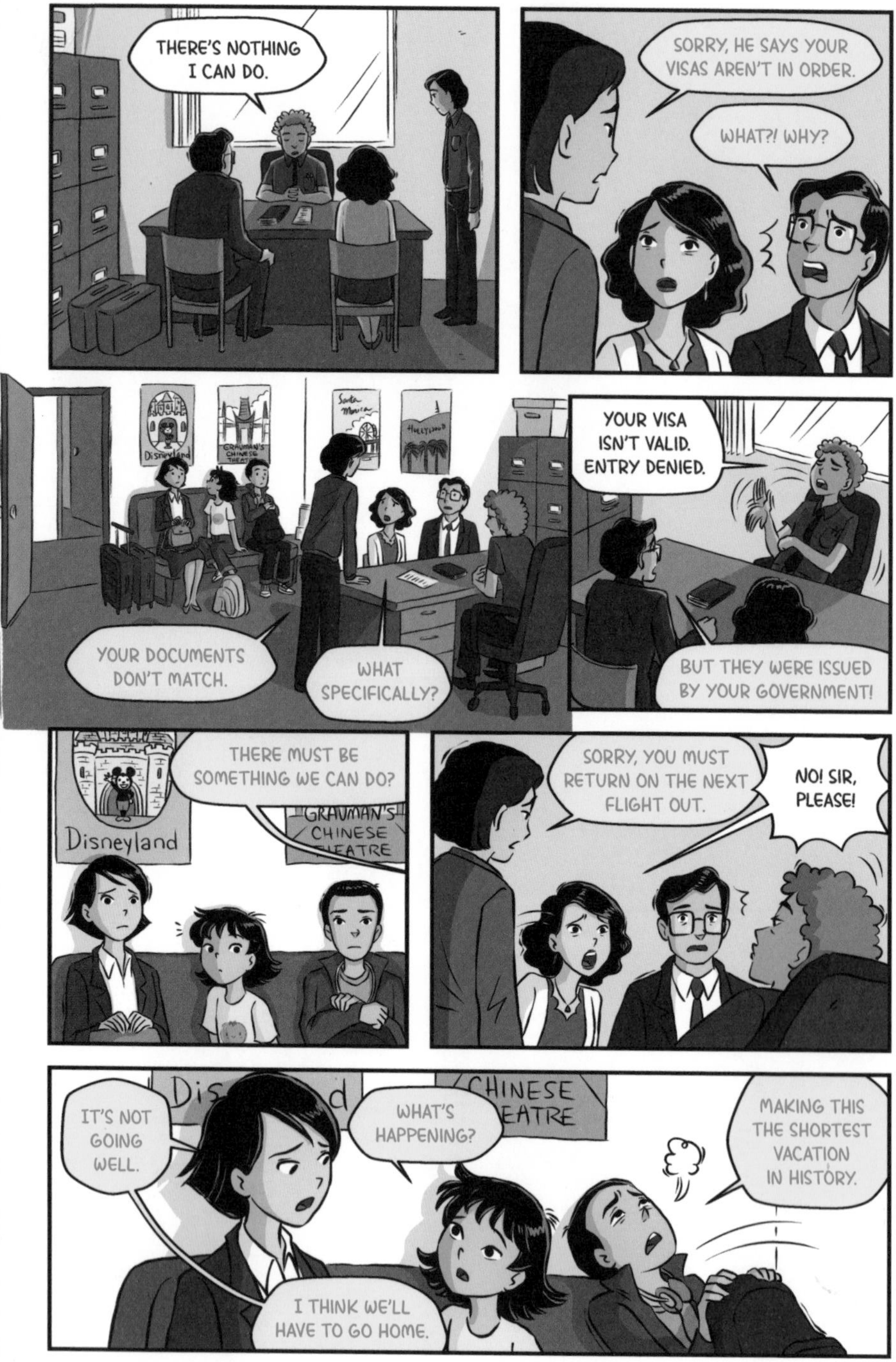
THERE'S NOTHING I CAN DO.
SORRY, HE SAYS YOUR VISAS AREN'T IN ORDER.
WHAT?! WHY?
Disneyland
GRAUMAN'S CHINESE THEATRE
Santa Monica
HOLLYWOOD
YOUR DOCUMENTS DON'T MATCH.
WHAT SPECIFICALLY?
YOUR VISA ISN'T VALID. ENTRY DENIED.
BUT THEY WERE ISSUED BY YOUR GOVERNMENT!
Disneyland
THERE MUST BE SOMETHING WE CAN DO?
GRAUMAN'S CHINESE THEATRE
SORRY, YOU MUST RETURN ON THE NEXT FLIGHT OUT.
NO! SIR, PLEASE!
IT'S NOT GOING WELL.
WHAT'S HAPPENING?
MAKING THIS THE SHORTEST VACATION IN HISTORY.
I THINK WE'LL HAVE TO GO HOME.

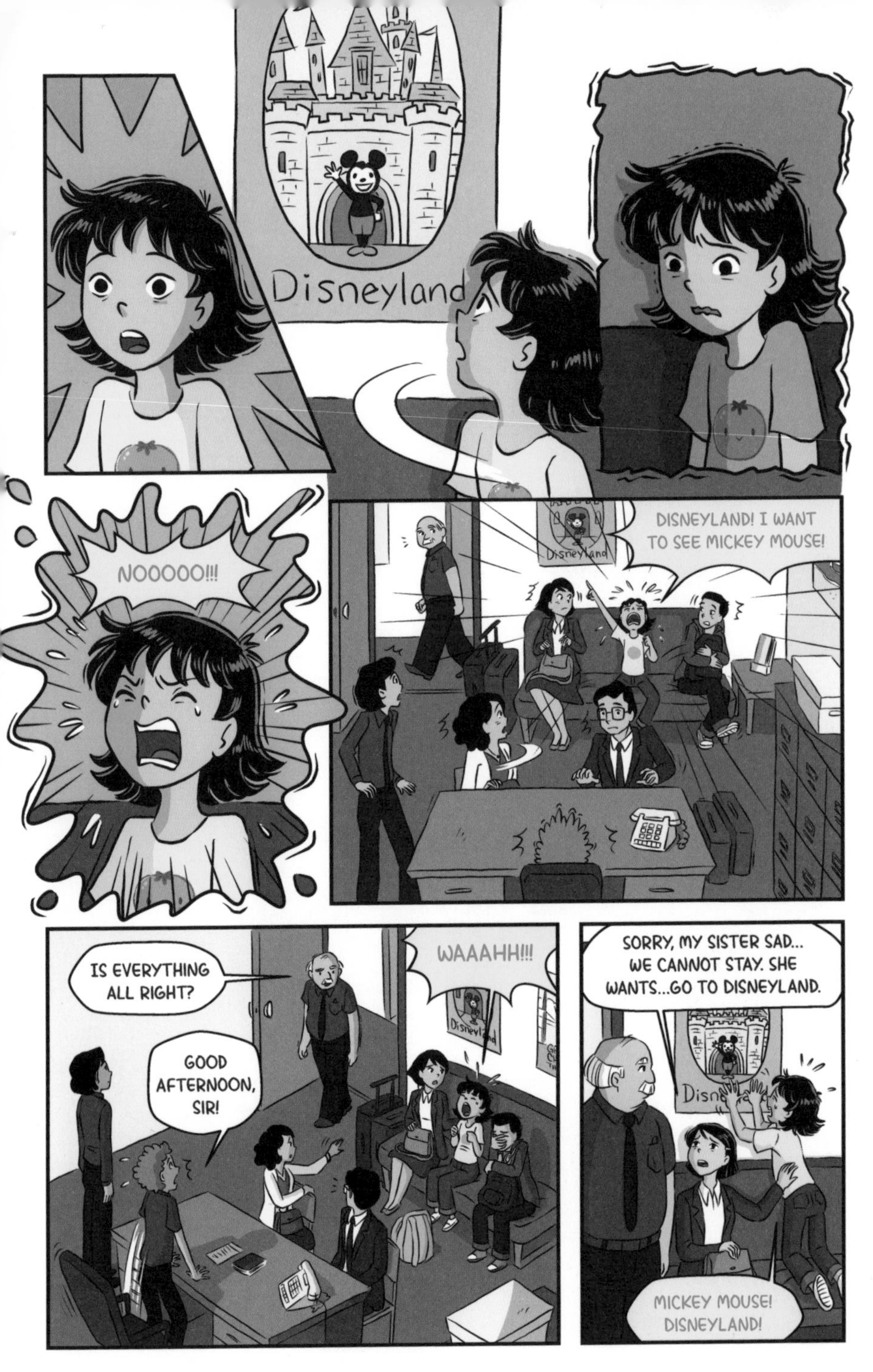
Disneyland
NOOOOO!!!
Disneyland
DISNEYLAND! I WANT TO SEE MICKEY MOUSE!
IS EVERYTHING ALL RIGHT?
GOOD AFTERNOON, SIR!
WAAAHH!!!
Disneyland
SORRY, MY SISTER SAD... WE CANNOT STAY. SHE WANTS...GO TO DISNEYLAND.
MICKEY MOUSE! DISNEYLAND!

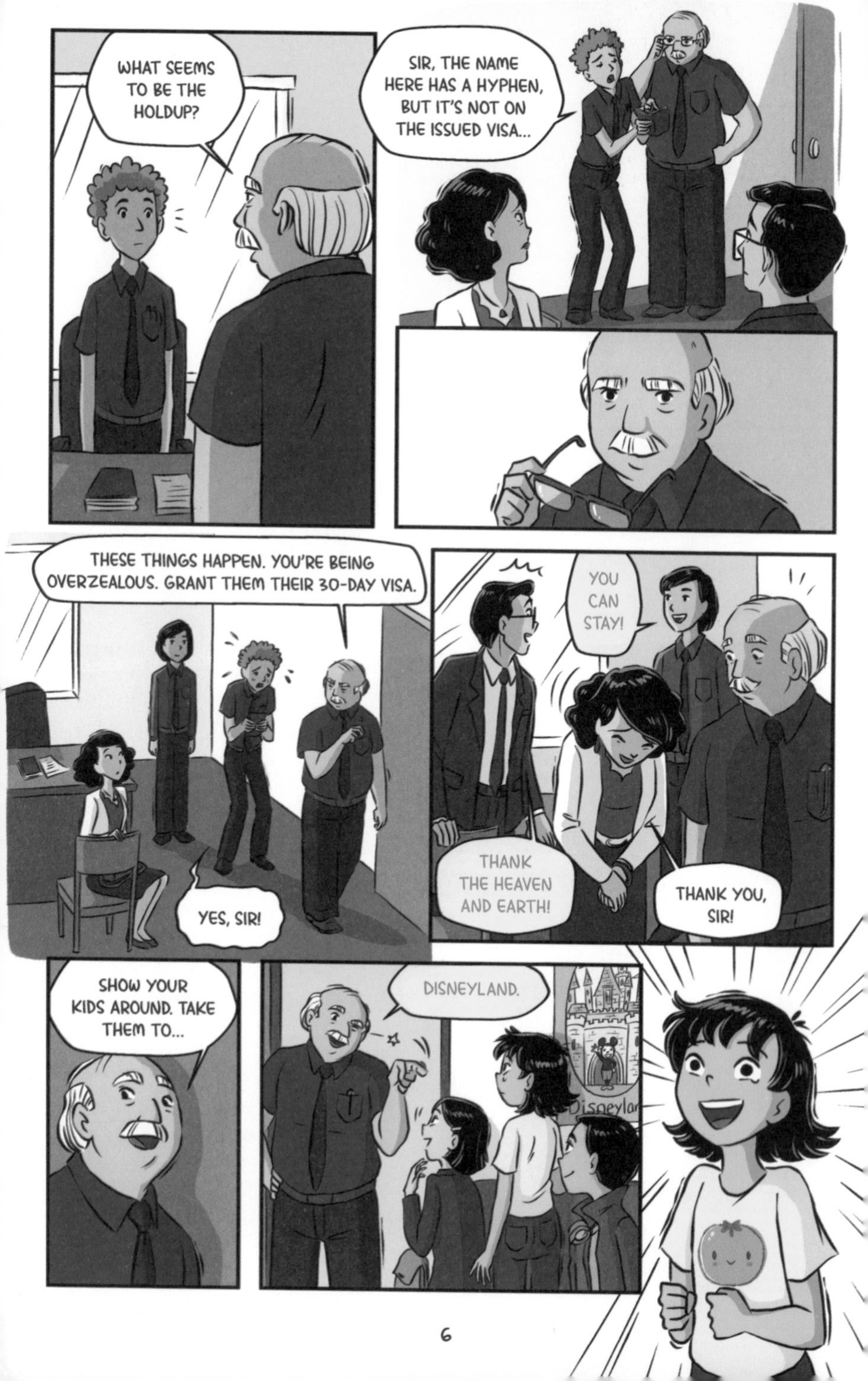
WHAT SEEMS TO BE THE HOLDUP?
SIR, THE NAME HERE HAS A HYPHEN, BUT IT'S NOT ON THE ISSUED VISA...
THESE THINGS HAPPEN. YOU'RE BEING OVERZEALOUS. GRANT THEM THEIR 30-DAY VISA.
YES, SIR!
YOU CAN STAY!
THANK THE HEAVEN AND EARTH!
THANK YOU, SIR!
SHOW YOUR KIDS AROUND. TAKE THEM TO...
DISNEYLAND.
Disneylan

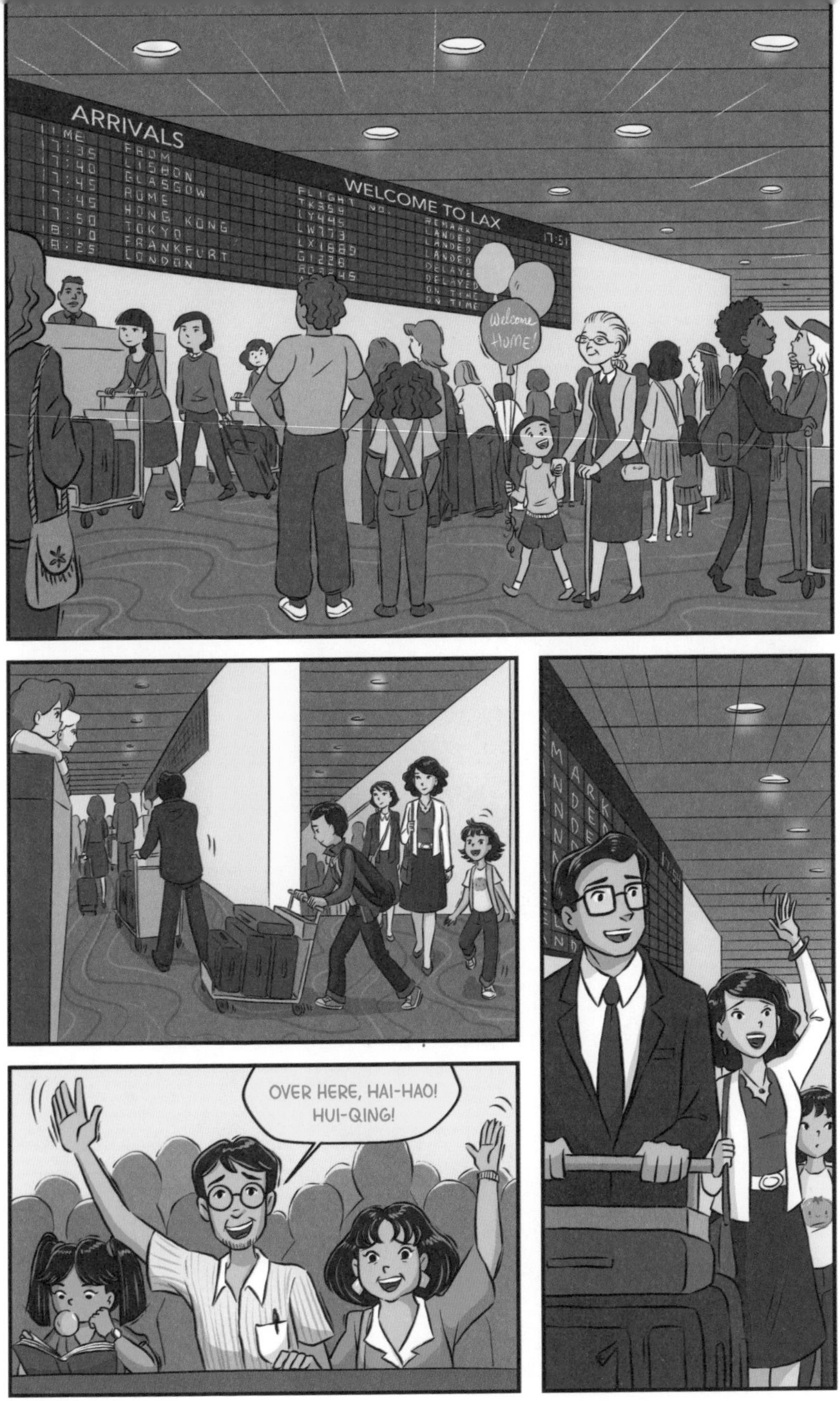
ARRIVALS
WELCOME TO LAX
LISBON
GLASGOW
ROME
HONG KONG
TOKYO
FRANKFURT
LONDON
Welcome Home!
OVER HERE, HAI-HAO! HUI-QING!

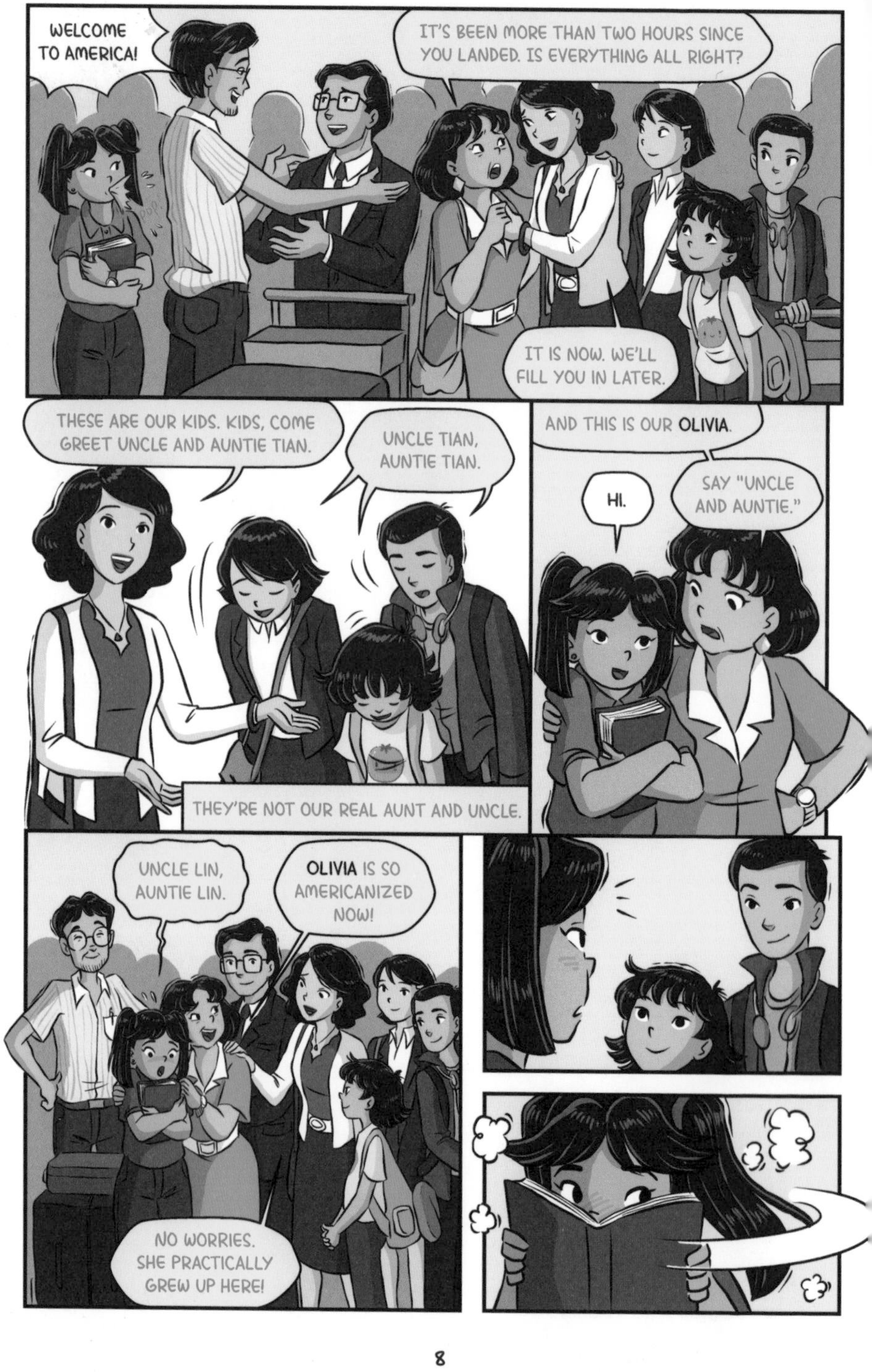
WELCOME TO AMERICA!
IT'S BEEN MORE THAN TWO HOURS SINCE YOU LANDED. IS EVERYTHING ALL RIGHT?
IT IS NOW. WE'LL FILL YOU IN LATER.
THESE ARE OUR KIDS. KIDS, COME GREET UNCLE AND AUNTIE TIAN.
UNCLE TIAN, AUNTIE TIAN.
THEY'RE NOT OUR REAL AUNT AND UNCLE.
AND THIS IS OUR **OLIVIA**.
HI.
SAY "UNCLE AND AUNTIE."
UNCLE LIN, AUNTIE LIN.
OLIVIA IS SO AMERICANIZED NOW!
NO WORRIES. SHE PRACTICALLY GREW UP HERE!

ME AT DISNEYLAND.

SIS AT THE HOLLYWOOD SIGN.

BRO ON THE
HOP ON HOP OFF BUS.

MAMA AT
STUDIOS

ALL OF US AT GRAUMAN'S
CHINESE THEATRE.

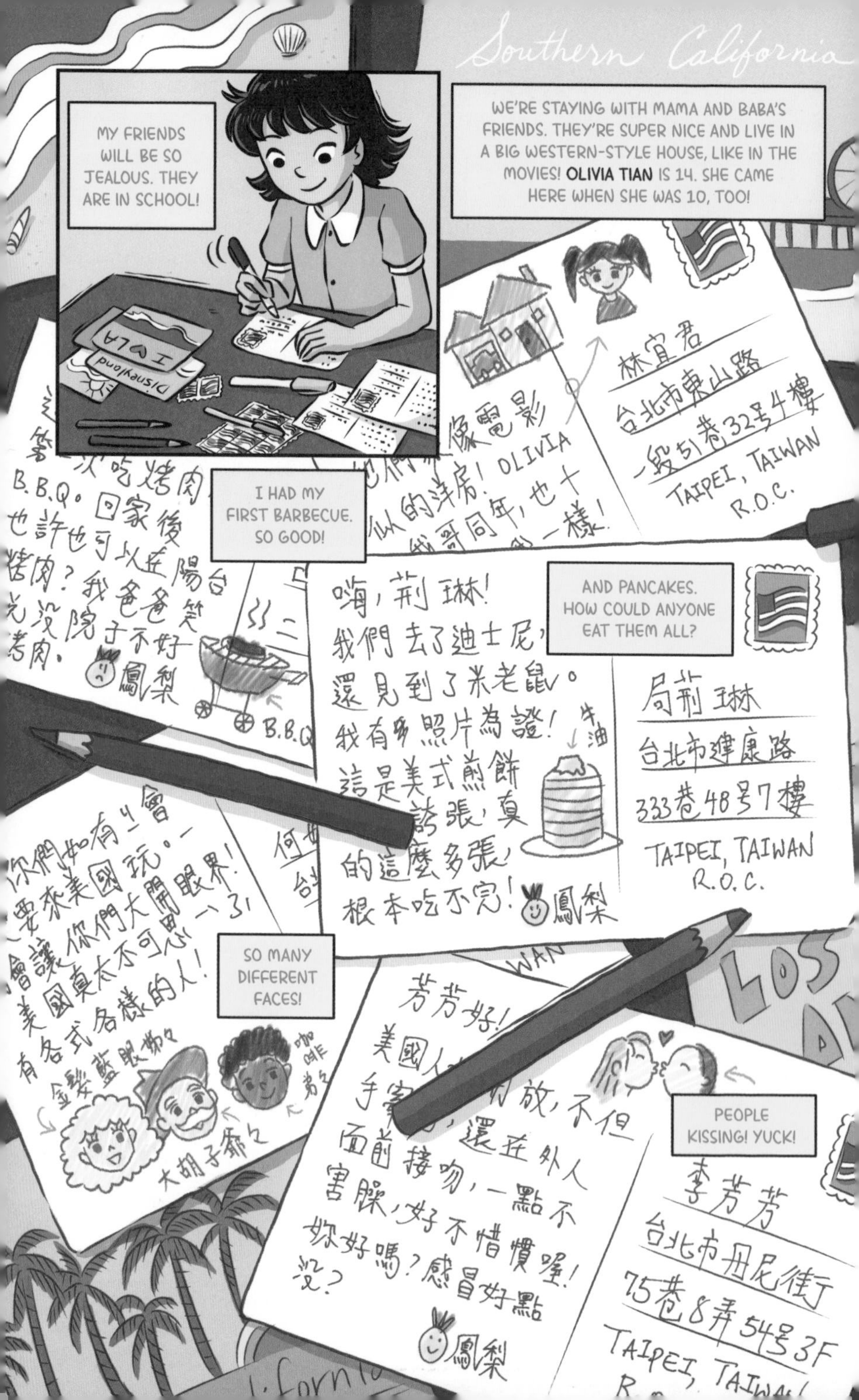
Southern California
MY FRIENDS WILL BE SO JEALOUS. THEY ARE IN SCHOOL!
WE'RE STAYING WITH MAMA AND BABA'S FRIENDS. THEY'RE SUPER NICE AND LIVE IN A BIG WESTERN-STYLE HOUSE, LIKE IN THE MOVIES! OLIVIA TIAN IS 14. SHE CAME HERE WHEN SHE WAS 10, TOO!
I ♥ LA
Disneyland
林宜君
台北市東山路
一段51巷32号4樓
TAIPEI, TAIWAN
R.O.C.
I HAD MY FIRST BARBECUE. SO GOOD!
B.B.Q
鳳梨
AND PANCAKES. HOW COULD ANYONE EAT THEM ALL?
嗨，荊琳！
我們去了迪士尼，
還見到了米老鼠。
我有照片為證！
這是美式煎餅
的這麼多張！
根本吃不完！鳳梨
牛油
周荊琳
台北市建康路
333巷48号7樓
TAIPEI, TAIWAN
R.O.C.
SO MANY DIFFERENT FACES!
有各式各樣的人！
金髮藍眼叔叔
咖啡弟弟
大胡子爺爺
芳芳好！
還在外人
面前接吻，一點不
害臊，好不習慣喔！
妳好嗎？感冒好點
沒？
鳳梨
PEOPLE KISSING! YUCK!
李芳芳
台北市丹尼街
75巷8弄54号3F
TAIPEI, TAIWAN

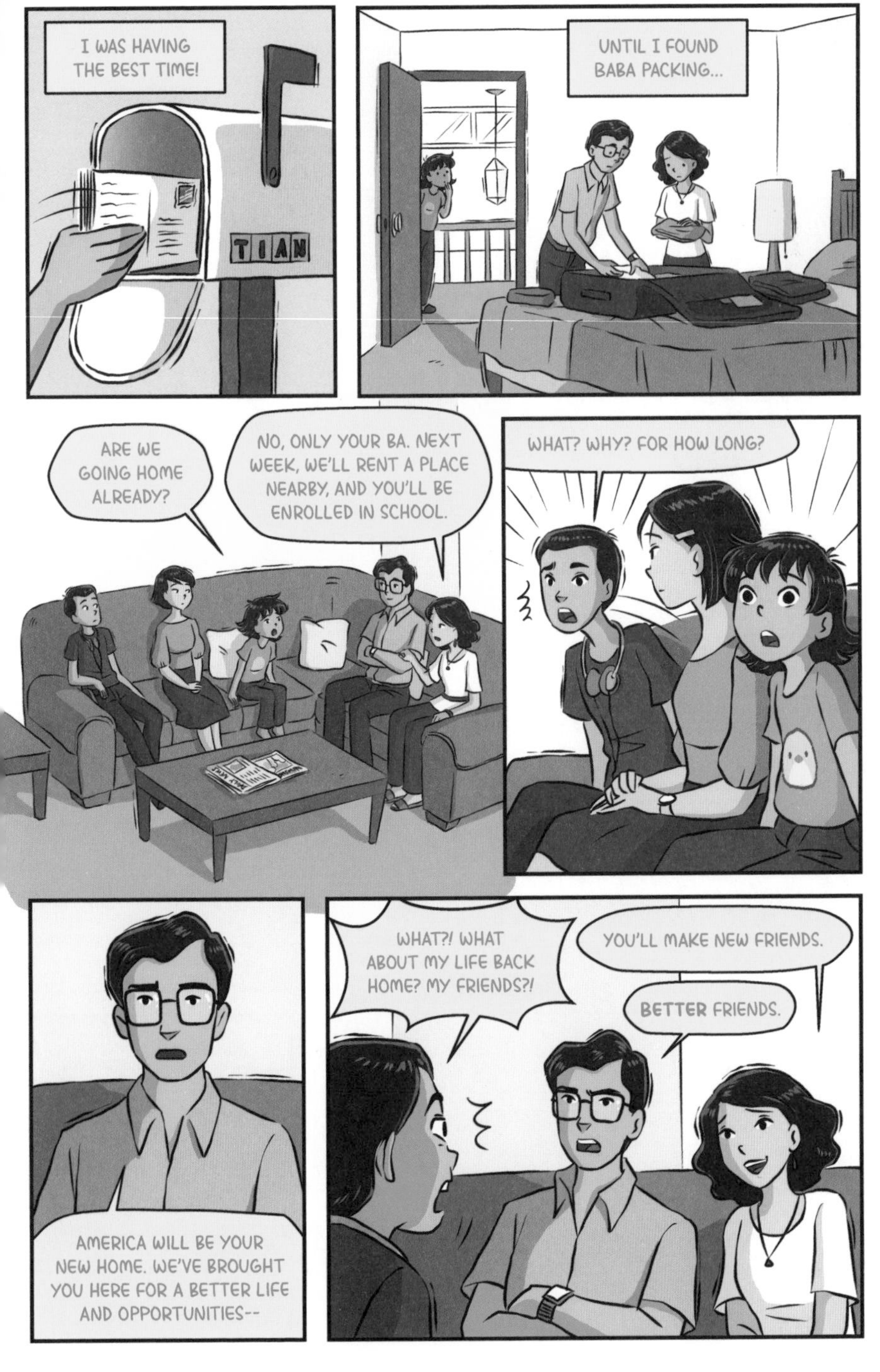
I WAS HAVING THE BEST TIME!
TIAN
UNTIL I FOUND BABA PACKING...
ARE WE GOING HOME ALREADY?
NO, ONLY YOUR BA. NEXT WEEK, WE'LL RENT A PLACE NEARBY, AND YOU'LL BE ENROLLED IN SCHOOL.
WHAT? WHY? FOR HOW LONG?
AMERICA WILL BE YOUR NEW HOME. WE'VE BROUGHT YOU HERE FOR A BETTER LIFE AND OPPORTUNITIES--
WHAT?! WHAT ABOUT MY LIFE BACK HOME? MY FRIENDS?!
YOU'LL MAKE NEW FRIENDS.
BETTER FRIENDS.

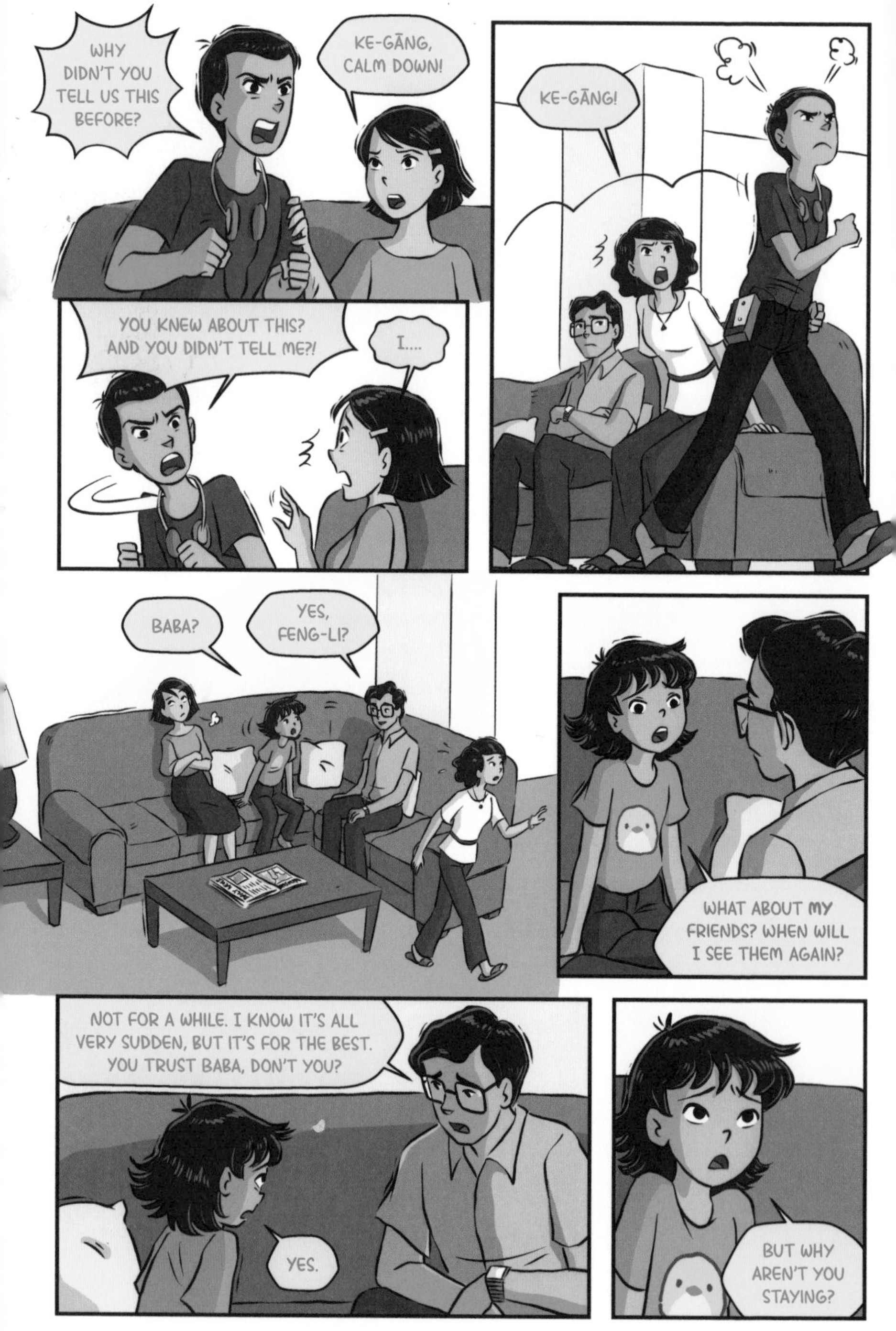
WHY DIDN'T YOU TELL US THIS BEFORE?
KE-GĀNG, CALM DOWN!
YOU KNEW ABOUT THIS? AND YOU DIDN'T TELL ME?!
I....
KE-GĀNG!
BABA?
YES, FENG-LI?
WHAT ABOUT MY FRIENDS? WHEN WILL I SEE THEM AGAIN?
NOT FOR A WHILE. I KNOW IT'S ALL VERY SUDDEN, BUT IT'S FOR THE BEST. YOU TRUST BABA, DON'T YOU?
YES.
BUT WHY AREN'T YOU STAYING?

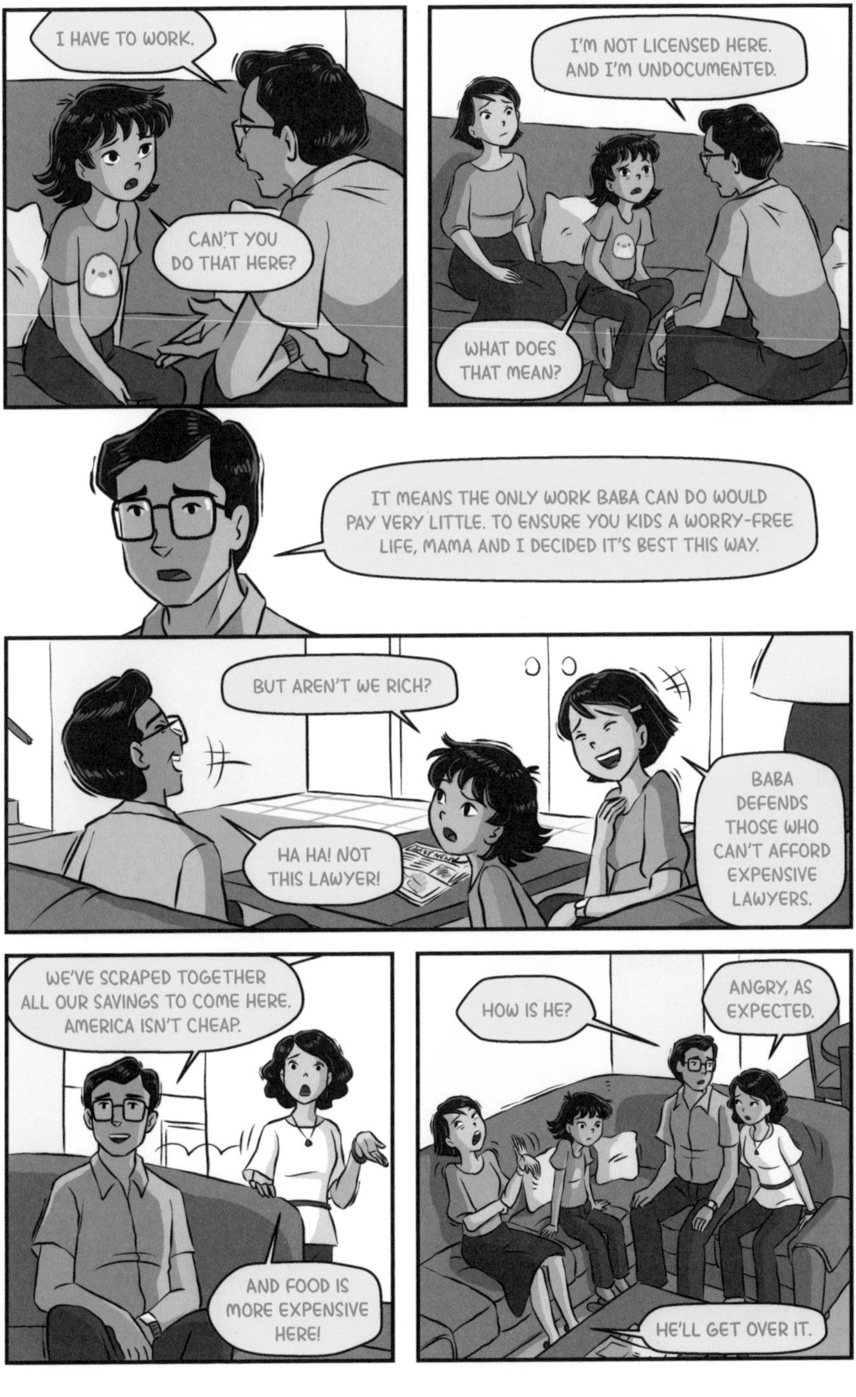
I HAVE TO WORK.
CAN'T YOU DO THAT HERE?
I'M NOT LICENSED HERE. AND I'M UNDOCUMENTED.
WHAT DOES THAT MEAN?
IT MEANS THE ONLY WORK BABA CAN DO WOULD PAY VERY LITTLE. TO ENSURE YOU KIDS A WORRY-FREE LIFE, MAMA AND I DECIDED IT'S BEST THIS WAY.
BUT AREN'T WE RICH?
HA HA! NOT THIS LAWYER!
BABA DEFENDS THOSE WHO CAN'T AFFORD EXPENSIVE LAWYERS.
WE'VE SCRAPED TOGETHER ALL OUR SAVINGS TO COME HERE. AMERICA ISN'T CHEAP.
AND FOOD IS MORE EXPENSIVE HERE!
HOW IS HE?
ANGRY, AS EXPECTED.
HE'LL GET OVER IT.

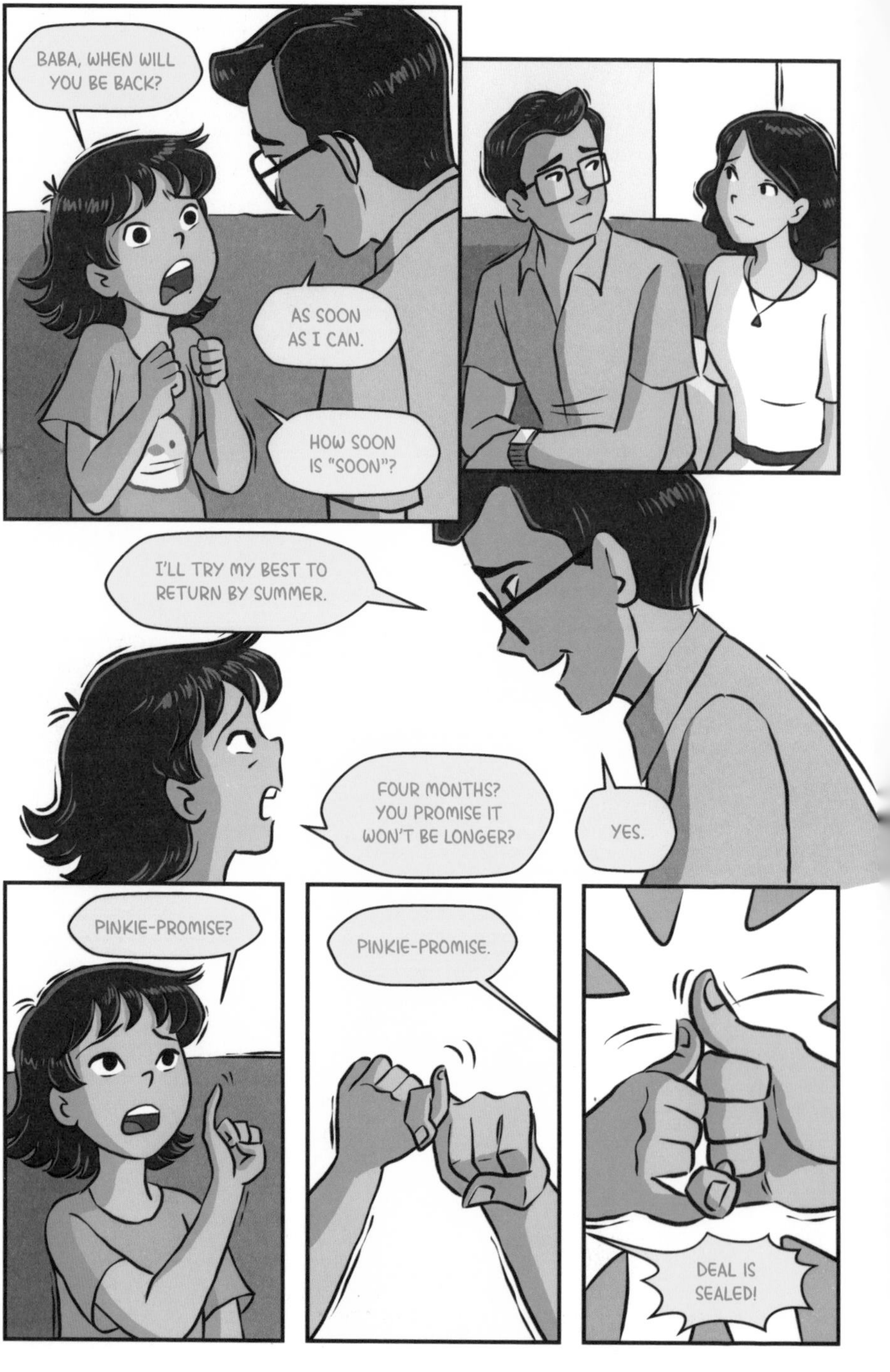
BABA, WHEN WILL YOU BE BACK?
AS SOON AS I CAN.
HOW SOON IS "SOON"?
I'LL TRY MY BEST TO RETURN BY SUMMER.
FOUR MONTHS? YOU PROMISE IT WON'T BE LONGER?
YES.
PINKIE-PROMISE?
PINKIE-PROMISE.
DEAL IS SEALED!

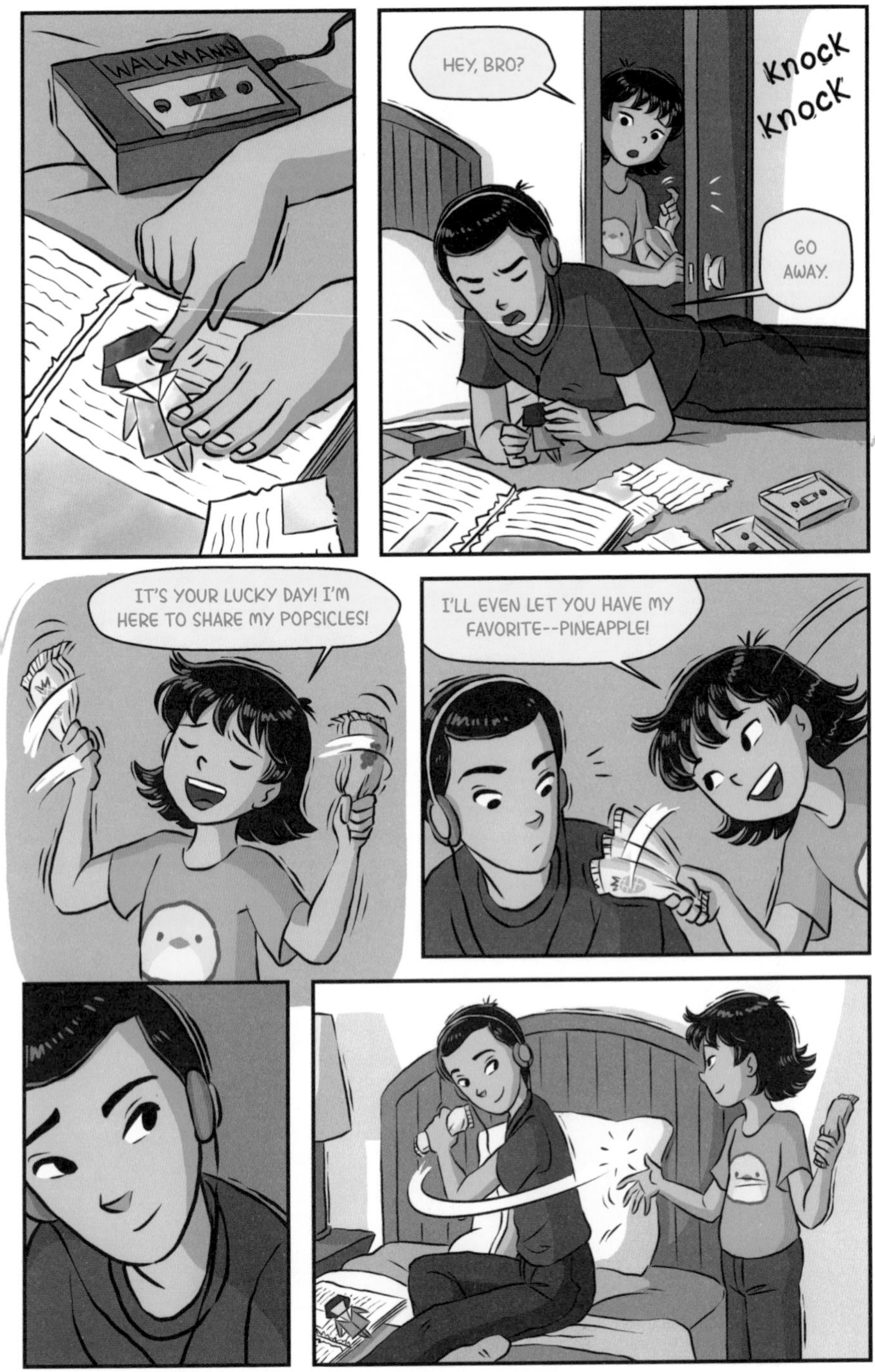
WALKMANN
HEY, BRO?
Knock Knock
GO AWAY.
IT'S YOUR LUCKY DAY! I'M HERE TO SHARE MY POPSICLES!
I'LL EVEN LET YOU HAVE MY FAVORITE--PINEAPPLE!

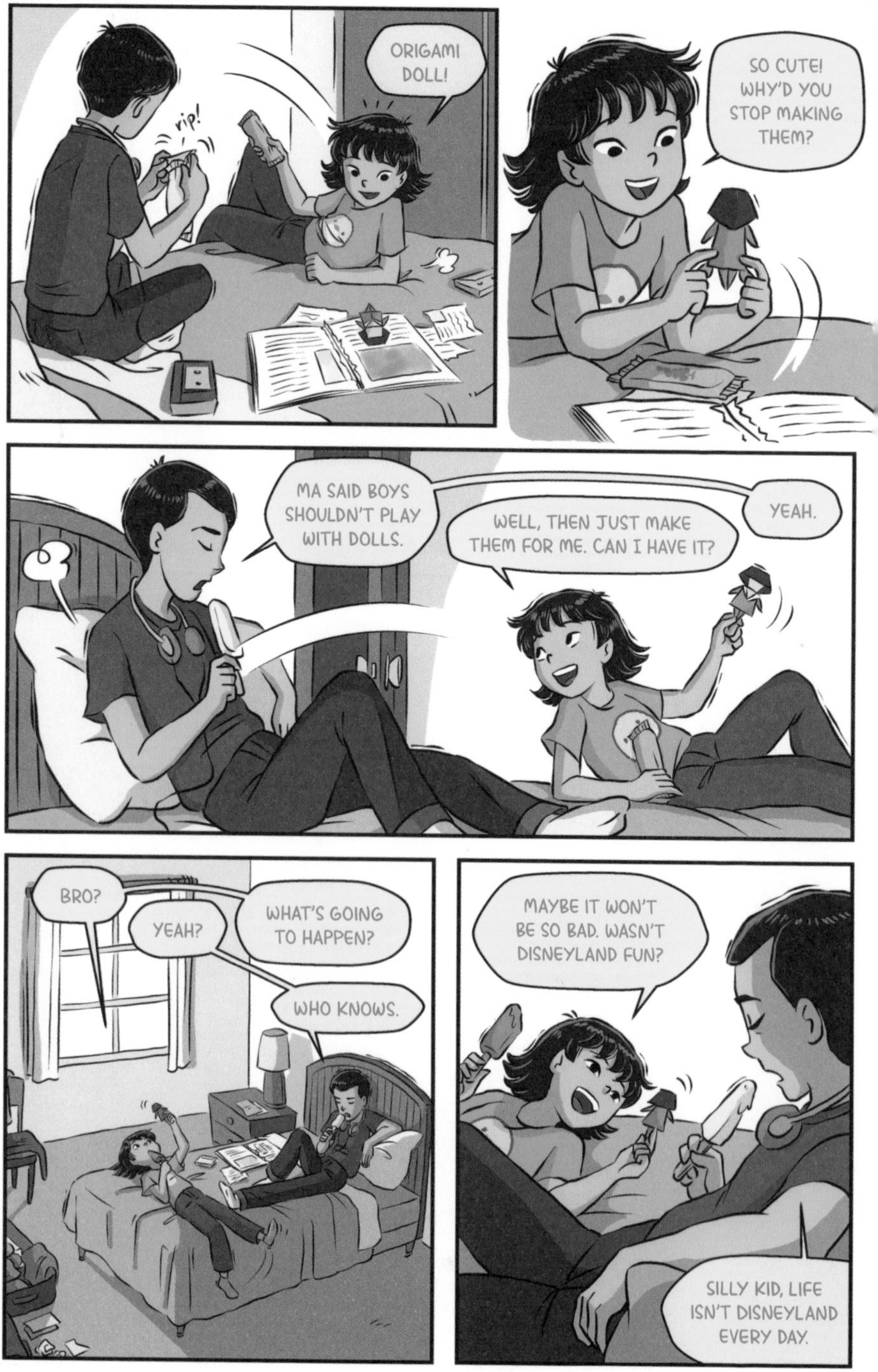
rip!
ORIGAMI DOLL!
SO CUTE! WHY'D YOU STOP MAKING THEM?
MA SAID BOYS SHOULDN'T PLAY WITH DOLLS.
WELL, THEN JUST MAKE THEM FOR ME. CAN I HAVE IT?
YEAH.
BRO?
YEAH?
WHAT'S GOING TO HAPPEN?
WHO KNOWS.
MAYBE IT WON'T BE SO BAD. WASN'T DISNEYLAND FUN?
SILLY KID, LIFE ISN'T DISNEYLAND EVERY DAY.

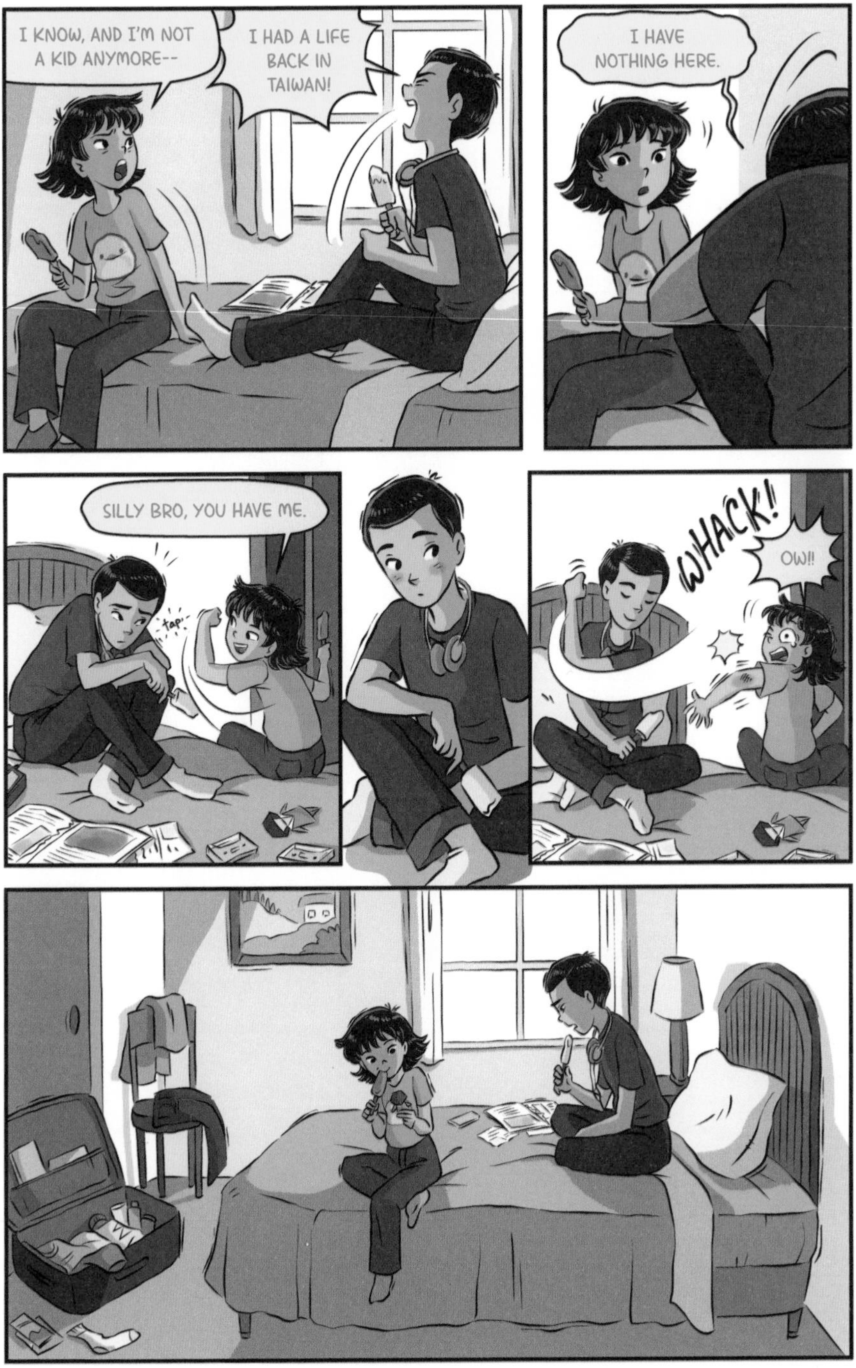
I KNOW, AND I'M NOT A KID ANYMORE--
I HAD A LIFE BACK IN TAIWAN!
I HAVE NOTHING HERE.
SILLY BRO, YOU HAVE ME.
tap
WHACK!
OW!!

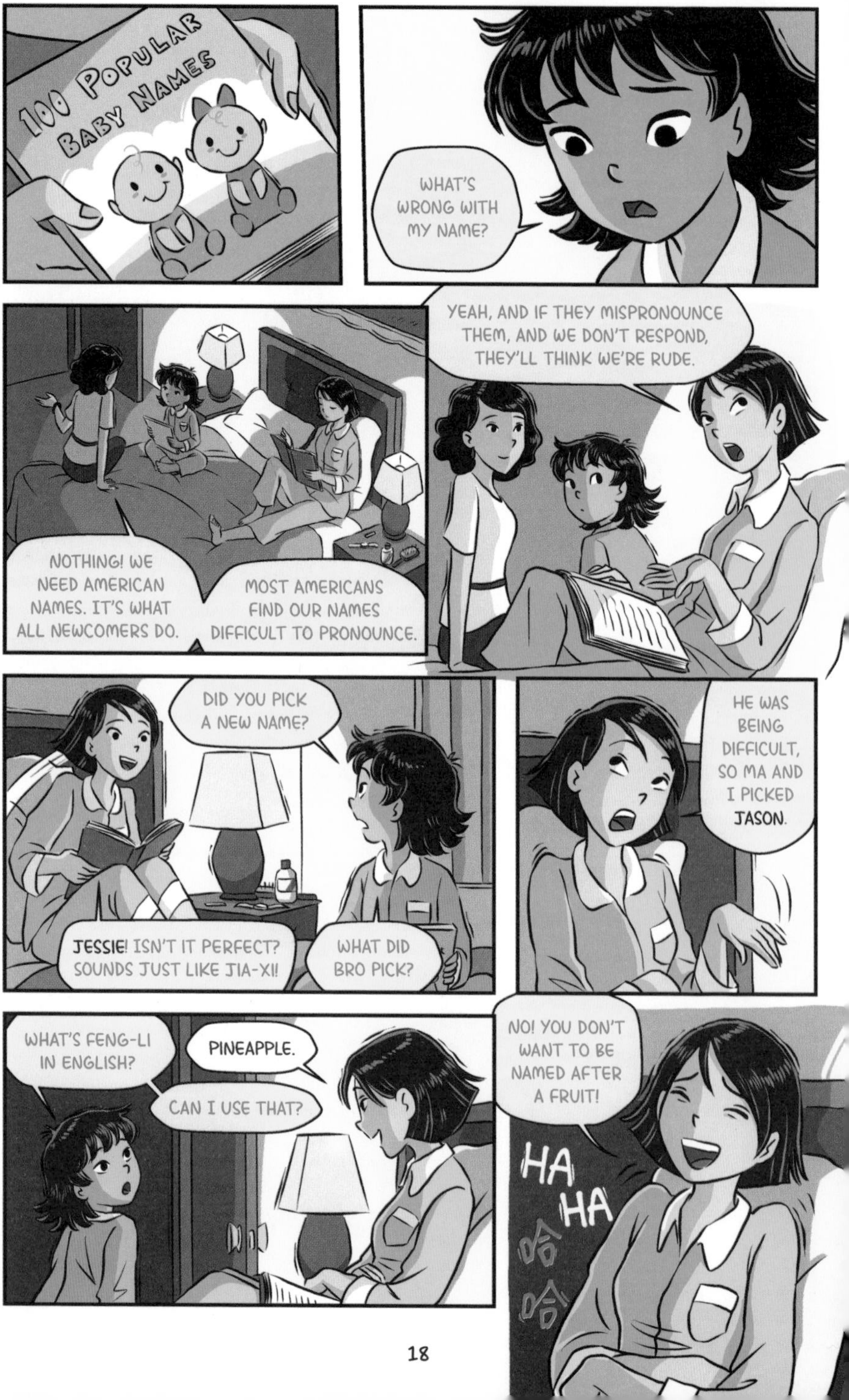
100 POPULAR BABY NAMES
WHAT'S WRONG WITH MY NAME?
NOTHING! WE NEED AMERICAN NAMES. IT'S WHAT ALL NEWCOMERS DO.
MOST AMERICANS FIND OUR NAMES DIFFICULT TO PRONOUNCE.
YEAH, AND IF THEY MISPRONOUNCE THEM, AND WE DON'T RESPOND, THEY'LL THINK WE'RE RUDE.
DID YOU PICK A NEW NAME?
JESSIE! ISN'T IT PERFECT? SOUNDS JUST LIKE JIA-XI!
WHAT DID BRO PICK?
HE WAS BEING DIFFICULT, SO MA AND I PICKED JASON.
WHAT'S FENG-LI IN ENGLISH?
PINEAPPLE.
CAN I USE THAT?
NO! YOU DON'T WANT TO BE NAMED AFTER A FRUIT!
HA HA
哈哈

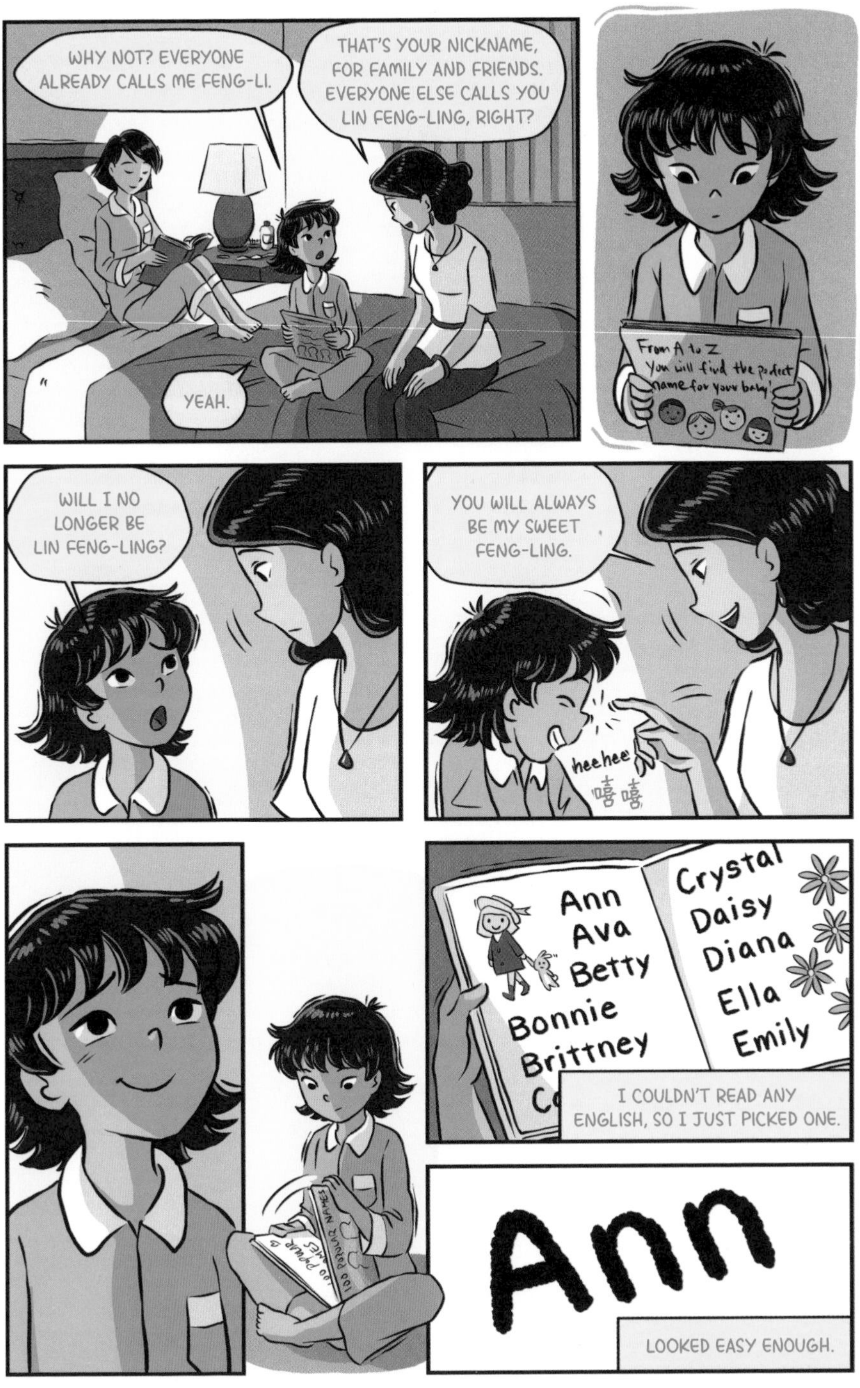
WHY NOT? EVERYONE ALREADY CALLS ME FENG-LI.
THAT'S YOUR NICKNAME, FOR FAMILY AND FRIENDS. EVERYONE ELSE CALLS YOU LIN FENG-LING, RIGHT?
YEAH.
From A to Z
You will find the perfect name for your baby!
WILL I NO LONGER BE LIN FENG-LING?
YOU WILL ALWAYS BE MY SWEET FENG-LING.
heehee
嘻嘻
Ann
Ava
Betty
Bonnie
Brittney
Crystal
Daisy
Diana
Ella
Emily
I COULDN'T READ ANY ENGLISH, SO I JUST PICKED ONE.
Ann
LOOKED EASY ENOUGH.

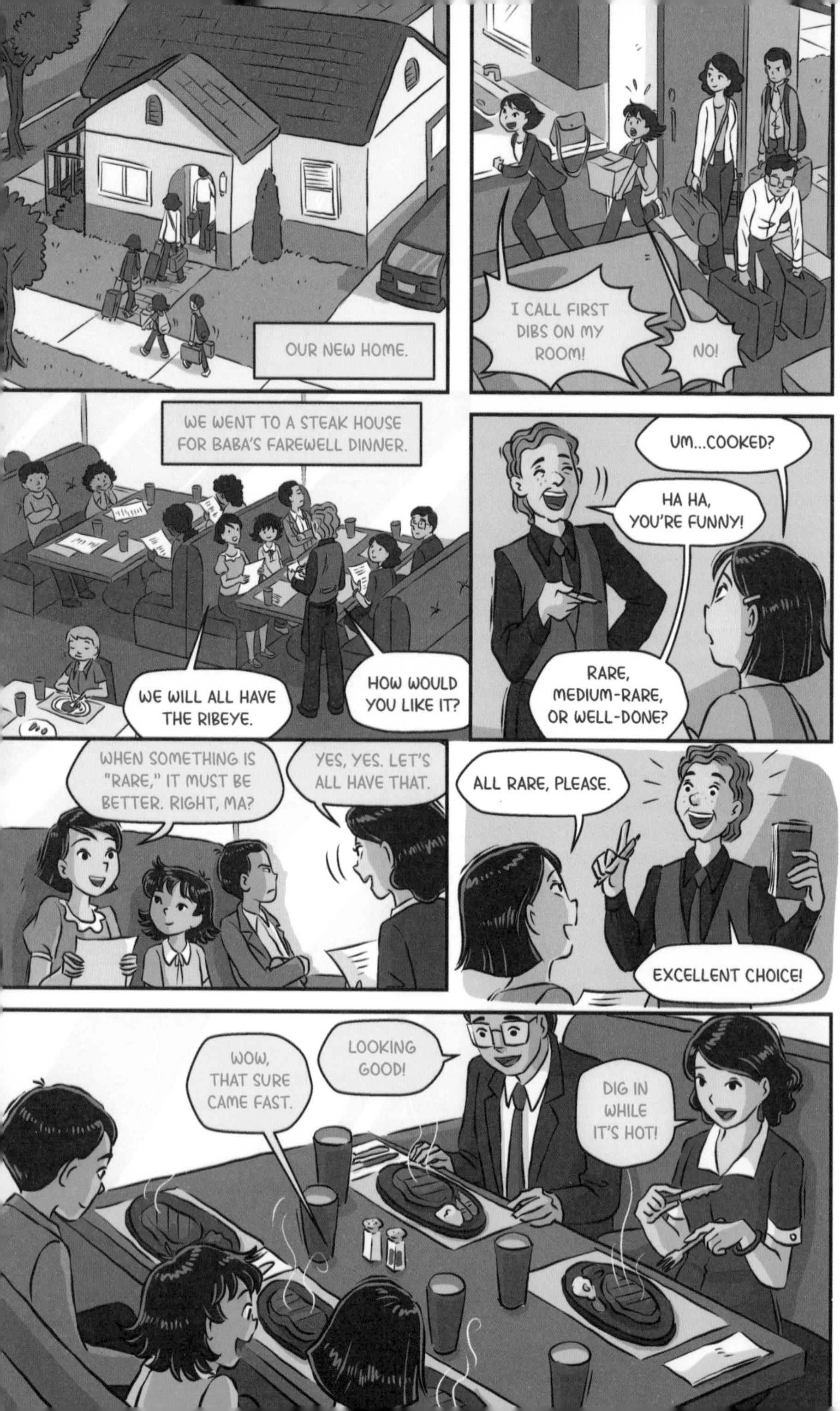
OUR NEW HOME.
I CALL FIRST DIBS ON MY ROOM!
NO!
WE WENT TO A STEAK HOUSE FOR BABA'S FAREWELL DINNER.
WE WILL ALL HAVE THE RIBEYE.
HOW WOULD YOU LIKE IT?
RARE, MEDIUM-RARE, OR WELL-DONE?
UM...COOKED?
HA HA, YOU'RE FUNNY!
WHEN SOMETHING IS "RARE," IT MUST BE BETTER. RIGHT, MA?
YES, YES. LET'S ALL HAVE THAT.
ALL RARE, PLEASE.
EXCELLENT CHOICE!
WOW, THAT SURE CAME FAST.
LOOKING GOOD!
DIG IN WHILE IT'S HOT!

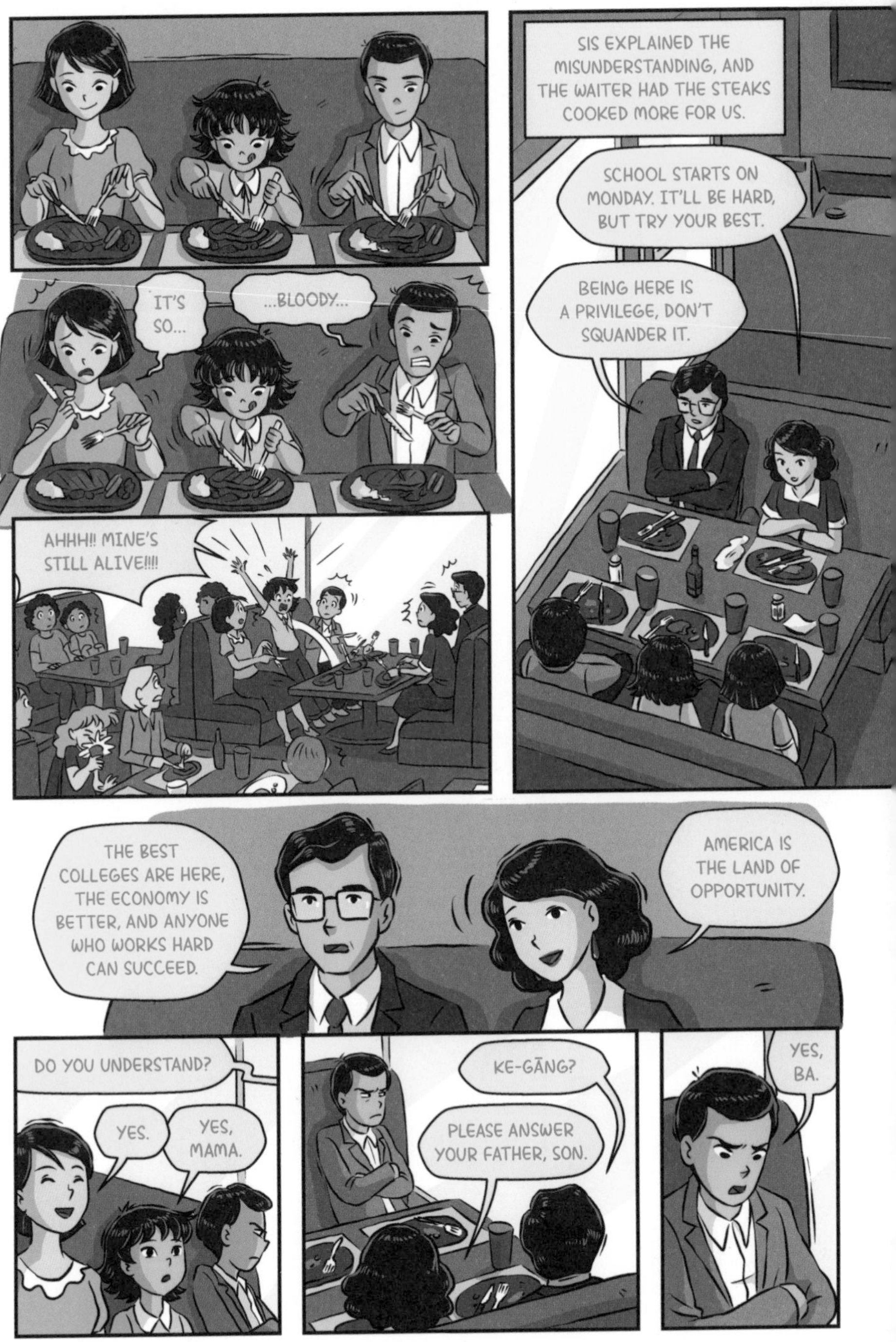
IT'S SO...
...BLOODY...
AHHH!! MINE'S STILL ALIVE!!!!
SIS EXPLAINED THE MISUNDERSTANDING, AND THE WAITER HAD THE STEAKS COOKED MORE FOR US.
SCHOOL STARTS ON MONDAY. IT'LL BE HARD, BUT TRY YOUR BEST.
BEING HERE IS A PRIVILEGE, DON'T SQUANDER IT.
THE BEST COLLEGES ARE HERE, THE ECONOMY IS BETTER, AND ANYONE WHO WORKS HARD CAN SUCCEED.
AMERICA IS THE LAND OF OPPORTUNITY.
DO YOU UNDERSTAND?
YES.
YES, MAMA.
KE-GĀNG?
PLEASE ANSWER YOUR FATHER, SON.
YES, BA.

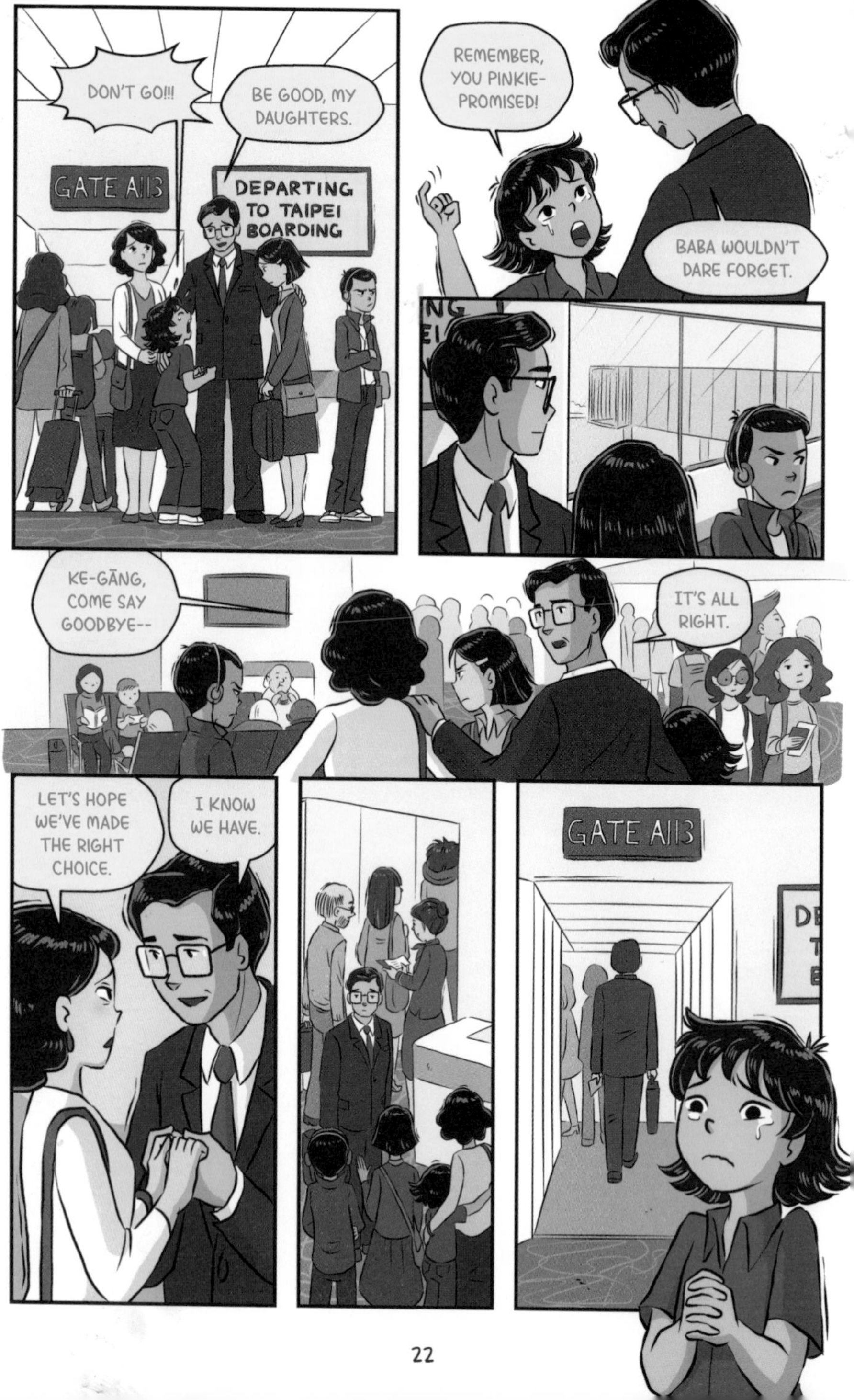
DON'T GO!!!
BE GOOD, MY DAUGHTERS.
GATE A113
DEPARTING TO TAIPEI BOARDING
REMEMBER, YOU PINKIE-PROMISED!
BABA WOULDN'T DARE FORGET.
KE-GĀNG, COME SAY GOODBYE--
IT'S ALL RIGHT.
LET'S HOPE WE'VE MADE THE RIGHT CHOICE.
I KNOW WE HAVE.
GATE A113

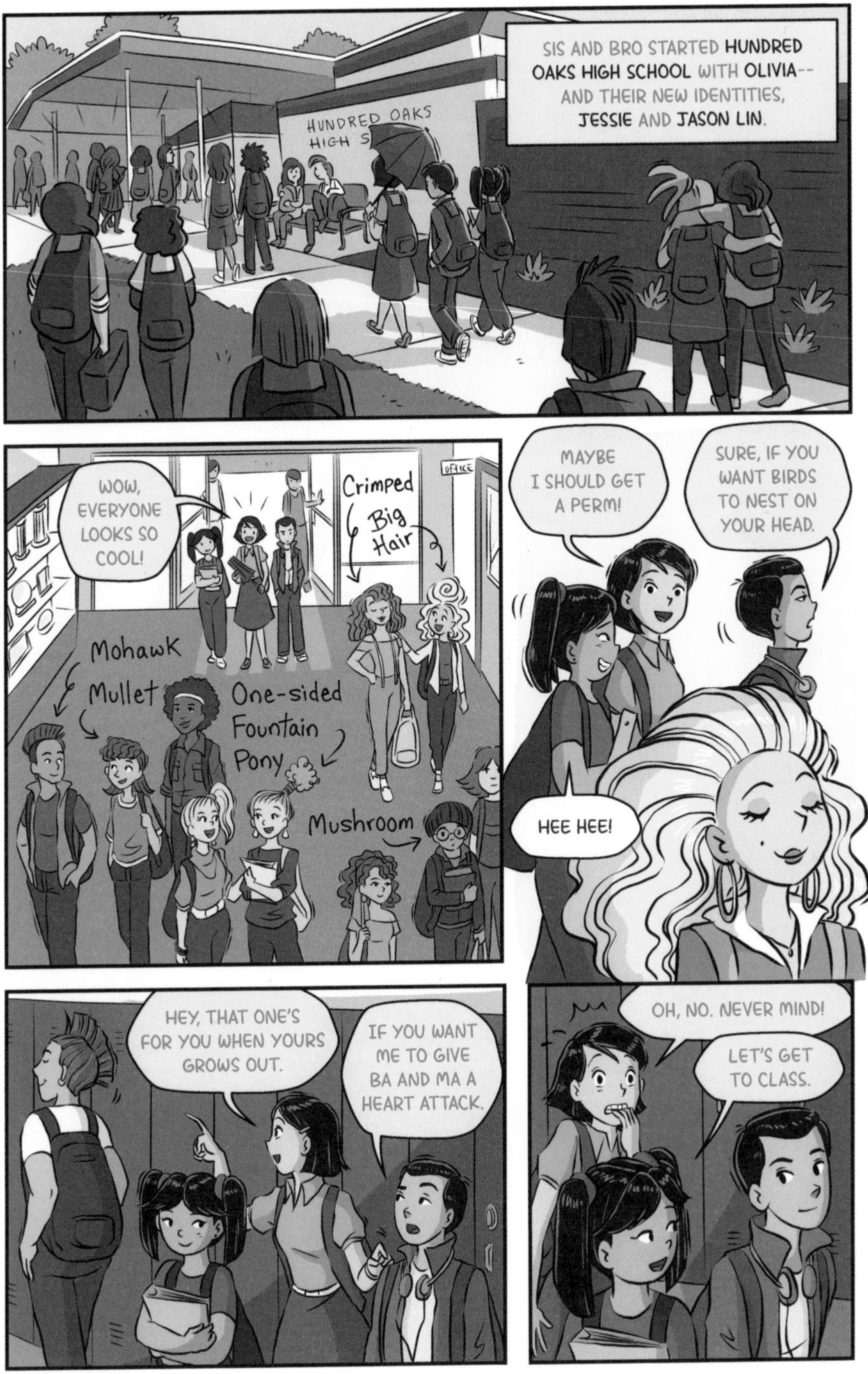
SIS AND BRO STARTED HUNDRED OAKS HIGH SCHOOL WITH OLIVIA-- AND THEIR NEW IDENTITIES, JESSIE AND JASON LIN.
HUNDRED OAKS HIGH S
OFFICE
WOW, EVERYONE LOOKS SO COOL!
Crimped
Big Hair
Mohawk
Mullet
One-sided Fountain Pony
Mushroom
MAYBE I SHOULD GET A PERM!
SURE, IF YOU WANT BIRDS TO NEST ON YOUR HEAD.
HEE HEE!
HEY, THAT ONE'S FOR YOU WHEN YOURS GROWS OUT.
IF YOU WANT ME TO GIVE BA AND MA A HEART ATTACK.
OH, NO. NEVER MIND!
LET'S GET TO CLASS.

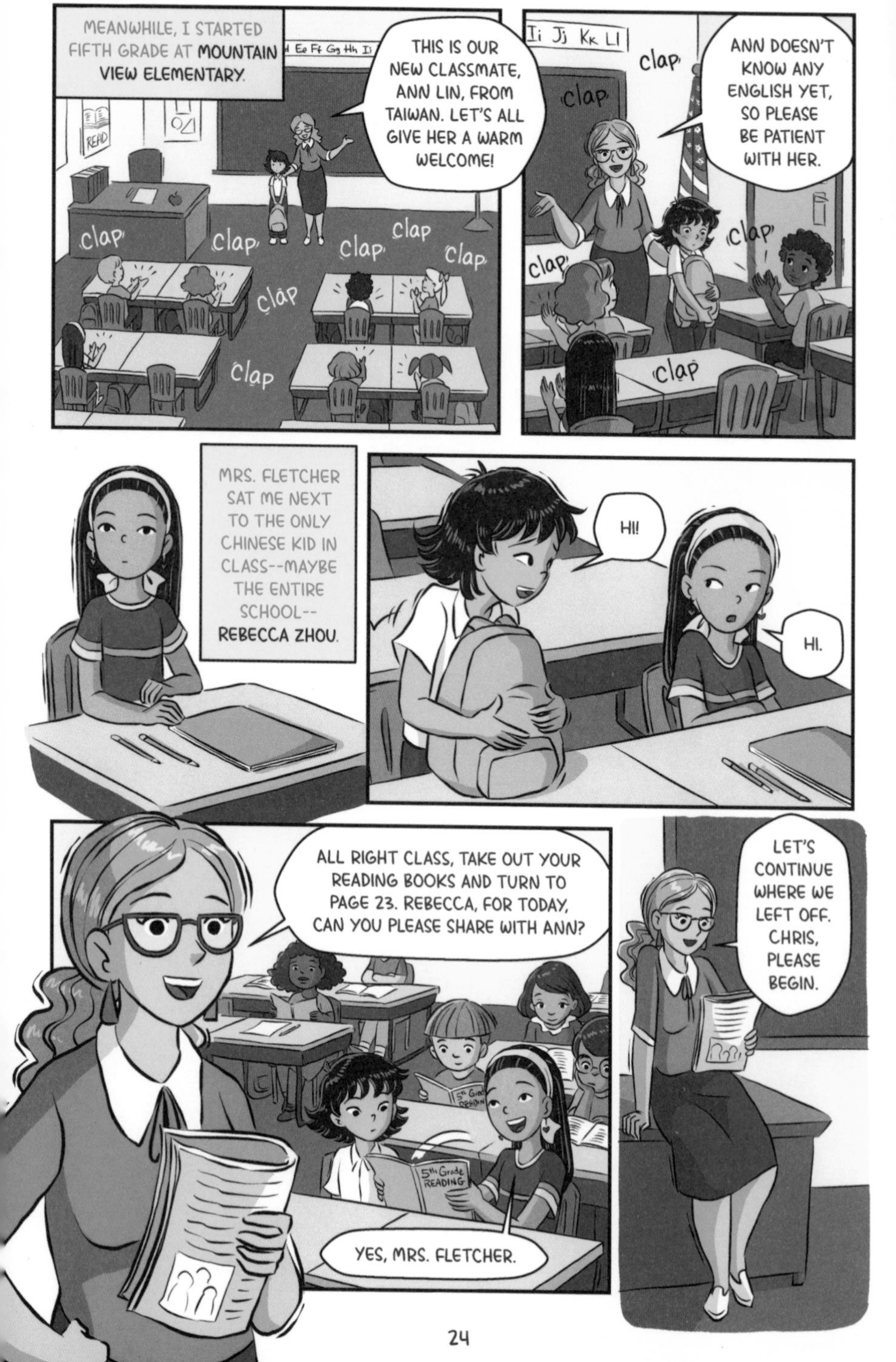
MEANWHILE, I STARTED FIFTH GRADE AT MOUNTAIN VIEW ELEMENTARY.
THIS IS OUR NEW CLASSMATE, ANN LIN, FROM TAIWAN. LET'S ALL GIVE HER A WARM WELCOME!
CLAP CLAP CLAP CLAP CLAP CLAP CLAP
ANN DOESN'T KNOW ANY ENGLISH YET, SO PLEASE BE PATIENT WITH HER.
CLAP CLAP CLAP CLAP CLAP
MRS. FLETCHER SAT ME NEXT TO THE ONLY CHINESE KID IN CLASS--MAYBE THE ENTIRE SCHOOL--REBECCA ZHOU.
HI!
HI.
ALL RIGHT CLASS, TAKE OUT YOUR READING BOOKS AND TURN TO PAGE 23. REBECCA, FOR TODAY, CAN YOU PLEASE SHARE WITH ANN?
5th Grade READING
YES, MRS. FLETCHER.
LET'S CONTINUE WHERE WE LEFT OFF. CHRIS, PLEASE BEGIN.

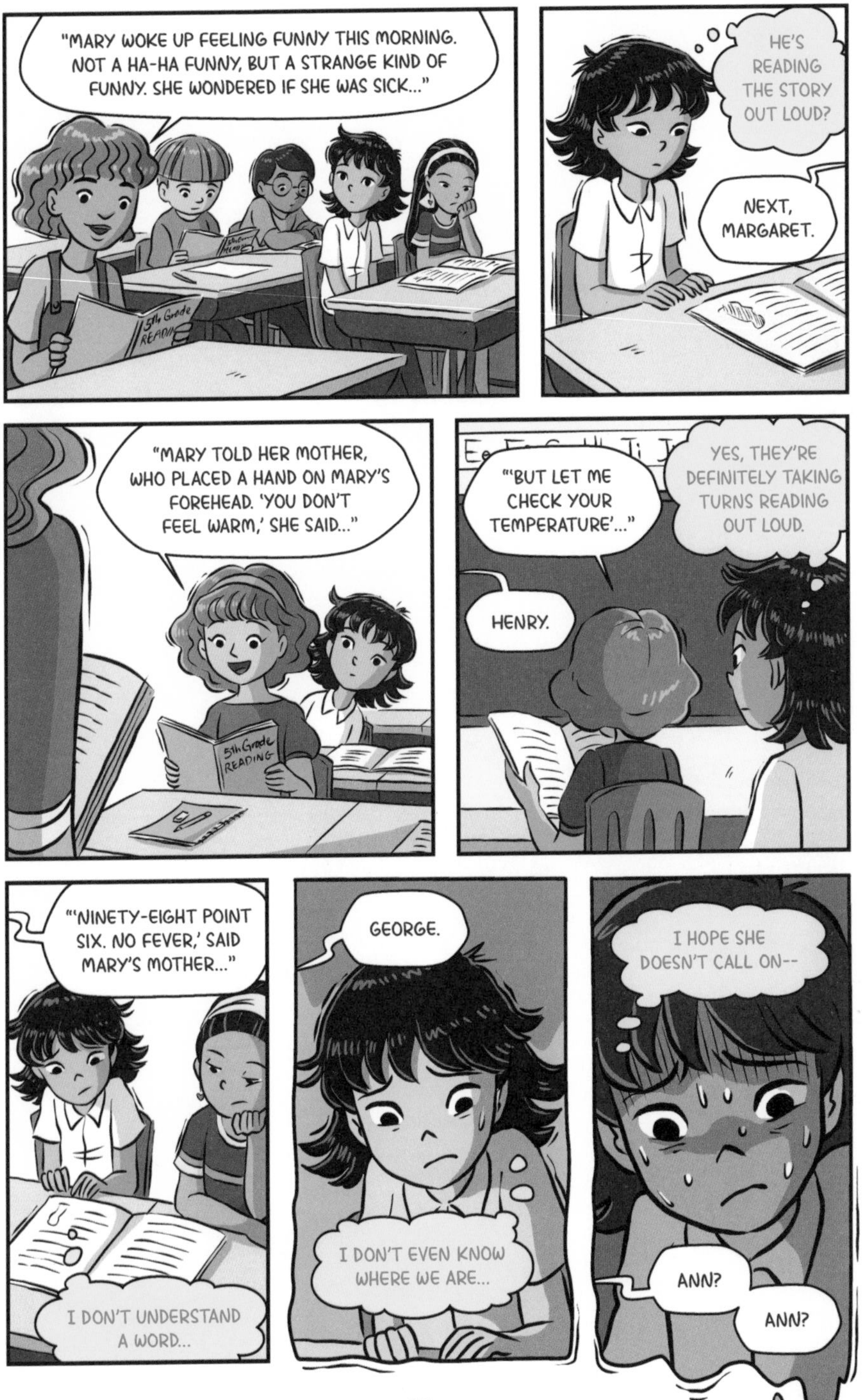
"MARY WOKE UP FEELING FUNNY THIS MORNING. NOT A HA-HA FUNNY, BUT A STRANGE KIND OF FUNNY. SHE WONDERED IF SHE WAS SICK..."
5th Grade READING
HE'S READING THE STORY OUT LOUD?
NEXT, MARGARET.
"MARY TOLD HER MOTHER, WHO PLACED A HAND ON MARY'S FOREHEAD. 'YOU DON'T FEEL WARM,' SHE SAID..."
5th Grade READING
"'BUT LET ME CHECK YOUR TEMPERATURE'..."
YES, THEY'RE DEFINITELY TAKING TURNS READING OUT LOUD.
HENRY.
"'NINETY-EIGHT POINT SIX. NO FEVER,' SAID MARY'S MOTHER..."
I DON'T UNDERSTAND A WORD...
GEORGE.
I DON'T EVEN KNOW WHERE WE ARE...
I HOPE SHE DOESN'T CALL ON--
ANN?
ANN?

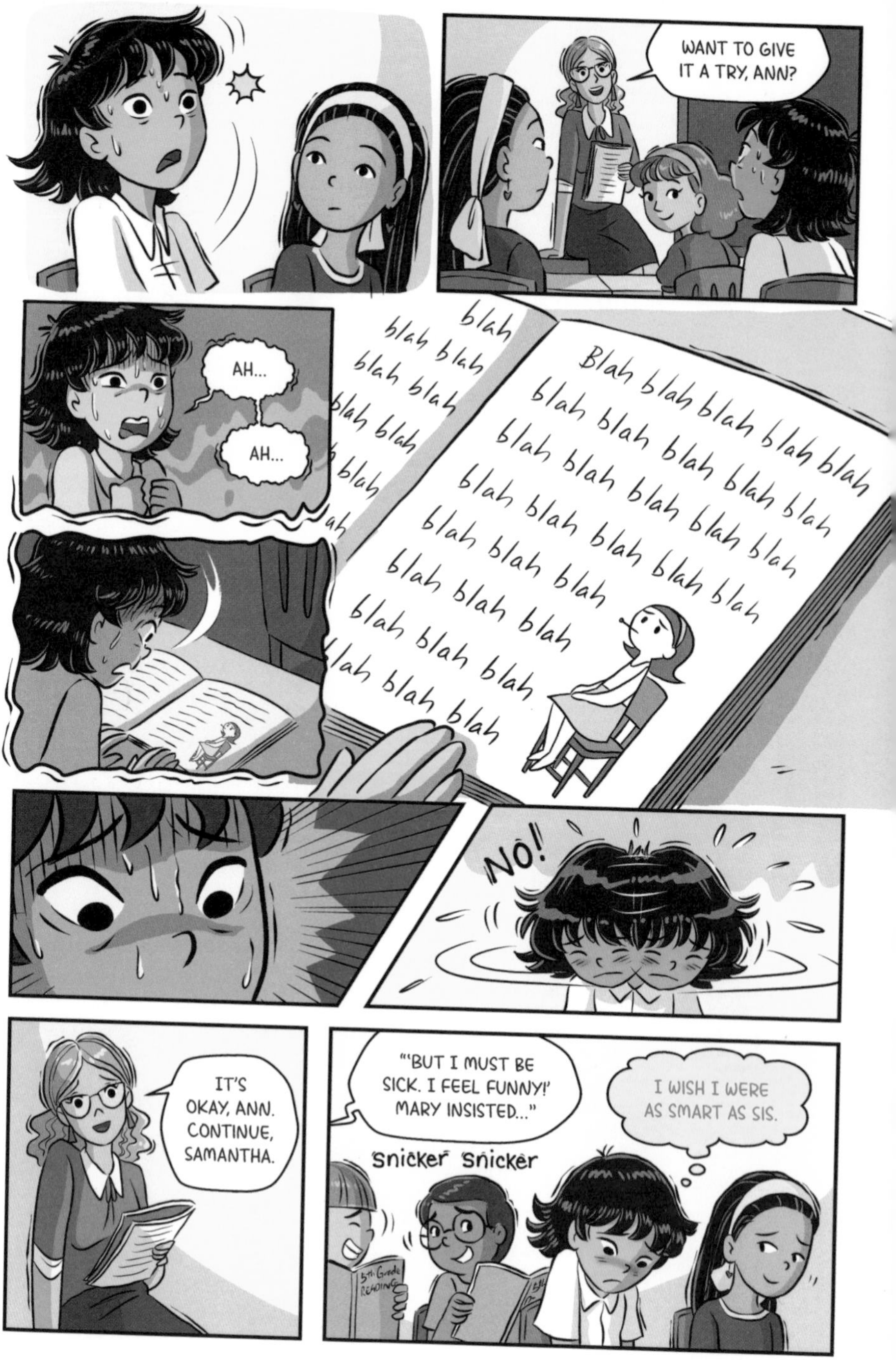
WANT TO GIVE IT A TRY, ANN?
AH...
AH...
blah blah blah blah blah blah blah blah
Blah blah blah blah blah
blah blah blah blah blah blah
blah blah blah blah blah blah
blah blah blah blah blah blah
blah blah blah blah blah blah
blah blah blah
blah blah blah
blah blah blah
blah blah blah
NO!
IT'S OKAY, ANN. CONTINUE, SAMANTHA.
"'BUT I MUST BE SICK. I FEEL FUNNY!' MARY INSISTED..."
I WISH I WERE AS SMART AS SIS.
snicker snicker
5th Grade READING

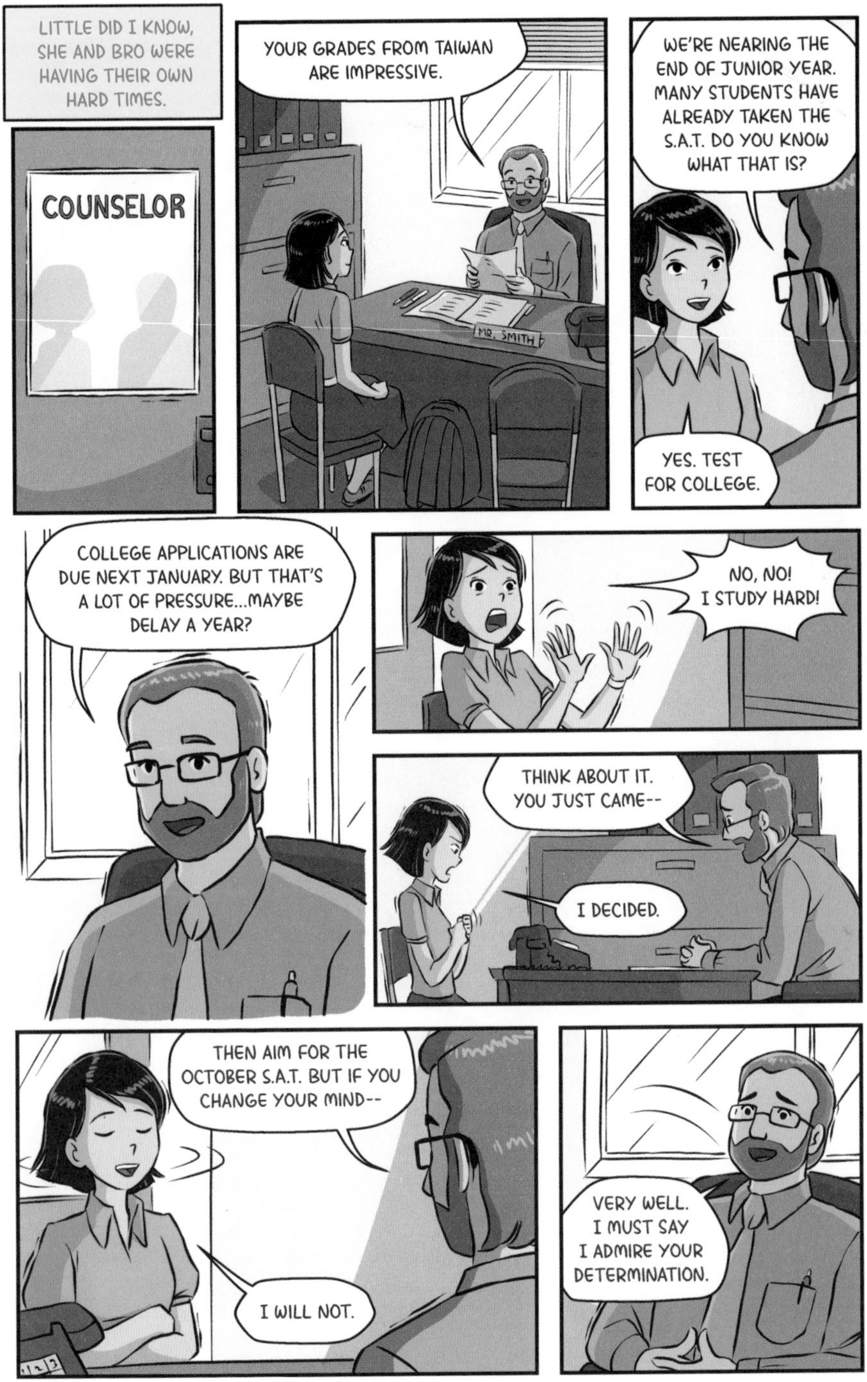
LITTLE DID I KNOW, SHE AND BRO WERE HAVING THEIR OWN HARD TIMES.
COUNSELOR
YOUR GRADES FROM TAIWAN ARE IMPRESSIVE.
MR. SMITH
WE'RE NEARING THE END OF JUNIOR YEAR. MANY STUDENTS HAVE ALREADY TAKEN THE S.A.T. DO YOU KNOW WHAT THAT IS?
YES. TEST FOR COLLEGE.
COLLEGE APPLICATIONS ARE DUE NEXT JANUARY. BUT THAT'S A LOT OF PRESSURE...MAYBE DELAY A YEAR?
NO, NO! I STUDY HARD!
THINK ABOUT IT. YOU JUST CAME--
I DECIDED.
THEN AIM FOR THE OCTOBER S.A.T. BUT IF YOU CHANGE YOUR MIND--
I WILL NOT.
VERY WELL. I MUST SAY I ADMIRE YOUR DETERMINATION.

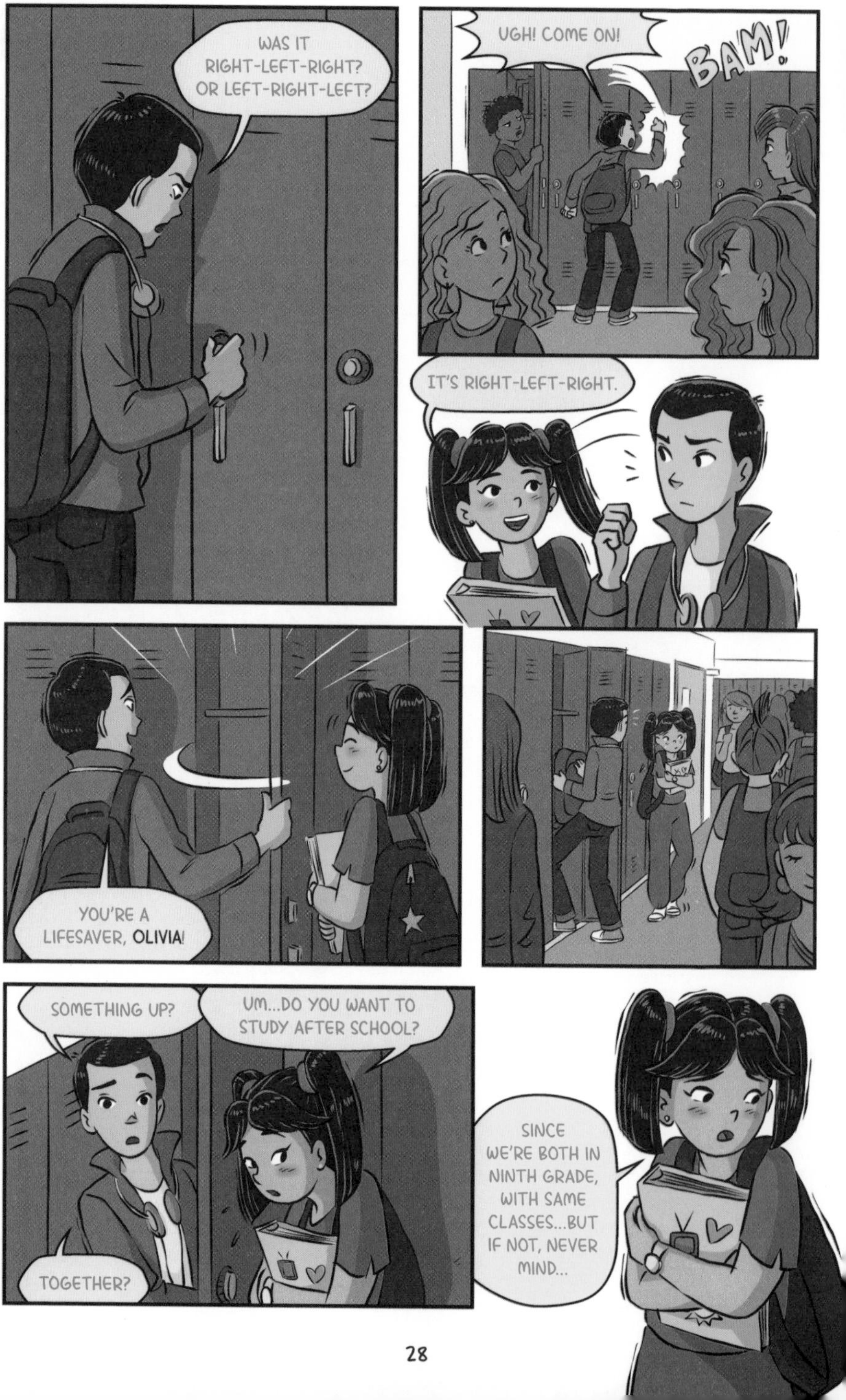
WAS IT RIGHT-LEFT-RIGHT? OR LEFT-RIGHT-LEFT?
UGH! COME ON!
BAM!
IT'S RIGHT-LEFT-RIGHT.
YOU'RE A LIFESAVER, **OLIVIA**!
SOMETHING UP?
UM...DO YOU WANT TO STUDY AFTER SCHOOL?
TOGETHER?
SINCE WE'RE BOTH IN NINTH GRADE, WITH SAME CLASSES...BUT IF NOT, NEVER MIND...

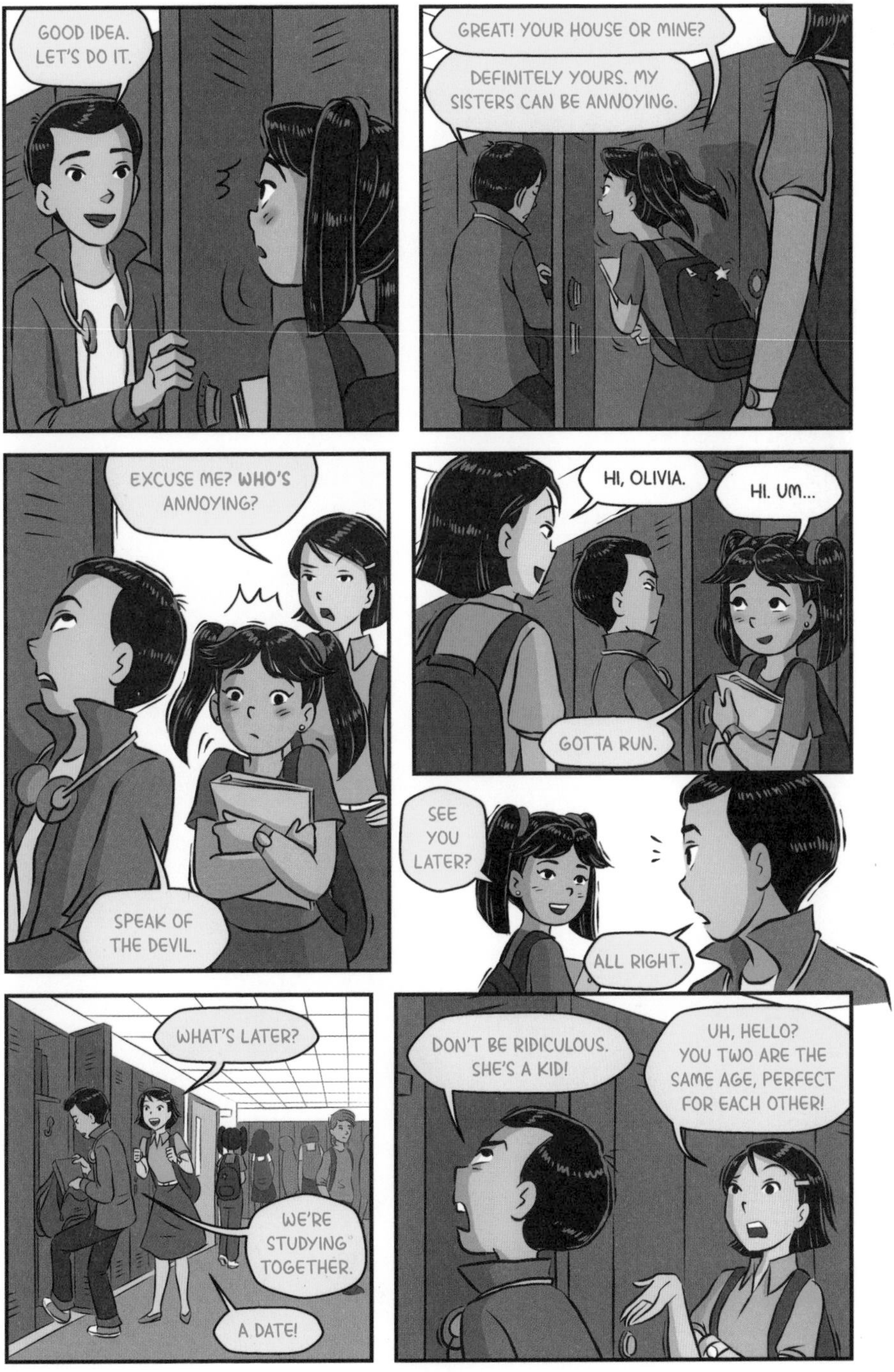
GOOD IDEA. LET'S DO IT.
GREAT! YOUR HOUSE OR MINE?
DEFINITELY YOURS. MY SISTERS CAN BE ANNOYING.
EXCUSE ME? WHO'S ANNOYING?
SPEAK OF THE DEVIL.
HI, OLIVIA.
HI. UM...
GOTTA RUN.
SEE YOU LATER?
ALL RIGHT.
WHAT'S LATER?
WE'RE STUDYING TOGETHER.
A DATE!
DON'T BE RIDICULOUS. SHE'S A KID!
UH, HELLO? YOU TWO ARE THE SAME AGE, PERFECT FOR EACH OTHER!

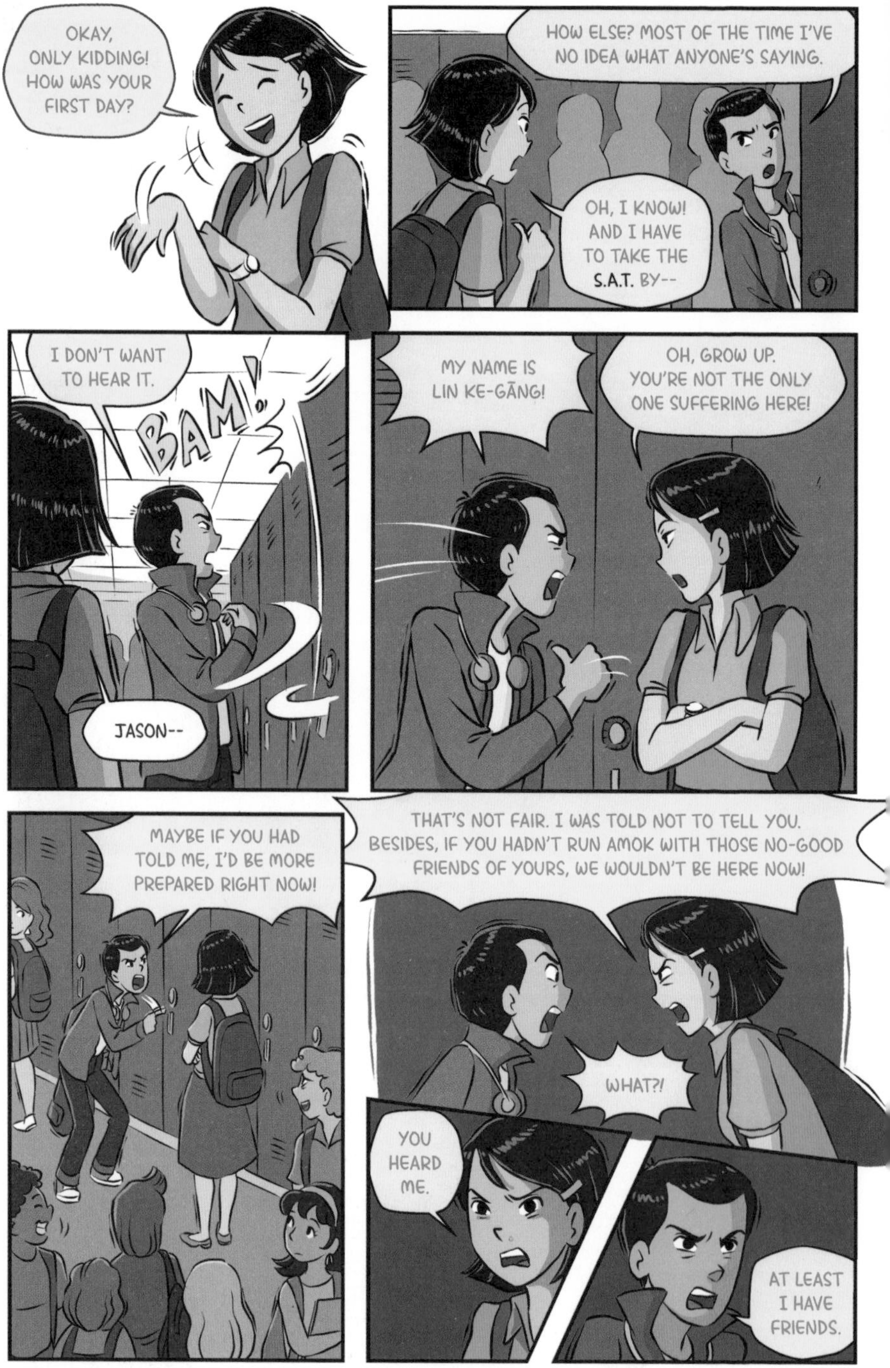
OKAY, ONLY KIDDING! HOW WAS YOUR FIRST DAY?
HOW ELSE? MOST OF THE TIME I'VE NO IDEA WHAT ANYONE'S SAYING.
OH, I KNOW! AND I HAVE TO TAKE THE S.A.T. BY--
I DON'T WANT TO HEAR IT.
BAM!
JASON--
MY NAME IS LIN KE-GĀNG!
OH, GROW UP. YOU'RE NOT THE ONLY ONE SUFFERING HERE!
MAYBE IF YOU HAD TOLD ME, I'D BE MORE PREPARED RIGHT NOW!
THAT'S NOT FAIR. I WAS TOLD NOT TO TELL YOU. BESIDES, IF YOU HADN'T RUN AMOK WITH THOSE NO-GOOD FRIENDS OF YOURS, WE WOULDN'T BE HERE NOW!
WHAT?!
YOU HEARD ME.
AT LEAST I HAVE FRIENDS.

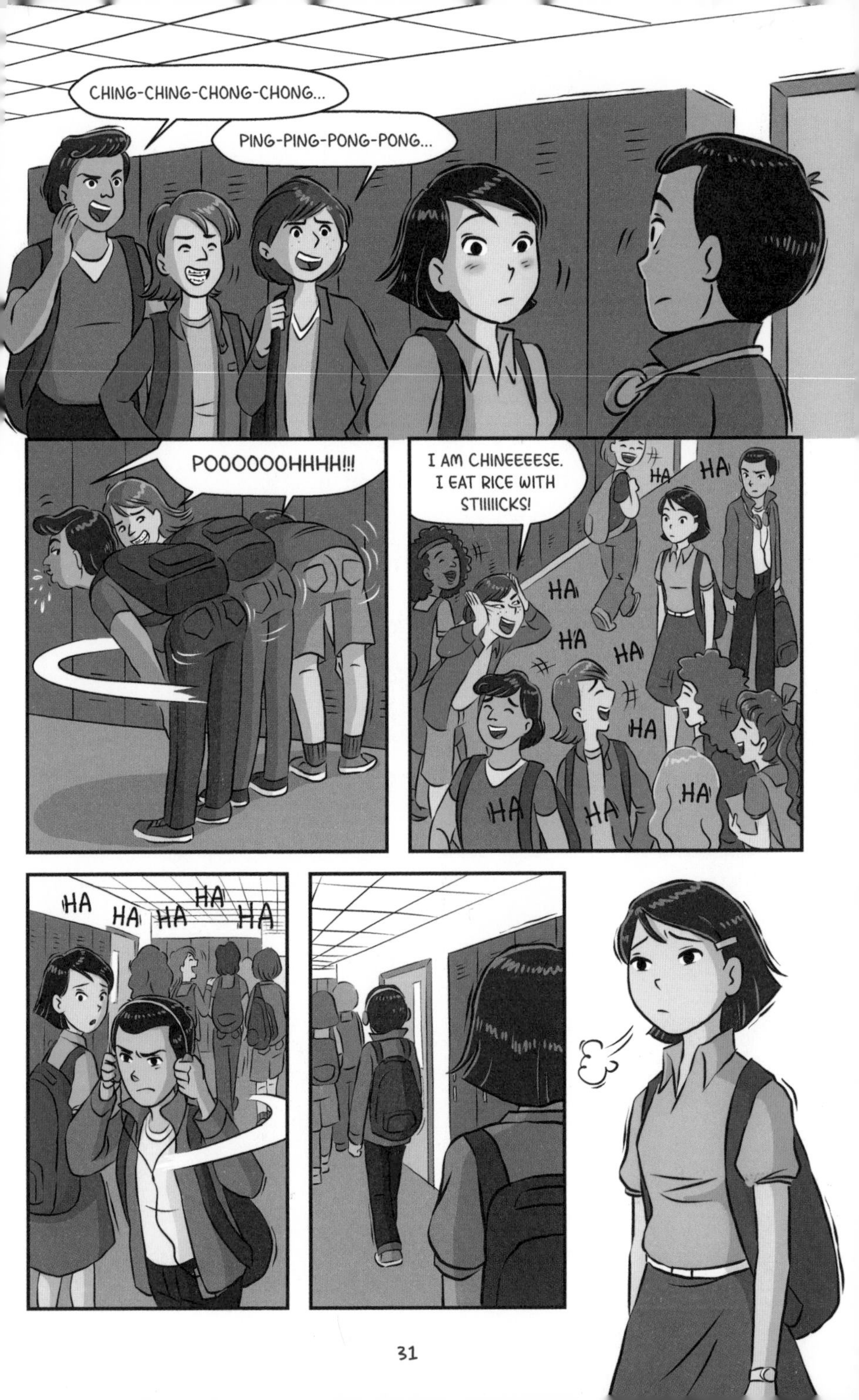
CHING-CHING-CHONG-CHONG...
PING-PING-PONG-PONG...
POOOOOOHHHH!!!
I AM CHINEEEESE. I EAT RICE WITH STIIIIICKS!
HA
HA
HA
HA
HA
HA
HA
HA
HA
HA
HA
HA
HA
HA

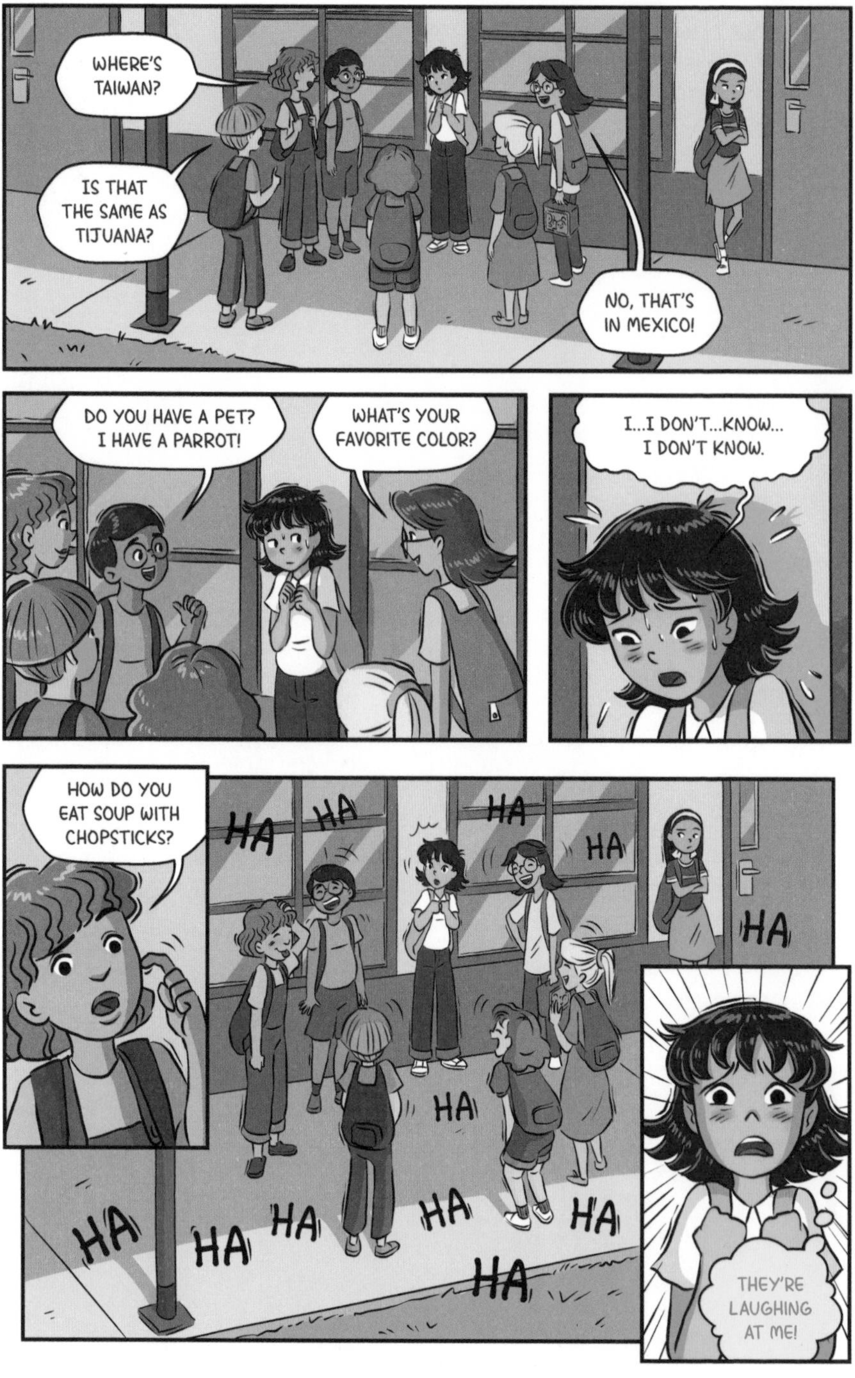
WHERE'S TAIWAN?
IS THAT THE SAME AS TIJUANA?
NO, THAT'S IN MEXICO!
DO YOU HAVE A PET? I HAVE A PARROT!
WHAT'S YOUR FAVORITE COLOR?
I...I DON'T...KNOW... I DON'T KNOW.
HOW DO YOU EAT SOUP WITH CHOPSTICKS?
HA HA HA HA HA HA HA HA HA HA HA HA HA
THEY'RE LAUGHING AT ME!

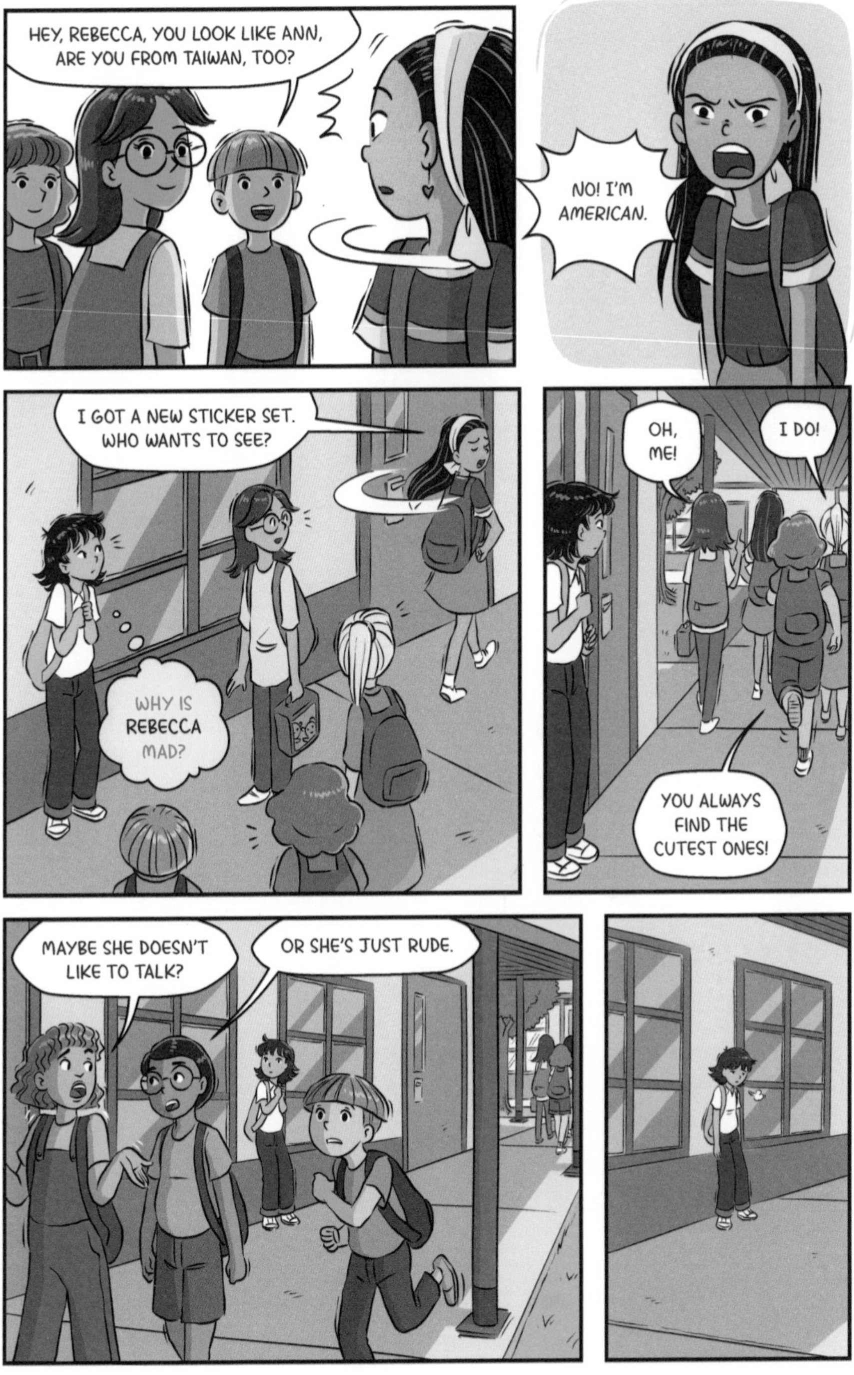
HEY, REBECCA, YOU LOOK LIKE ANN, ARE YOU FROM TAIWAN, TOO?
NO! I'M AMERICAN.
I GOT A NEW STICKER SET. WHO WANTS TO SEE?
WHY IS REBECCA MAD?
OH, ME!
I DO!
YOU ALWAYS FIND THE CUTEST ONES!
MAYBE SHE DOESN'T LIKE TO TALK?
OR SHE'S JUST RUDE.

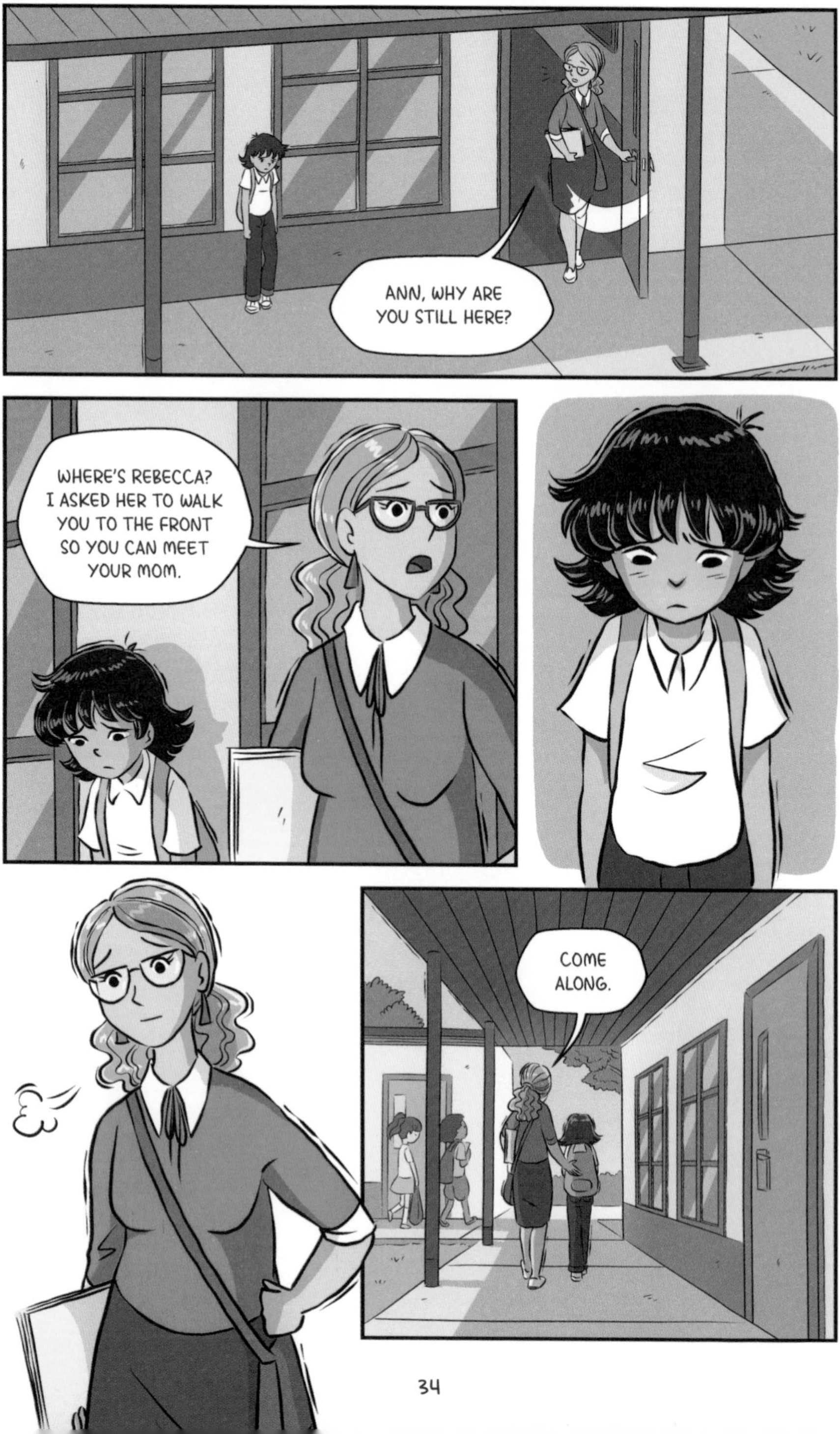
ANN, WHY ARE YOU STILL HERE?
WHERE'S REBECCA? I ASKED HER TO WALK YOU TO THE FRONT SO YOU CAN MEET YOUR MOM.
COME ALONG.

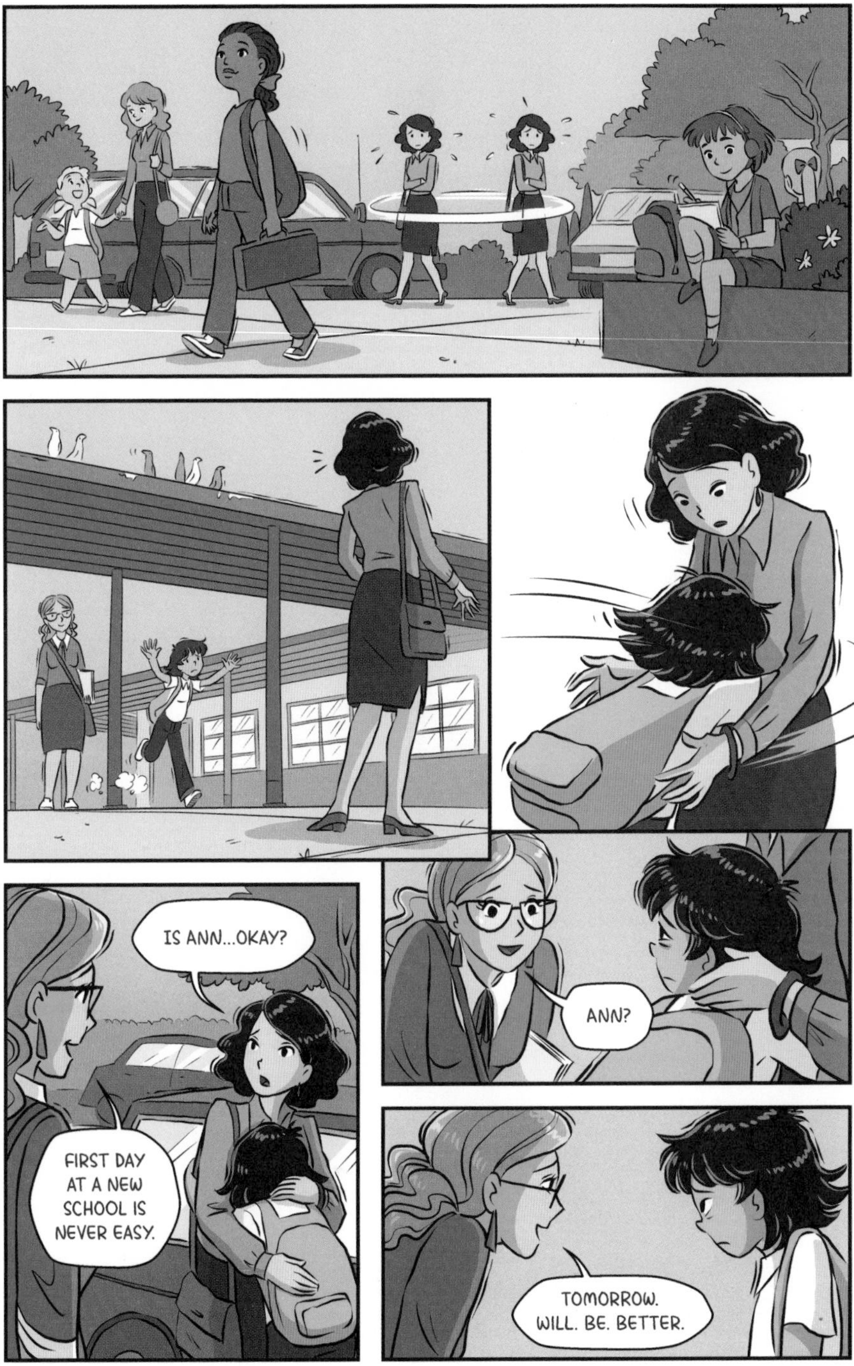
IS ANN...OKAY?
FIRST DAY AT A NEW SCHOOL IS NEVER EASY.
ANN?
TOMORROW. WILL. BE. BETTER.

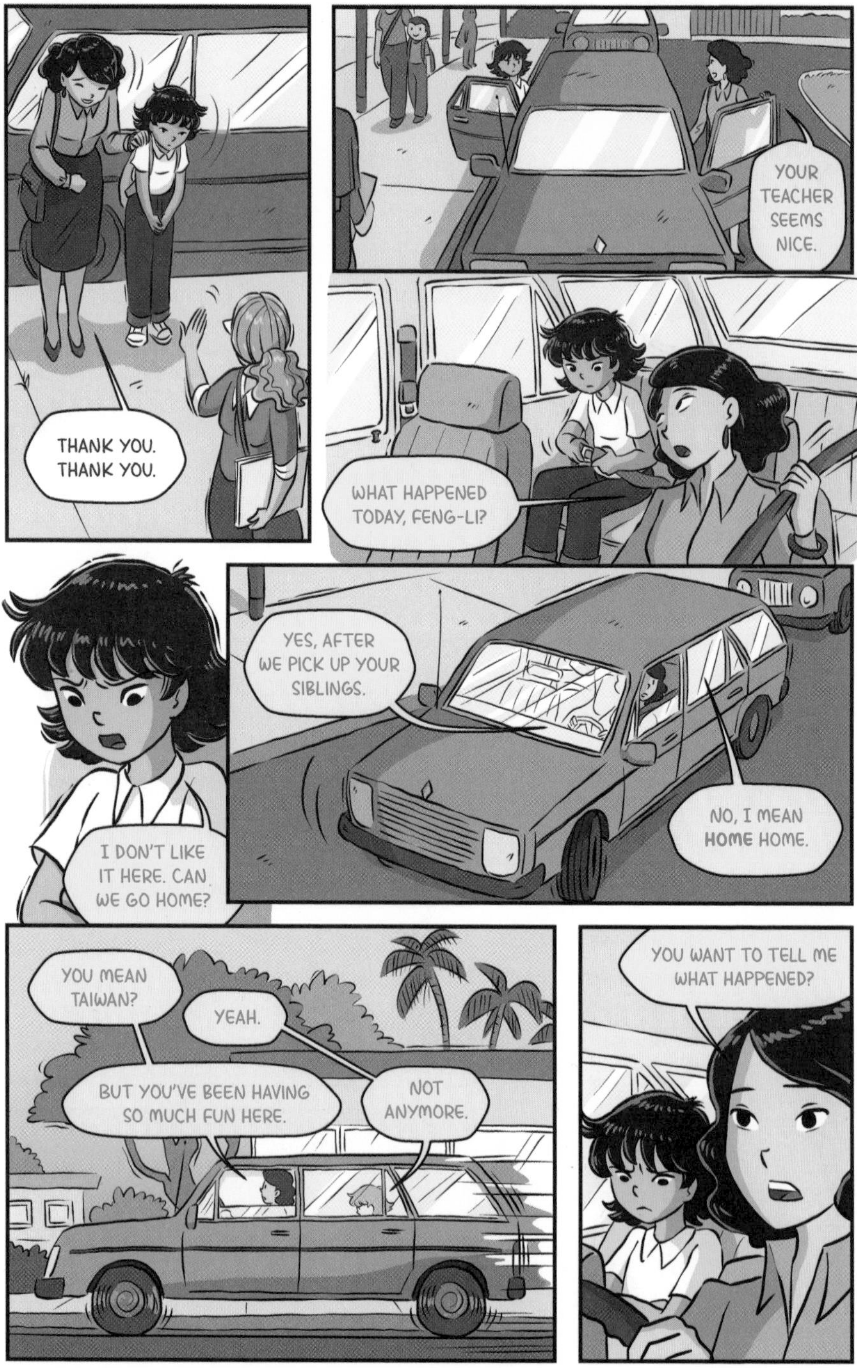
THANK YOU. THANK YOU.
YOUR TEACHER SEEMS NICE.
WHAT HAPPENED TODAY, FENG-LI?
I DON'T LIKE IT HERE. CAN WE GO HOME?
YES, AFTER WE PICK UP YOUR SIBLINGS.
NO, I MEAN **HOME** HOME.
YOU MEAN TAIWAN?
YEAH.
BUT YOU'VE BEEN HAVING SO MUCH FUN HERE.
NOT ANYMORE.
YOU WANT TO TELL ME WHAT HAPPENED?

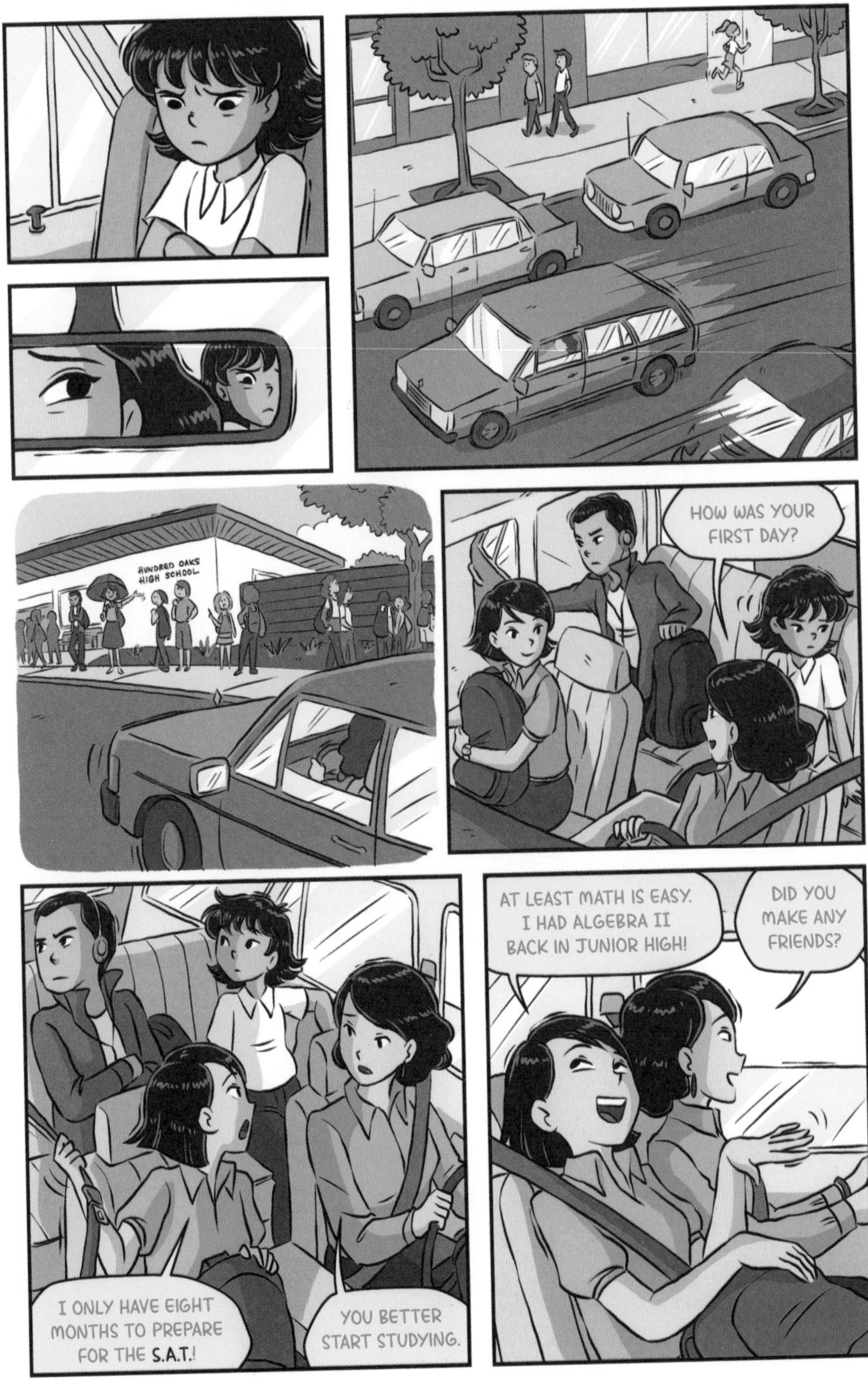
HUNDRED OAKS HIGH SCHOOL
HOW WAS YOUR FIRST DAY?
I ONLY HAVE EIGHT MONTHS TO PREPARE FOR THE S.A.T.!
YOU BETTER START STUDYING.
AT LEAST MATH IS EASY. I HAD ALGEBRA II BACK IN JUNIOR HIGH!
DID YOU MAKE ANY FRIENDS?

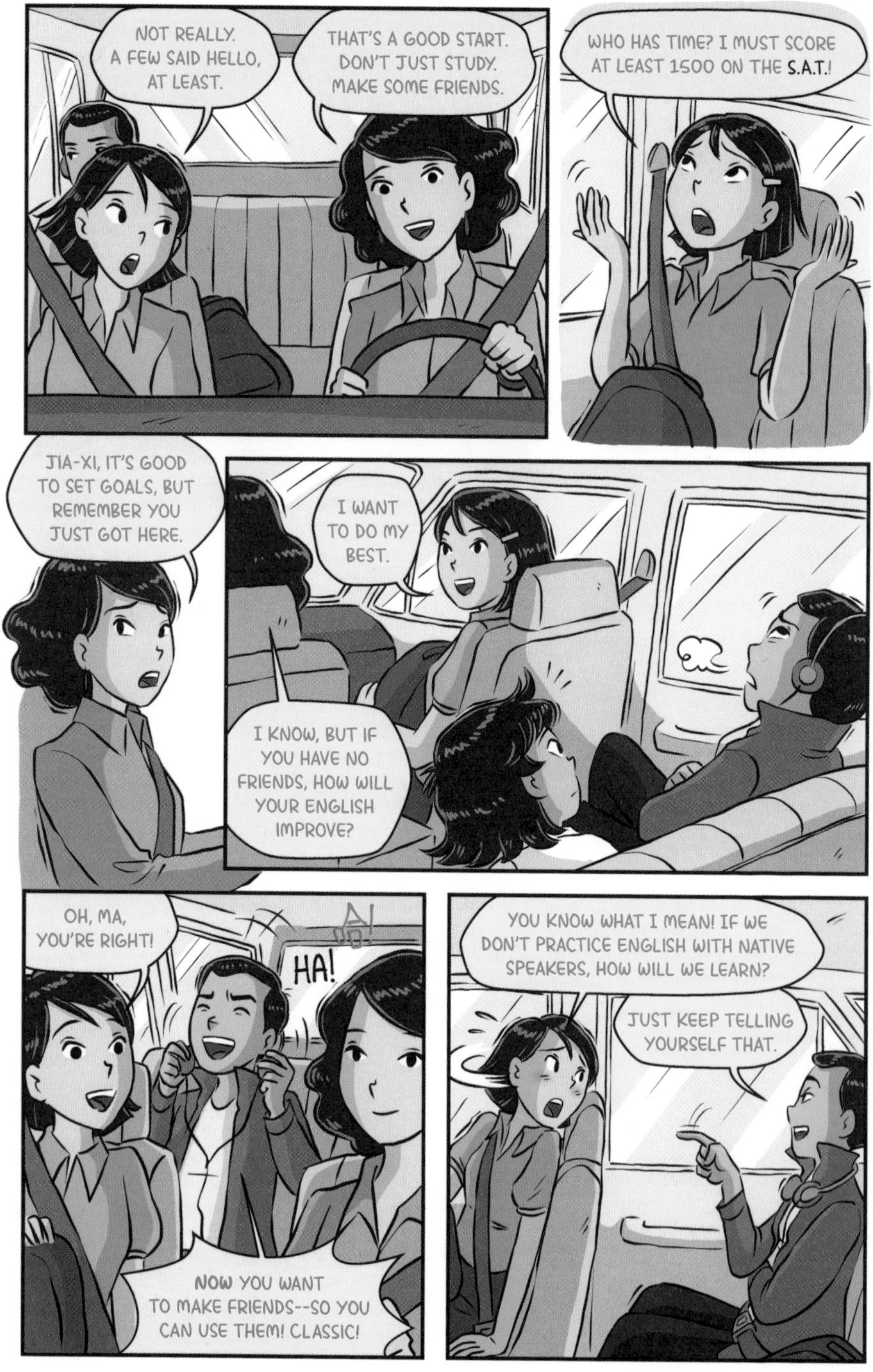
NOT REALLY. A FEW SAID HELLO, AT LEAST.
THAT'S A GOOD START. DON'T JUST STUDY. MAKE SOME FRIENDS.
WHO HAS TIME? I MUST SCORE AT LEAST 1500 ON THE S.A.T.!
JIA-XI, IT'S GOOD TO SET GOALS, BUT REMEMBER YOU JUST GOT HERE.
I WANT TO DO MY BEST.
I KNOW, BUT IF YOU HAVE NO FRIENDS, HOW WILL YOUR ENGLISH IMPROVE?
OH, MA, YOU'RE RIGHT!
HA!
NOW YOU WANT TO MAKE FRIENDS--SO YOU CAN USE THEM! CLASSIC!
YOU KNOW WHAT I MEAN! IF WE DON'T PRACTICE ENGLISH WITH NATIVE SPEAKERS, HOW WILL WE LEARN?
JUST KEEP TELLING YOURSELF THAT.

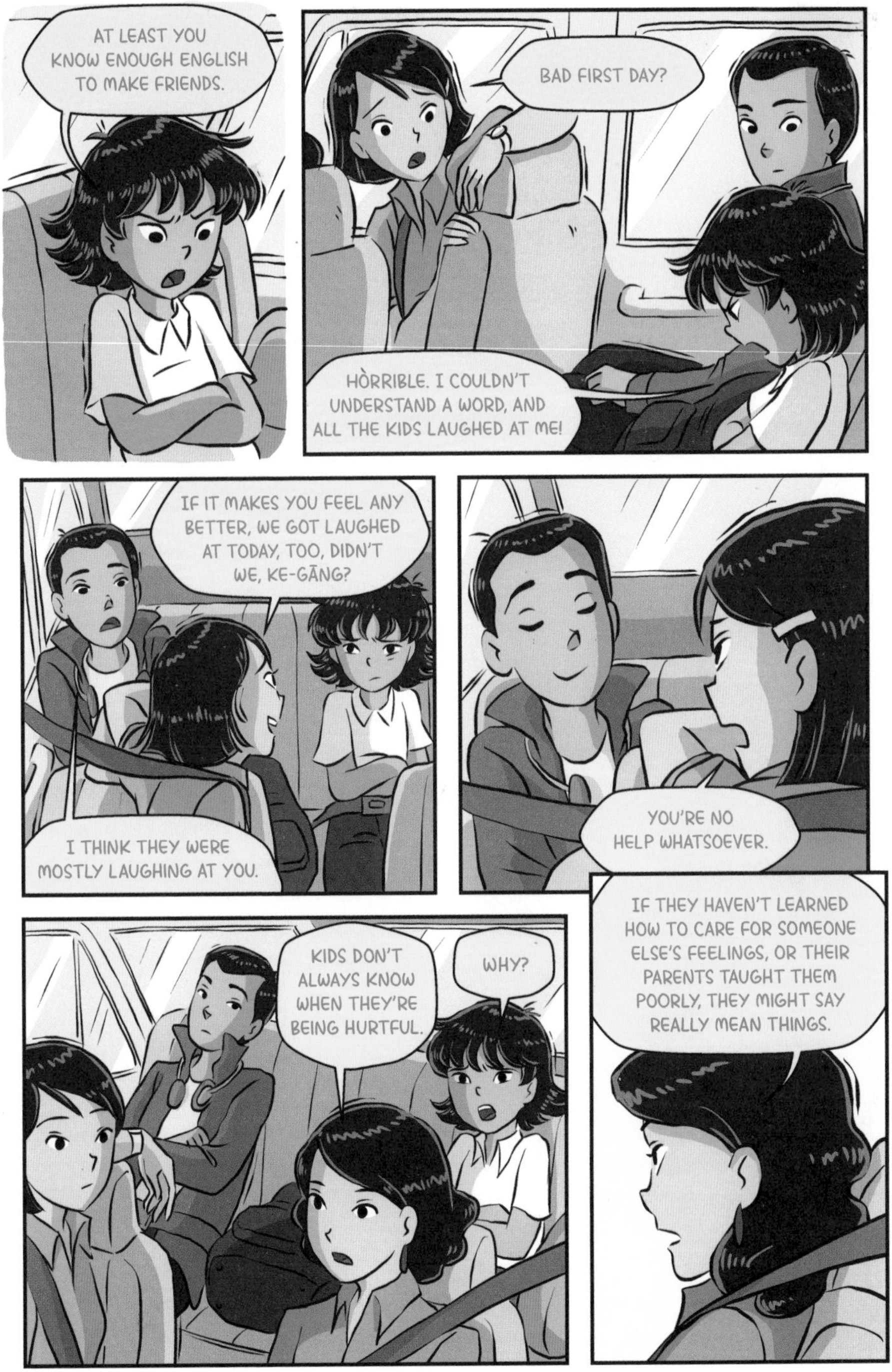
AT LEAST YOU KNOW ENOUGH ENGLISH TO MAKE FRIENDS.
BAD FIRST DAY?
HÒRRIBLE. I COULDN'T UNDERSTAND A WORD, AND ALL THE KIDS LAUGHED AT ME!
IF IT MAKES YOU FEEL ANY BETTER, WE GOT LAUGHED AT TODAY, TOO, DIDN'T WE, KE-GĀNG?
I THINK THEY WERE MOSTLY LAUGHING AT YOU.
YOU'RE NO HELP WHATSOEVER.
KIDS DON'T ALWAYS KNOW WHEN THEY'RE BEING HURTFUL.
WHY?
IF THEY HAVEN'T LEARNED HOW TO CARE FOR SOMEONE ELSE'S FEELINGS, OR THEIR PARENTS TAUGHT THEM POORLY, THEY MIGHT SAY REALLY MEAN THINGS.

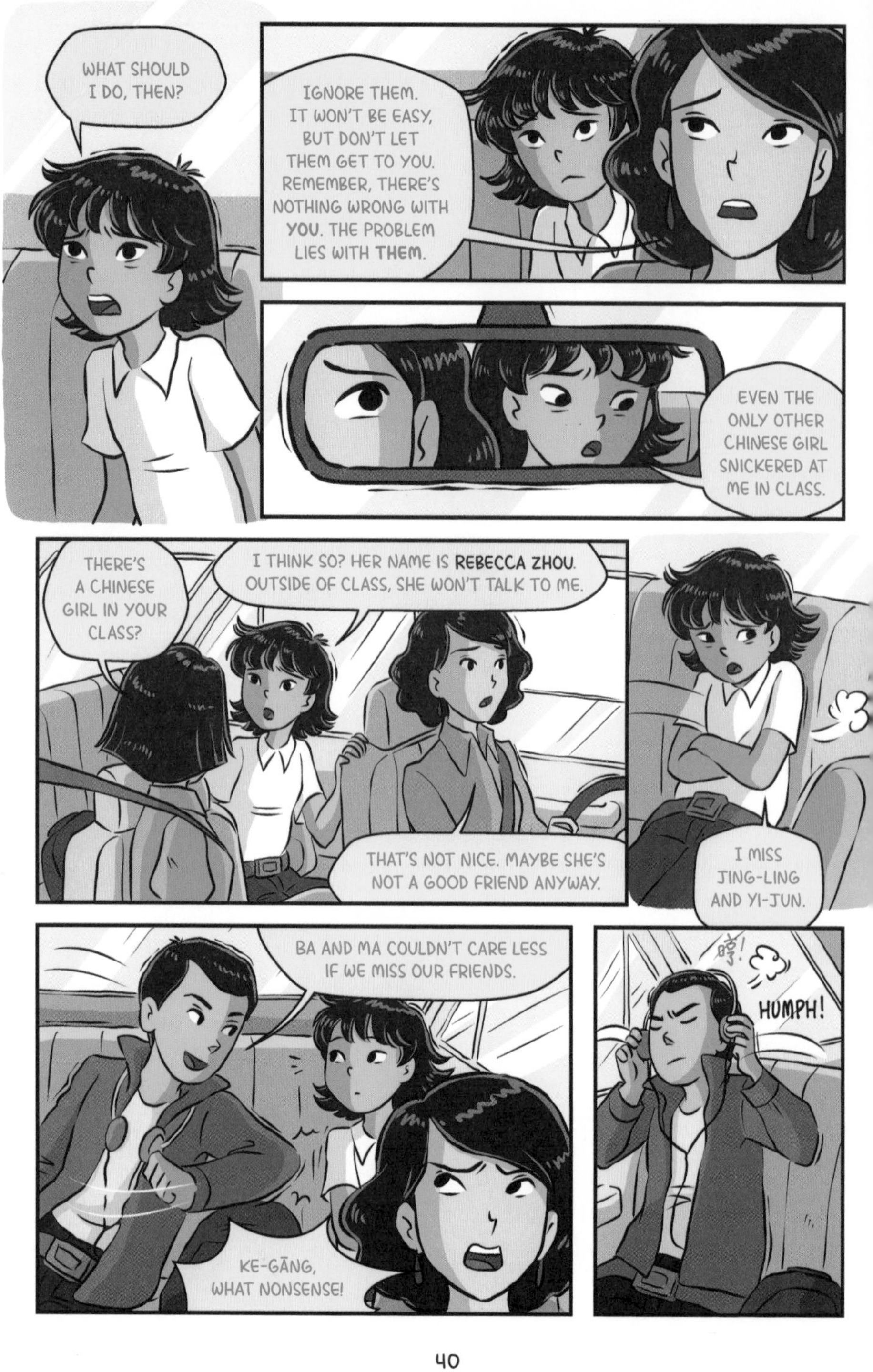
WHAT SHOULD I DO, THEN?
IGNORE THEM. IT WON'T BE EASY, BUT DON'T LET THEM GET TO YOU. REMEMBER, THERE'S NOTHING WRONG WITH **YOU**. THE PROBLEM LIES WITH **THEM**.
EVEN THE ONLY OTHER CHINESE GIRL SNICKERED AT ME IN CLASS.
THERE'S A CHINESE GIRL IN YOUR CLASS?
I THINK SO? HER NAME IS **REBECCA ZHOU**. OUTSIDE OF CLASS, SHE WON'T TALK TO ME.
THAT'S NOT NICE. MAYBE SHE'S NOT A GOOD FRIEND ANYWAY.
I MISS JING-LING AND YI-JUN.
BA AND MA COULDN'T CARE LESS IF WE MISS OUR FRIENDS.
KE-GĀNG, WHAT NONSENSE!
哼!
HUMPH!

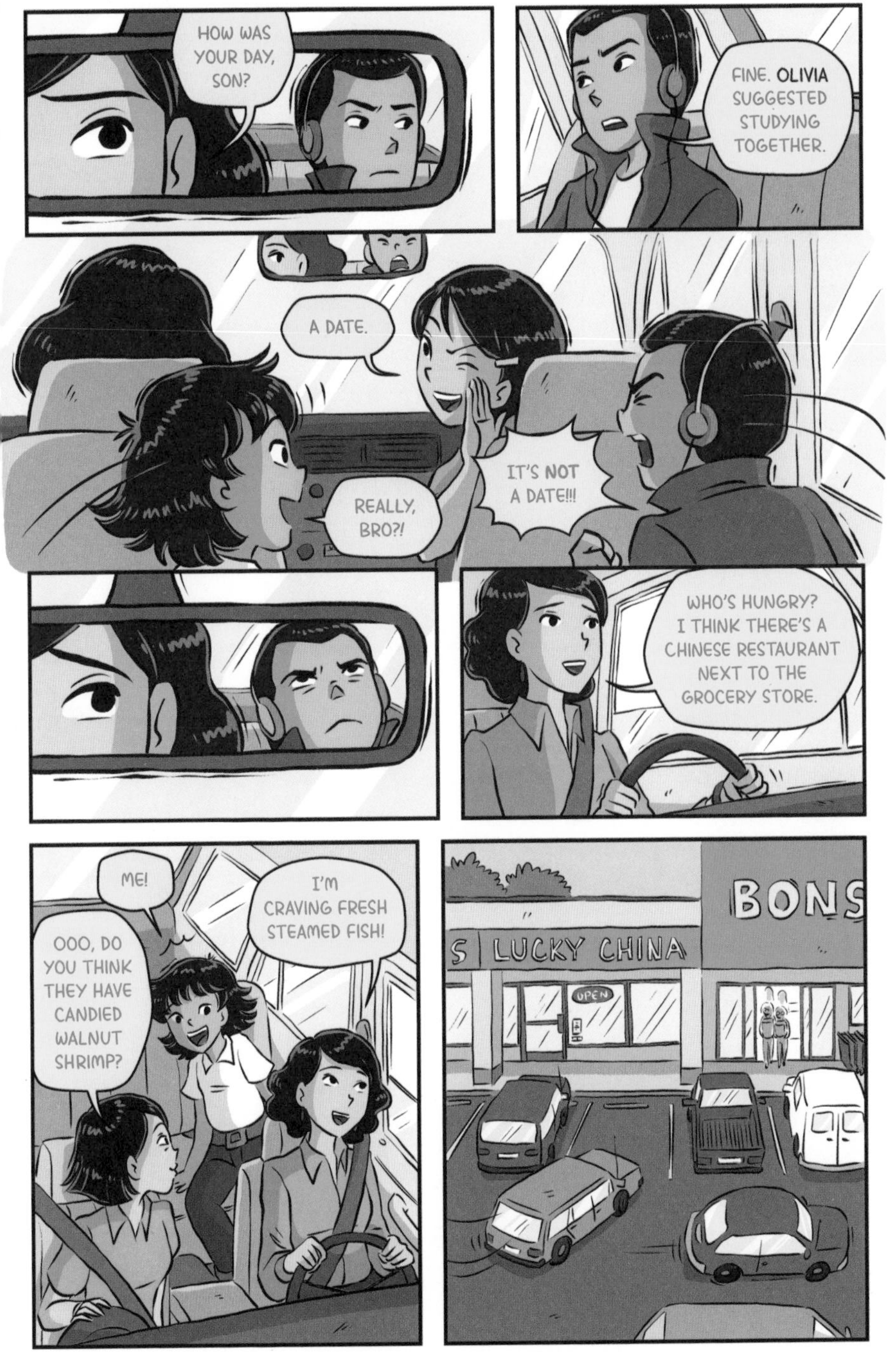
HOW WAS YOUR DAY, SON?
FINE. OLIVIA SUGGESTED STUDYING TOGETHER.
A DATE.
REALLY, BRO?!
IT'S NOT A DATE!!!
WHO'S HUNGRY? I THINK THERE'S A CHINESE RESTAURANT NEXT TO THE GROCERY STORE.
ME!
I'M CRAVING FRESH STEAMED FISH!
OOO, DO YOU THINK THEY HAVE CANDIED WALNUT SHRIMP?
S LUCKY CHINA
OPEN
BONS

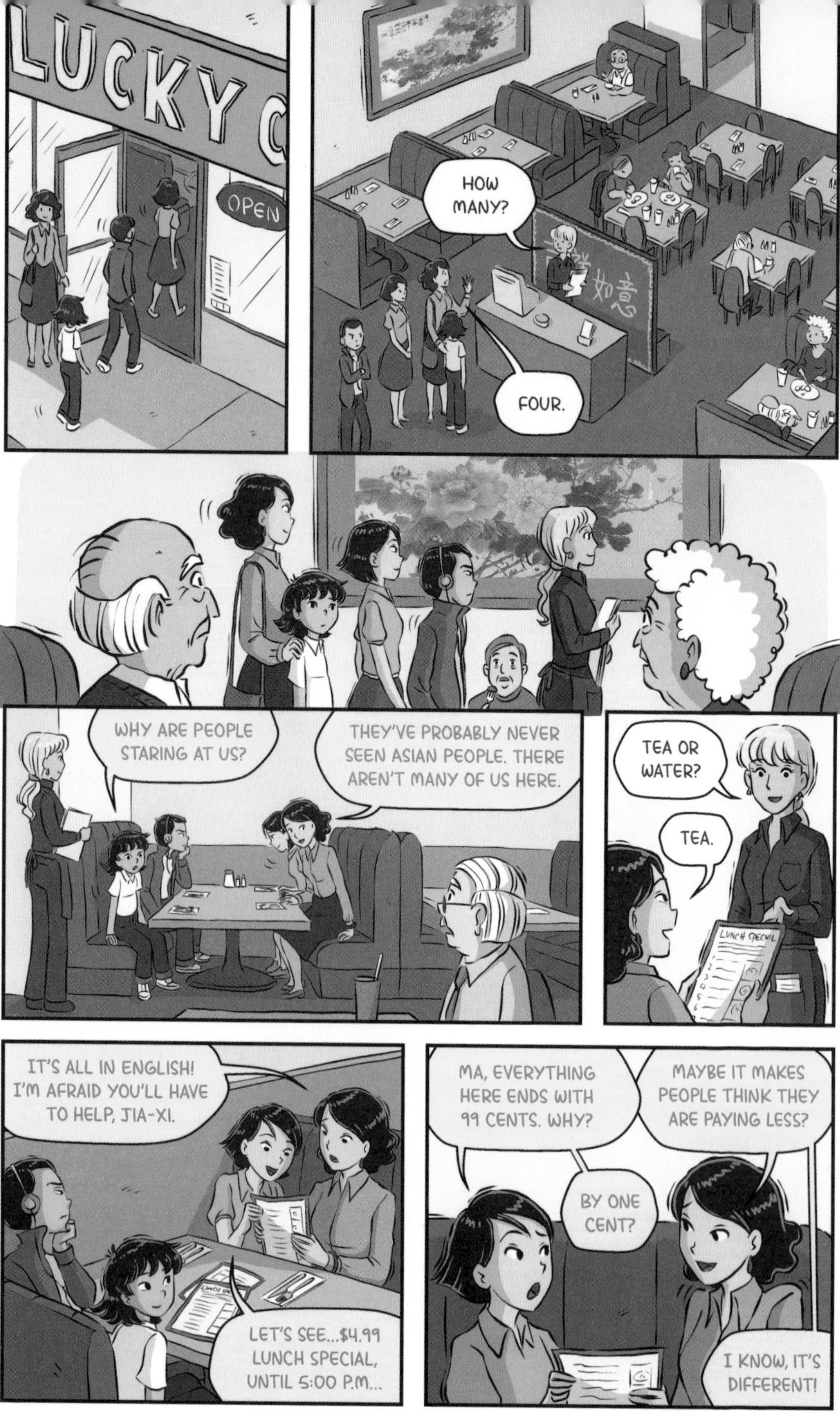
LUCKY C
OPEN
HOW MANY?
FOUR.
如意
WHY ARE PEOPLE STARING AT US?
THEY'VE PROBABLY NEVER SEEN ASIAN PEOPLE. THERE AREN'T MANY OF US HERE.
TEA OR WATER?
TEA.
LUNCH SPECIAL
IT'S ALL IN ENGLISH! I'M AFRAID YOU'LL HAVE TO HELP, JIA-XI.
LET'S SEE...$4.99 LUNCH SPECIAL, UNTIL 5:00 P.M...
MA, EVERYTHING HERE ENDS WITH 99 CENTS. WHY?
BY ONE CENT?
MAYBE IT MAKES PEOPLE THINK THEY ARE PAYING LESS?
I KNOW, IT'S DIFFERENT!

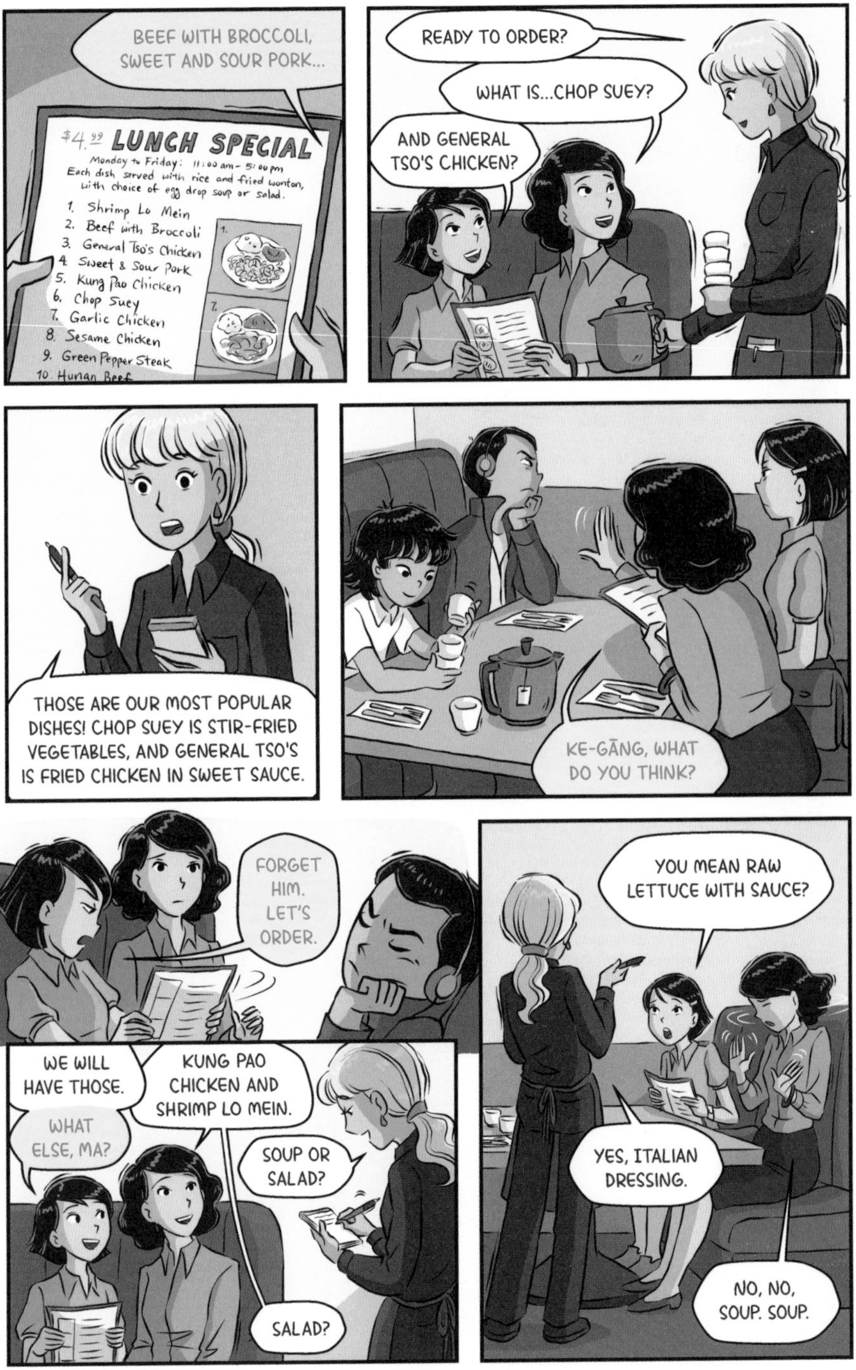

BEEF WITH BROCCOLI, SWEET AND SOUR PORK...
$4.99 LUNCH SPECIAL
Monday to Friday: 11:00 am - 5:00 pm
Each dish served with rice and fried wonton, with choice of egg drop soup or salad.
1. Shrimp Lo Mein
2. Beef with Broccoli
3. General Tso's Chicken
4. Sweet & Sour Pork
5. Kung Pao Chicken
6. Chop Suey
7. Garlic Chicken
8. Sesame Chicken
9. Green Pepper Steak
10. Hunan Beef
READY TO ORDER?
WHAT IS...CHOP SUEY?
AND GENERAL TSO'S CHICKEN?
THOSE ARE OUR MOST POPULAR DISHES! CHOP SUEY IS STIR-FRIED VEGETABLES, AND GENERAL TSO'S IS FRIED CHICKEN IN SWEET SAUCE.
KE-GĀNG, WHAT DO YOU THINK?
FORGET HIM. LET'S ORDER.
WE WILL HAVE THOSE.
WHAT ELSE, MA?
KUNG PAO CHICKEN AND SHRIMP LO MEIN.
SOUP OR SALAD?
SALAD?
YOU MEAN RAW LETTUCE WITH SAUCE?
YES, ITALIAN DRESSING.
NO, NO, SOUP. SOUP.

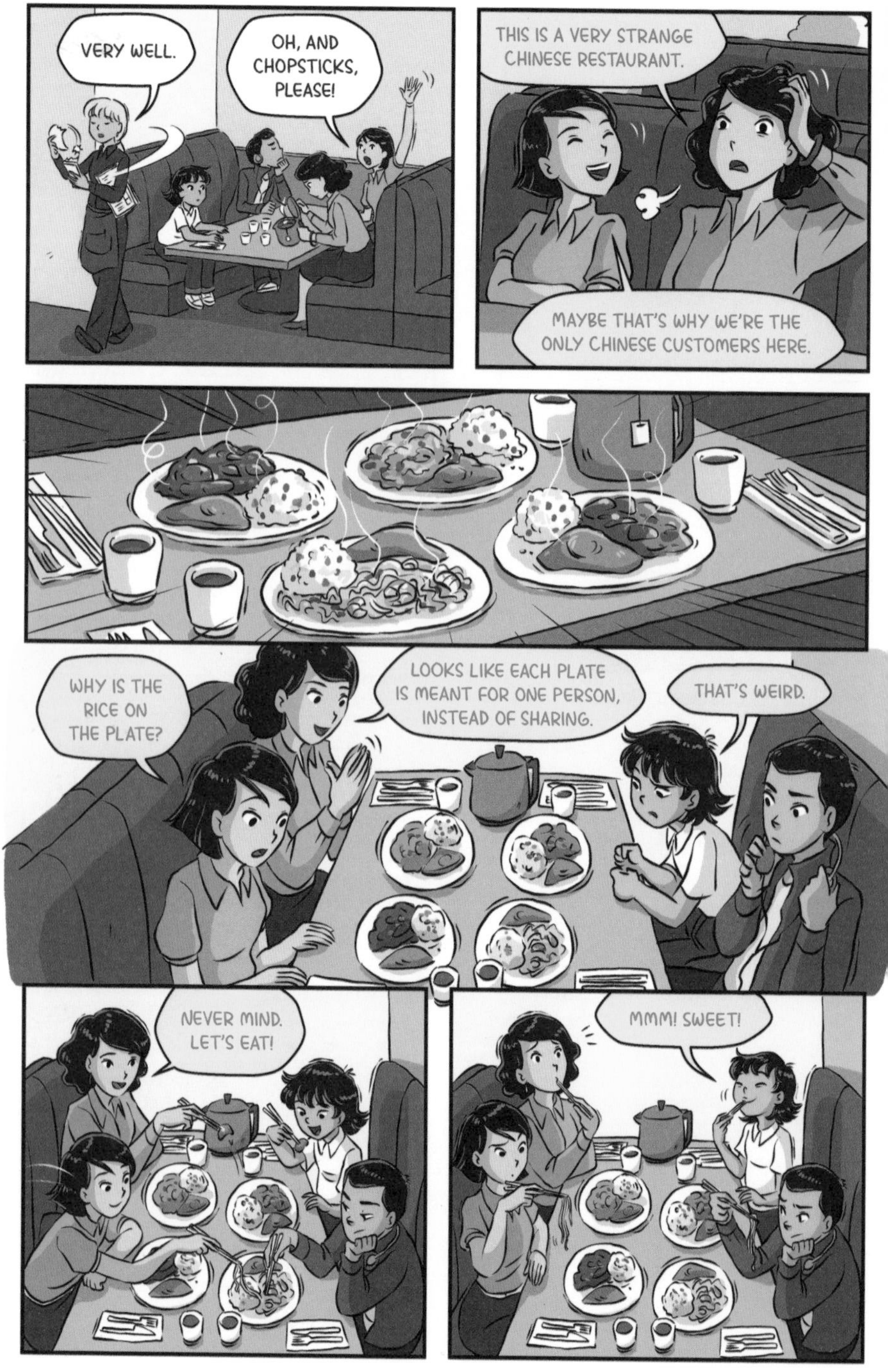
VERY WELL.
OH, AND CHOPSTICKS, PLEASE!
THIS IS A VERY STRANGE CHINESE RESTAURANT.
MAYBE THAT'S WHY WE'RE THE ONLY CHINESE CUSTOMERS HERE.
WHY IS THE RICE ON THE PLATE?
LOOKS LIKE EACH PLATE IS MEANT FOR ONE PERSON, INSTEAD OF SHARING.
THAT'S WEIRD.
NEVER MIND. LET'S EAT!
MMM! SWEET!

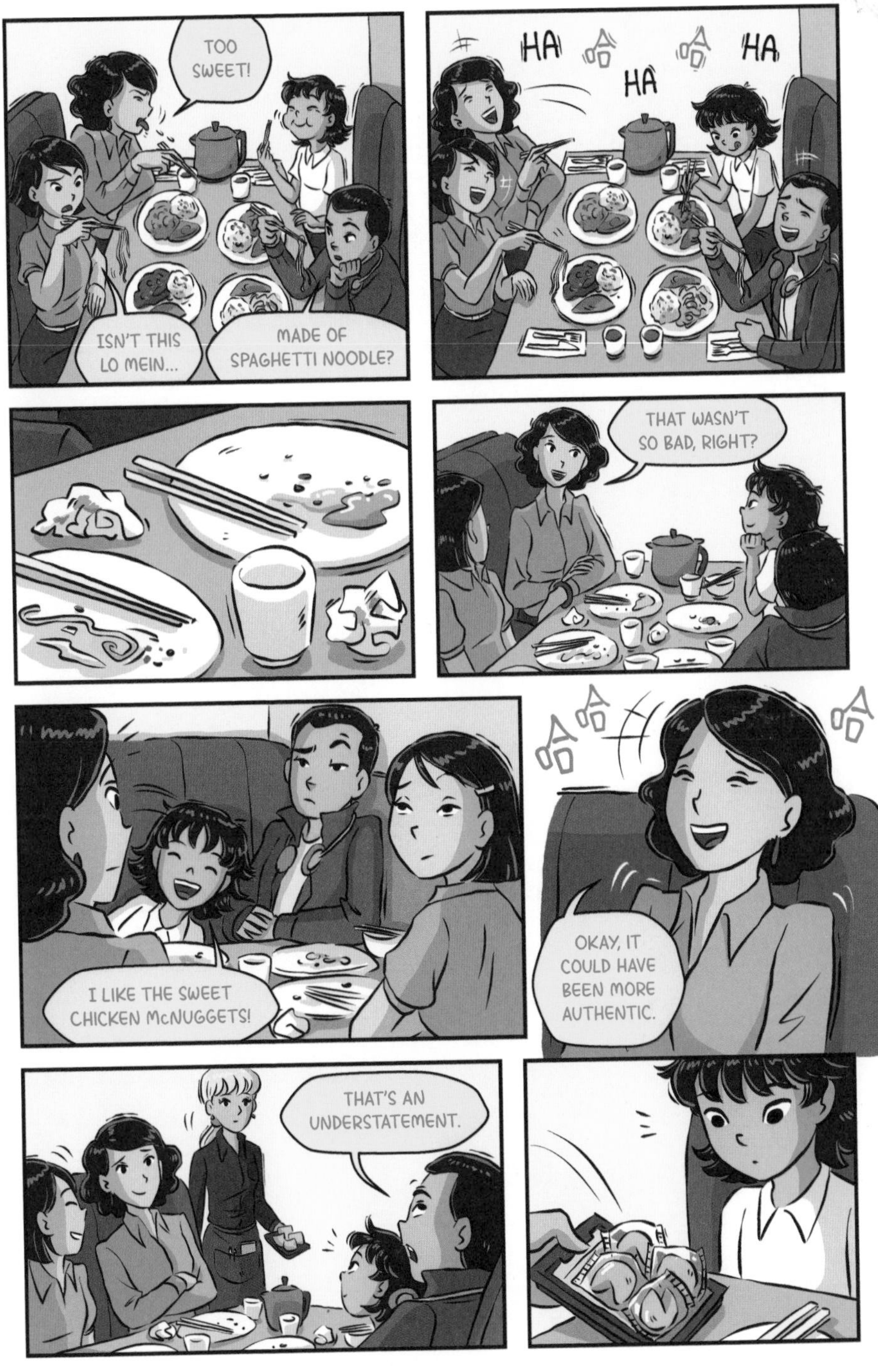

TOO SWEET!
ISN'T THIS LO MEIN...
MADE OF SPAGHETTI NOODLE?
HA
哈
HA
哈
HA
THAT WASN'T SO BAD, RIGHT?
I LIKE THE SWEET CHICKEN McNUGGETS!
哈
哈
哈
OKAY, IT COULD HAVE BEEN MORE AUTHENTIC.
THAT'S AN UNDERSTATEMENT.

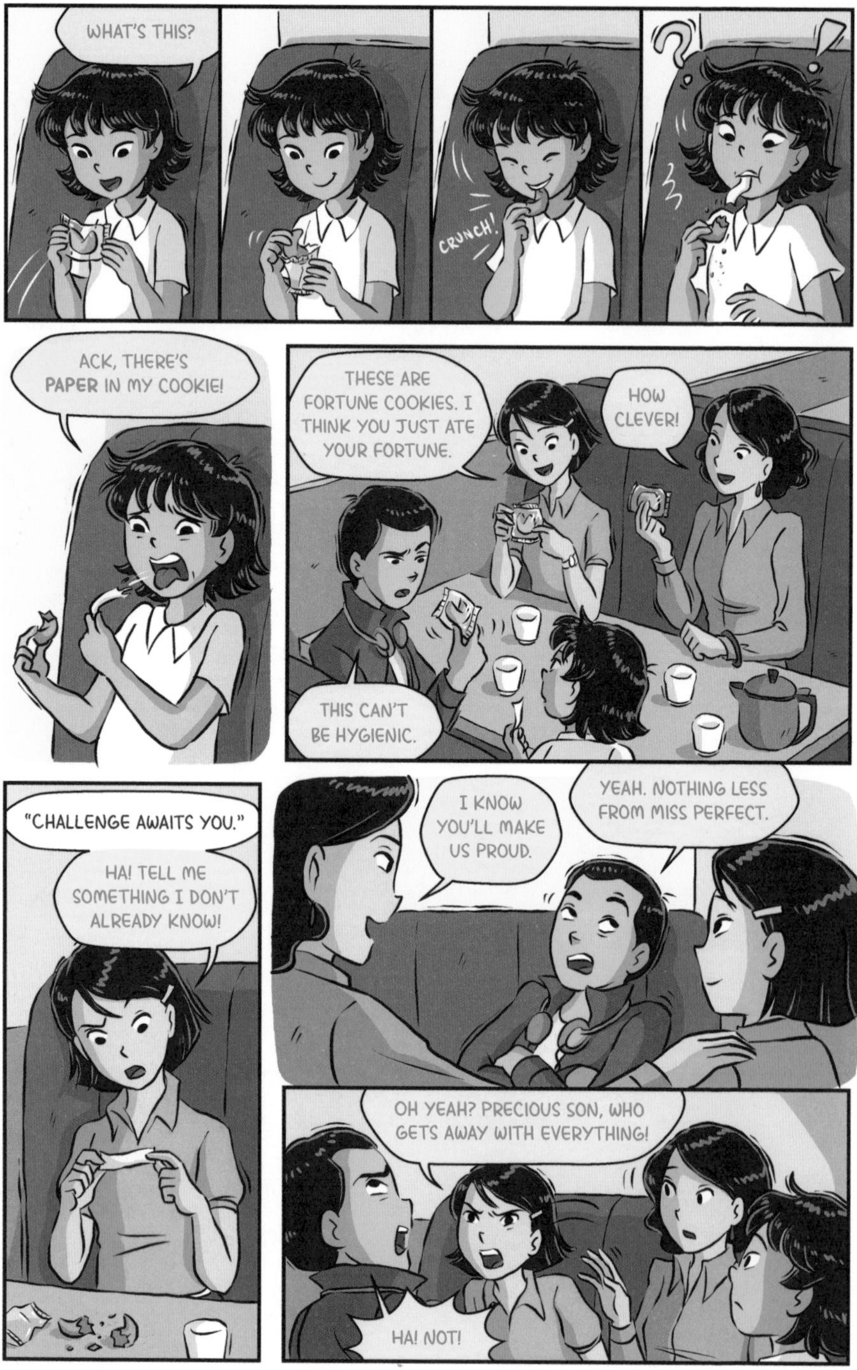
WHAT'S THIS?
?
!
CRUNCH!
ACK, THERE'S PAPER IN MY COOKIE!
THESE ARE FORTUNE COOKIES. I THINK YOU JUST ATE YOUR FORTUNE.
HOW CLEVER!
THIS CAN'T BE HYGIENIC.
"CHALLENGE AWAITS YOU."
HA! TELL ME SOMETHING I DON'T ALREADY KNOW!
I KNOW YOU'LL MAKE US PROUD.
YEAH. NOTHING LESS FROM MISS PERFECT.
OH YEAH? PRECIOUS SON, WHO GETS AWAY WITH EVERYTHING!
HA! NOT!

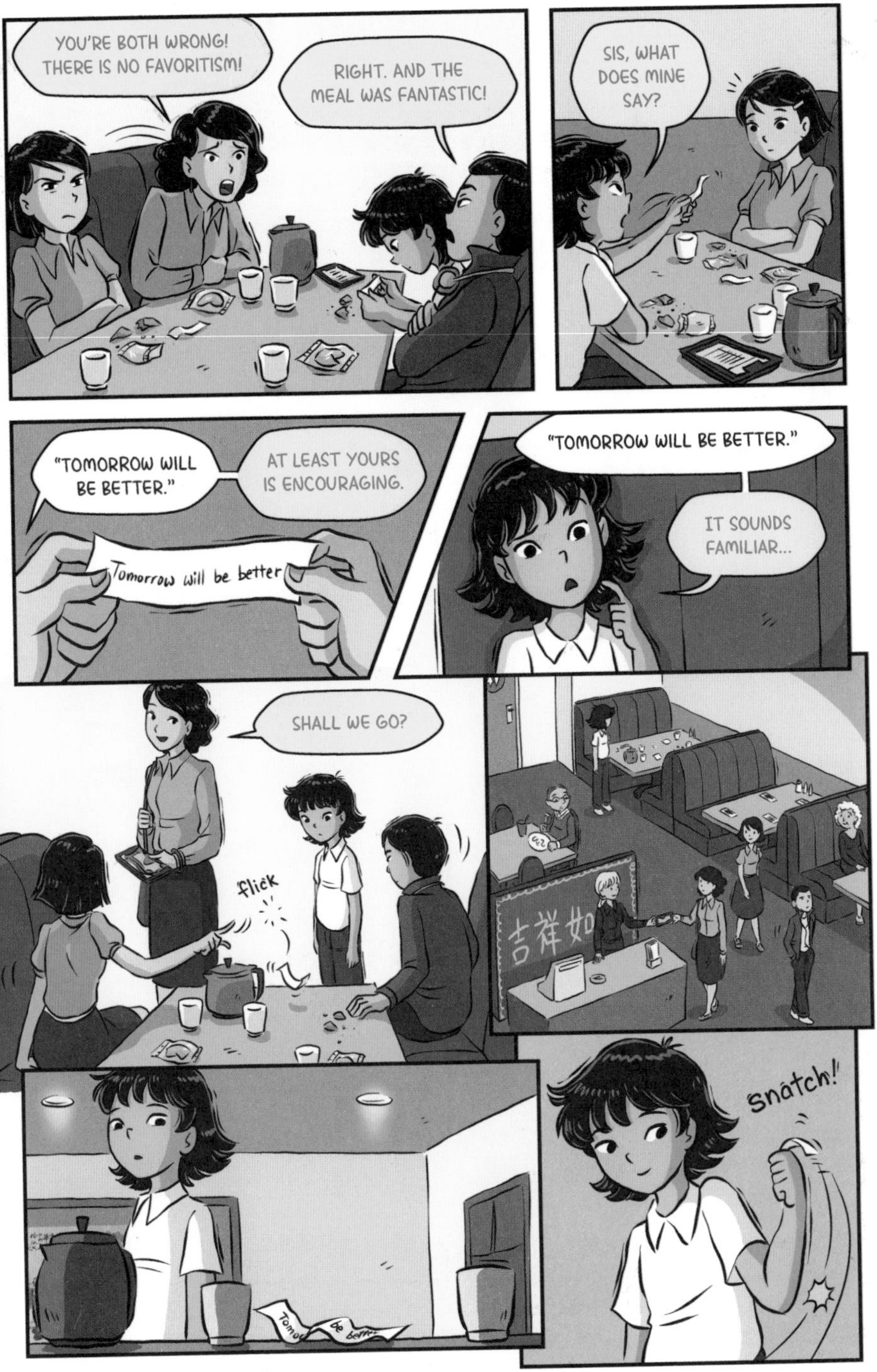
YOU'RE BOTH WRONG! THERE IS NO FAVORITISM!
RIGHT. AND THE MEAL WAS FANTASTIC!
SIS, WHAT DOES MINE SAY?
"TOMORROW WILL BE BETTER."
AT LEAST YOURS IS ENCOURAGING.
Tomorrow will be better
"TOMORROW WILL BE BETTER."
IT SOUNDS FAMILIAR...
SHALL WE GO?
flick
吉祥如
Snatch!

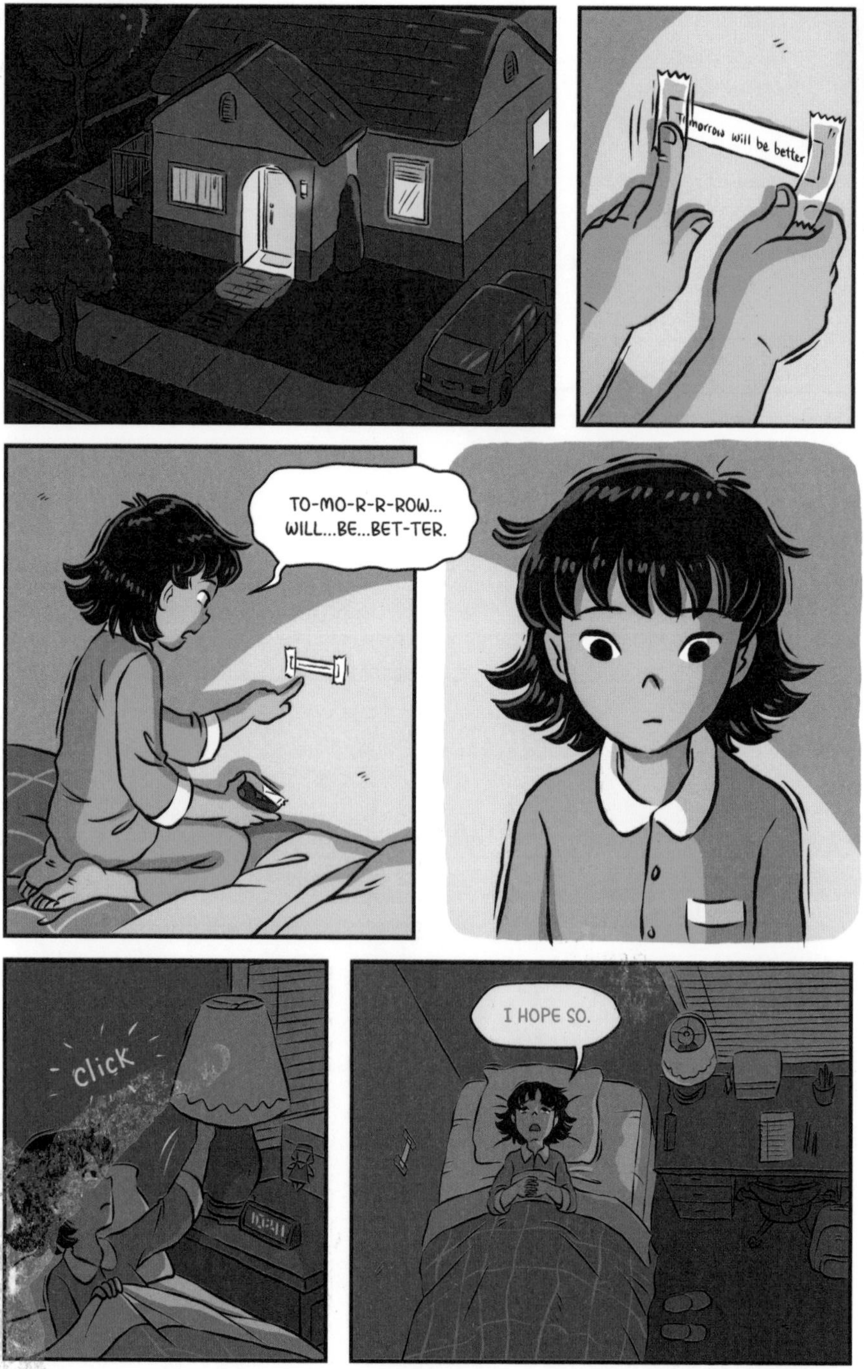
morrow will be better
TO-MO-R-R-ROW... WILL...BE...BET-TER.
click
I HOPE SO.

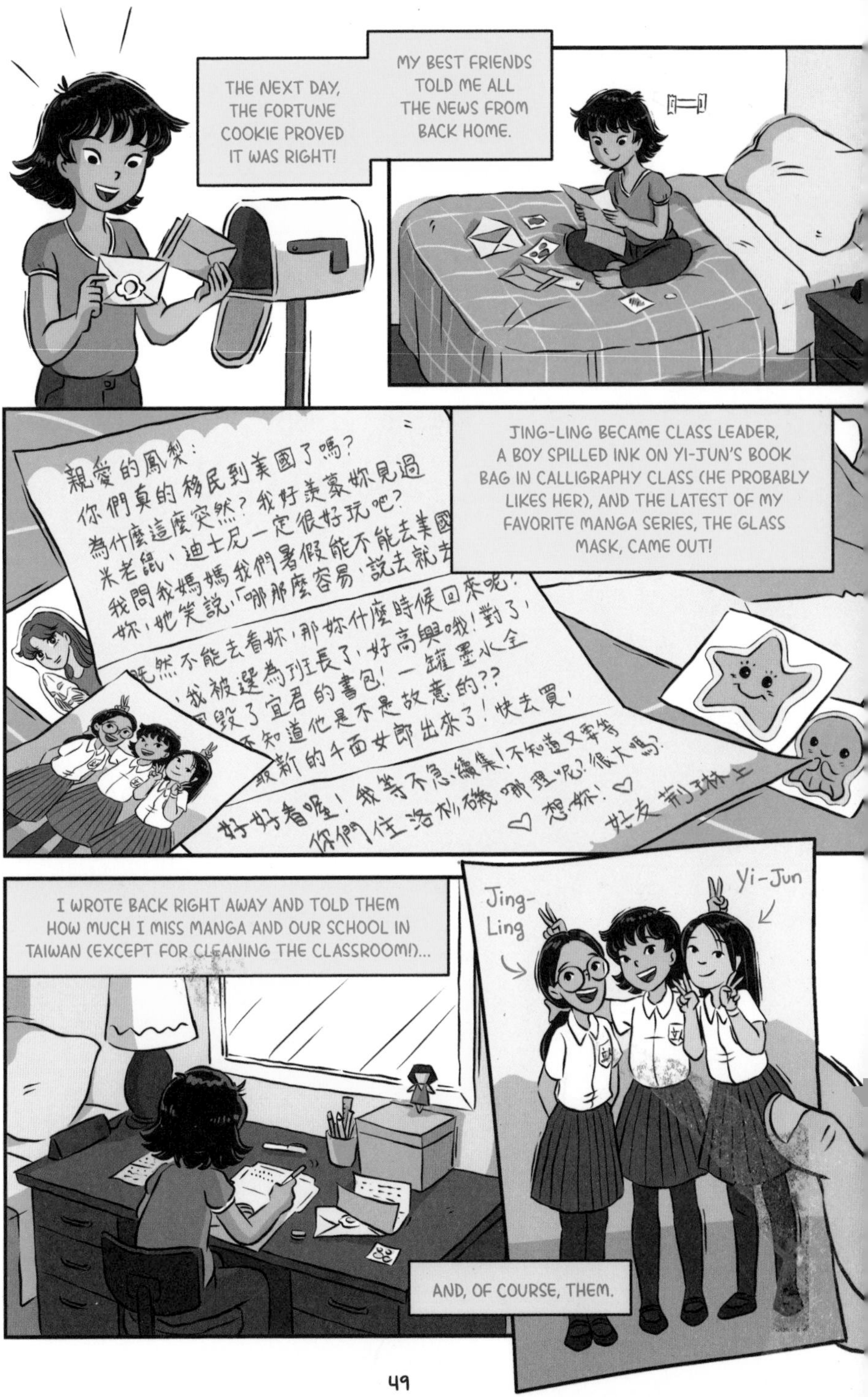
THE NEXT DAY, THE FORTUNE COOKIE PROVED IT WAS RIGHT!
MY BEST FRIENDS TOLD ME ALL THE NEWS FROM BACK HOME.
親愛的鳳梨：
你們真的移民到美國了嗎？
為什麼這麼突然？我好羨慕妳見過
米老鼠、迪士尼一定很好玩吧？
我問我媽媽我們暑假能不能去美國
妳，她笑說「哪那麼容易，說去就去
既然不能去看妳，那妳什麼時候回來呢？
，我被選為班長了，好高興哦！對了，
毀了宜君的書包！一罐墨水全
不知道他是不是故意的？？
最新的千面女郎出來了！快去買，
好好看喔！我等不急續集！不知道又要等
你們住洛杉磯哪裡呢？很大嗎？
♡ 想妳！♡
好友 荊琳 上
JING-LING BECAME CLASS LEADER, A BOY SPILLED INK ON YI-JUN'S BOOK BAG IN CALLIGRAPHY CLASS (HE PROBABLY LIKES HER), AND THE LATEST OF MY FAVORITE MANGA SERIES, THE GLASS MASK, CAME OUT!
I WROTE BACK RIGHT AWAY AND TOLD THEM HOW MUCH I MISS MANGA AND OUR SCHOOL IN TAIWAN (EXCEPT FOR CLEANING THE CLASSROOM!)...
Jing-Ling
Yi-Jun
AND, OF COURSE, THEM.

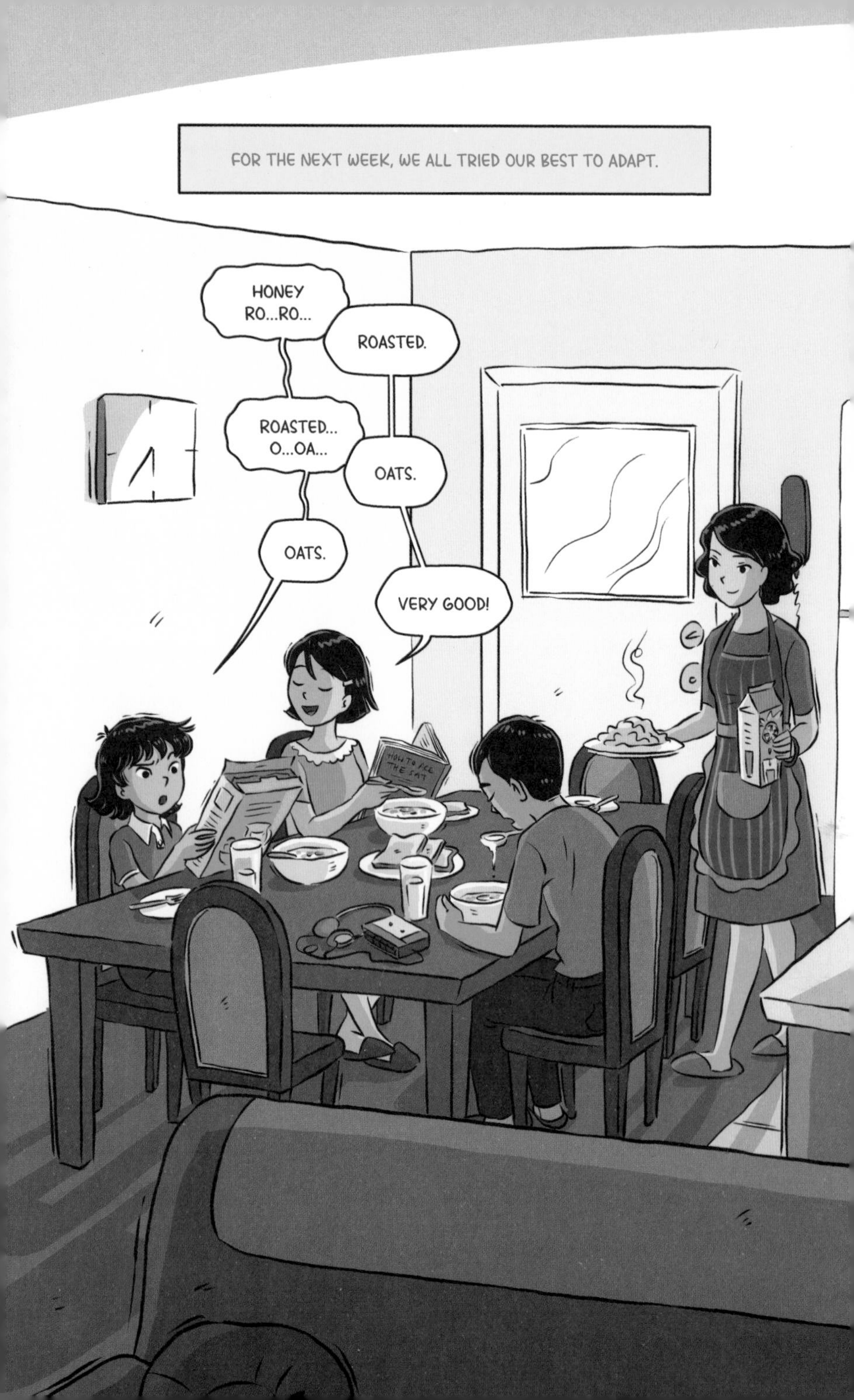
FOR THE NEXT WEEK, WE ALL TRIED OUR BEST TO ADAPT.
HONEY RO...RO...
ROASTED.
ROASTED... O...OA...
OATS.
OATS.
VERY GOOD!

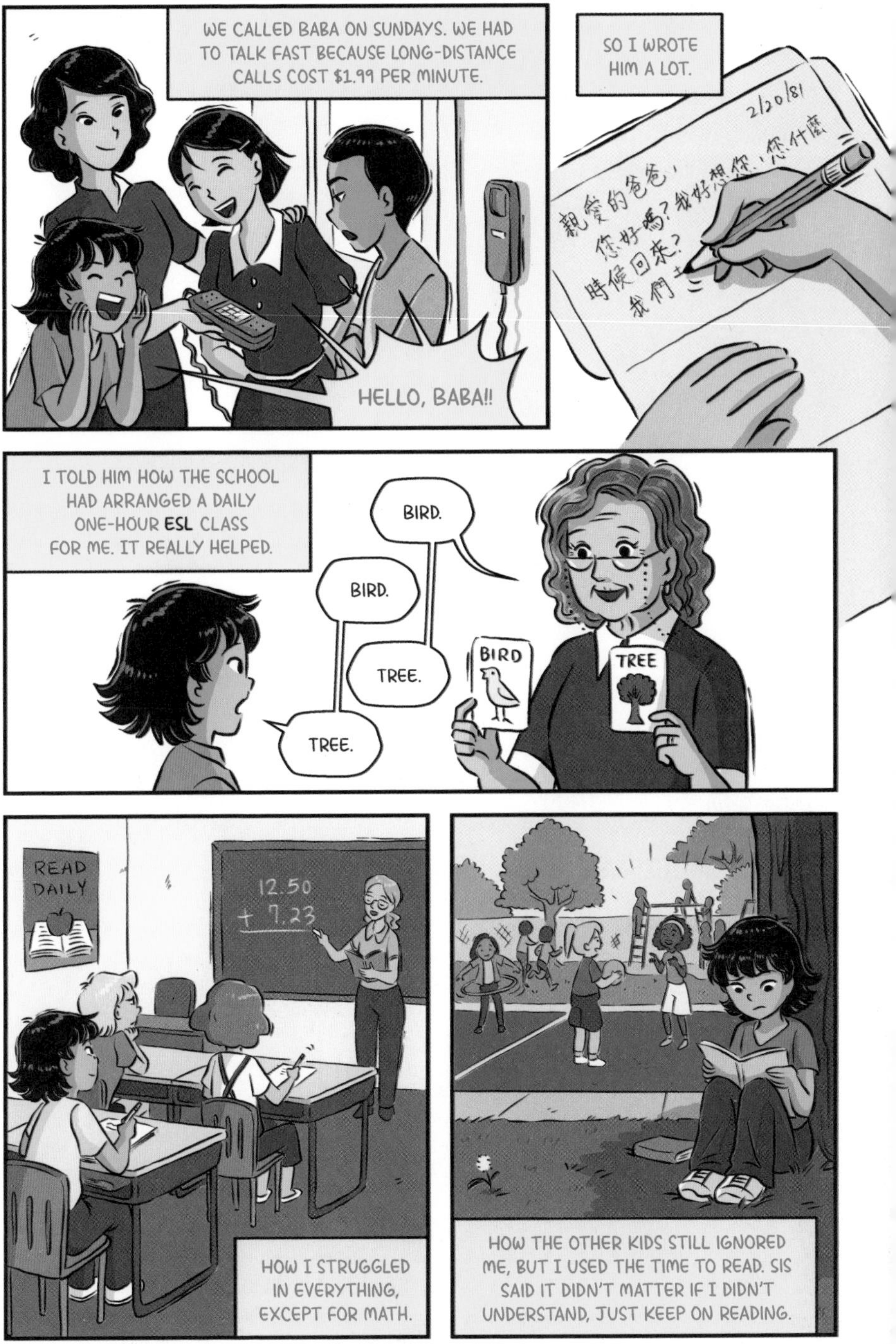
WE CALLED BABA ON SUNDAYS. WE HAD TO TALK FAST BECAUSE LONG-DISTANCE CALLS COST $1.99 PER MINUTE.
HELLO, BABA!!
SO I WROTE HIM A LOT.
2/20/81
親愛的爸爸，
您好嗎？我好想您，您什麼
時候回來？
我們
I TOLD HIM HOW THE SCHOOL HAD ARRANGED A DAILY ONE-HOUR **ESL** CLASS FOR ME. IT REALLY HELPED.
BIRD.
BIRD.
TREE.
TREE.
BIRD
TREE
READ DAILY
12.50
+ 7.23
HOW I STRUGGLED IN EVERYTHING, EXCEPT FOR MATH.
HOW THE OTHER KIDS STILL IGNORED ME, BUT I USED THE TIME TO READ. SIS SAID IT DIDN'T MATTER IF I DIDN'T UNDERSTAND, JUST KEEP ON READING.

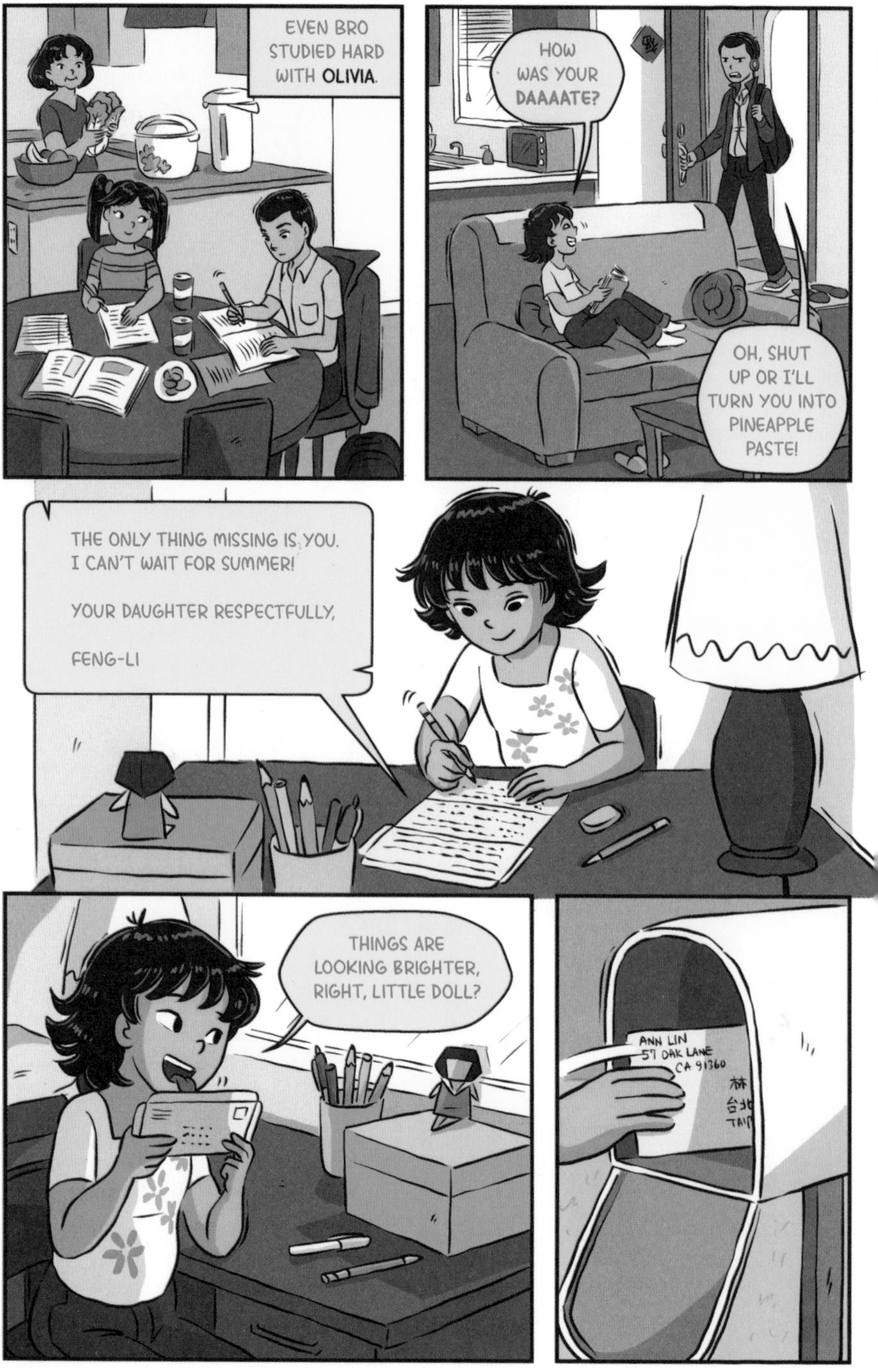
EVEN BRO STUDIED HARD WITH **OLIVIA**.
HOW WAS YOUR **DAAAATE?**
OH, SHUT UP OR I'LL TURN YOU INTO PINEAPPLE PASTE!
THE ONLY THING MISSING IS YOU. I CAN'T WAIT FOR SUMMER!
YOUR DAUGHTER RESPECTFULLY,
FENG-LI
THINGS ARE LOOKING BRIGHTER, RIGHT, LITTLE DOLL?
ANN LIN
57 OAK LANE
CA 91360
林
台北

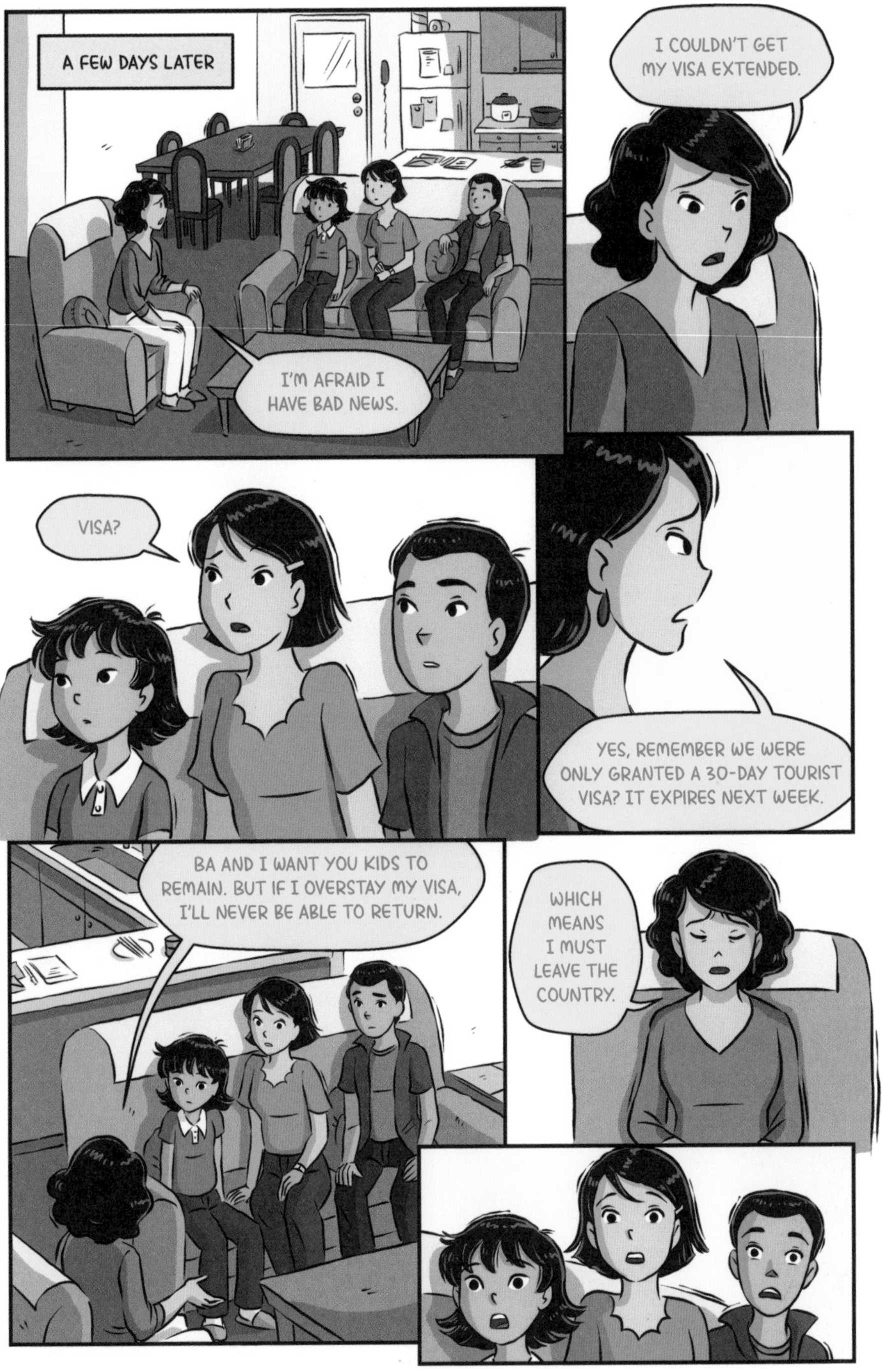
A FEW DAYS LATER
I'M AFRAID I HAVE BAD NEWS.
I COULDN'T GET MY VISA EXTENDED.
VISA?
YES, REMEMBER WE WERE ONLY GRANTED A 30-DAY TOURIST VISA? IT EXPIRES NEXT WEEK.
BA AND I WANT YOU KIDS TO REMAIN. BUT IF I OVERSTAY MY VISA, I'LL NEVER BE ABLE TO RETURN.
WHICH MEANS I MUST LEAVE THE COUNTRY.

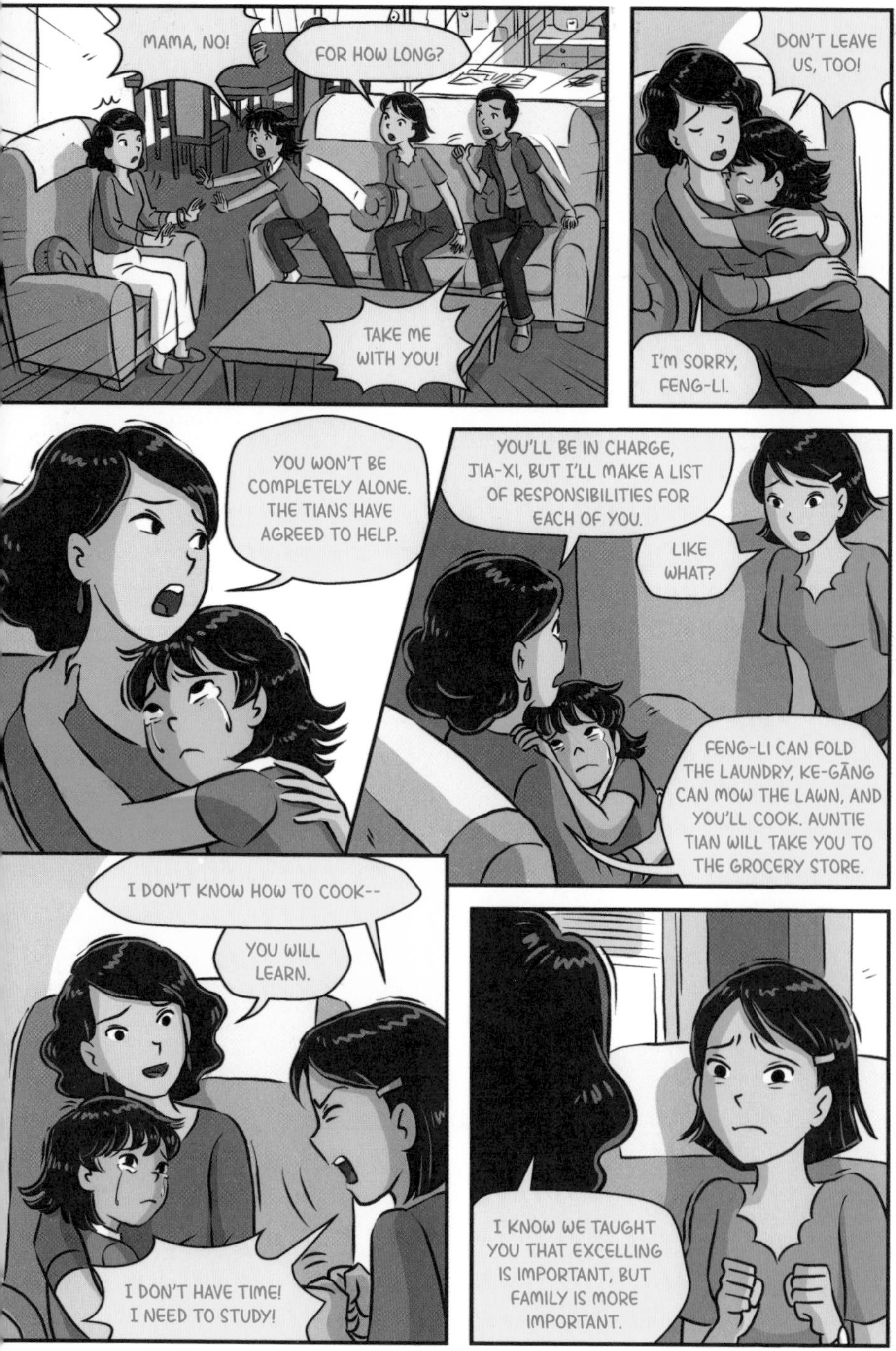
MAMA, NO!
FOR HOW LONG?
TAKE ME WITH YOU!
DON'T LEAVE US, TOO!
I'M SORRY, FENG-LI.
YOU WON'T BE COMPLETELY ALONE. THE TIANS HAVE AGREED TO HELP.
YOU'LL BE IN CHARGE, JIA-XI, BUT I'LL MAKE A LIST OF RESPONSIBILITIES FOR EACH OF YOU.
LIKE WHAT?
FENG-LI CAN FOLD THE LAUNDRY, KE-GĀNG CAN MOW THE LAWN, AND YOU'LL COOK. AUNTIE TIAN WILL TAKE YOU TO THE GROCERY STORE.
I DON'T KNOW HOW TO COOK--
YOU WILL LEARN.
I DON'T HAVE TIME! I NEED TO STUDY!
I KNOW WE TAUGHT YOU THAT EXCELLING IS IMPORTANT, BUT FAMILY IS MORE IMPORTANT.

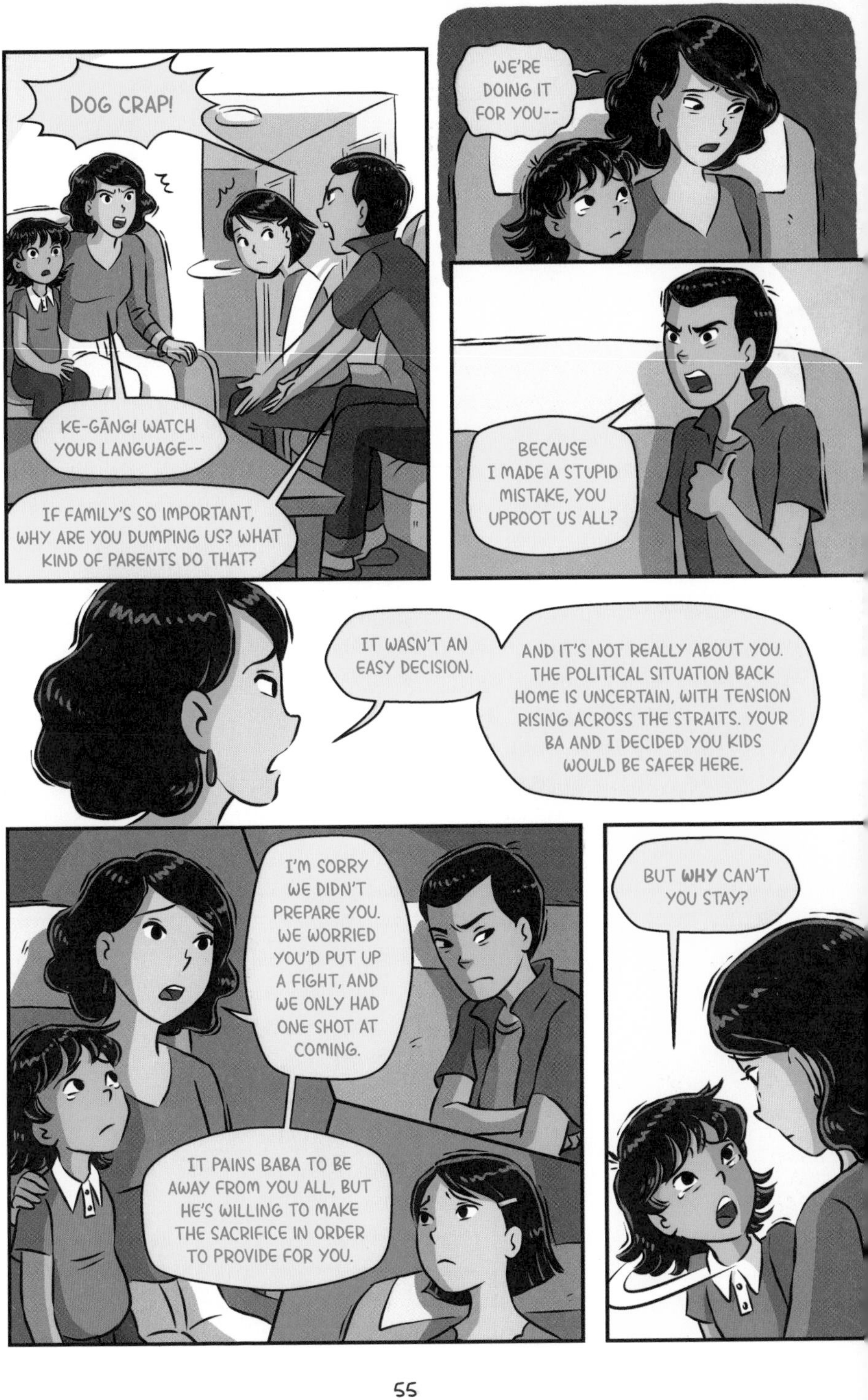
DOG CRAP!
KE-GĀNG! WATCH YOUR LANGUAGE--
IF FAMILY'S SO IMPORTANT, WHY ARE YOU DUMPING US? WHAT KIND OF PARENTS DO THAT?
WE'RE DOING IT FOR YOU--
BECAUSE I MADE A STUPID MISTAKE, YOU UPROOT US ALL?
IT WASN'T AN EASY DECISION.
AND IT'S NOT REALLY ABOUT YOU. THE POLITICAL SITUATION BACK HOME IS UNCERTAIN, WITH TENSION RISING ACROSS THE STRAITS. YOUR BA AND I DECIDED YOU KIDS WOULD BE SAFER HERE.
I'M SORRY WE DIDN'T PREPARE YOU. WE WORRIED YOU'D PUT UP A FIGHT, AND WE ONLY HAD ONE SHOT AT COMING.
IT PAINS BABA TO BE AWAY FROM YOU ALL, BUT HE'S WILLING TO MAKE THE SACRIFICE IN ORDER TO PROVIDE FOR YOU.
BUT WHY CAN'T YOU STAY?

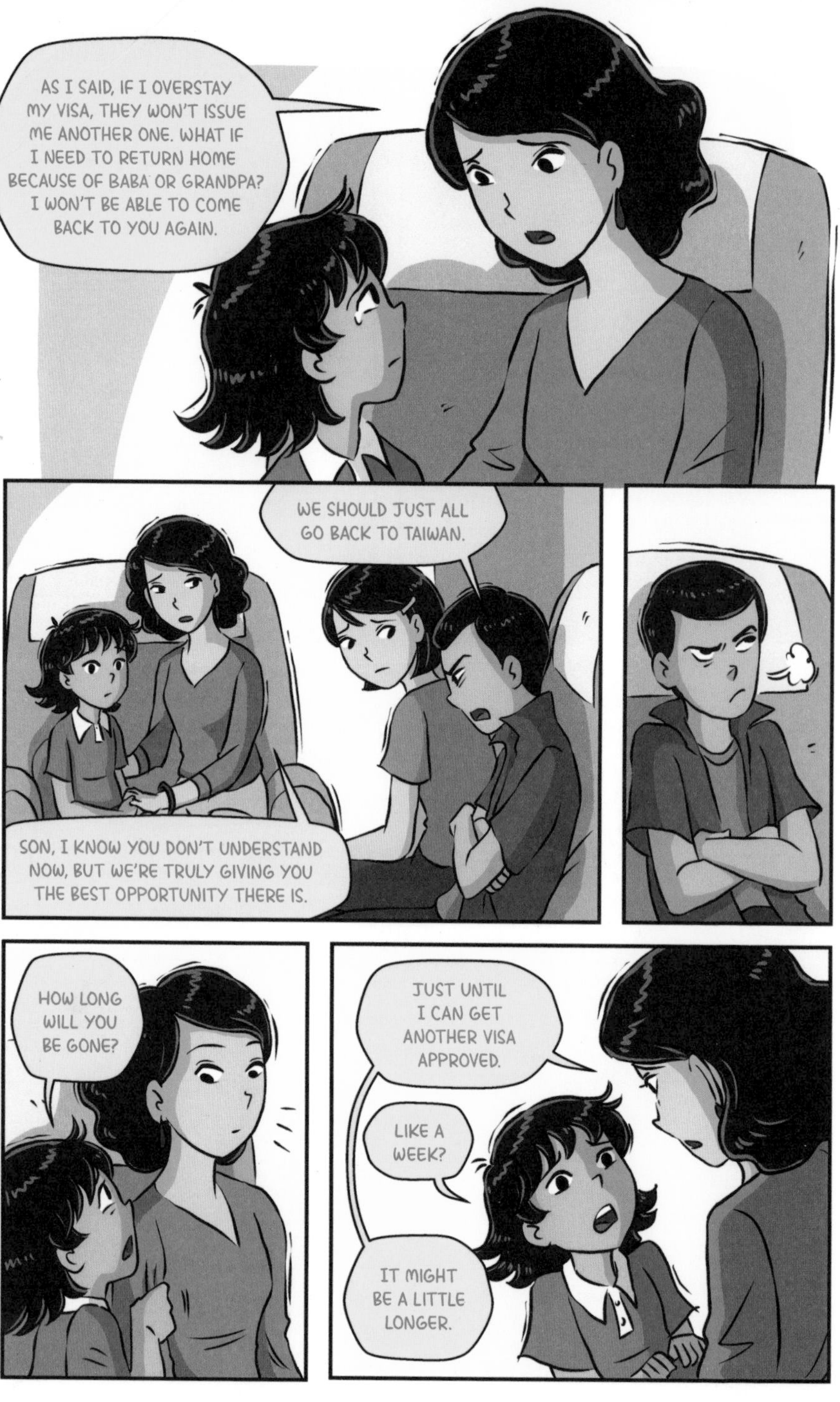
AS I SAID, IF I OVERSTAY MY VISA, THEY WON'T ISSUE ME ANOTHER ONE. WHAT IF I NEED TO RETURN HOME BECAUSE OF BABA OR GRANDPA? I WON'T BE ABLE TO COME BACK TO YOU AGAIN.
WE SHOULD JUST ALL GO BACK TO TAIWAN.
SON, I KNOW YOU DON'T UNDERSTAND NOW, BUT WE'RE TRULY GIVING YOU THE BEST OPPORTUNITY THERE IS.
HOW LONG WILL YOU BE GONE?
JUST UNTIL I CAN GET ANOTHER VISA APPROVED.
LIKE A WEEK?
IT MIGHT BE A LITTLE LONGER.

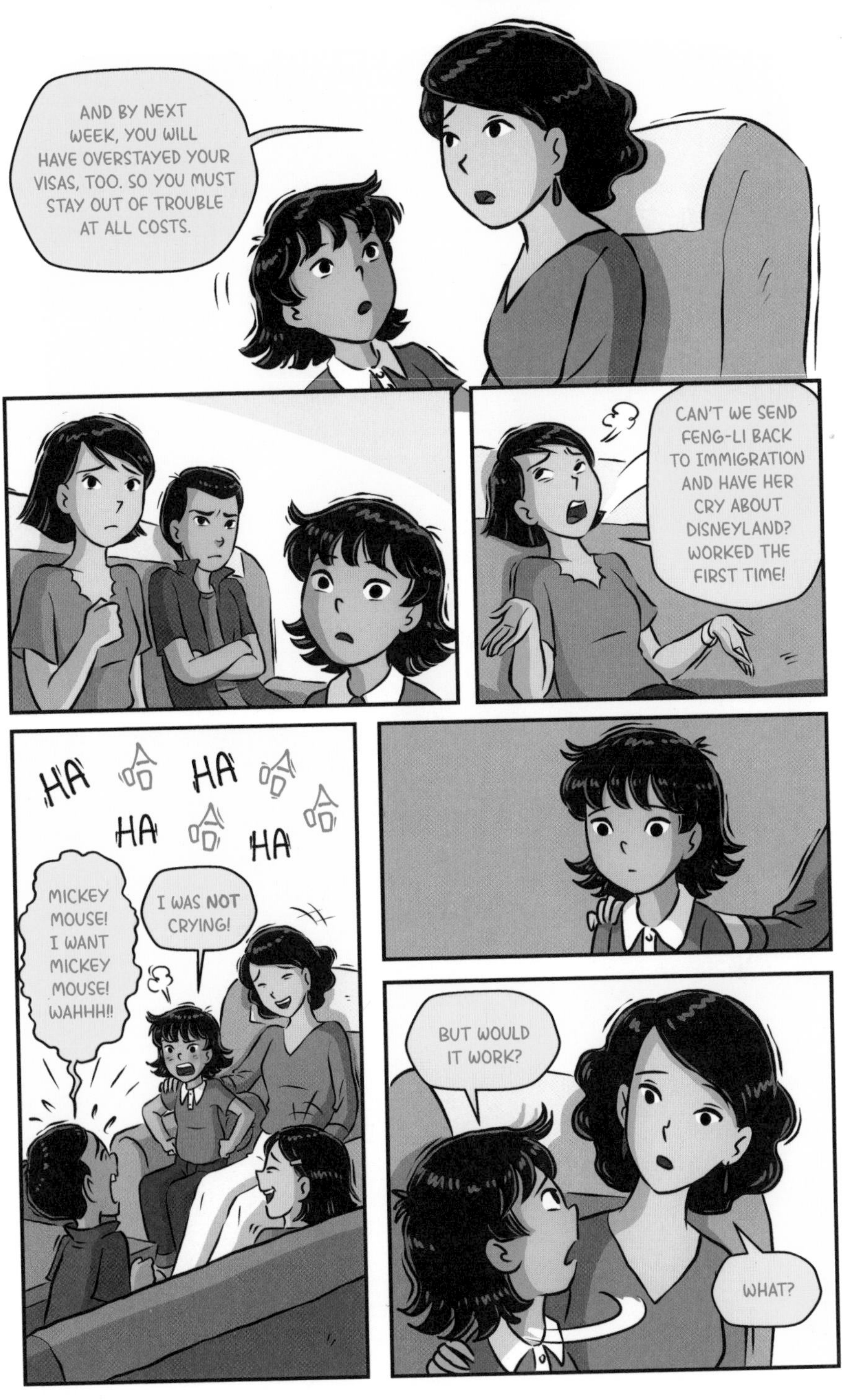
AND BY NEXT WEEK, YOU WILL HAVE OVERSTAYED YOUR VISAS, TOO. SO YOU MUST STAY OUT OF TROUBLE AT ALL COSTS.
CAN'T WE SEND FENG-LI BACK TO IMMIGRATION AND HAVE HER CRY ABOUT DISNEYLAND? WORKED THE FIRST TIME!
HA HA HA HA
MICKEY MOUSE! I WANT MICKEY MOUSE! WAHHH!!
I WAS NOT CRYING!
BUT WOULD IT WORK?
WHAT?

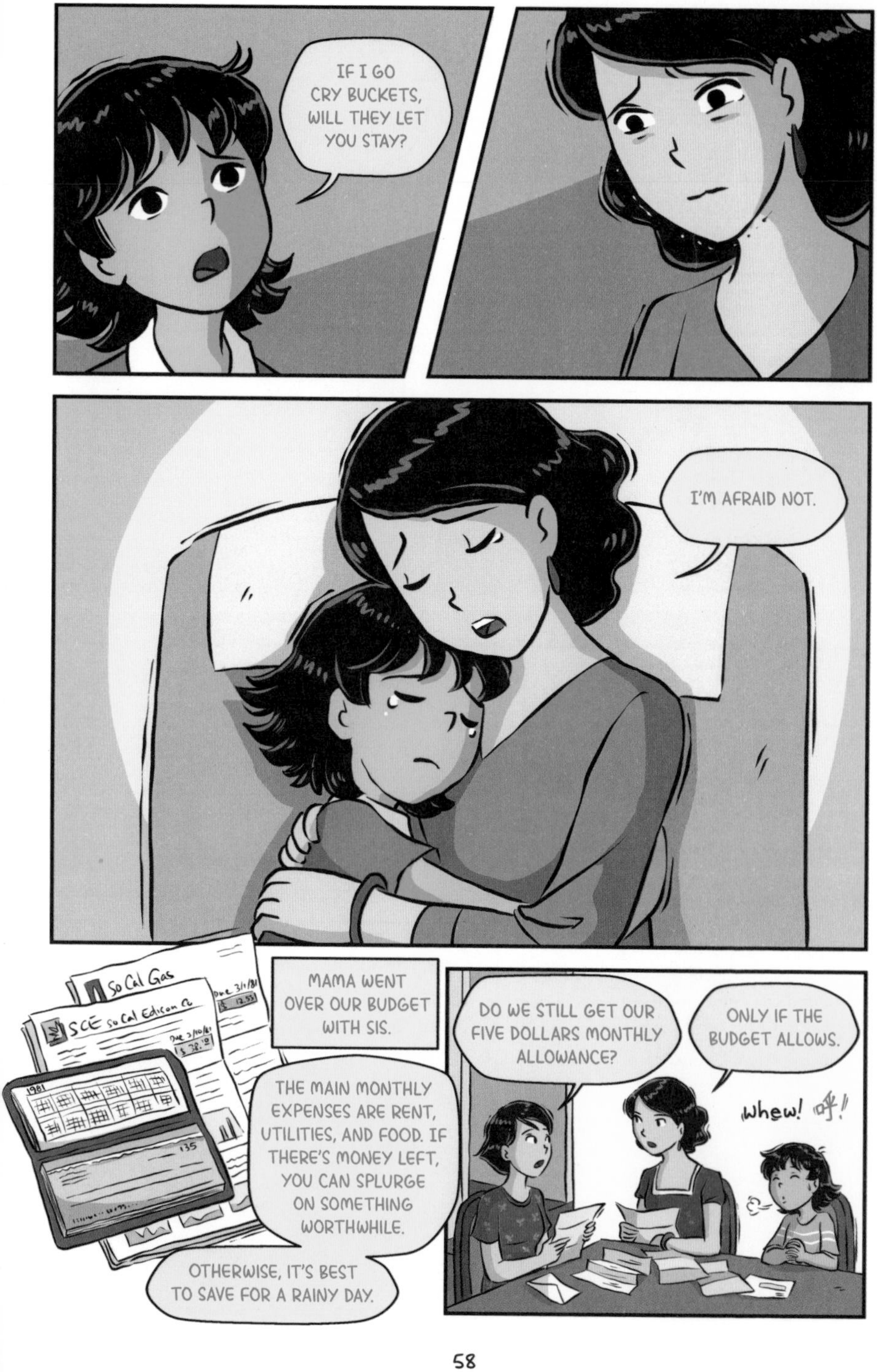

IF I GO CRY BUCKETS, WILL THEY LET YOU STAY?
I'M AFRAID NOT.
So Cal Gas
SCE So Cal Edison Co
1981
MAMA WENT OVER OUR BUDGET WITH SIS.
THE MAIN MONTHLY EXPENSES ARE RENT, UTILITIES, AND FOOD. IF THERE'S MONEY LEFT, YOU CAN SPLURGE ON SOMETHING WORTHWHILE.
OTHERWISE, IT'S BEST TO SAVE FOR A RAINY DAY.
DO WE STILL GET OUR FIVE DOLLARS MONTHLY ALLOWANCE?
ONLY IF THE BUDGET ALLOWS.
Whew! 呼!

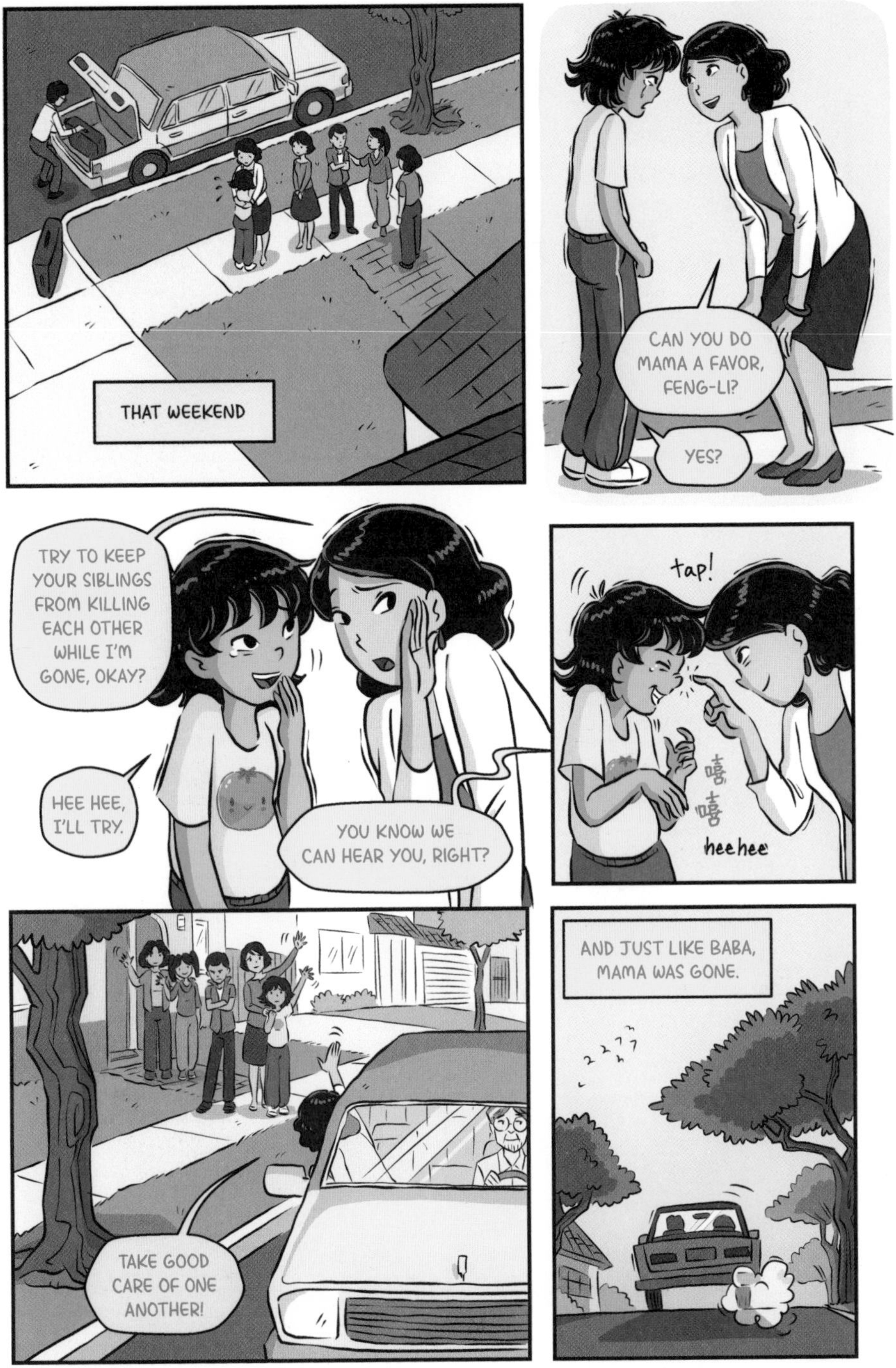
THAT WEEKEND
CAN YOU DO MAMA A FAVOR, FENG-LI?
YES?
TRY TO KEEP YOUR SIBLINGS FROM KILLING EACH OTHER WHILE I'M GONE, OKAY?
HEE HEE, I'LL TRY.
YOU KNOW WE CAN HEAR YOU, RIGHT?
tap!
嘻嘻
heehee
TAKE GOOD CARE OF ONE ANOTHER!
AND JUST LIKE BABA, MAMA WAS GONE.

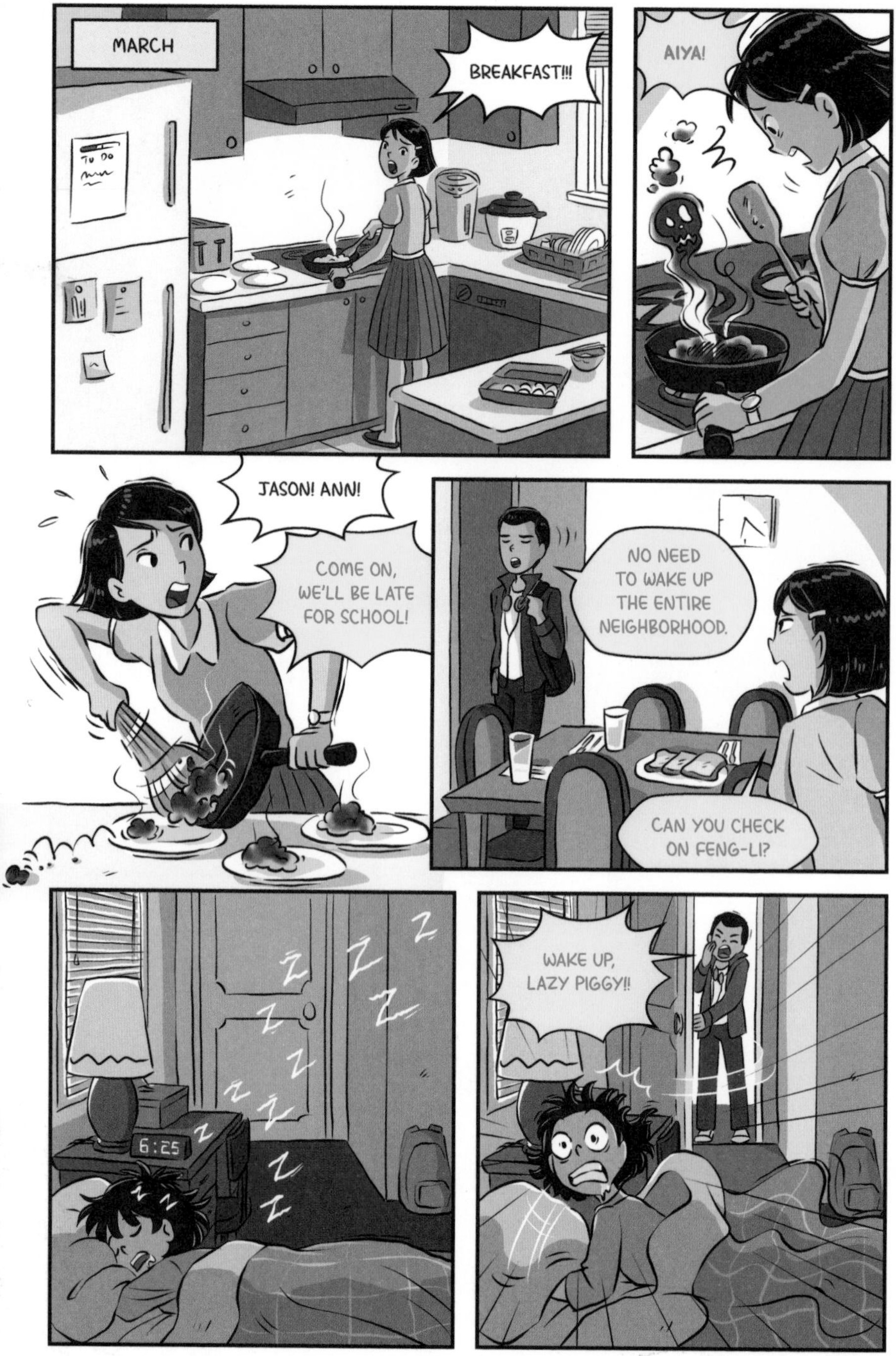
MARCH
BREAKFAST!!!
TO DO
AIYA!
JASON! ANN!
COME ON, WE'LL BE LATE FOR SCHOOL!
NO NEED TO WAKE UP THE ENTIRE NEIGHBORHOOD.
CAN YOU CHECK ON FENG-LI?
6:25
WAKE UP, LAZY PIGGY!!

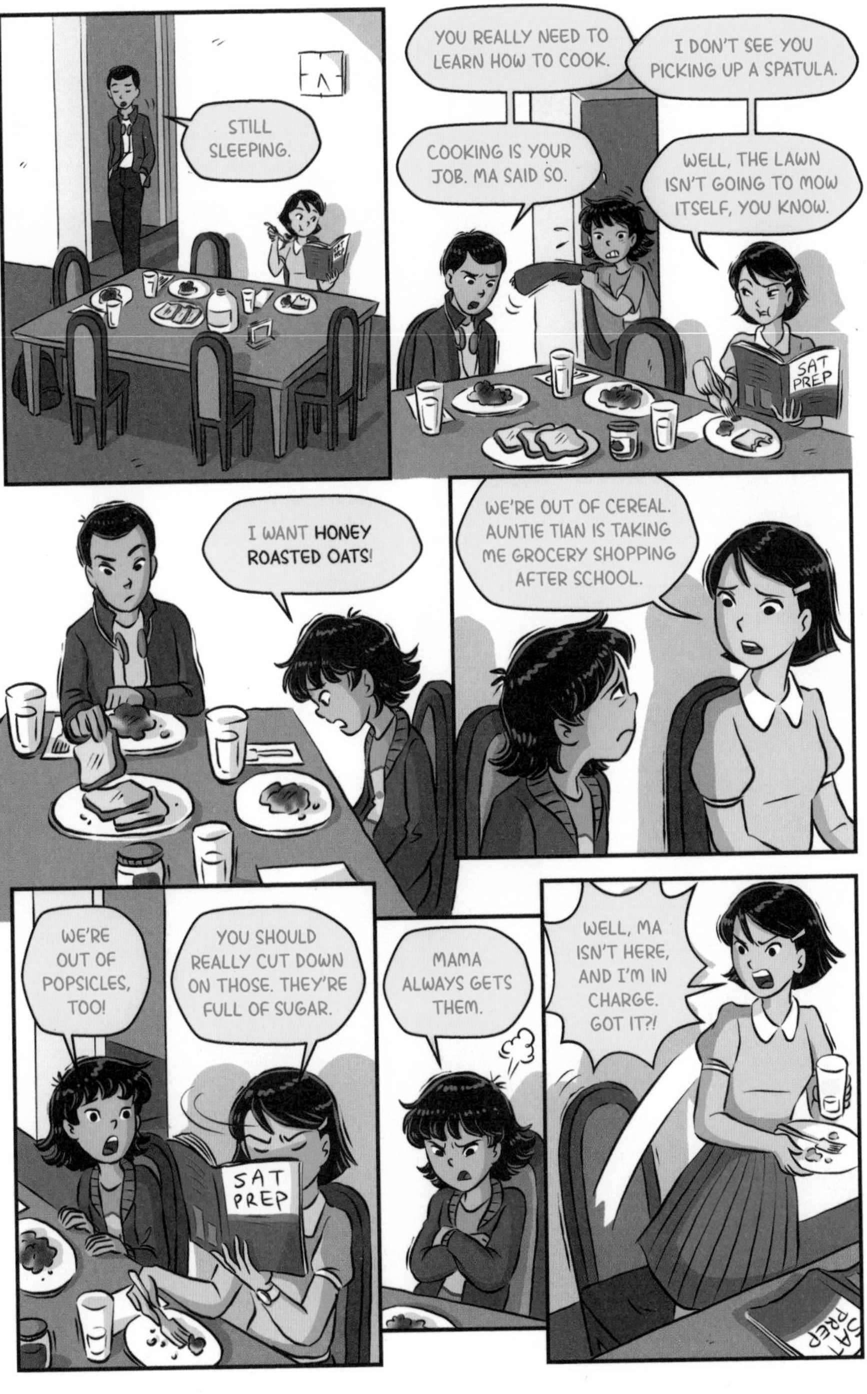
STILL SLEEPING.
YOU REALLY NEED TO LEARN HOW TO COOK.
COOKING IS YOUR JOB. MA SAID SO.
I DON'T SEE YOU PICKING UP A SPATULA.
WELL, THE LAWN ISN'T GOING TO MOW ITSELF, YOU KNOW.
SAT PREP
I WANT **HONEY ROASTED OATS**!
WE'RE OUT OF CEREAL. AUNTIE TIAN IS TAKING ME GROCERY SHOPPING AFTER SCHOOL.
WE'RE OUT OF POPSICLES, TOO!
YOU SHOULD REALLY CUT DOWN ON THOSE. THEY'RE FULL OF SUGAR.
SAT PREP
MAMA ALWAYS GETS THEM.
WELL, MA ISN'T HERE, AND I'M IN CHARGE. GOT IT?!

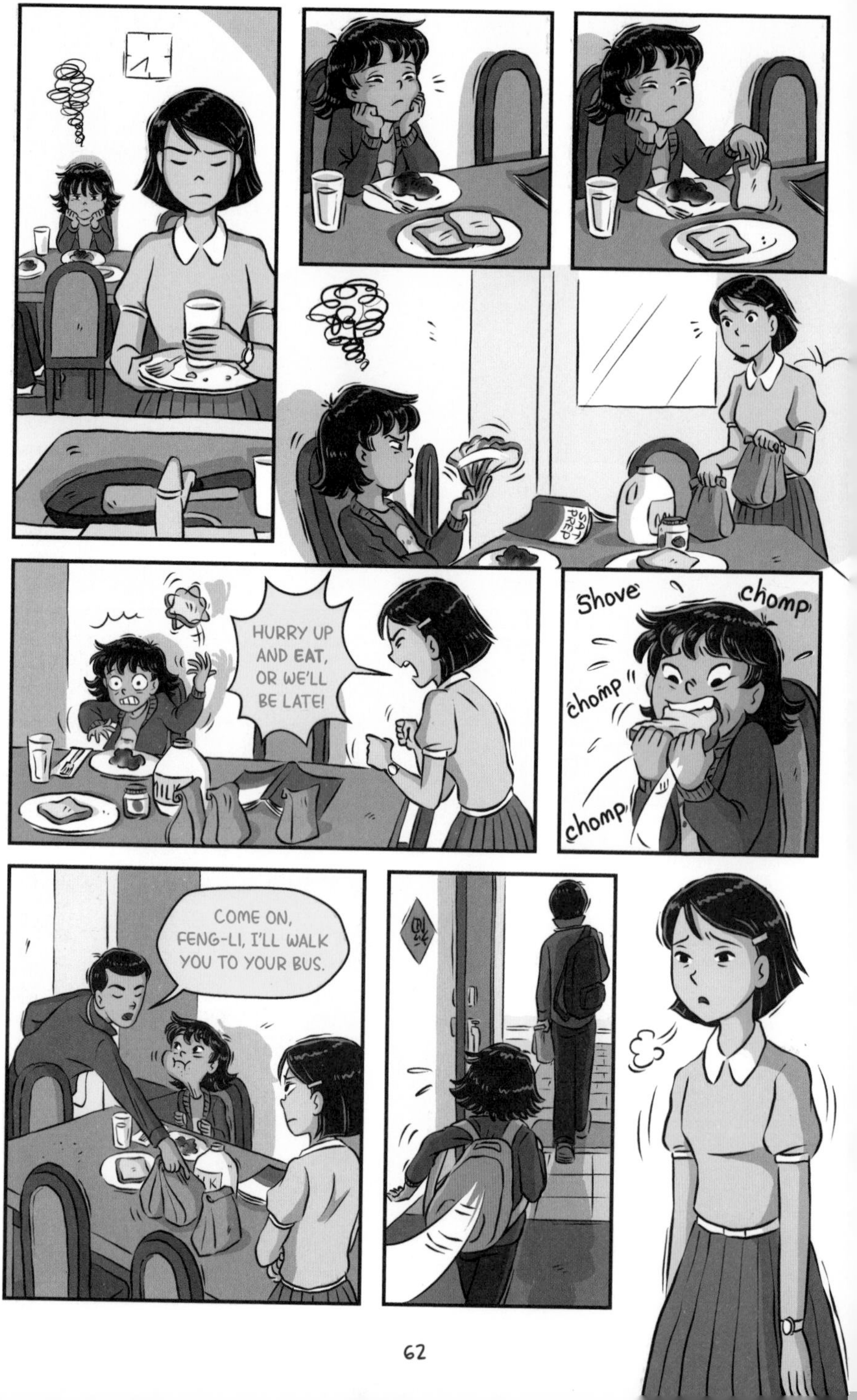
SAT PREP
HURRY UP AND EAT, OR WE'LL BE LATE!
Shove
chomp
chomp
chomp
COME ON, FENG-LI, I'LL WALK YOU TO YOUR BUS.

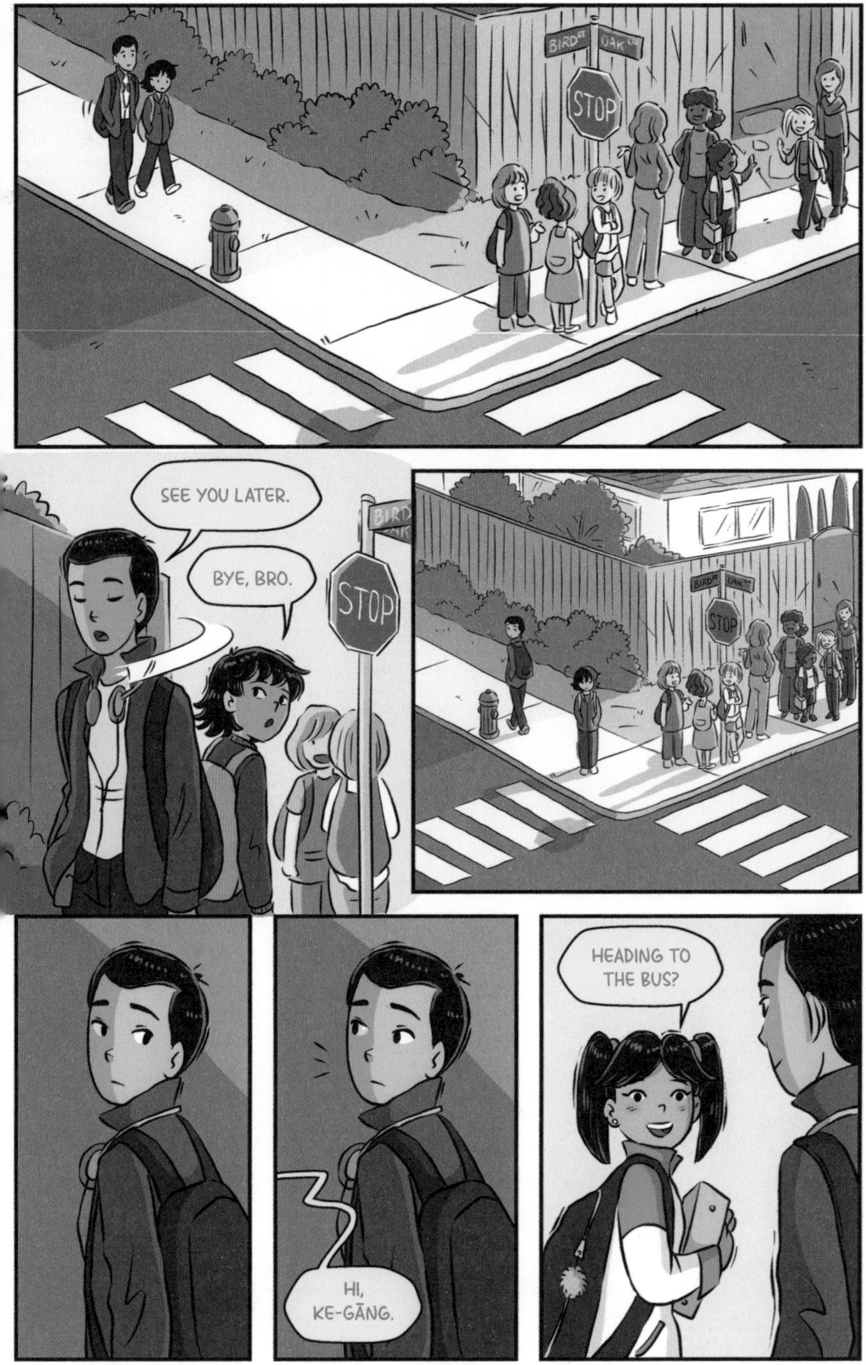
BIRD ST
OAK ST
STOP
SEE YOU LATER.
BYE, BRO.
HI,
KE-GĀNG.
HEADING TO
THE BUS?

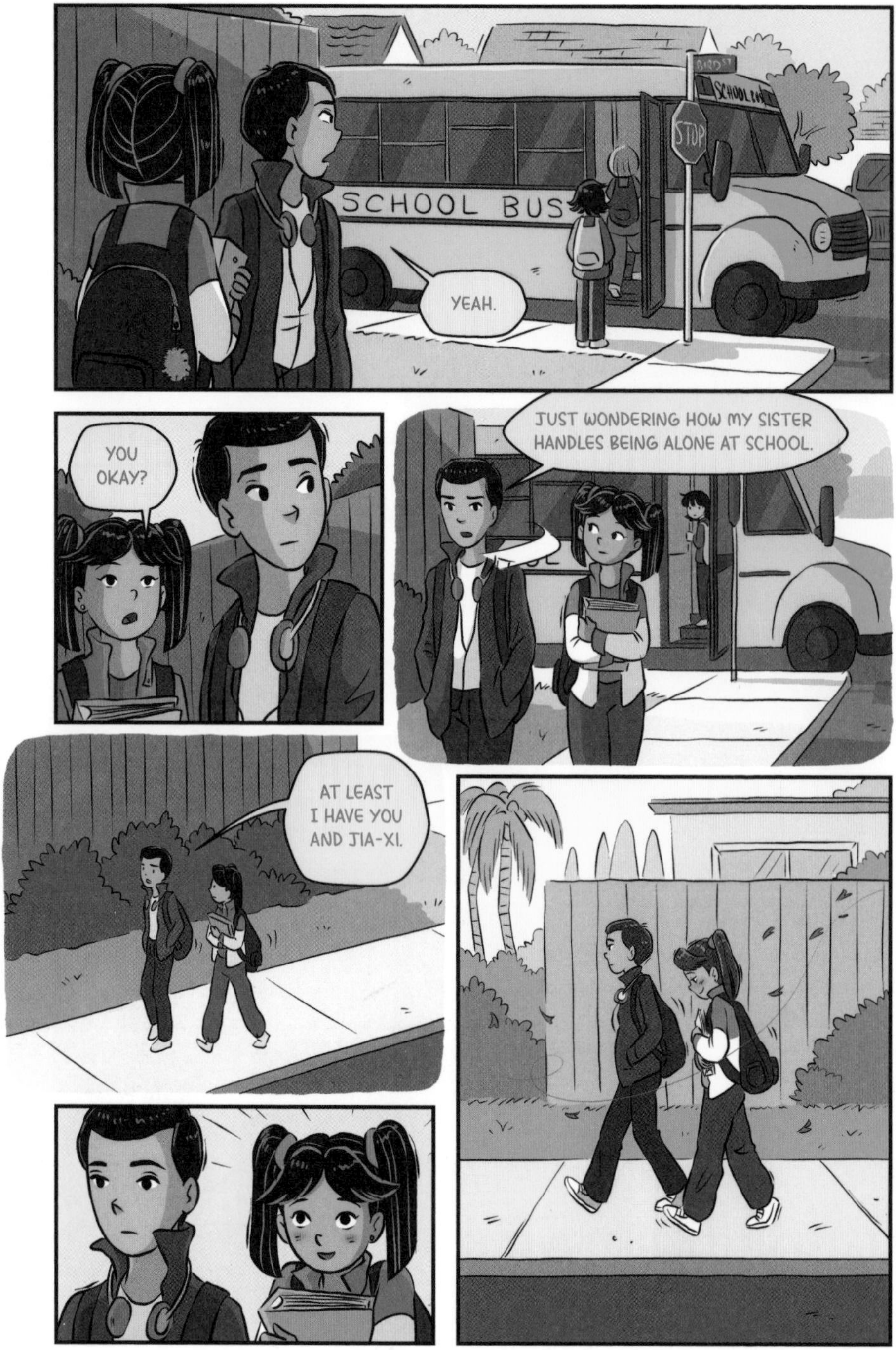
BIRD ST
SCHOOL BUS
STOP
SCHOOL BUS
YEAH.
YOU OKAY?
JUST WONDERING HOW MY SISTER HANDLES BEING ALONE AT SCHOOL.
AT LEAST I HAVE YOU AND JIA-XI.

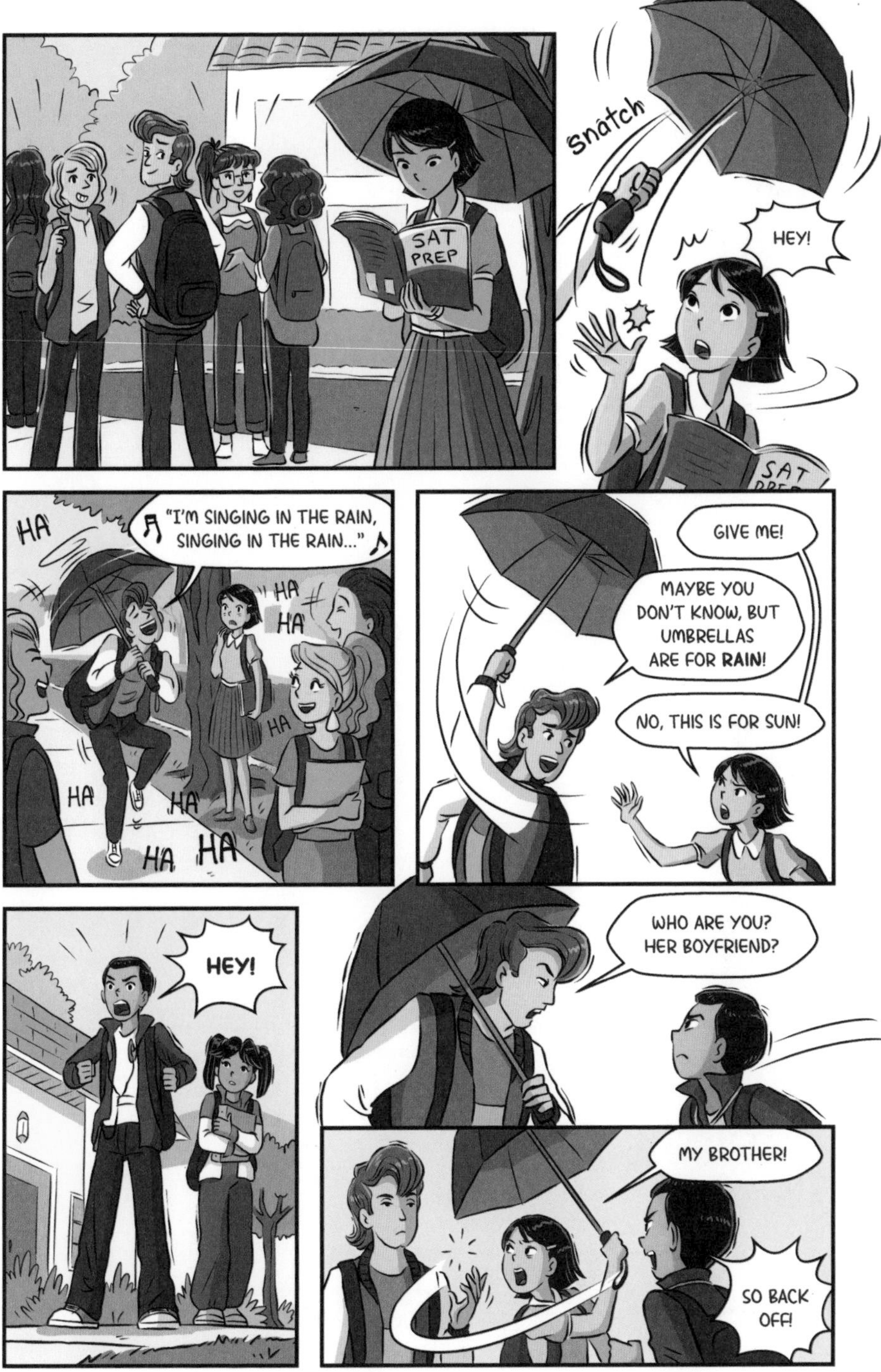
Snatch
HEY!
HA
"I'M SINGING IN THE RAIN, SINGING IN THE RAIN..."
HA
HA
HA
HA
HA
HA
HA
GIVE ME!
MAYBE YOU DON'T KNOW, BUT UMBRELLAS ARE FOR RAIN!
NO, THIS IS FOR SUN!
HEY!
WHO ARE YOU? HER BOYFRIEND?
MY BROTHER!
SO BACK OFF!

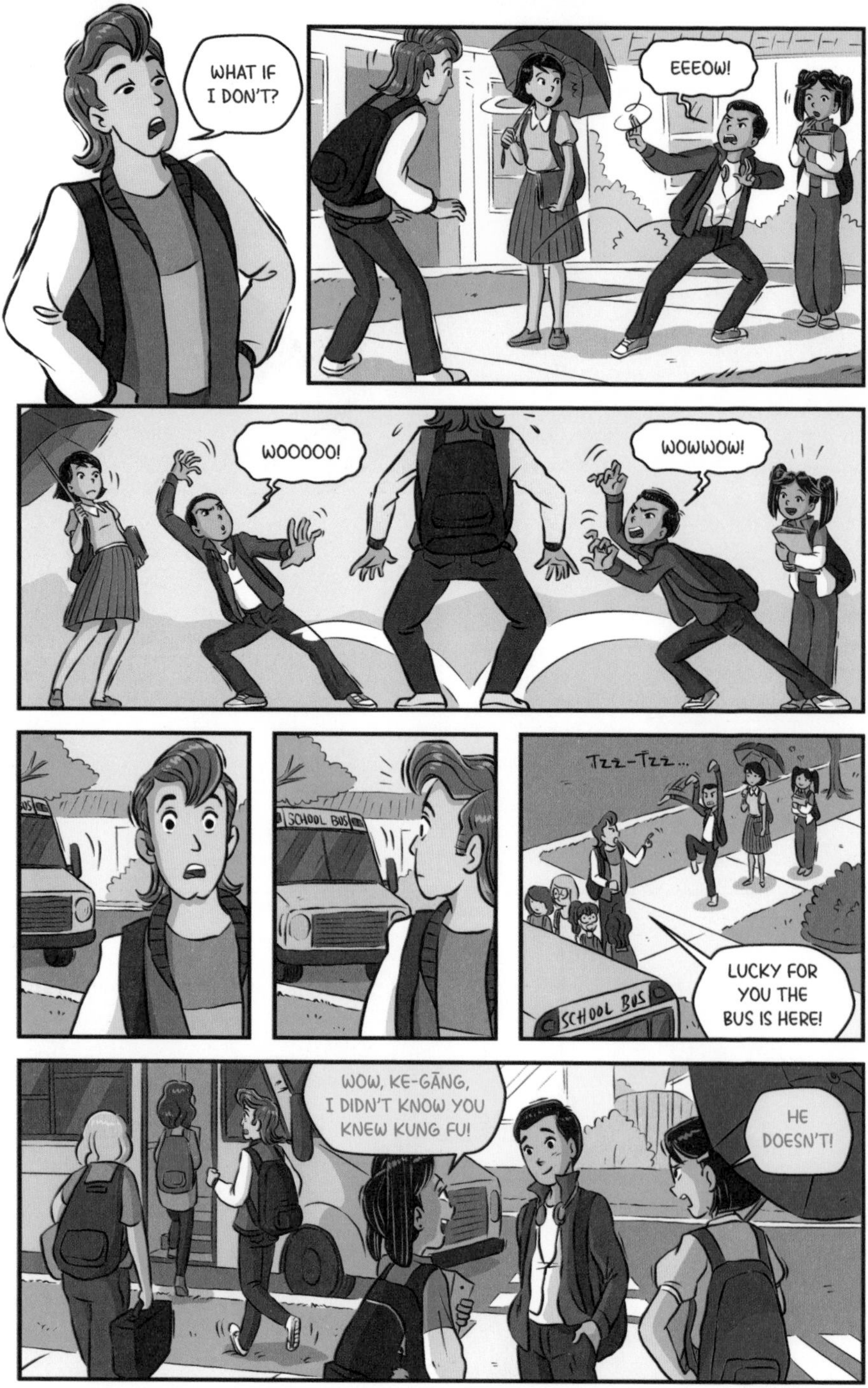
WHAT IF I DON'T?
EEEOW!
WOOOOO!
WOWWOW!
TZZ-TZZ...
LUCKY FOR YOU THE BUS IS HERE!
SCHOOL BUS
WOW, KE-GĀNG, I DIDN'T KNOW YOU KNEW KUNG FU!
HE DOESN'T!

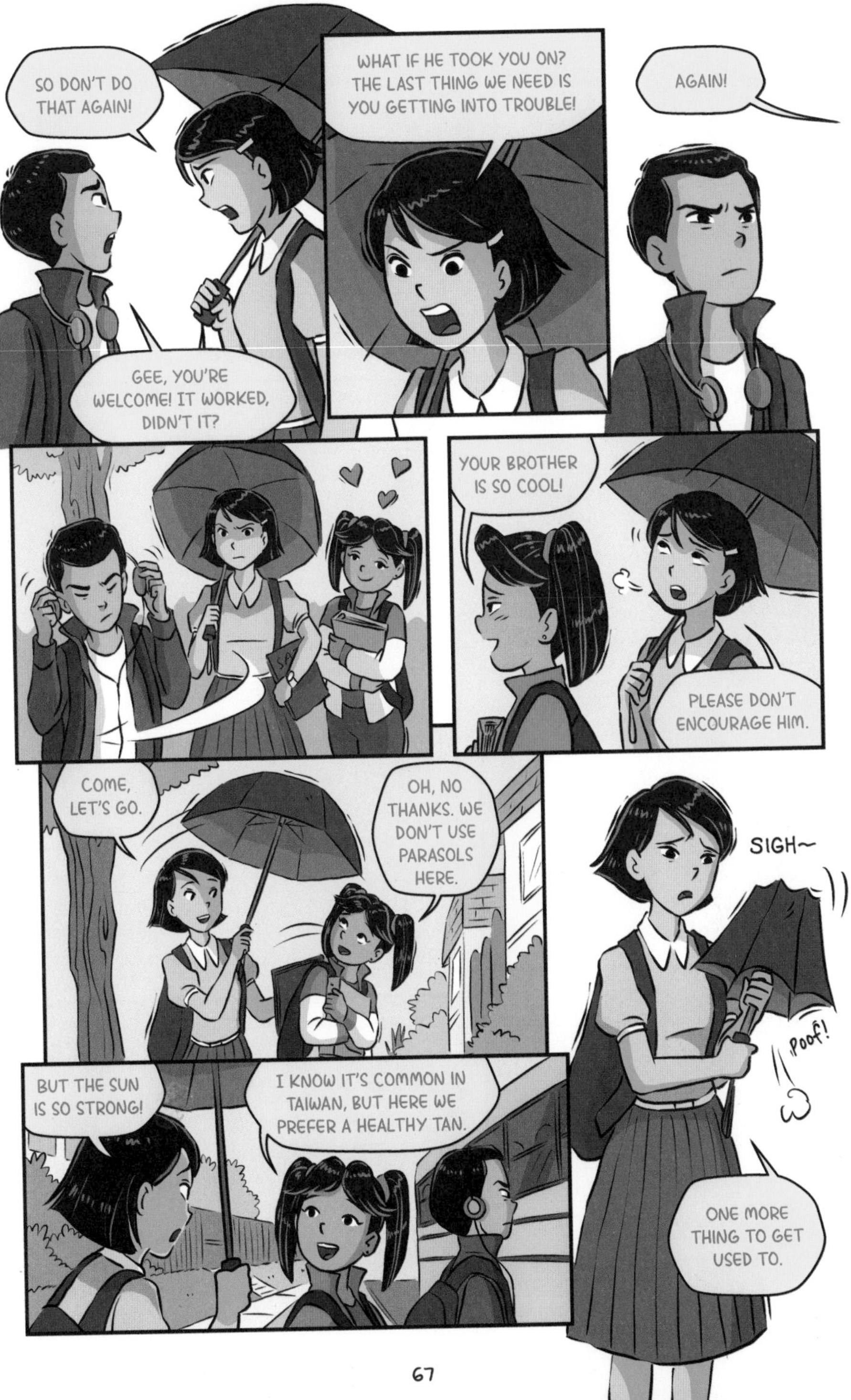
SO DON'T DO THAT AGAIN!
GEE, YOU'RE WELCOME! IT WORKED, DIDN'T IT?
WHAT IF HE TOOK YOU ON? THE LAST THING WE NEED IS YOU GETTING INTO TROUBLE!
AGAIN!
YOUR BROTHER IS SO COOL!
PLEASE DON'T ENCOURAGE HIM.
COME, LET'S GO.
OH, NO THANKS. WE DON'T USE PARASOLS HERE.
BUT THE SUN IS SO STRONG!
I KNOW IT'S COMMON IN TAIWAN, BUT HERE WE PREFER A HEALTHY TAN.
SIGH~
Poof!
ONE MORE THING TO GET USED TO.

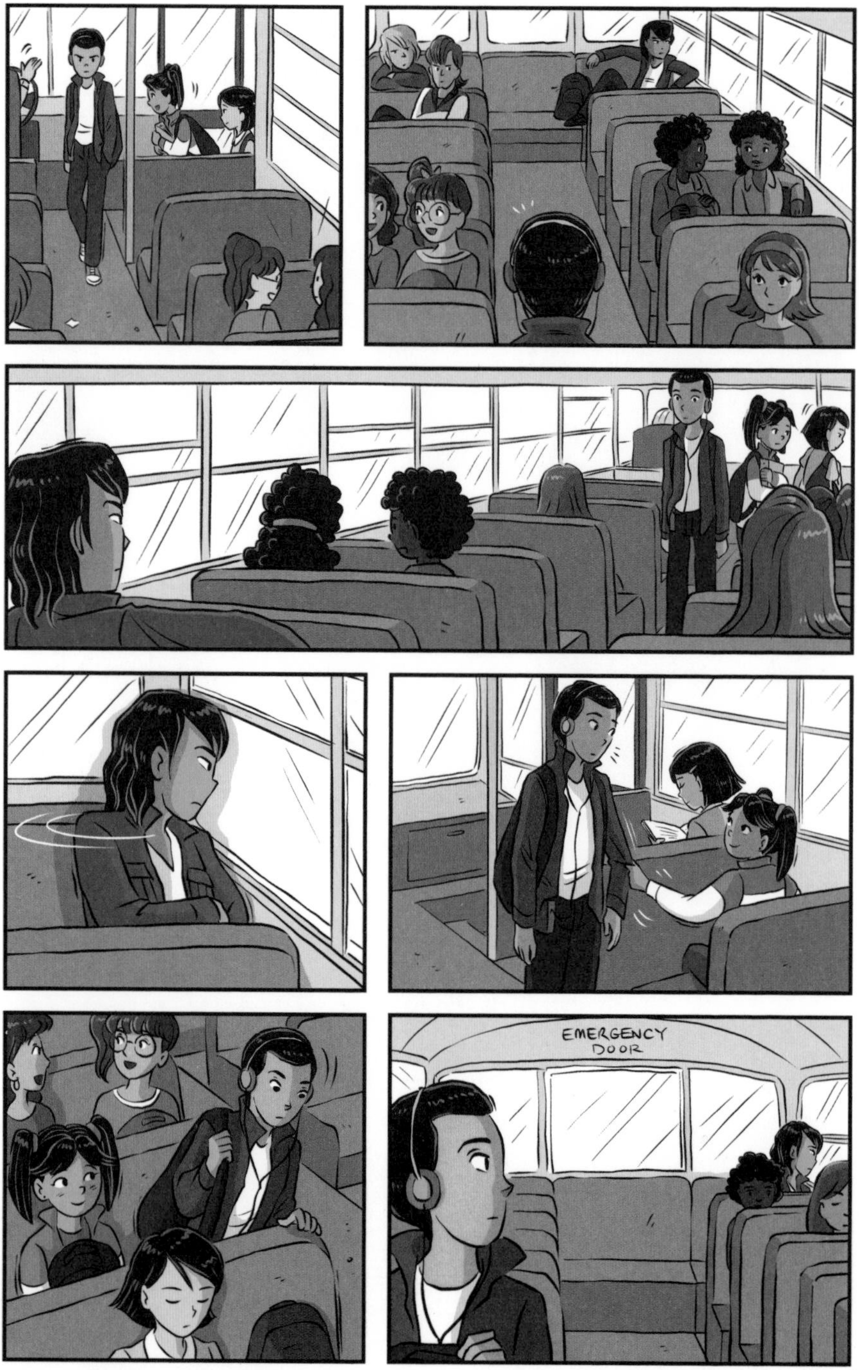
EMERGENCY
DOOR

THE NEXT SPELLING WORD IS:

"RECOGNIZE."

Scribble

Scribble

Scribble

Scribble

Scribble

Scribble

"RECOGNITION."

WAIT, IS THAT A NEW WORD? IT SOUNDS LIKE THE LAST ONE.

TAKE A MINUTE TO CHECK YOUR SPELLING.

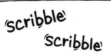

Scribble

Scribble

OKAY, TIME'S UP. PLEASE PASS YOUR PAPERS UP TO THE FRONT.

ANN LIN

1. SUT
2. POWR
3. APLOD
4. SPRIN
5. RELEF
6. SIBOLIZM
7. PRAKTIZ
8. AKTIEN
9. REKONICE
10. REKONICE

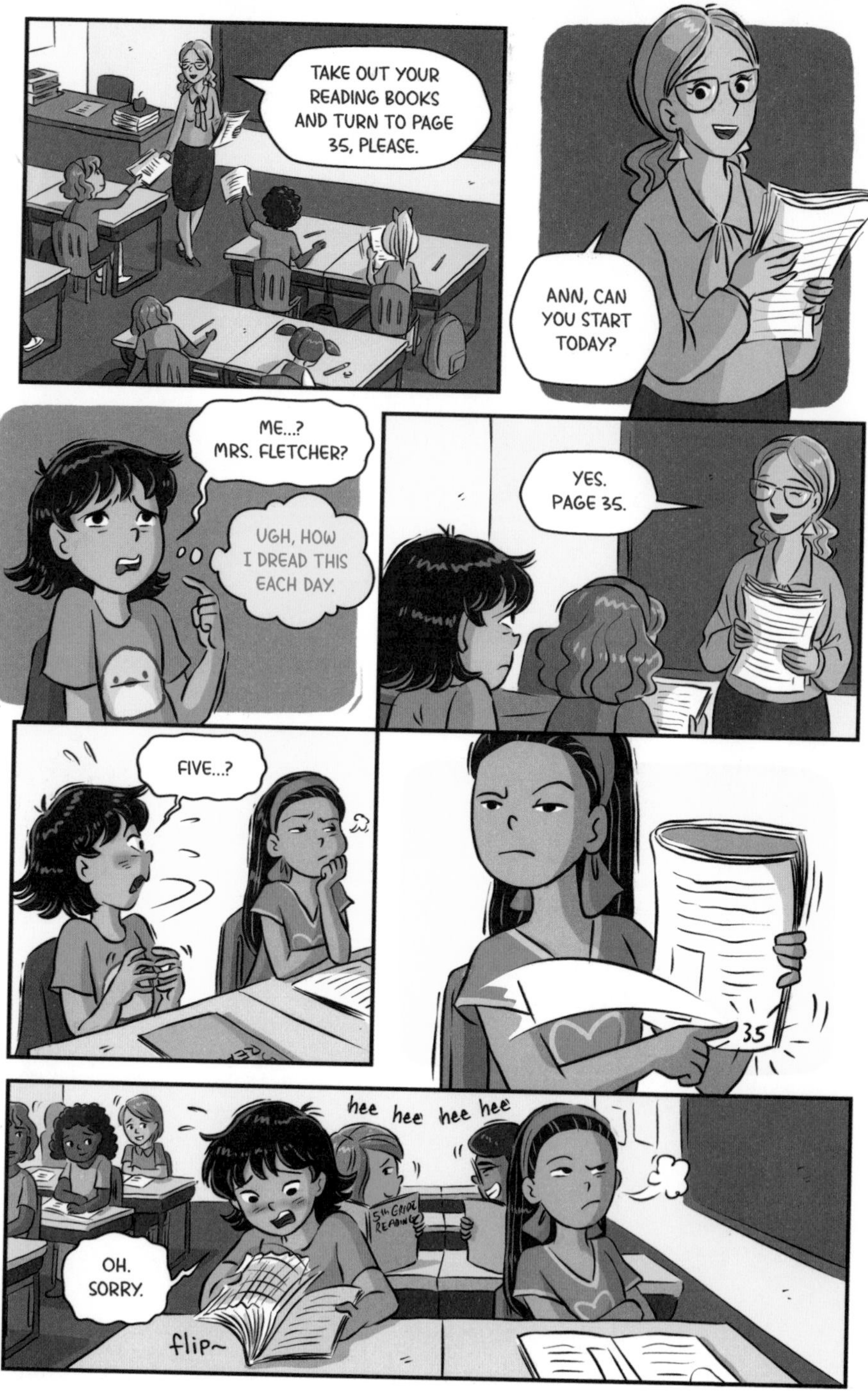
TAKE OUT YOUR READING BOOKS AND TURN TO PAGE 35, PLEASE.
ANN, CAN YOU START TODAY?
ME...? MRS. FLETCHER?
UGH, HOW I DREAD THIS EACH DAY.
YES. PAGE 35.
FIVE...?
35
hee hee hee hee
5th GRADE READING
OH. SORRY.
flip~

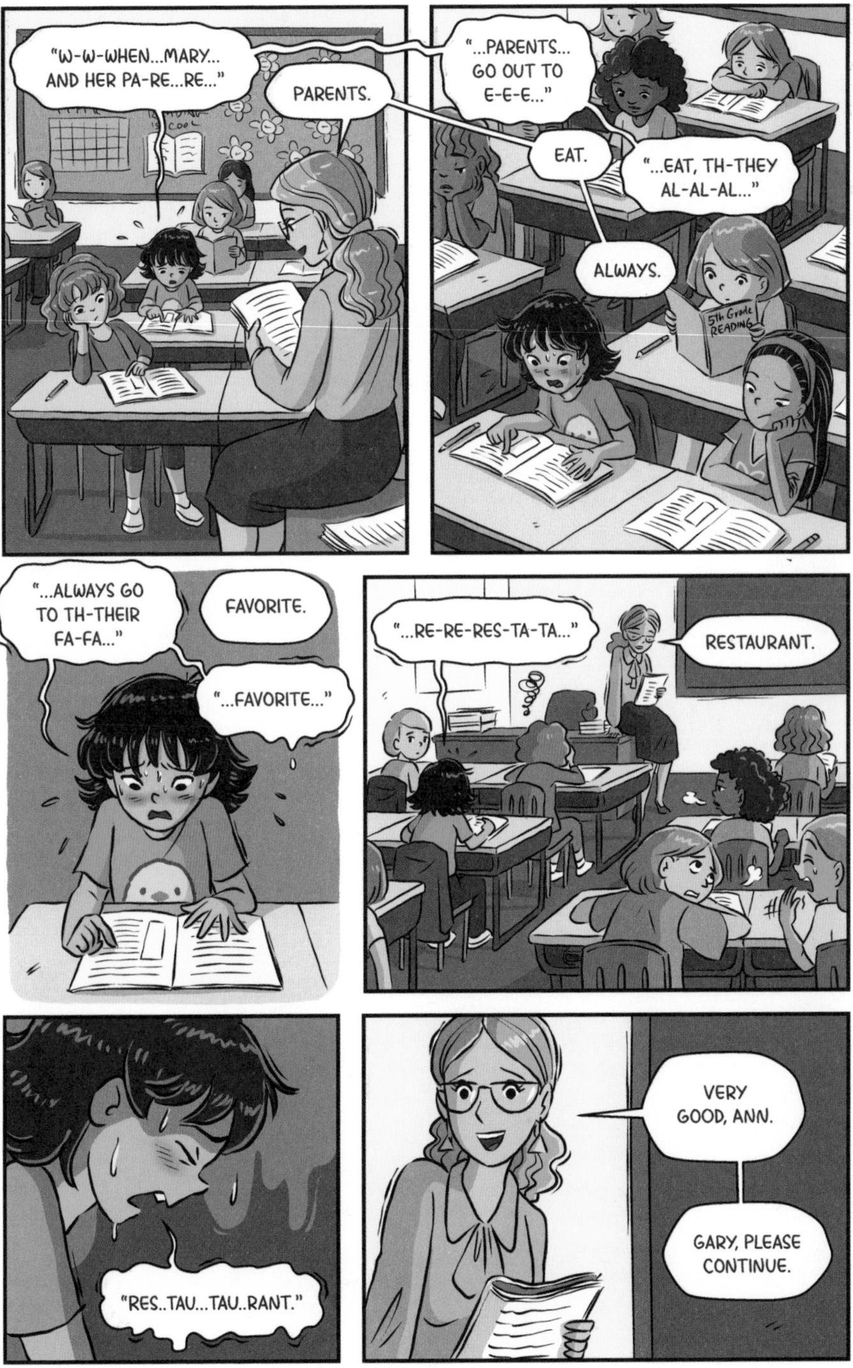
"W-W-WHEN...MARY... AND HER PA-RE...RE..."
PARENTS.
"...PARENTS... GO OUT TO E-E-E..."
EAT.
"...EAT, TH-THEY AL-AL-AL..."
ALWAYS.
5th Grade READING
"...ALWAYS GO TO TH-THEIR FA-FA..."
FAVORITE.
"...FAVORITE..."
"...RE-RE-RES-TA-TA..."
RESTAURANT.
"RES..TAU...TAU..RANT."
VERY GOOD, ANN.
GARY, PLEASE CONTINUE.

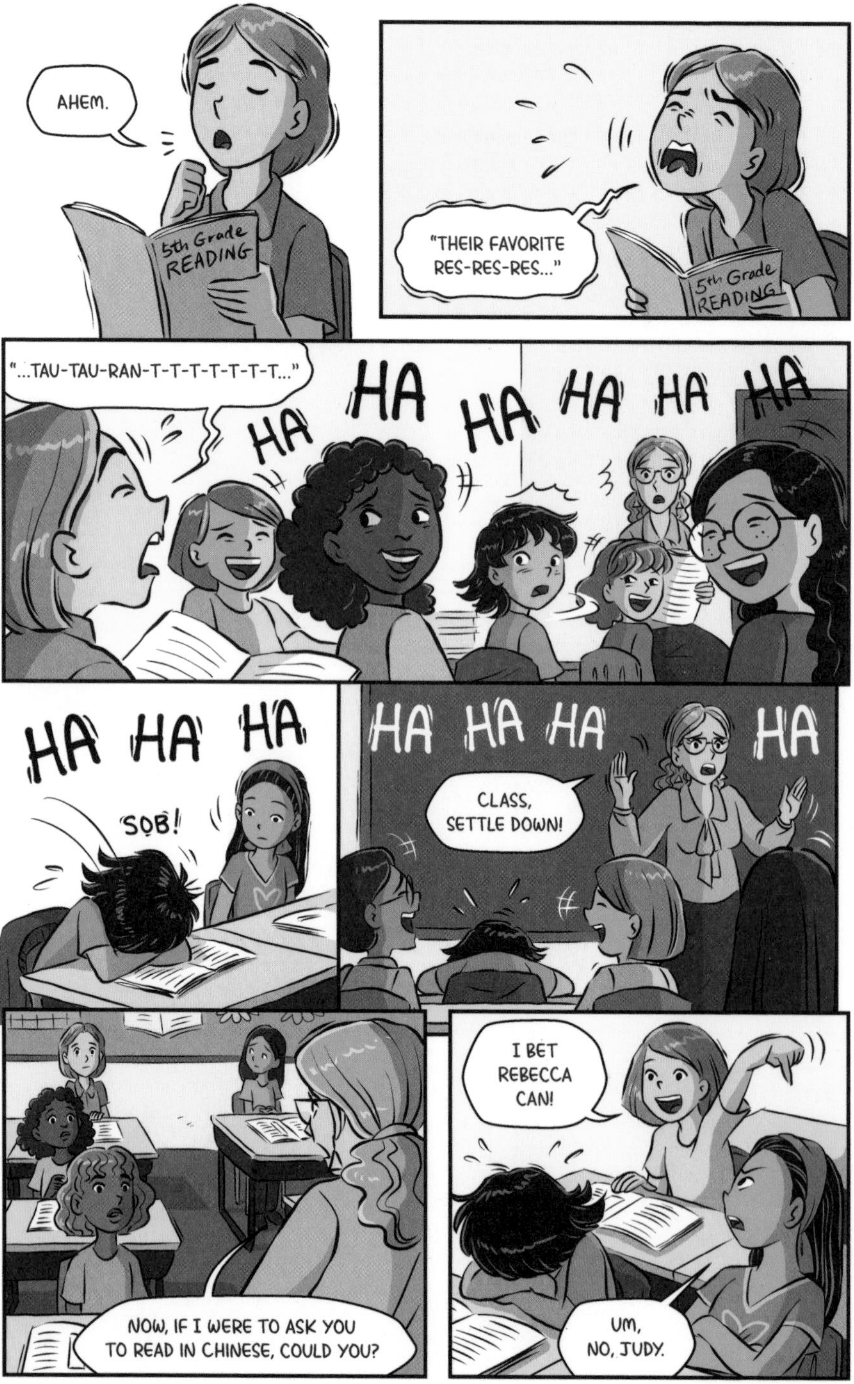
AHEM.
"THEIR FAVORITE RES-RES-RES..."
"...TAU-TAU-RAN-T-T-T-T-T-T-T..."
HA HA HA HA HA HA
HA HA HA
SOB!
HA HA HA HA
CLASS, SETTLE DOWN!
NOW, IF I WERE TO ASK YOU TO READ IN CHINESE, COULD YOU?
I BET REBECCA CAN!
UM, NO, JUDY.

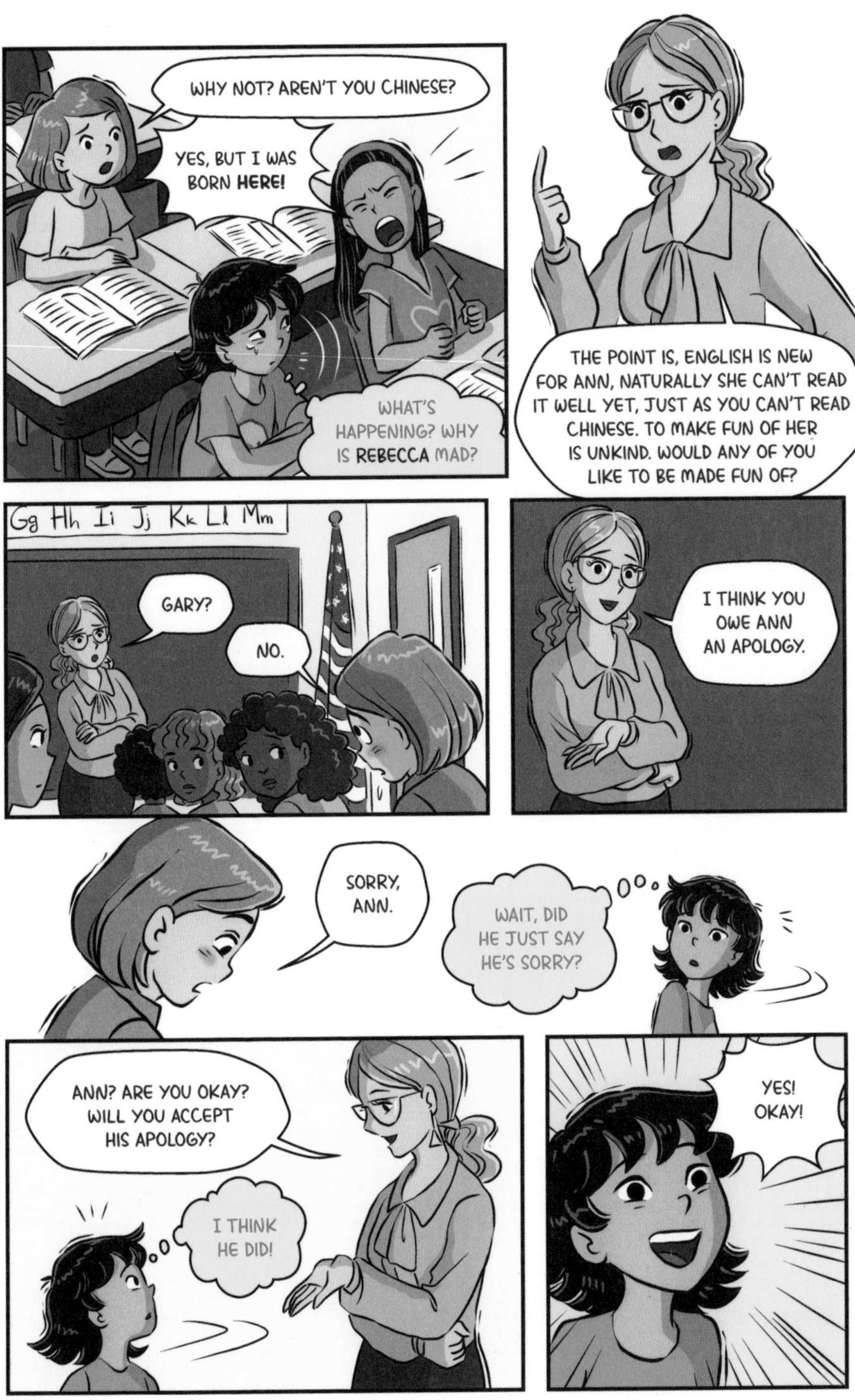
WHY NOT? AREN'T YOU CHINESE?
YES, BUT I WAS BORN **HERE!**
WHAT'S HAPPENING? WHY IS **REBECCA** MAD?
THE POINT IS, ENGLISH IS NEW FOR ANN, NATURALLY SHE CAN'T READ IT WELL YET, JUST AS YOU CAN'T READ CHINESE. TO MAKE FUN OF HER IS UNKIND. WOULD ANY OF YOU LIKE TO BE MADE FUN OF?
Gg Hh Ii Jj Kk Ll Mm
GARY?
NO.
I THINK YOU OWE ANN AN APOLOGY.
SORRY, ANN.
WAIT, DID HE JUST SAY HE'S SORRY?
ANN? ARE YOU OKAY? WILL YOU ACCEPT HIS APOLOGY?
I THINK HE DID!
YES! OKAY!

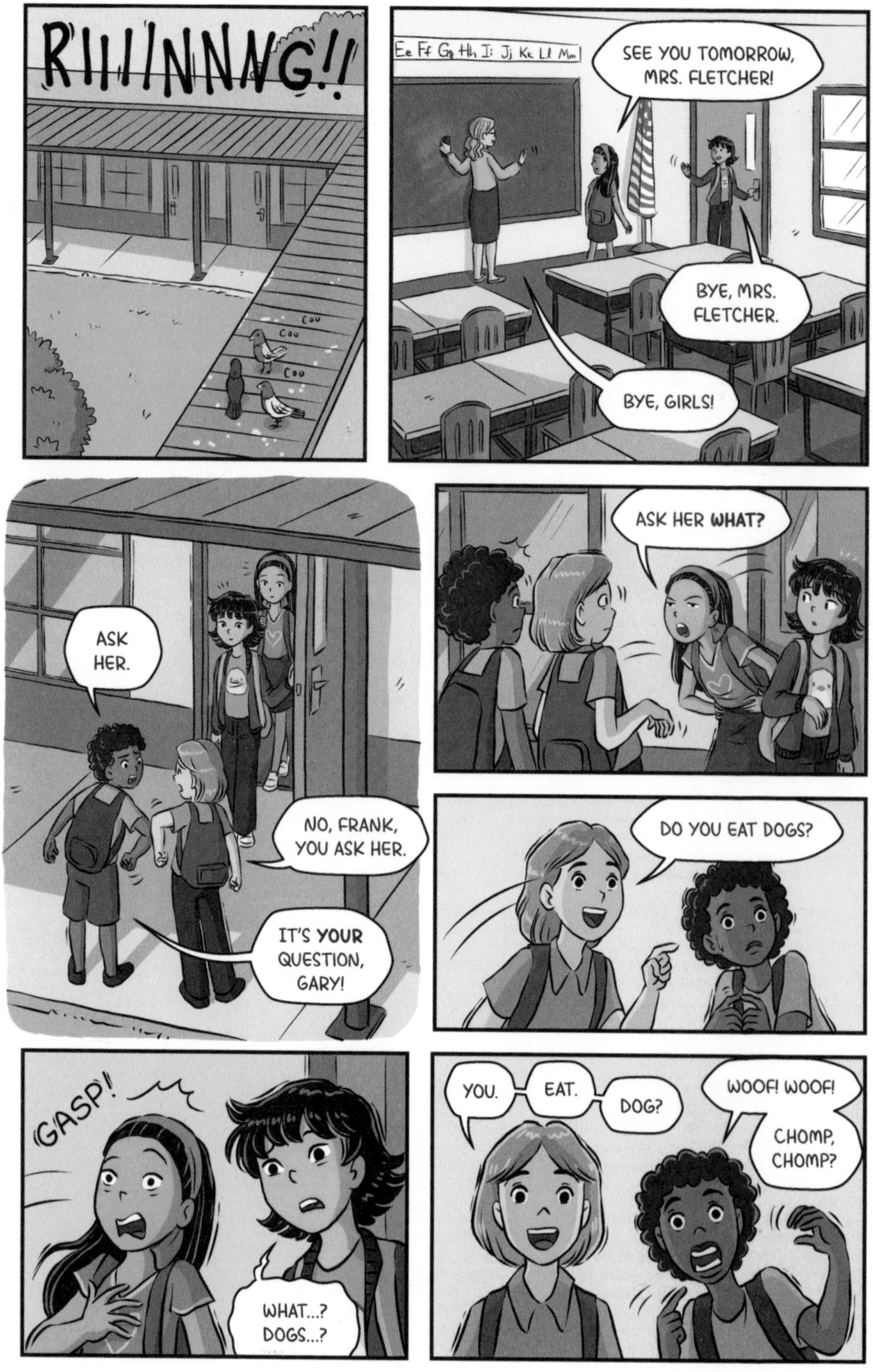
RIIIINNNG!!
COO
COO
COO
Ee Ff Gg Hh Ii Jj Kk Ll Mm
SEE YOU TOMORROW, MRS. FLETCHER!
BYE, MRS. FLETCHER.
BYE, GIRLS!
ASK HER.
NO, FRANK, YOU ASK HER.
IT'S **YOUR** QUESTION, GARY!
ASK HER **WHAT?**
DO YOU EAT DOGS?
GASP!
WHAT...? DOGS...?
YOU.
EAT.
DOG?
WOOF! WOOF!
CHOMP, CHOMP?

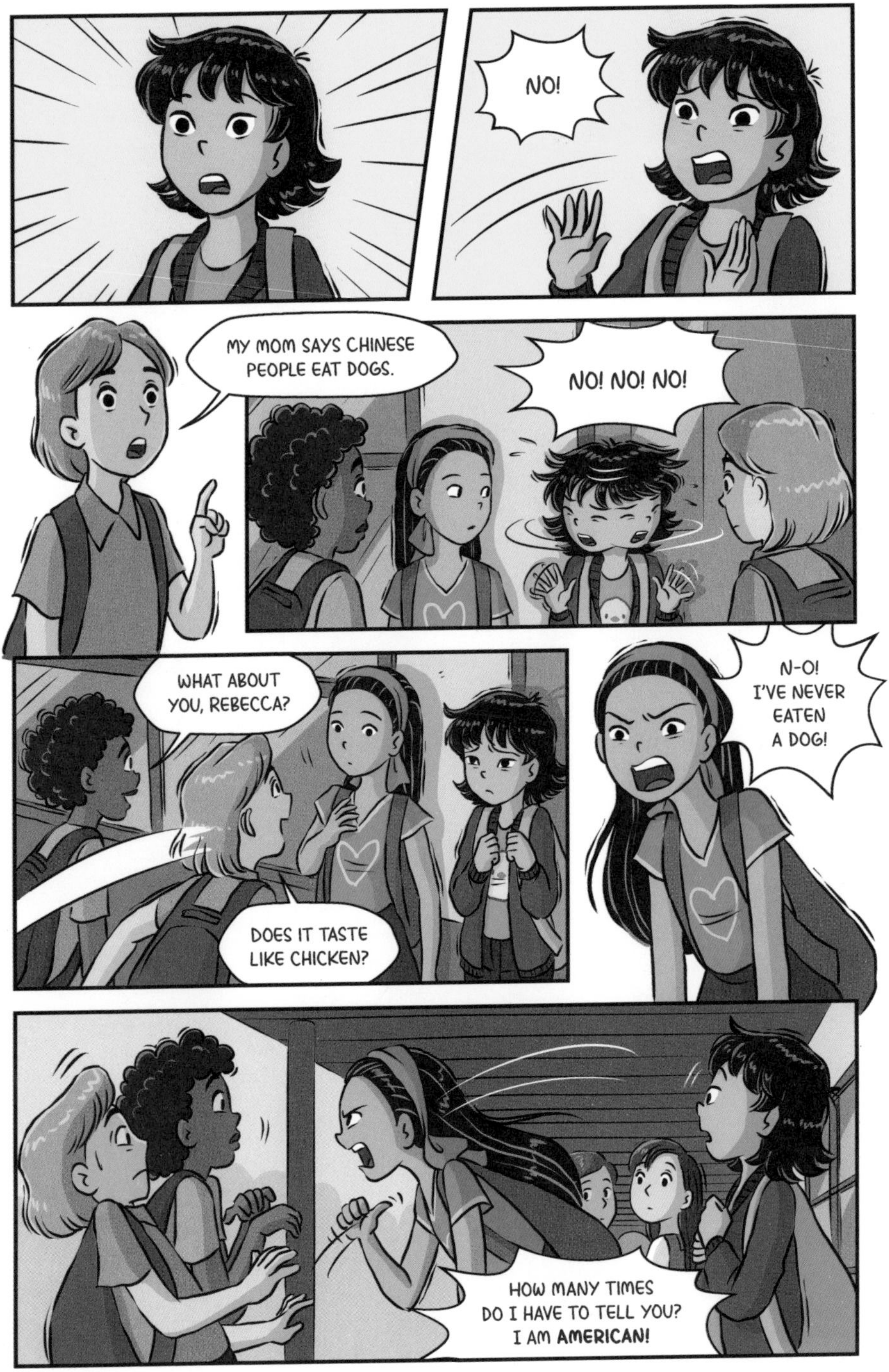
NO!
MY MOM SAYS CHINESE PEOPLE EAT DOGS.
NO! NO! NO!
WHAT ABOUT YOU, REBECCA?
DOES IT TASTE LIKE CHICKEN?
N-O! I'VE NEVER EATEN A DOG!
HOW MANY TIMES DO I HAVE TO TELL YOU? I AM AMERICAN!

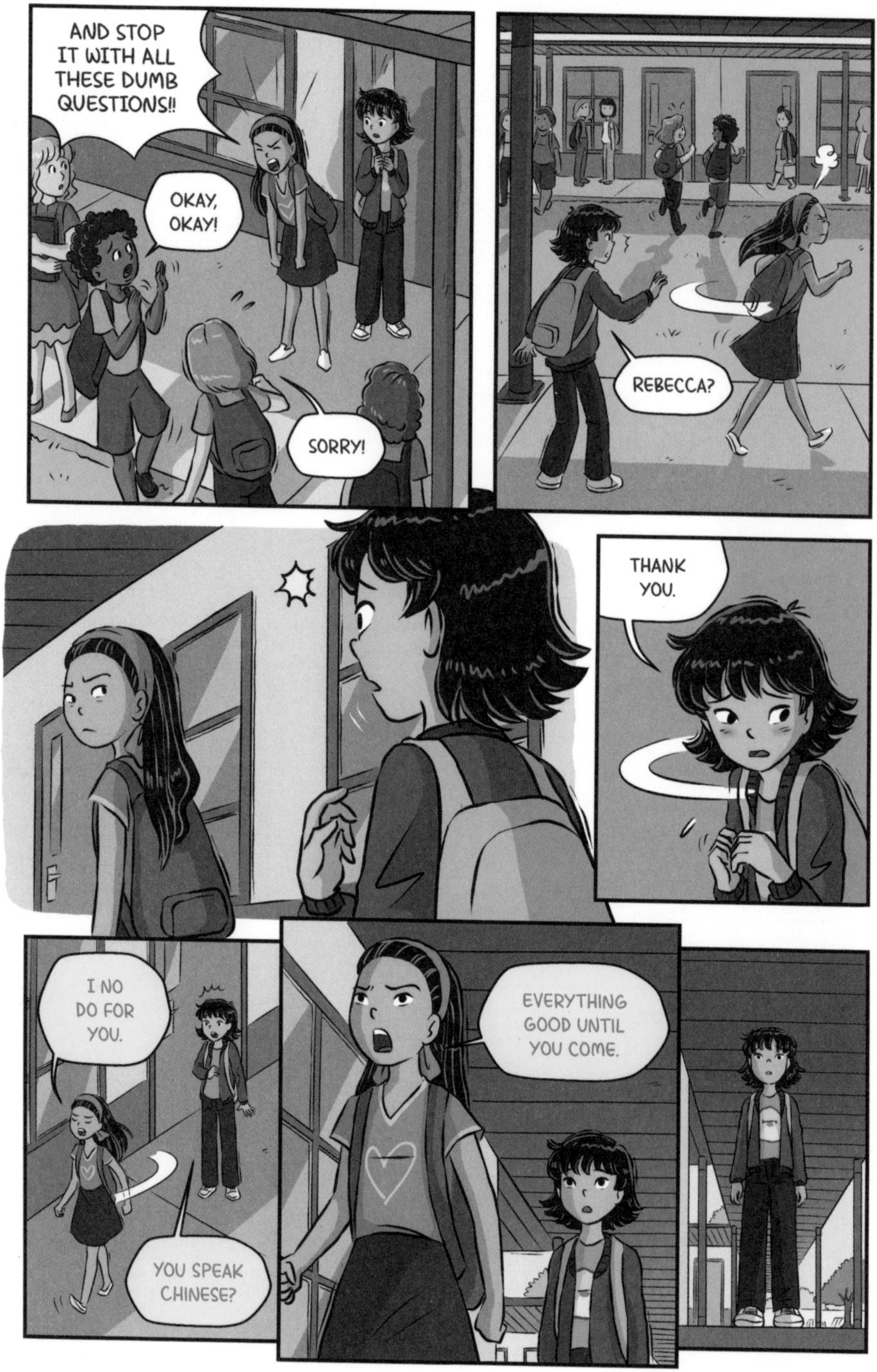
AND STOP IT WITH ALL THESE DUMB QUESTIONS!!
OKAY, OKAY!
SORRY!
REBECCA?
THANK YOU.
I NO DO FOR YOU.
YOU SPEAK CHINESE?
EVERYTHING GOOD UNTIL YOU COME.

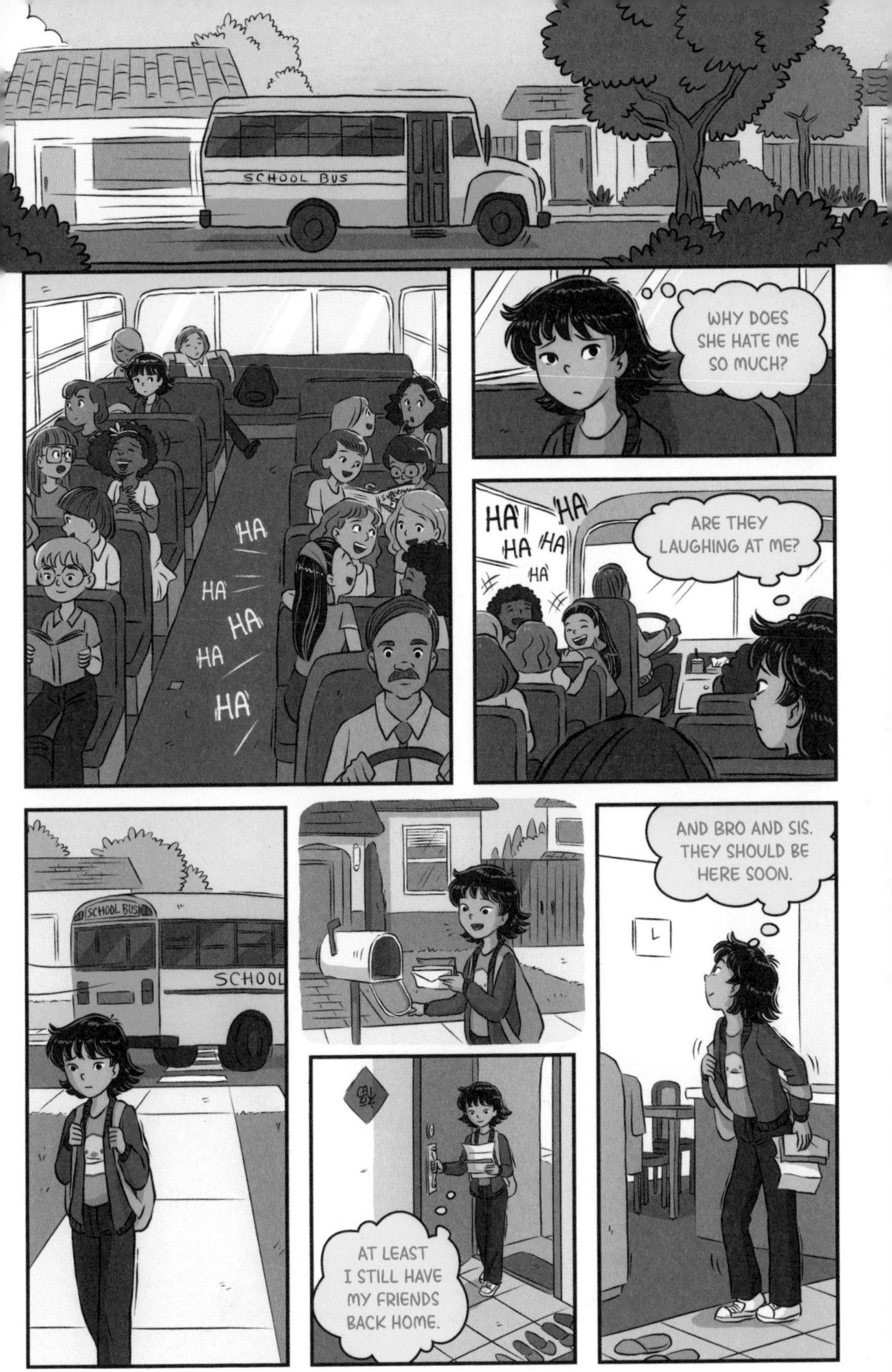
SCHOOL BUS
HA HA HA HA HA HA
WHY DOES SHE HATE ME SO MUCH?
HA HA HA HA HA
ARE THEY LAUGHING AT ME?
SCHOOL BUS
SCHOOL
AT LEAST I STILL HAVE MY FRIENDS BACK HOME.
AND BRO AND SIS. THEY SHOULD BE HERE SOON.

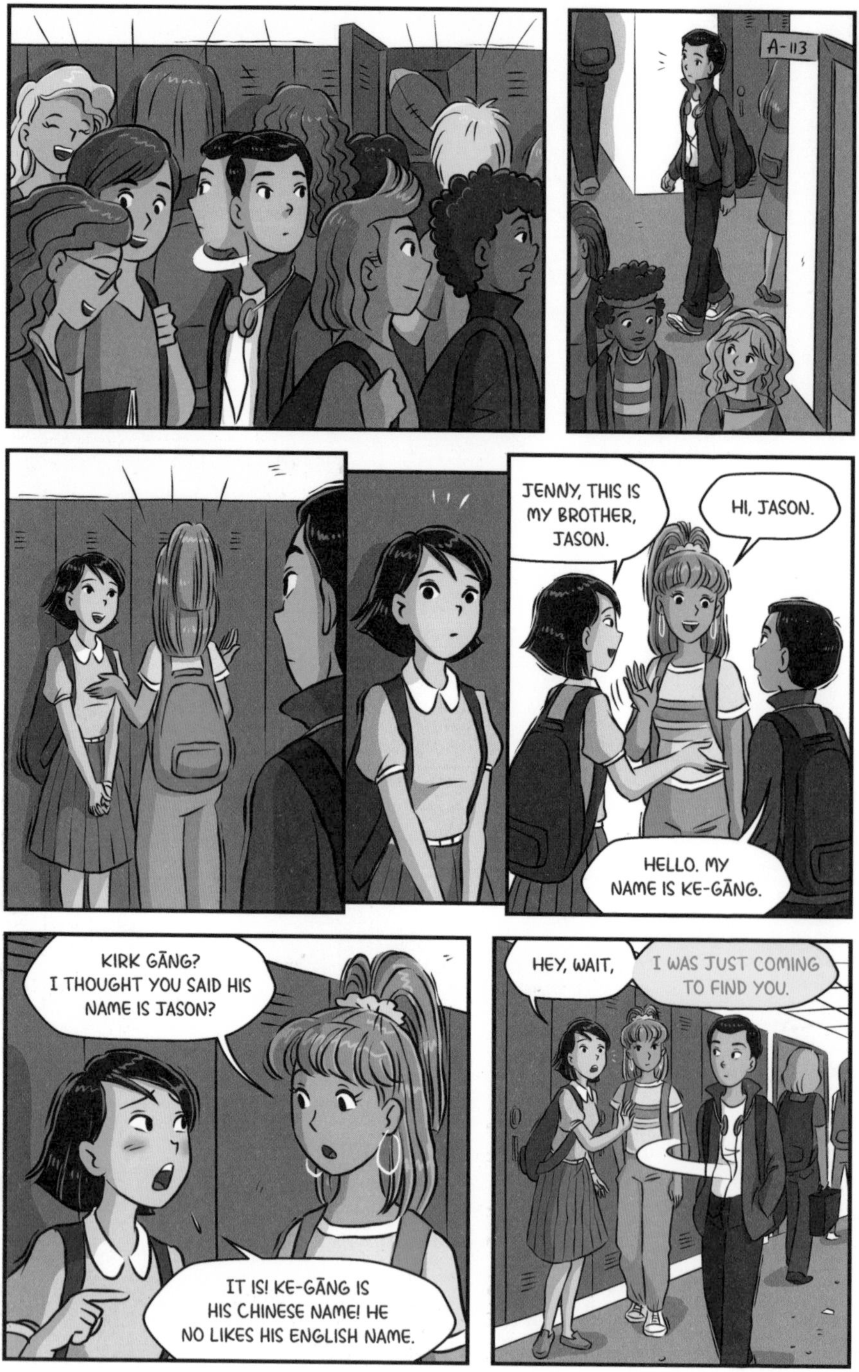
A-113
JENNY, THIS IS MY BROTHER, JASON.
HI, JASON.
HELLO. MY NAME IS KE-GĀNG.
KIRK GĀNG? I THOUGHT YOU SAID HIS NAME IS JASON?
IT IS! KE-GĀNG IS HIS CHINESE NAME! HE NO LIKES HIS ENGLISH NAME.
HEY, WAIT,
I WAS JUST COMING TO FIND YOU.

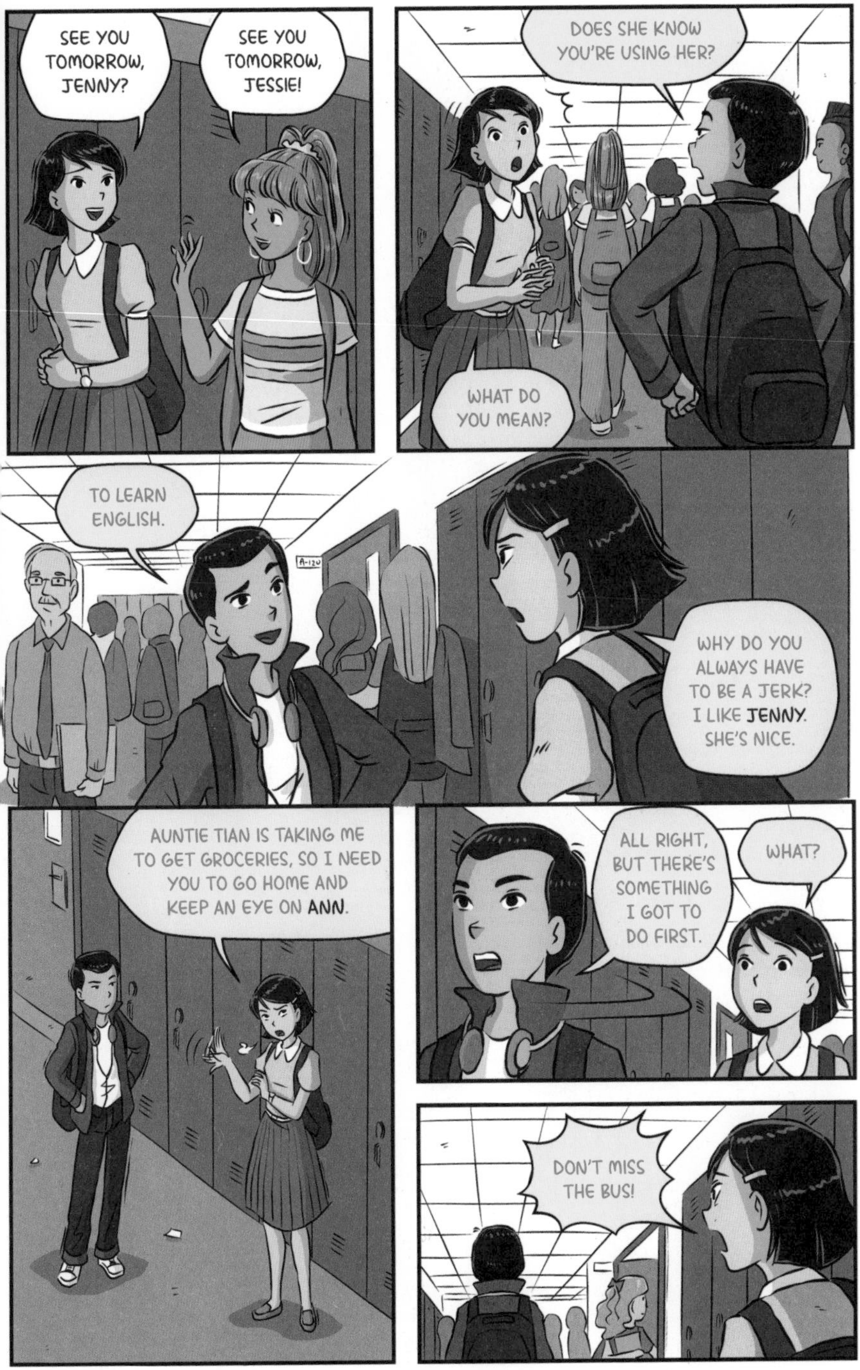
SEE YOU TOMORROW, JENNY?
SEE YOU TOMORROW, JESSIE!
DOES SHE KNOW YOU'RE USING HER?
WHAT DO YOU MEAN?
TO LEARN ENGLISH.
A-12U
WHY DO YOU ALWAYS HAVE TO BE A JERK? I LIKE JENNY. SHE'S NICE.
AUNTIE TIAN IS TAKING ME TO GET GROCERIES, SO I NEED YOU TO GO HOME AND KEEP AN EYE ON ANN.
ALL RIGHT, BUT THERE'S SOMETHING I GOT TO DO FIRST.
WHAT?
DON'T MISS THE BUS!

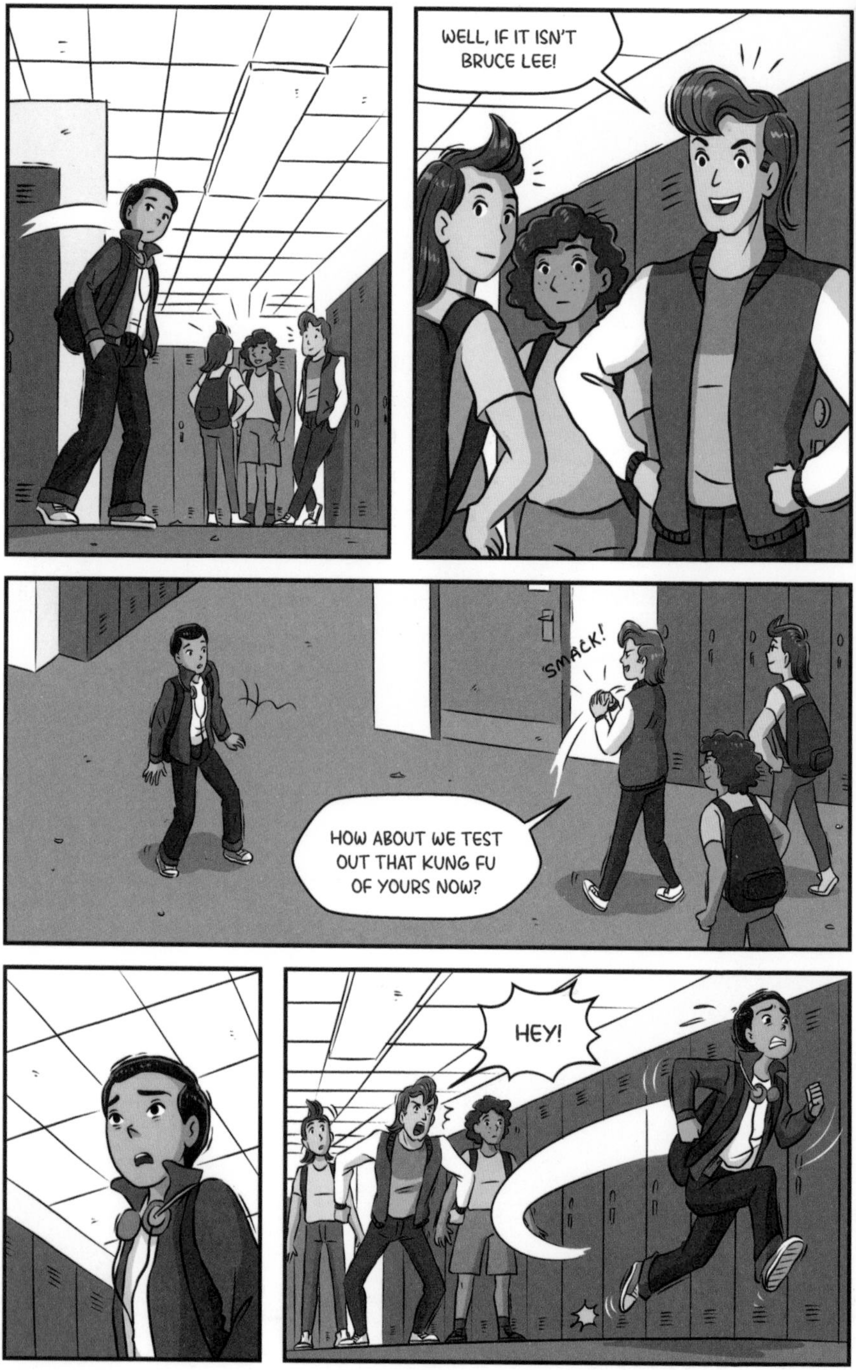
WELL, IF IT ISN'T BRUCE LEE!
SMACK!
HOW ABOUT WE TEST OUT THAT KUNG FU OF YOURS NOW?
HEY!

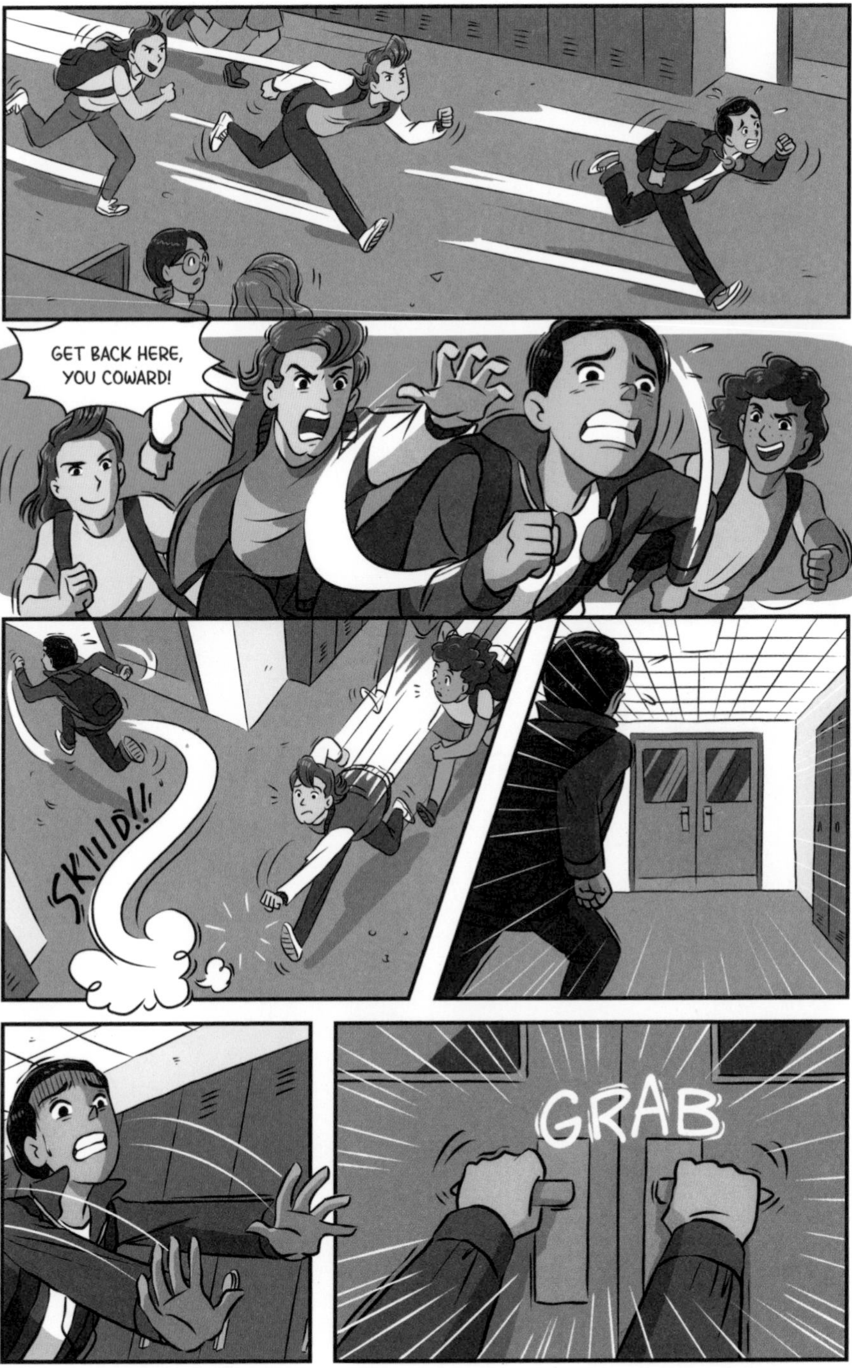
GET BACK HERE, YOU COWARD!
SKIIID!!
GRAB

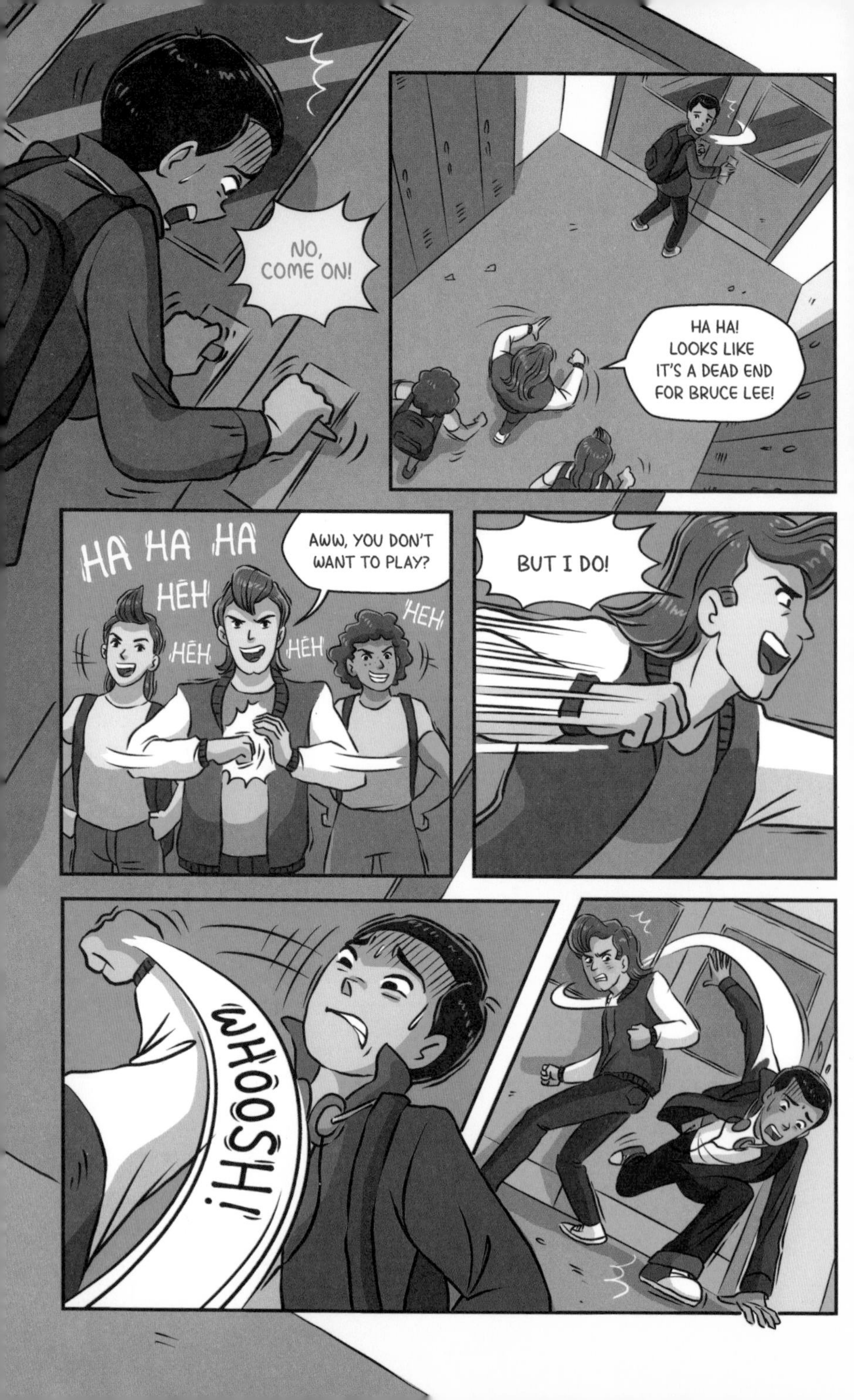
NO, COME ON!
HA HA! LOOKS LIKE IT'S A DEAD END FOR BRUCE LEE!
HA HA HA
HEH
HEH
HEH
HEH
AWW, YOU DON'T WANT TO PLAY?
BUT I DO!
WHOOSH!

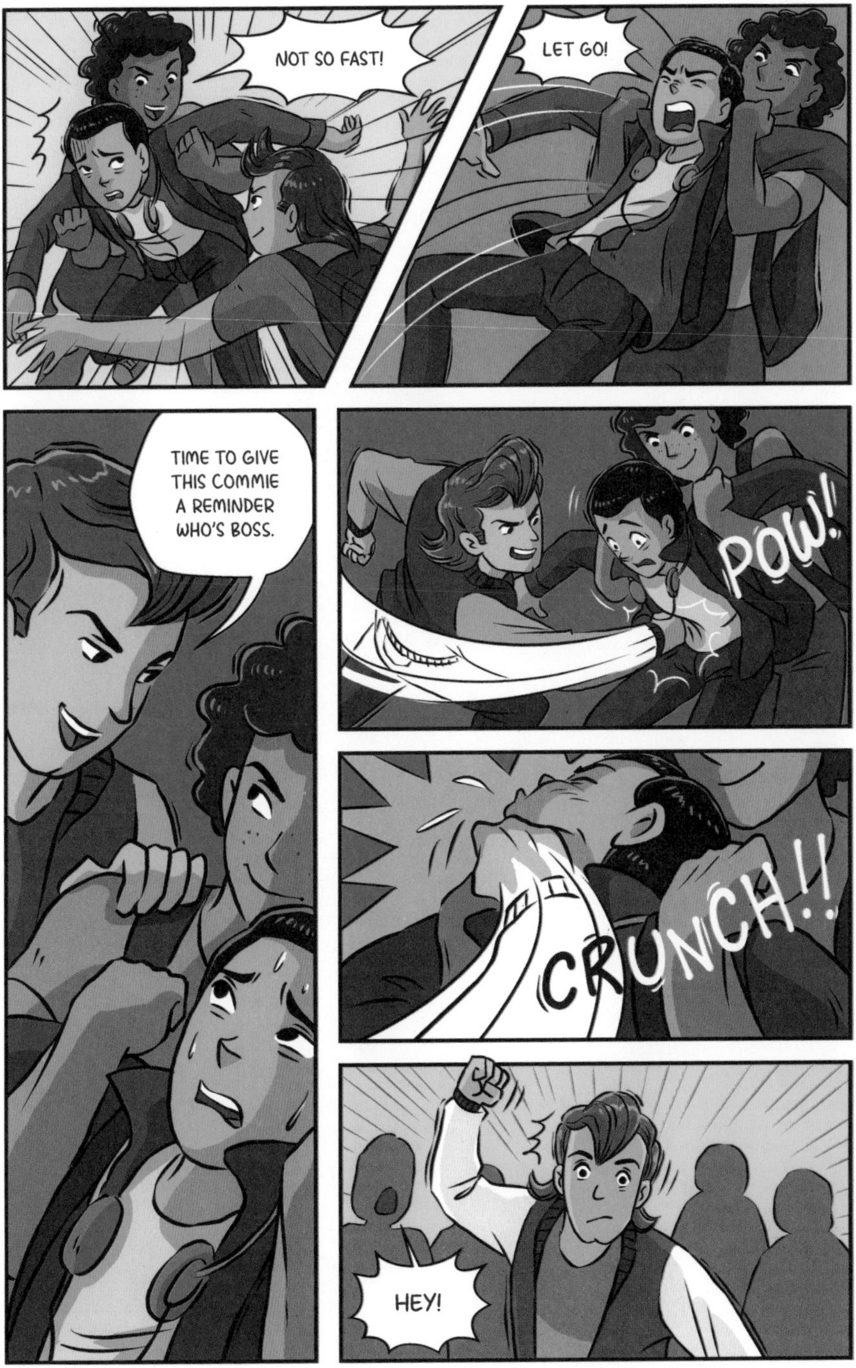
NOT SO FAST!
LET GO!
TIME TO GIVE THIS COMMIE A REMINDER WHO'S BOSS.
POW!!
CRUNCH!!
HEY!

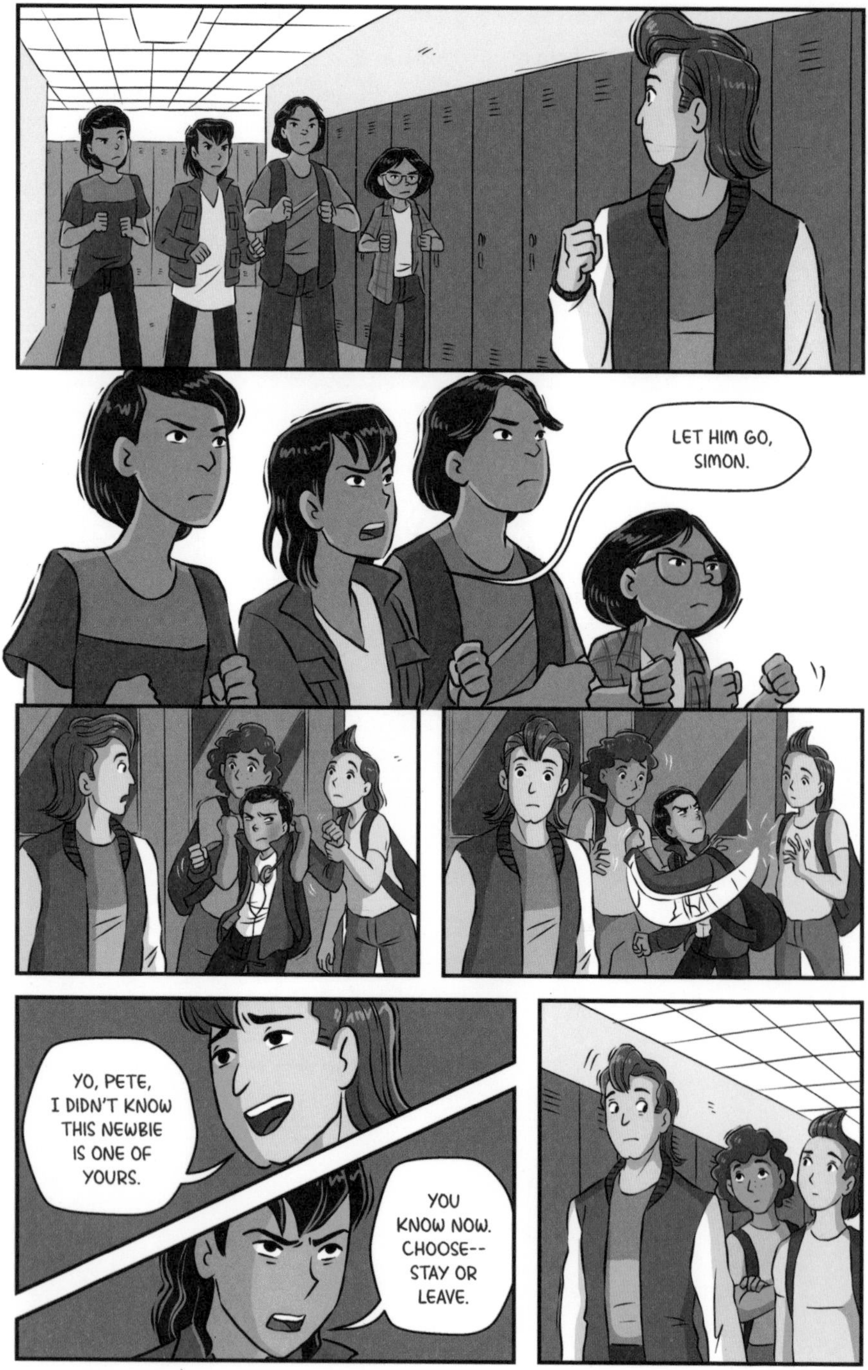
LET HIM GO, SIMON.
YO, PETE, I DIDN'T KNOW THIS NEWBIE IS ONE OF YOURS.
YOU KNOW NOW. CHOOSE-- STAY OR LEAVE.

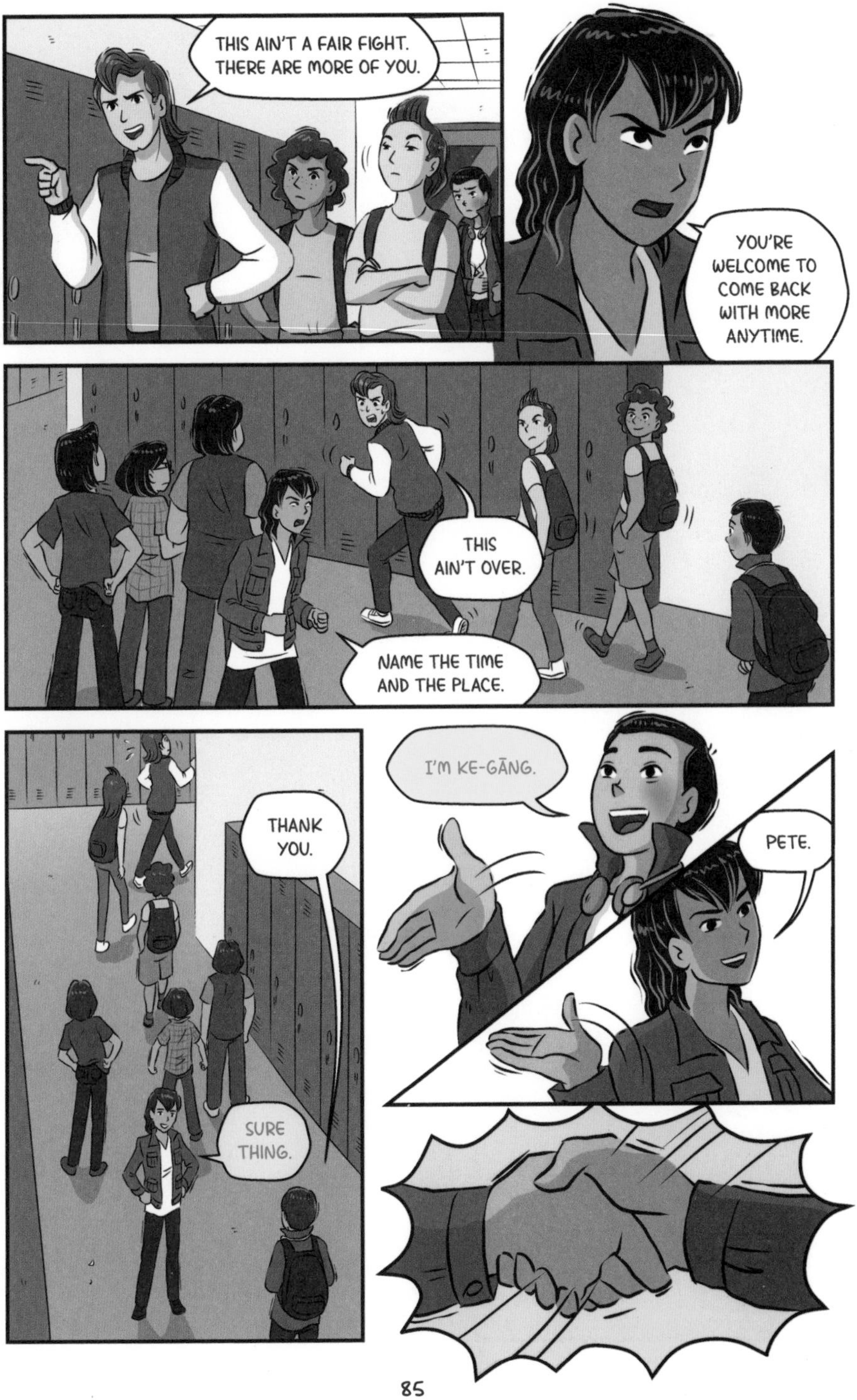
THIS AIN'T A FAIR FIGHT. THERE ARE MORE OF YOU.
YOU'RE WELCOME TO COME BACK WITH MORE ANYTIME.
THIS AIN'T OVER.
NAME THE TIME AND THE PLACE.
THANK YOU.
SURE THING.
I'M KE-GĀNG.
PETE.

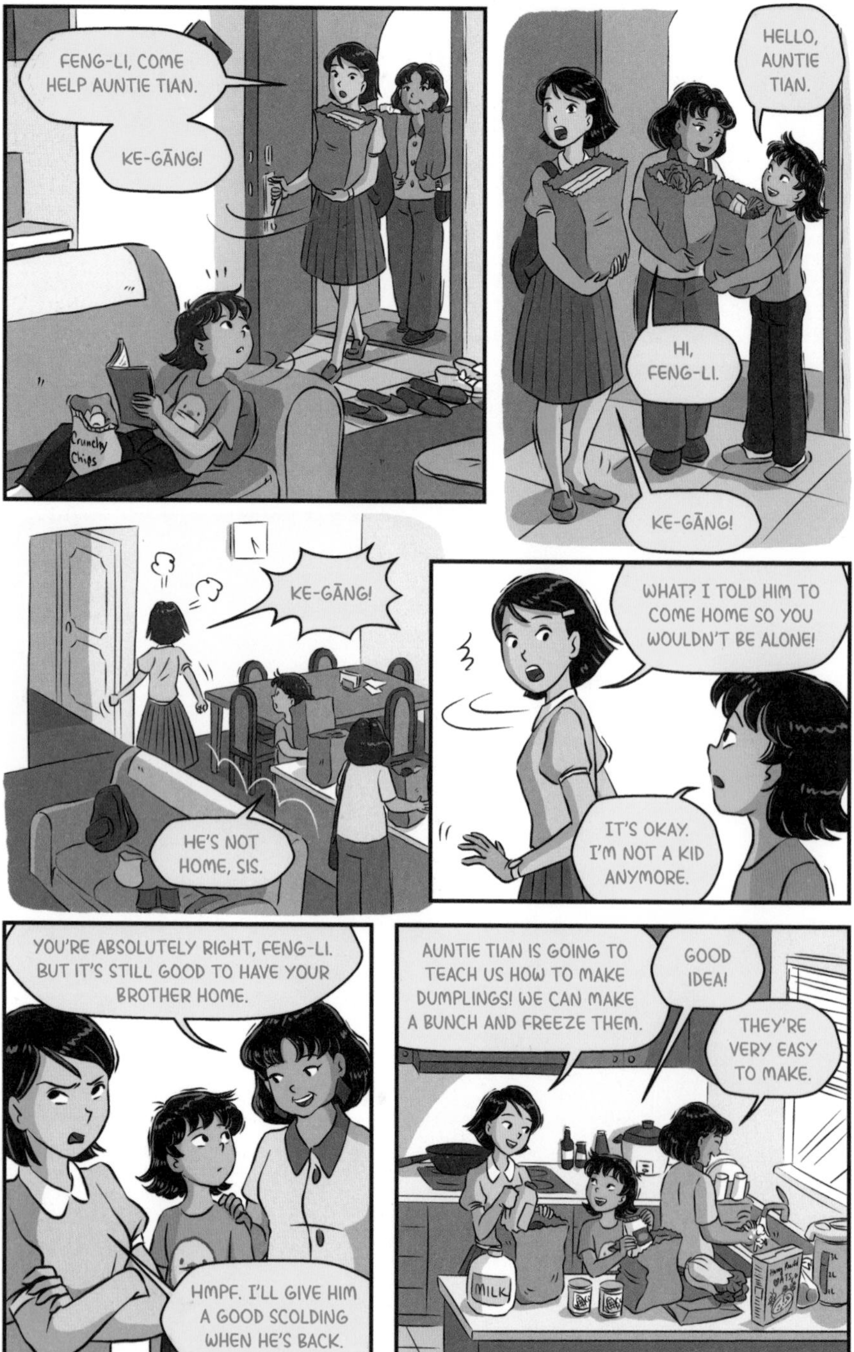
FENG-LI, COME HELP AUNTIE TIAN.
KE-GĀNG!
HELLO, AUNTIE TIAN.
HI, FENG-LI.
KE-GĀNG!
KE-GĀNG!
HE'S NOT HOME, SIS.
WHAT? I TOLD HIM TO COME HOME SO YOU WOULDN'T BE ALONE!
IT'S OKAY. I'M NOT A KID ANYMORE.
YOU'RE ABSOLUTELY RIGHT, FENG-LI. BUT IT'S STILL GOOD TO HAVE YOUR BROTHER HOME.
HMPF. I'LL GIVE HIM A GOOD SCOLDING WHEN HE'S BACK.
AUNTIE TIAN IS GOING TO TEACH US HOW TO MAKE DUMPLINGS! WE CAN MAKE A BUNCH AND FREEZE THEM.
GOOD IDEA!
THEY'RE VERY EASY TO MAKE.

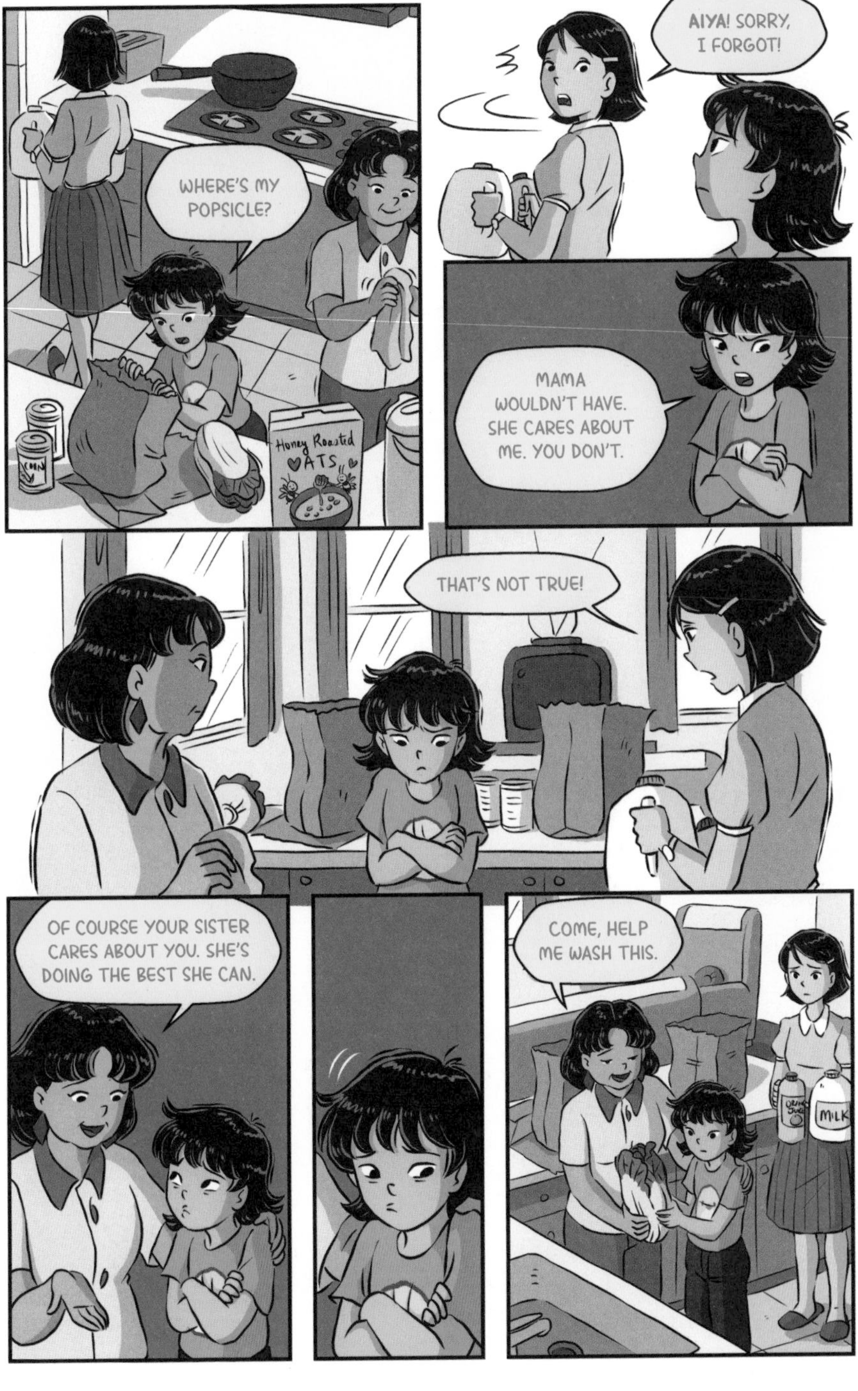
WHERE'S MY POPSICLE?
AIYA! SORRY, I FORGOT!
MAMA WOULDN'T HAVE. SHE CARES ABOUT ME. YOU DON'T.
THAT'S NOT TRUE!
OF COURSE YOUR SISTER CARES ABOUT YOU. SHE'S DOING THE BEST SHE CAN.
COME, HELP ME WASH THIS.
Honey Roasted OATS
MILK

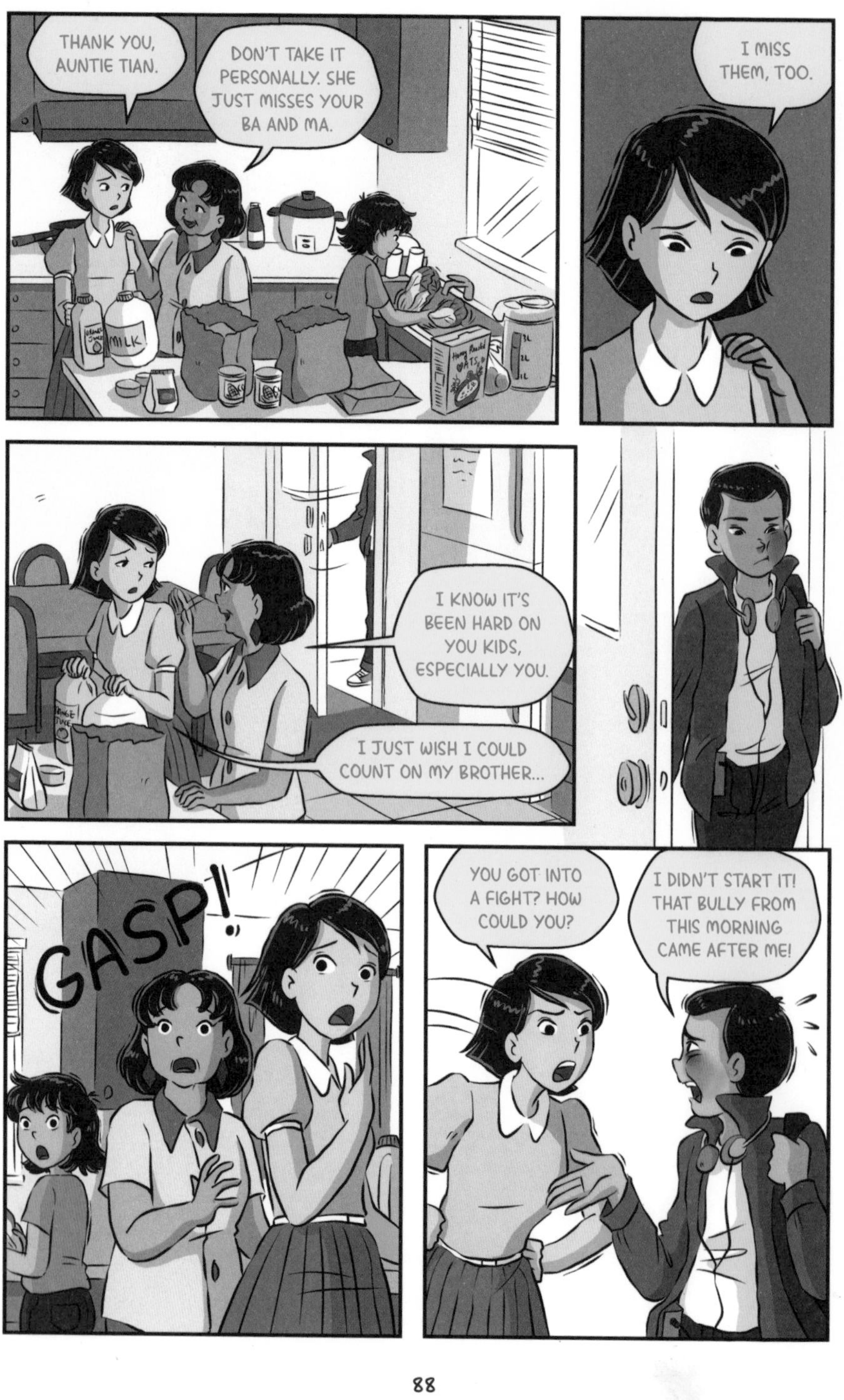
THANK YOU, AUNTIE TIAN.
DON'T TAKE IT PERSONALLY. SHE JUST MISSES YOUR BA AND MA.
MILK
I MISS THEM, TOO.
I KNOW IT'S BEEN HARD ON YOU KIDS, ESPECIALLY YOU.
I JUST WISH I COULD COUNT ON MY BROTHER...
GASP!
YOU GOT INTO A FIGHT? HOW COULD YOU?
I DIDN'T START IT! THAT BULLY FROM THIS MORNING CAME AFTER ME!

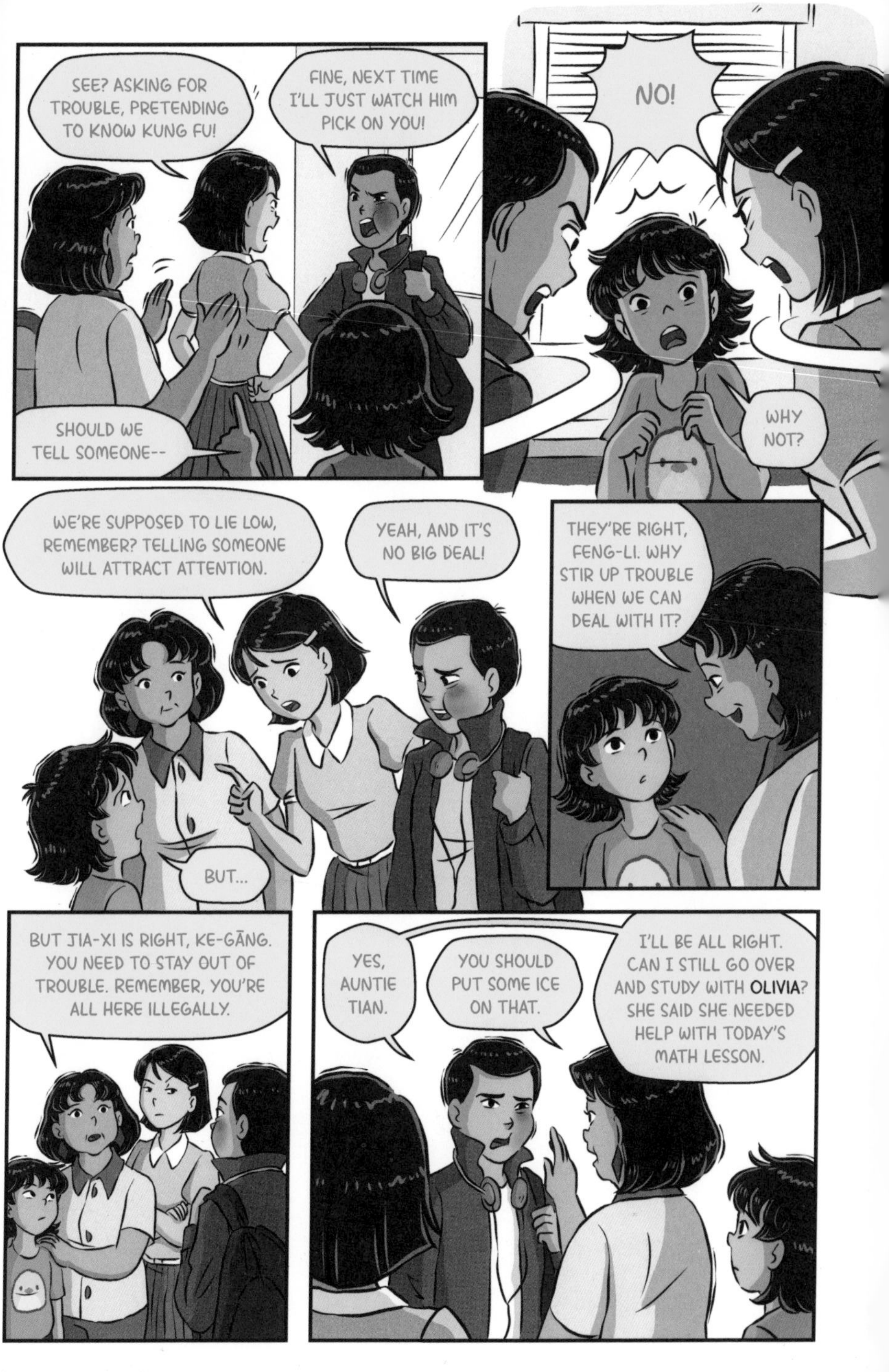
SEE? ASKING FOR TROUBLE, PRETENDING TO KNOW KUNG FU!
SHOULD WE TELL SOMEONE--
FINE, NEXT TIME I'LL JUST WATCH HIM PICK ON YOU!
NO!
WHY NOT?
WE'RE SUPPOSED TO LIE LOW, REMEMBER? TELLING SOMEONE WILL ATTRACT ATTENTION.
BUT...
YEAH, AND IT'S NO BIG DEAL!
THEY'RE RIGHT, FENG-LI. WHY STIR UP TROUBLE WHEN WE CAN DEAL WITH IT?
BUT JIA-XI IS RIGHT, KE-GĀNG. YOU NEED TO STAY OUT OF TROUBLE. REMEMBER, YOU'RE ALL HERE ILLEGALLY.
YES, AUNTIE TIAN.
YOU SHOULD PUT SOME ICE ON THAT.
I'LL BE ALL RIGHT. CAN I STILL GO OVER AND STUDY WITH OLIVIA? SHE SAID SHE NEEDED HELP WITH TODAY'S MATH LESSON.

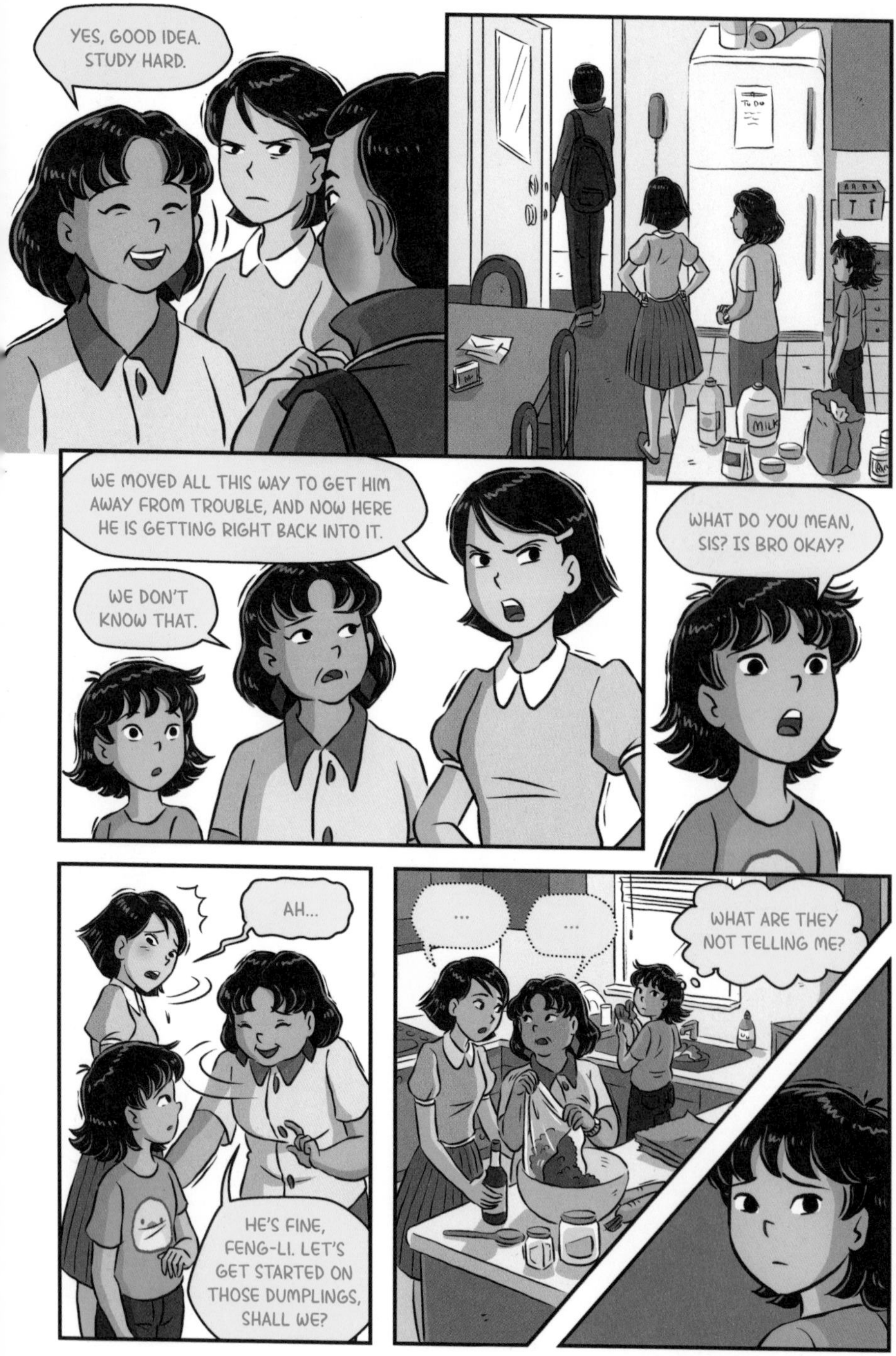
YES, GOOD IDEA. STUDY HARD.
TO DO
MILK
WE MOVED ALL THIS WAY TO GET HIM AWAY FROM TROUBLE, AND NOW HERE HE IS GETTING RIGHT BACK INTO IT.
WE DON'T KNOW THAT.
WHAT DO YOU MEAN, SIS? IS BRO OKAY?
AH...
HE'S FINE, FENG-LI. LET'S GET STARTED ON THOSE DUMPLINGS, SHALL WE?
...
...
WHAT ARE THEY NOT TELLING ME?

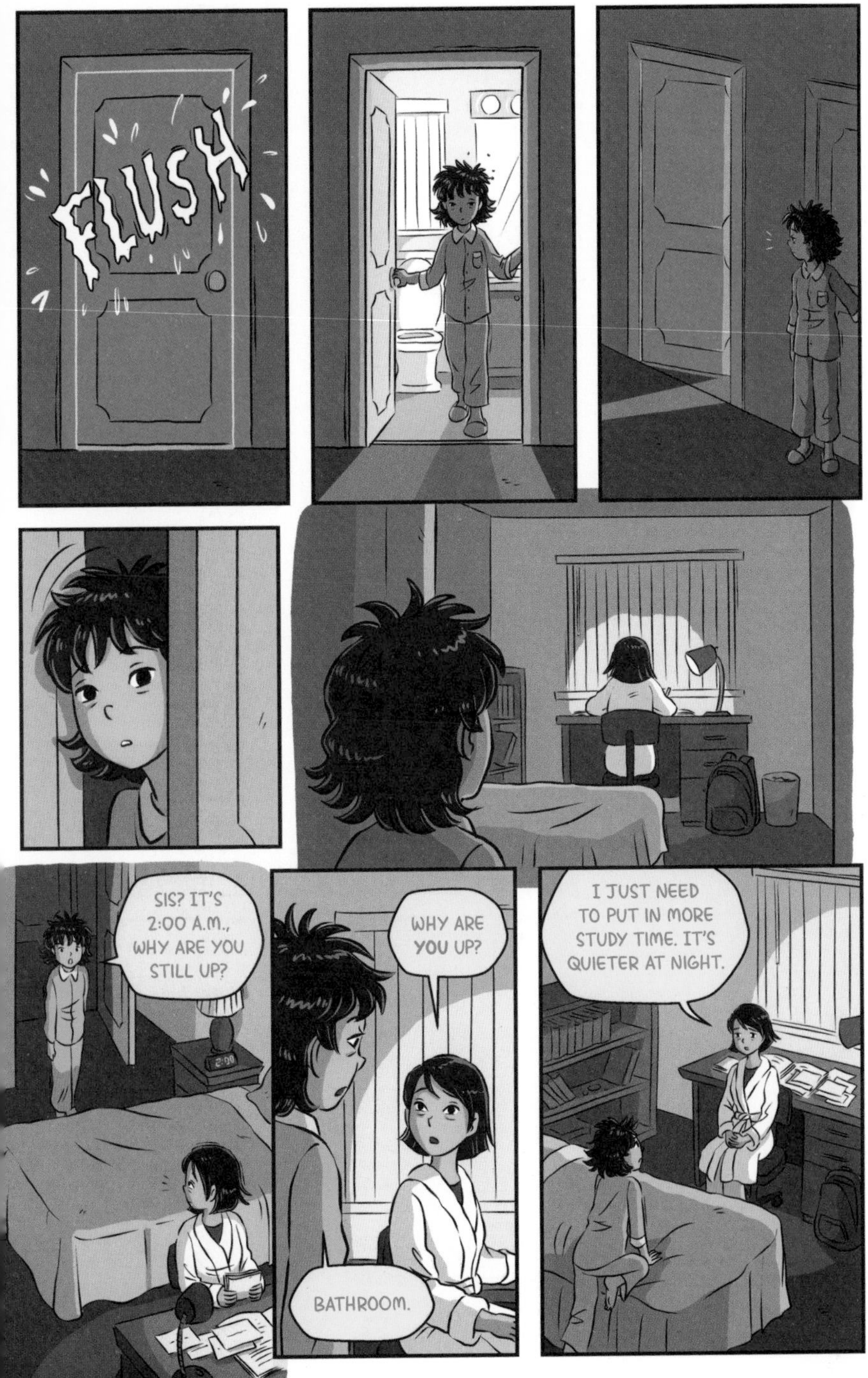
FLUSH
SIS? IT'S 2:00 A.M., WHY ARE YOU STILL UP?
WHY ARE YOU UP?
BATHROOM.
I JUST NEED TO PUT IN MORE STUDY TIME. IT'S QUIETER AT NIGHT.

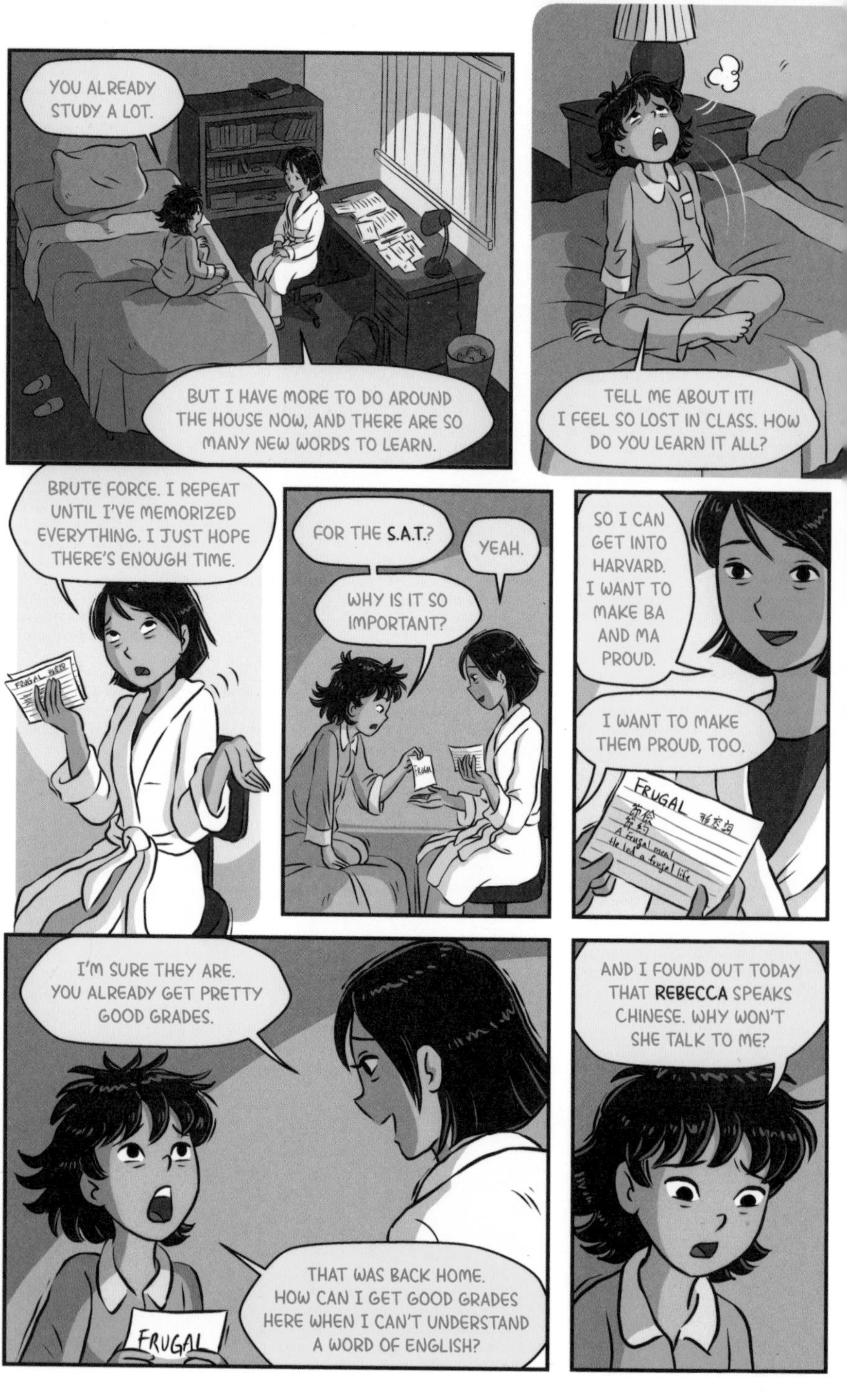
YOU ALREADY STUDY A LOT.
BUT I HAVE MORE TO DO AROUND THE HOUSE NOW, AND THERE ARE SO MANY NEW WORDS TO LEARN.
TELL ME ABOUT IT! I FEEL SO LOST IN CLASS. HOW DO YOU LEARN IT ALL?
BRUTE FORCE. I REPEAT UNTIL I'VE MEMORIZED EVERYTHING. I JUST HOPE THERE'S ENOUGH TIME.
FOR THE S.A.T.?
YEAH.
WHY IS IT SO IMPORTANT?
FRUGAL
SO I CAN GET INTO HARVARD. I WANT TO MAKE BA AND MA PROUD.
I WANT TO MAKE THEM PROUD, TOO.
FRUGAL 形容词
节俭
节约
A frugal meal
He led a frugal life
I'M SURE THEY ARE. YOU ALREADY GET PRETTY GOOD GRADES.
FRUGAL
THAT WAS BACK HOME. HOW CAN I GET GOOD GRADES HERE WHEN I CAN'T UNDERSTAND A WORD OF ENGLISH?
AND I FOUND OUT TODAY THAT REBECCA SPEAKS CHINESE. WHY WON'T SHE TALK TO ME?

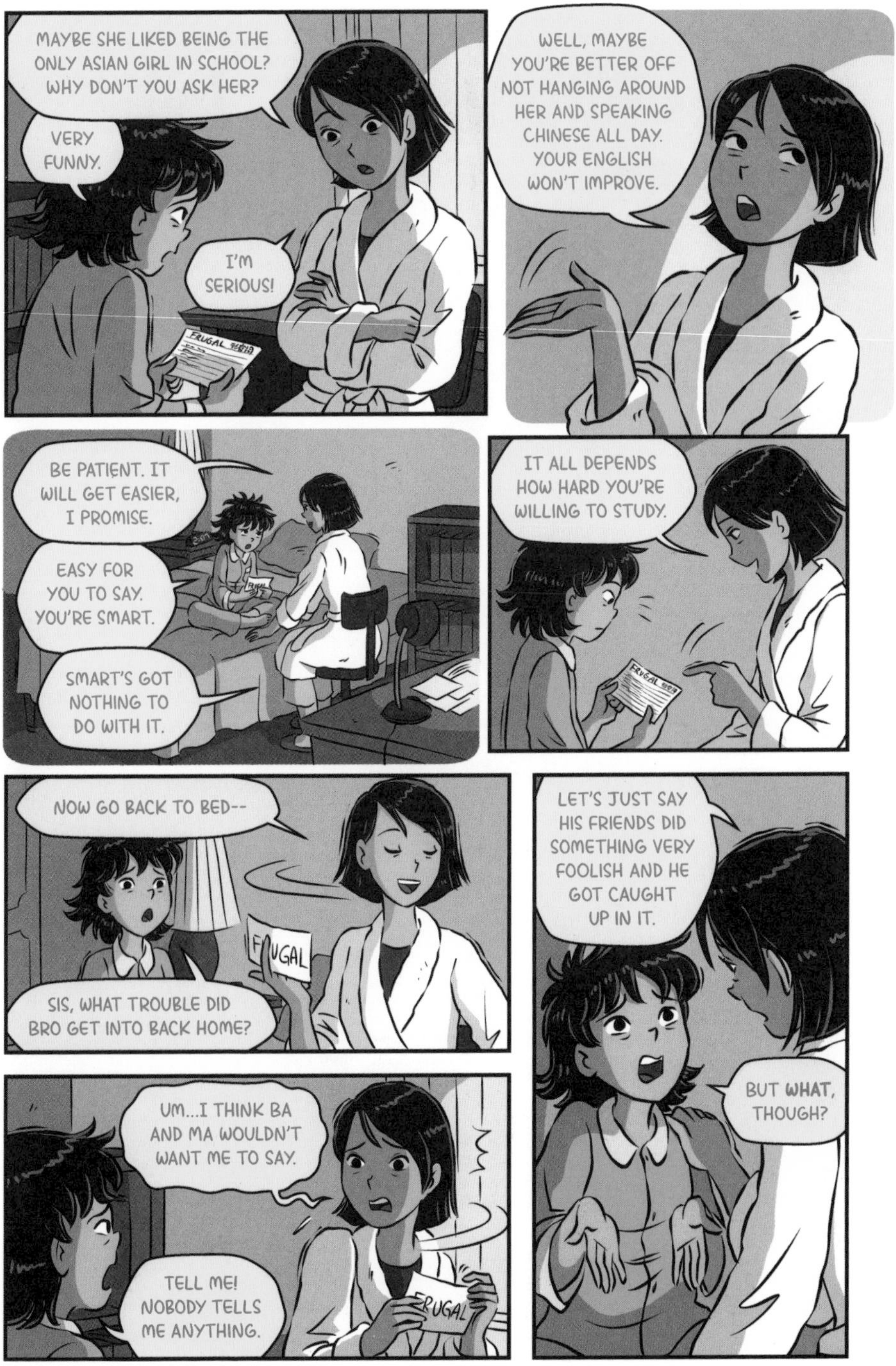

MAYBE SHE LIKED BEING THE ONLY ASIAN GIRL IN SCHOOL? WHY DON'T YOU ASK HER?
VERY FUNNY.
I'M SERIOUS!
FRUGAL
WELL, MAYBE YOU'RE BETTER OFF NOT HANGING AROUND HER AND SPEAKING CHINESE ALL DAY. YOUR ENGLISH WON'T IMPROVE.
BE PATIENT. IT WILL GET EASIER, I PROMISE.
EASY FOR YOU TO SAY. YOU'RE SMART.
SMART'S GOT NOTHING TO DO WITH IT.
IT ALL DEPENDS HOW HARD YOU'RE WILLING TO STUDY.
FRUGAL
NOW GO BACK TO BED--
FRUGAL
SIS, WHAT TROUBLE DID BRO GET INTO BACK HOME?
UM...I THINK BA AND MA WOULDN'T WANT ME TO SAY.
TELL ME! NOBODY TELLS ME ANYTHING.
FRUGAL
LET'S JUST SAY HIS FRIENDS DID SOMETHING VERY FOOLISH AND HE GOT CAUGHT UP IN IT.
BUT **WHAT**, THOUGH?

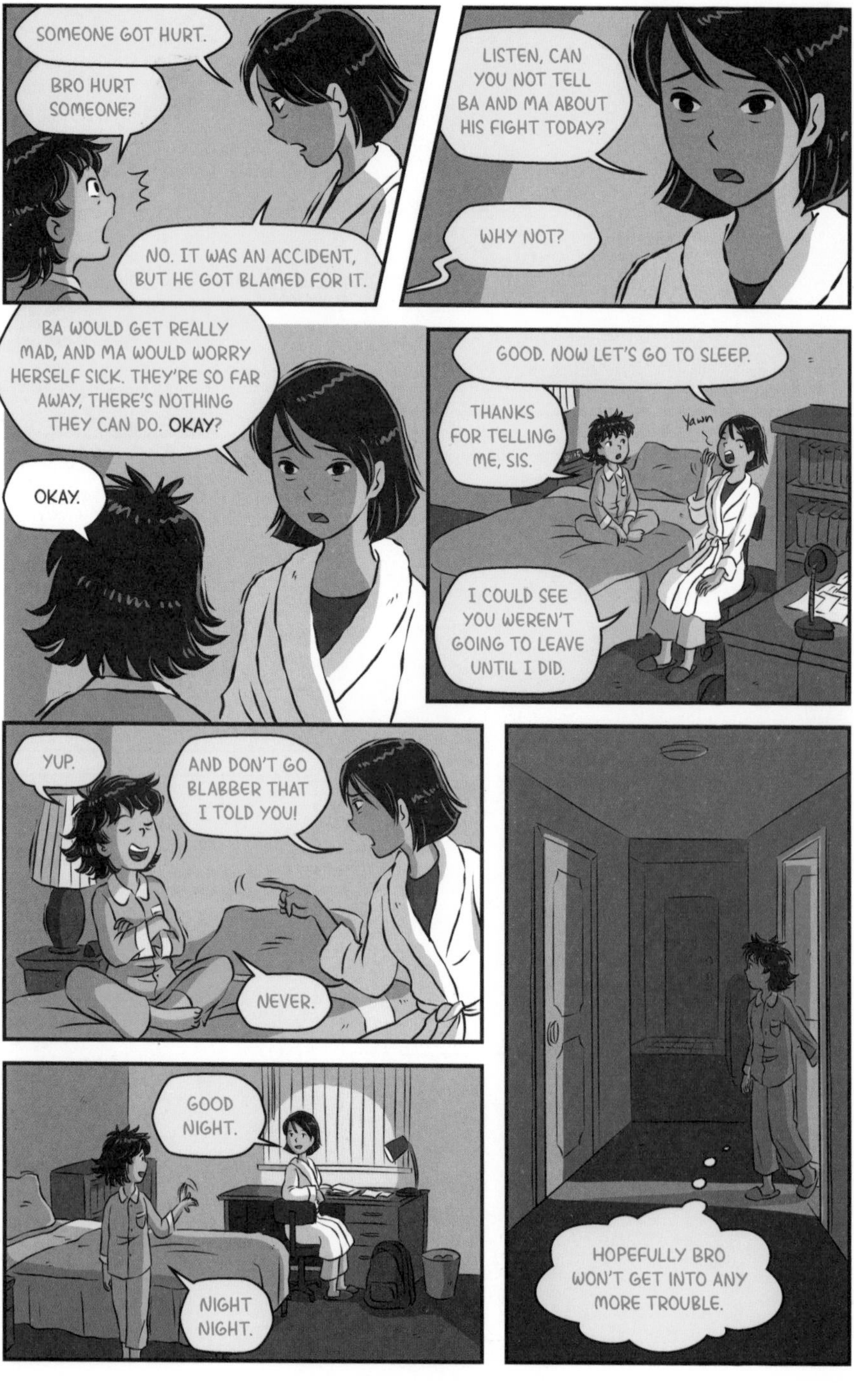
SOMEONE GOT HURT.
BRO HURT SOMEONE?
NO. IT WAS AN ACCIDENT, BUT HE GOT BLAMED FOR IT.
LISTEN, CAN YOU NOT TELL BA AND MA ABOUT HIS FIGHT TODAY?
WHY NOT?
BA WOULD GET REALLY MAD, AND MA WOULD WORRY HERSELF SICK. THEY'RE SO FAR AWAY, THERE'S NOTHING THEY CAN DO. OKAY?
OKAY.
GOOD. NOW LET'S GO TO SLEEP.
THANKS FOR TELLING ME, SIS.
Yawn
I COULD SEE YOU WEREN'T GOING TO LEAVE UNTIL I DID.
YUP.
AND DON'T GO BLABBER THAT I TOLD YOU!
NEVER.
GOOD NIGHT.
NIGHT NIGHT.
HOPEFULLY BRO WON'T GET INTO ANY MORE TROUBLE.

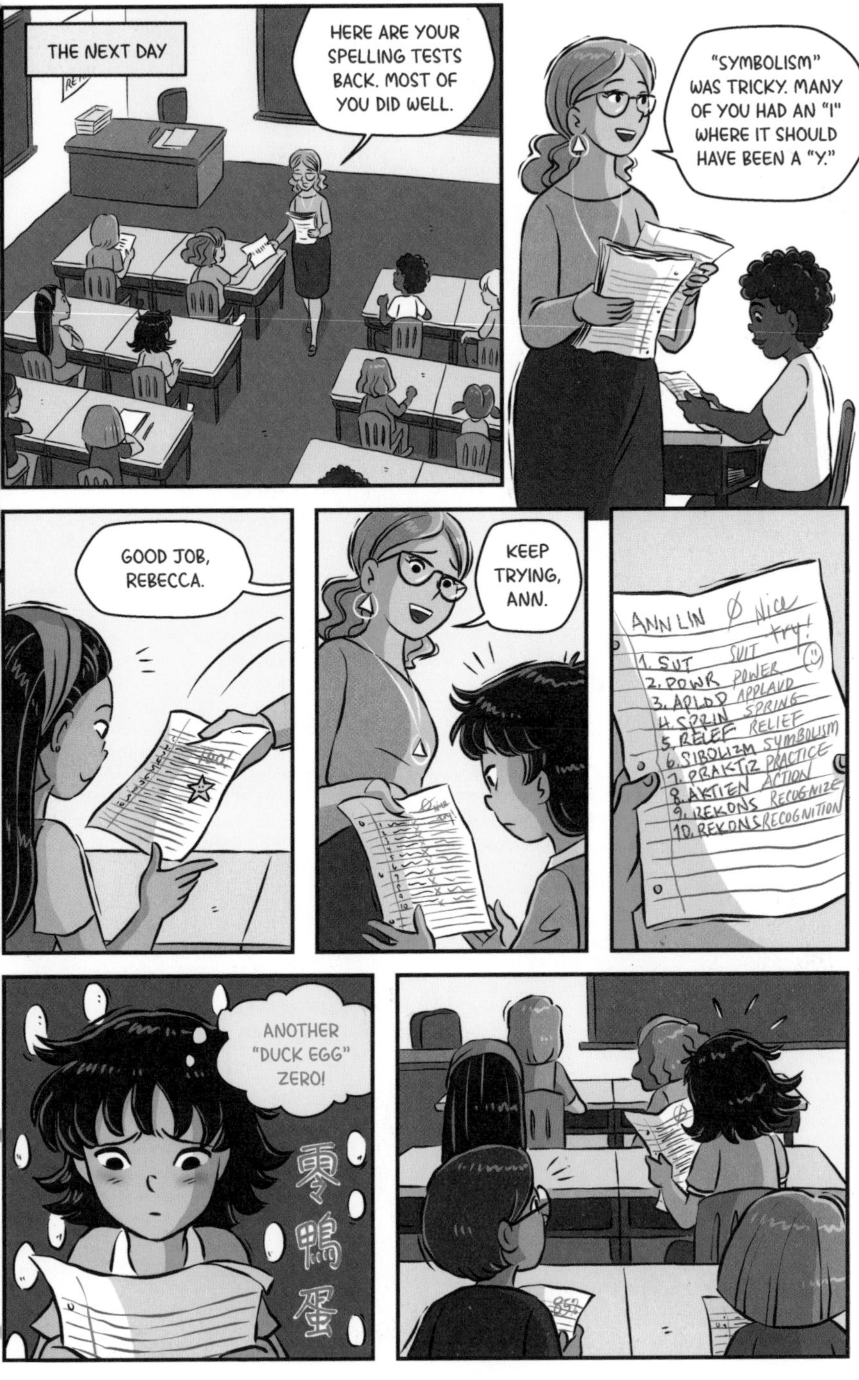

THE NEXT DAY
HERE ARE YOUR SPELLING TESTS BACK. MOST OF YOU DID WELL.
"SYMBOLISM" WAS TRICKY. MANY OF YOU HAD AN "I" WHERE IT SHOULD HAVE BEEN A "Y."
GOOD JOB, REBECCA.
KEEP TRYING, ANN.
ANN LIN Ø Nice try!
1. SUT SUIT
2. POWR POWER
3. APLOD APPLAUD
4. SPRIN SPRING
5. RELEF RELIEF
6. SIBOLIZM SYMBOLISM
7. PRAKTIZ PRACTICE
8. AKTIEN ACTION
9. REKONS RECOGNIZE
10. REKONS RECOGNITION
ANOTHER "DUCK EGG" ZERO!
零鴨蛋

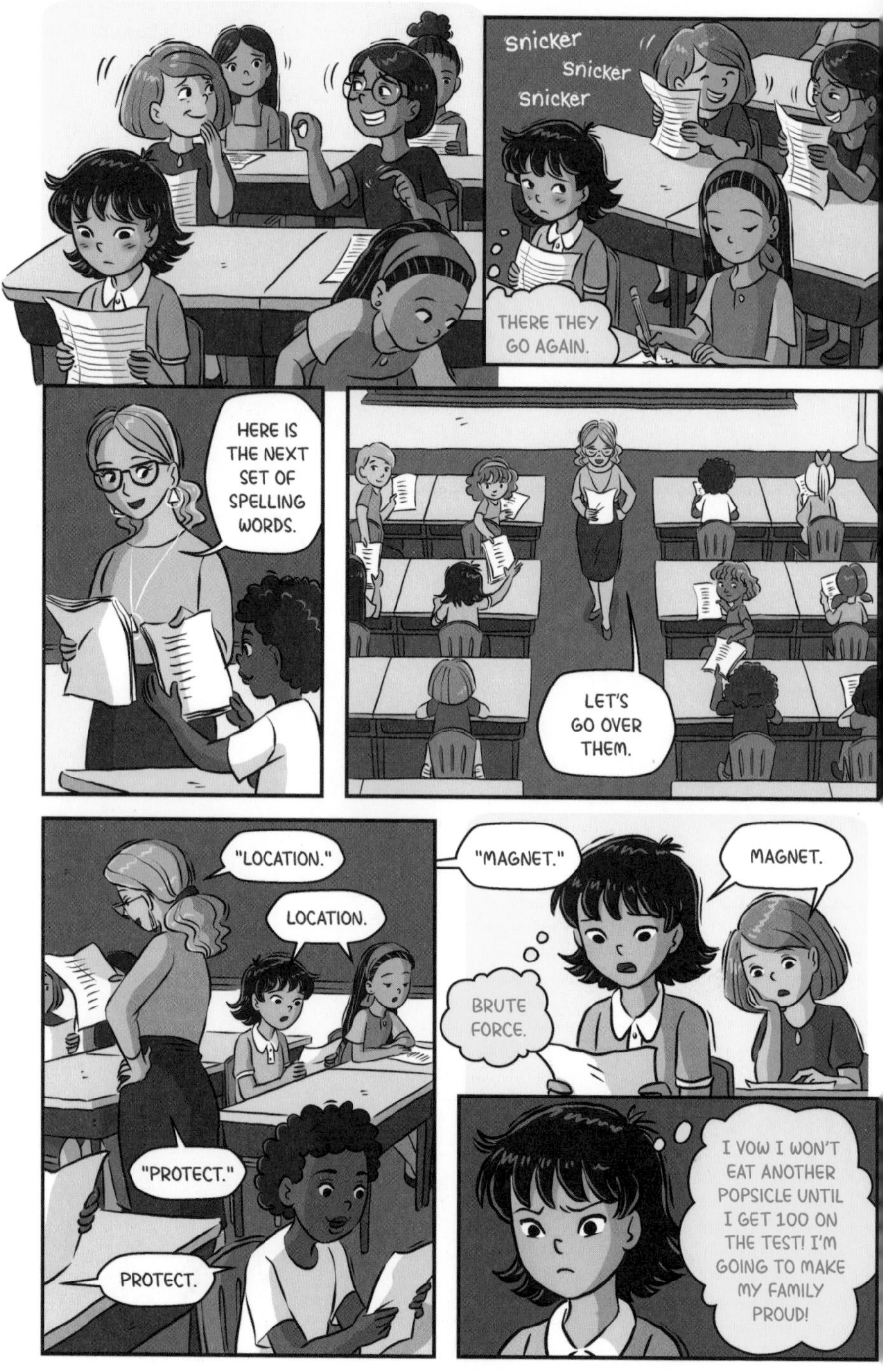
snicker
snicker
snicker
THERE THEY GO AGAIN.
HERE IS THE NEXT SET OF SPELLING WORDS.
LET'S GO OVER THEM.
"LOCATION."
LOCATION.
"PROTECT."
PROTECT.
"MAGNET."
MAGNET.
BRUTE FORCE.
I VOW I WON'T EAT ANOTHER POPSICLE UNTIL I GET 100 ON THE TEST! I'M GOING TO MAKE MY FAMILY PROUD!

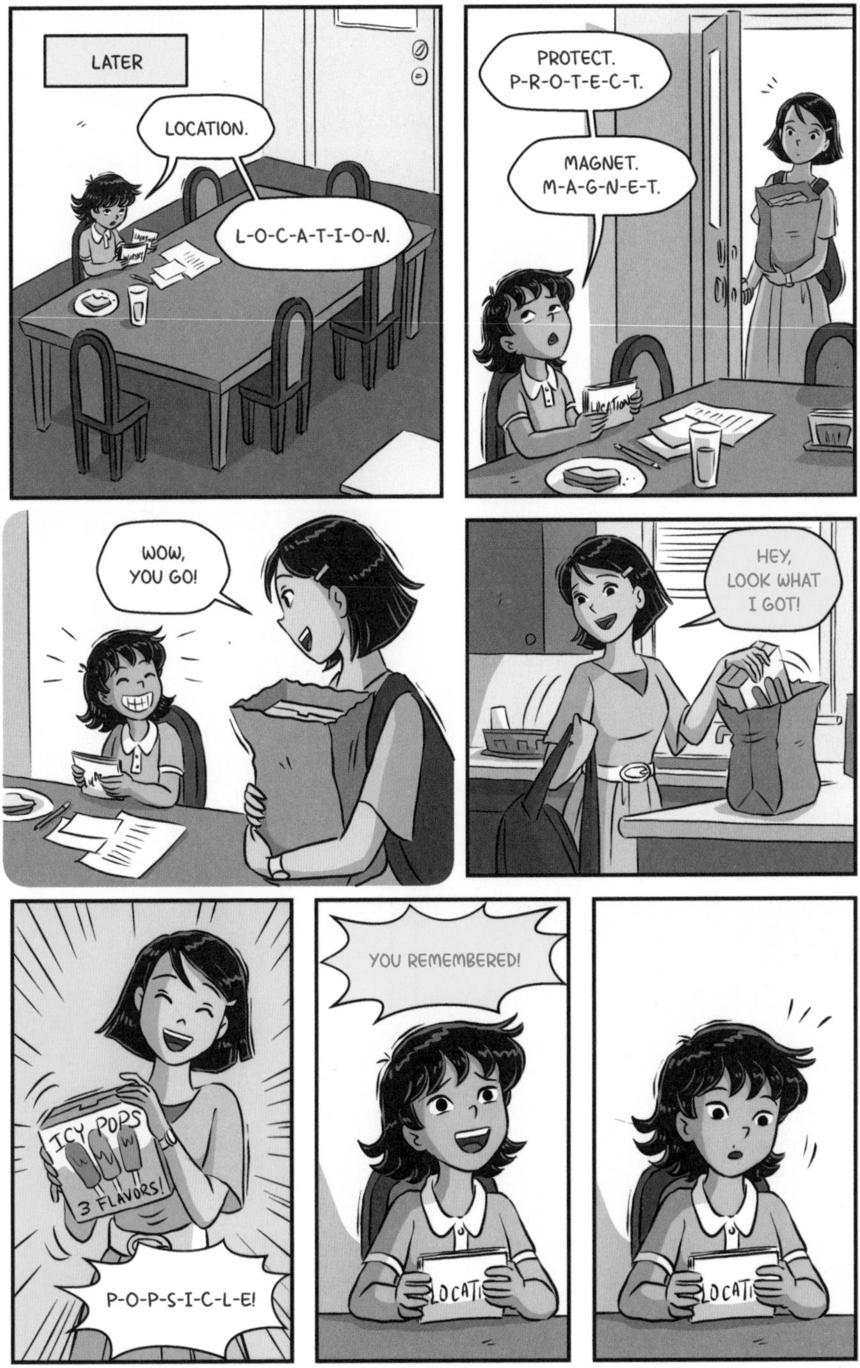
LATER
LOCATION.
L-O-C-A-T-I-O-N.
PROTECT.
P-R-O-T-E-C-T.
MAGNET.
M-A-G-N-E-T.
WOW,
YOU GO!
HEY,
LOOK WHAT
I GOT!
ICY POPS
3 FLAVORS!
P-O-P-S-I-C-L-E!
YOU REMEMBERED!

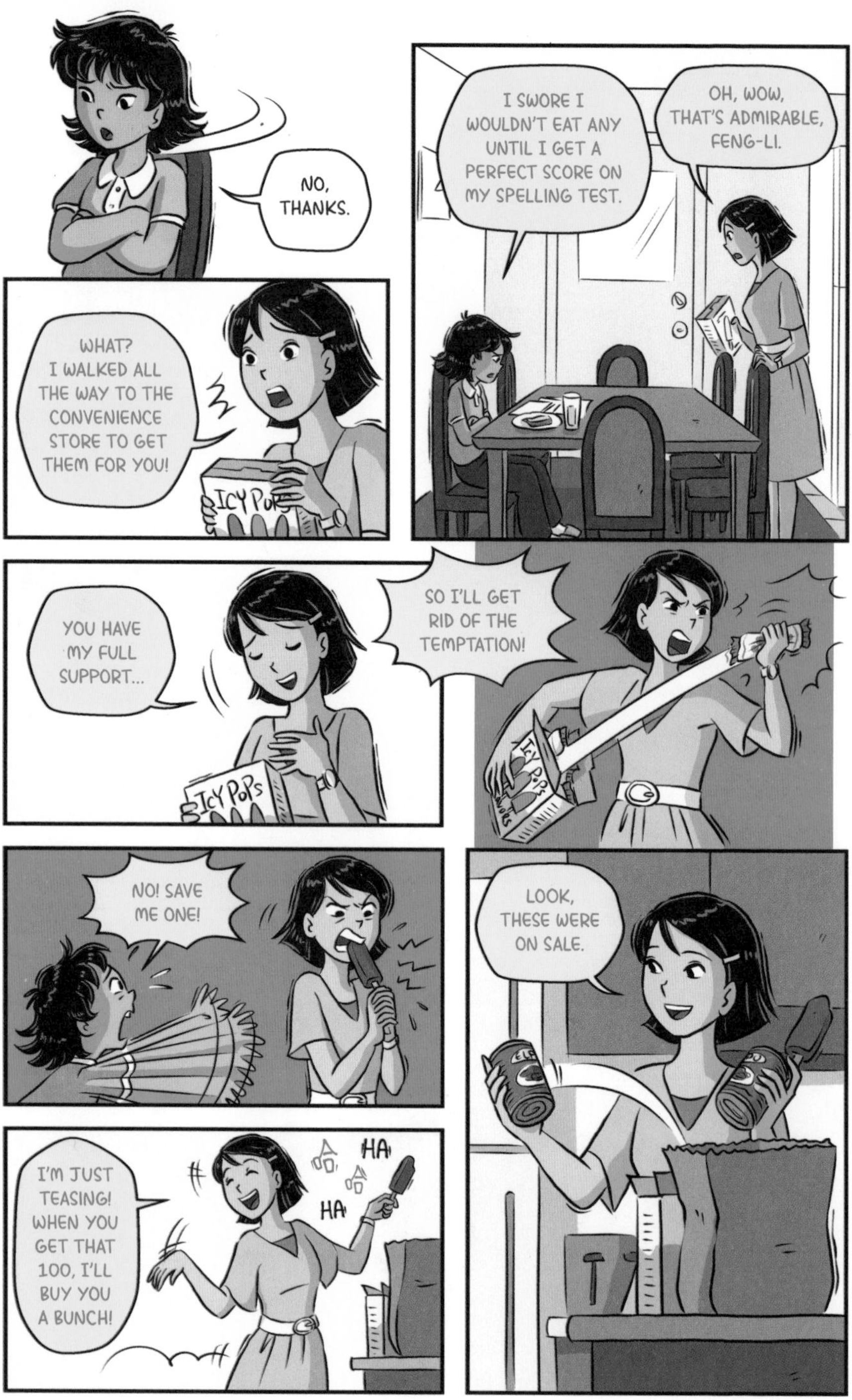
NO, THANKS.
I SWORE I WOULDN'T EAT ANY UNTIL I GET A PERFECT SCORE ON MY SPELLING TEST.
OH, WOW, THAT'S ADMIRABLE, FENG-LI.
WHAT? I WALKED ALL THE WAY TO THE CONVENIENCE STORE TO GET THEM FOR YOU!
ICY POPS
YOU HAVE MY FULL SUPPORT...
ICY POPS
SO I'LL GET RID OF THE TEMPTATION!
NO! SAVE ME ONE!
LOOK, THESE WERE ON SALE.
I'M JUST TEASING! WHEN YOU GET THAT 100, I'LL BUY YOU A BUNCH!
HA
HA

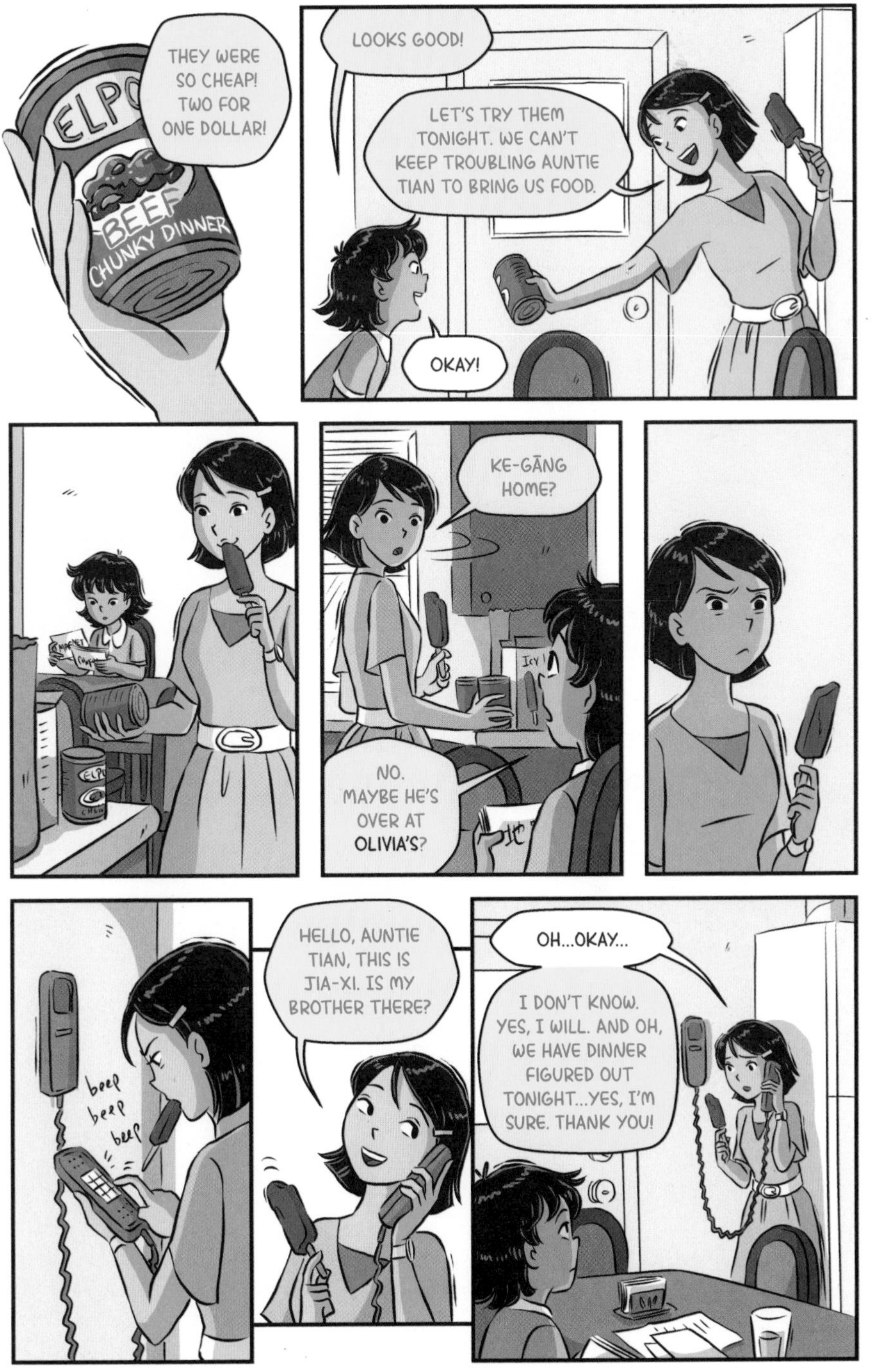
ELPO
BEEF
CHUNKY DINNER
THEY WERE SO CHEAP! TWO FOR ONE DOLLAR!
LOOKS GOOD!
LET'S TRY THEM TONIGHT. WE CAN'T KEEP TROUBLING AUNTIE TIAN TO BRING US FOOD.
OKAY!
KE-GĀNG HOME?
NO. MAYBE HE'S OVER AT OLIVIA'S?
beep beep beep
HELLO, AUNTIE TIAN, THIS IS JIA-XI. IS MY BROTHER THERE?
OH...OKAY...
I DON'T KNOW. YES, I WILL. AND OH, WE HAVE DINNER FIGURED OUT TONIGHT...YES, I'M SURE. THANK YOU!

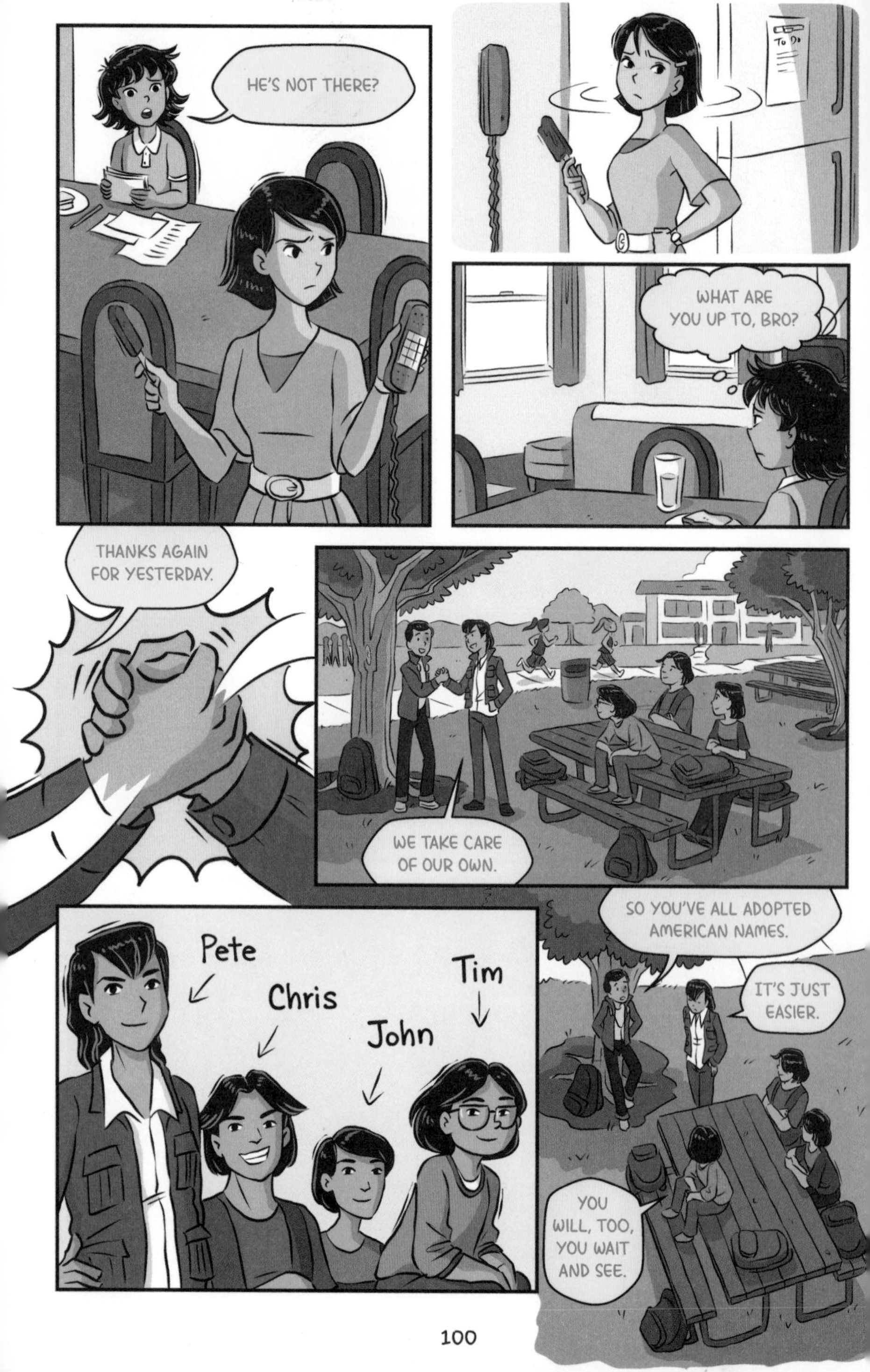

HE'S NOT THERE?
WHAT ARE YOU UP TO, BRO?
THANKS AGAIN FOR YESTERDAY.
WE TAKE CARE OF OUR OWN.
Pete
Chris
John
Tim
SO YOU'VE ALL ADOPTED AMERICAN NAMES.
IT'S JUST EASIER.
YOU WILL, TOO, YOU WAIT AND SEE.

HOW COME I'M ONLY FINDING YOU GUYS NOW? I'VE BEEN AT THE SCHOOL FOR WELL OVER A MONTH!

THAT'S BECAUSE YOUR **GIRLFRIEND** HAS YOU ON A SHORT LEASH.

GIRLFRIEND?

THE DOUBLE-PONYTAILED ONE. ALWAYS TAILING YOU.

"OH, KE-GĀNG, ARE YOU COMING OVER LATER?"

嘻 嘻 hee hee

HA HA HA

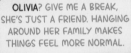

OLIVIA? GIVE ME A BREAK, SHE'S JUST A FRIEND. HANGING AROUND HER FAMILY MAKES THINGS FEEL MORE NORMAL.

flick

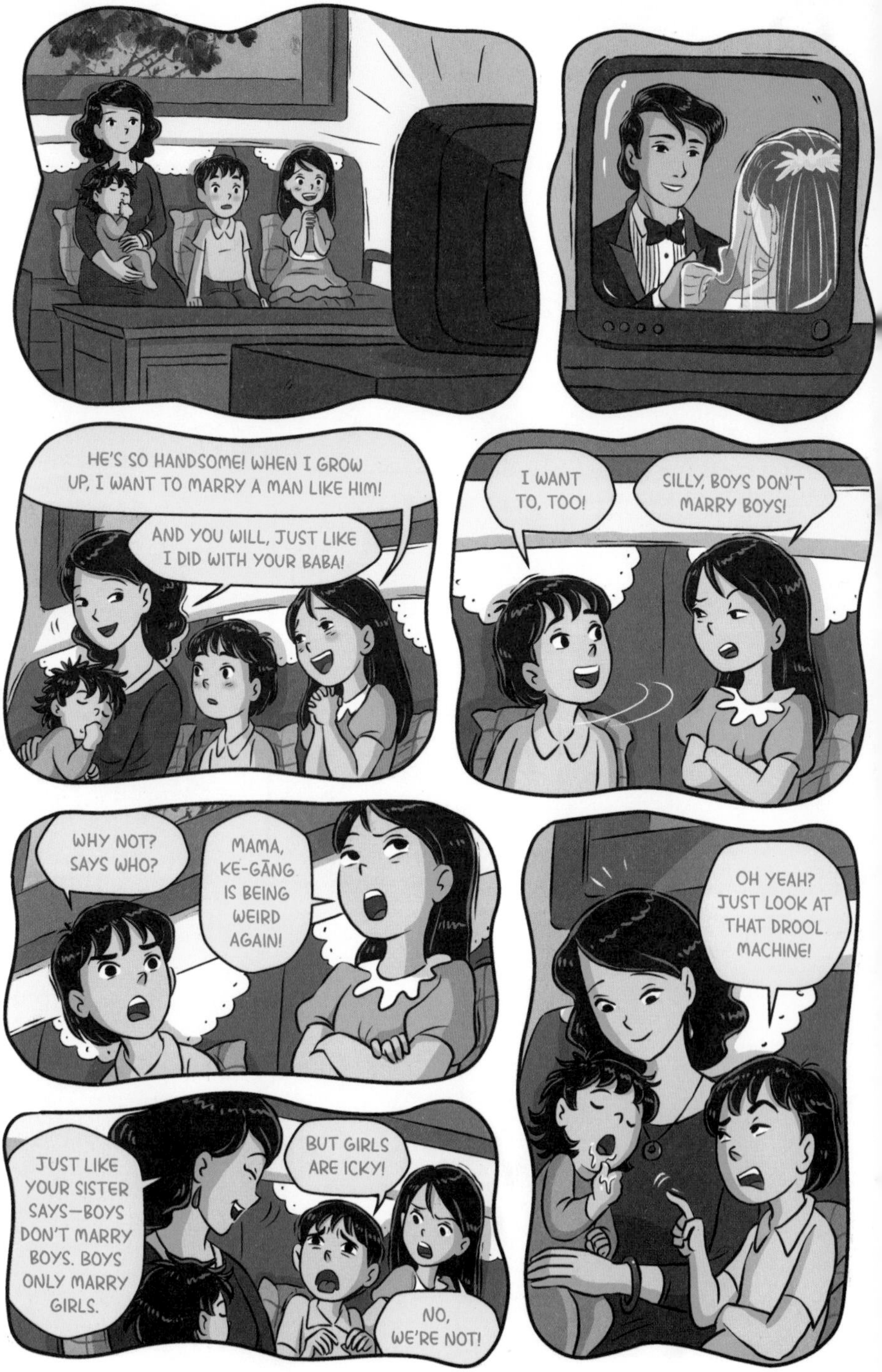
HE'S SO HANDSOME! WHEN I GROW UP, I WANT TO MARRY A MAN LIKE HIM!
AND YOU WILL, JUST LIKE I DID WITH YOUR BABA!
I WANT TO, TOO!
SILLY, BOYS DON'T MARRY BOYS!
WHY NOT? SAYS WHO?
MAMA, KE-GĀNG IS BEING WEIRD AGAIN!
JUST LIKE YOUR SISTER SAYS—BOYS DON'T MARRY BOYS. BOYS ONLY MARRY GIRLS.
BUT GIRLS ARE ICKY!
NO, WE'RE NOT!
OH YEAH? JUST LOOK AT THAT DROOL MACHINE!

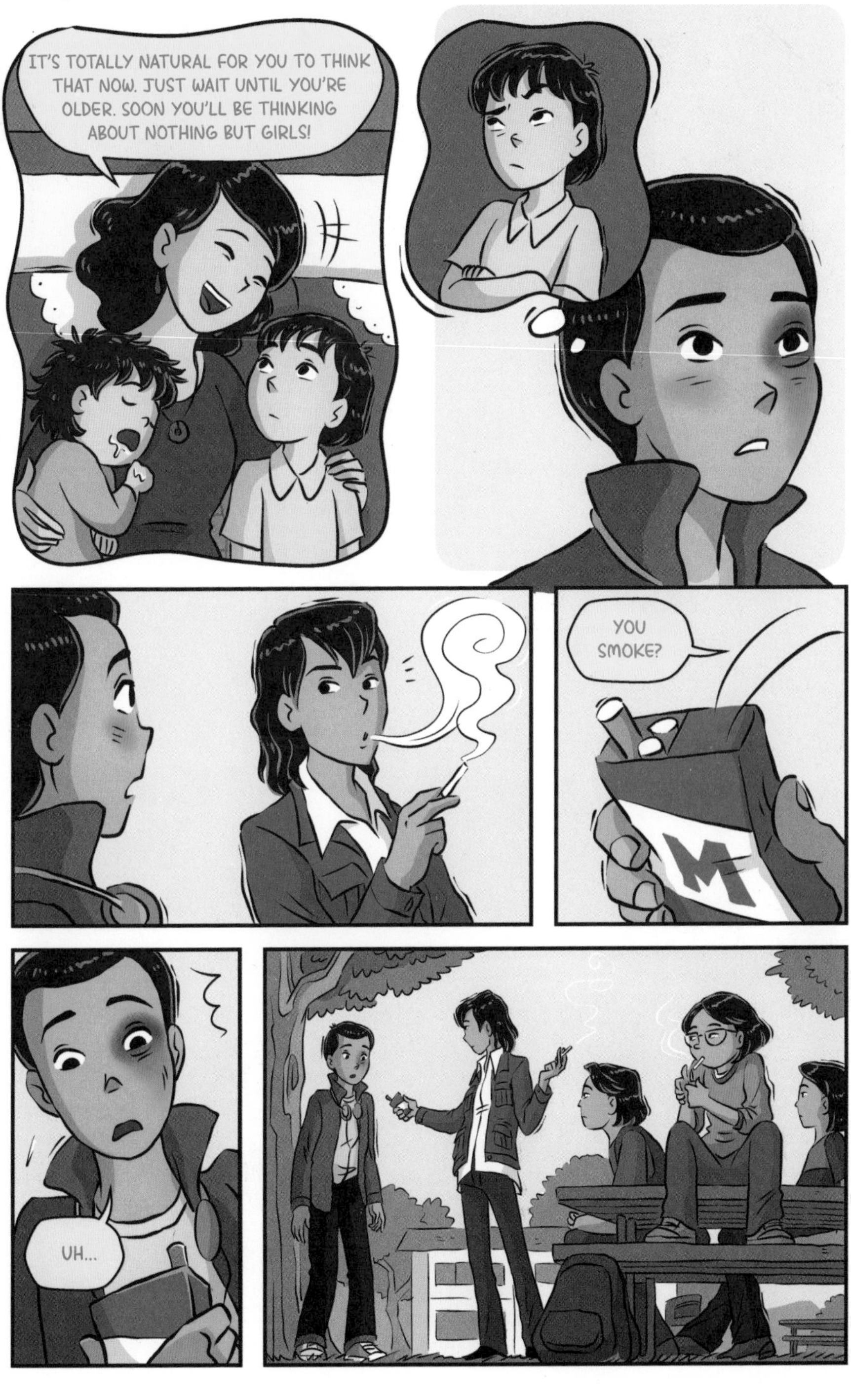
IT'S TOTALLY NATURAL FOR YOU TO THINK THAT NOW. JUST WAIT UNTIL YOU'RE OLDER. SOON YOU'LL BE THINKING ABOUT NOTHING BUT GIRLS!
YOU SMOKE?
UH...

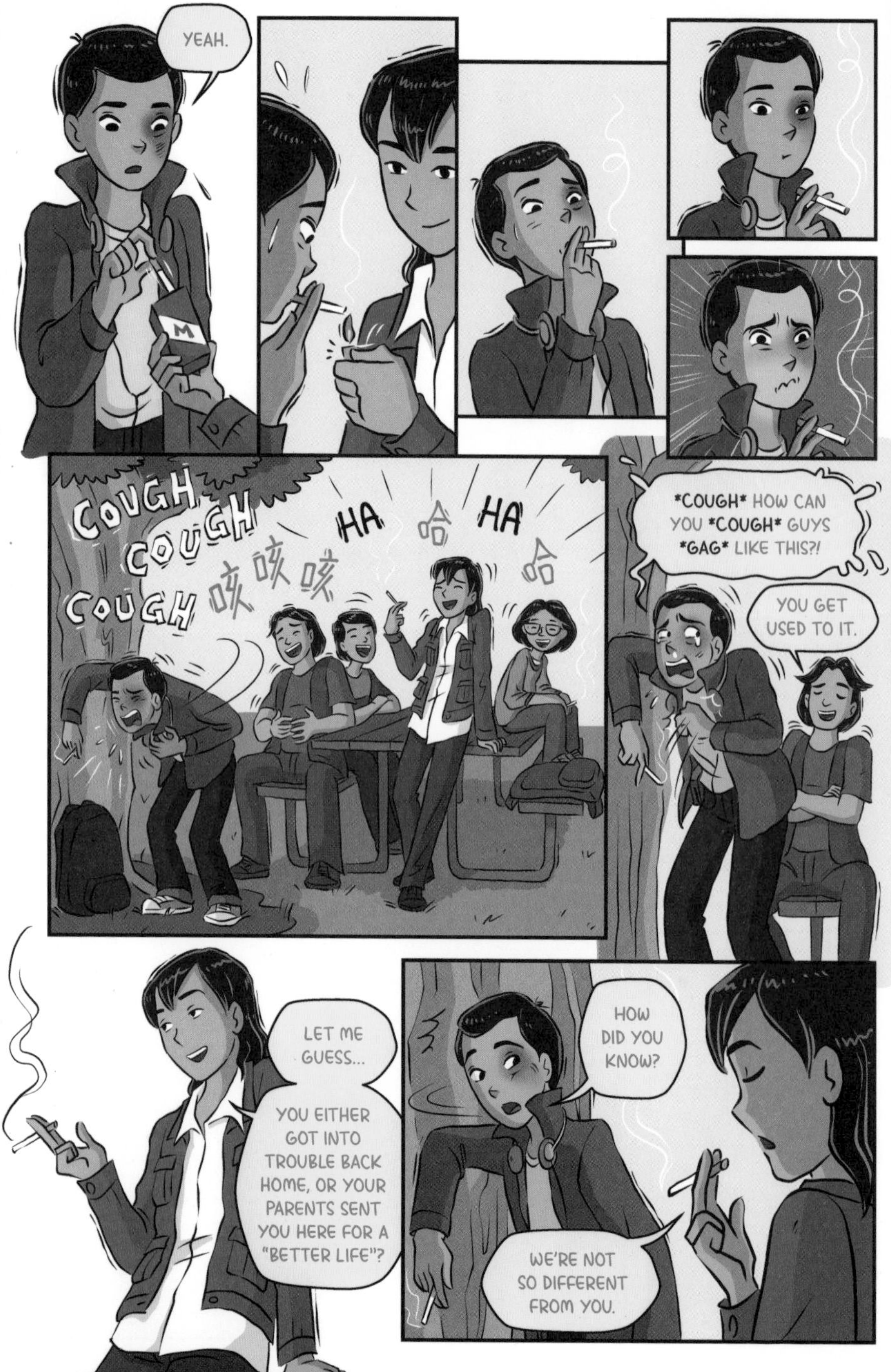
YEAH.
COUGH COUGH COUGH 咳咳咳
HA 哈 HA 哈
COUGH HOW CAN YOU *COUGH* GUYS *GAG* LIKE THIS?!
YOU GET USED TO IT.
LET ME GUESS...
YOU EITHER GOT INTO TROUBLE BACK HOME, OR YOUR PARENTS SENT YOU HERE FOR A "BETTER LIFE"?
HOW DID YOU KNOW?
WE'RE NOT SO DIFFERENT FROM YOU.

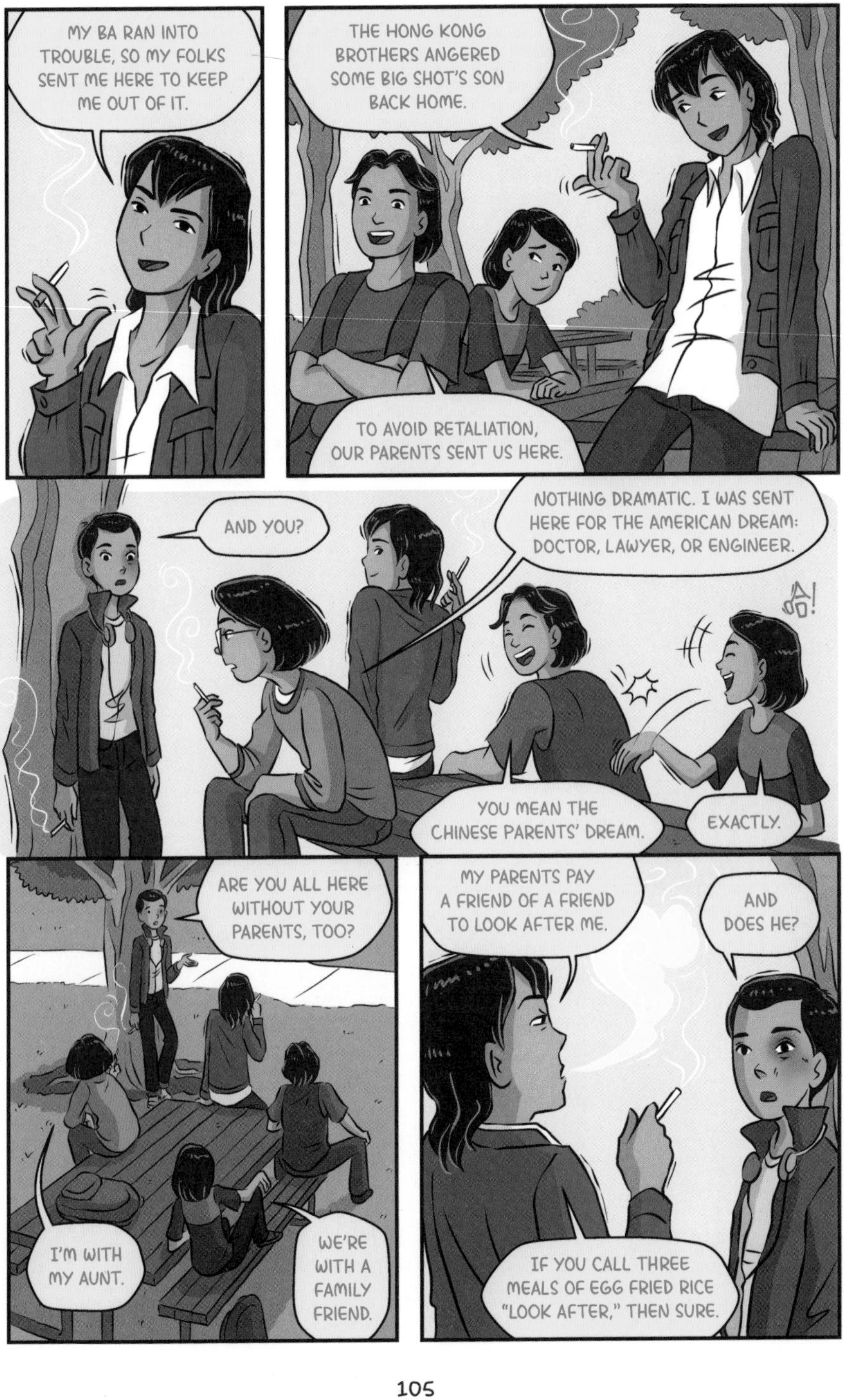
MY BA RAN INTO TROUBLE, SO MY FOLKS SENT ME HERE TO KEEP ME OUT OF IT.
THE HONG KONG BROTHERS ANGERED SOME BIG SHOT'S SON BACK HOME.
TO AVOID RETALIATION, OUR PARENTS SENT US HERE.
AND YOU?
NOTHING DRAMATIC. I WAS SENT HERE FOR THE AMERICAN DREAM: DOCTOR, LAWYER, OR ENGINEER.
YOU MEAN THE CHINESE PARENTS' DREAM.
EXACTLY.
ARE YOU ALL HERE WITHOUT YOUR PARENTS, TOO?
I'M WITH MY AUNT.
WE'RE WITH A FAMILY FRIEND.
MY PARENTS PAY A FRIEND OF A FRIEND TO LOOK AFTER ME.
AND DOES HE?
IF YOU CALL THREE MEALS OF EGG FRIED RICE "LOOK AFTER," THEN SURE.

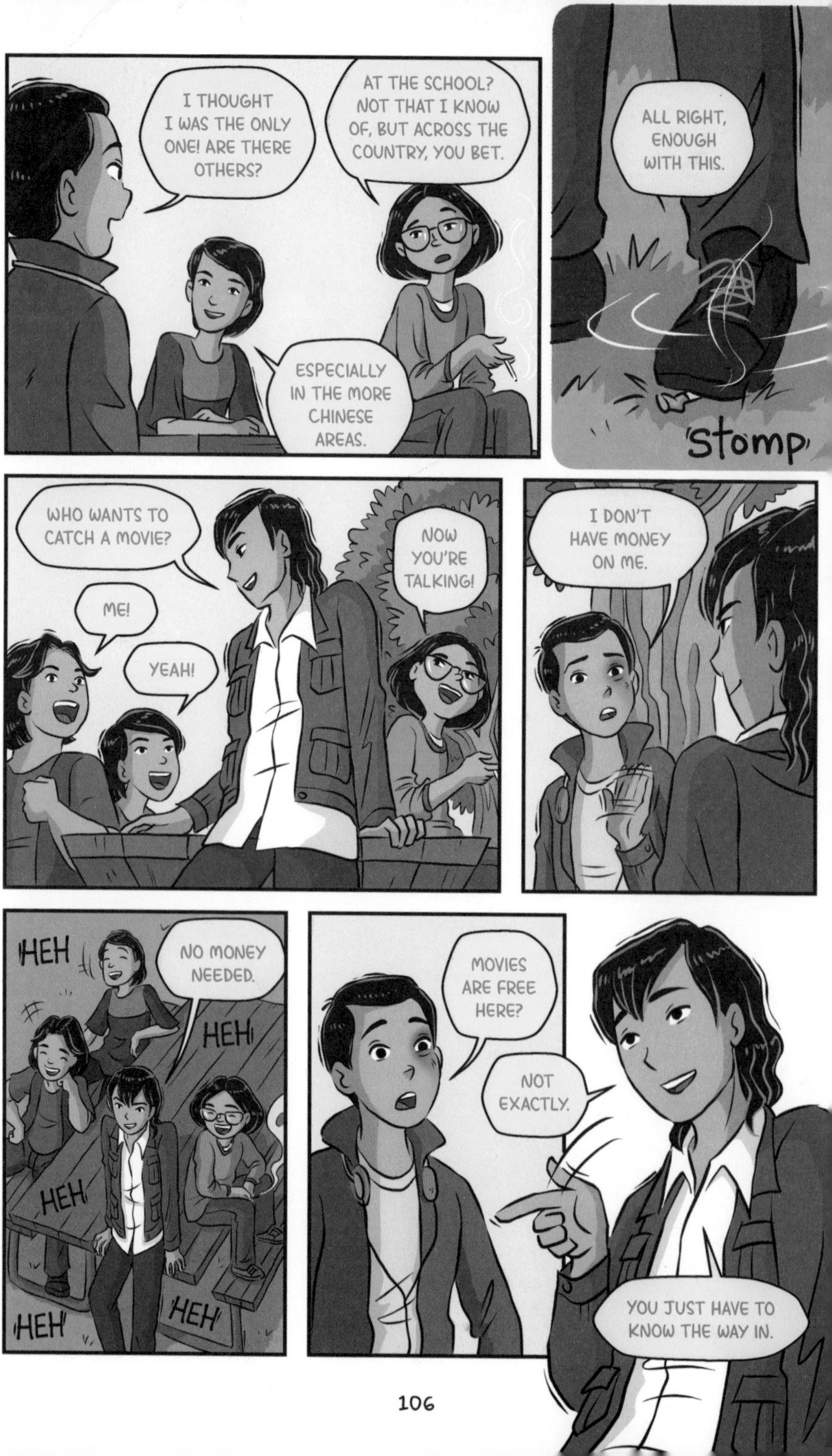
I THOUGHT I WAS THE ONLY ONE! ARE THERE OTHERS?
AT THE SCHOOL? NOT THAT I KNOW OF, BUT ACROSS THE COUNTRY, YOU BET.
ESPECIALLY IN THE MORE CHINESE AREAS.
ALL RIGHT, ENOUGH WITH THIS.
STOMP
WHO WANTS TO CATCH A MOVIE?
ME!
YEAH!
NOW YOU'RE TALKING!
I DON'T HAVE MONEY ON ME.
HEH
NO MONEY NEEDED.
HEH
HEH
HEH
HEH
MOVIES ARE FREE HERE?
NOT EXACTLY.
YOU JUST HAVE TO KNOW THE WAY IN.

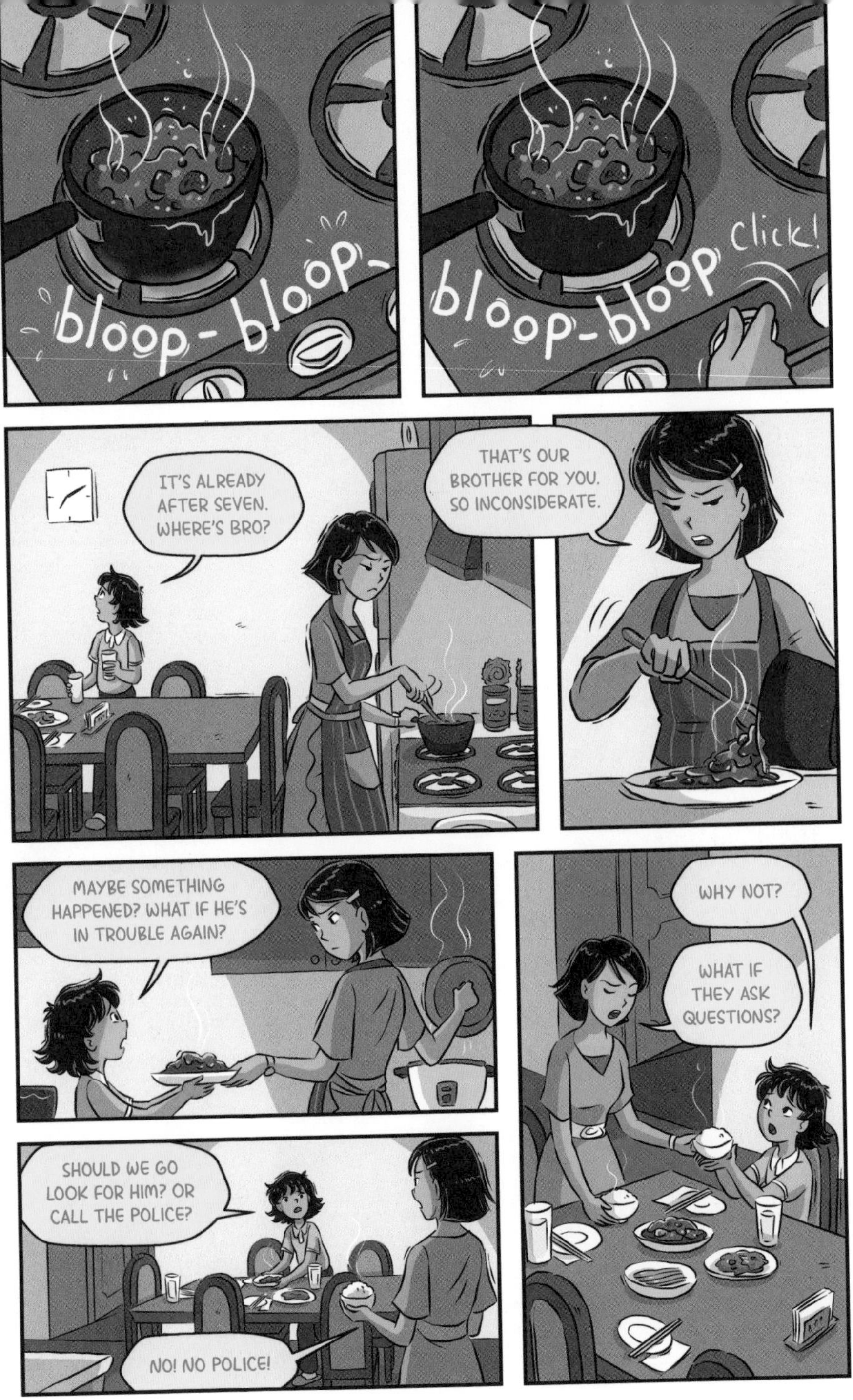
bloop-bloop-
bloop-bloop
Click!
IT'S ALREADY AFTER SEVEN. WHERE'S BRO?
THAT'S OUR BROTHER FOR YOU. SO INCONSIDERATE.
MAYBE SOMETHING HAPPENED? WHAT IF HE'S IN TROUBLE AGAIN?
SHOULD WE GO LOOK FOR HIM? OR CALL THE POLICE?
NO! NO POLICE!
WHY NOT?
WHAT IF THEY ASK QUESTIONS?

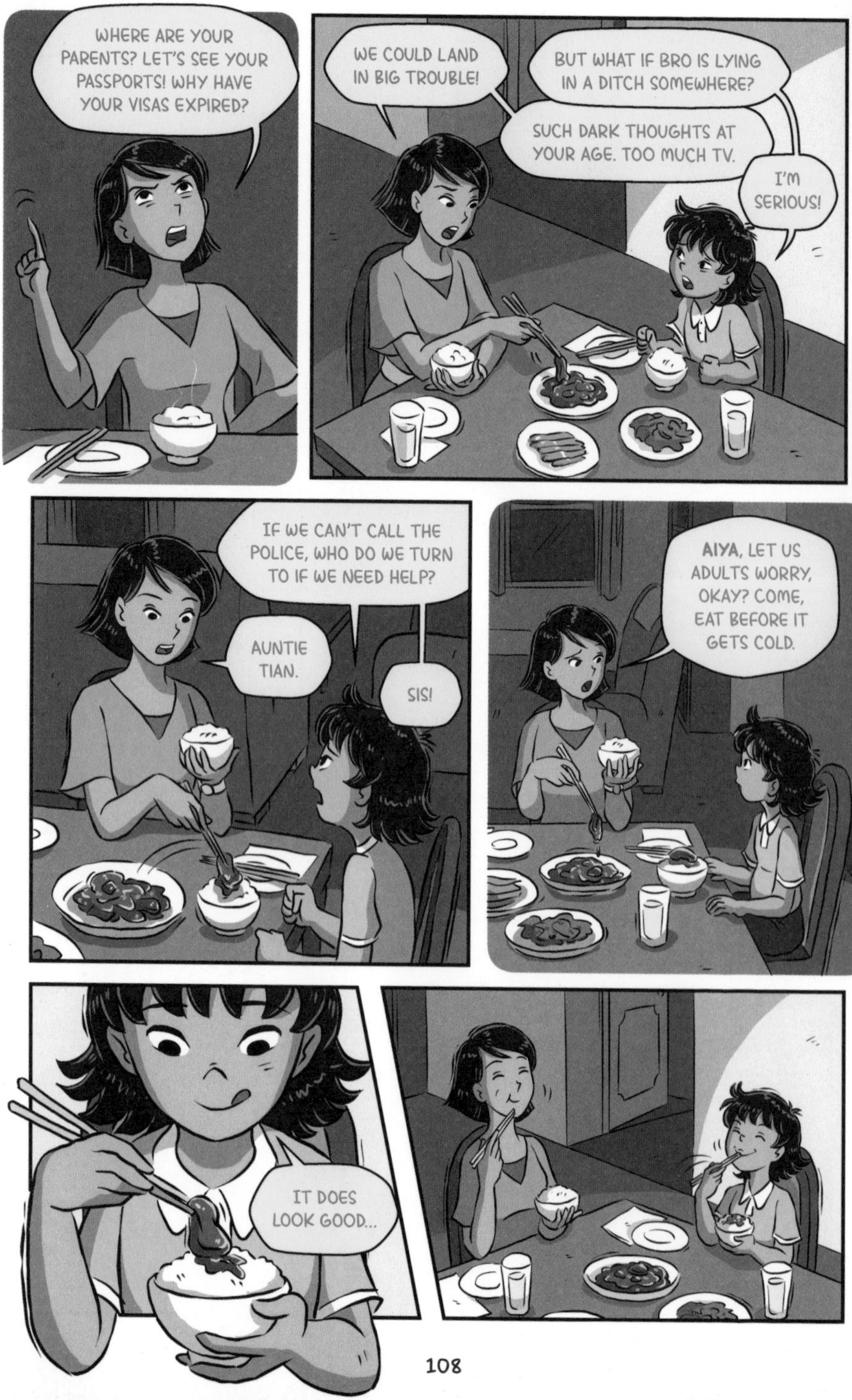
WHERE ARE YOUR PARENTS? LET'S SEE YOUR PASSPORTS! WHY HAVE YOUR VISAS EXPIRED?
WE COULD LAND IN BIG TROUBLE!
BUT WHAT IF BRO IS LYING IN A DITCH SOMEWHERE?
SUCH DARK THOUGHTS AT YOUR AGE. TOO MUCH TV.
I'M SERIOUS!
IF WE CAN'T CALL THE POLICE, WHO DO WE TURN TO IF WE NEED HELP?
AUNTIE TIAN.
SIS!
AIYA, LET US ADULTS WORRY, OKAY? COME, EAT BEFORE IT GETS COLD.
IT DOES LOOK GOOD...

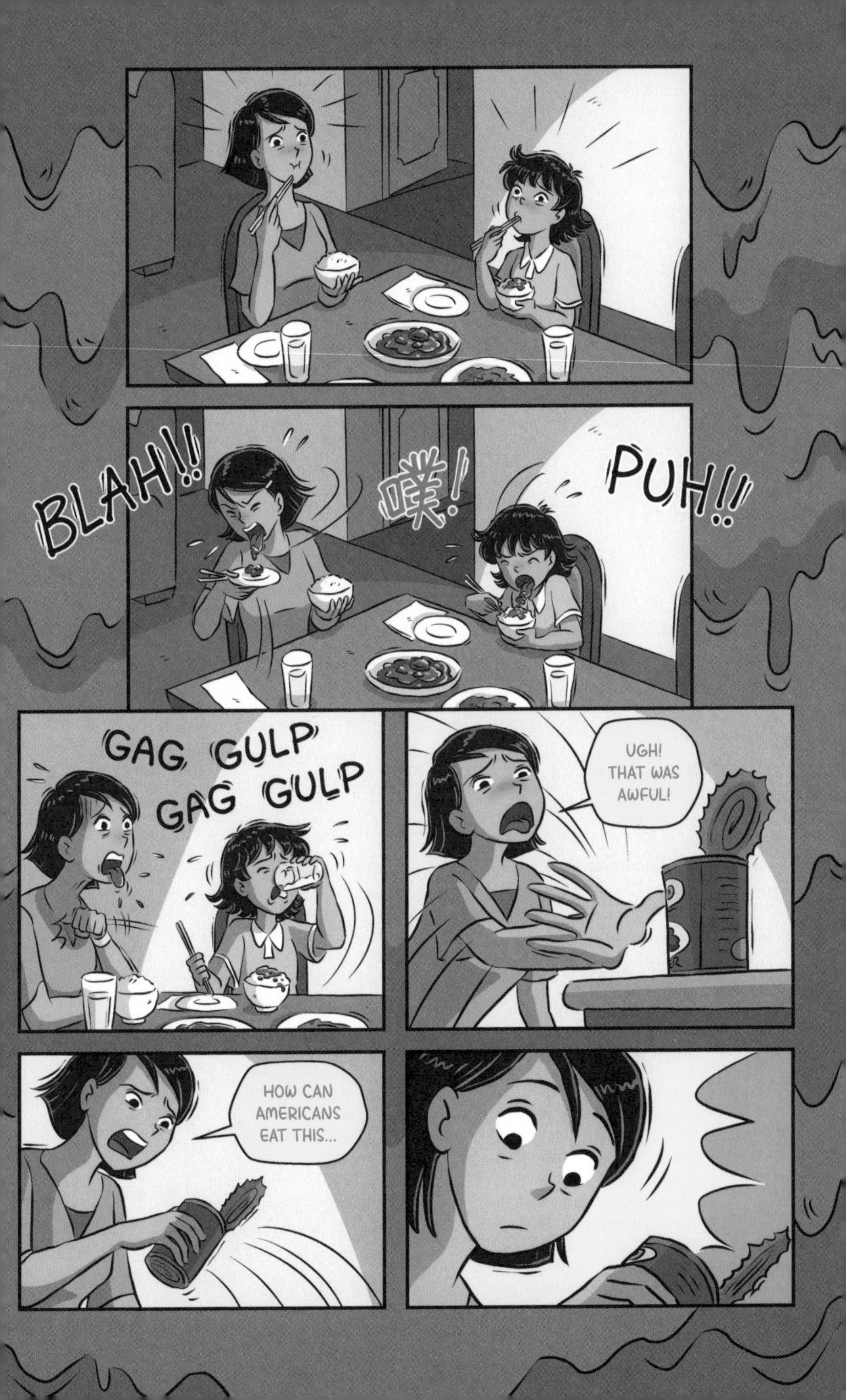
BLAH!!
噗!
PUH!!
GAG GULP
GAG GULP
UGH! THAT WAS AWFUL!
HOW CAN AMERICANS EAT THIS...

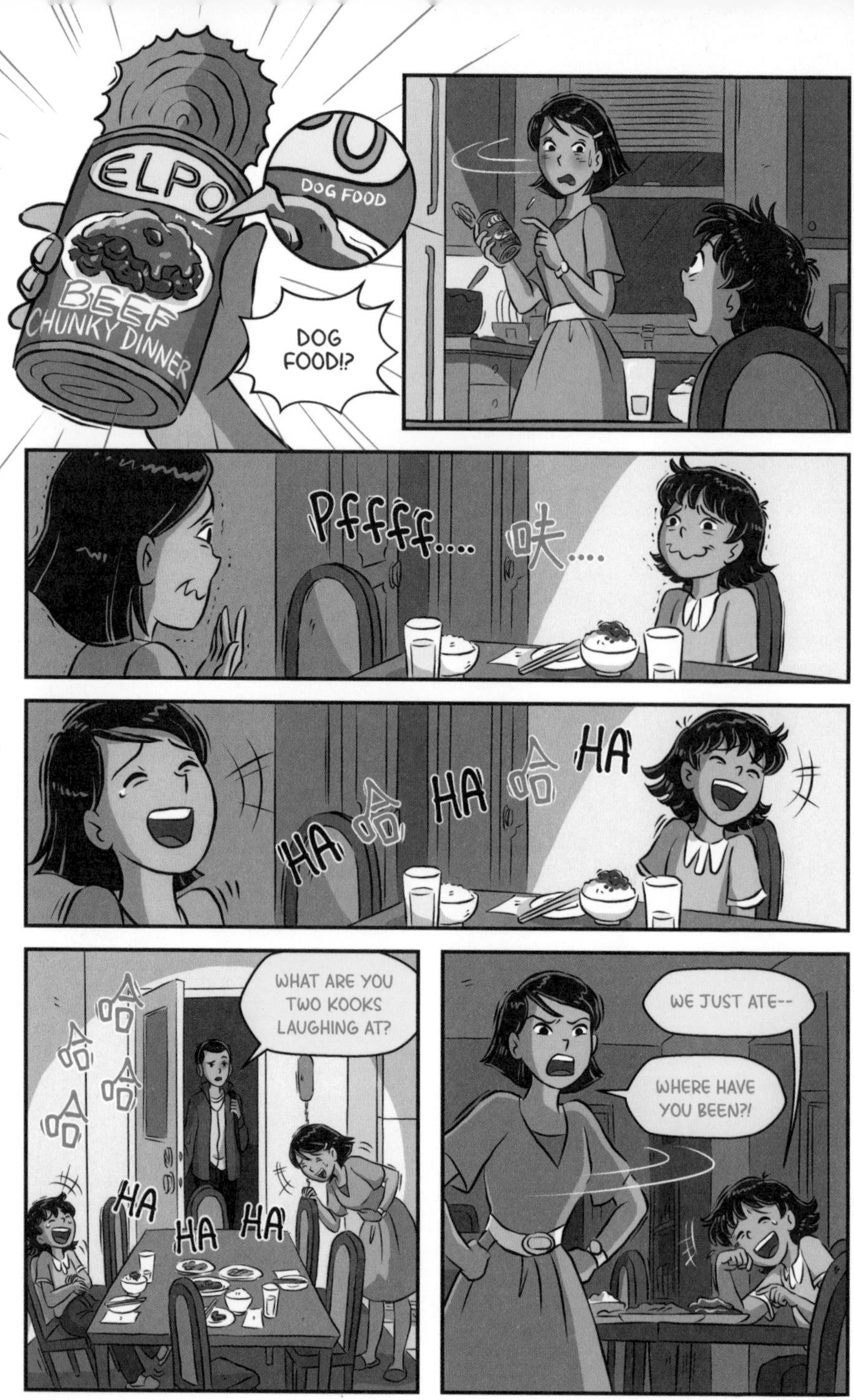
ELPO
BEEF CHUNKY DINNER
DOG FOOD
DOG FOOD!?
Pfffff....
呋....
HA
哈
HA
哈
HA
哈
哈
哈
哈
HA
HA
HA
WHAT ARE YOU TWO KOOKS LAUGHING AT?
WE JUST ATE--
WHERE HAVE YOU BEEN?!

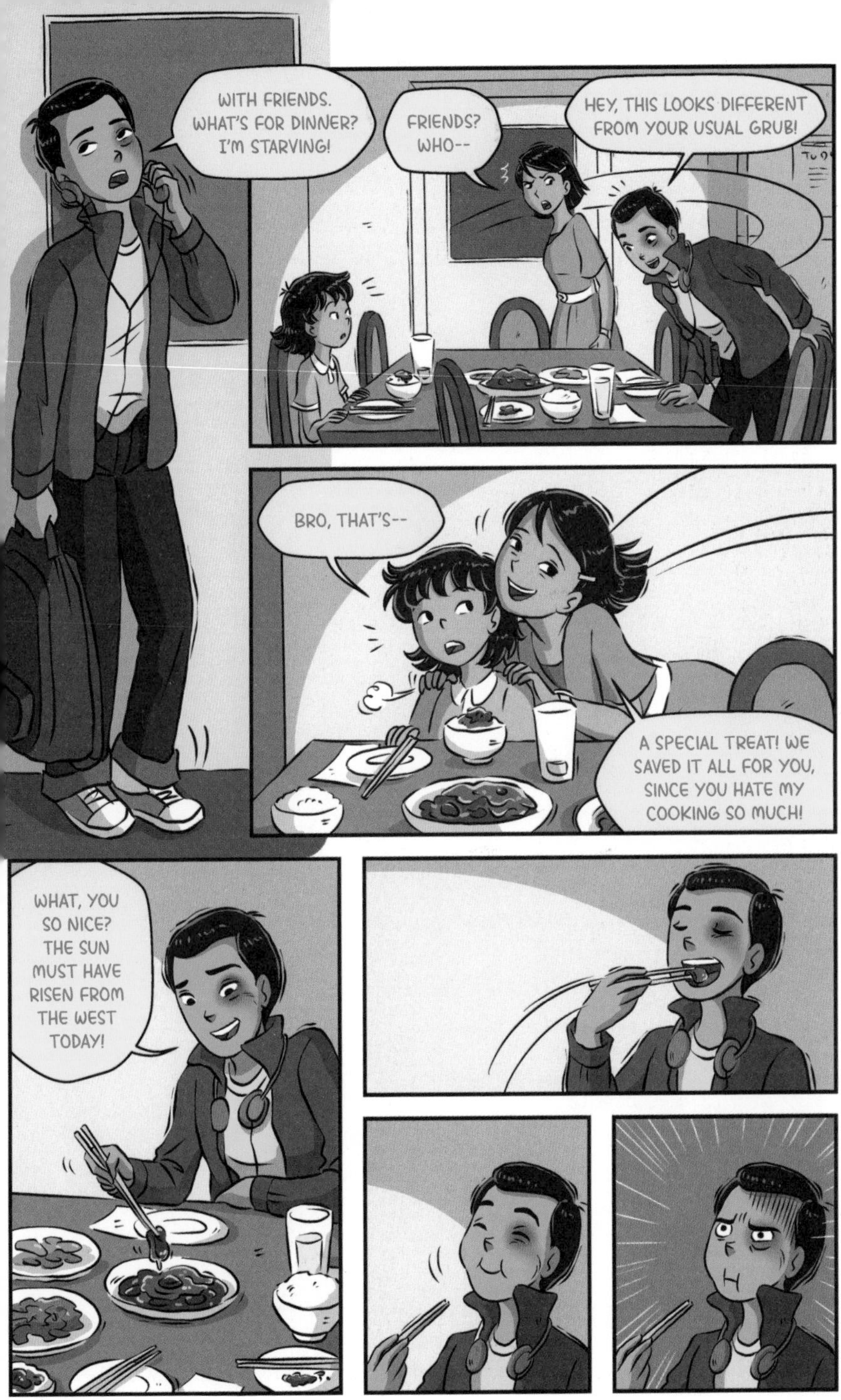
WITH FRIENDS.
WHAT'S FOR DINNER?
I'M STARVING!
FRIENDS?
WHO--
HEY, THIS LOOKS DIFFERENT
FROM YOUR USUAL GRUB!
BRO, THAT'S--
A SPECIAL TREAT! WE
SAVED IT ALL FOR YOU,
SINCE YOU HATE MY
COOKING SO MUCH!
WHAT, YOU
SO NICE?
THE SUN
MUST HAVE
RISEN FROM
THE WEST
TODAY!

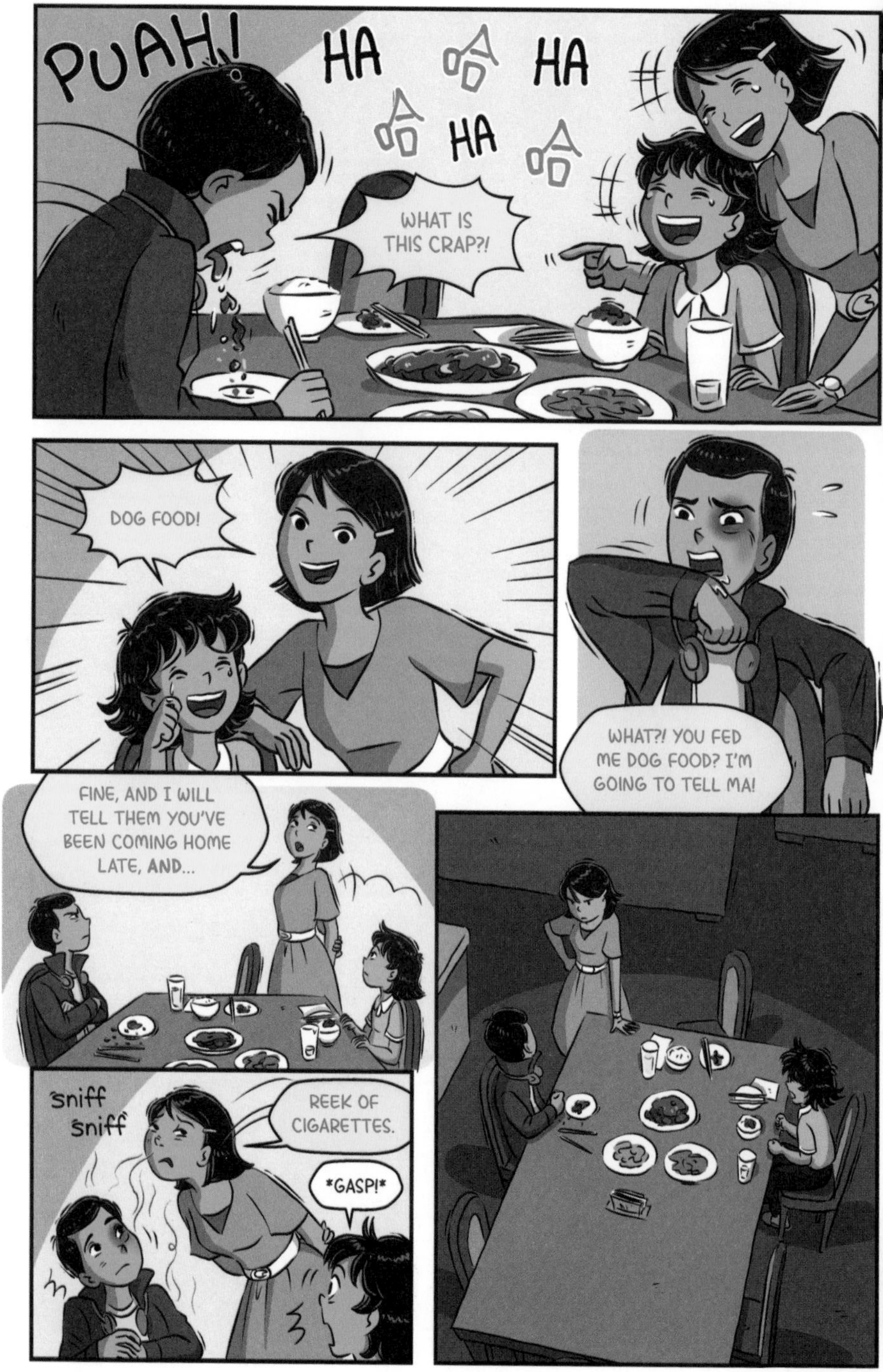

PUAH!
HA 哈 HA 哈 HA 哈
WHAT IS THIS CRAP?!
DOG FOOD!
WHAT?! YOU FED ME DOG FOOD? I'M GOING TO TELL MA!
FINE, AND I WILL TELL THEM YOU'VE BEEN COMING HOME LATE, AND...
sniff sniff
REEK OF CIGARETTES.
GASP!

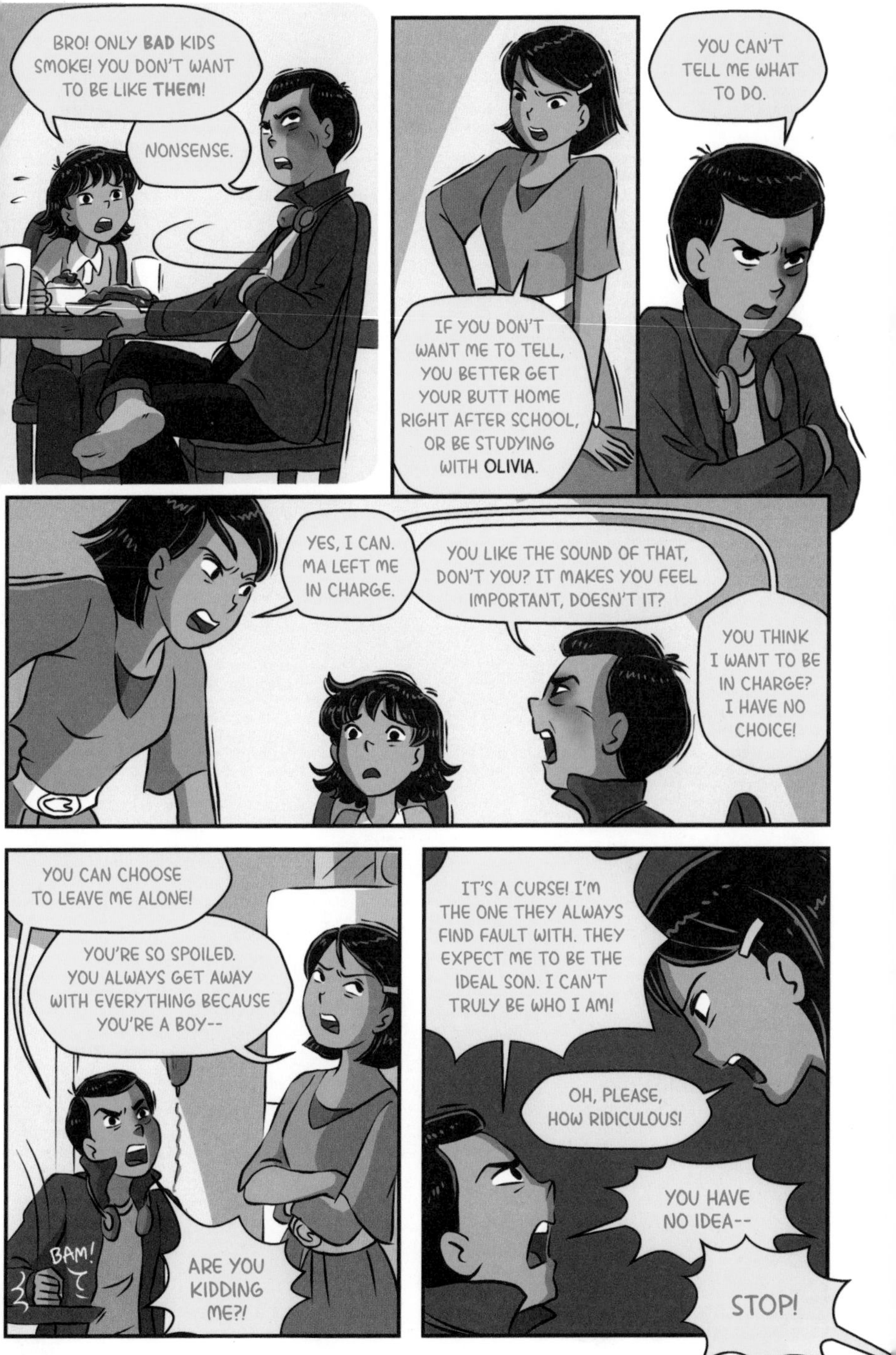

BRO! ONLY **BAD** KIDS SMOKE! YOU DON'T WANT TO BE LIKE **THEM**!
NONSENSE.
IF YOU DON'T WANT ME TO TELL, YOU BETTER GET YOUR BUTT HOME RIGHT AFTER SCHOOL, OR BE STUDYING WITH **OLIVIA**.
YOU CAN'T TELL ME WHAT TO DO.
YES, I CAN. MA LEFT ME IN CHARGE.
YOU LIKE THE SOUND OF THAT, DON'T YOU? IT MAKES YOU FEEL IMPORTANT, DOESN'T IT?
YOU THINK I WANT TO BE IN CHARGE? I HAVE NO CHOICE!
YOU CAN CHOOSE TO LEAVE ME ALONE!
YOU'RE SO SPOILED. YOU ALWAYS GET AWAY WITH EVERYTHING BECAUSE YOU'RE A BOY--
BAM!
ARE YOU KIDDING ME?!
IT'S A CURSE! I'M THE ONE THEY ALWAYS FIND FAULT WITH. THEY EXPECT ME TO BE THE IDEAL SON. I CAN'T TRULY BE WHO I AM!
OH, PLEASE, HOW RIDICULOUS!
YOU HAVE NO IDEA--
STOP!

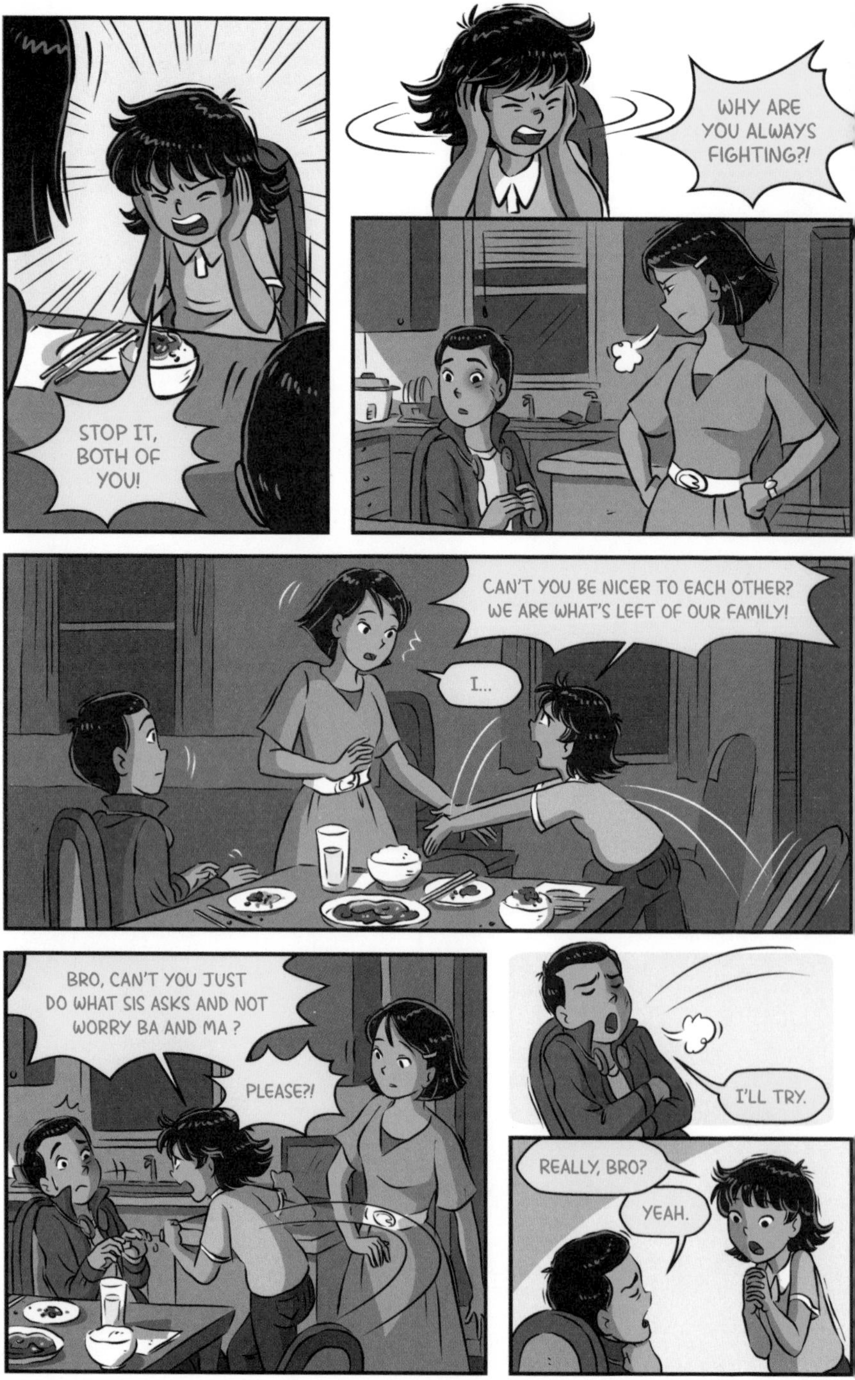
STOP IT, BOTH OF YOU!
WHY ARE YOU ALWAYS FIGHTING?!
CAN'T YOU BE NICER TO EACH OTHER? WE ARE WHAT'S LEFT OF OUR FAMILY!
I...
BRO, CAN'T YOU JUST DO WHAT SIS ASKS AND NOT WORRY BA AND MA ?
PLEASE?!
I'LL TRY.
REALLY, BRO?
YEAH.

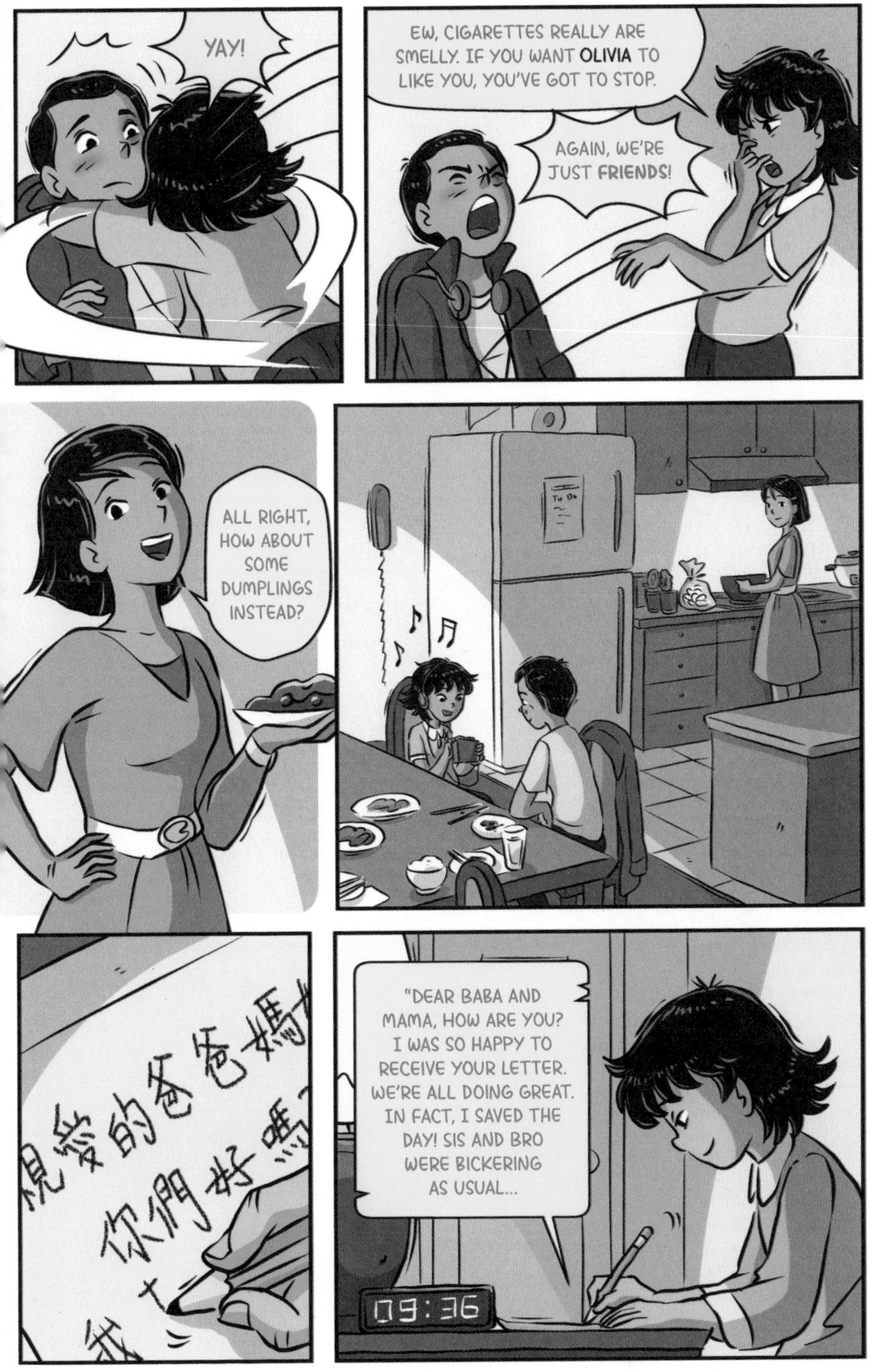
YAY!
EW, CIGARETTES REALLY ARE SMELLY. IF YOU WANT **OLIVIA** TO LIKE YOU, YOU'VE GOT TO STOP.
AGAIN, WE'RE JUST **FRIENDS**!
ALL RIGHT, HOW ABOUT SOME DUMPLINGS INSTEAD?
TO DO
愛的爸爸媽
你們好嗎
"DEAR BABA AND MAMA, HOW ARE YOU? I WAS SO HAPPY TO RECEIVE YOUR LETTER. WE'RE ALL DOING GREAT. IN FACT, I SAVED THE DAY! SIS AND BRO WERE BICKERING AS USUAL...
09:36

APRIL

AS PROMISED, BRO CONTINUED TO COME HOME AFTER SCHOOL.

OR HE'D GO OVER TO THE TIANS'.

SIS SEEMED TO HAVE GOTTEN THE HANG OF JUGGLING CHORES AND STUDIES.

GEOGRAPHY. G-E-O-G-R-A-P-H-Y.

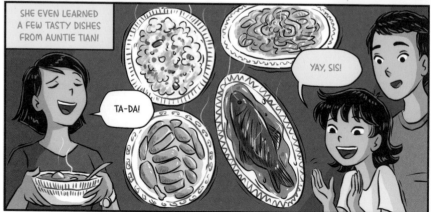

SHE EVEN LEARNED A FEW TASTY DISHES FROM AUNTIE TIAN!

TA-DA!

YAY, SIS!

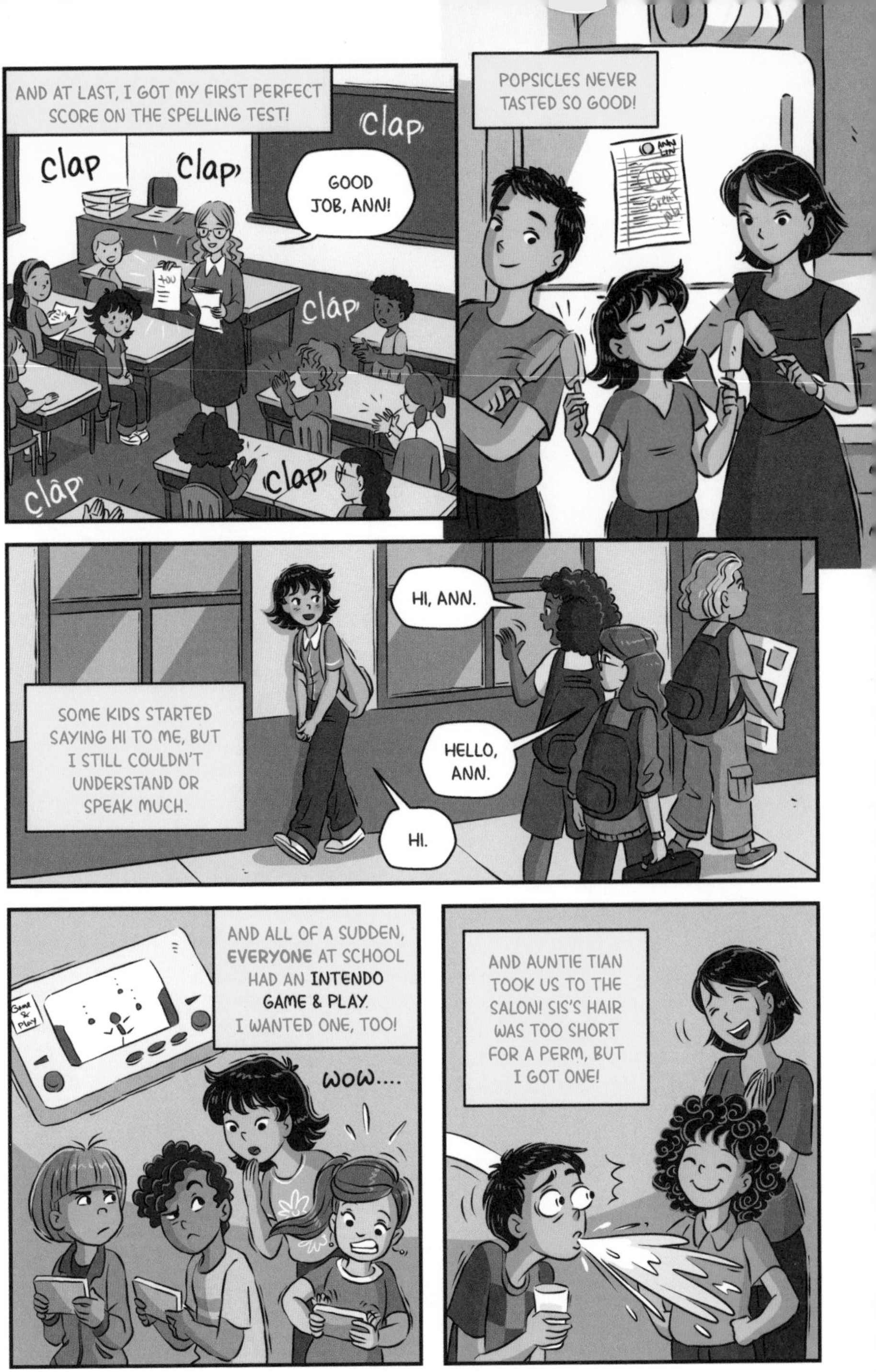
AND AT LAST, I GOT MY FIRST PERFECT SCORE ON THE SPELLING TEST!
clap
clap
clap
GOOD JOB, ANN!
clap
clap
clap
POPSICLES NEVER TASTED SO GOOD!
SOME KIDS STARTED SAYING HI TO ME, BUT I STILL COULDN'T UNDERSTAND OR SPEAK MUCH.
HI, ANN.
HELLO, ANN.
HI.
AND ALL OF A SUDDEN, **EVERYONE** AT SCHOOL HAD AN **INTENDO GAME & PLAY**. I WANTED ONE, TOO!
Game & Play
WOW....
AND AUNTIE TIAN TOOK US TO THE SALON! SIS'S HAIR WAS TOO SHORT FOR A PERM, BUT I GOT ONE!

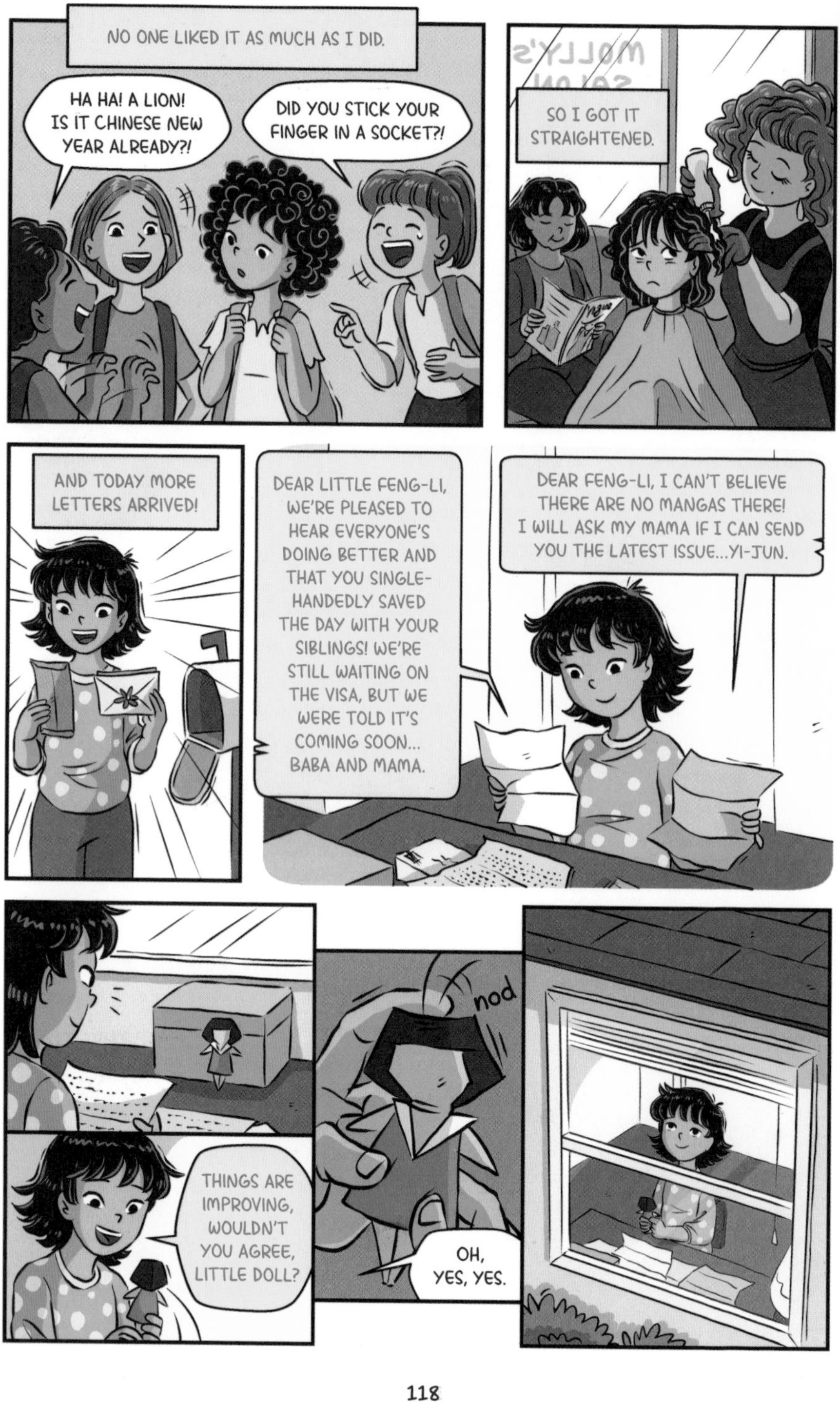
NO ONE LIKED IT AS MUCH AS I DID.
HA HA! A LION! IS IT CHINESE NEW YEAR ALREADY?!
DID YOU STICK YOUR FINGER IN A SOCKET?!
MOLLY'S SALON
SO I GOT IT STRAIGHTENED.
AND TODAY MORE LETTERS ARRIVED!
DEAR LITTLE FENG-LI, WE'RE PLEASED TO HEAR EVERYONE'S DOING BETTER AND THAT YOU SINGLE-HANDEDLY SAVED THE DAY WITH YOUR SIBLINGS! WE'RE STILL WAITING ON THE VISA, BUT WE WERE TOLD IT'S COMING SOON... BABA AND MAMA.
DEAR FENG-LI, I CAN'T BELIEVE THERE ARE NO MANGAS THERE! I WILL ASK MY MAMA IF I CAN SEND YOU THE LATEST ISSUE...YI-JUN.
THINGS ARE IMPROVING, WOULDN'T YOU AGREE, LITTLE DOLL?
nod
OH, YES, YES.

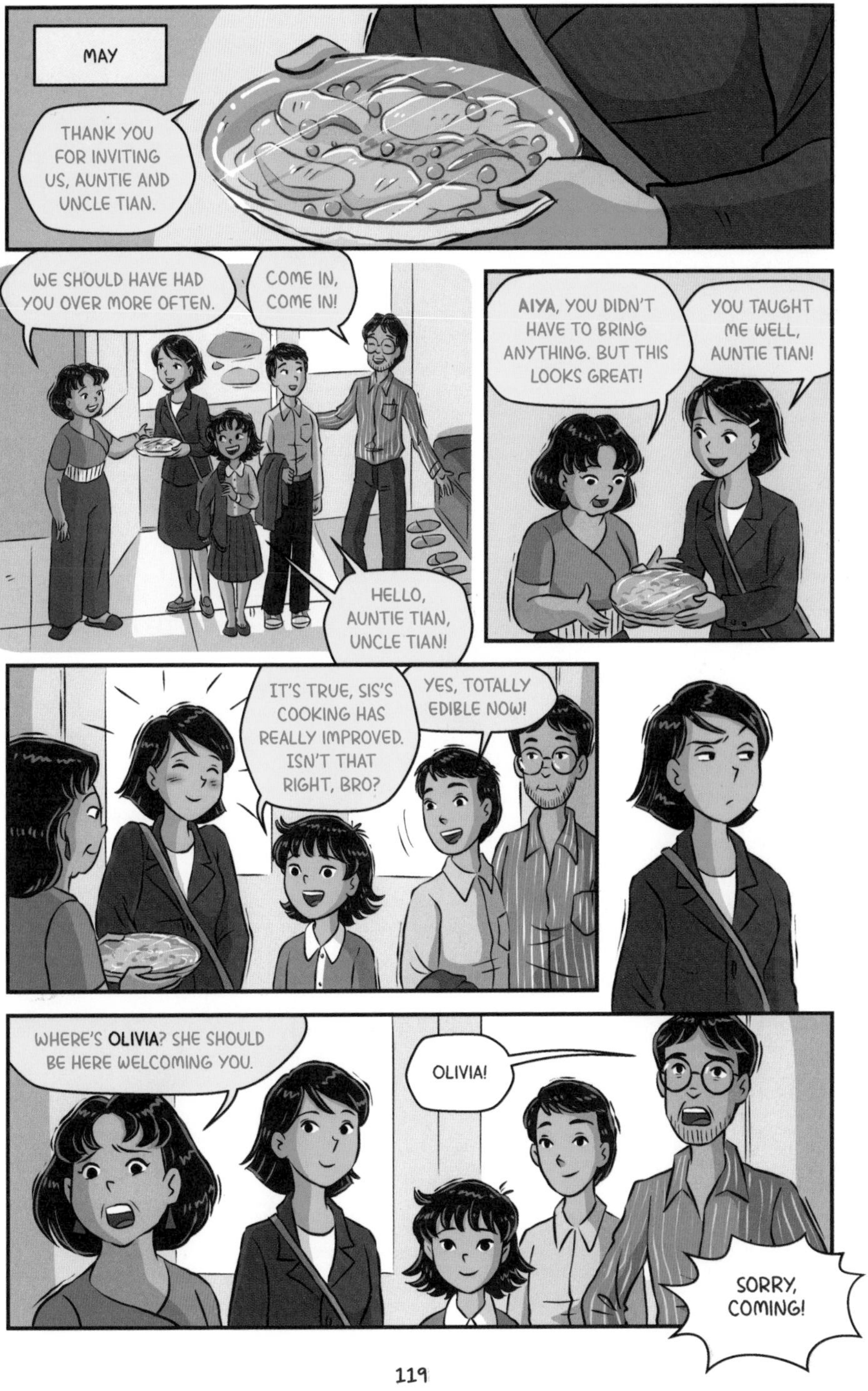
MAY
THANK YOU FOR INVITING US, AUNTIE AND UNCLE TIAN.
WE SHOULD HAVE HAD YOU OVER MORE OFTEN.
COME IN, COME IN!
HELLO, AUNTIE TIAN, UNCLE TIAN!
AIYA, YOU DIDN'T HAVE TO BRING ANYTHING. BUT THIS LOOKS GREAT!
YOU TAUGHT ME WELL, AUNTIE TIAN!
IT'S TRUE, SIS'S COOKING HAS REALLY IMPROVED. ISN'T THAT RIGHT, BRO?
YES, TOTALLY EDIBLE NOW!
WHERE'S OLIVIA? SHE SHOULD BE HERE WELCOMING YOU.
OLIVIA!
SORRY, COMING!

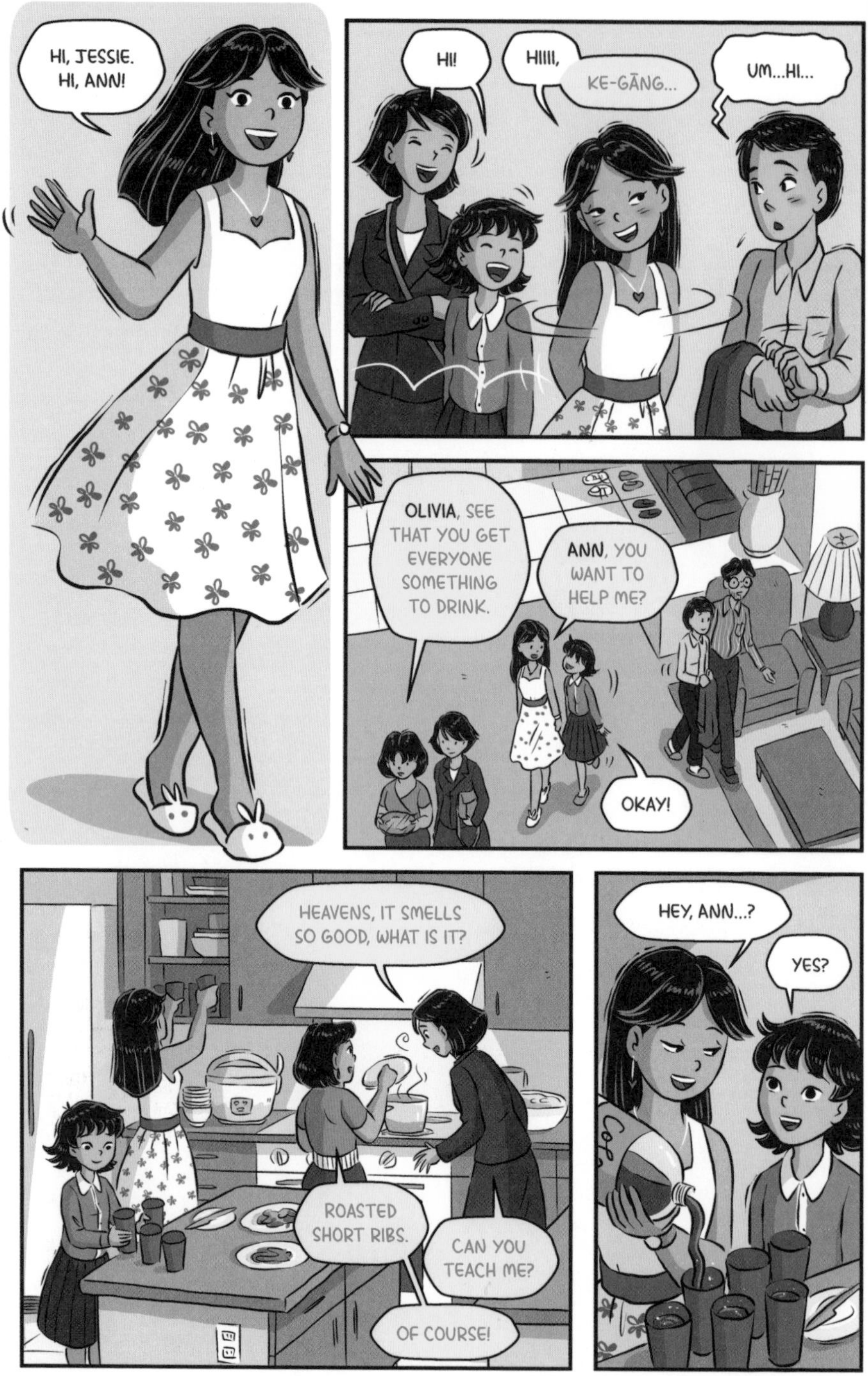
HI, JESSIE.
HI, ANN!
HI!
HIIII,
KE-GĀNG...
UM...HI...
OLIVIA, SEE THAT YOU GET EVERYONE SOMETHING TO DRINK.
ANN, YOU WANT TO HELP ME?
OKAY!
HEAVENS, IT SMELLS SO GOOD, WHAT IS IT?
ROASTED SHORT RIBS.
CAN YOU TEACH ME?
OF COURSE!
HEY, ANN...?
YES?

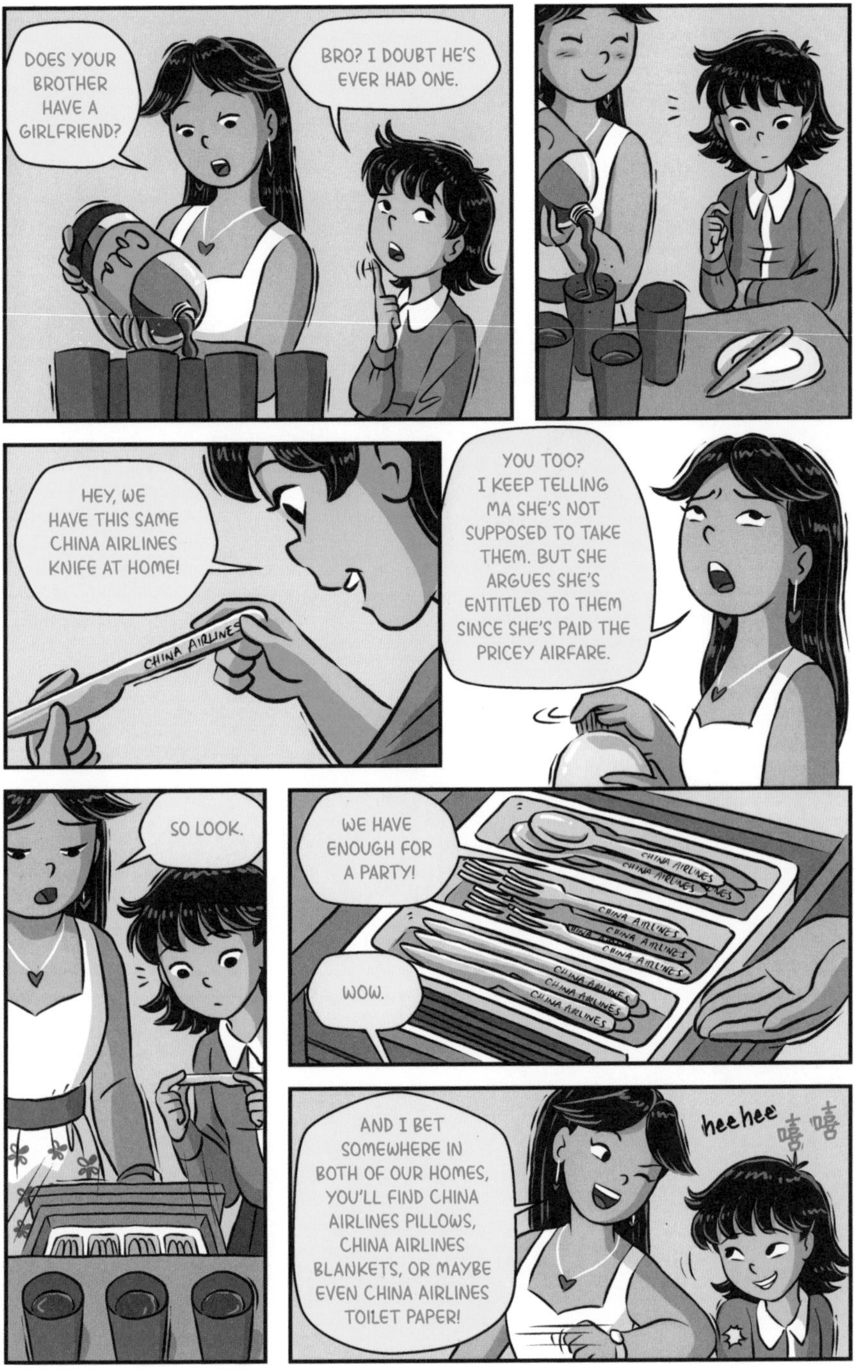
DOES YOUR BROTHER HAVE A GIRLFRIEND?
BRO? I DOUBT HE'S EVER HAD ONE.
HEY, WE HAVE THIS SAME CHINA AIRLINES KNIFE AT HOME!
CHINA AIRLINES
YOU TOO? I KEEP TELLING MA SHE'S NOT SUPPOSED TO TAKE THEM. BUT SHE ARGUES SHE'S ENTITLED TO THEM SINCE SHE'S PAID THE PRICEY AIRFARE.
SO LOOK.
WE HAVE ENOUGH FOR A PARTY!
WOW.
AND I BET SOMEWHERE IN BOTH OF OUR HOMES, YOU'LL FIND CHINA AIRLINES PILLOWS, CHINA AIRLINES BLANKETS, OR MAYBE EVEN CHINA AIRLINES TOILET PAPER!
hee hee 嘻嘻

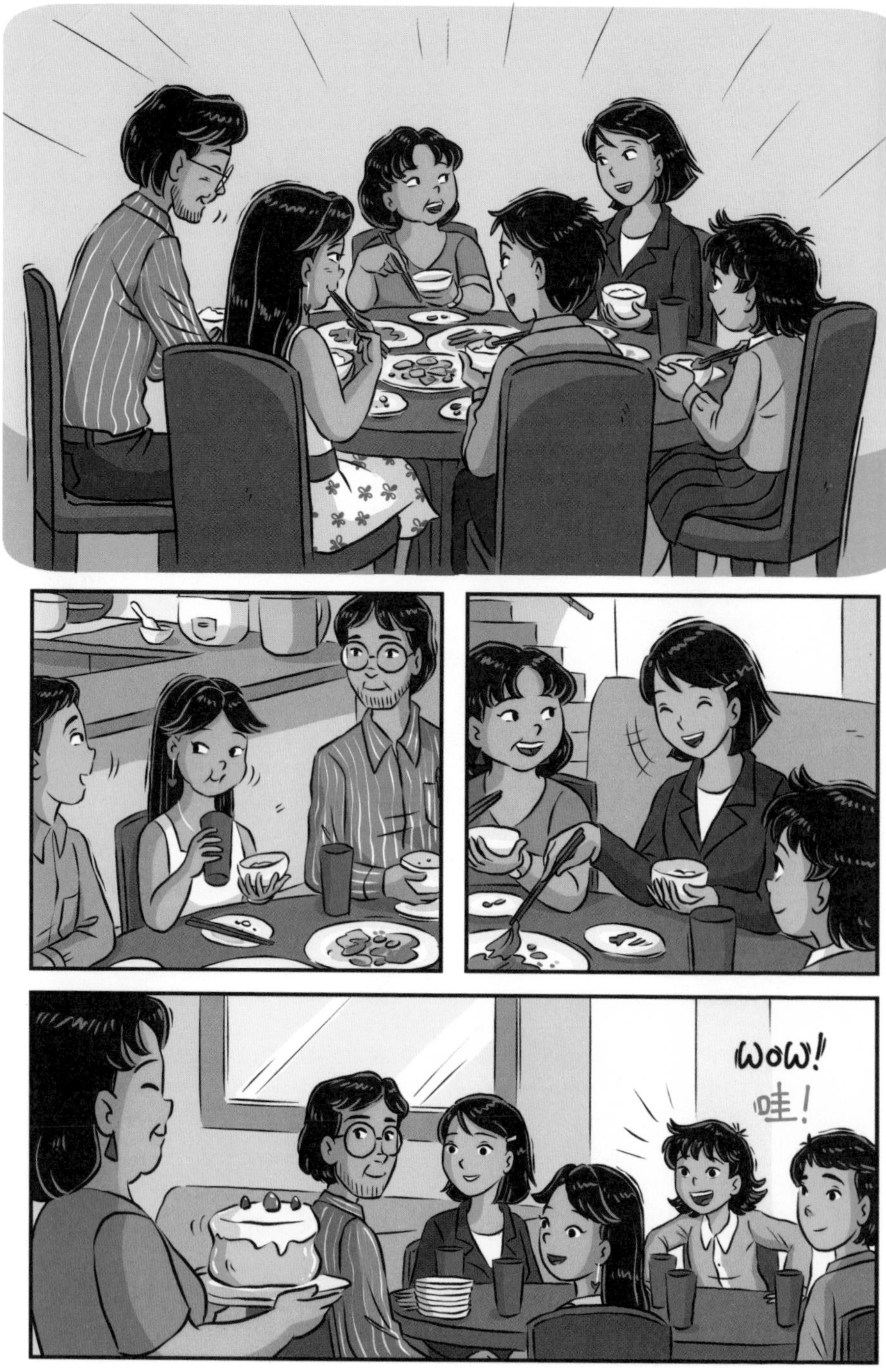
WOW!
哇!

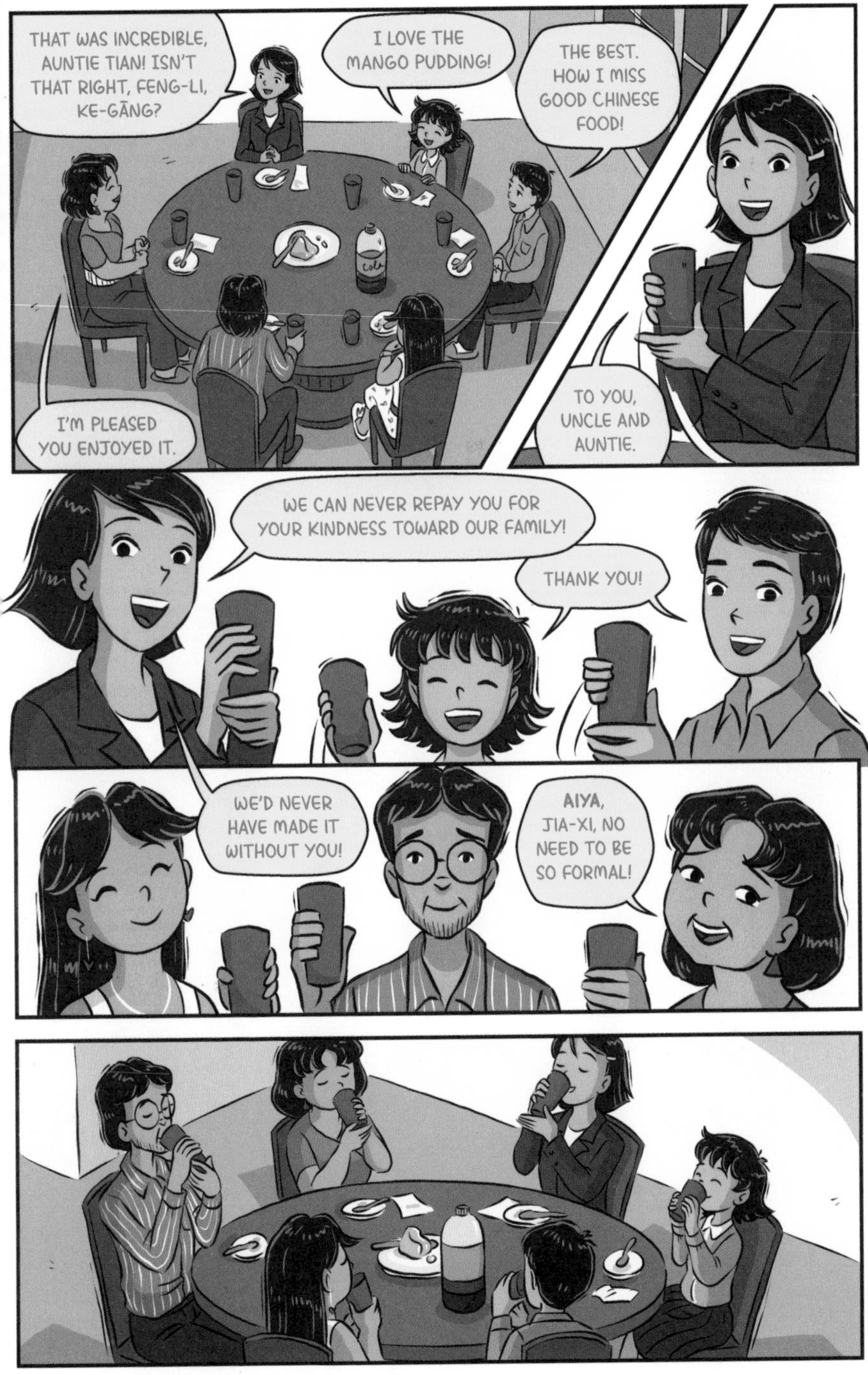
THAT WAS INCREDIBLE, AUNTIE TIAN! ISN'T THAT RIGHT, FENG-LI, KE-GĀNG?
I LOVE THE MANGO PUDDING!
THE BEST. HOW I MISS GOOD CHINESE FOOD!
I'M PLEASED YOU ENJOYED IT.
TO YOU, UNCLE AND AUNTIE.
WE CAN NEVER REPAY YOU FOR YOUR KINDNESS TOWARD OUR FAMILY!
THANK YOU!
WE'D NEVER HAVE MADE IT WITHOUT YOU!
AIYA, JIA-XI, NO NEED TO BE SO FORMAL!

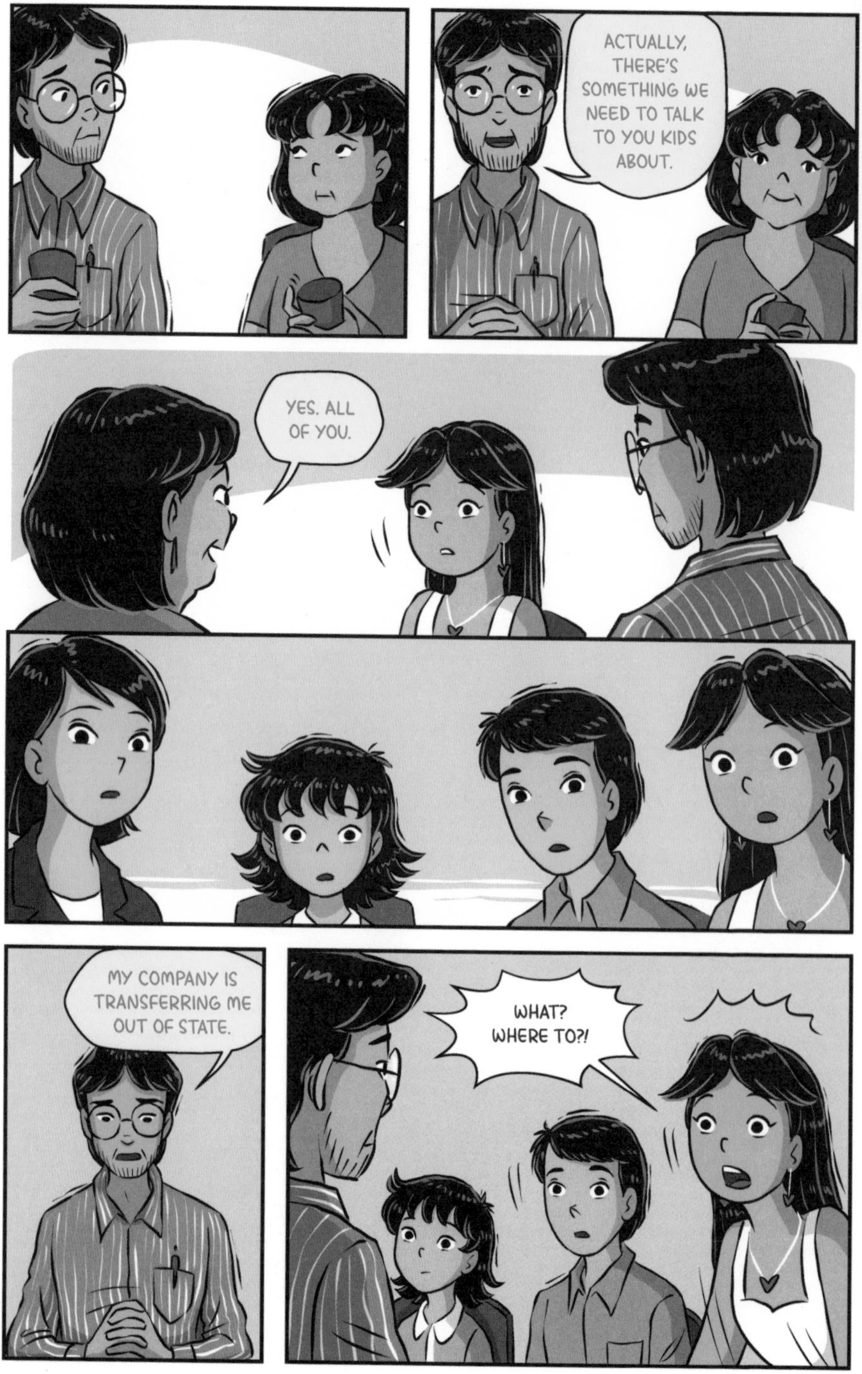
ACTUALLY, THERE'S SOMETHING WE NEED TO TALK TO YOU KIDS ABOUT.
YES. ALL OF YOU.
MY COMPANY IS TRANSFERRING ME OUT OF STATE.
WHAT? WHERE TO?!

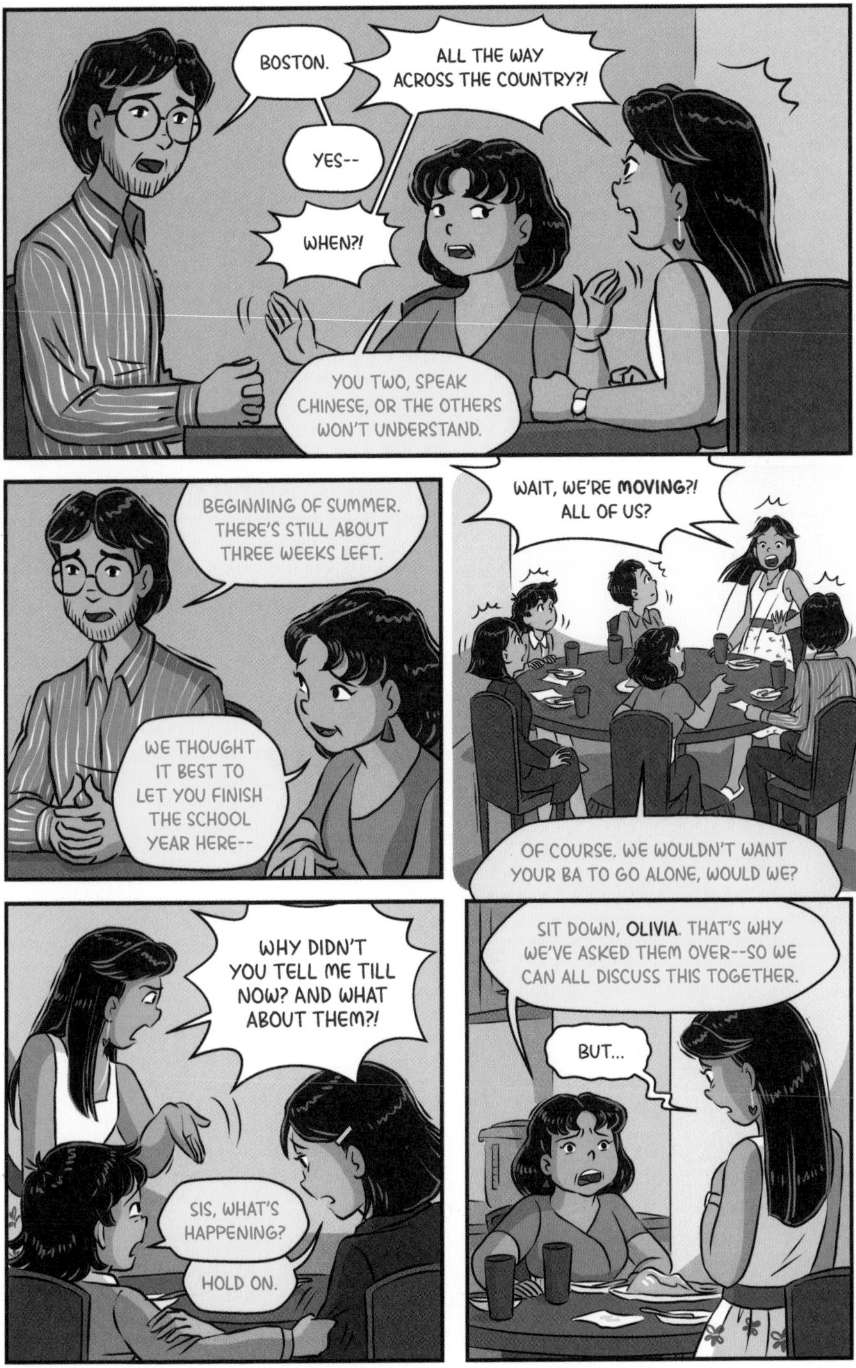
BOSTON.
ALL THE WAY ACROSS THE COUNTRY?!
YES--
WHEN?!
YOU TWO, SPEAK CHINESE, OR THE OTHERS WON'T UNDERSTAND.
BEGINNING OF SUMMER. THERE'S STILL ABOUT THREE WEEKS LEFT.
WE THOUGHT IT BEST TO LET YOU FINISH THE SCHOOL YEAR HERE--
WAIT, WE'RE MOVING?! ALL OF US?
OF COURSE. WE WOULDN'T WANT YOUR BA TO GO ALONE, WOULD WE?
WHY DIDN'T YOU TELL ME TILL NOW? AND WHAT ABOUT THEM?!
SIS, WHAT'S HAPPENING?
HOLD ON.
SIT DOWN, OLIVIA. THAT'S WHY WE'VE ASKED THEM OVER--SO WE CAN ALL DISCUSS THIS TOGETHER.
BUT...

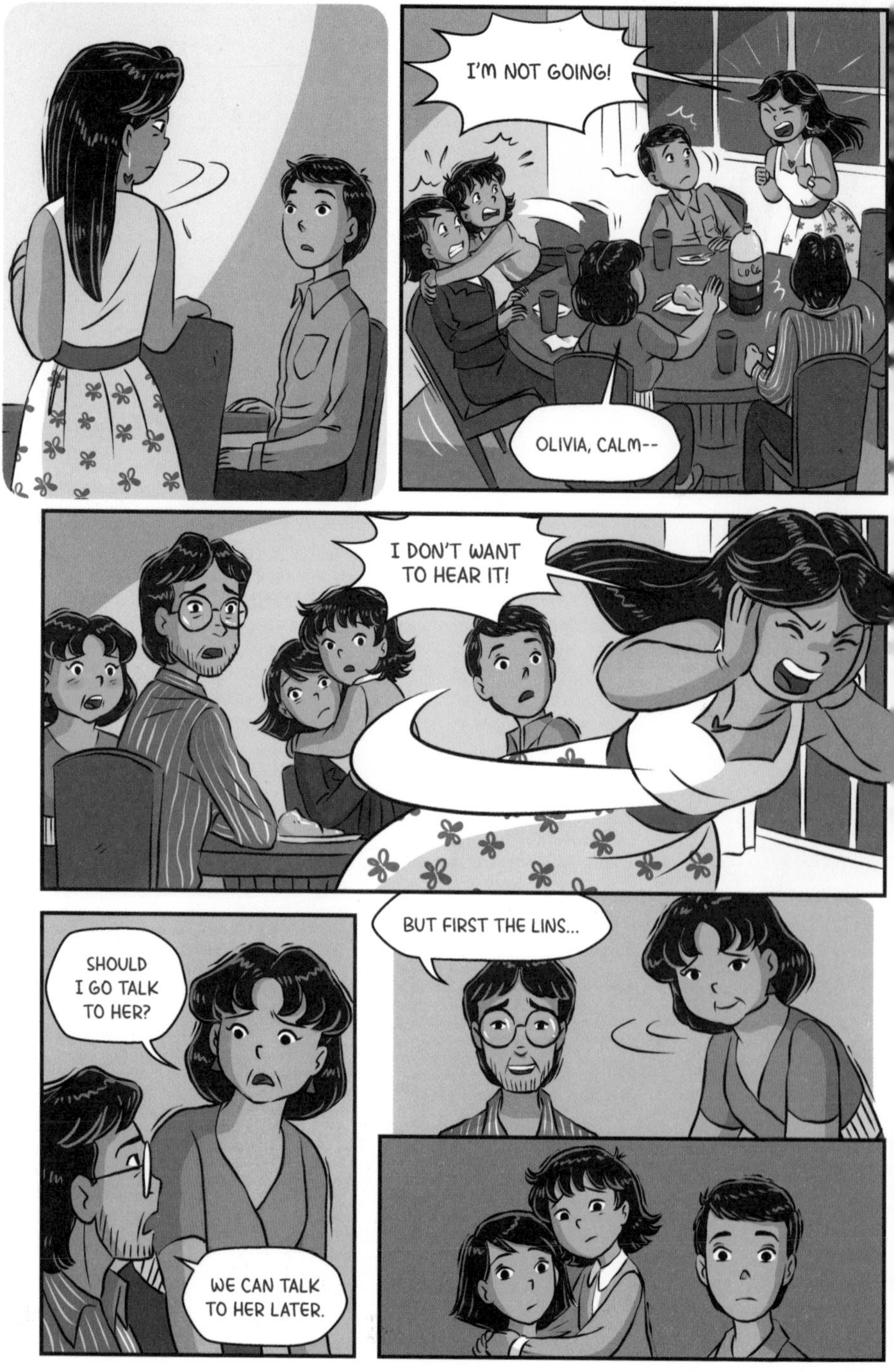
I'M NOT GOING!
OLIVIA, CALM--
I DON'T WANT TO HEAR IT!
SHOULD I GO TALK TO HER?
WE CAN TALK TO HER LATER.
BUT FIRST THE LINS...

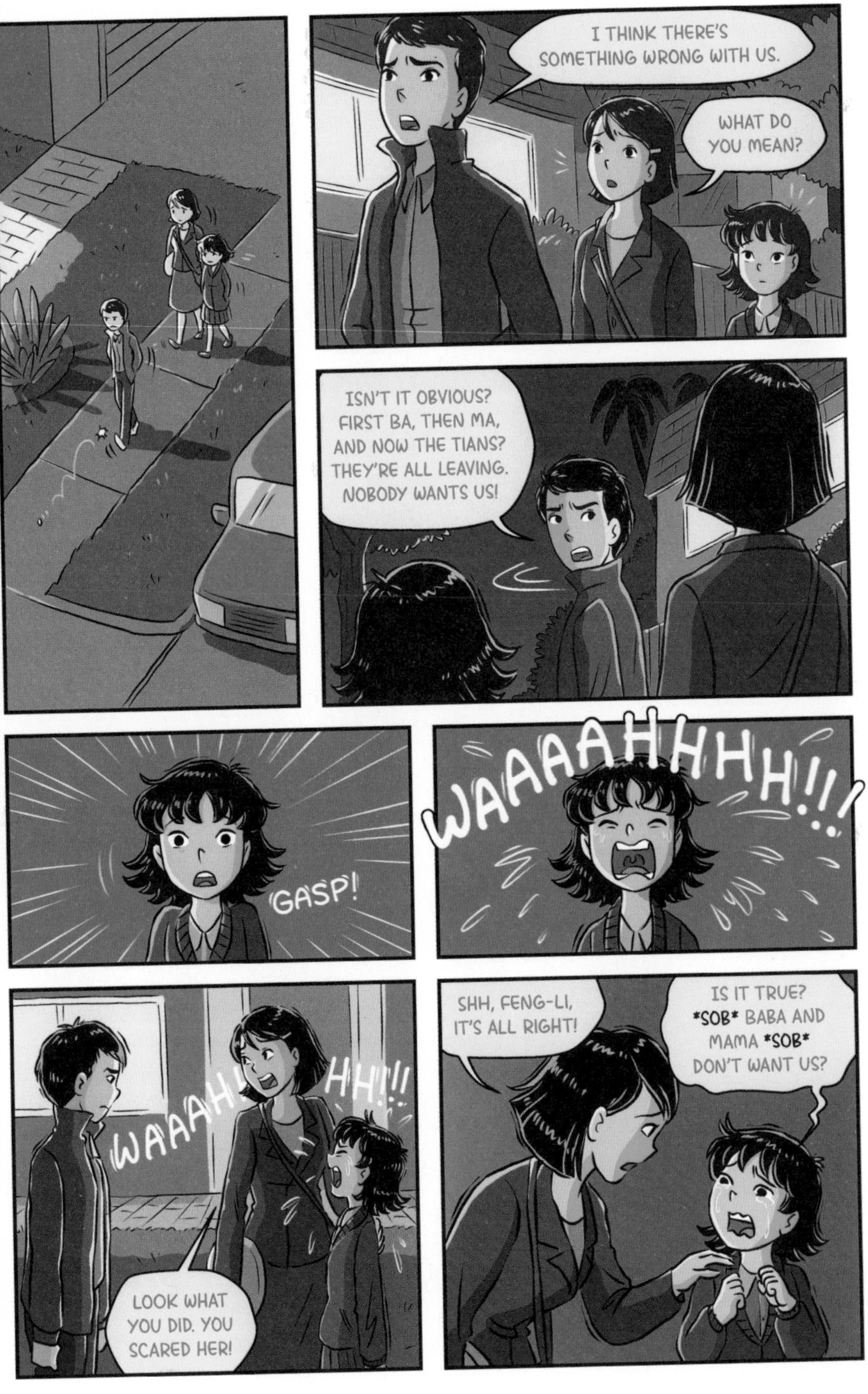
I THINK THERE'S SOMETHING WRONG WITH US.
WHAT DO YOU MEAN?
ISN'T IT OBVIOUS? FIRST BA, THEN MA, AND NOW THE TIANS? THEY'RE ALL LEAVING. NOBODY WANTS US!
GASP!
WAAAAHHHHH!!!
WAAAH! HH!!!
LOOK WHAT YOU DID. YOU SCARED HER!
SHH, FENG-LI, IT'S ALL RIGHT!
IS IT TRUE? *SOB* BABA AND MAMA *SOB* DON'T WANT US?

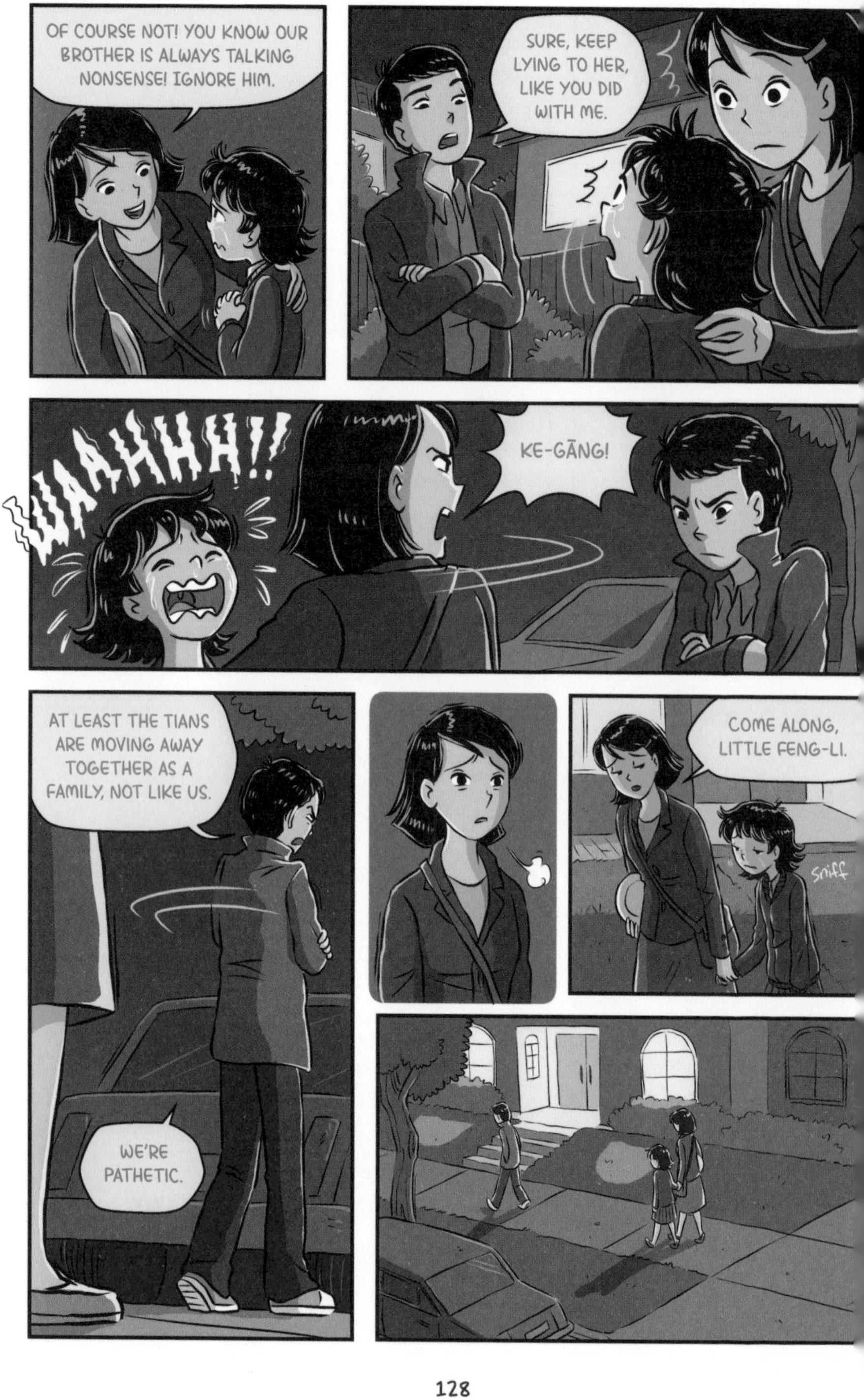
OF COURSE NOT! YOU KNOW OUR BROTHER IS ALWAYS TALKING NONSENSE! IGNORE HIM.
SURE, KEEP LYING TO HER, LIKE YOU DID WITH ME.
WAAHHH!!
KE-GĀNG!
AT LEAST THE TIANS ARE MOVING AWAY TOGETHER AS A FAMILY, NOT LIKE US.
WE'RE PATHETIC.
COME ALONG, LITTLE FENG-LI.
sniff

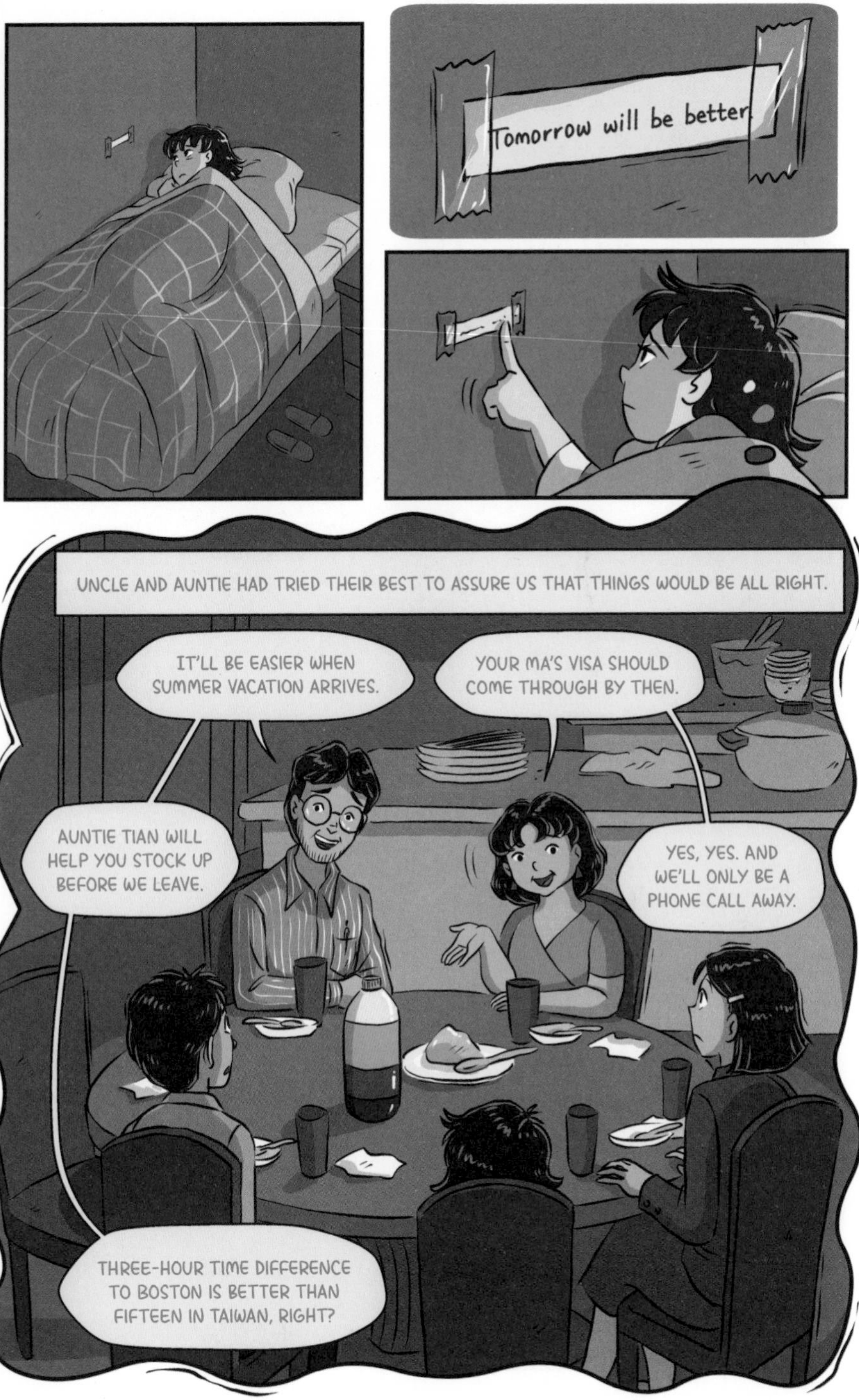
Tomorrow will be better
UNCLE AND AUNTIE HAD TRIED THEIR BEST TO ASSURE US THAT THINGS WOULD BE ALL RIGHT.
IT'LL BE EASIER WHEN SUMMER VACATION ARRIVES.
YOUR MA'S VISA SHOULD COME THROUGH BY THEN.
AUNTIE TIAN WILL HELP YOU STOCK UP BEFORE WE LEAVE.
YES, YES. AND WE'LL ONLY BE A PHONE CALL AWAY.
THREE-HOUR TIME DIFFERENCE TO BOSTON IS BETTER THAN FIFTEEN IN TAIWAN, RIGHT?

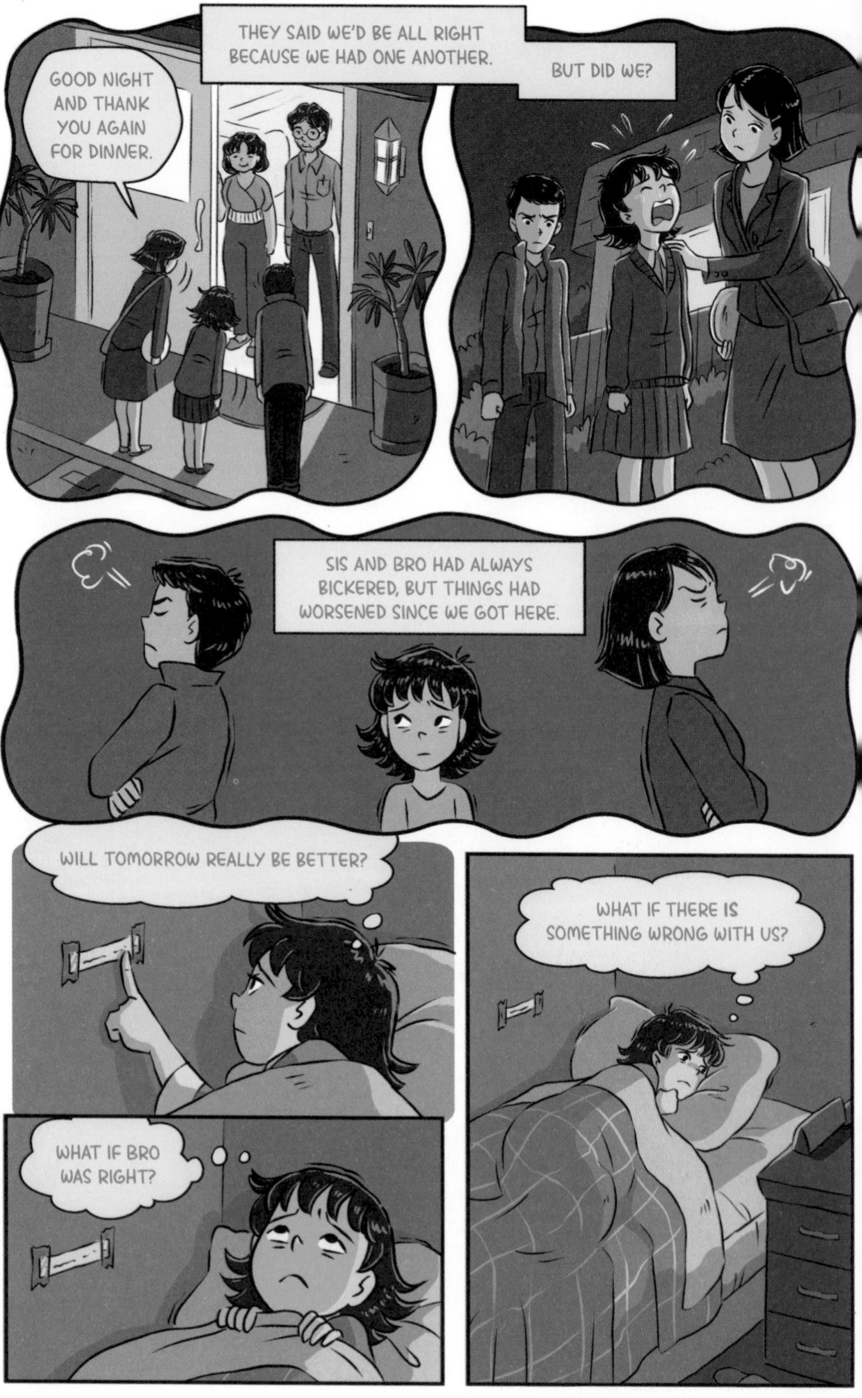
THEY SAID WE'D BE ALL RIGHT BECAUSE WE HAD ONE ANOTHER.
GOOD NIGHT AND THANK YOU AGAIN FOR DINNER.
BUT DID WE?
SIS AND BRO HAD ALWAYS BICKERED, BUT THINGS HAD WORSENED SINCE WE GOT HERE.
WILL TOMORROW REALLY BE BETTER?
WHAT IF BRO WAS RIGHT?
WHAT IF THERE IS SOMETHING WRONG WITH US?

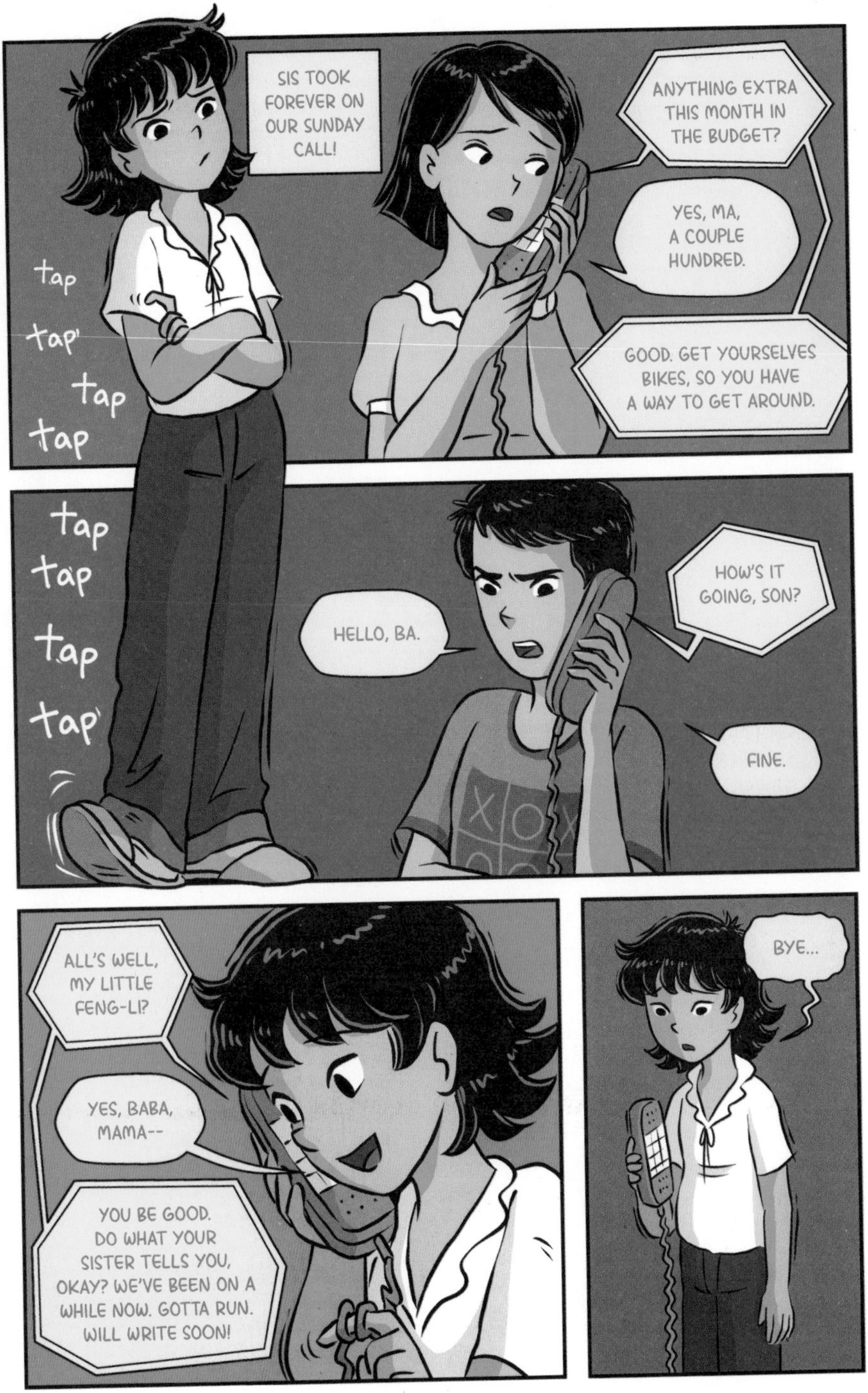
SIS TOOK FOREVER ON OUR SUNDAY CALL!
ANYTHING EXTRA THIS MONTH IN THE BUDGET?
YES, MA, A COUPLE HUNDRED.
GOOD. GET YOURSELVES BIKES, SO YOU HAVE A WAY TO GET AROUND.
tap
tap
tap
tap
tap
tap
tap
tap
HELLO, BA.
HOW'S IT GOING, SON?
FINE.
ALL'S WELL, MY LITTLE FENG-LI?
YES, BABA, MAMA--
YOU BE GOOD. DO WHAT YOUR SISTER TELLS YOU, OKAY? WE'VE BEEN ON A WHILE NOW. GOTTA RUN. WILL WRITE SOON!
BYE...

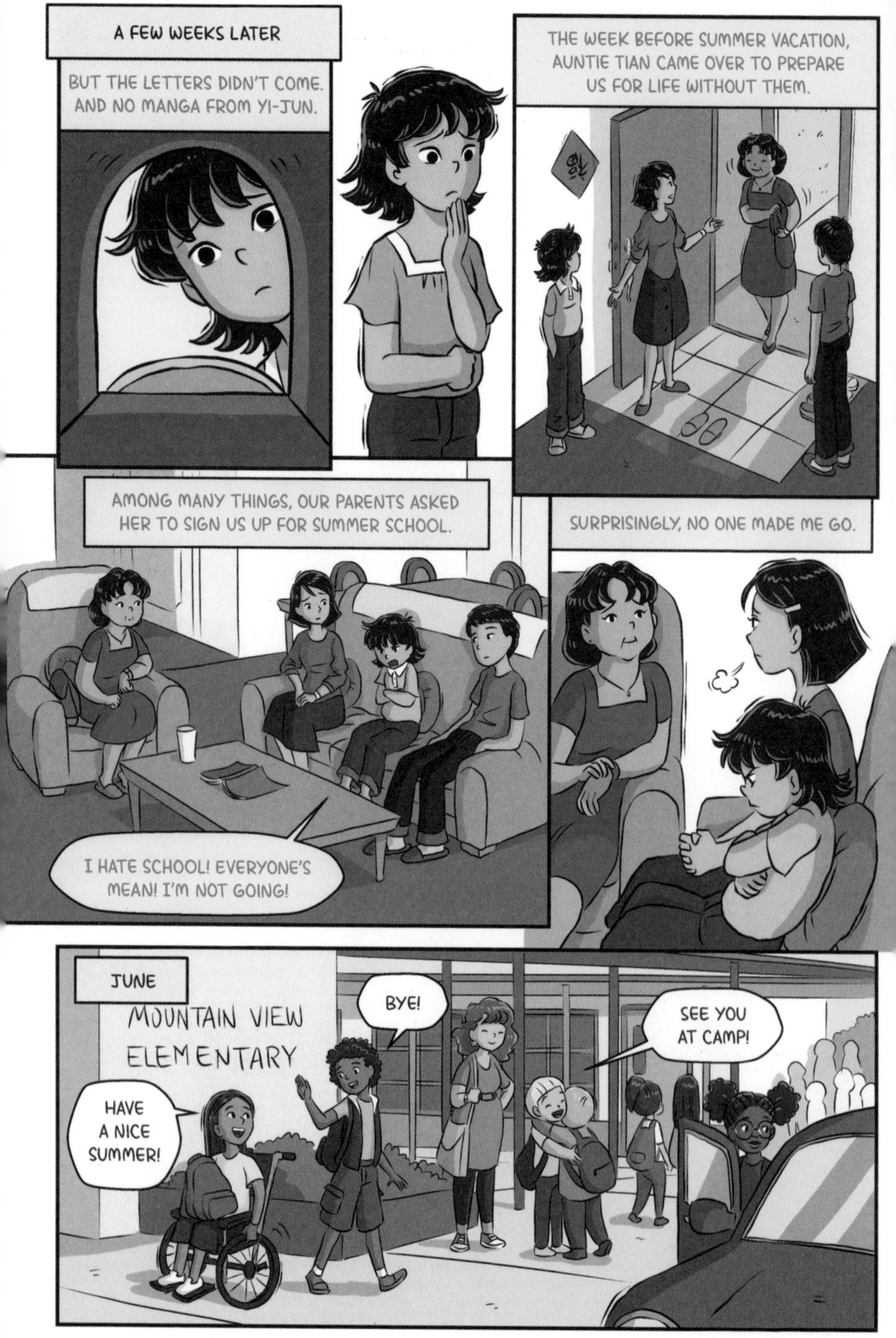
A FEW WEEKS LATER
BUT THE LETTERS DIDN'T COME. AND NO MANGA FROM YI-JUN.
THE WEEK BEFORE SUMMER VACATION, AUNTIE TIAN CAME OVER TO PREPARE US FOR LIFE WITHOUT THEM.
AMONG MANY THINGS, OUR PARENTS ASKED HER TO SIGN US UP FOR SUMMER SCHOOL.
I HATE SCHOOL! EVERYONE'S MEAN! I'M NOT GOING!
SURPRISINGLY, NO ONE MADE ME GO.
JUNE
MOUNTAIN VIEW ELEMENTARY
HAVE A NICE SUMMER!
BYE!
SEE YOU AT CAMP!

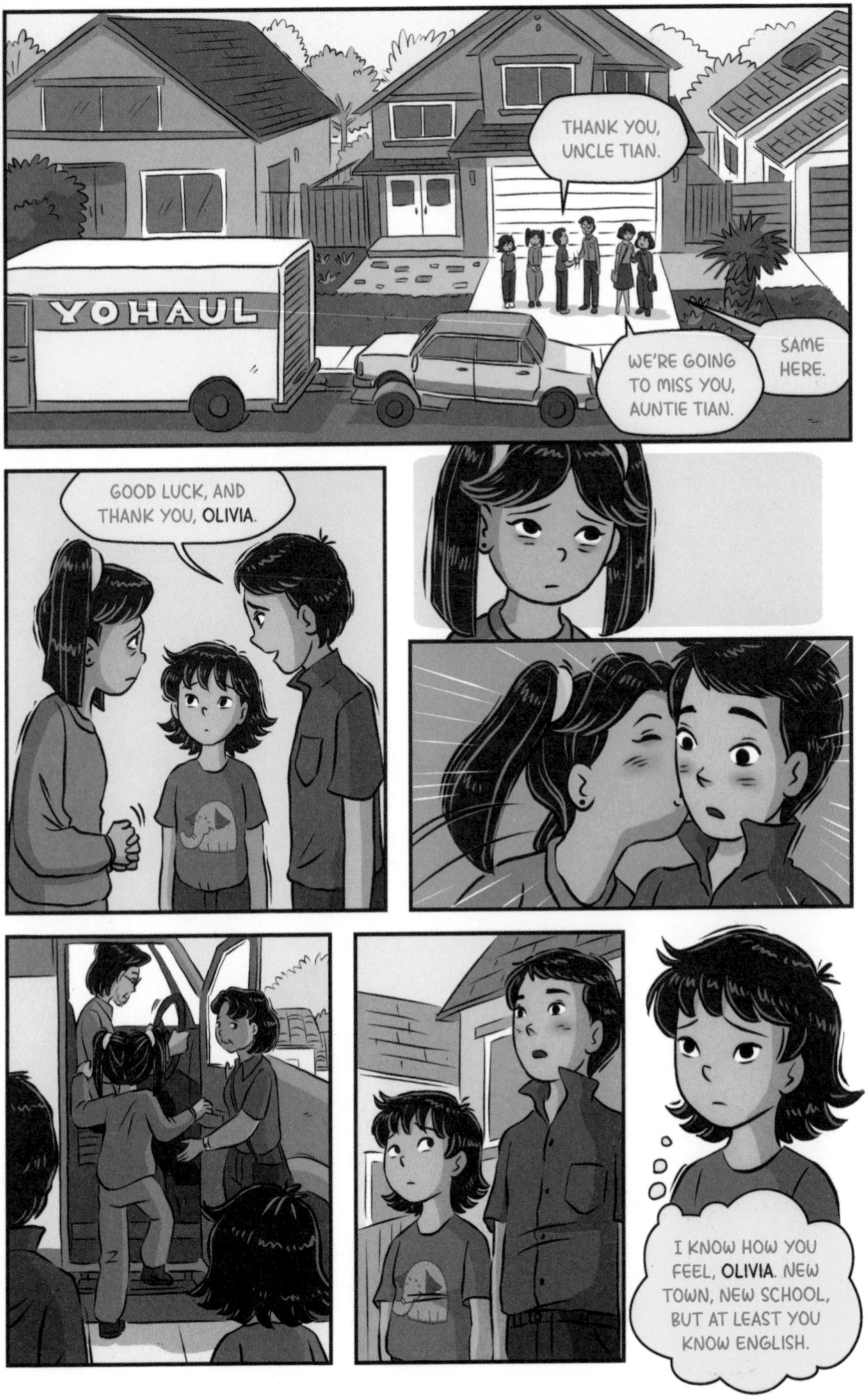
THANK YOU, UNCLE TIAN.
YOHAUL
WE'RE GOING TO MISS YOU, AUNTIE TIAN.
SAME HERE.
GOOD LUCK, AND THANK YOU, OLIVIA.
I KNOW HOW YOU FEEL, OLIVIA. NEW TOWN, NEW SCHOOL, BUT AT LEAST YOU KNOW ENGLISH.

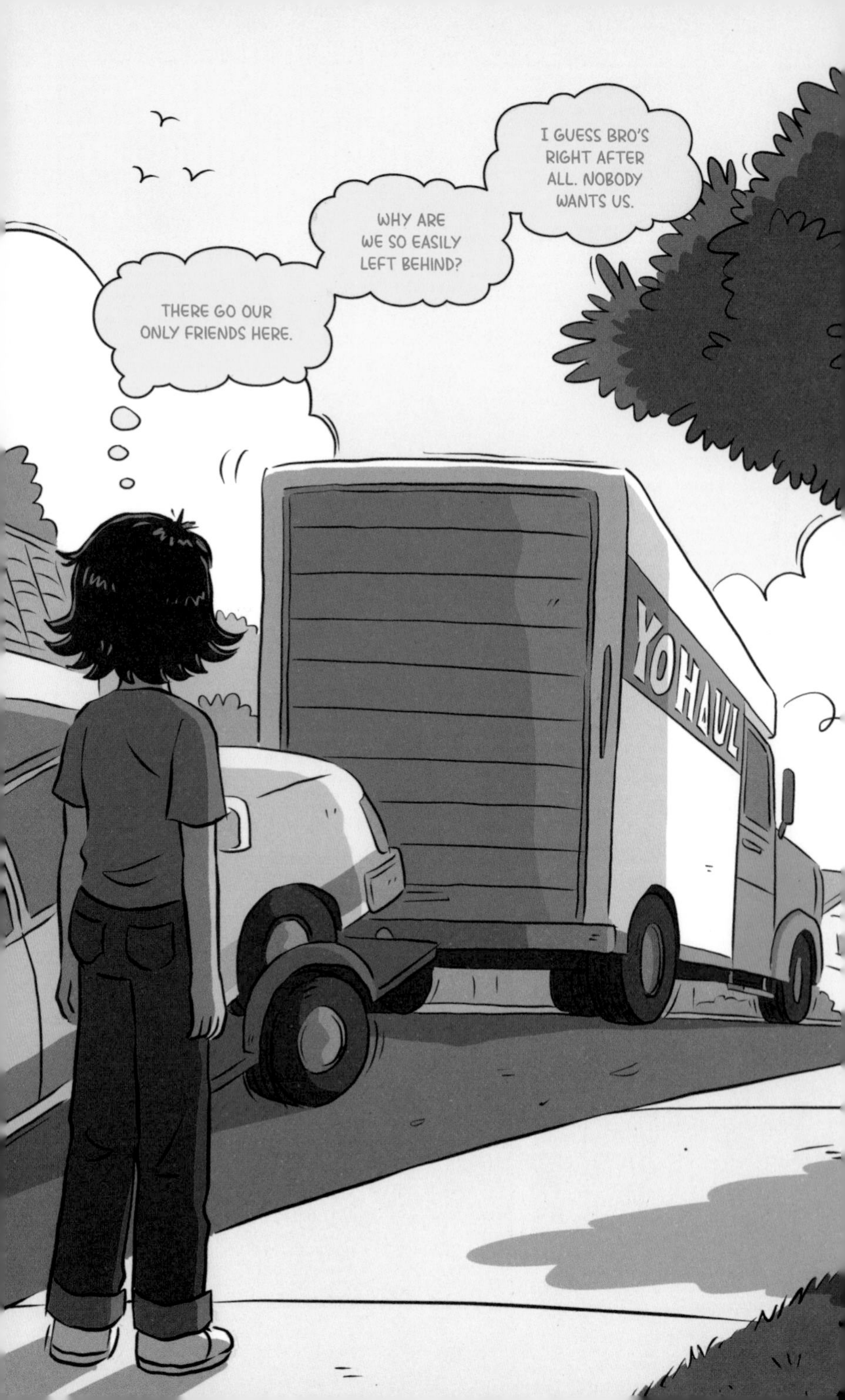
THERE GO OUR ONLY FRIENDS HERE.
WHY ARE WE SO EASILY LEFT BEHIND?
I GUESS BRO'S RIGHT AFTER ALL. NOBODY WANTS US.
YOHAUL

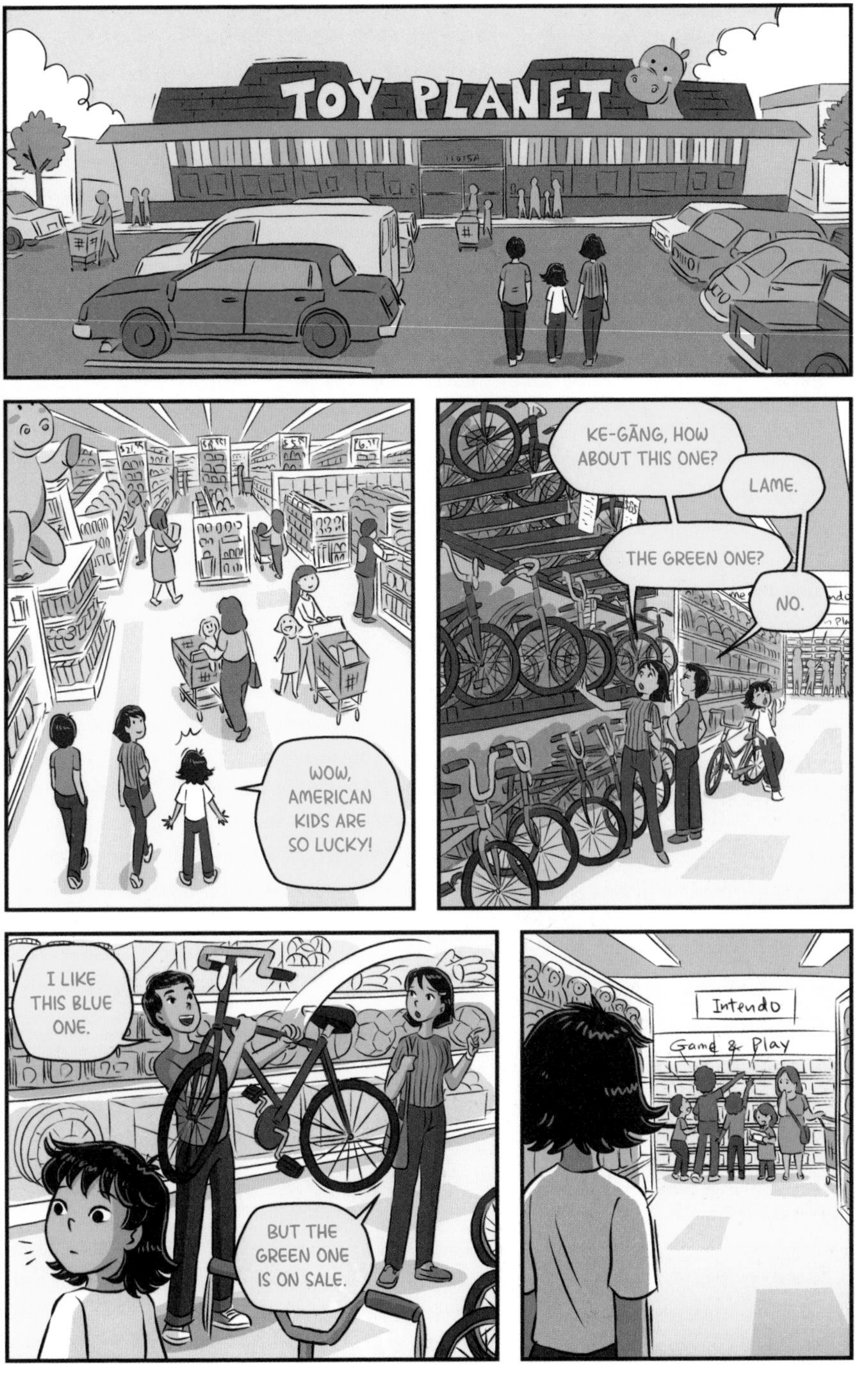
TOY PLANET
WOW, AMERICAN KIDS ARE SO LUCKY!
KE-GĀNG, HOW ABOUT THIS ONE?
LAME.
THE GREEN ONE?
NO.
I LIKE THIS BLUE ONE.
BUT THE GREEN ONE IS ON SALE.
Intendo
Game & Play

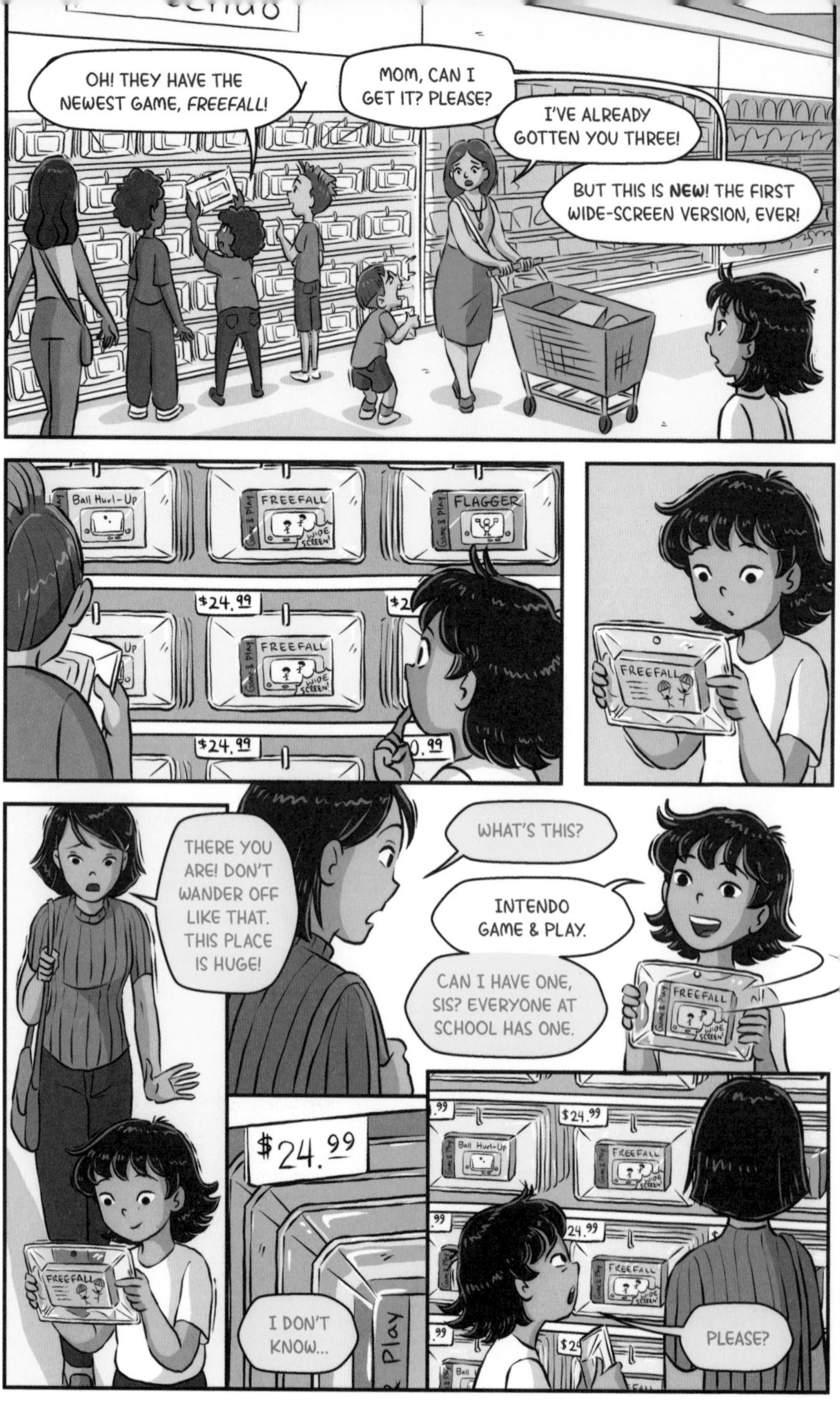

OH! THEY HAVE THE NEWEST GAME, *FREEFALL*!
MOM, CAN I GET IT? PLEASE?
I'VE ALREADY GOTTEN YOU THREE!
BUT THIS IS **NEW**! THE FIRST WIDE-SCREEN VERSION, EVER!
Ball Hurl-Up
FREEFALL
WIDE SCREEN!
FLAGGER
$24.99
$24.99
FREEFALL
THERE YOU ARE! DON'T WANDER OFF LIKE THAT. THIS PLACE IS HUGE!
WHAT'S THIS?
INTENDO GAME & PLAY.
CAN I HAVE ONE, SIS? EVERYONE AT SCHOOL HAS ONE.
$24.99
I DON'T KNOW...
Play
PLEASE?

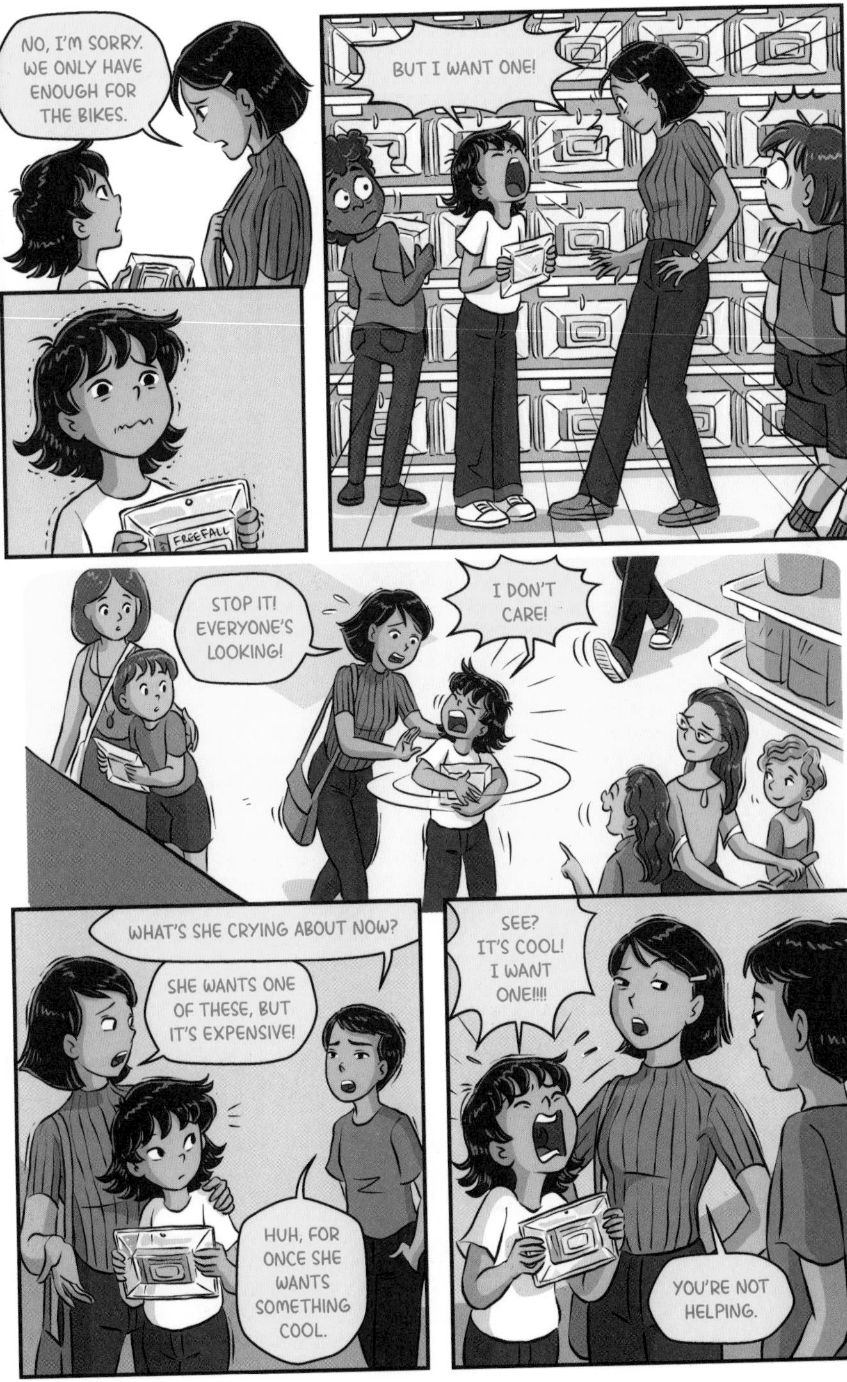
NO, I'M SORRY. WE ONLY HAVE ENOUGH FOR THE BIKES.
FREEFALL
BUT I WANT ONE!
STOP IT! EVERYONE'S LOOKING!
I DON'T CARE!
WHAT'S SHE CRYING ABOUT NOW?
SHE WANTS ONE OF THESE, BUT IT'S EXPENSIVE!
HUH, FOR ONCE SHE WANTS SOMETHING COOL.
SEE? IT'S COOL! I WANT ONE!!!!
YOU'RE NOT HELPING.

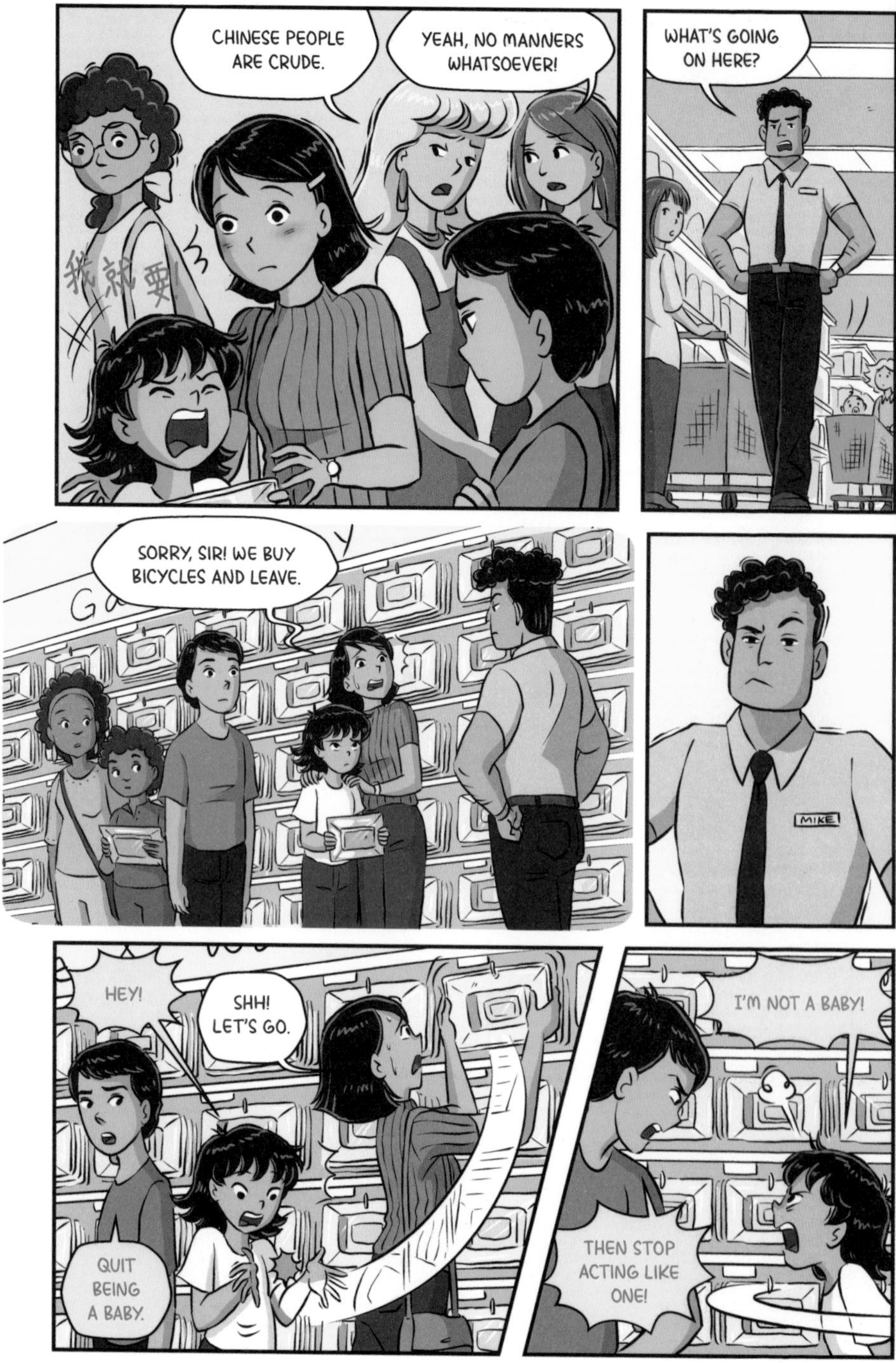
CHINESE PEOPLE ARE CRUDE.
YEAH, NO MANNERS WHATSOEVER!
我就要
WHAT'S GOING ON HERE?
SORRY, SIR! WE BUY BICYCLES AND LEAVE.
MIKE
HEY!
SHH! LET'S GO.
QUIT BEING A BABY.
I'M NOT A BABY!
THEN STOP ACTING LIKE ONE!

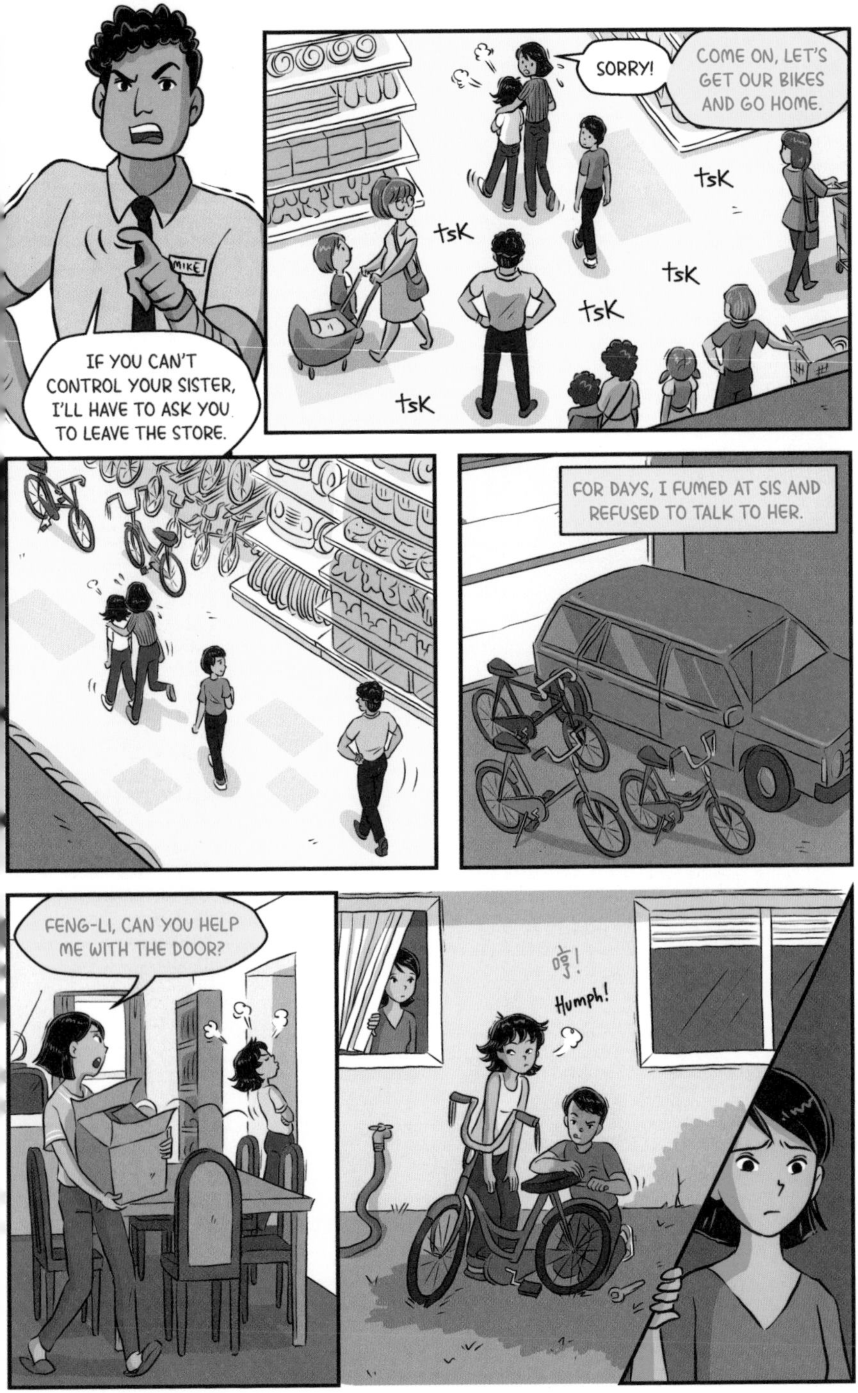
IF YOU CAN'T CONTROL YOUR SISTER, I'LL HAVE TO ASK YOU TO LEAVE THE STORE.
MIKE
SORRY!
COME ON, LET'S GET OUR BIKES AND GO HOME.
tsK
tsK
tsK
tsK
tsK
FOR DAYS, I FUMED AT SIS AND REFUSED TO TALK TO HER.
FENG-LI, CAN YOU HELP ME WITH THE DOOR?
哼!
Humph!

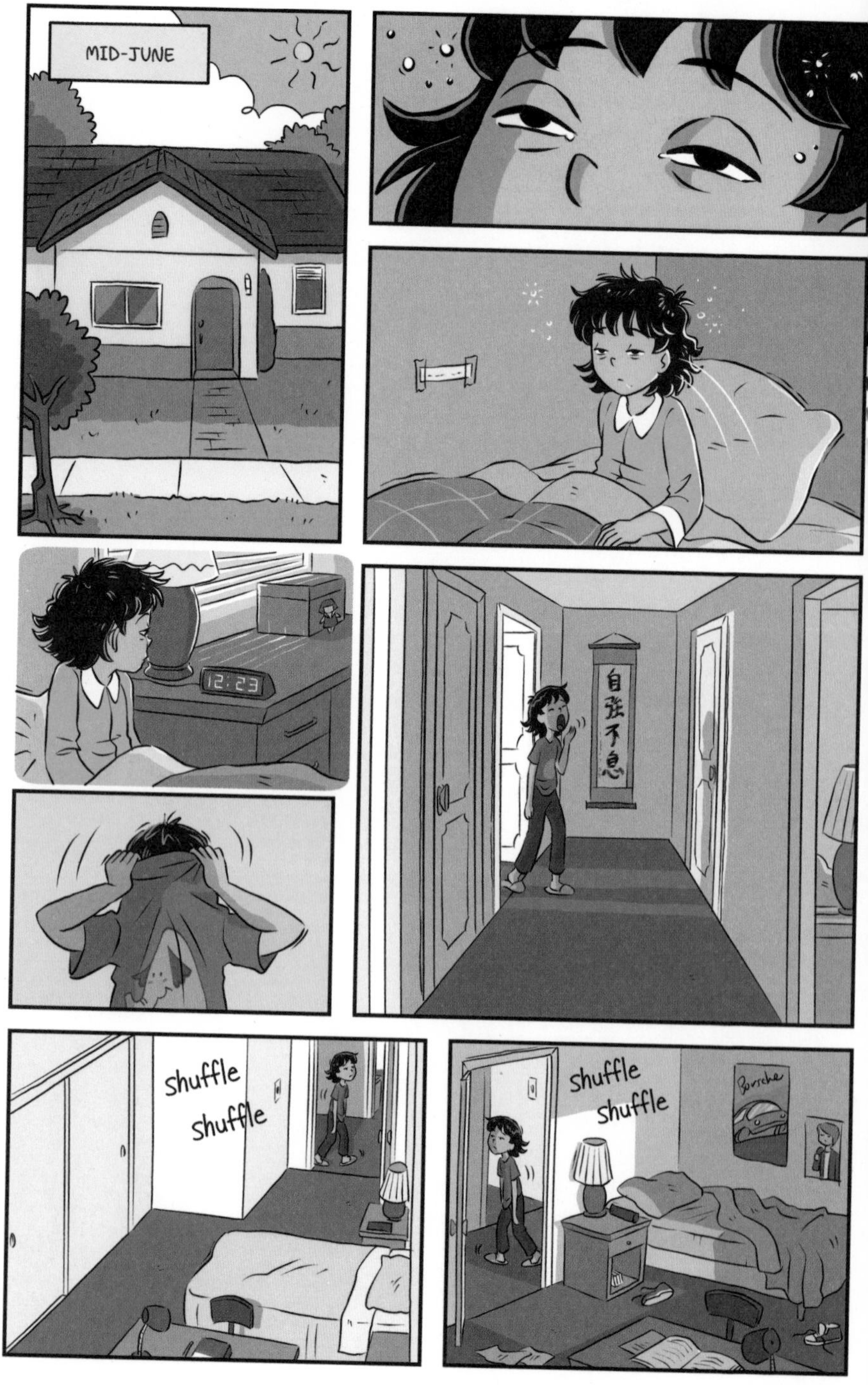
MID-JUNE
12:23
自强不息
shuffle
shuffle
shuffle
shuffle
Porsche

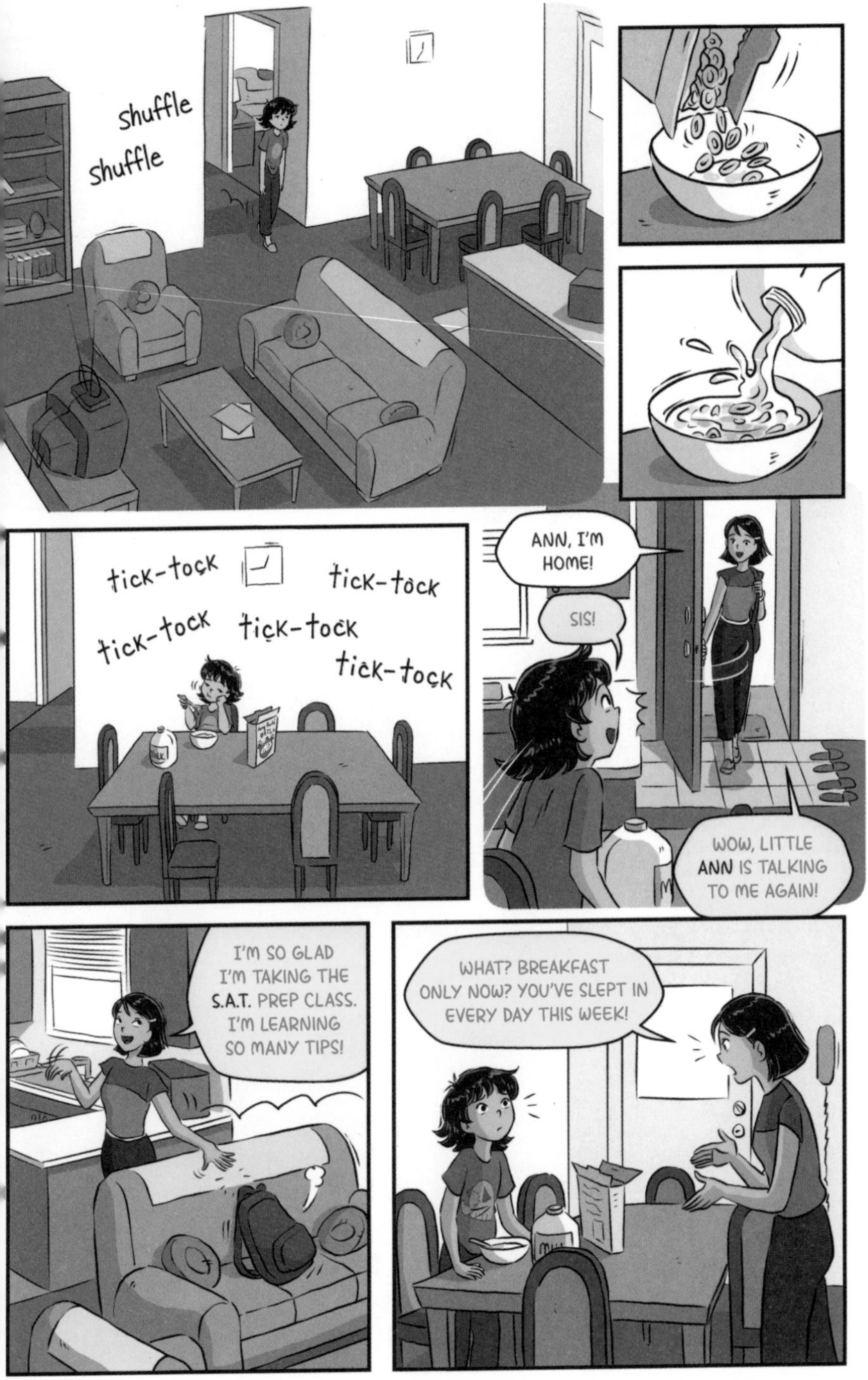
shuffle
shuffle
tick-tock
tick-tock
tick-tock
tick-tock
tick-tock
ANN, I'M HOME!
SIS!
WOW, LITTLE ANN IS TALKING TO ME AGAIN!
I'M SO GLAD I'M TAKING THE S.A.T. PREP CLASS. I'M LEARNING SO MANY TIPS!
WHAT? BREAKFAST ONLY NOW? YOU'VE SLEPT IN EVERY DAY THIS WEEK!

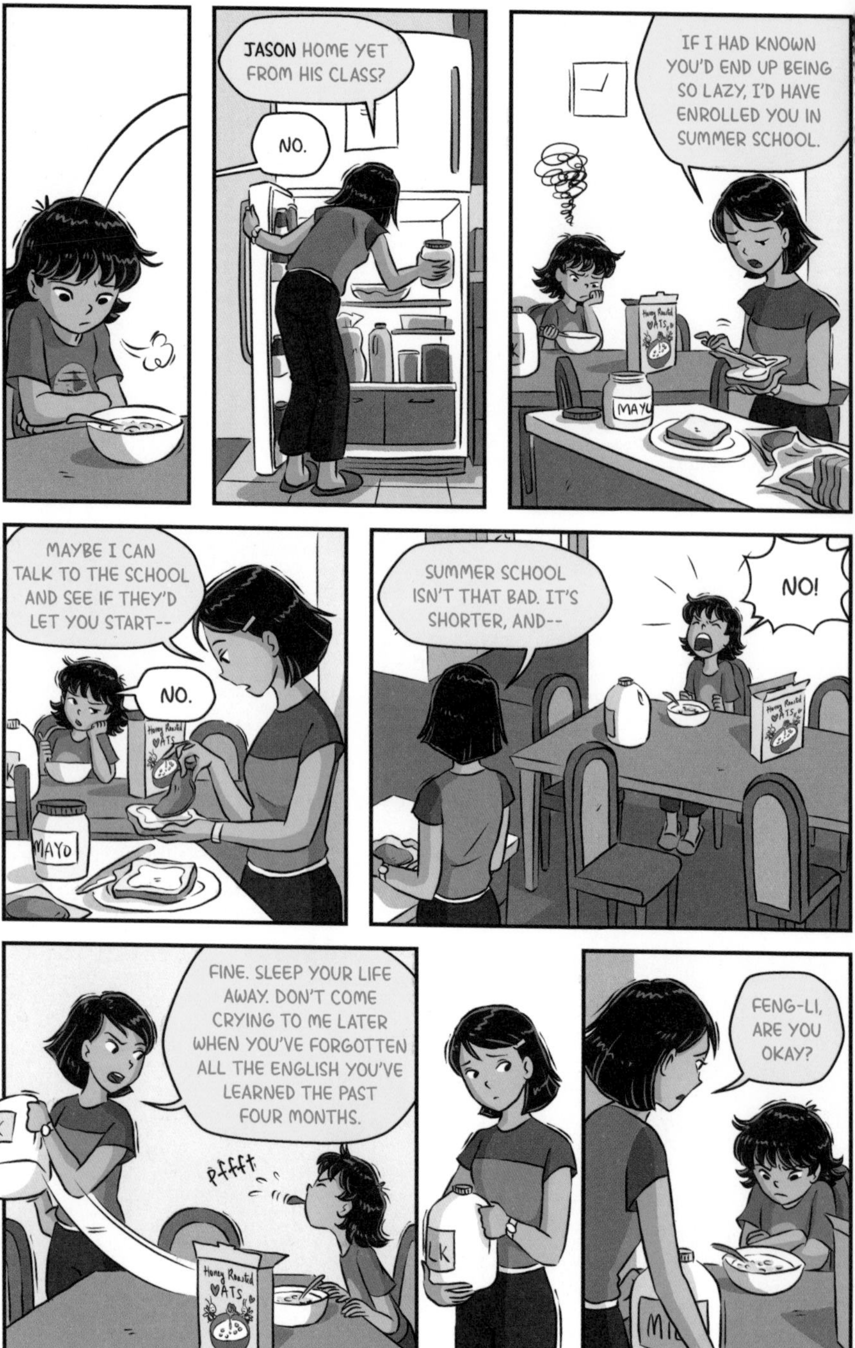
JASON HOME YET FROM HIS CLASS?
NO.
IF I HAD KNOWN YOU'D END UP BEING SO LAZY, I'D HAVE ENROLLED YOU IN SUMMER SCHOOL.
MAYO
Honey Roasted OATS
MAYBE I CAN TALK TO THE SCHOOL AND SEE IF THEY'D LET YOU START--
NO.
MAYO
SUMMER SCHOOL ISN'T THAT BAD. IT'S SHORTER, AND--
NO!
FINE. SLEEP YOUR LIFE AWAY. DON'T COME CRYING TO ME LATER WHEN YOU'VE FORGOTTEN ALL THE ENGLISH YOU'VE LEARNED THE PAST FOUR MONTHS.
pffft
Honey Roasted OATS
FENG-LI, ARE YOU OKAY?

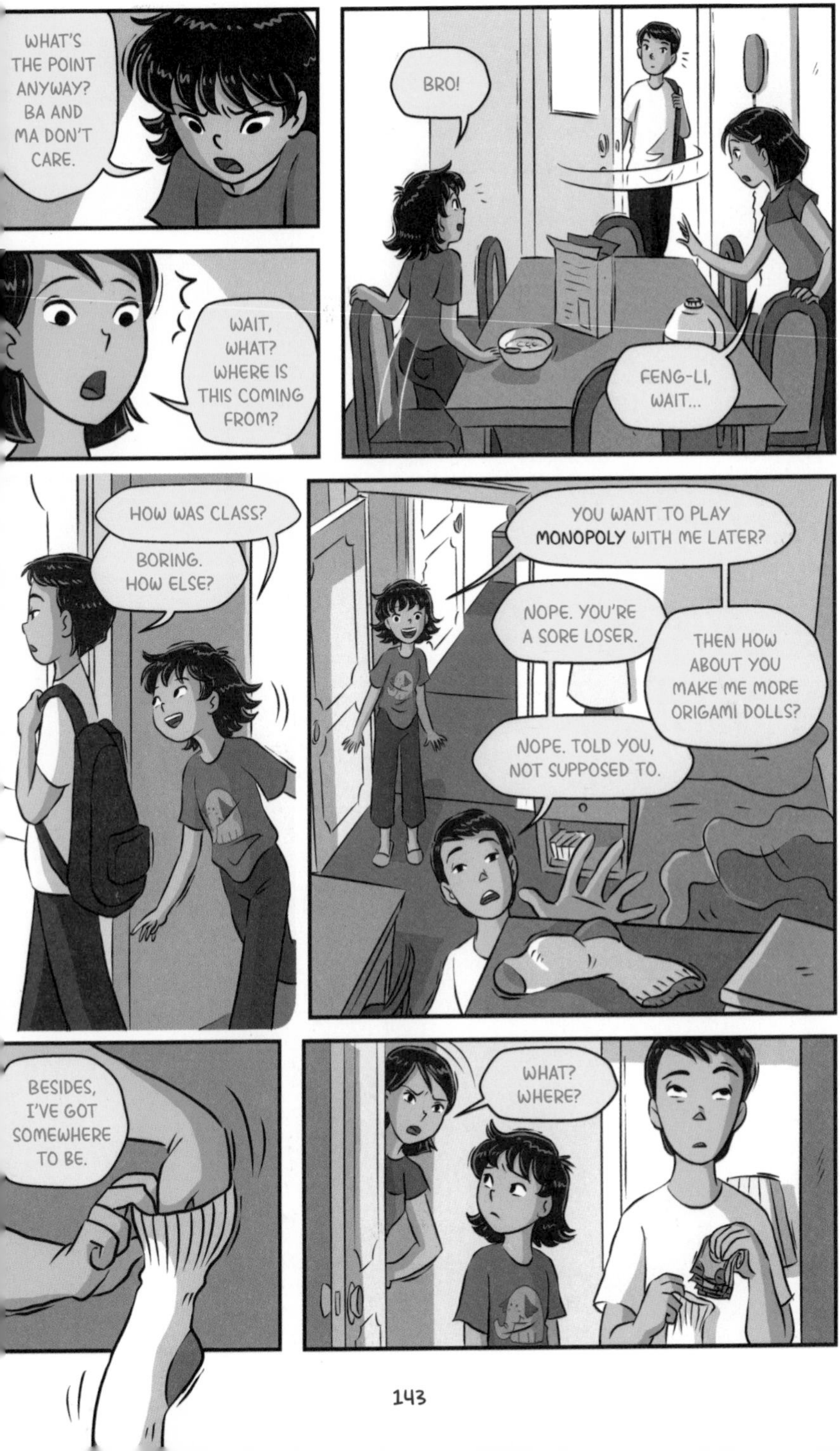
WHAT'S THE POINT ANYWAY? BA AND MA DON'T CARE.
BRO!
WAIT, WHAT? WHERE IS THIS COMING FROM?
FENG-LI, WAIT...
HOW WAS CLASS?
BORING. HOW ELSE?
YOU WANT TO PLAY MONOPOLY WITH ME LATER?
NOPE. YOU'RE A SORE LOSER.
THEN HOW ABOUT YOU MAKE ME MORE ORIGAMI DOLLS?
NOPE. TOLD YOU, NOT SUPPOSED TO.
BESIDES, I'VE GOT SOMEWHERE TO BE.
WHAT? WHERE?

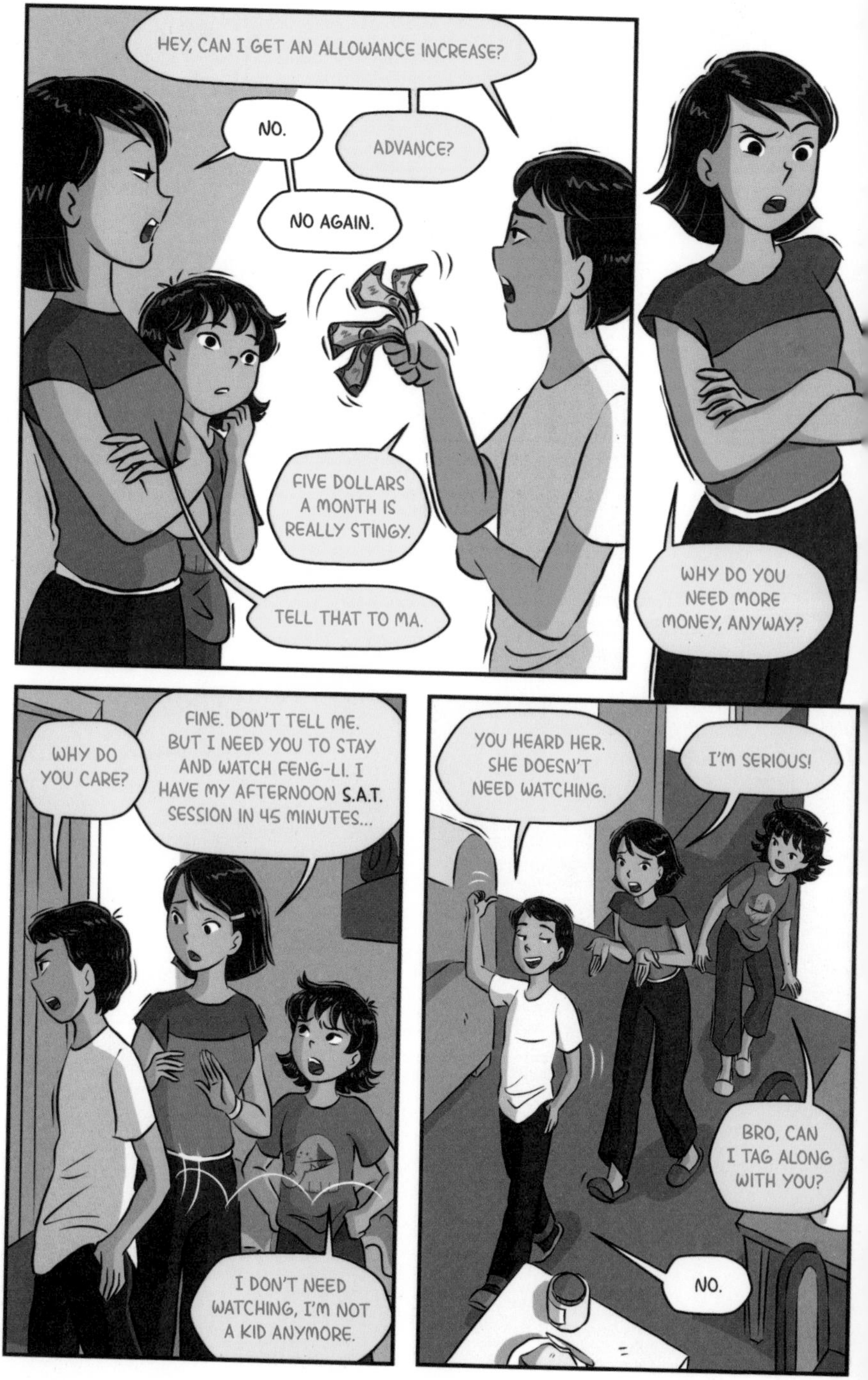
HEY, CAN I GET AN ALLOWANCE INCREASE?
NO.
ADVANCE?
NO AGAIN.
FIVE DOLLARS A MONTH IS REALLY STINGY.
TELL THAT TO MA.
WHY DO YOU NEED MORE MONEY, ANYWAY?
WHY DO YOU CARE?
FINE. DON'T TELL ME. BUT I NEED YOU TO STAY AND WATCH FENG-LI. I HAVE MY AFTERNOON S.A.T. SESSION IN 45 MINUTES...
I DON'T NEED WATCHING, I'M NOT A KID ANYMORE.
YOU HEARD HER. SHE DOESN'T NEED WATCHING.
I'M SERIOUS!
BRO, CAN I TAG ALONG WITH YOU?
NO.

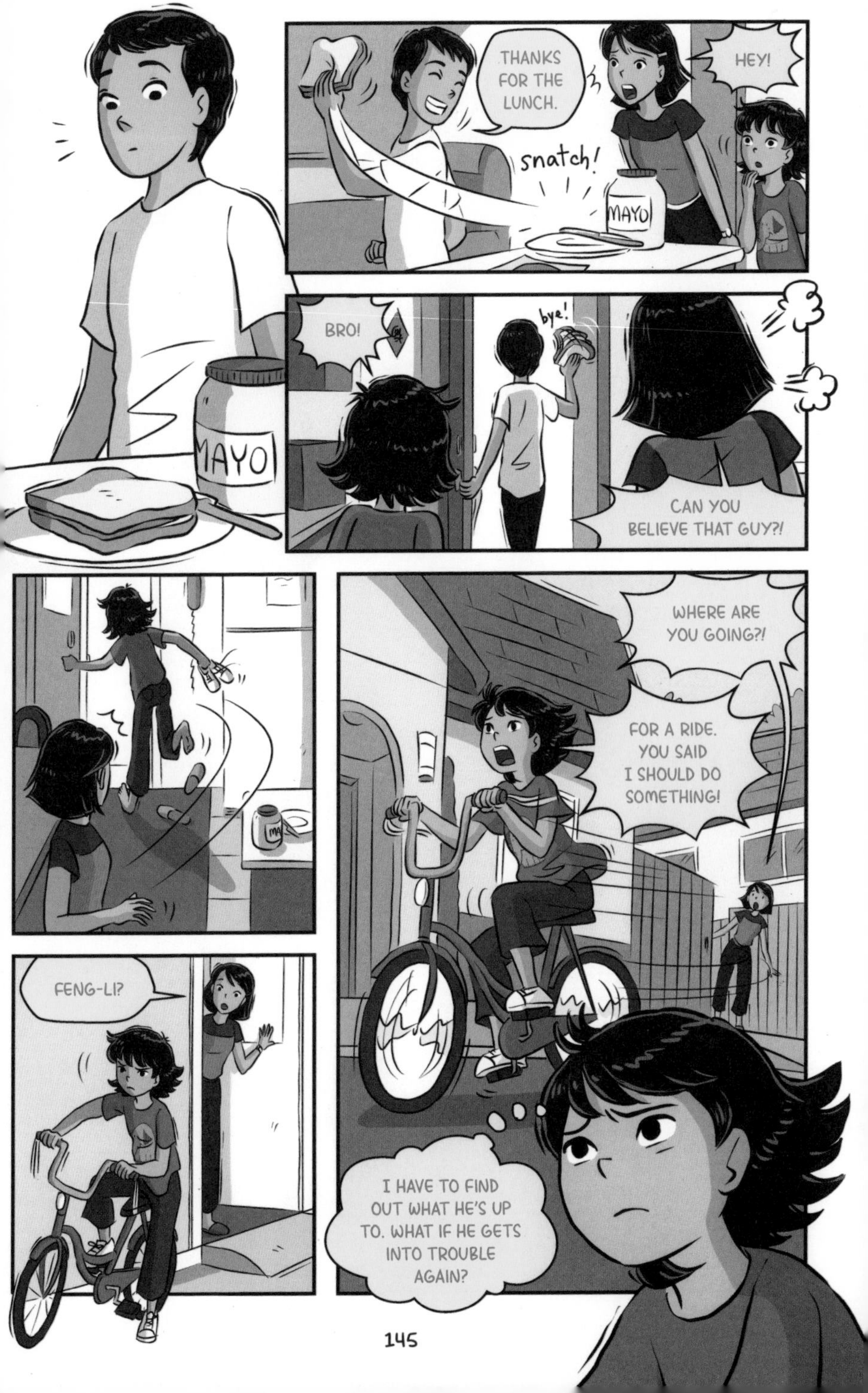
THANKS FOR THE LUNCH.
snatch!
HEY!
MAYO
BRO!
bye!
CAN YOU BELIEVE THAT GUY?!
WHERE ARE YOU GOING?!
FOR A RIDE. YOU SAID I SHOULD DO SOMETHING!
FENG-LI?
I HAVE TO FIND OUT WHAT HE'S UP TO. WHAT IF HE GETS INTO TROUBLE AGAIN?

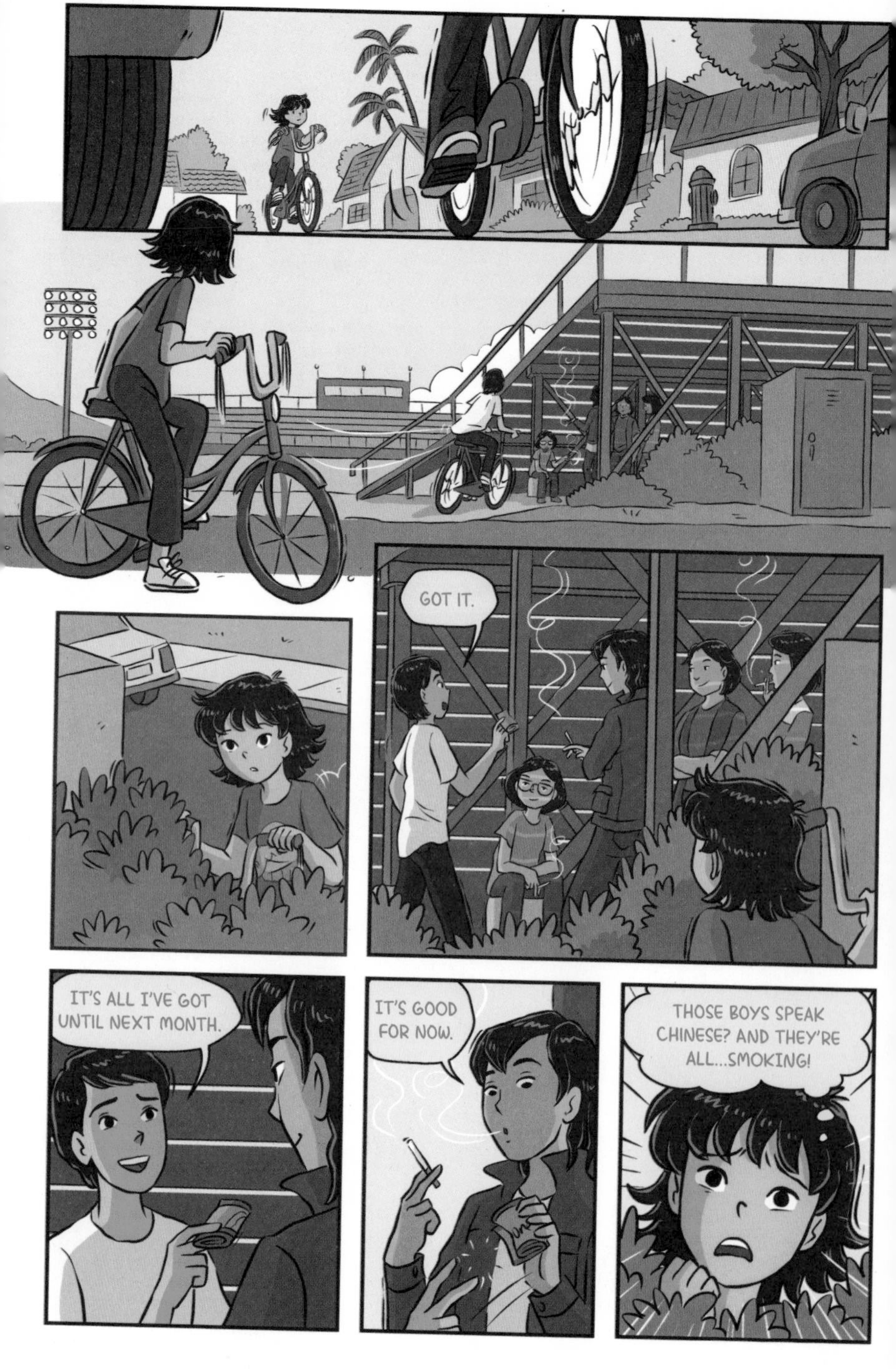
GOT IT.
IT'S ALL I'VE GOT UNTIL NEXT MONTH.
IT'S GOOD FOR NOW.
THOSE BOYS SPEAK CHINESE? AND THEY'RE ALL...SMOKING!

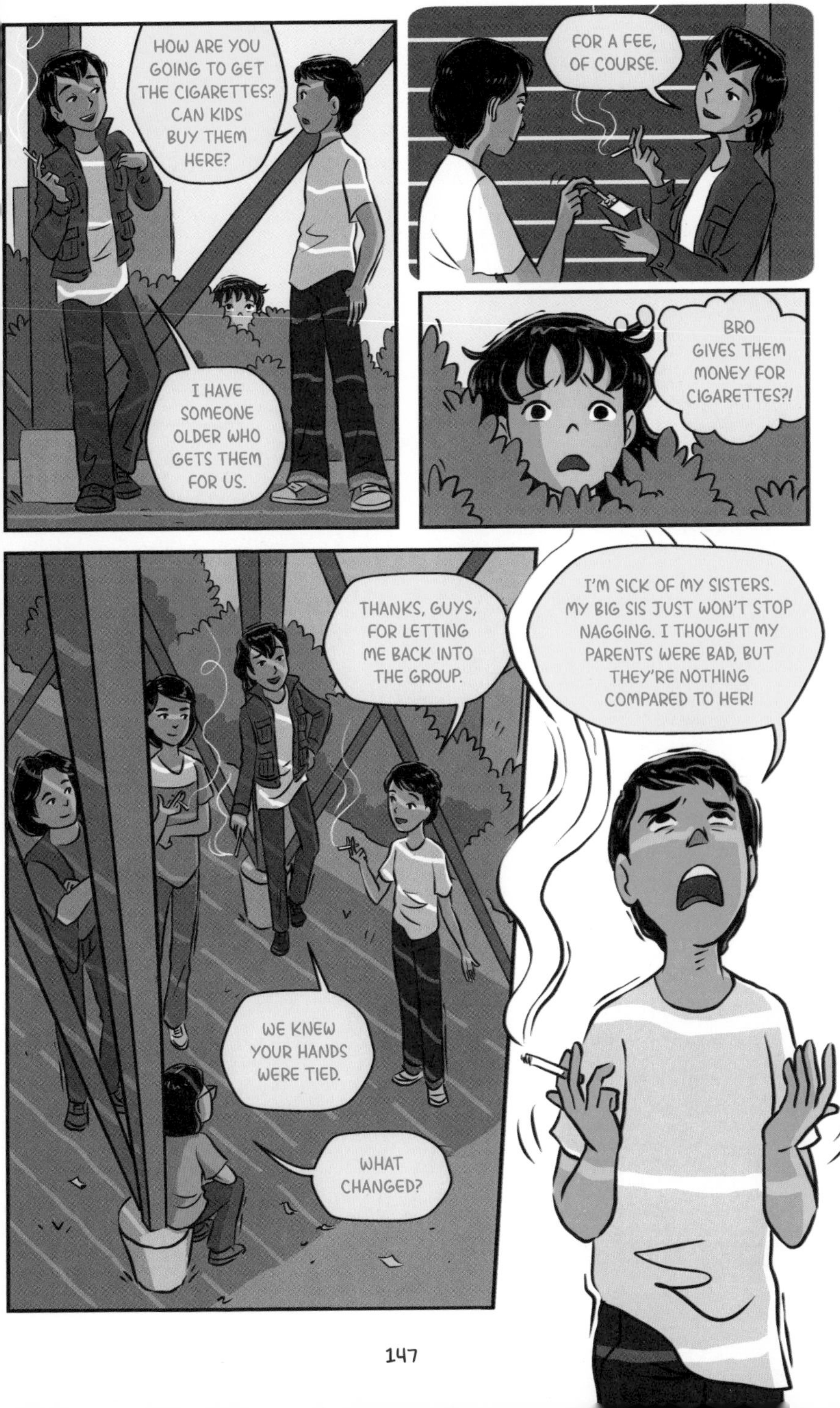
HOW ARE YOU GOING TO GET THE CIGARETTES? CAN KIDS BUY THEM HERE?
I HAVE SOMEONE OLDER WHO GETS THEM FOR US.
FOR A FEE, OF COURSE.
BRO GIVES THEM MONEY FOR CIGARETTES?!
THANKS, GUYS, FOR LETTING ME BACK INTO THE GROUP.
WE KNEW YOUR HANDS WERE TIED.
WHAT CHANGED?
I'M SICK OF MY SISTERS. MY BIG SIS JUST WON'T STOP NAGGING. I THOUGHT MY PARENTS WERE BAD, BUT THEY'RE NOTHING COMPARED TO HER!

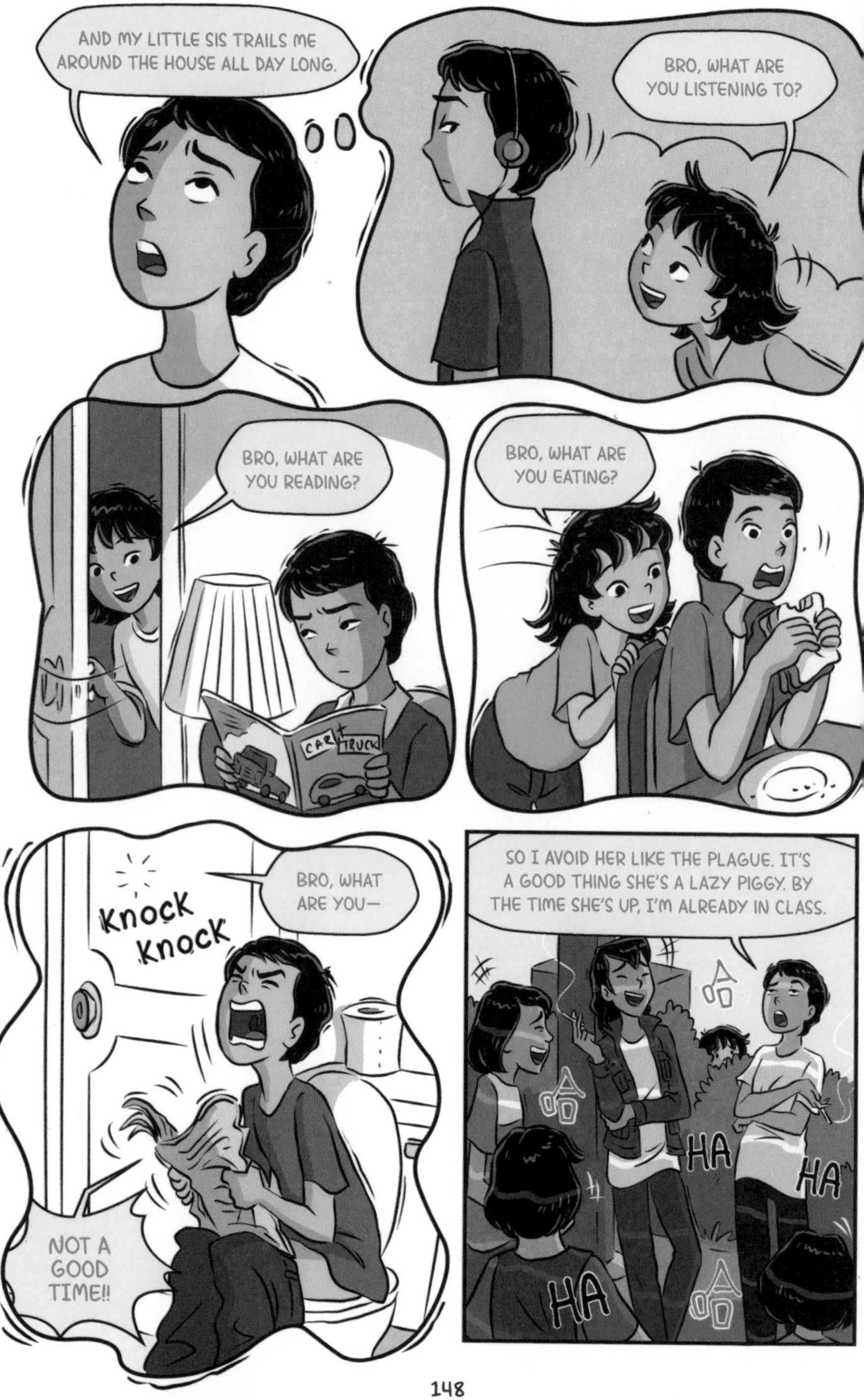
AND MY LITTLE SIS TRAILS ME AROUND THE HOUSE ALL DAY LONG.
BRO, WHAT ARE YOU LISTENING TO?
BRO, WHAT ARE YOU READING?
CAR TRUCK
BRO, WHAT ARE YOU EATING?
BRO, WHAT ARE YOU—
Knock Knock
NOT A GOOD TIME!!
SO I AVOID HER LIKE THE PLAGUE. IT'S A GOOD THING SHE'S A LAZY PIGGY. BY THE TIME SHE'S UP, I'M ALREADY IN CLASS.
HA
HA
HA

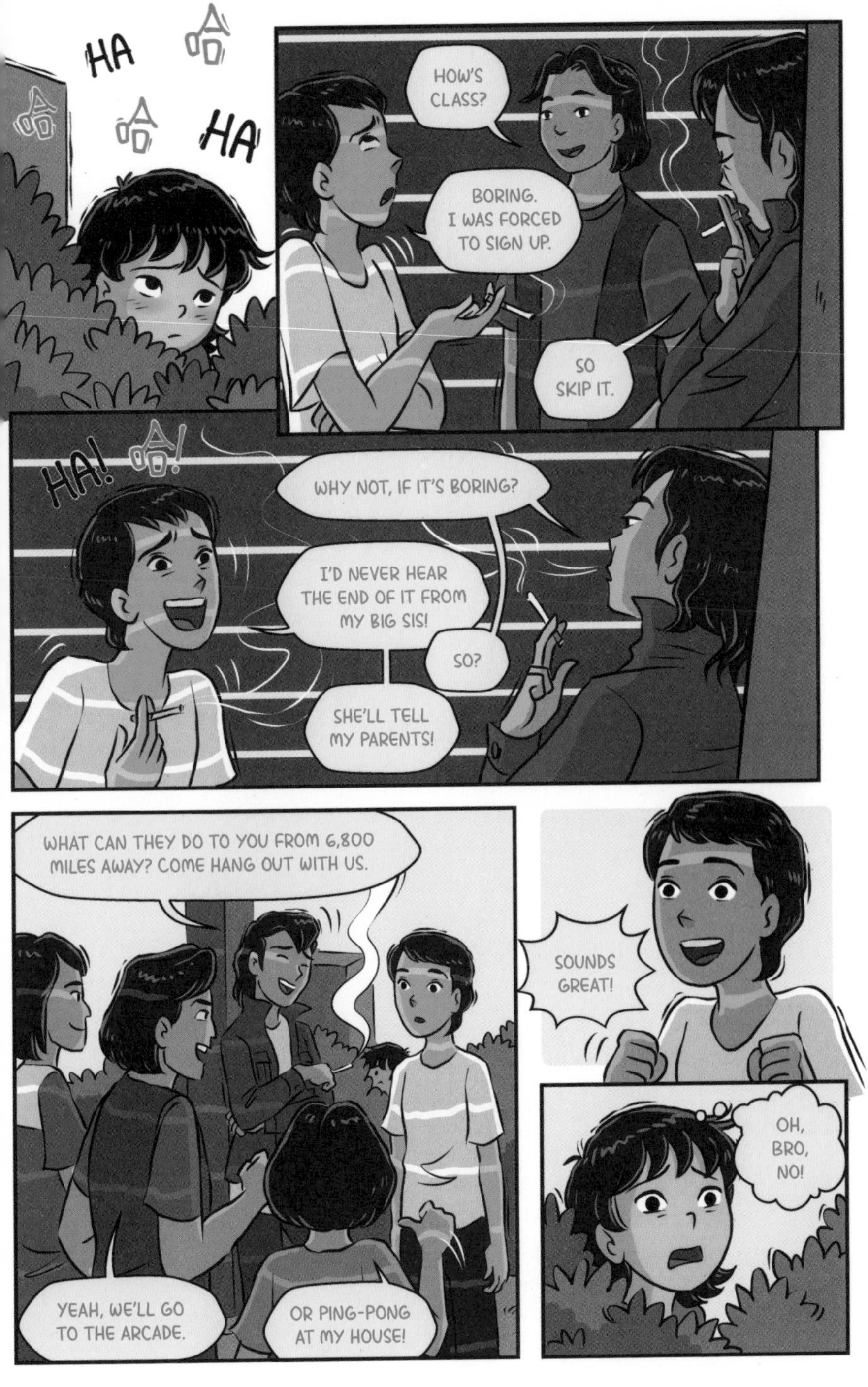

HA
哈
哈
HA
HOW'S CLASS?
BORING. I WAS FORCED TO SIGN UP.
SO SKIP IT.
HA! 哈!
WHY NOT, IF IT'S BORING?
I'D NEVER HEAR THE END OF IT FROM MY BIG SIS!
SO?
SHE'LL TELL MY PARENTS!
WHAT CAN THEY DO TO YOU FROM 6,800 MILES AWAY? COME HANG OUT WITH US.
YEAH, WE'LL GO TO THE ARCADE.
OR PING-PONG AT MY HOUSE!
SOUNDS GREAT!
OH, BRO, NO!

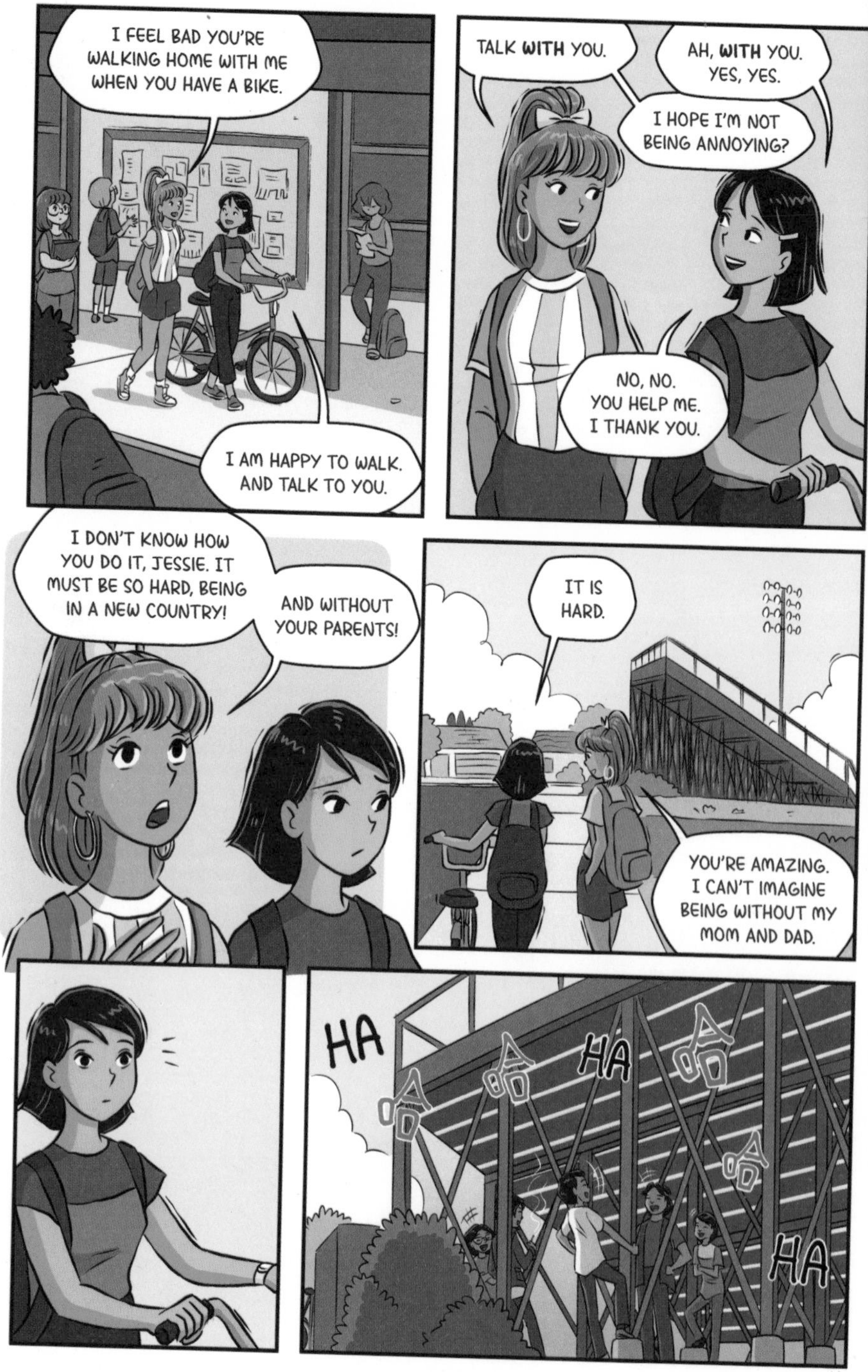
I FEEL BAD YOU'RE WALKING HOME WITH ME WHEN YOU HAVE A BIKE.
I AM HAPPY TO WALK. AND TALK TO YOU.
TALK **WITH** YOU.
AH, **WITH** YOU. YES, YES.
I HOPE I'M NOT BEING ANNOYING?
NO, NO. YOU HELP ME. I THANK YOU.
I DON'T KNOW HOW YOU DO IT, JESSIE. IT MUST BE SO HARD, BEING IN A NEW COUNTRY!
AND WITHOUT YOUR PARENTS!
IT IS HARD.
YOU'RE AMAZING. I CAN'T IMAGINE BEING WITHOUT MY MOM AND DAD.
HA
HA
HA

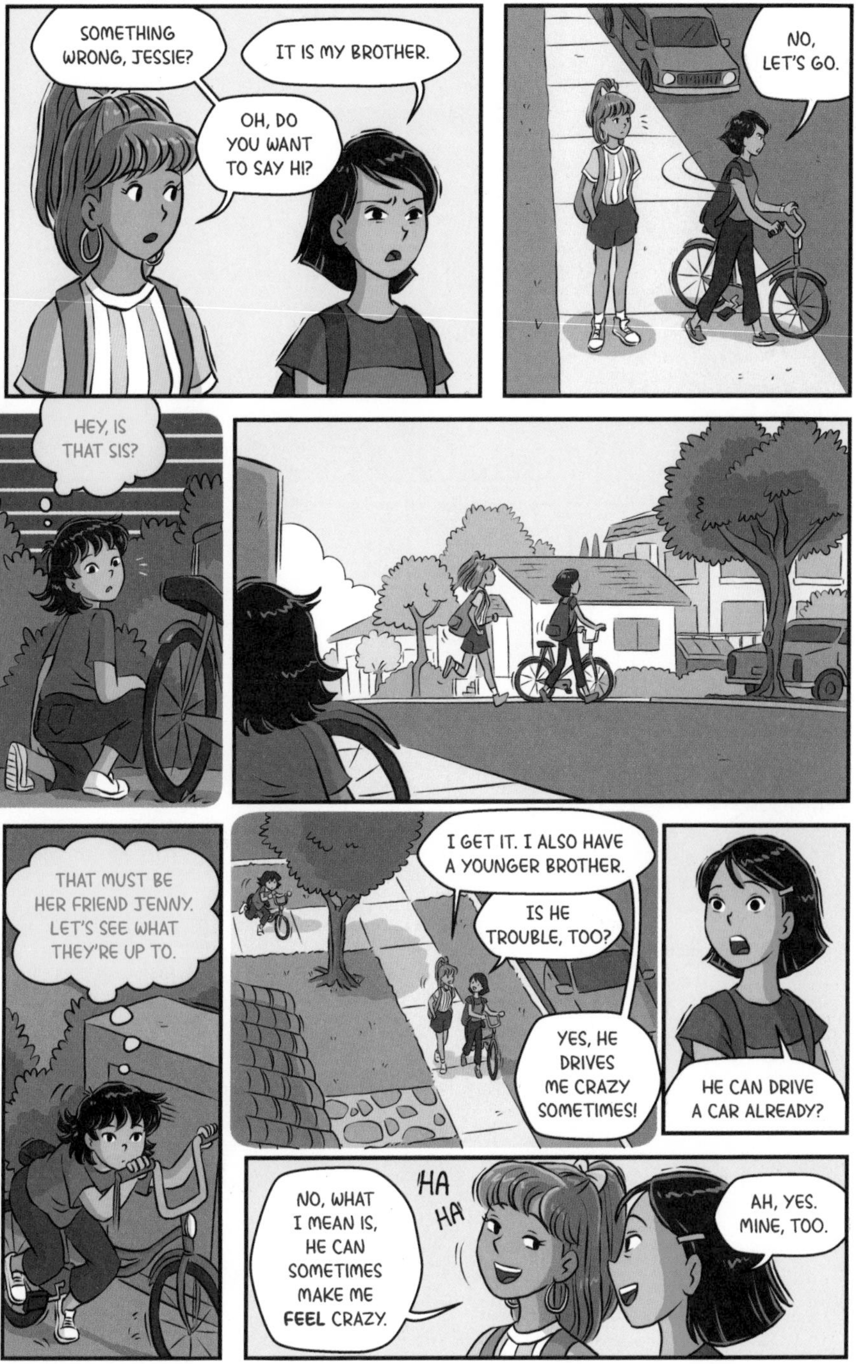
SOMETHING WRONG, JESSIE?
IT IS MY BROTHER.
OH, DO YOU WANT TO SAY HI?
NO, LET'S GO.
HEY, IS THAT SIS?
THAT MUST BE HER FRIEND JENNY. LET'S SEE WHAT THEY'RE UP TO.
I GET IT. I ALSO HAVE A YOUNGER BROTHER.
IS HE TROUBLE, TOO?
YES, HE DRIVES ME CRAZY SOMETIMES!
HE CAN DRIVE A CAR ALREADY?
NO, WHAT I MEAN IS, HE CAN SOMETIMES MAKE ME FEEL CRAZY.
HA HA
AH, YES. MINE, TOO.

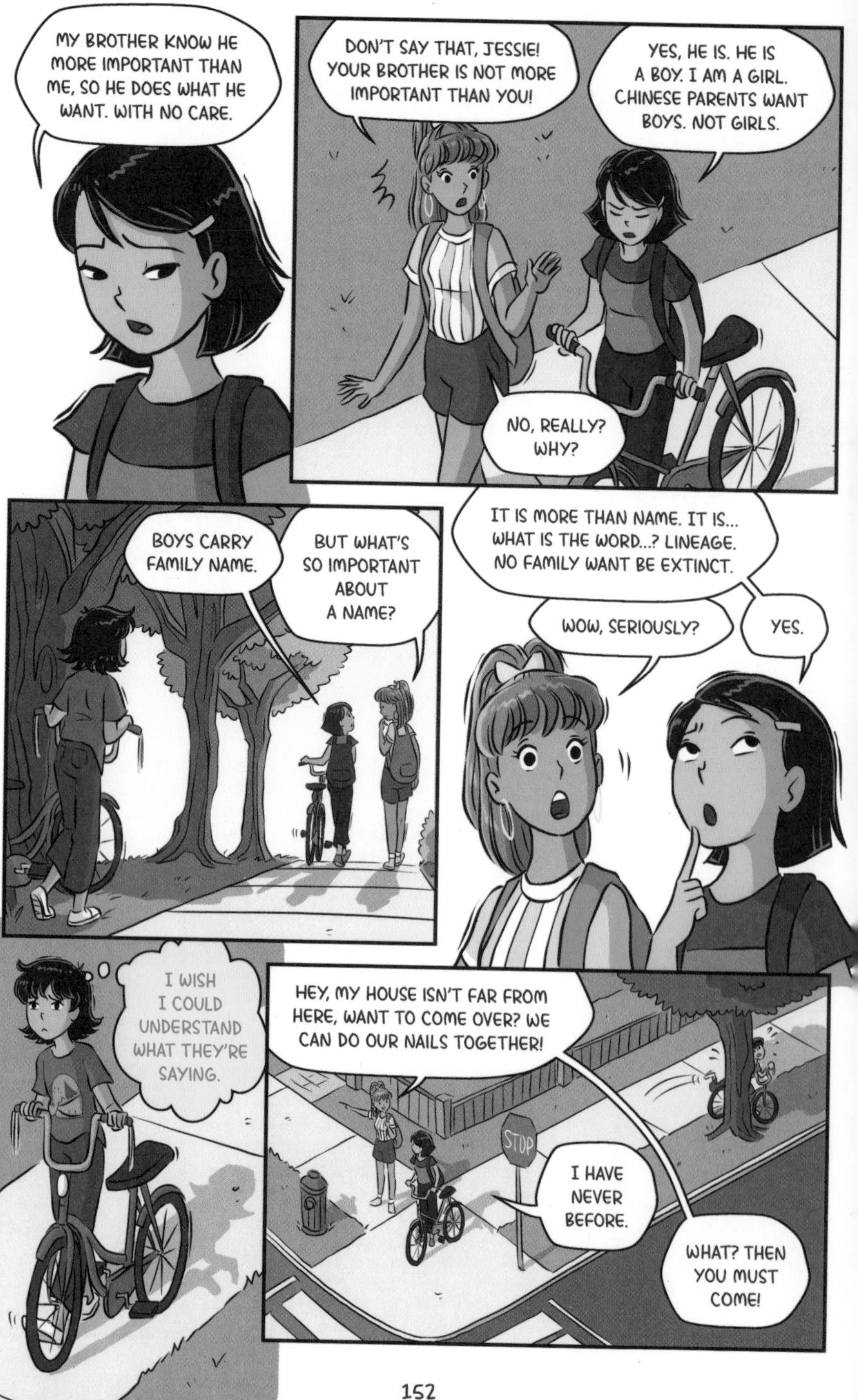
MY BROTHER KNOW HE MORE IMPORTANT THAN ME, SO HE DOES WHAT HE WANT. WITH NO CARE.
DON'T SAY THAT, JESSIE! YOUR BROTHER IS NOT MORE IMPORTANT THAN YOU!
YES, HE IS. HE IS A BOY. I AM A GIRL. CHINESE PARENTS WANT BOYS. NOT GIRLS.
NO, REALLY? WHY?
BOYS CARRY FAMILY NAME.
BUT WHAT'S SO IMPORTANT ABOUT A NAME?
IT IS MORE THAN NAME. IT IS... WHAT IS THE WORD...? LINEAGE. NO FAMILY WANT BE EXTINCT.
WOW, SERIOUSLY?
YES.
I WISH I COULD UNDERSTAND WHAT THEY'RE SAYING.
HEY, MY HOUSE ISN'T FAR FROM HERE, WANT TO COME OVER? WE CAN DO OUR NAILS TOGETHER!
STOP
I HAVE NEVER BEFORE.
WHAT? THEN YOU MUST COME!

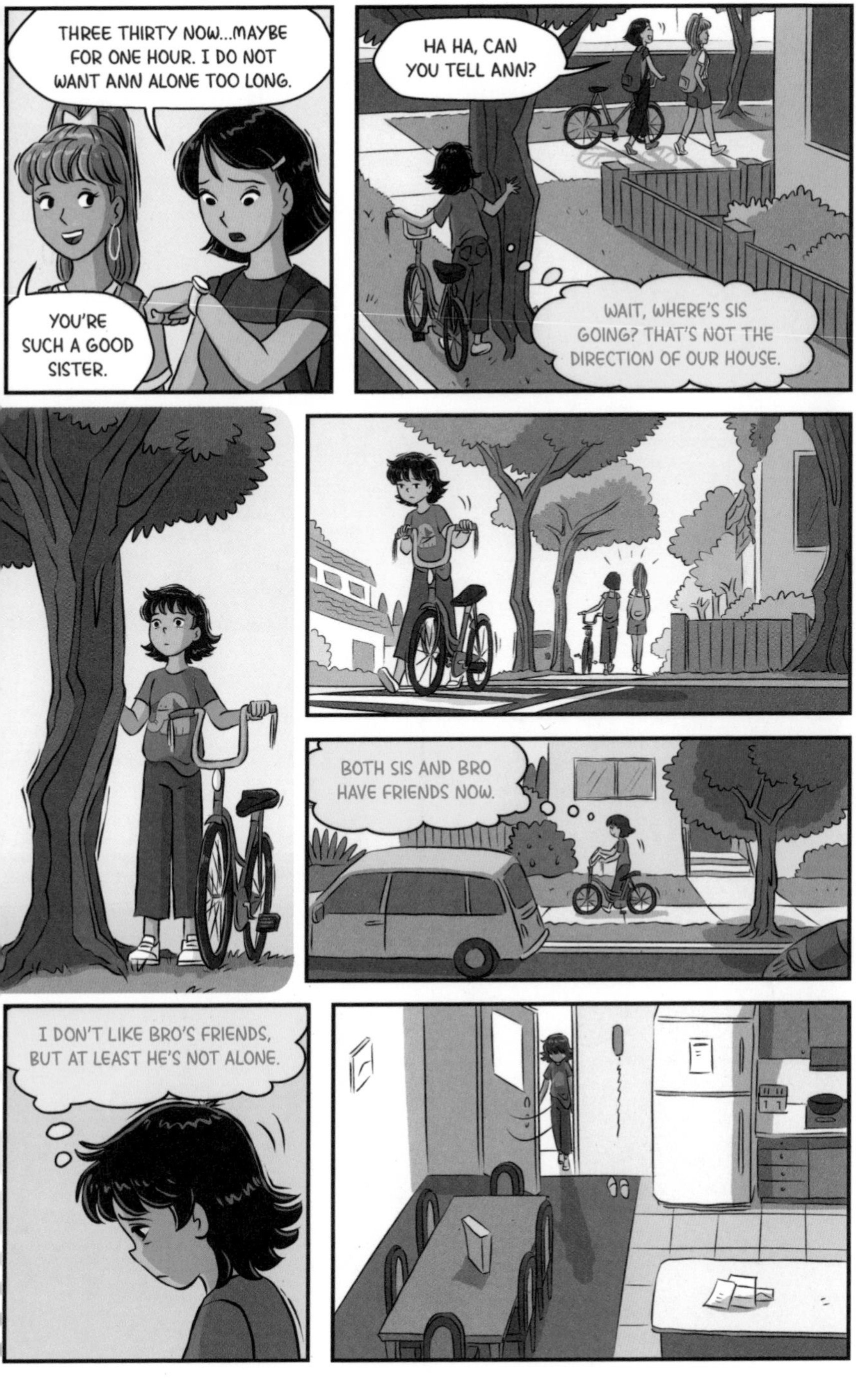
THREE THIRTY NOW...MAYBE FOR ONE HOUR. I DO NOT WANT ANN ALONE TOO LONG.
YOU'RE SUCH A GOOD SISTER.
HA HA, CAN YOU TELL ANN?
WAIT, WHERE'S SIS GOING? THAT'S NOT THE DIRECTION OF OUR HOUSE.
BOTH SIS AND BRO HAVE FRIENDS NOW.
I DON'T LIKE BRO'S FRIENDS, BUT AT LEAST HE'S NOT ALONE.

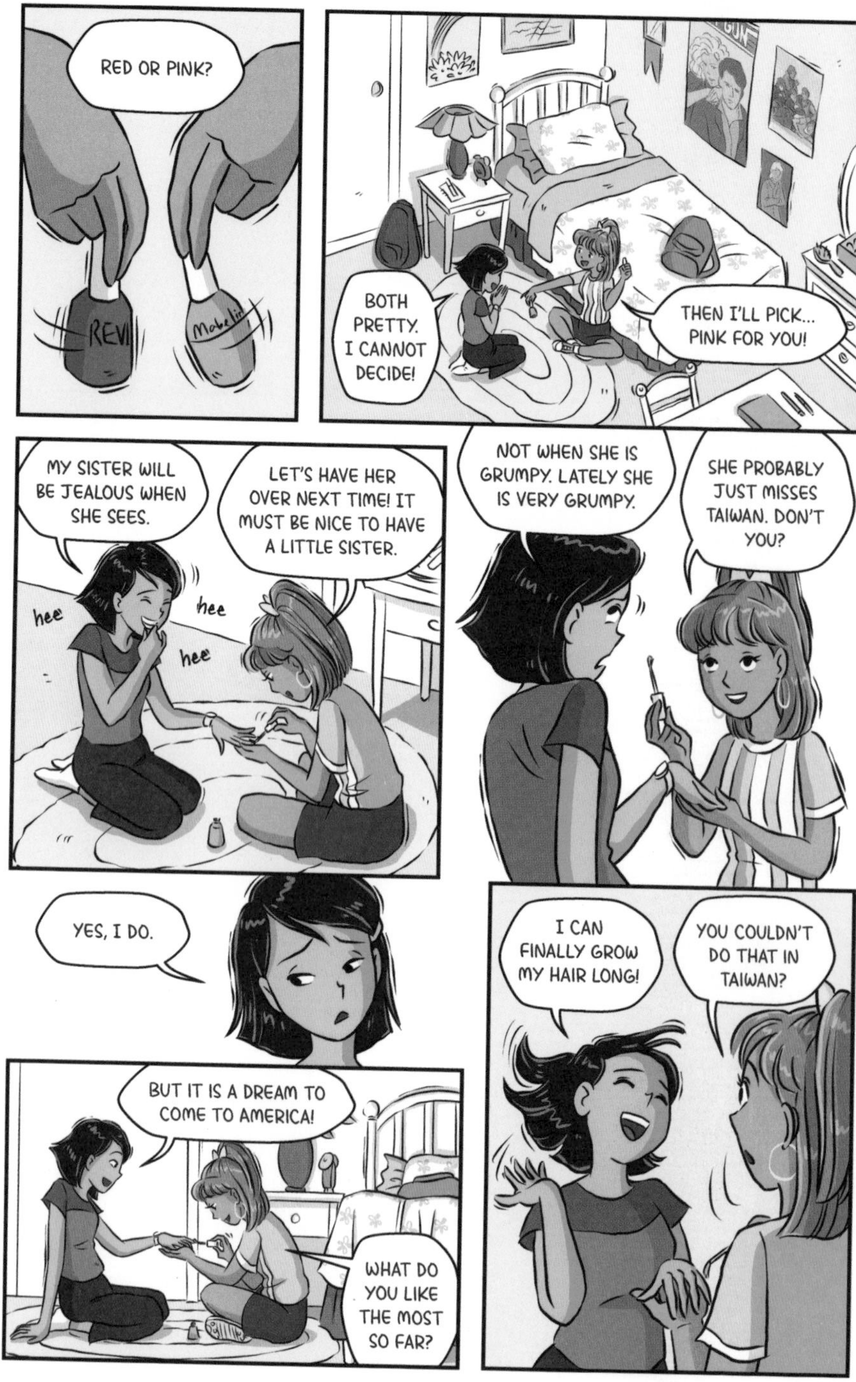
RED OR PINK?
REVI
Mabelin
BOTH PRETTY. I CANNOT DECIDE!
THEN I'LL PICK... PINK FOR YOU!
MY SISTER WILL BE JEALOUS WHEN SHE SEES.
LET'S HAVE HER OVER NEXT TIME! IT MUST BE NICE TO HAVE A LITTLE SISTER.
hee
hee
hee
NOT WHEN SHE IS GRUMPY. LATELY SHE IS VERY GRUMPY.
SHE PROBABLY JUST MISSES TAIWAN. DON'T YOU?
YES, I DO.
BUT IT IS A DREAM TO COME TO AMERICA!
WHAT DO YOU LIKE THE MOST SO FAR?
I CAN FINALLY GROW MY HAIR LONG!
YOU COULDN'T DO THAT IN TAIWAN?

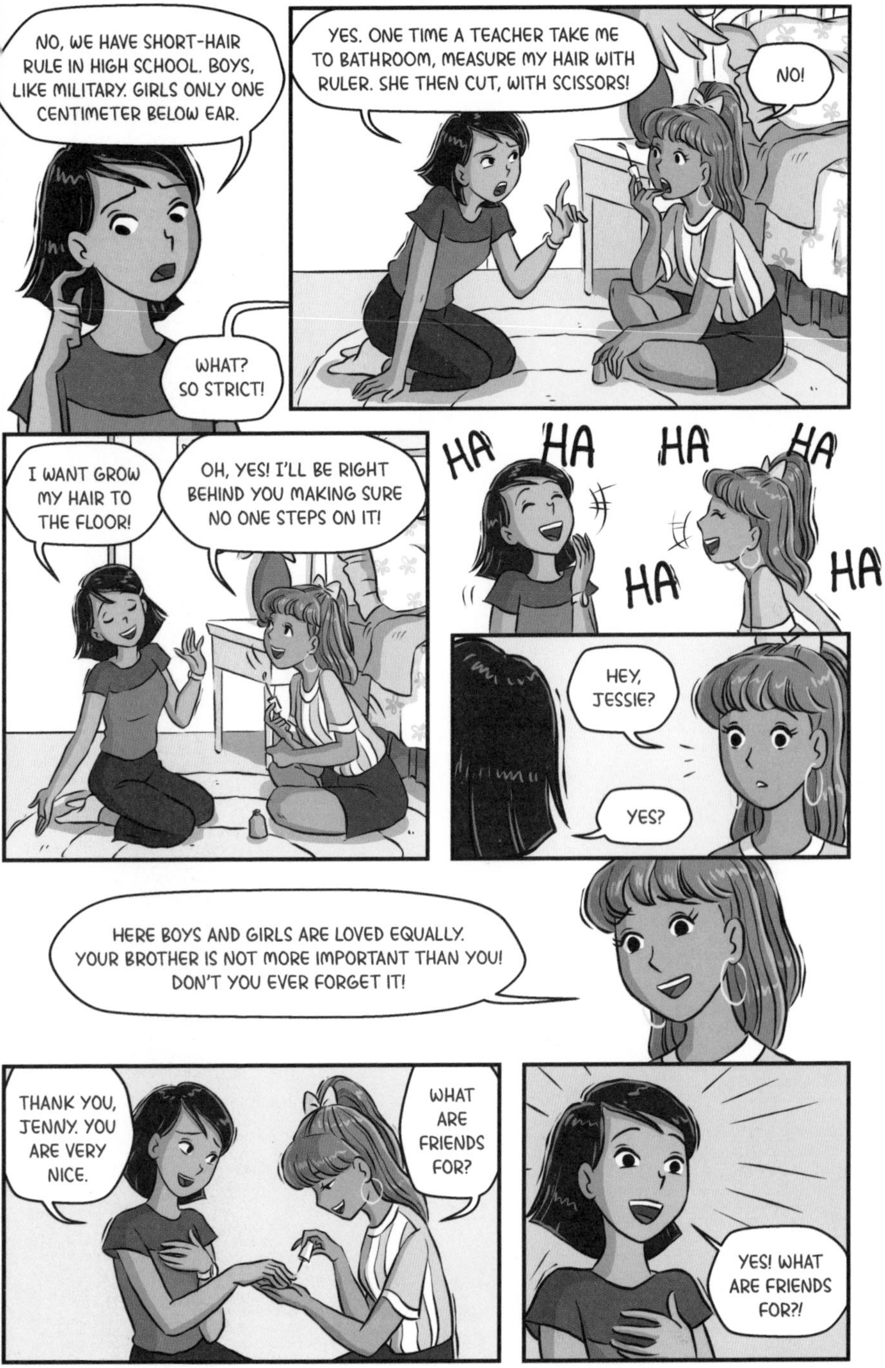
NO, WE HAVE SHORT-HAIR RULE IN HIGH SCHOOL. BOYS, LIKE MILITARY. GIRLS ONLY ONE CENTIMETER BELOW EAR.
WHAT? SO STRICT!
YES. ONE TIME A TEACHER TAKE ME TO BATHROOM, MEASURE MY HAIR WITH RULER. SHE THEN CUT, WITH SCISSORS!
NO!
I WANT GROW MY HAIR TO THE FLOOR!
OH, YES! I'LL BE RIGHT BEHIND YOU MAKING SURE NO ONE STEPS ON IT!
HA HA HA HA HA HA
HEY, JESSIE?
YES?
HERE BOYS AND GIRLS ARE LOVED EQUALLY. YOUR BROTHER IS NOT MORE IMPORTANT THAN YOU! DON'T YOU EVER FORGET IT!
THANK YOU, JENNY. YOU ARE VERY NICE.
WHAT ARE FRIENDS FOR?
YES! WHAT ARE FRIENDS FOR?!

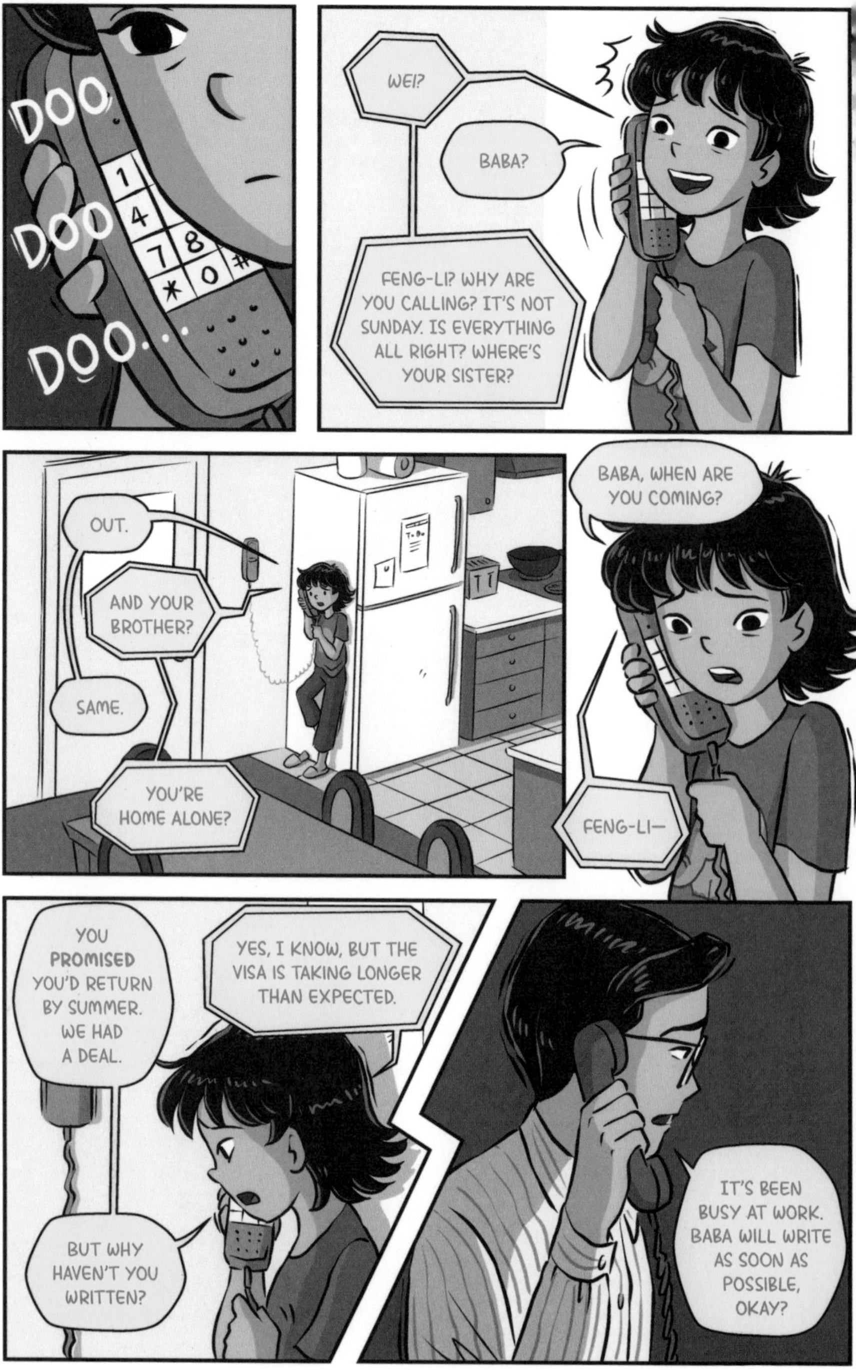
DOO
DOO
DOO...
WEI?
BABA?
FENG-LI? WHY ARE YOU CALLING? IT'S NOT SUNDAY. IS EVERYTHING ALL RIGHT? WHERE'S YOUR SISTER?
OUT.
AND YOUR BROTHER?
SAME.
YOU'RE HOME ALONE?
BABA, WHEN ARE YOU COMING?
FENG-LI—
YOU **PROMISED** YOU'D RETURN BY SUMMER. WE HAD A DEAL.
YES, I KNOW, BUT THE VISA IS TAKING LONGER THAN EXPECTED.
BUT WHY HAVEN'T YOU WRITTEN?
IT'S BEEN BUSY AT WORK. BABA WILL WRITE AS SOON AS POSSIBLE, OKAY?

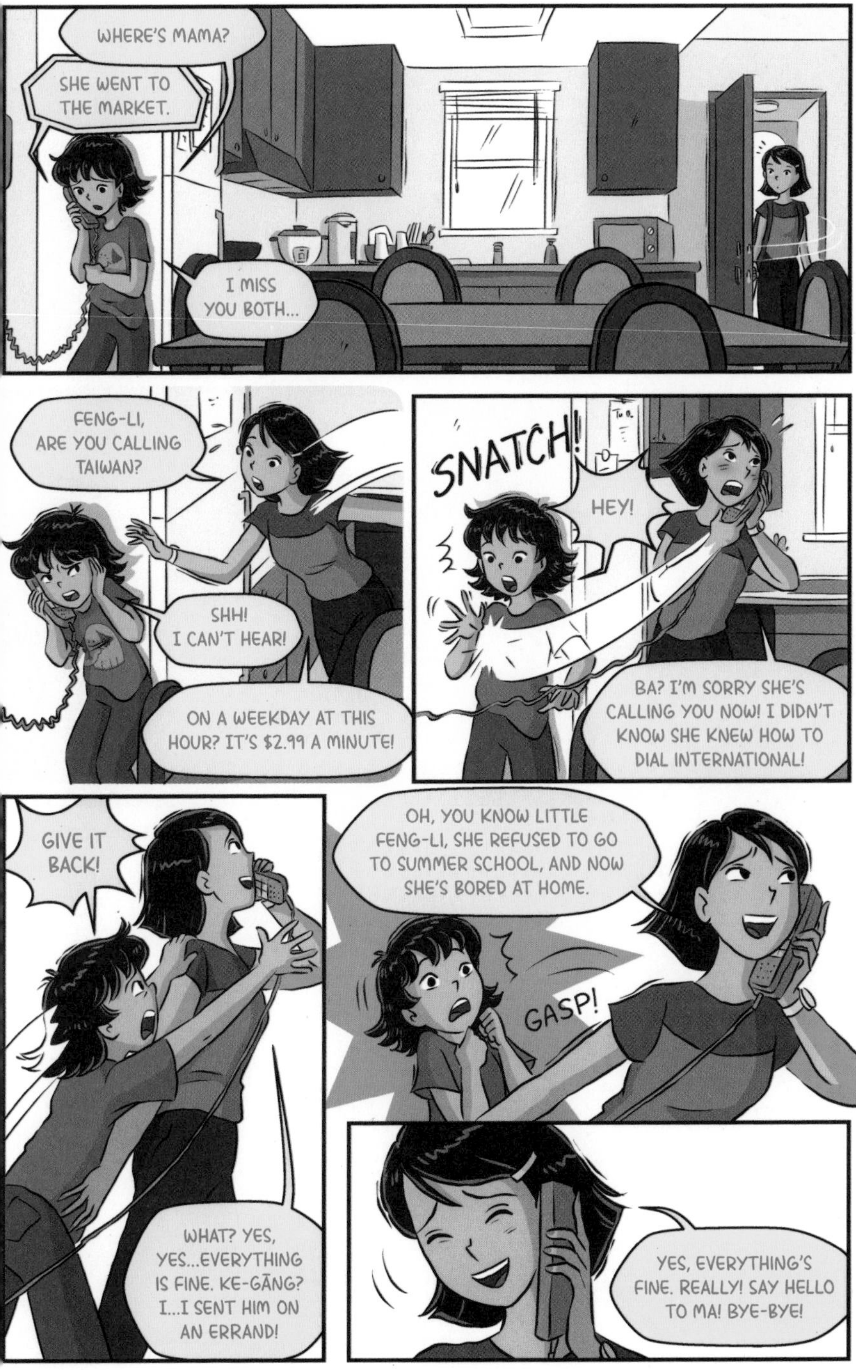
WHERE'S MAMA?
SHE WENT TO THE MARKET.
I MISS YOU BOTH...
FENG-LI, ARE YOU CALLING TAIWAN?
SHH! I CAN'T HEAR!
ON A WEEKDAY AT THIS HOUR? IT'S $2.99 A MINUTE!
SNATCH!
HEY!
BA? I'M SORRY SHE'S CALLING YOU NOW! I DIDN'T KNOW SHE KNEW HOW TO DIAL INTERNATIONAL!
GIVE IT BACK!
WHAT? YES, YES...EVERYTHING IS FINE. KE-GĀNG? I...I SENT HIM ON AN ERRAND!
OH, YOU KNOW LITTLE FENG-LI, SHE REFUSED TO GO TO SUMMER SCHOOL, AND NOW SHE'S BORED AT HOME.
GASP!
YES, EVERYTHING'S FINE. REALLY! SAY HELLO TO MA! BYE-BYE!

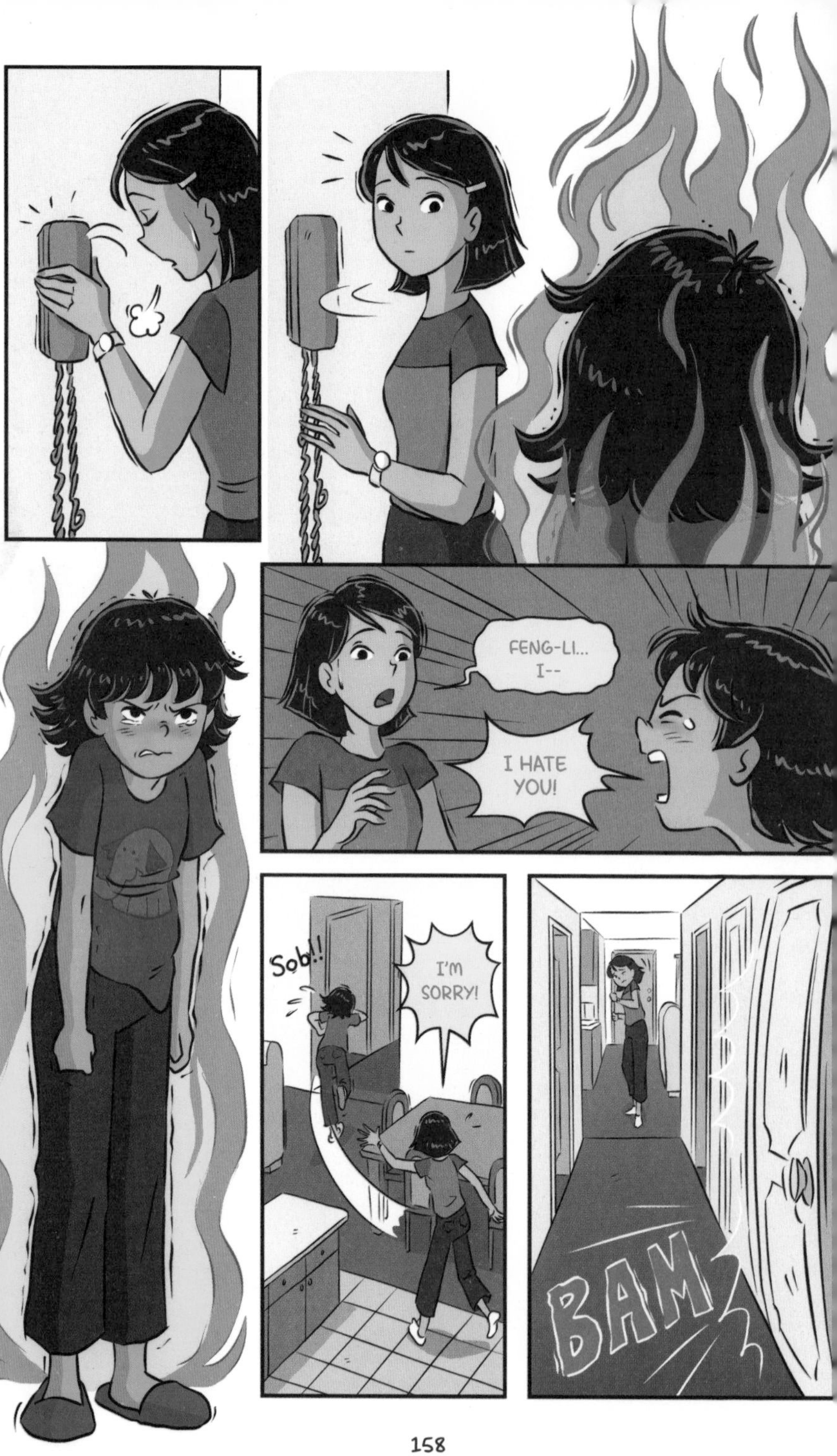
FENG-LI...
I--
I HATE YOU!
Sob!!
I'M SORRY!
BAM

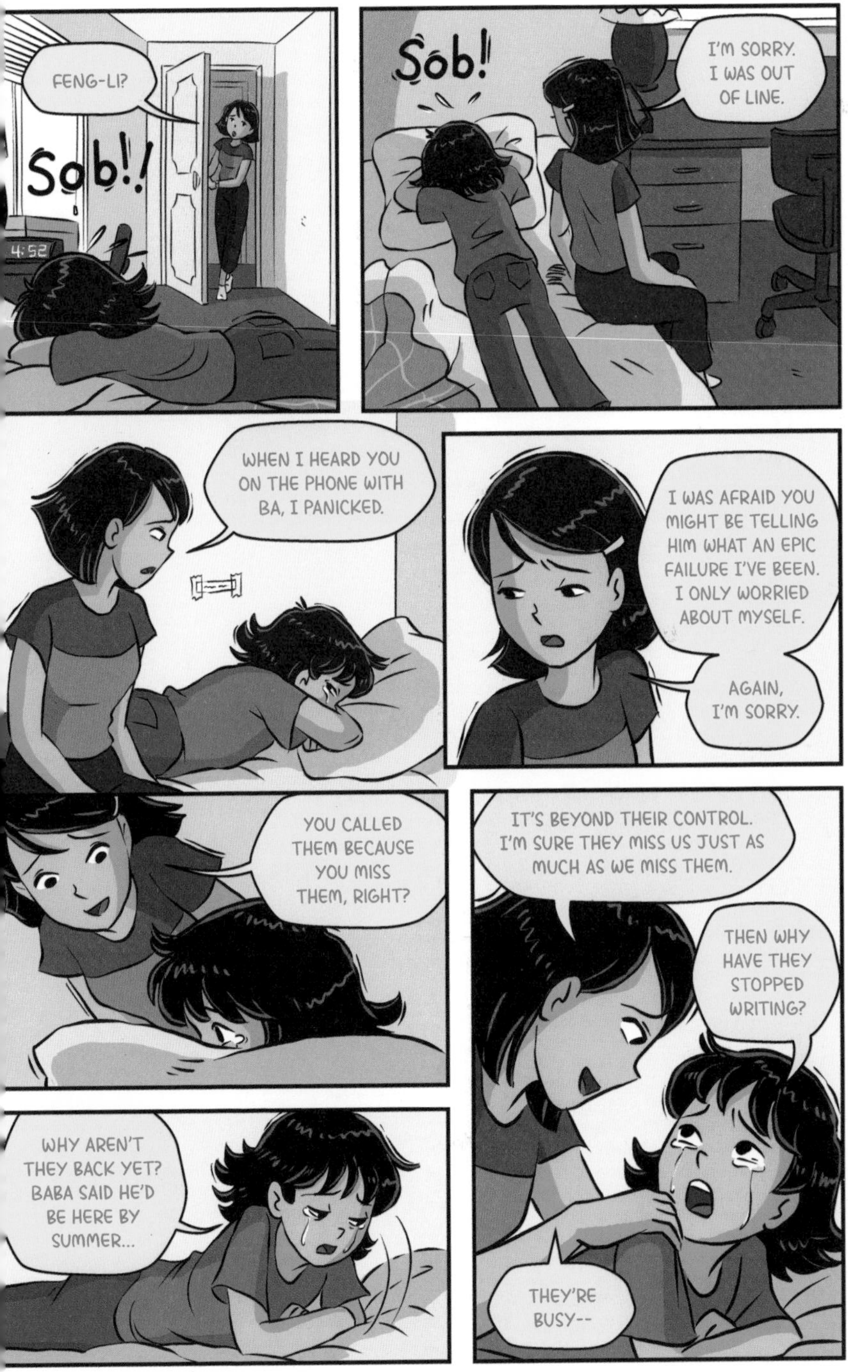
FENG-LI?
SOB!!
SOB!
I'M SORRY. I WAS OUT OF LINE.
WHEN I HEARD YOU ON THE PHONE WITH BA, I PANICKED.
I WAS AFRAID YOU MIGHT BE TELLING HIM WHAT AN EPIC FAILURE I'VE BEEN. I ONLY WORRIED ABOUT MYSELF.
AGAIN, I'M SORRY.
YOU CALLED THEM BECAUSE YOU MISS THEM, RIGHT?
WHY AREN'T THEY BACK YET? BABA SAID HE'D BE HERE BY SUMMER...
THEY'RE BUSY--
IT'S BEYOND THEIR CONTROL. I'M SURE THEY MISS US JUST AS MUCH AS WE MISS THEM.
THEN WHY HAVE THEY STOPPED WRITING?

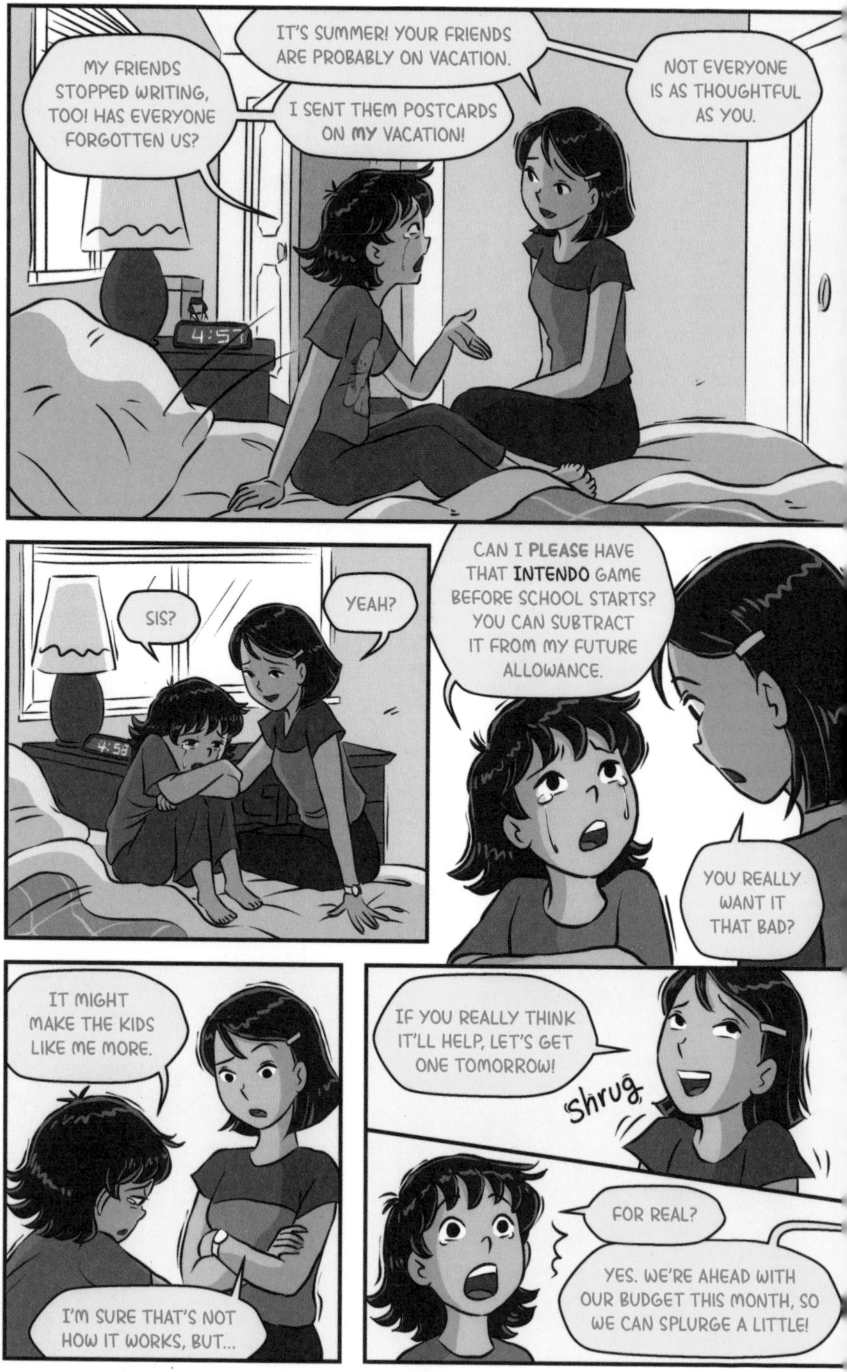
MY FRIENDS STOPPED WRITING, TOO! HAS EVERYONE FORGOTTEN US?
IT'S SUMMER! YOUR FRIENDS ARE PROBABLY ON VACATION.
I SENT THEM POSTCARDS ON MY VACATION!
NOT EVERYONE IS AS THOUGHTFUL AS YOU.
4:57
SIS?
YEAH?
4:58
CAN I PLEASE HAVE THAT INTENDO GAME BEFORE SCHOOL STARTS? YOU CAN SUBTRACT IT FROM MY FUTURE ALLOWANCE.
YOU REALLY WANT IT THAT BAD?
IT MIGHT MAKE THE KIDS LIKE ME MORE.
I'M SURE THAT'S NOT HOW IT WORKS, BUT...
IF YOU REALLY THINK IT'LL HELP, LET'S GET ONE TOMORROW!
Shrug
FOR REAL?
YES. WE'RE AHEAD WITH OUR BUDGET THIS MONTH, SO WE CAN SPLURGE A LITTLE!

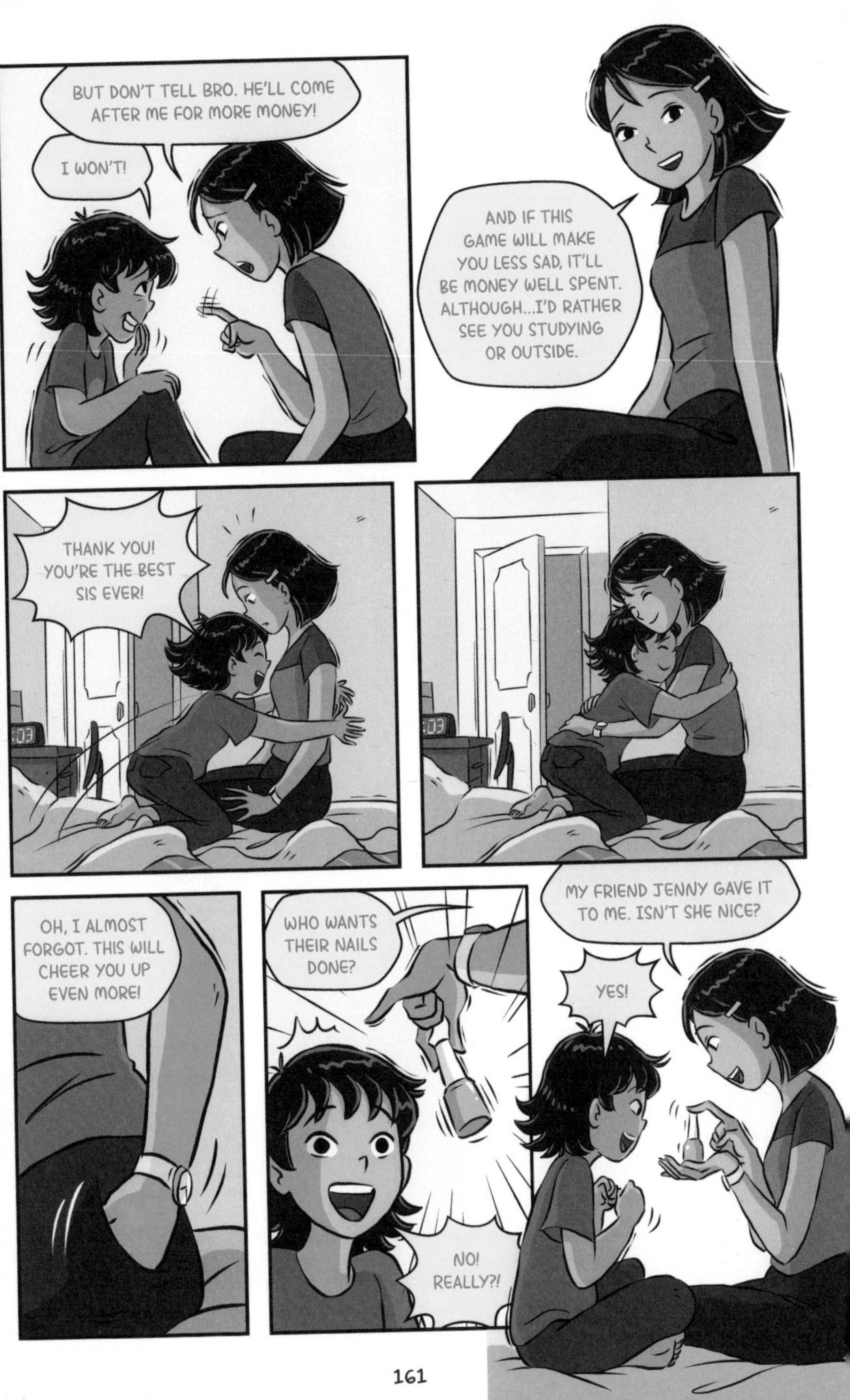
BUT DON'T TELL BRO. HE'LL COME AFTER ME FOR MORE MONEY!
I WON'T!
AND IF THIS GAME WILL MAKE YOU LESS SAD, IT'LL BE MONEY WELL SPENT. ALTHOUGH...I'D RATHER SEE YOU STUDYING OR OUTSIDE.
THANK YOU! YOU'RE THE BEST SIS EVER!
OH, I ALMOST FORGOT. THIS WILL CHEER YOU UP EVEN MORE!
WHO WANTS THEIR NAILS DONE?
NO! REALLY?!
MY FRIEND JENNY GAVE IT TO ME. ISN'T SHE NICE?
YES!

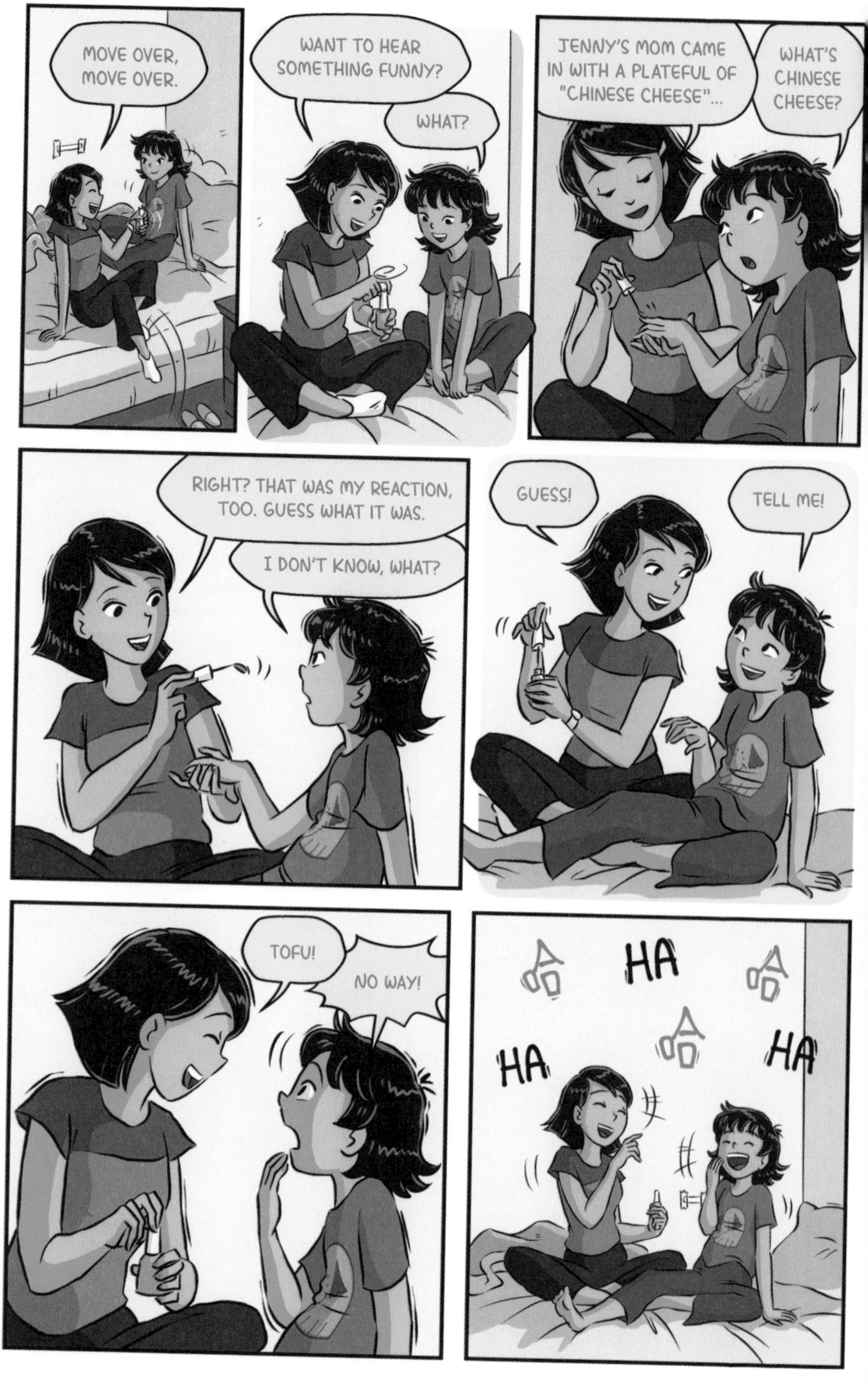
MOVE OVER, MOVE OVER.
WANT TO HEAR SOMETHING FUNNY?
WHAT?
JENNY'S MOM CAME IN WITH A PLATEFUL OF "CHINESE CHEESE"...
WHAT'S CHINESE CHEESE?
RIGHT? THAT WAS MY REACTION, TOO. GUESS WHAT IT WAS.
I DON'T KNOW, WHAT?
GUESS!
TELL ME!
TOFU!
NO WAY!
HA
HA
HA

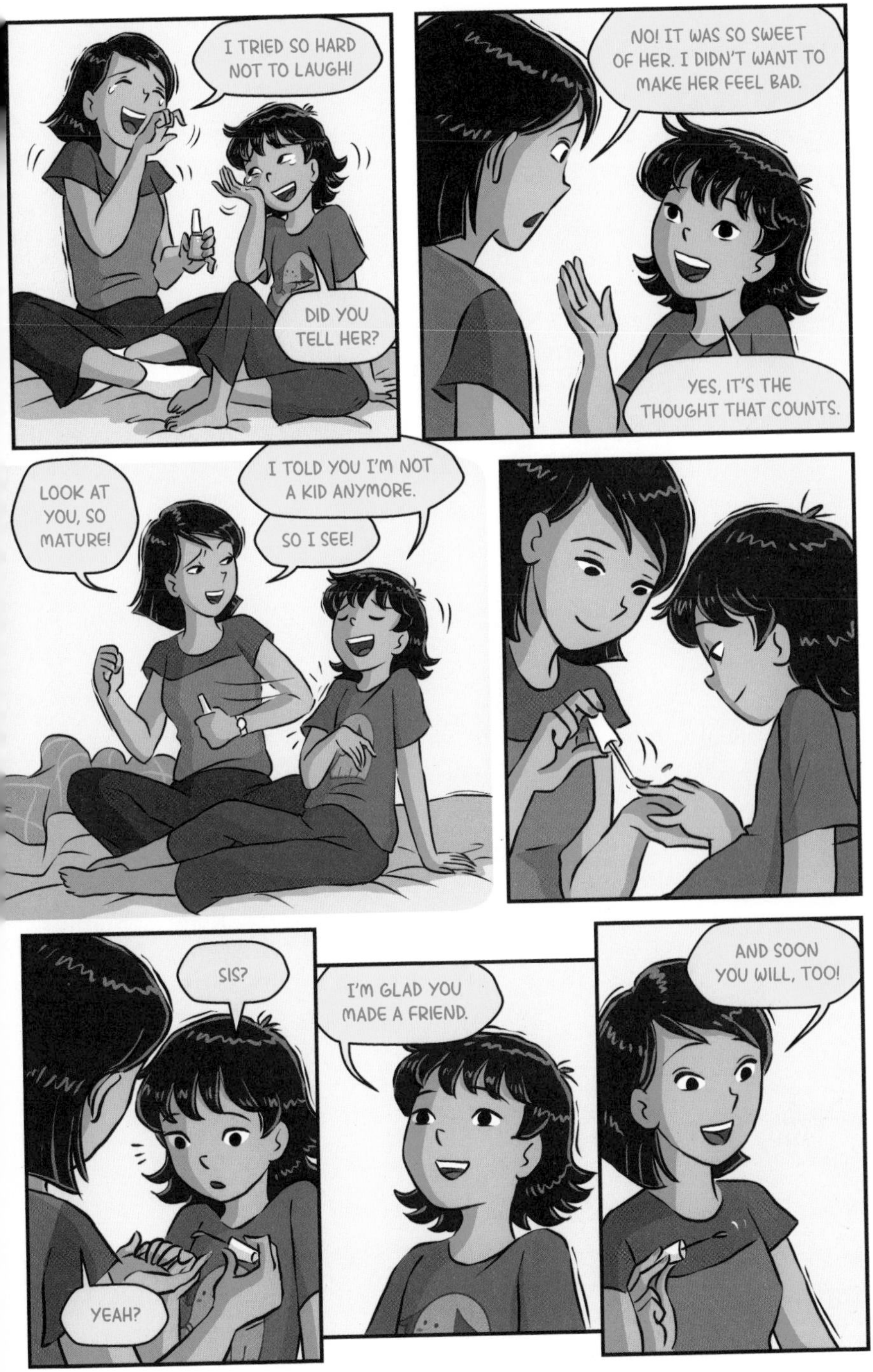
I TRIED SO HARD NOT TO LAUGH!
DID YOU TELL HER?
NO! IT WAS SO SWEET OF HER. I DIDN'T WANT TO MAKE HER FEEL BAD.
YES, IT'S THE THOUGHT THAT COUNTS.
LOOK AT YOU, SO MATURE!
I TOLD YOU I'M NOT A KID ANYMORE.
SO I SEE!
SIS?
YEAH?
I'M GLAD YOU MADE A FRIEND.
AND SOON YOU WILL, TOO!

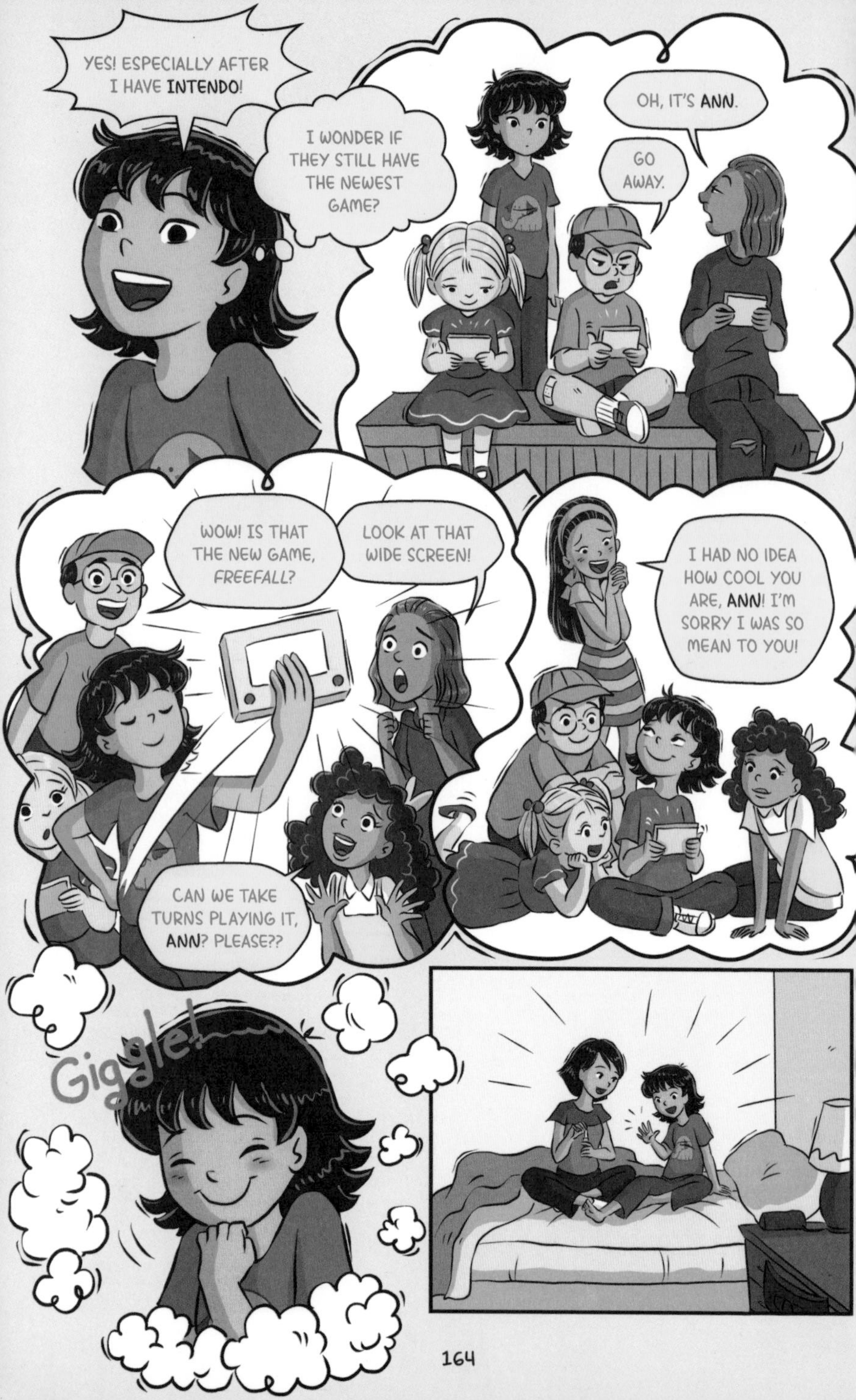
YES! ESPECIALLY AFTER I HAVE INTENDO!
I WONDER IF THEY STILL HAVE THE NEWEST GAME?
OH, IT'S ANN.
GO AWAY.
WOW! IS THAT THE NEW GAME, FREEFALL?
LOOK AT THAT WIDE SCREEN!
CAN WE TAKE TURNS PLAYING IT, ANN? PLEASE??
I HAD NO IDEA HOW COOL YOU ARE, ANN! I'M SORRY I WAS SO MEAN TO YOU!
Giggle!

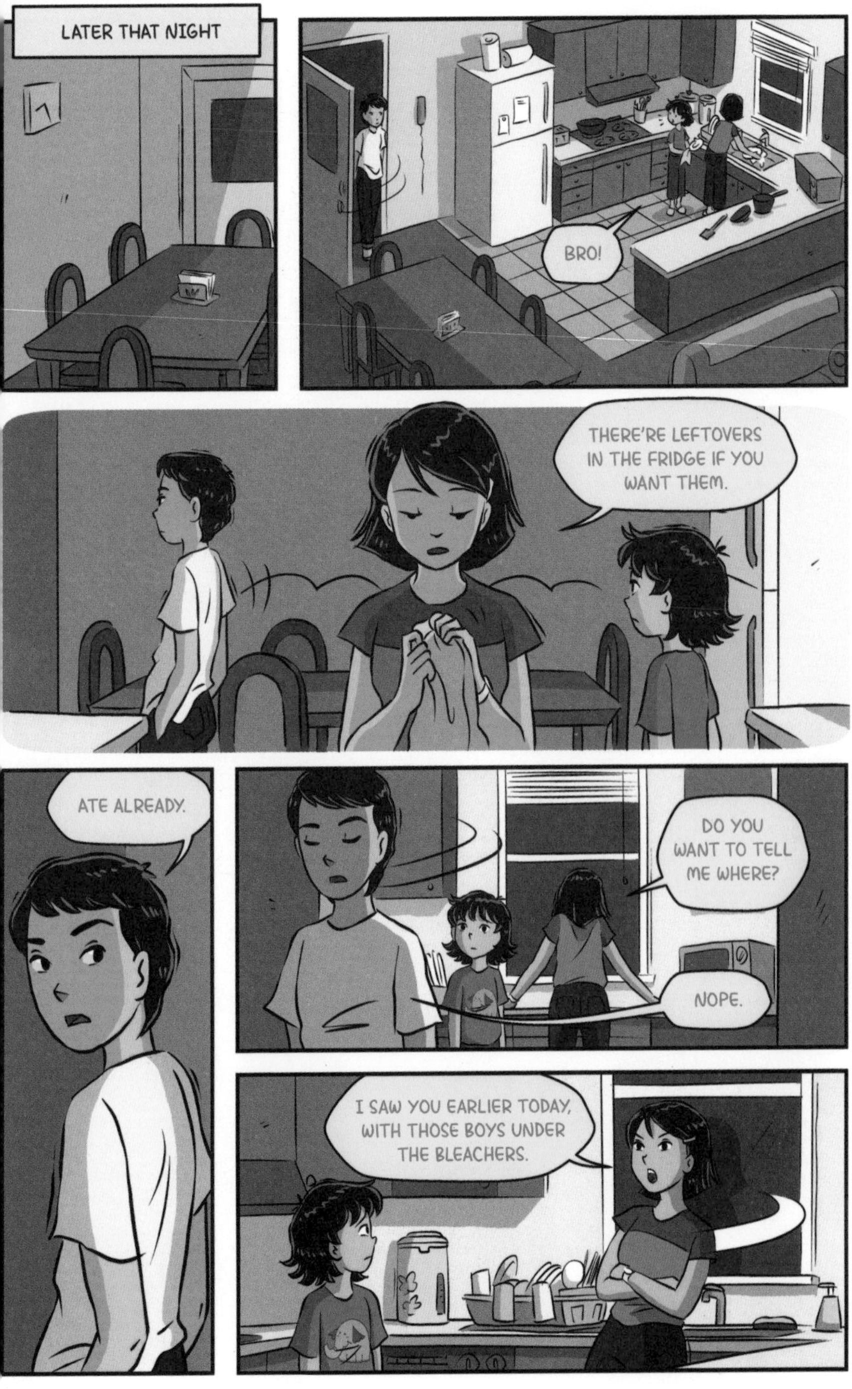
LATER THAT NIGHT
BRO!
THERE'RE LEFTOVERS IN THE FRIDGE IF YOU WANT THEM.
ATE ALREADY.
DO YOU WANT TO TELL ME WHERE?
NOPE.
I SAW YOU EARLIER TODAY, WITH THOSE BOYS UNDER THE BLEACHERS.

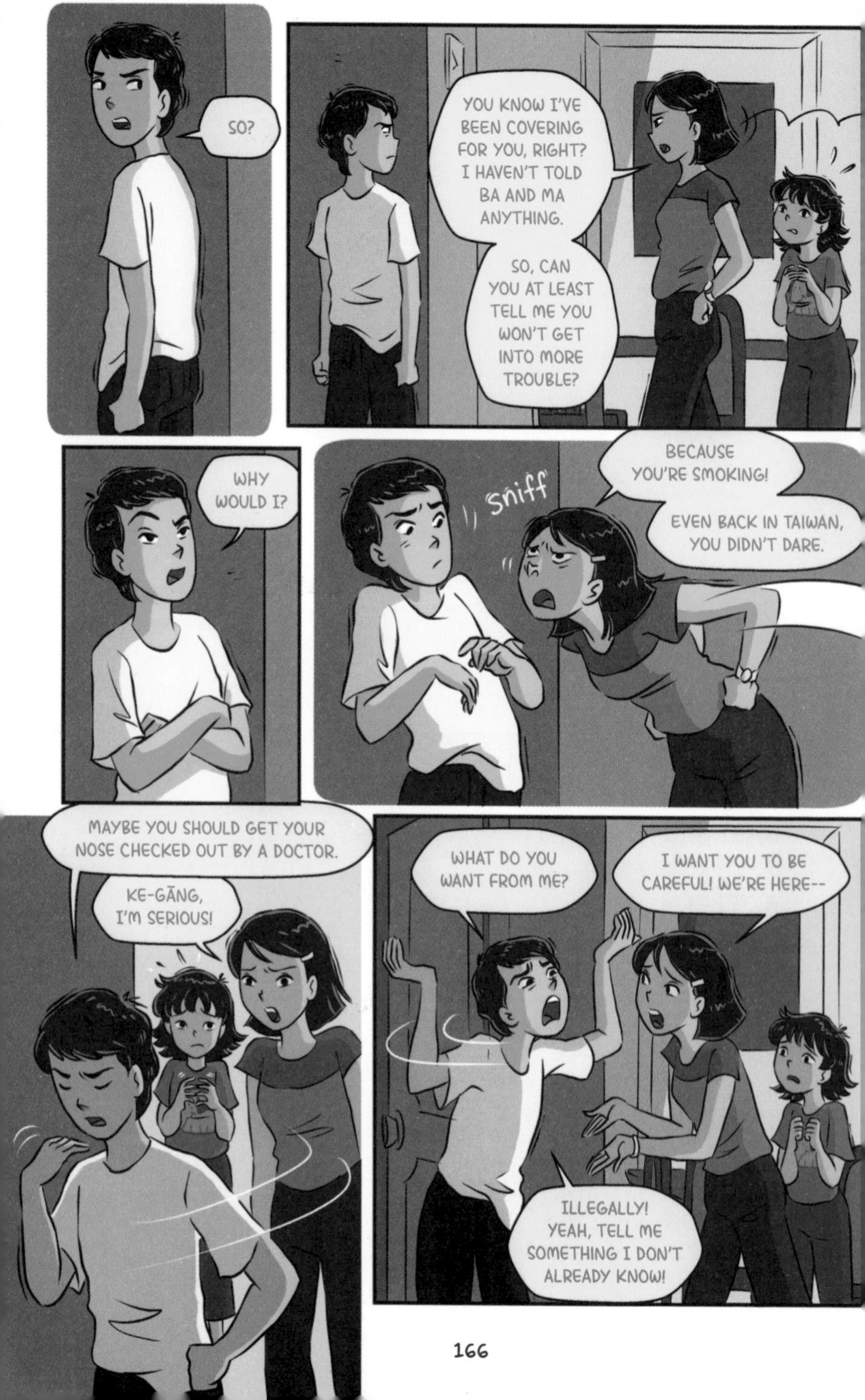
SO?
YOU KNOW I'VE BEEN COVERING FOR YOU, RIGHT? I HAVEN'T TOLD BA AND MA ANYTHING.
SO, CAN YOU AT LEAST TELL ME YOU WON'T GET INTO MORE TROUBLE?
WHY WOULD I?
SNIFF
BECAUSE YOU'RE SMOKING!
EVEN BACK IN TAIWAN, YOU DIDN'T DARE.
MAYBE YOU SHOULD GET YOUR NOSE CHECKED OUT BY A DOCTOR.
KE-GĀNG, I'M SERIOUS!
WHAT DO YOU WANT FROM ME?
I WANT YOU TO BE CAREFUL! WE'RE HERE--
ILLEGALLY! YEAH, TELL ME SOMETHING I DON'T ALREADY KNOW!

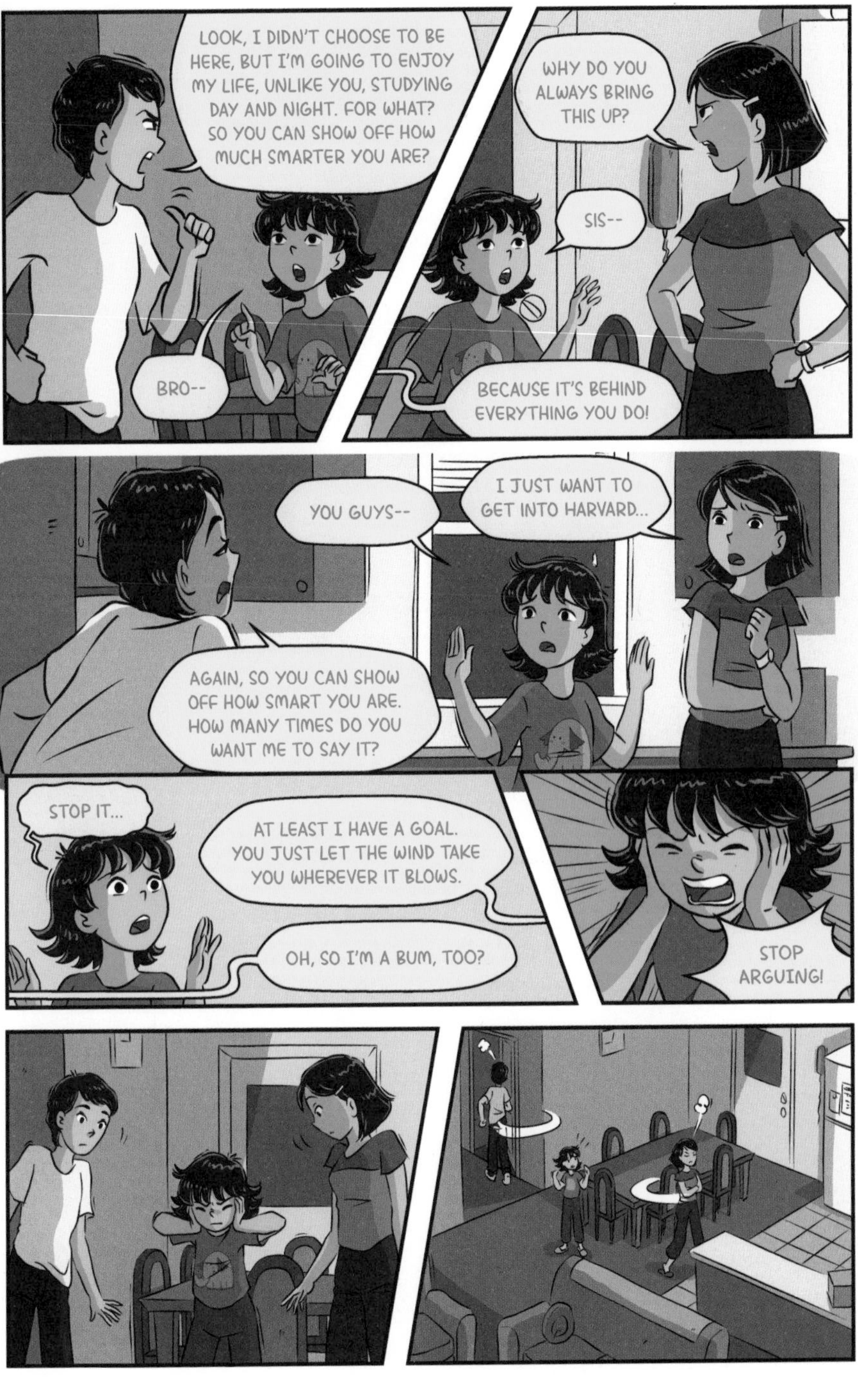
LOOK, I DIDN'T CHOOSE TO BE HERE, BUT I'M GOING TO ENJOY MY LIFE, UNLIKE YOU, STUDYING DAY AND NIGHT. FOR WHAT? SO YOU CAN SHOW OFF HOW MUCH SMARTER YOU ARE?
BRO--
WHY DO YOU ALWAYS BRING THIS UP?
SIS--
BECAUSE IT'S BEHIND EVERYTHING YOU DO!
YOU GUYS--
I JUST WANT TO GET INTO HARVARD...
AGAIN, SO YOU CAN SHOW OFF HOW SMART YOU ARE. HOW MANY TIMES DO YOU WANT ME TO SAY IT?
STOP IT...
AT LEAST I HAVE A GOAL. YOU JUST LET THE WIND TAKE YOU WHEREVER IT BLOWS.
OH, SO I'M A BUM, TOO?
STOP ARGUING!

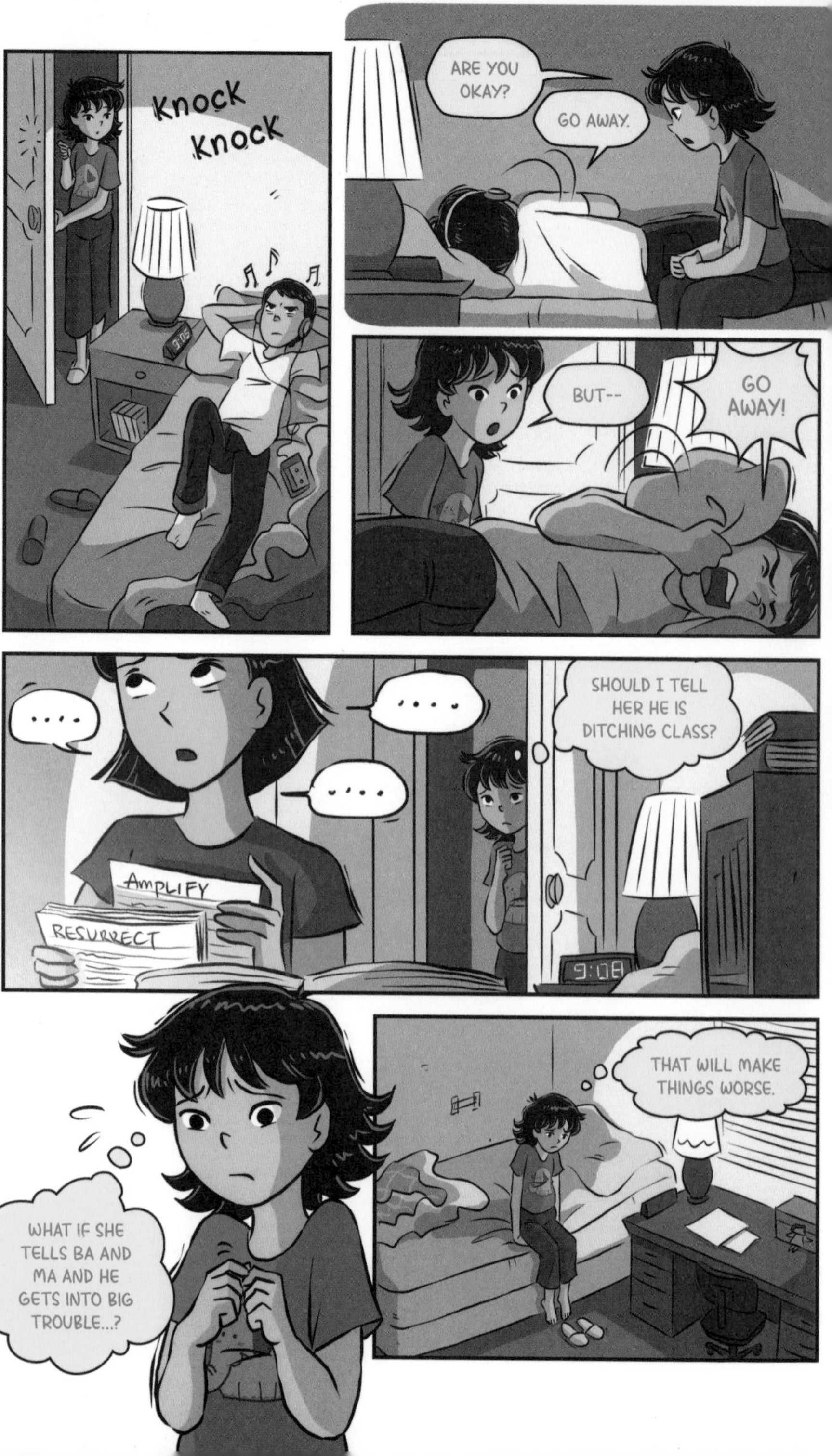

Knock
Knock
ARE YOU OKAY?
GO AWAY.
BUT--
GO AWAY!
AMPLIFY
RESURRECT
SHOULD I TELL HER HE IS DITCHING CLASS?
9:08
WHAT IF SHE TELLS BA AND MA AND HE GETS INTO BIG TROUBLE...?
THAT WILL MAKE THINGS WORSE.

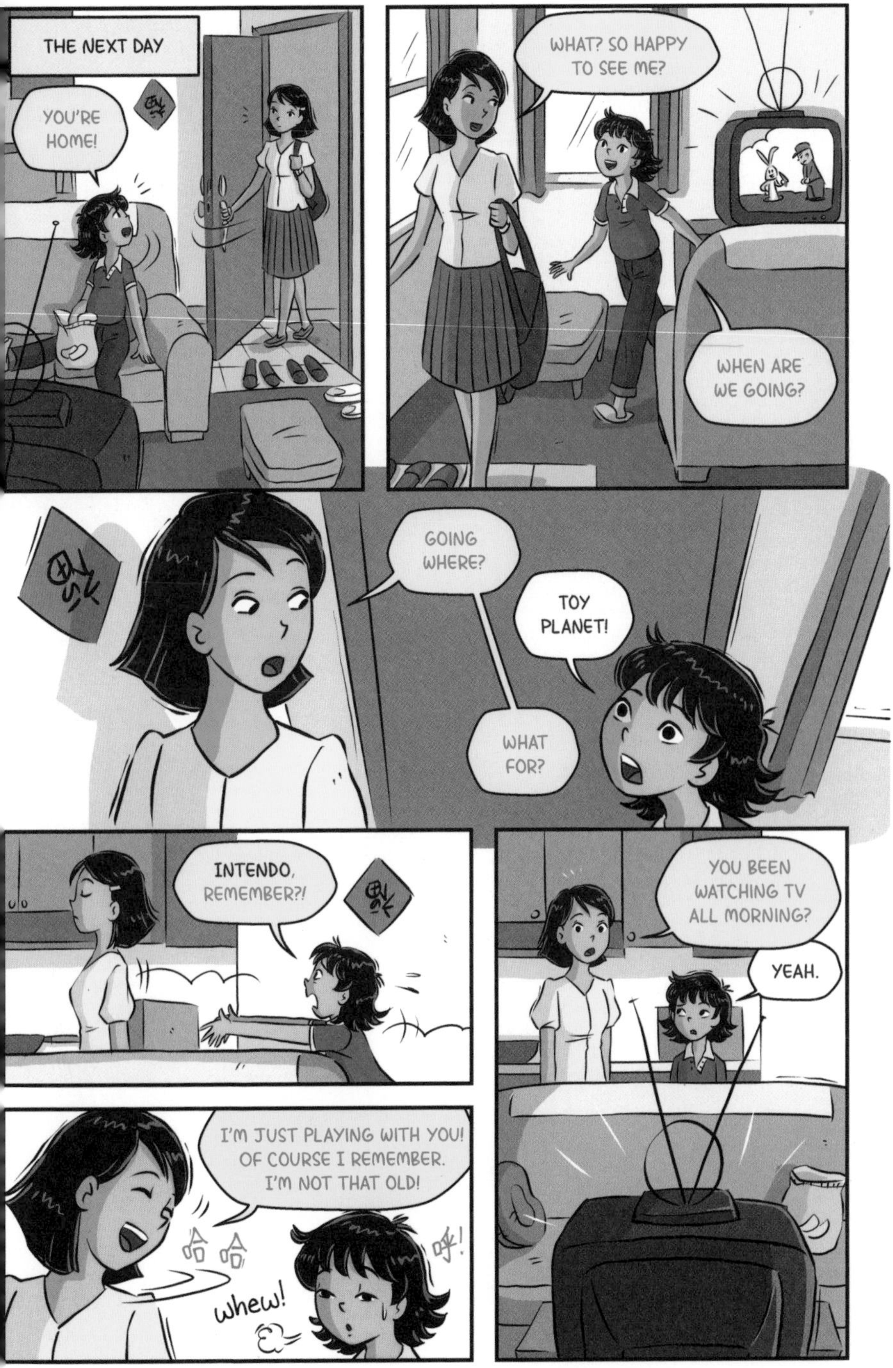
THE NEXT DAY
YOU'RE HOME!
WHAT? SO HAPPY TO SEE ME?
WHEN ARE WE GOING?
GOING WHERE?
TOY PLANET!
WHAT FOR?
INTENDO, REMEMBER?!
I'M JUST PLAYING WITH YOU! OF COURSE I REMEMBER. I'M NOT THAT OLD!
哈 哈
呼!
whew!
YOU BEEN WATCHING TV ALL MORNING?
YEAH.

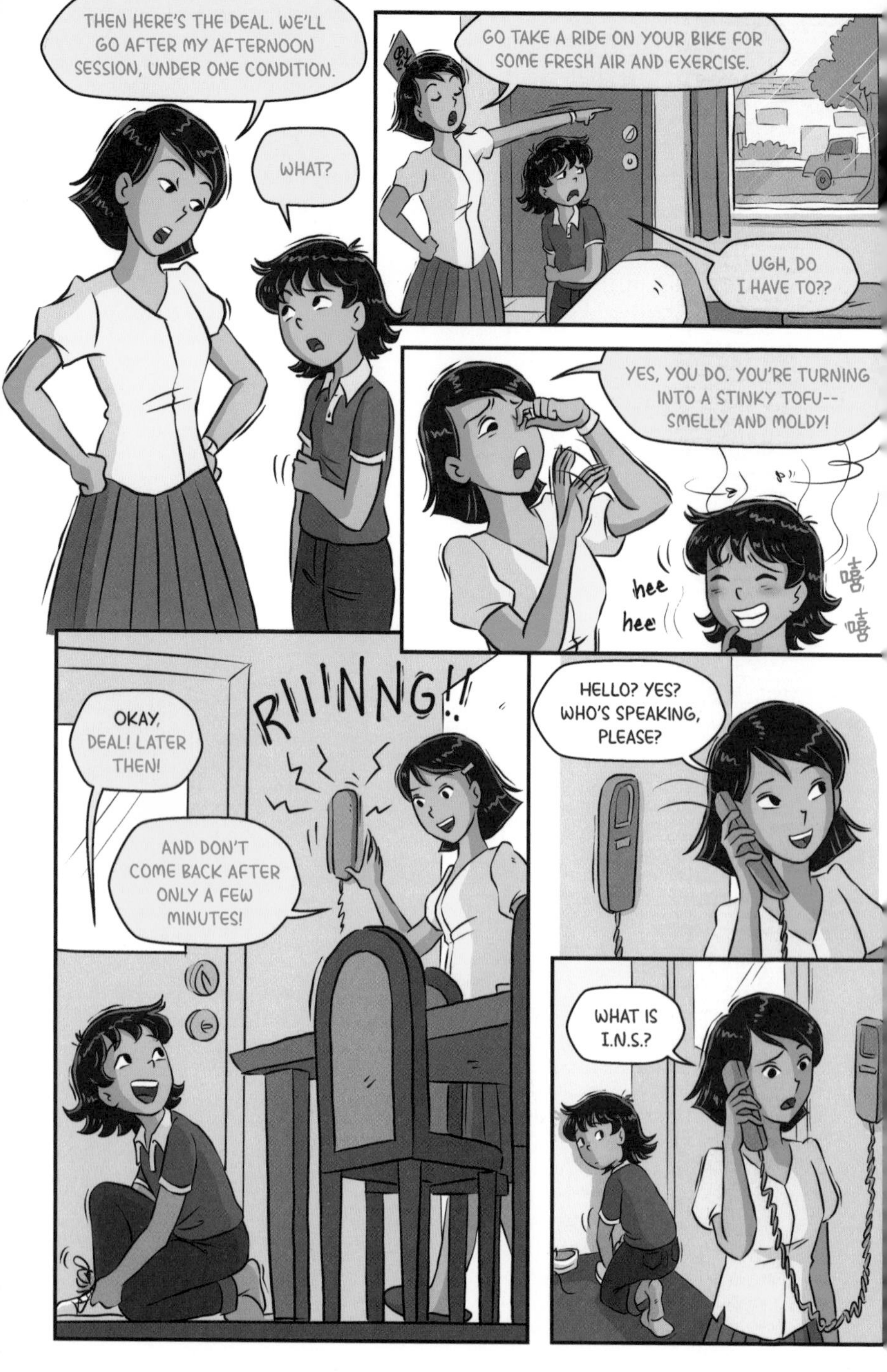
THEN HERE'S THE DEAL. WE'LL GO AFTER MY AFTERNOON SESSION, UNDER ONE CONDITION.
WHAT?
GO TAKE A RIDE ON YOUR BIKE FOR SOME FRESH AIR AND EXERCISE.
UGH, DO I HAVE TO??
YES, YOU DO. YOU'RE TURNING INTO A STINKY TOFU-- SMELLY AND MOLDY!
hee hee
嘻嘻
OKAY, DEAL! LATER THEN!
AND DON'T COME BACK AFTER ONLY A FEW MINUTES!
RIIINNG!!
HELLO? YES? WHO'S SPEAKING, PLEASE?
WHAT IS I.N.S.?

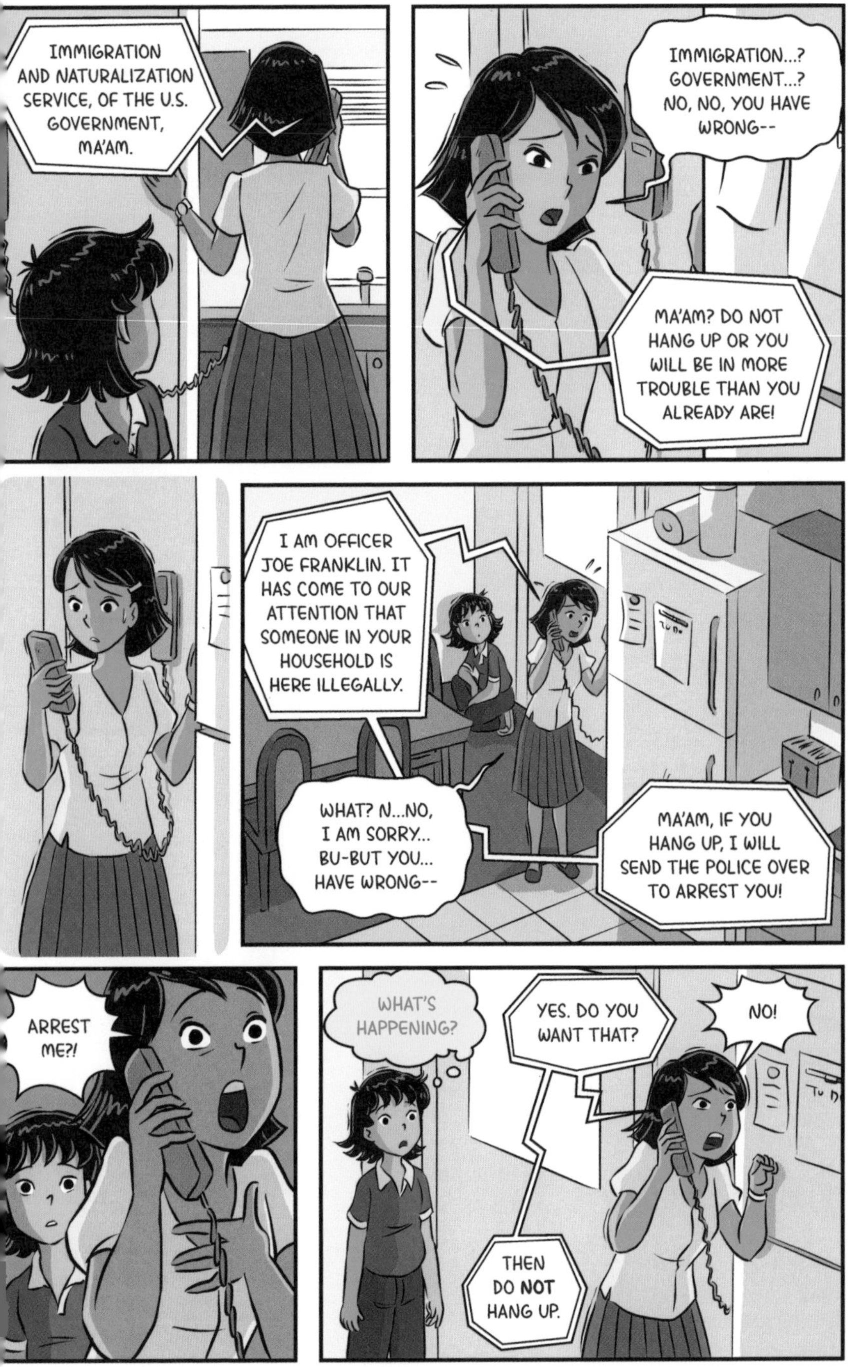
IMMIGRATION AND NATURALIZATION SERVICE, OF THE U.S. GOVERNMENT, MA'AM.
IMMIGRATION...? GOVERNMENT...? NO, NO, YOU HAVE WRONG--
MA'AM? DO NOT HANG UP OR YOU WILL BE IN MORE TROUBLE THAN YOU ALREADY ARE!
I AM OFFICER JOE FRANKLIN. IT HAS COME TO OUR ATTENTION THAT SOMEONE IN YOUR HOUSEHOLD IS HERE ILLEGALLY.
WHAT? N...NO, I AM SORRY... BU-BUT YOU... HAVE WRONG--
MA'AM, IF YOU HANG UP, I WILL SEND THE POLICE OVER TO ARREST YOU!
ARREST ME?!
WHAT'S HAPPENING?
YES. DO YOU WANT THAT?
NO!
THEN DO **NOT** HANG UP.

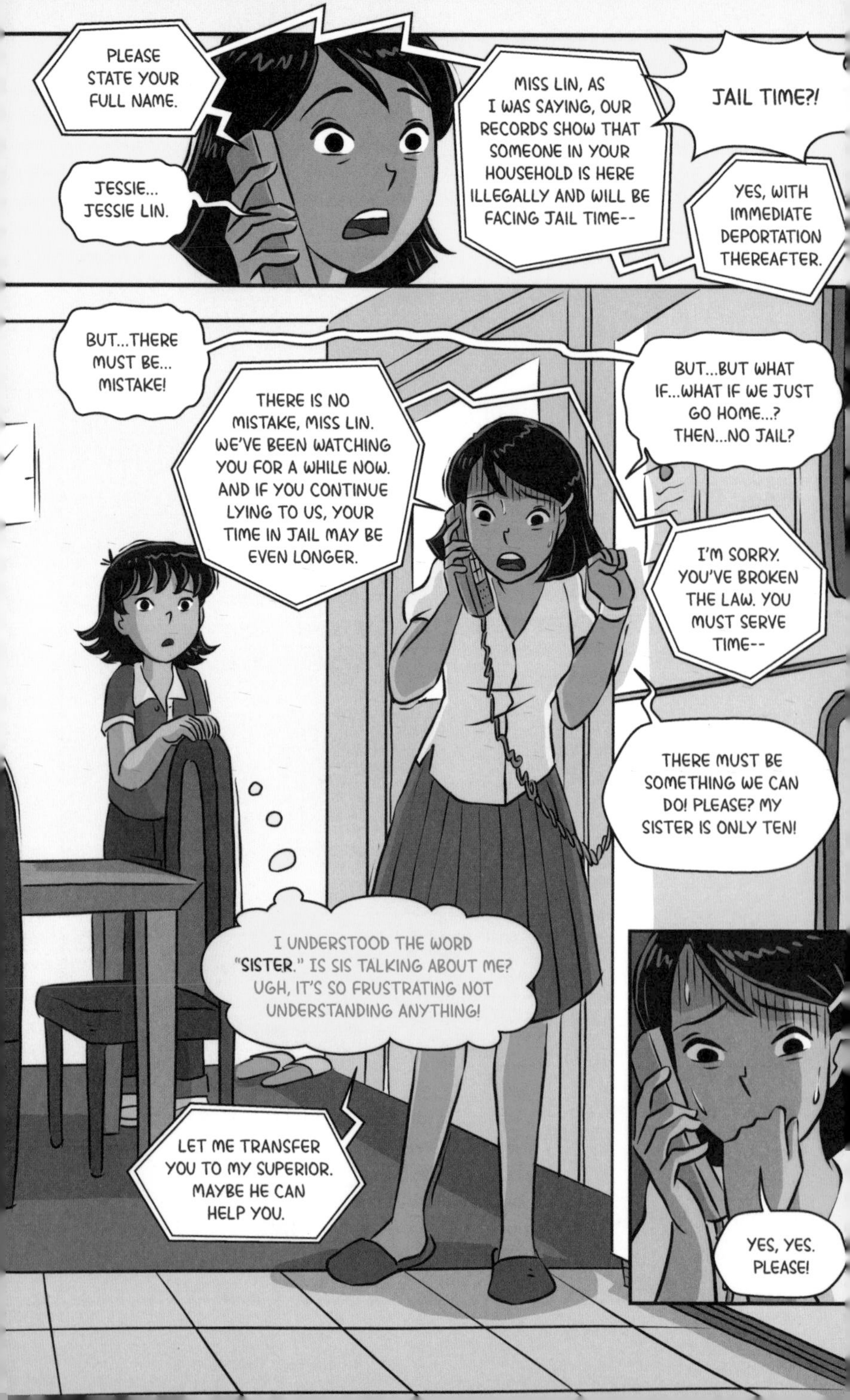
PLEASE STATE YOUR FULL NAME.
JESSIE... JESSIE LIN.
MISS LIN, AS I WAS SAYING, OUR RECORDS SHOW THAT SOMEONE IN YOUR HOUSEHOLD IS HERE ILLEGALLY AND WILL BE FACING JAIL TIME--
JAIL TIME?!
YES, WITH IMMEDIATE DEPORTATION THEREAFTER.
BUT...THERE MUST BE... MISTAKE!
THERE IS NO MISTAKE, MISS LIN. WE'VE BEEN WATCHING YOU FOR A WHILE NOW. AND IF YOU CONTINUE LYING TO US, YOUR TIME IN JAIL MAY BE EVEN LONGER.
BUT...BUT WHAT IF...WHAT IF WE JUST GO HOME...? THEN...NO JAIL?
I'M SORRY. YOU'VE BROKEN THE LAW. YOU MUST SERVE TIME--
THERE MUST BE SOMETHING WE CAN DO! PLEASE? MY SISTER IS ONLY TEN!
I UNDERSTOOD THE WORD "SISTER." IS SIS TALKING ABOUT ME? UGH, IT'S SO FRUSTRATING NOT UNDERSTANDING ANYTHING!
LET ME TRANSFER YOU TO MY SUPERIOR. MAYBE HE CAN HELP YOU.
YES, YES. PLEASE!

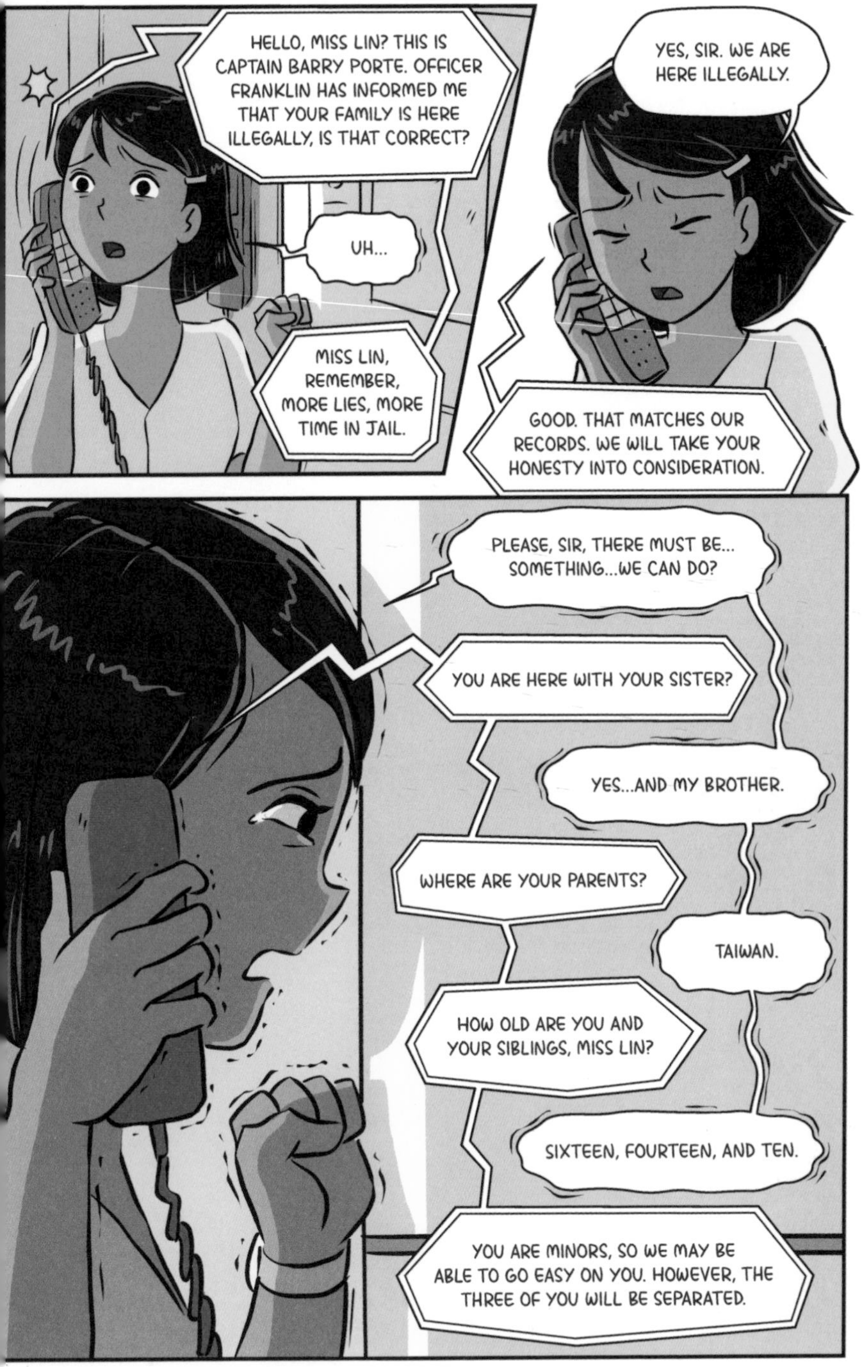
HELLO, MISS LIN? THIS IS CAPTAIN BARRY PORTE. OFFICER FRANKLIN HAS INFORMED ME THAT YOUR FAMILY IS HERE ILLEGALLY, IS THAT CORRECT?
UH...
MISS LIN, REMEMBER, MORE LIES, MORE TIME IN JAIL.
YES, SIR. WE ARE HERE ILLEGALLY.
GOOD. THAT MATCHES OUR RECORDS. WE WILL TAKE YOUR HONESTY INTO CONSIDERATION.
PLEASE, SIR, THERE MUST BE... SOMETHING...WE CAN DO?
YOU ARE HERE WITH YOUR SISTER?
YES...AND MY BROTHER.
WHERE ARE YOUR PARENTS?
TAIWAN.
HOW OLD ARE YOU AND YOUR SIBLINGS, MISS LIN?
SIXTEEN, FOURTEEN, AND TEN.
YOU ARE MINORS, SO WE MAY BE ABLE TO GO EASY ON YOU. HOWEVER, THE THREE OF YOU WILL BE SEPARATED.

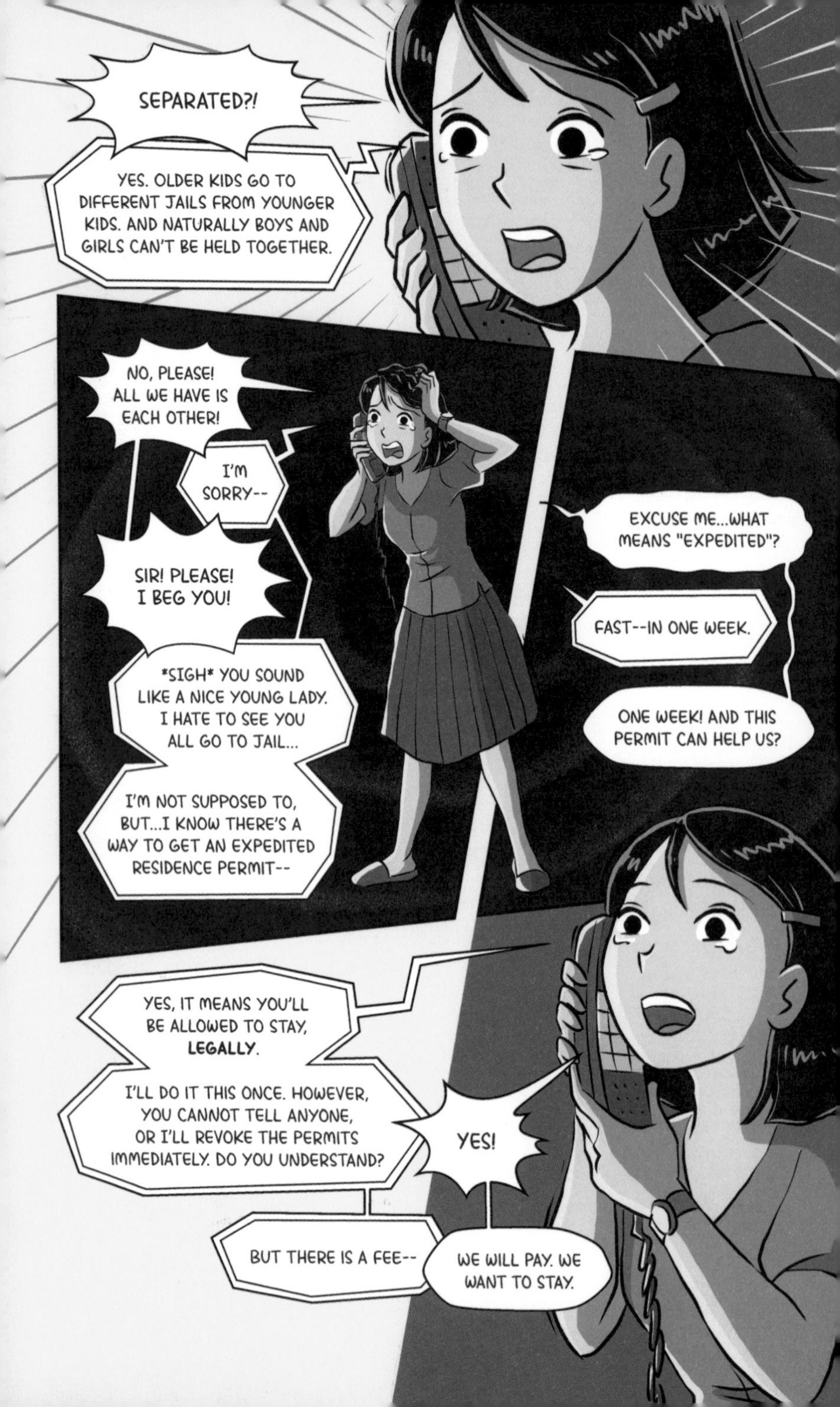

SEPARATED?!
YES. OLDER KIDS GO TO DIFFERENT JAILS FROM YOUNGER KIDS. AND NATURALLY BOYS AND GIRLS CAN'T BE HELD TOGETHER.
NO, PLEASE! ALL WE HAVE IS EACH OTHER!
I'M SORRY--
SIR! PLEASE! I BEG YOU!
SIGH YOU SOUND LIKE A NICE YOUNG LADY. I HATE TO SEE YOU ALL GO TO JAIL...
I'M NOT SUPPOSED TO, BUT...I KNOW THERE'S A WAY TO GET AN EXPEDITED RESIDENCE PERMIT--
EXCUSE ME...WHAT MEANS "EXPEDITED"?
FAST--IN ONE WEEK.
ONE WEEK! AND THIS PERMIT CAN HELP US?
YES, IT MEANS YOU'LL BE ALLOWED TO STAY, **LEGALLY**.
I'LL DO IT THIS ONCE. HOWEVER, YOU CANNOT TELL ANYONE, OR I'LL REVOKE THE PERMITS IMMEDIATELY. DO YOU UNDERSTAND?
YES!
BUT THERE IS A FEE--
WE WILL PAY. WE WANT TO STAY.

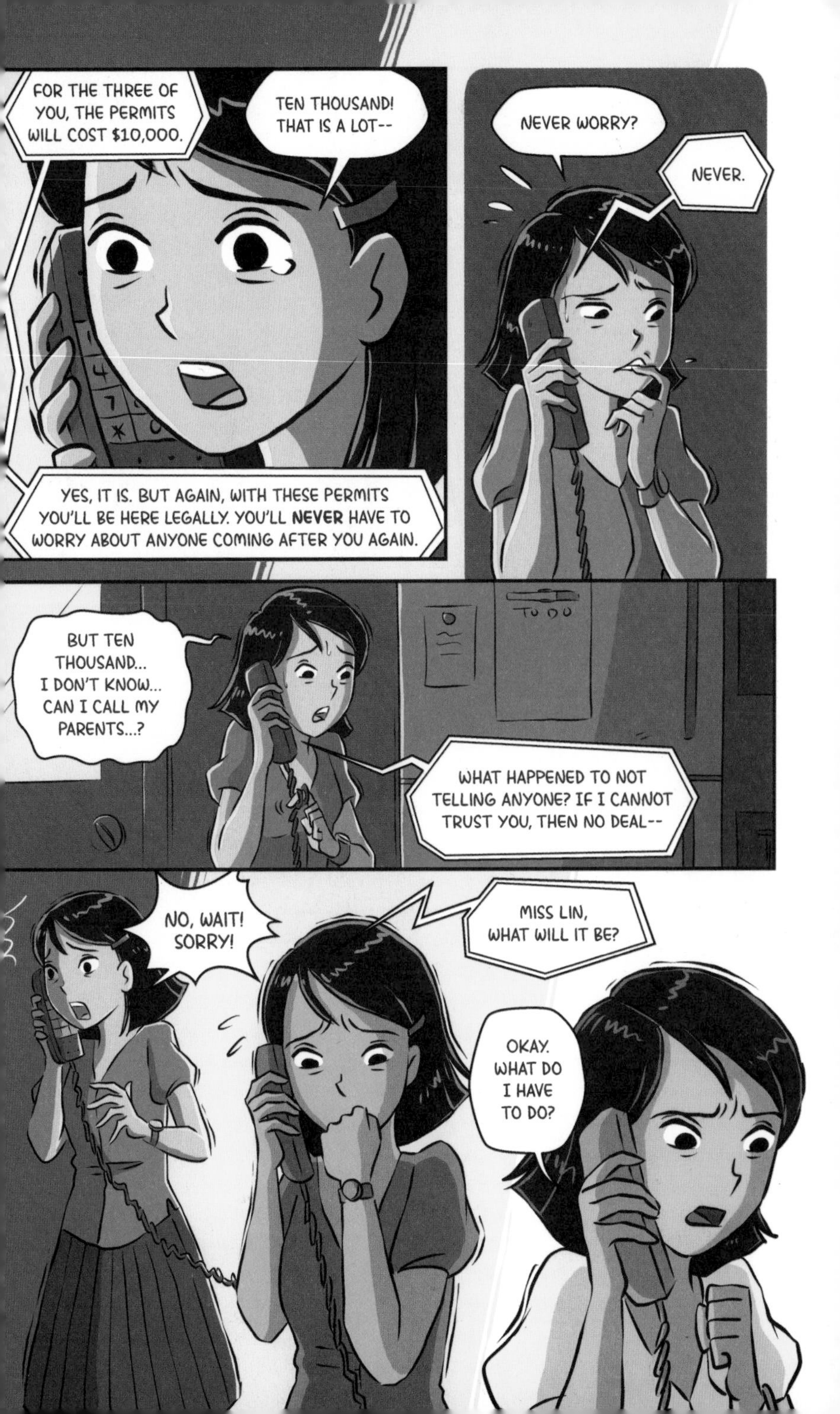
FOR THE THREE OF YOU, THE PERMITS WILL COST $10,000.
TEN THOUSAND! THAT IS A LOT--
YES, IT IS. BUT AGAIN, WITH THESE PERMITS YOU'LL BE HERE LEGALLY. YOU'LL **NEVER** HAVE TO WORRY ABOUT ANYONE COMING AFTER YOU AGAIN.
NEVER WORRY?
NEVER.
TO DO
BUT TEN THOUSAND... I DON'T KNOW... CAN I CALL MY PARENTS...?
WHAT HAPPENED TO NOT TELLING ANYONE? IF I CANNOT TRUST YOU, THEN NO DEAL--
NO, WAIT! SORRY!
MISS LIN, WHAT WILL IT BE?
OKAY. WHAT DO I HAVE TO DO?

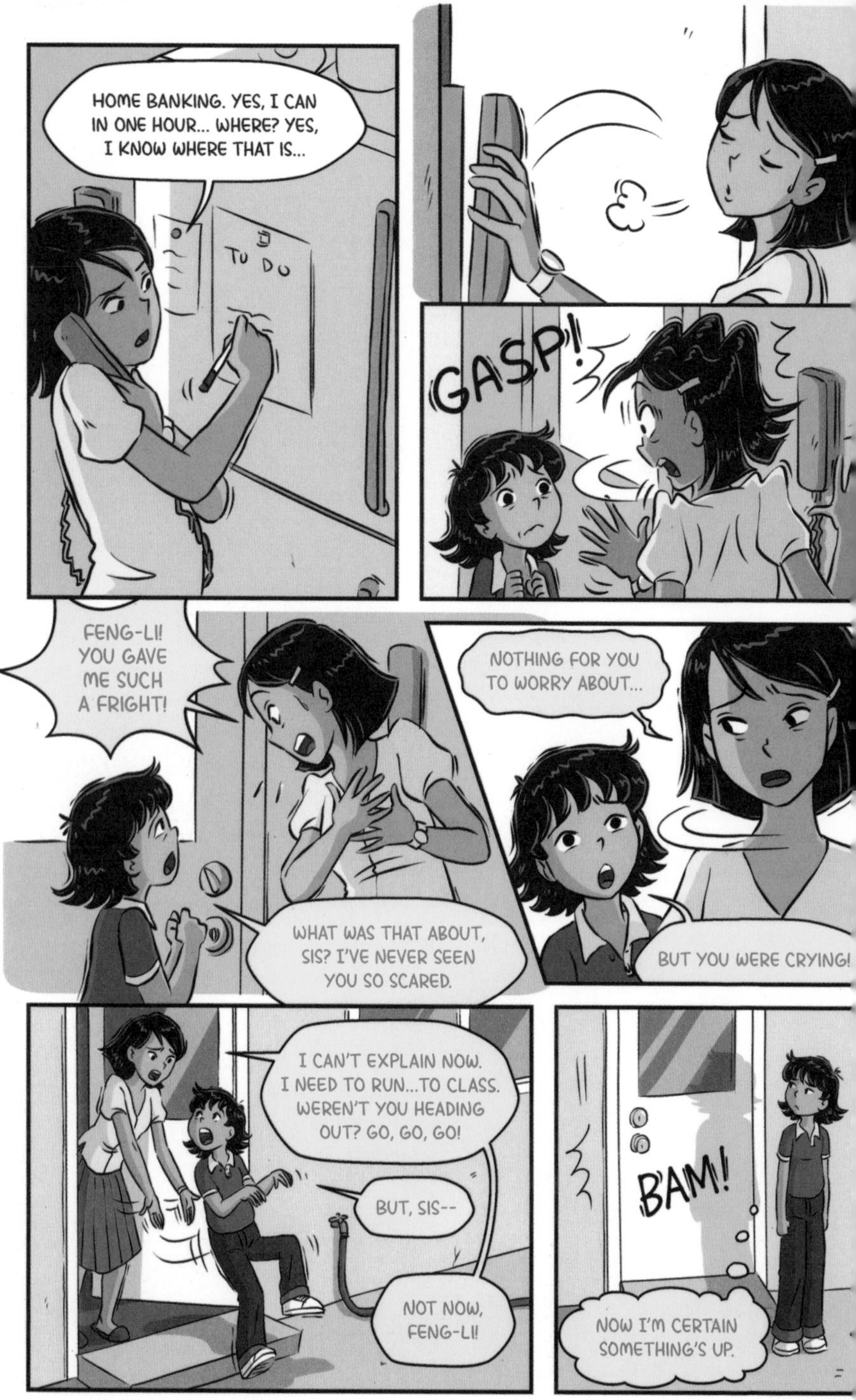
HOME BANKING. YES, I CAN IN ONE HOUR... WHERE? YES, I KNOW WHERE THAT IS...
TO DO
GASP!
FENG-LI! YOU GAVE ME SUCH A FRIGHT!
WHAT WAS THAT ABOUT, SIS? I'VE NEVER SEEN YOU SO SCARED.
NOTHING FOR YOU TO WORRY ABOUT...
BUT YOU WERE CRYING!
I CAN'T EXPLAIN NOW. I NEED TO RUN...TO CLASS. WEREN'T YOU HEADING OUT? GO, GO, GO!
BUT, SIS--
NOT NOW, FENG-LI!
BAM!
NOW I'M CERTAIN SOMETHING'S UP.

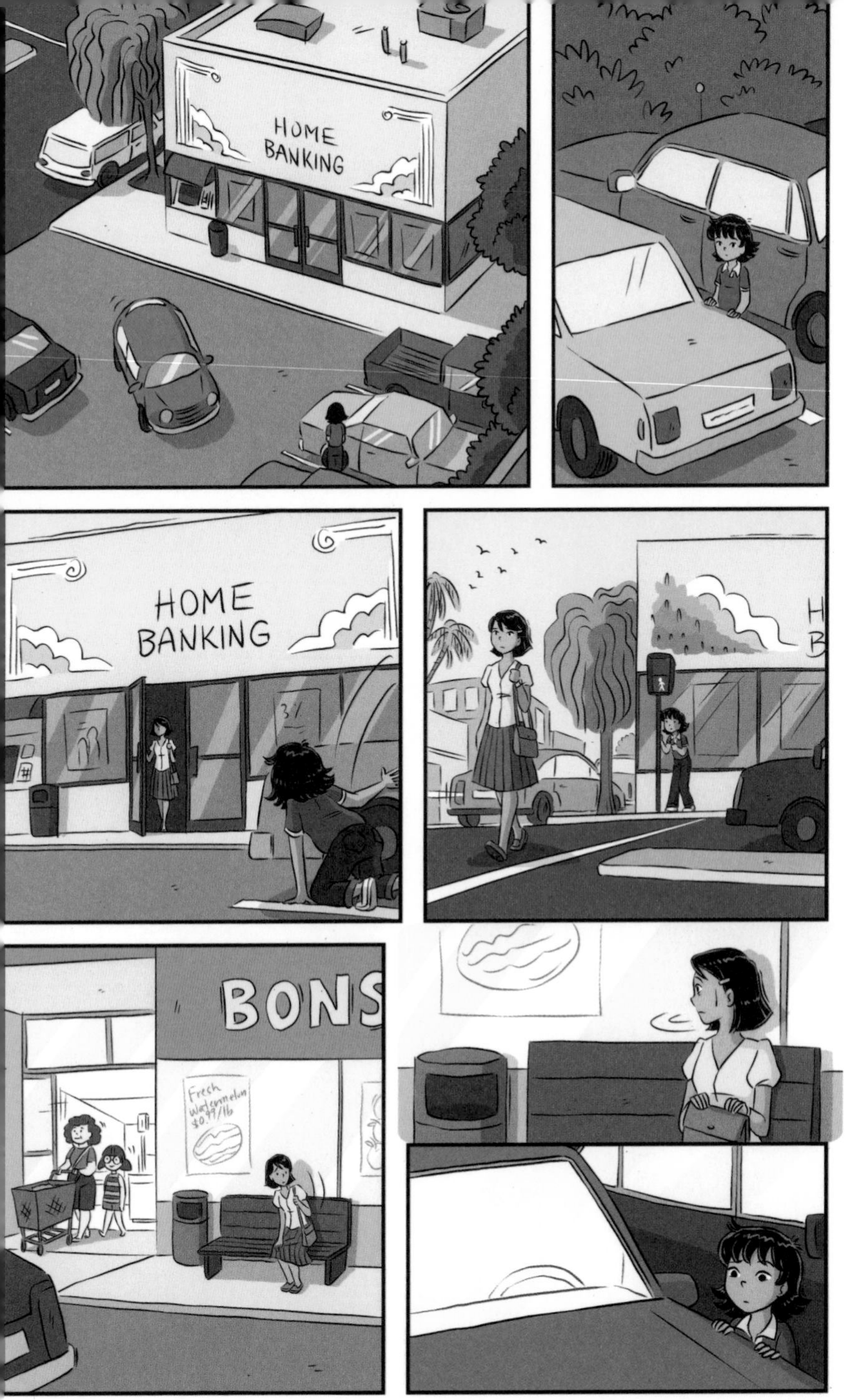
HOME BANKING
HOME BANKING
BONS
Fresh Watermelon $0.99/lb

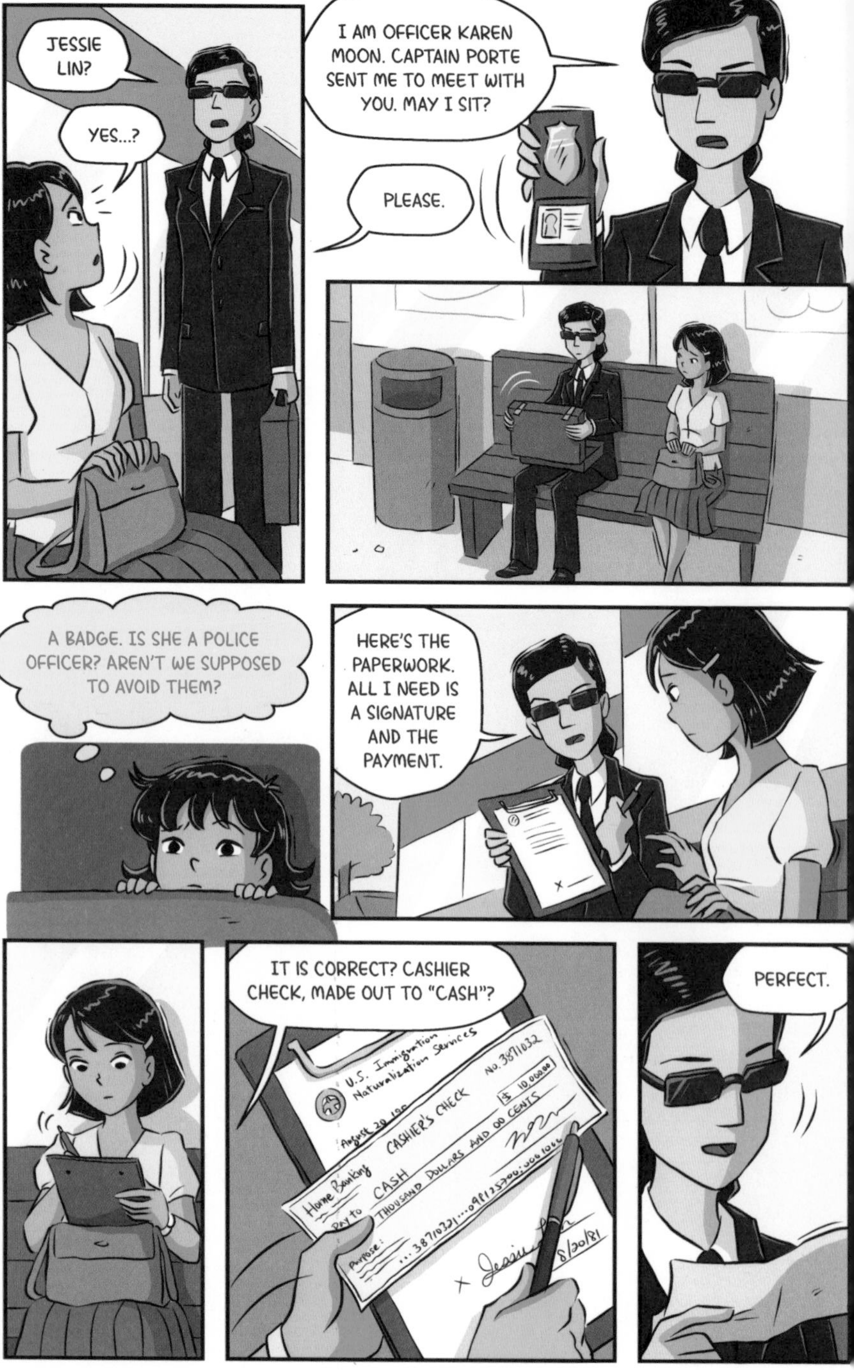
JESSIE LIN?
YES...?
I AM OFFICER KAREN MOON. CAPTAIN PORTE SENT ME TO MEET WITH YOU. MAY I SIT?
PLEASE.
A BADGE. IS SHE A POLICE OFFICER? AREN'T WE SUPPOSED TO AVOID THEM?
HERE'S THE PAPERWORK. ALL I NEED IS A SIGNATURE AND THE PAYMENT.
IT IS CORRECT? CASHIER CHECK, MADE OUT TO "CASH"?
U.S. Immigration Naturalization Services
CASHIER'S CHECK
Pay to CASH
THOUSAND DOLLARS AND 00 CENTS
8/20/81
PERFECT.

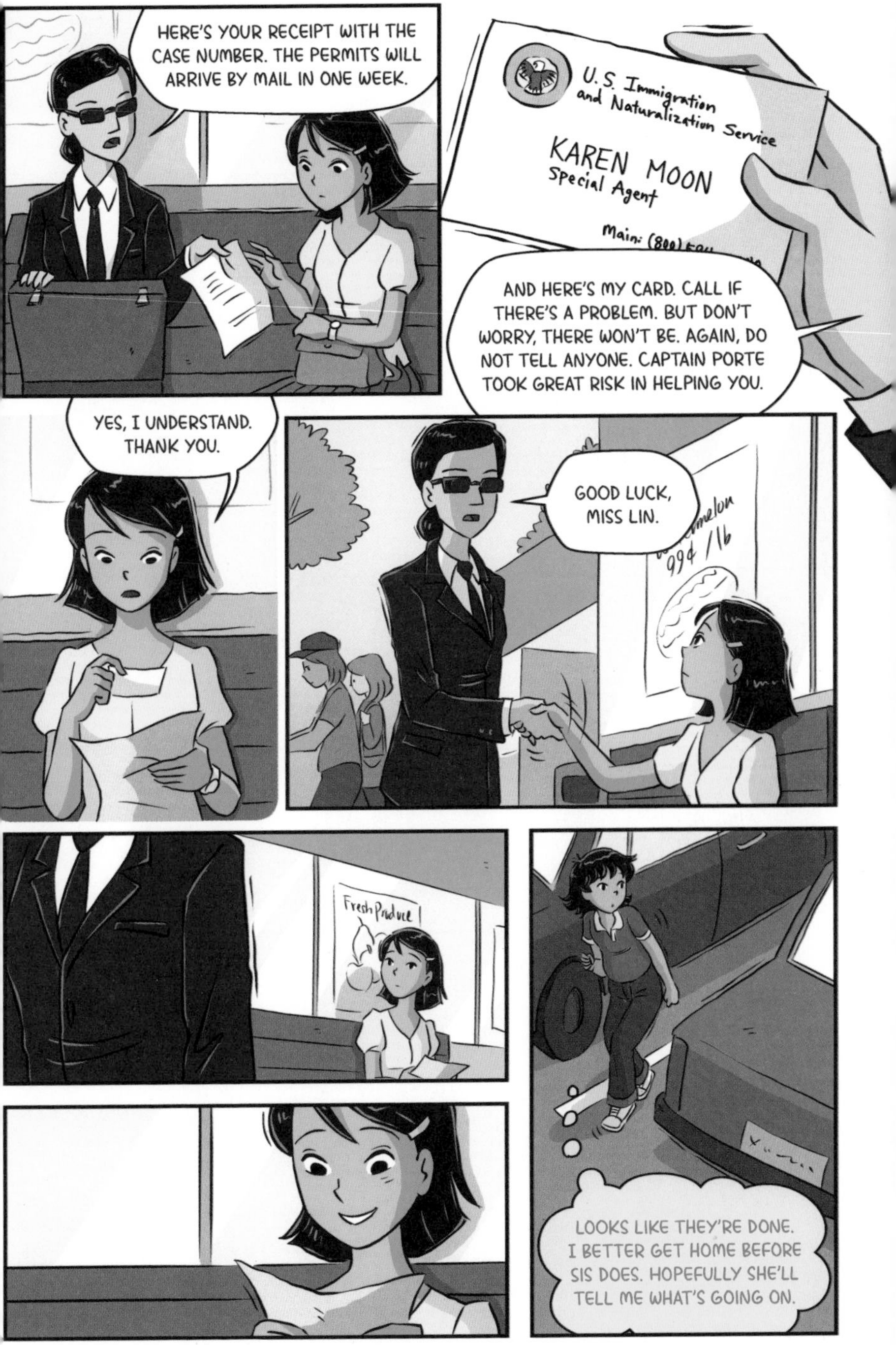
HERE'S YOUR RECEIPT WITH THE CASE NUMBER. THE PERMITS WILL ARRIVE BY MAIL IN ONE WEEK.
U.S. Immigration and Naturalization Service
KAREN MOON
Special Agent
Main:
AND HERE'S MY CARD. CALL IF THERE'S A PROBLEM. BUT DON'T WORRY, THERE WON'T BE. AGAIN, DO NOT TELL ANYONE. CAPTAIN PORTE TOOK GREAT RISK IN HELPING YOU.
YES, I UNDERSTAND. THANK YOU.
GOOD LUCK, MISS LIN.
Fresh Produce!
LOOKS LIKE THEY'RE DONE. I BETTER GET HOME BEFORE SIS DOES. HOPEFULLY SHE'LL TELL ME WHAT'S GOING ON.

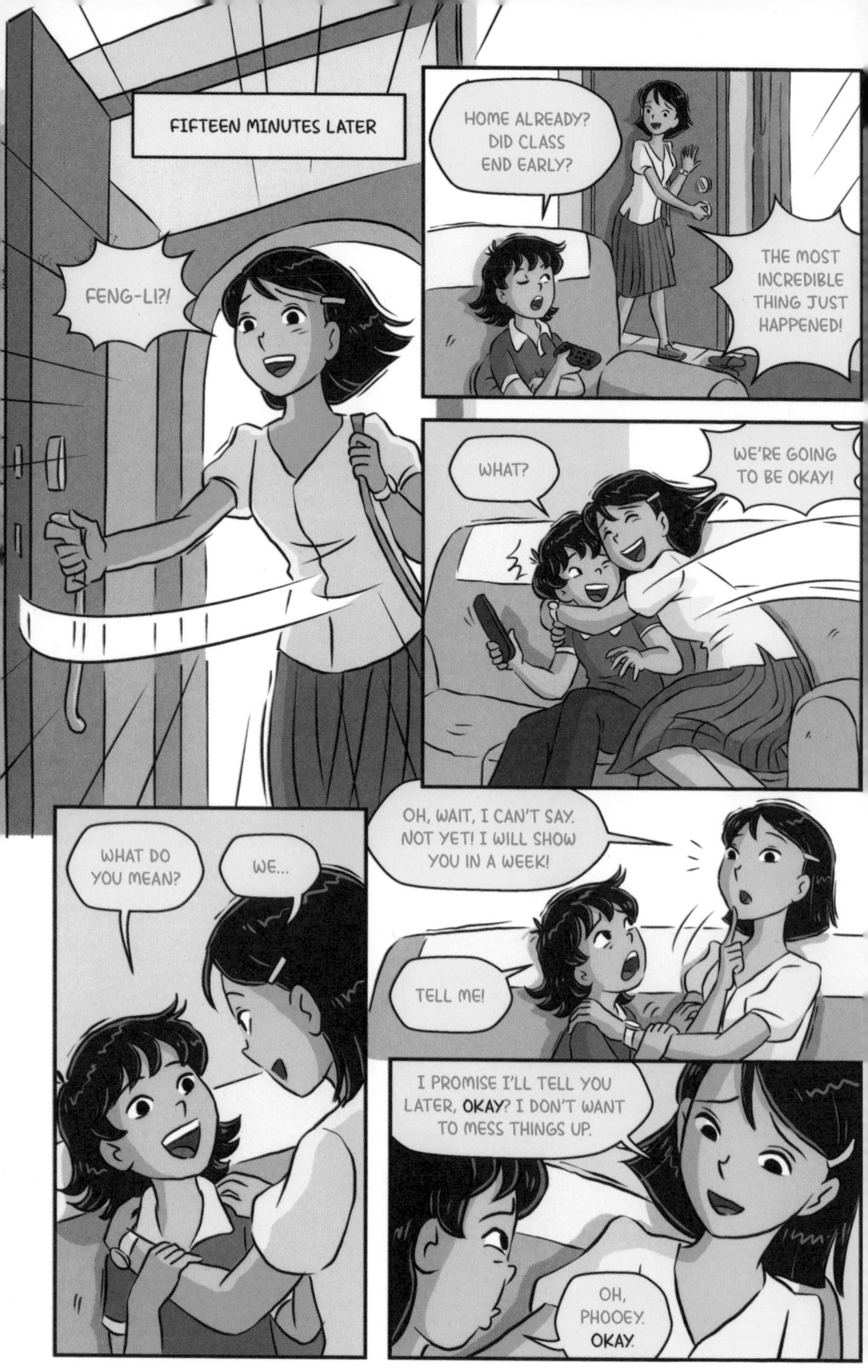

FIFTEEN MINUTES LATER
FENG-LI?!
HOME ALREADY? DID CLASS END EARLY?
THE MOST INCREDIBLE THING JUST HAPPENED!
WHAT?
WE'RE GOING TO BE OKAY!
WHAT DO YOU MEAN?
WE...
OH, WAIT, I CAN'T SAY. NOT YET! I WILL SHOW YOU IN A WEEK!
TELL ME!
I PROMISE I'LL TELL YOU LATER, **OKAY**? I DON'T WANT TO MESS THINGS UP.
OH, PHOOEY. **OKAY**.

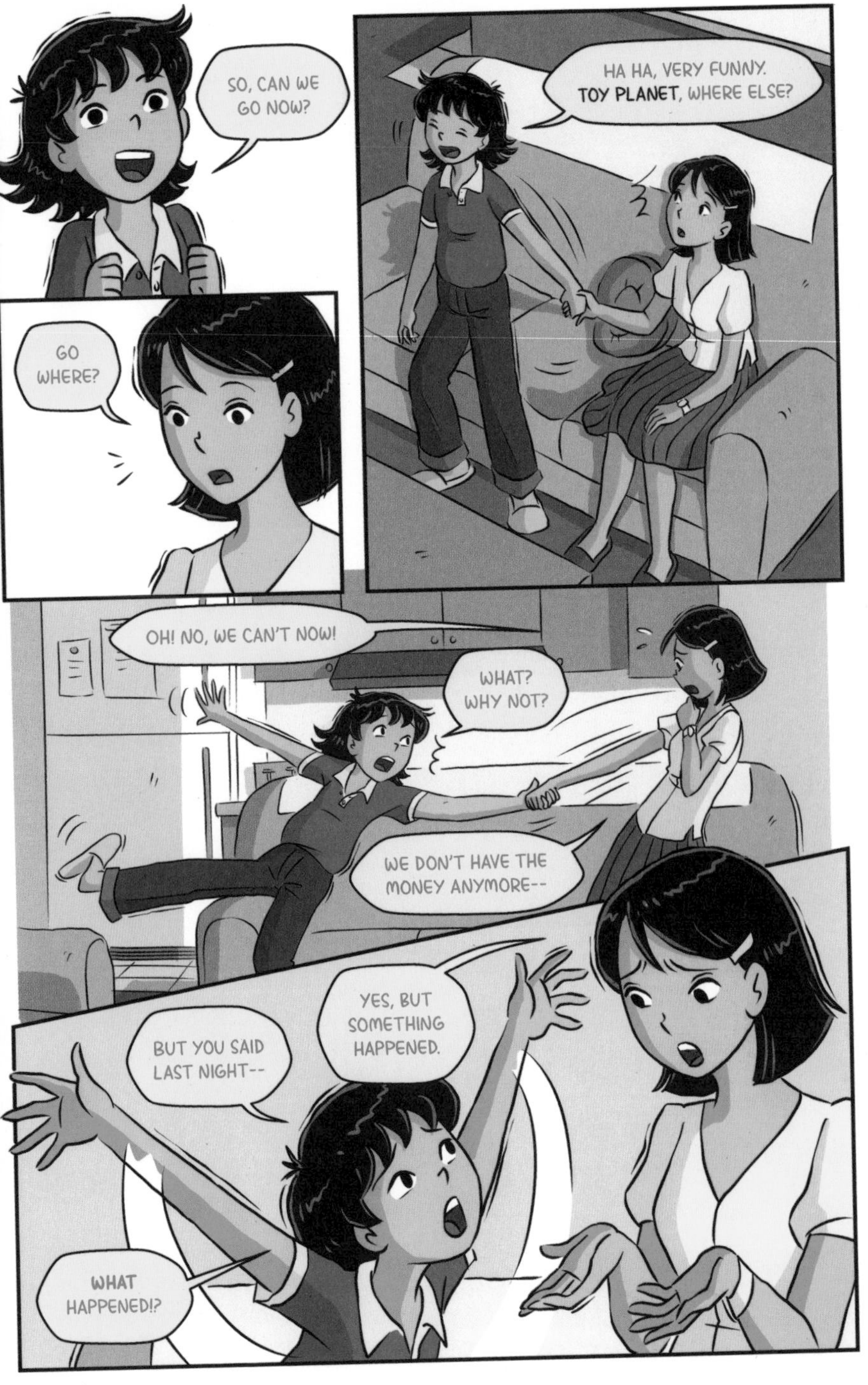
SO, CAN WE GO NOW?
GO WHERE?
HA HA, VERY FUNNY. TOY PLANET, WHERE ELSE?
OH! NO, WE CAN'T NOW!
WHAT? WHY NOT?
WE DON'T HAVE THE MONEY ANYMORE--
BUT YOU SAID LAST NIGHT--
YES, BUT SOMETHING HAPPENED.
WHAT HAPPENED!?

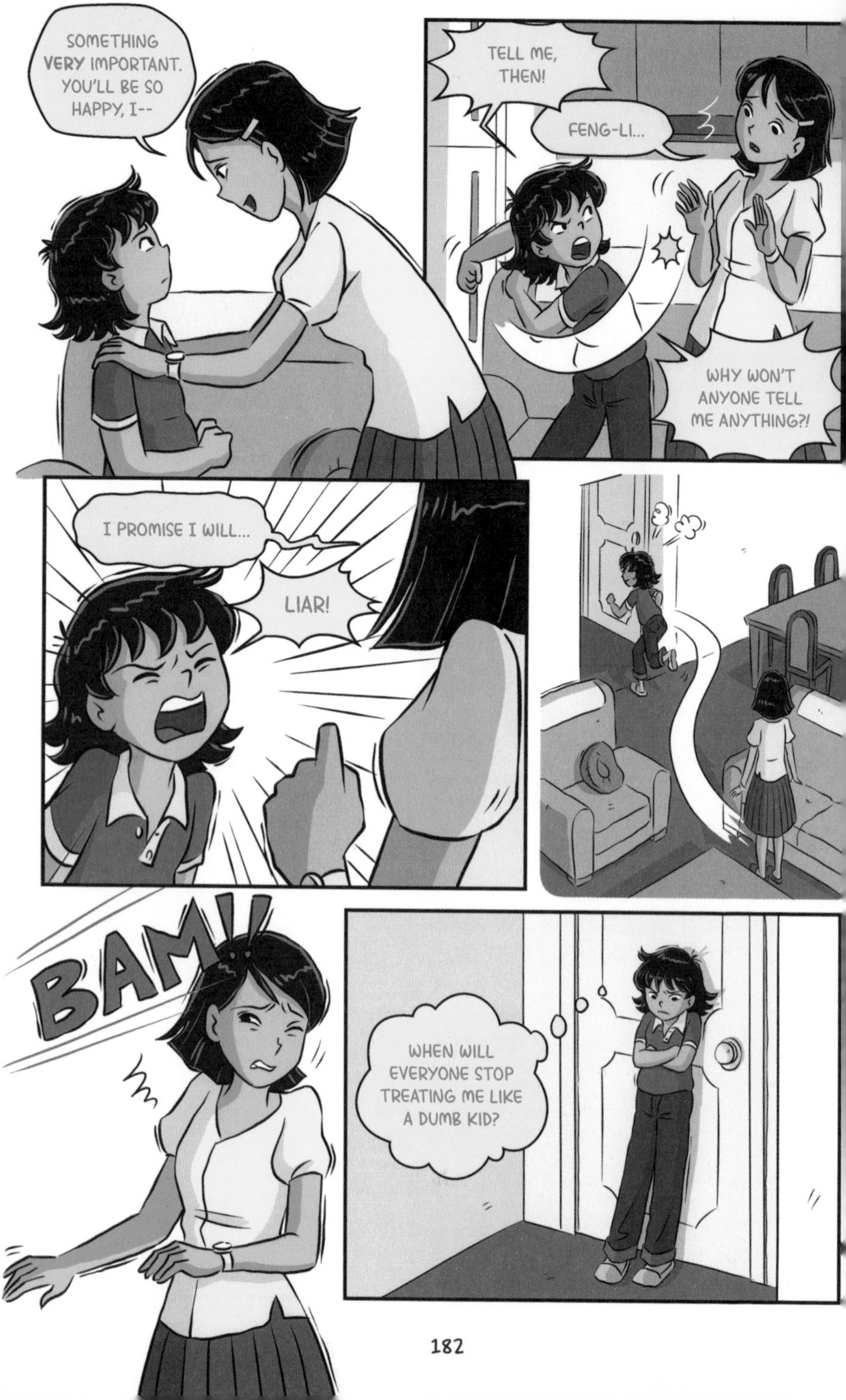
SOMETHING **VERY** IMPORTANT. YOU'LL BE SO HAPPY, I--
TELL ME, THEN!
FENG-LI...
WHY WON'T ANYONE TELL ME ANYTHING?!
I PROMISE I WILL...
LIAR!
BAM!!
WHEN WILL EVERYONE STOP TREATING ME LIKE A DUMB KID?

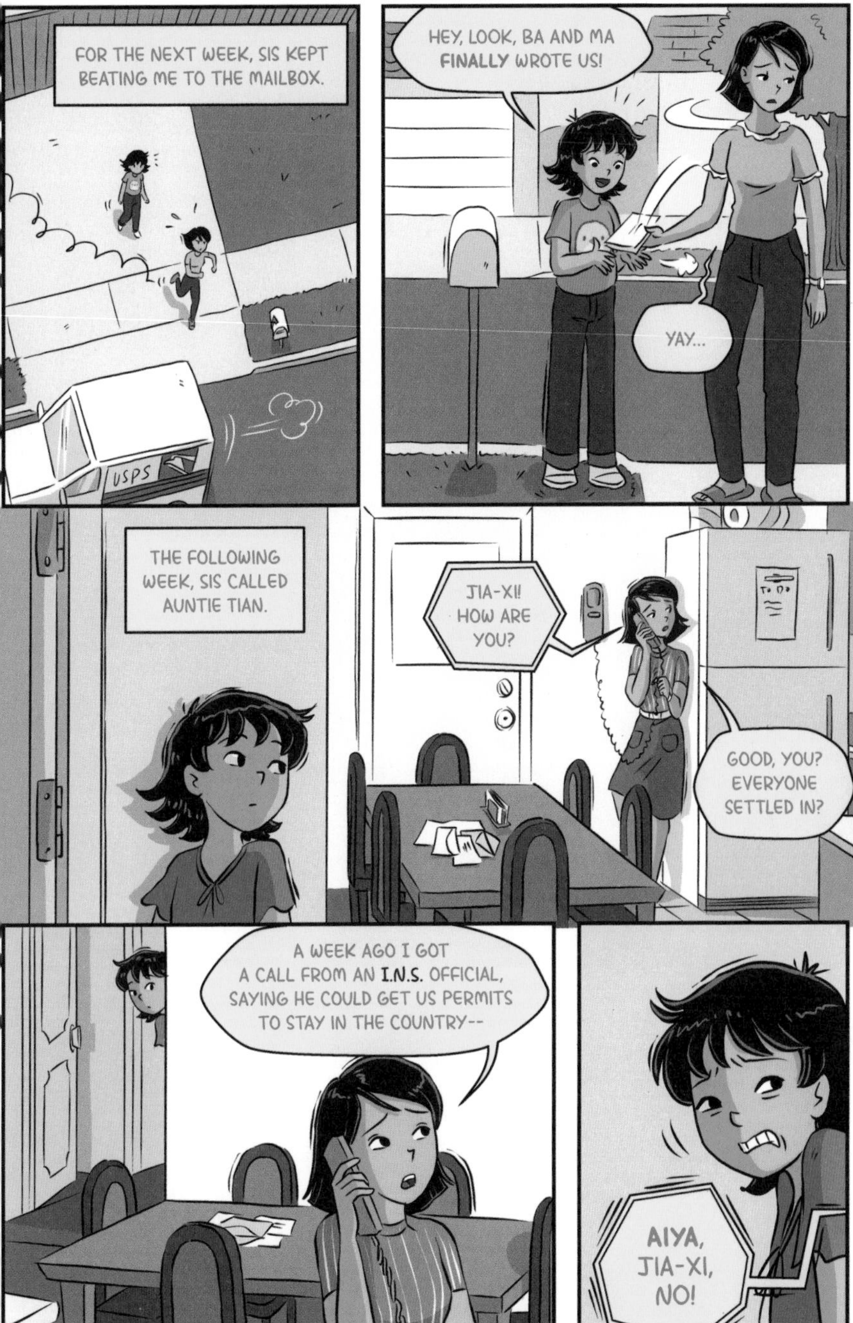
FOR THE NEXT WEEK, SIS KEPT BEATING ME TO THE MAILBOX.
USPS
HEY, LOOK, BA AND MA FINALLY WROTE US!
YAY...
THE FOLLOWING WEEK, SIS CALLED AUNTIE TIAN.
JIA-XI! HOW ARE YOU?
GOOD, YOU? EVERYONE SETTLED IN?
A WEEK AGO I GOT A CALL FROM AN I.N.S. OFFICIAL, SAYING HE COULD GET US PERMITS TO STAY IN THE COUNTRY--
AIYA, JIA-XI, NO!

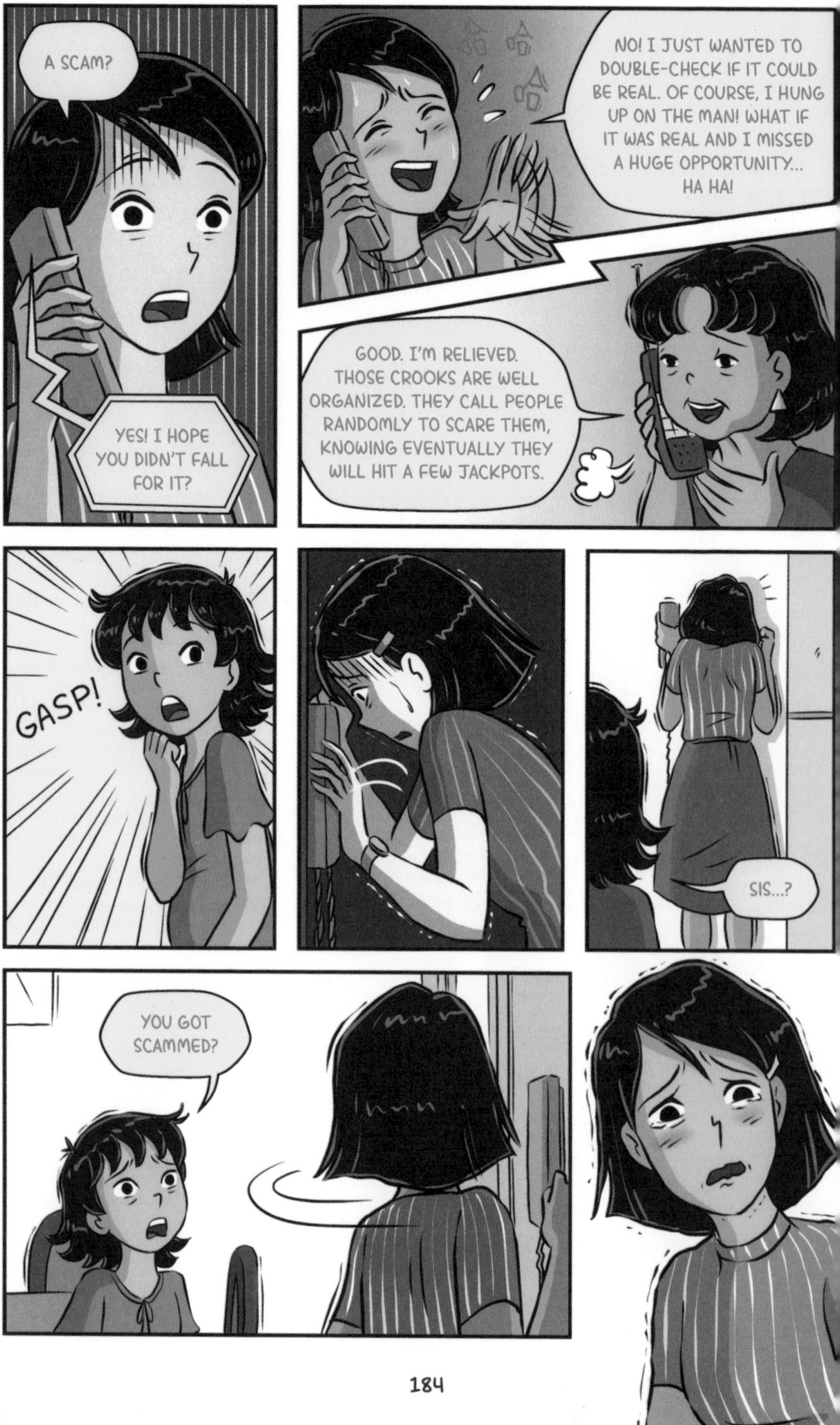
A SCAM?
YES! I HOPE YOU DIDN'T FALL FOR IT?
NO! I JUST WANTED TO DOUBLE-CHECK IF IT COULD BE REAL. OF COURSE, I HUNG UP ON THE MAN! WHAT IF IT WAS REAL AND I MISSED A HUGE OPPORTUNITY... HA HA!
GOOD. I'M RELIEVED. THOSE CROOKS ARE WELL ORGANIZED. THEY CALL PEOPLE RANDOMLY TO SCARE THEM, KNOWING EVENTUALLY THEY WILL HIT A FEW JACKPOTS.
GASP!
SIS...?
YOU GOT SCAMMED?

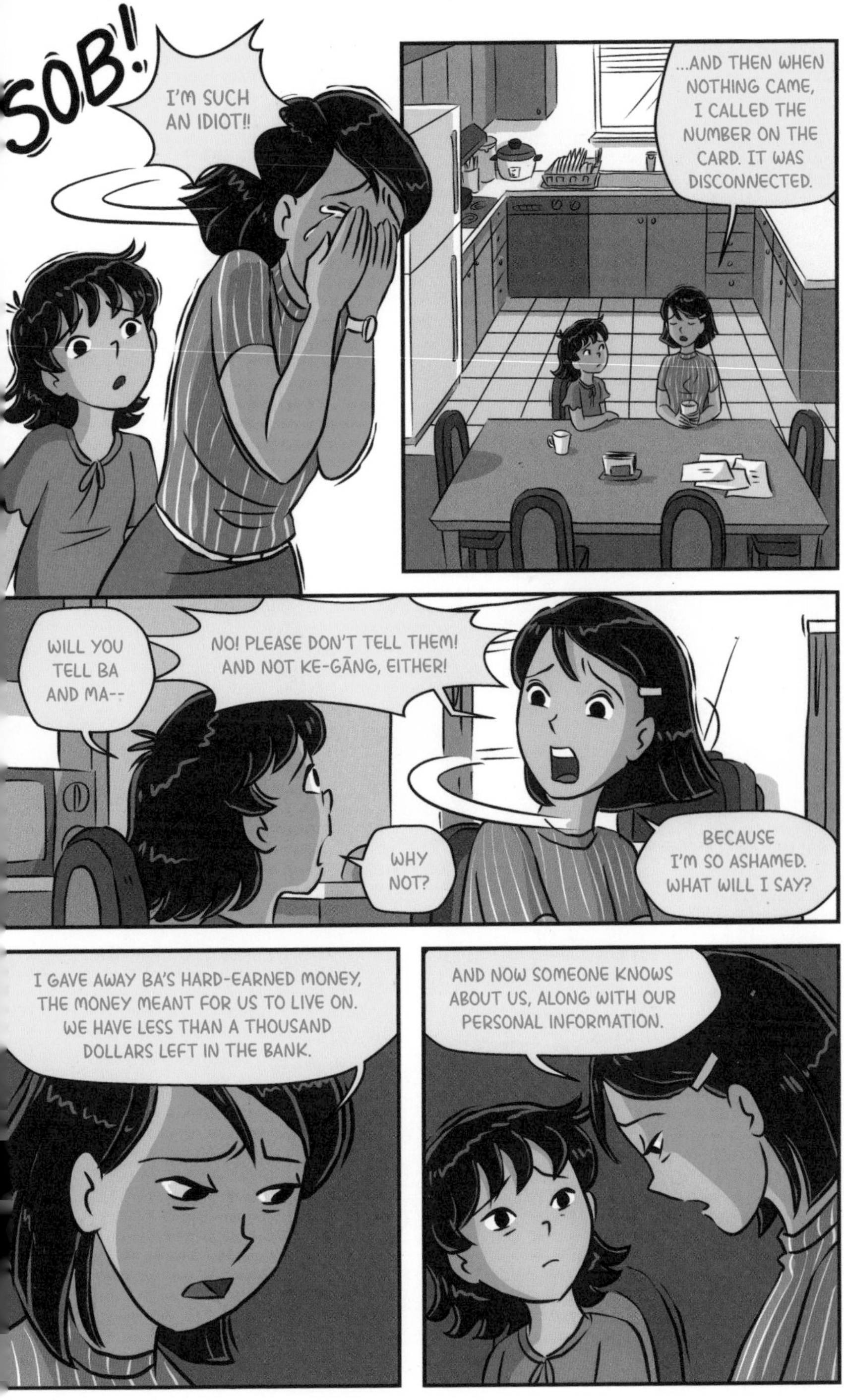
SOB!
I'M SUCH AN IDIOT!!
...AND THEN WHEN NOTHING CAME, I CALLED THE NUMBER ON THE CARD. IT WAS DISCONNECTED.
WILL YOU TELL BA AND MA--
NO! PLEASE DON'T TELL THEM! AND NOT KE-GĀNG, EITHER!
WHY NOT?
BECAUSE I'M SO ASHAMED. WHAT WILL I SAY?
I GAVE AWAY BA'S HARD-EARNED MONEY, THE MONEY MEANT FOR US TO LIVE ON. WE HAVE LESS THAN A THOUSAND DOLLARS LEFT IN THE BANK.
AND NOW SOMEONE KNOWS ABOUT US, ALONG WITH OUR PERSONAL INFORMATION.

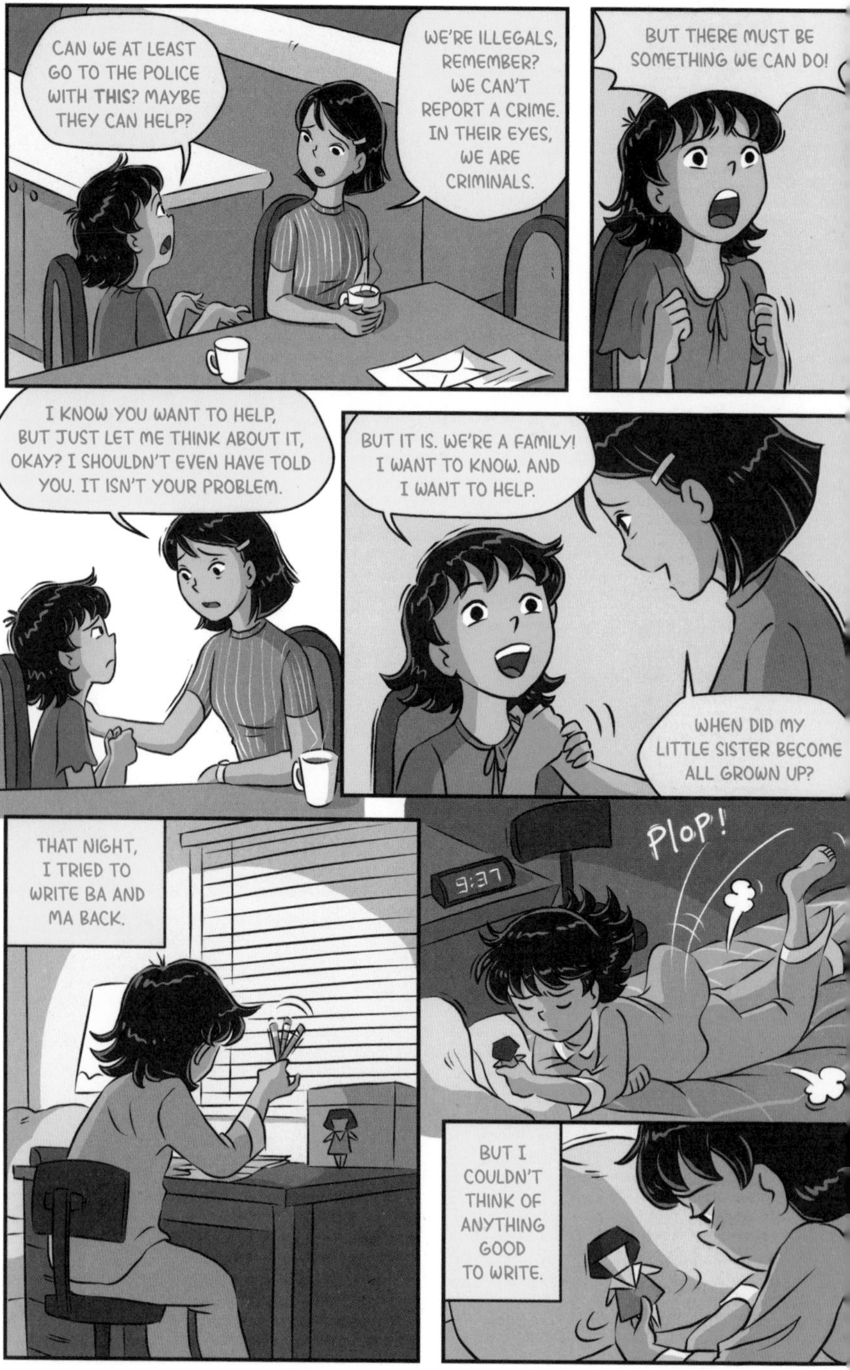
CAN WE AT LEAST GO TO THE POLICE WITH THIS? MAYBE THEY CAN HELP?
WE'RE ILLEGALS, REMEMBER? WE CAN'T REPORT A CRIME. IN THEIR EYES, WE ARE CRIMINALS.
BUT THERE MUST BE SOMETHING WE CAN DO!
I KNOW YOU WANT TO HELP, BUT JUST LET ME THINK ABOUT IT, OKAY? I SHOULDN'T EVEN HAVE TOLD YOU. IT ISN'T YOUR PROBLEM.
BUT IT IS. WE'RE A FAMILY! I WANT TO KNOW. AND I WANT TO HELP.
WHEN DID MY LITTLE SISTER BECOME ALL GROWN UP?
THAT NIGHT, I TRIED TO WRITE BA AND MA BACK.
9:37
PLOP!
BUT I COULDN'T THINK OF ANYTHING GOOD TO WRITE.

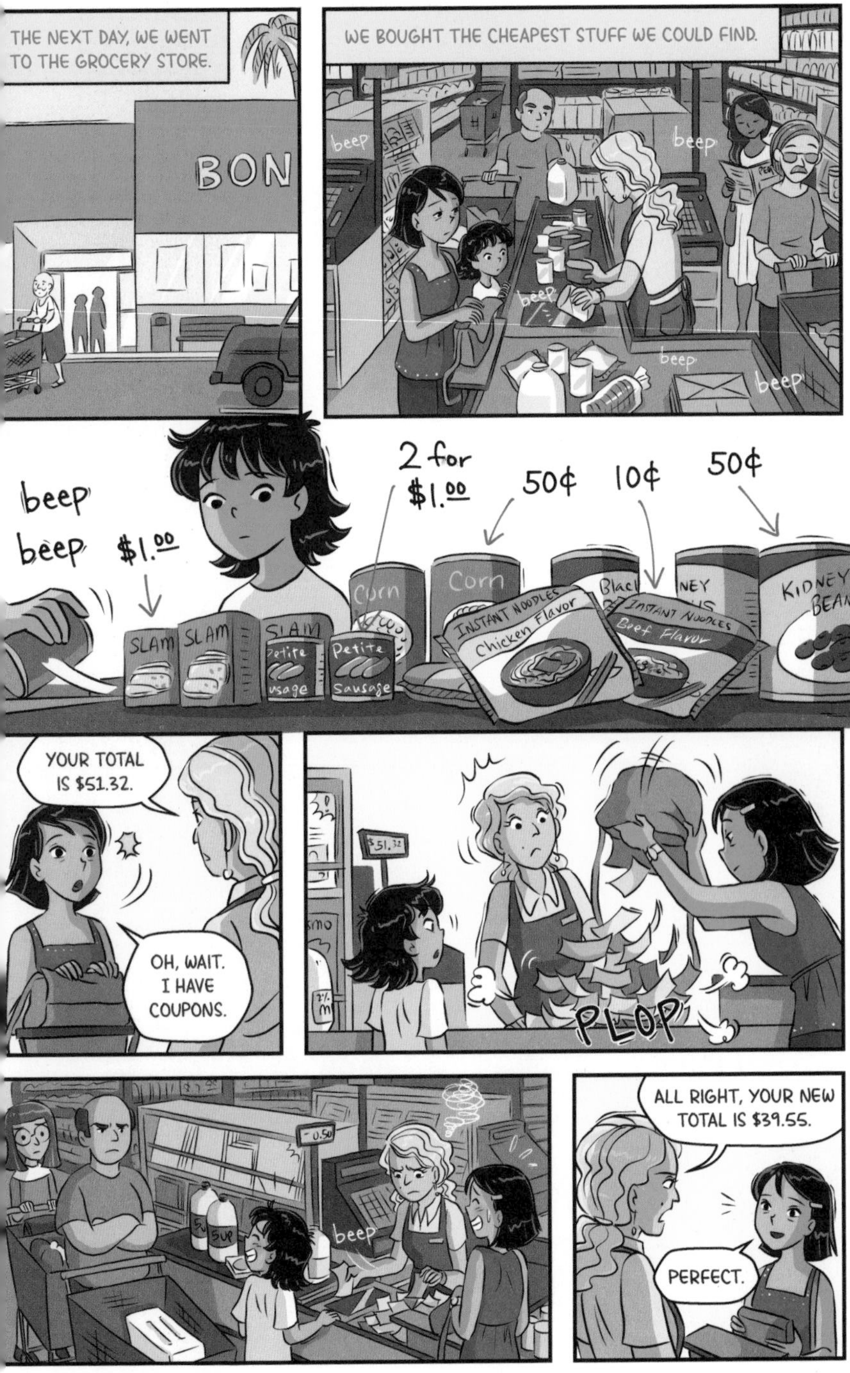
THE NEXT DAY, WE WENT TO THE GROCERY STORE.
BON
WE BOUGHT THE CHEAPEST STUFF WE COULD FIND.
beep
beep
beep
beep
beep
beep
beep
$1.00
2 for $1.00
50¢
10¢
50¢
SLAM
SLAM
SLAM
Petite Sausage
Petite Sausage
Corn
Corn
INSTANT NOODLES Chicken Flavor
INSTANT NOODLES Beef Flavor
KIDNEY BEANS
YOUR TOTAL IS $51.32.
OH, WAIT. I HAVE COUPONS.
$51.32
PLOP
beep
ALL RIGHT, YOUR NEW TOTAL IS $39.55.
PERFECT.

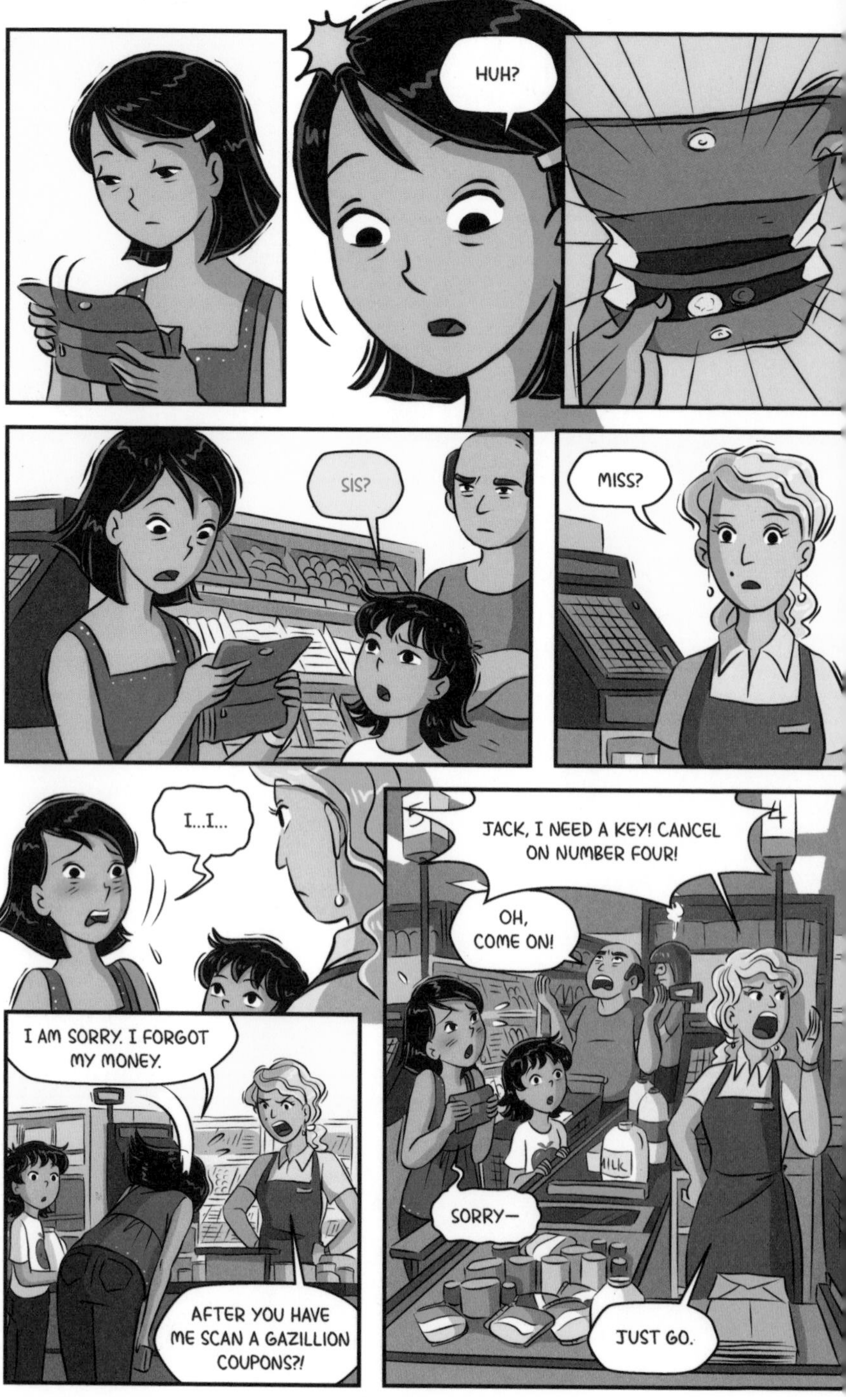
HUH?
SIS?
MISS?
I...I...
I AM SORRY. I FORGOT MY MONEY.
AFTER YOU HAVE ME SCAN A GAZILLION COUPONS?!
JACK, I NEED A KEY! CANCEL ON NUMBER FOUR!
OH, COME ON!
SORRY—
MILK
JUST GO.

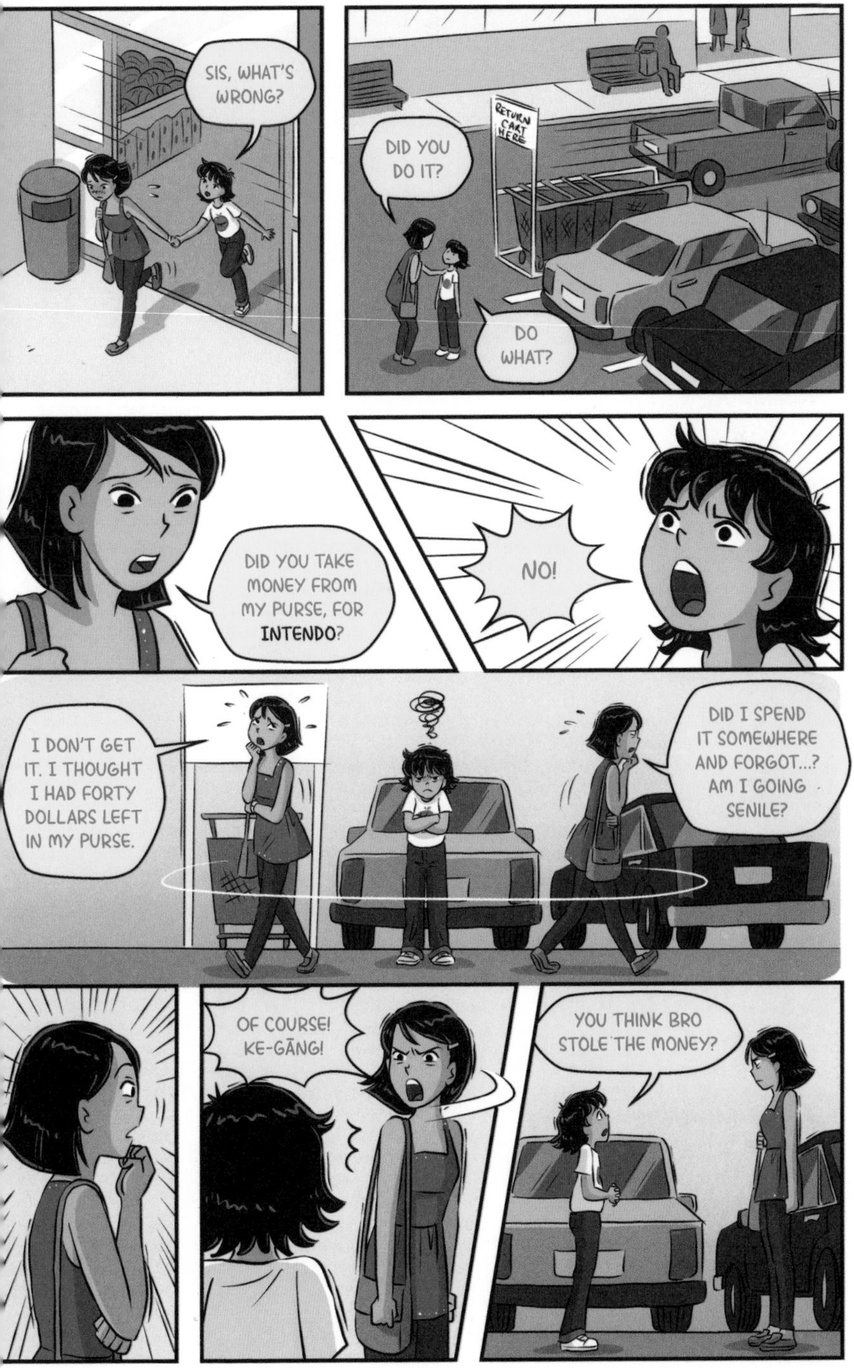
SIS, WHAT'S WRONG?
DID YOU DO IT?
RETURN CART HERE
DO WHAT?
DID YOU TAKE MONEY FROM MY PURSE, FOR INTENDO?
NO!
I DON'T GET IT. I THOUGHT I HAD FORTY DOLLARS LEFT IN MY PURSE.
DID I SPEND IT SOMEWHERE AND FORGOT...? AM I GOING SENILE?
OF COURSE! KE-GĀNG!
YOU THINK BRO STOLE THE MONEY?

KE-GĀNG!

KE-GĀNG!

OF COURSE HE ISN'T HOME!

RIIIINNNG

RIIIINNGG!

RIIIINNGG!!

RIIIINNG!!

SHOULD I?

NO!

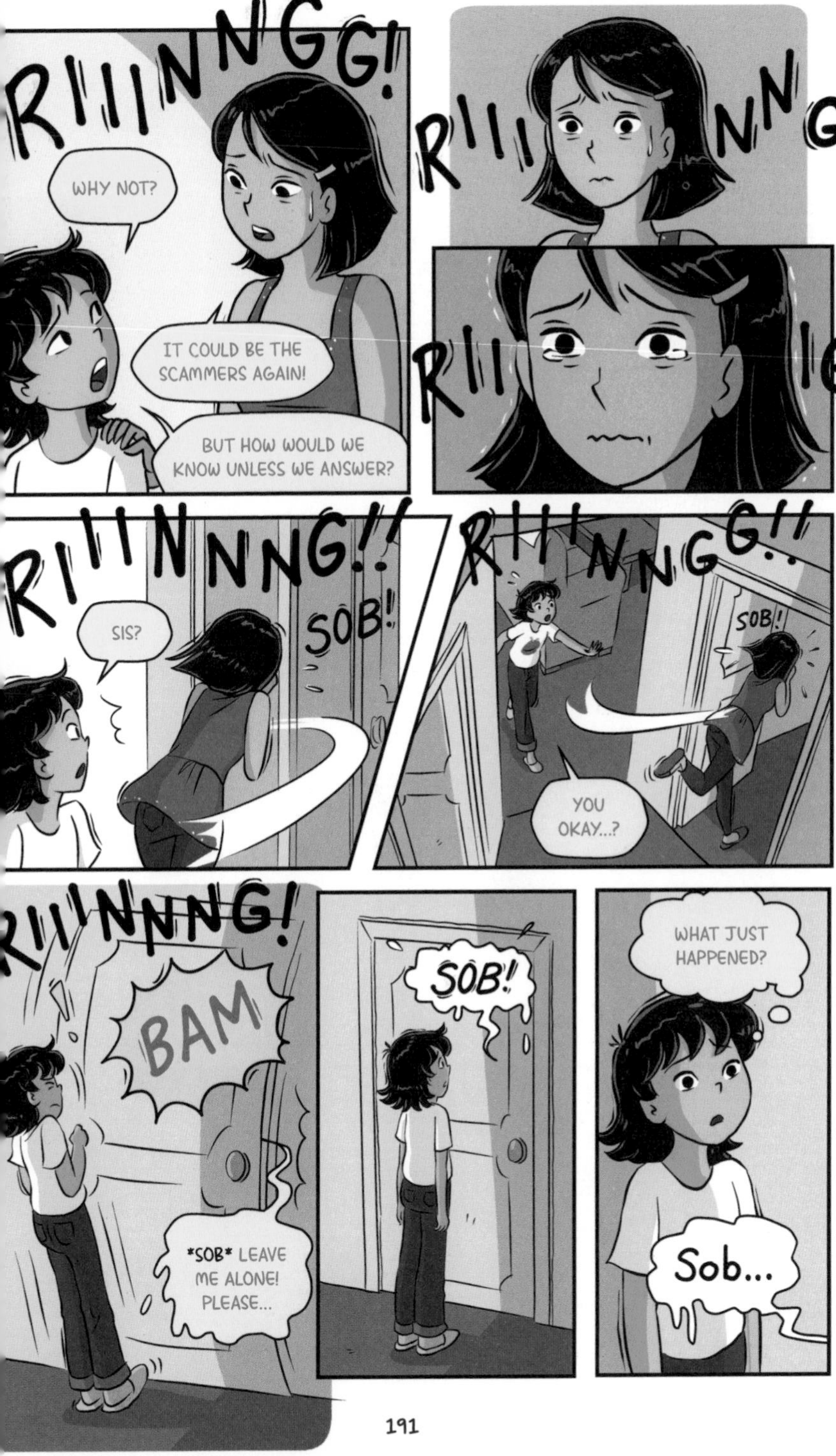
RIIINNGG!
WHY NOT?
IT COULD BE THE SCAMMERS AGAIN!
BUT HOW WOULD WE KNOW UNLESS WE ANSWER?
RIIINNG!
RIIIG!
RIIINNNG!!
SIS?
SOB!
RIIINNGG!!
SOB!
YOU OKAY...?
RIIINNNG!
BAM
SOB LEAVE ME ALONE! PLEASE...
SOB!
WHAT JUST HAPPENED?
Sob...

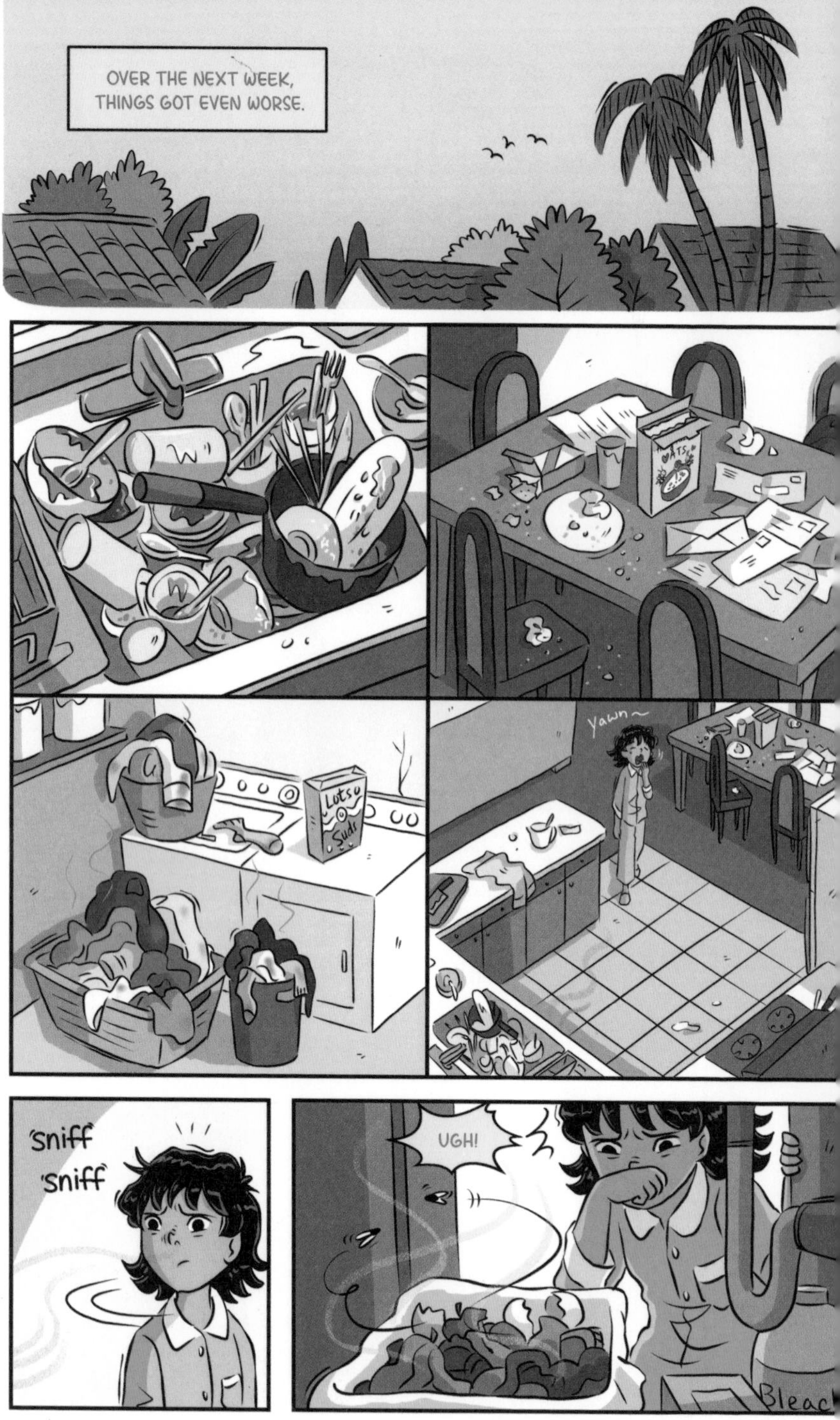
OVER THE NEXT WEEK, THINGS GOT EVEN WORSE.
OATS
Lots o Suds
Yawn~
Sniff
Sniff
UGH!
Bleac

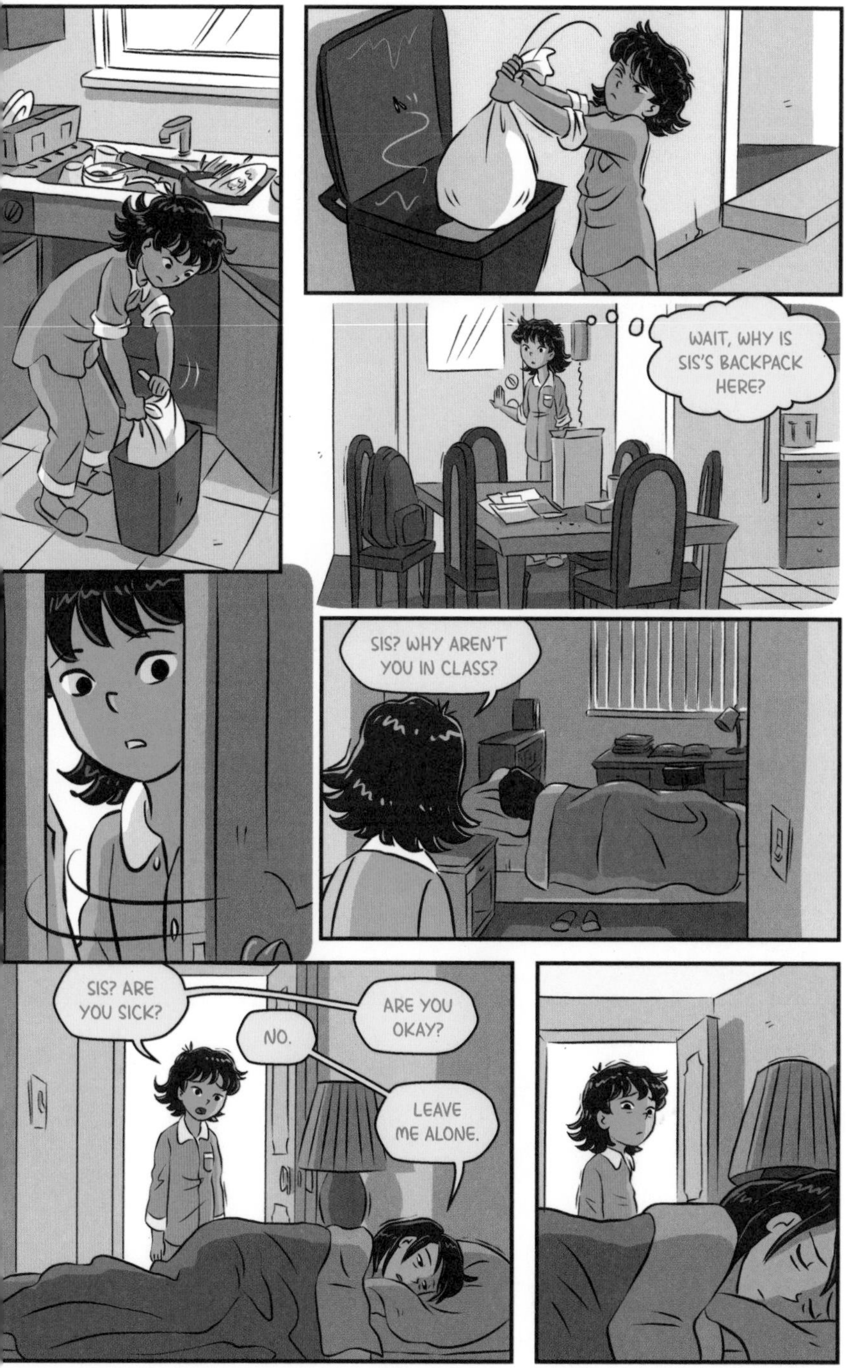
WAIT, WHY IS SIS'S BACKPACK HERE?
SIS? WHY AREN'T YOU IN CLASS?
SIS? ARE YOU SICK?
ARE YOU OKAY?
NO.
LEAVE ME ALONE.

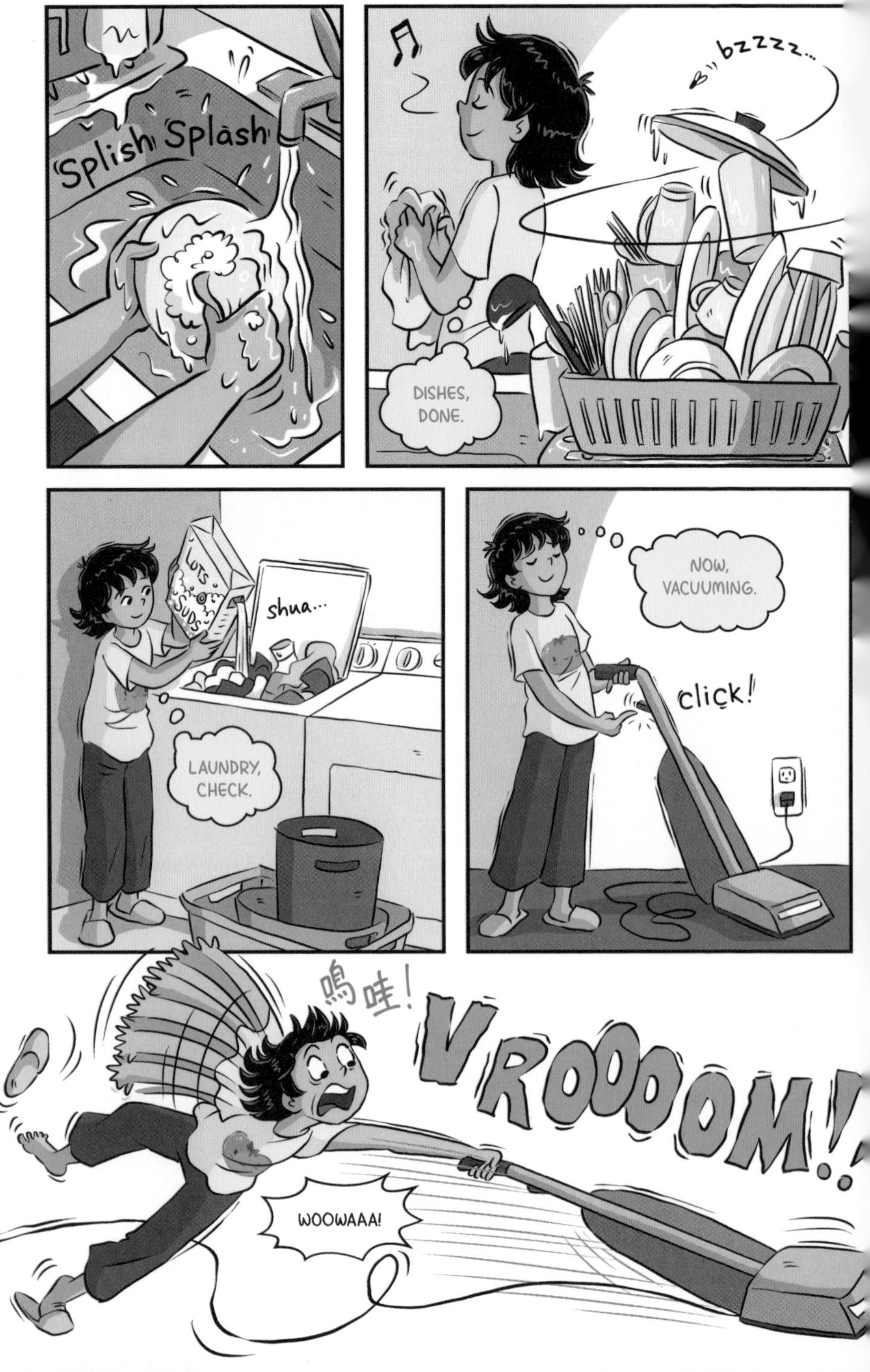

Splish Splash
bzzzz...
DISHES, DONE.
LOTS O SUDS
shua...
LAUNDRY, CHECK.
NOW, VACUUMING.
click!
嗚哇!
VROOOOM!!
WOOWAAA!

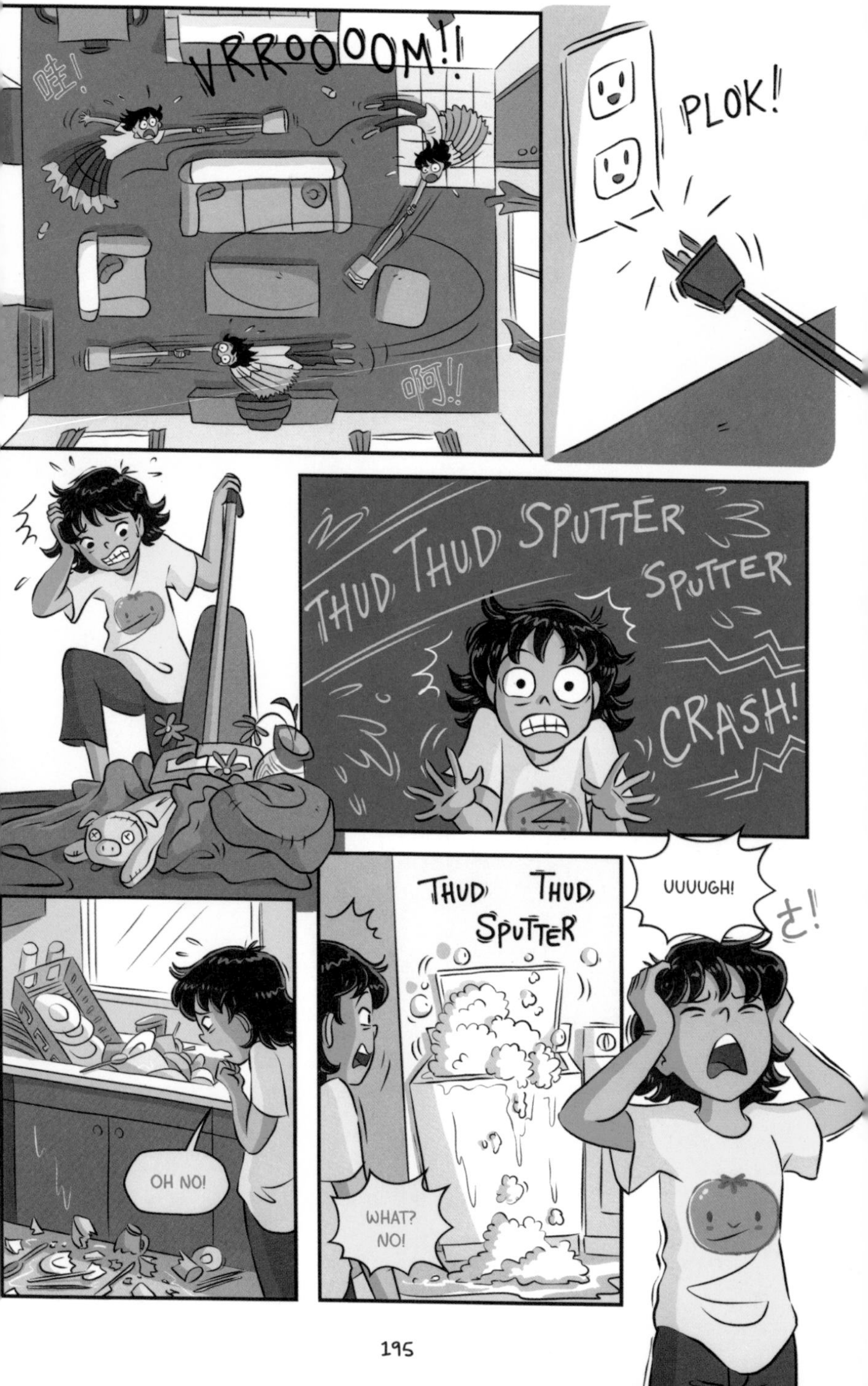
VRROOOOM!!
哇!
啊!!
PLOK!
THUD THUD SPUTTER
SPUTTER
CRASH!
UUUUGH!
さ!
OH NO!
THUD THUD
SPUTTER
WHAT? NO!

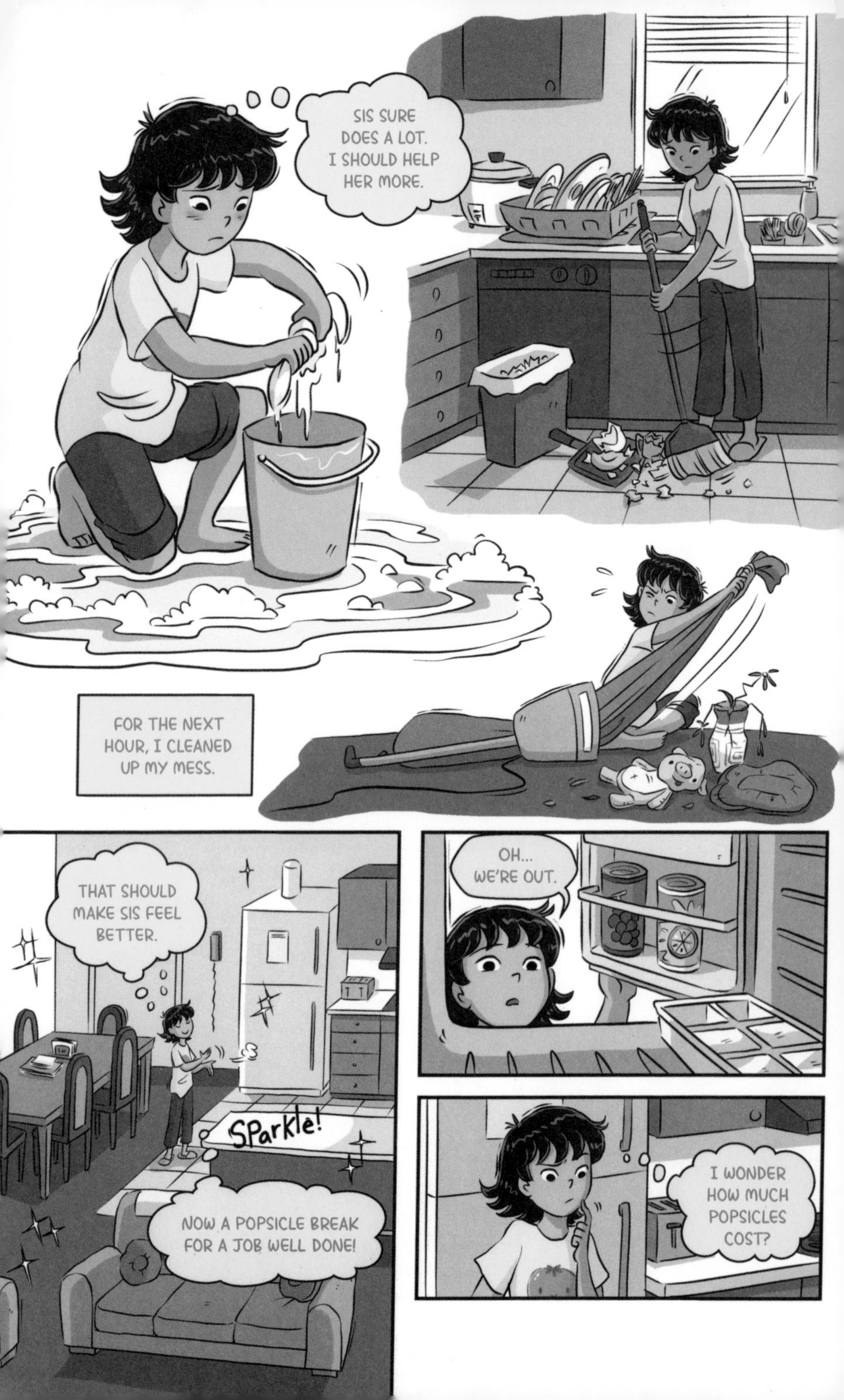
SIS SURE DOES A LOT. I SHOULD HELP HER MORE.
FOR THE NEXT HOUR, I CLEANED UP MY MESS.
THAT SHOULD MAKE SIS FEEL BETTER.
SPARKLE!
NOW A POPSICLE BREAK FOR A JOB WELL DONE!
OH... WE'RE OUT.
I WONDER HOW MUCH POPSICLES COST?

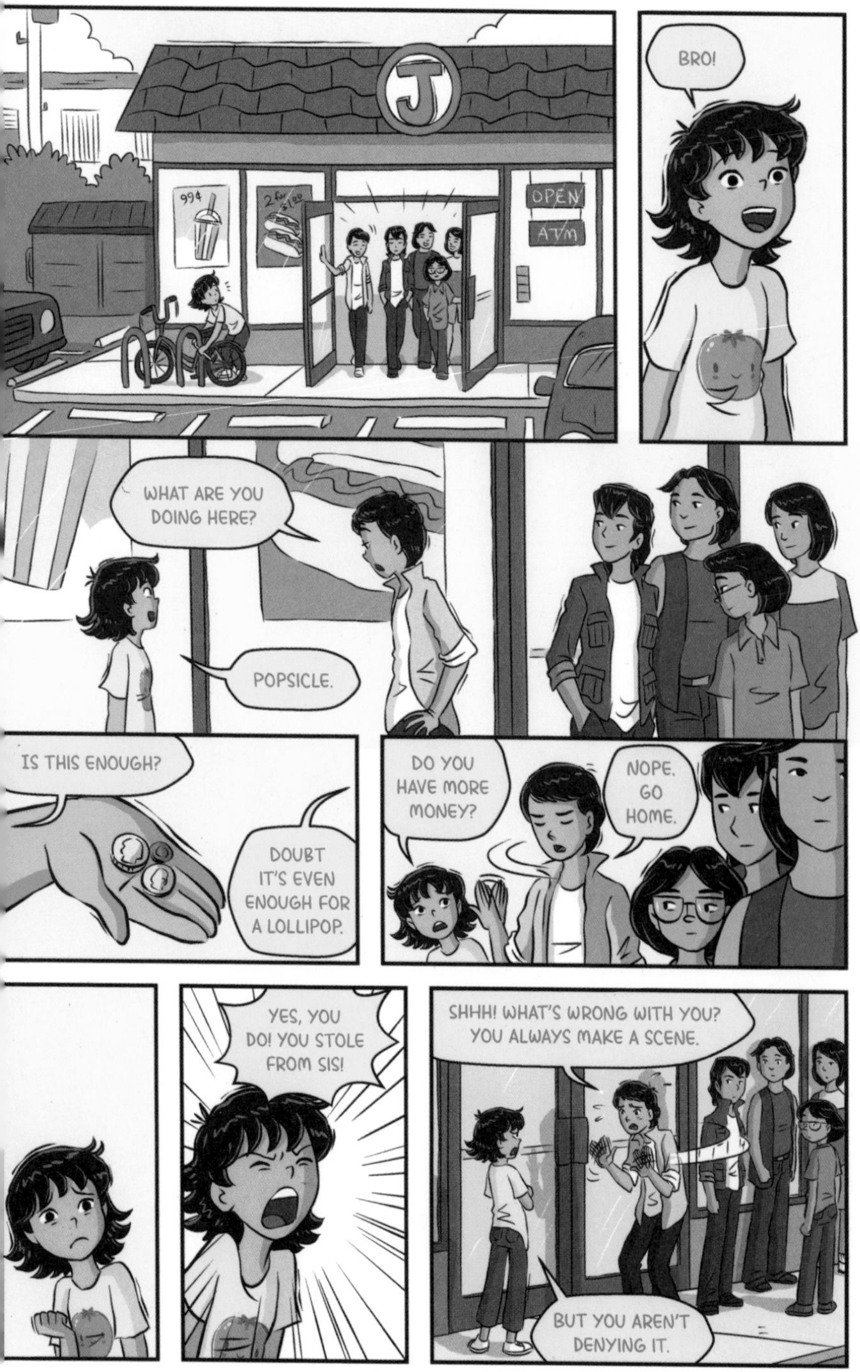

OPEN
ATM
99¢
2 for $1.00
BRO!
WHAT ARE YOU DOING HERE?
POPSICLE.
IS THIS ENOUGH?
DOUBT IT'S EVEN ENOUGH FOR A LOLLIPOP.
DO YOU HAVE MORE MONEY?
NOPE. GO HOME.
YES, YOU DO! YOU STOLE FROM SIS!
SHHH! WHAT'S WRONG WITH YOU? YOU ALWAYS MAKE A SCENE.
BUT YOU AREN'T DENYING IT.

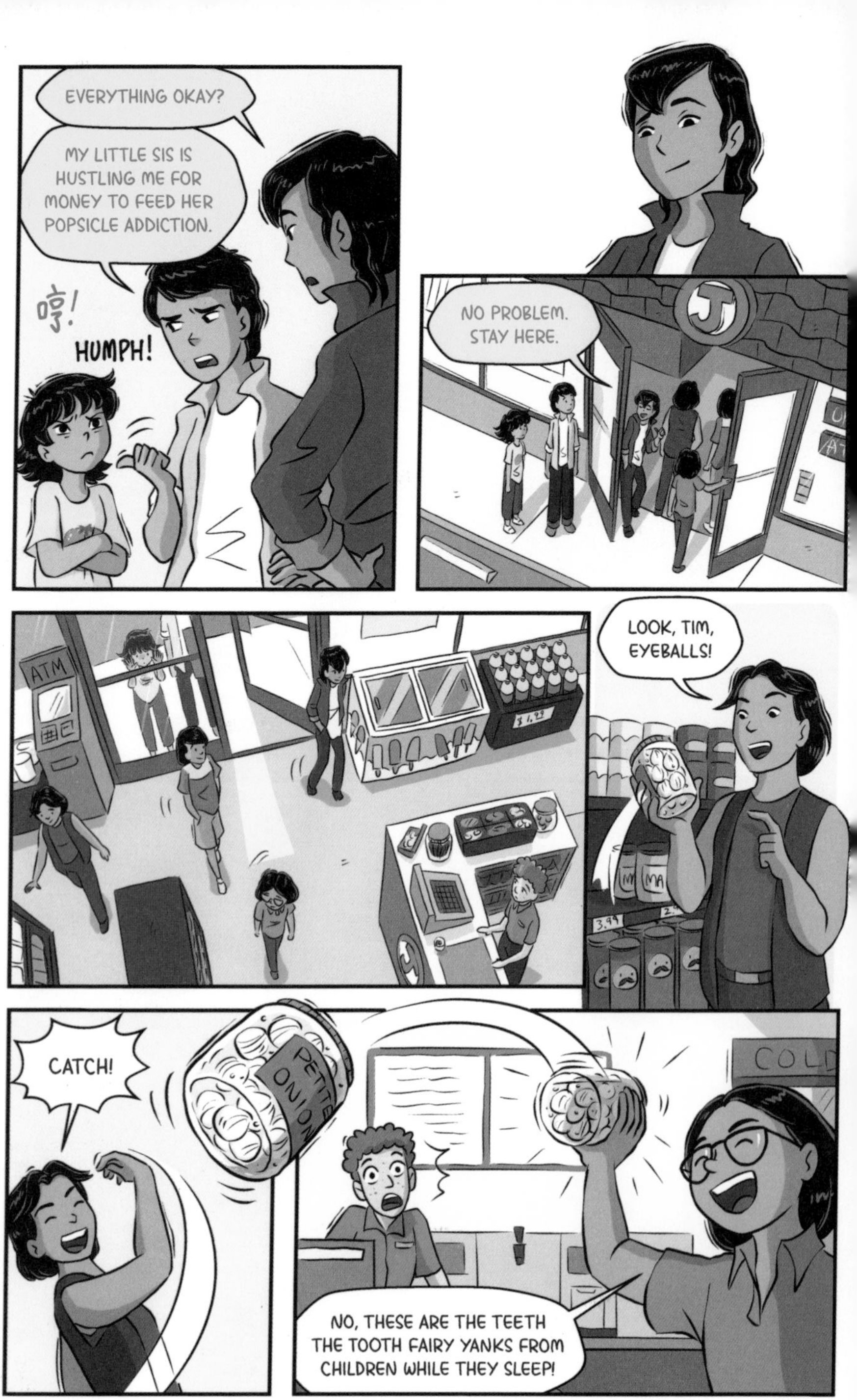
EVERYTHING OKAY?
MY LITTLE SIS IS HUSTLING ME FOR MONEY TO FEED HER POPSICLE ADDICTION.
哼!
HUMPH!
NO PROBLEM. STAY HERE.
ATM
$1.99
LOOK, TIM, EYEBALLS!
3.99
CATCH!
PETITE ONION
COLD
NO, THESE ARE THE TEETH THE TOOTH FAIRY YANKS FROM CHILDREN WHILE THEY SLEEP!

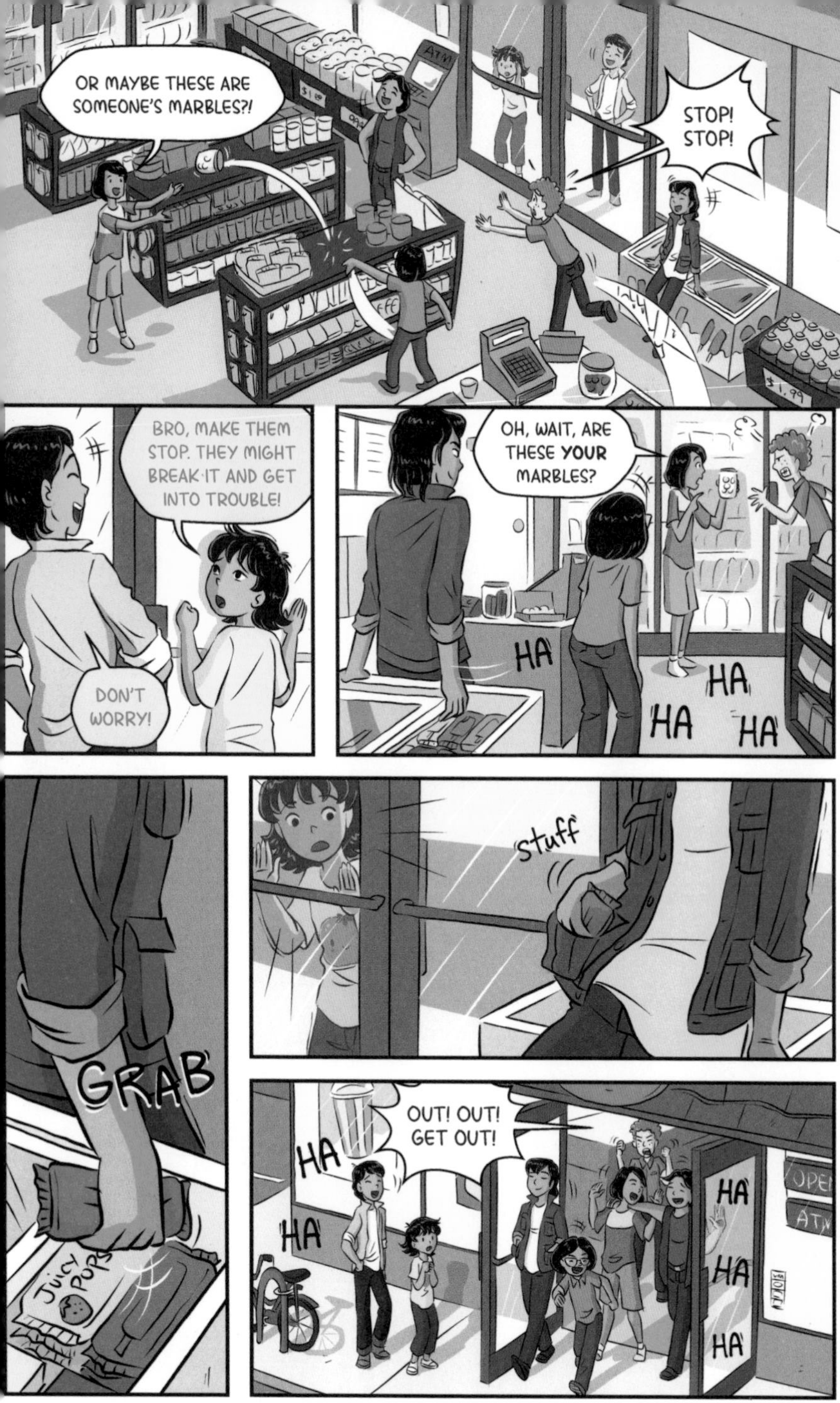

OR MAYBE THESE ARE SOMEONE'S MARBLES?!
STOP! STOP!
ATM
$1.99
BRO, MAKE THEM STOP. THEY MIGHT BREAK IT AND GET INTO TROUBLE!
DON'T WORRY!
OH, WAIT, ARE THESE **YOUR** MARBLES?
HA
HA
HA
HA
GRAB
Juicy POPS
stuff
OUT! OUT! GET OUT!
HA
HA
HA
HA
HA
OPEN
ATM

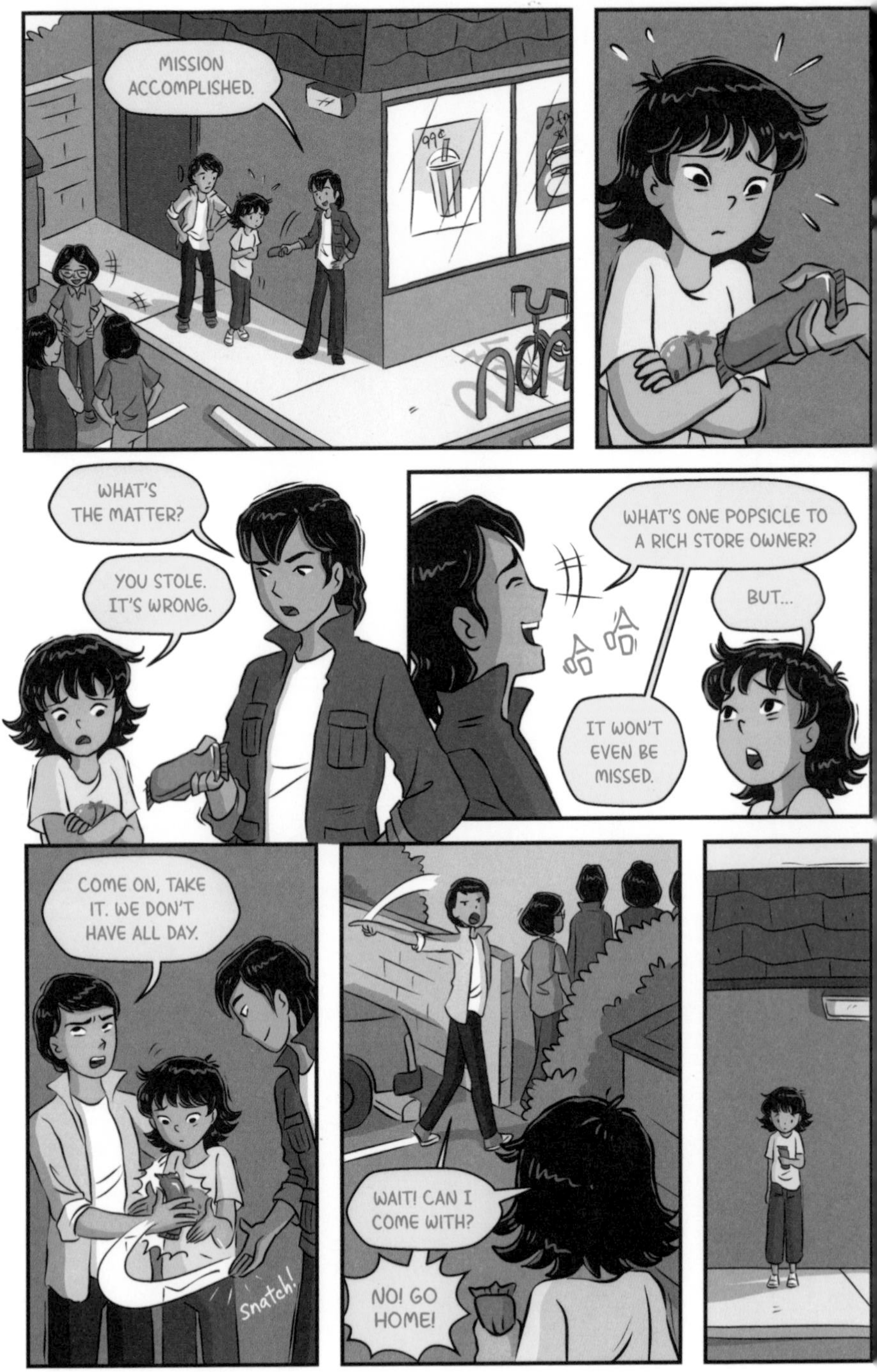
MISSION ACCOMPLISHED.
WHAT'S THE MATTER?
YOU STOLE. IT'S WRONG.
WHAT'S ONE POPSICLE TO A RICH STORE OWNER?
IT WON'T EVEN BE MISSED.
BUT...
COME ON, TAKE IT. WE DON'T HAVE ALL DAY.
Snatch!
WAIT! CAN I COME WITH?
NO! GO HOME!

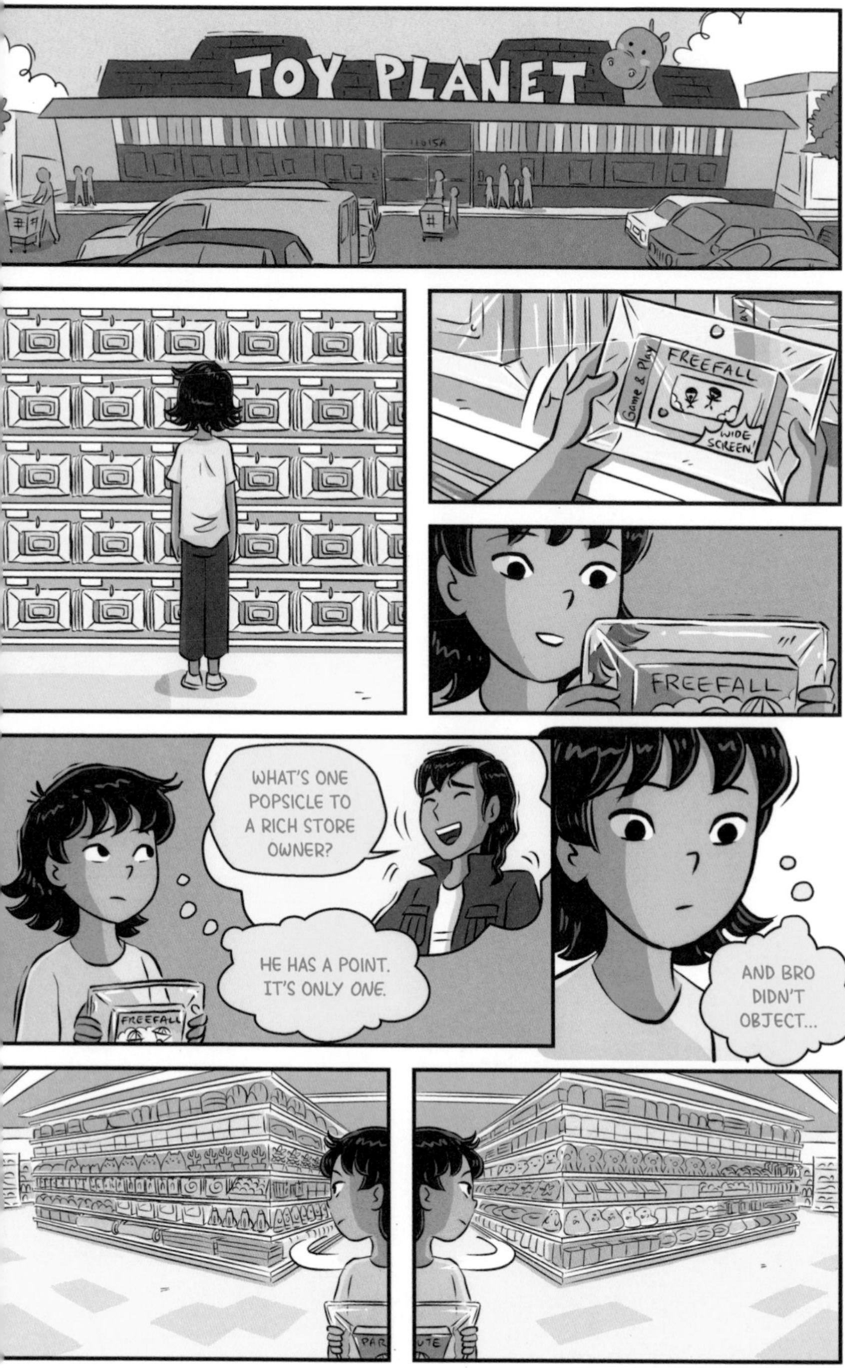
TOY PLANET
FREEFALL
Game & Play
WIDE SCREEN!
FREEFALL
WHAT'S ONE POPSICLE TO A RICH STORE OWNER?
HE HAS A POINT. IT'S ONLY ONE.
FREEFALL
AND BRO DIDN'T OBJECT...

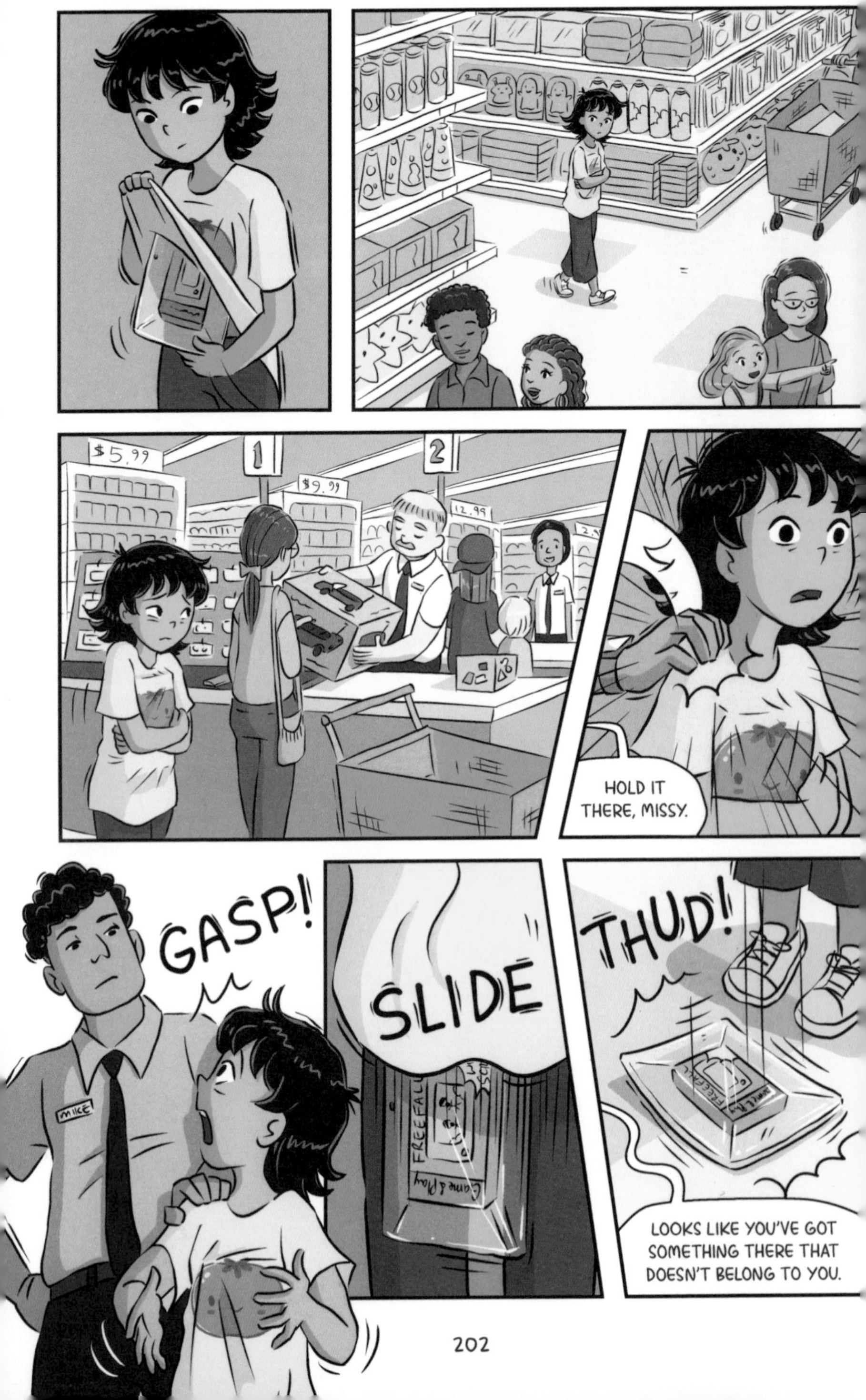
$5.99
1
2
$9.99
12.99
HOLD IT THERE, MISSY.
MIKE
GASP!
SLIDE
FREEFALL
Game & Play
THUD!
LOOKS LIKE YOU'VE GOT SOMETHING THERE THAT DOESN'T BELONG TO YOU.

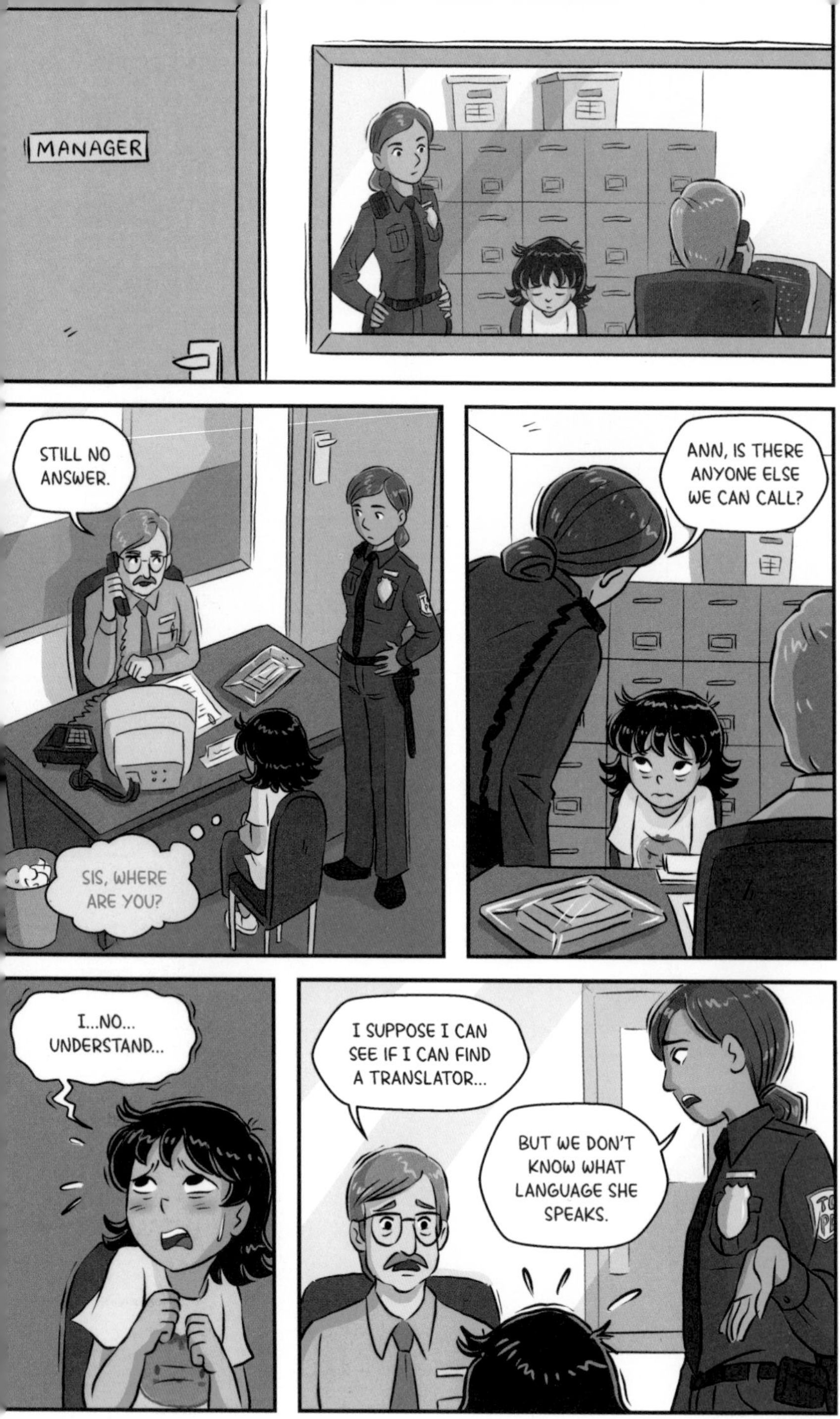
MANAGER
STILL NO ANSWER.
SIS, WHERE ARE YOU?
ANN, IS THERE ANYONE ELSE WE CAN CALL?
I...NO... UNDERSTAND...
I SUPPOSE I CAN SEE IF I CAN FIND A TRANSLATOR...
BUT WE DON'T KNOW WHAT LANGUAGE SHE SPEAKS.

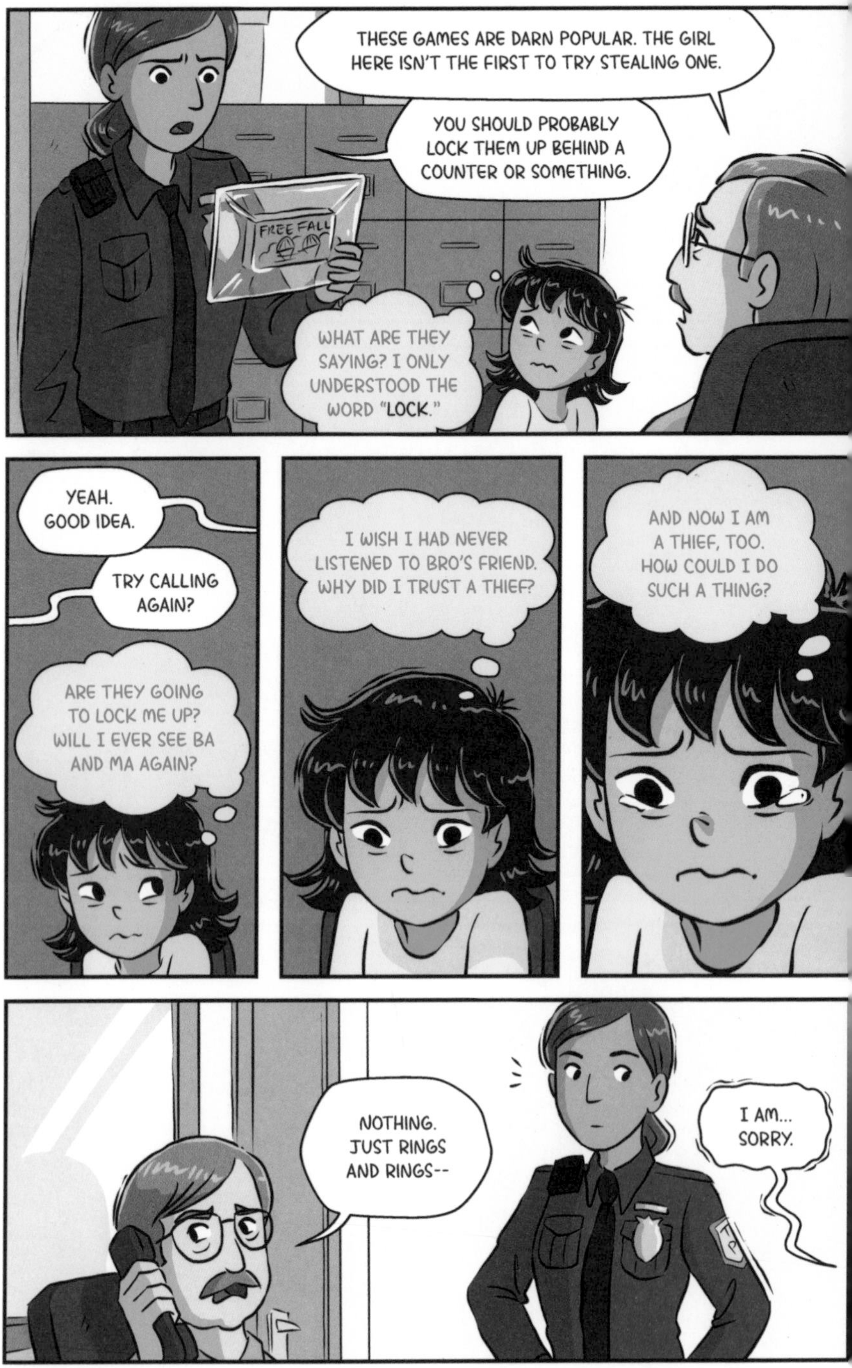
THESE GAMES ARE DARN POPULAR. THE GIRL HERE ISN'T THE FIRST TO TRY STEALING ONE.
YOU SHOULD PROBABLY LOCK THEM UP BEHIND A COUNTER OR SOMETHING.
FREE FALL
WHAT ARE THEY SAYING? I ONLY UNDERSTOOD THE WORD "LOCK."
YEAH. GOOD IDEA.
TRY CALLING AGAIN?
ARE THEY GOING TO LOCK ME UP? WILL I EVER SEE BA AND MA AGAIN?
I WISH I HAD NEVER LISTENED TO BRO'S FRIEND. WHY DID I TRUST A THIEF?
AND NOW I AM A THIEF, TOO. HOW COULD I DO SUCH A THING?
NOTHING. JUST RINGS AND RINGS--
I AM... SORRY.

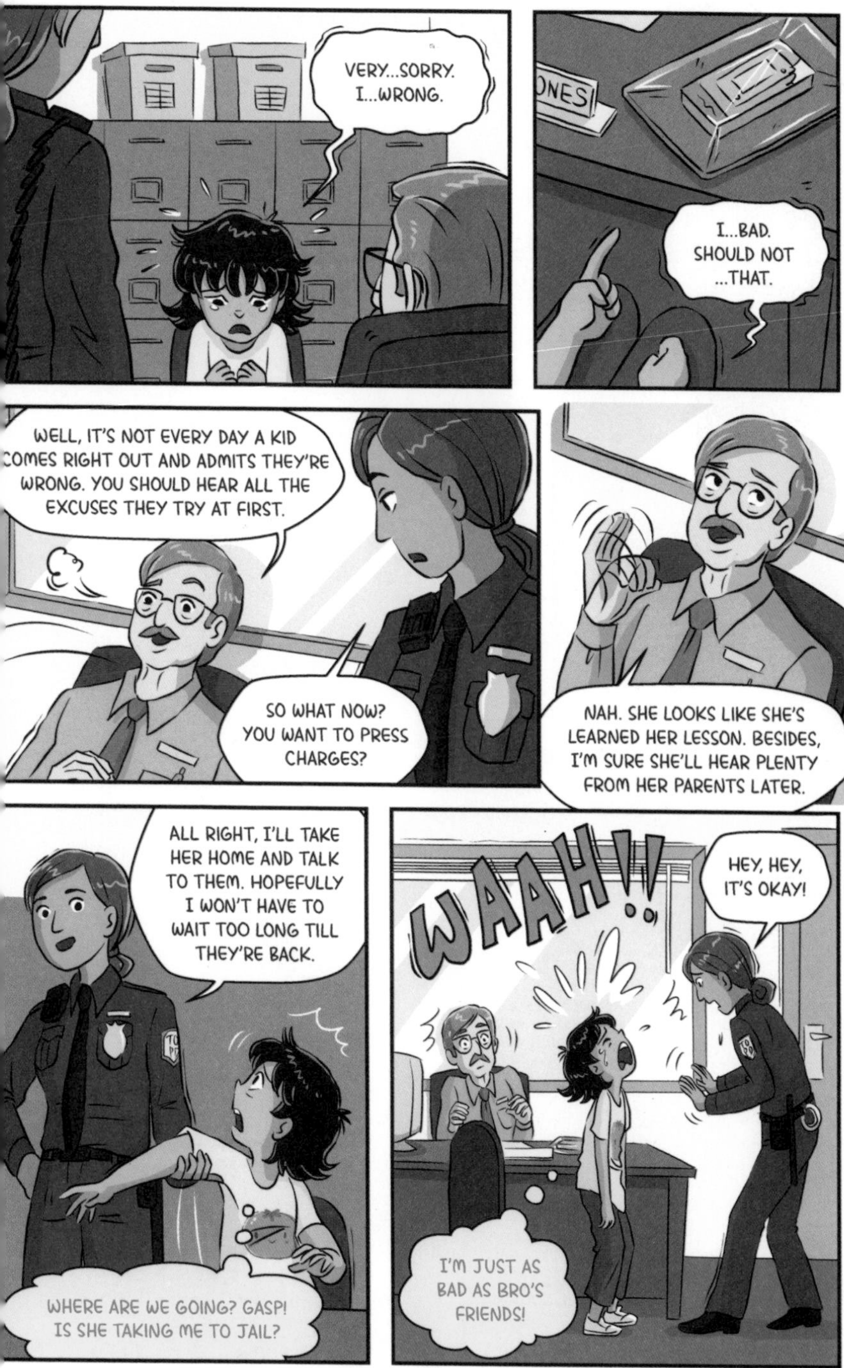
VERY...SORRY.
I...WRONG.
ONES
I...BAD.
SHOULD NOT
...THAT.
WELL, IT'S NOT EVERY DAY A KID COMES RIGHT OUT AND ADMITS THEY'RE WRONG. YOU SHOULD HEAR ALL THE EXCUSES THEY TRY AT FIRST.
SO WHAT NOW? YOU WANT TO PRESS CHARGES?
NAH. SHE LOOKS LIKE SHE'S LEARNED HER LESSON. BESIDES, I'M SURE SHE'LL HEAR PLENTY FROM HER PARENTS LATER.
ALL RIGHT, I'LL TAKE HER HOME AND TALK TO THEM. HOPEFULLY I WON'T HAVE TO WAIT TOO LONG TILL THEY'RE BACK.
WHERE ARE WE GOING? GASP! IS SHE TAKING ME TO JAIL?
WAAH!!
HEY, HEY, IT'S OKAY!
I'M JUST AS BAD AS BRO'S FRIENDS!

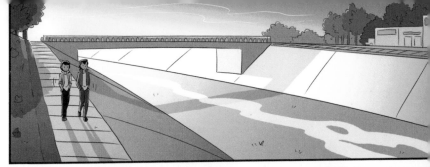

DO YOU MISS HOME, **PETE**?

DON'T START. IT'LL JUST DRAG YOU DOWN.

DO YOU?

ALL THE TIME.

I MISS THE PEOPLE, THE CROWDS, AND THE HUSTLE AND BUSTLE OF LIFE. HERE IT'S LIKE A GHOST TOWN IN THE EVENINGS, WITH EVERYONE HIDING INSIDE THEIR HOMES.

YEAH.

I MISS THE STREET FOOD VENDORS, THE NIGHTLIFE, THE RAIN, AND, I CAN'T BELIEVE I'M SAYING THIS, BUT I EVEN MISS THE HUMIDITY.

THAT'S ONE THING I'LL NEVER MISS.

HEY, SO WHY DID YOUR PARENTS BRING YOU HERE?

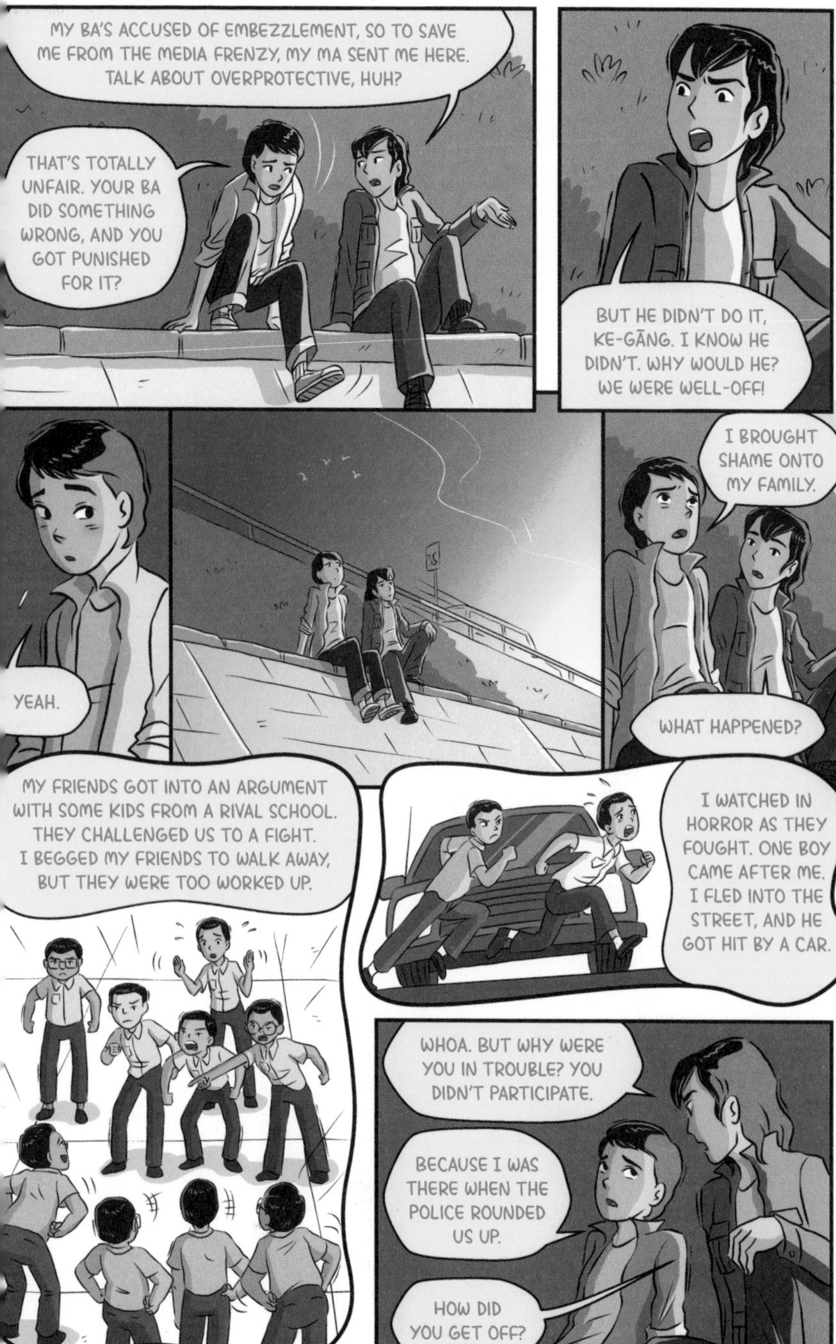
MY BA'S ACCUSED OF EMBEZZLEMENT, SO TO SAVE ME FROM THE MEDIA FRENZY, MY MA SENT ME HERE. TALK ABOUT OVERPROTECTIVE, HUH?
THAT'S TOTALLY UNFAIR. YOUR BA DID SOMETHING WRONG, AND YOU GOT PUNISHED FOR IT?
BUT HE DIDN'T DO IT, KE-GĀNG. I KNOW HE DIDN'T. WHY WOULD HE? WE WERE WELL-OFF!
YEAH.
I BROUGHT SHAME ONTO MY FAMILY.
WHAT HAPPENED?
MY FRIENDS GOT INTO AN ARGUMENT WITH SOME KIDS FROM A RIVAL SCHOOL. THEY CHALLENGED US TO A FIGHT. I BEGGED MY FRIENDS TO WALK AWAY, BUT THEY WERE TOO WORKED UP.
I WATCHED IN HORROR AS THEY FOUGHT. ONE BOY CAME AFTER ME. I FLED INTO THE STREET, AND HE GOT HIT BY A CAR.
WHOA. BUT WHY WERE YOU IN TROUBLE? YOU DIDN'T PARTICIPATE.
BECAUSE I WAS THERE WHEN THE POLICE ROUNDED US UP.
HOW DID YOU GET OFF?

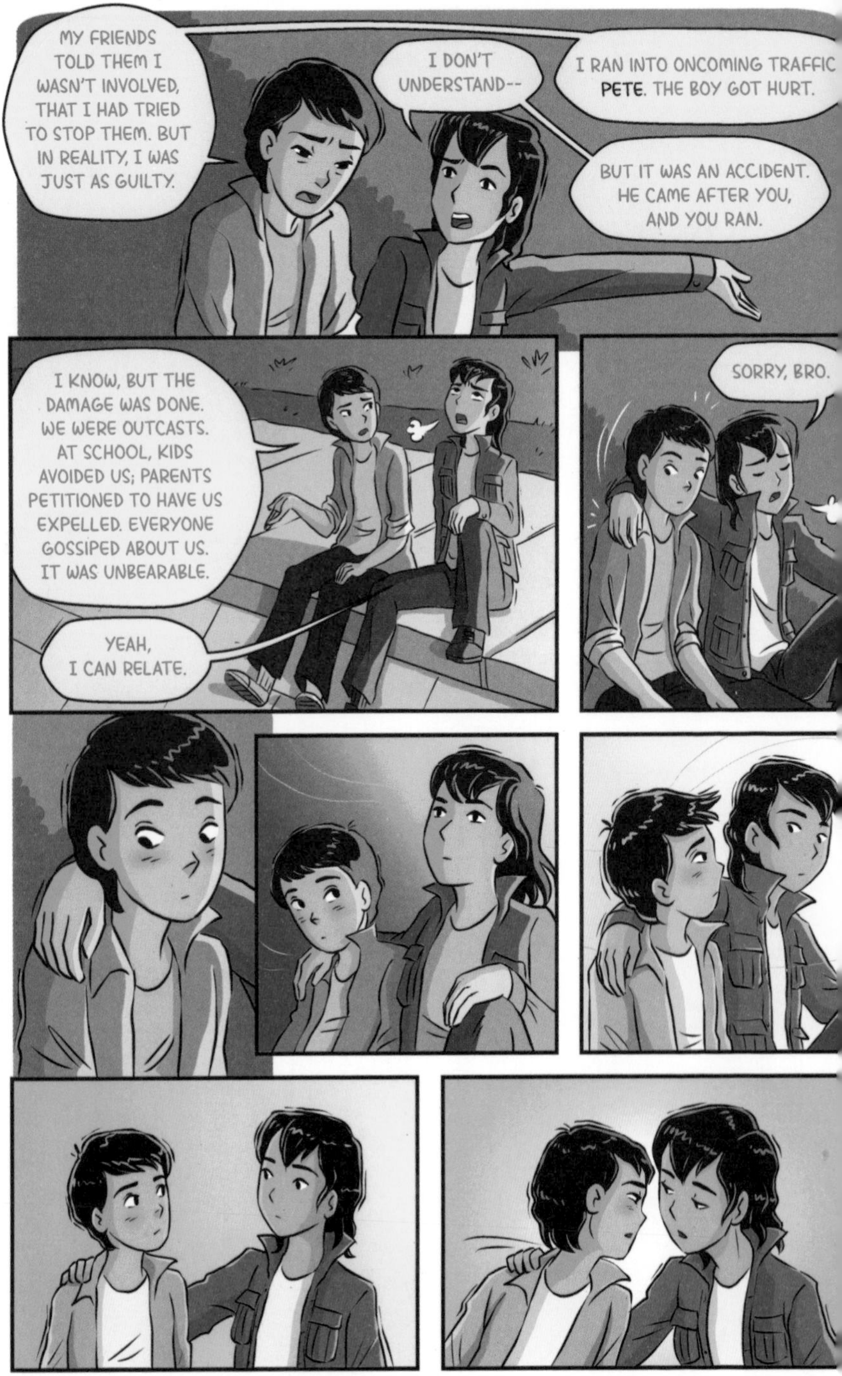
MY FRIENDS TOLD THEM I WASN'T INVOLVED, THAT I HAD TRIED TO STOP THEM. BUT IN REALITY, I WAS JUST AS GUILTY.
I DON'T UNDERSTAND--
I RAN INTO ONCOMING TRAFFIC PETE. THE BOY GOT HURT.
BUT IT WAS AN ACCIDENT. HE CAME AFTER YOU, AND YOU RAN.
I KNOW, BUT THE DAMAGE WAS DONE. WE WERE OUTCASTS. AT SCHOOL, KIDS AVOIDED US; PARENTS PETITIONED TO HAVE US EXPELLED. EVERYONE GOSSIPED ABOUT US. IT WAS UNBEARABLE.
YEAH, I CAN RELATE.
SORRY, BRO.

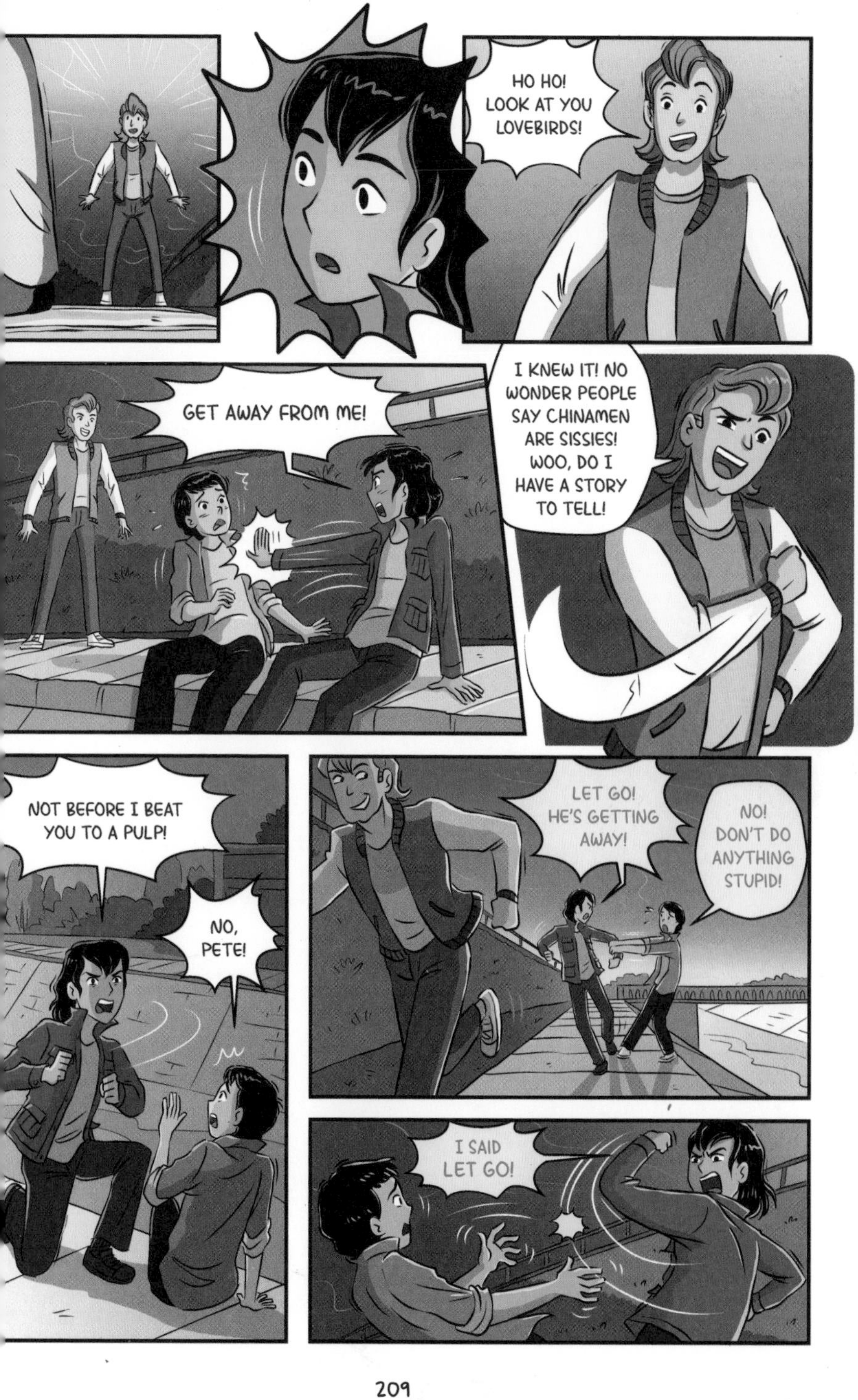
HO HO!
LOOK AT YOU
LOVEBIRDS!
GET AWAY FROM ME!
I KNEW IT! NO WONDER PEOPLE SAY CHINAMEN ARE SISSIES! WOO, DO I HAVE A STORY TO TELL!
NOT BEFORE I BEAT YOU TO A PULP!
NO, PETE!
LET GO! HE'S GETTING AWAY!
NO! DON'T DO ANYTHING STUPID!
I SAID LET GO!

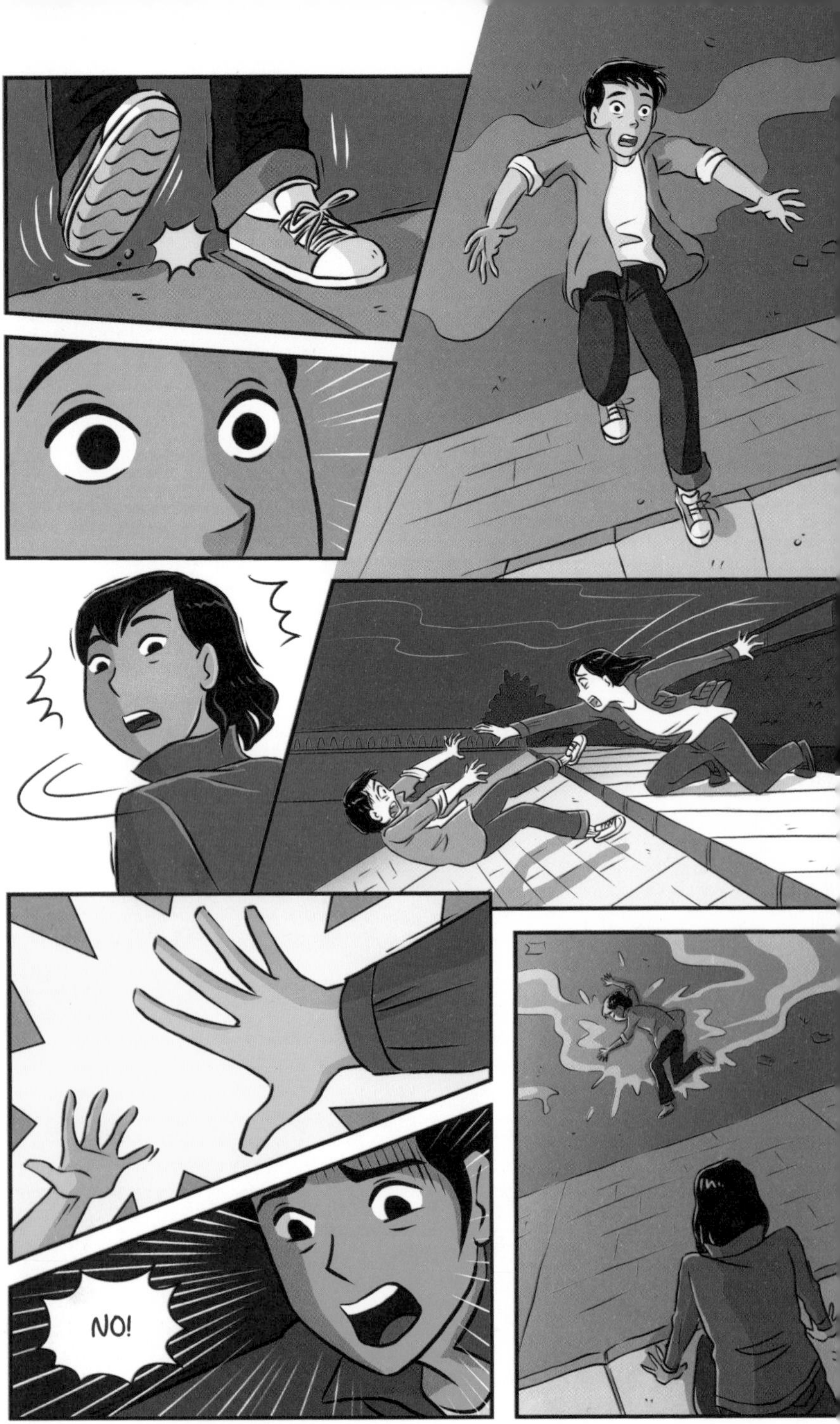
NO!

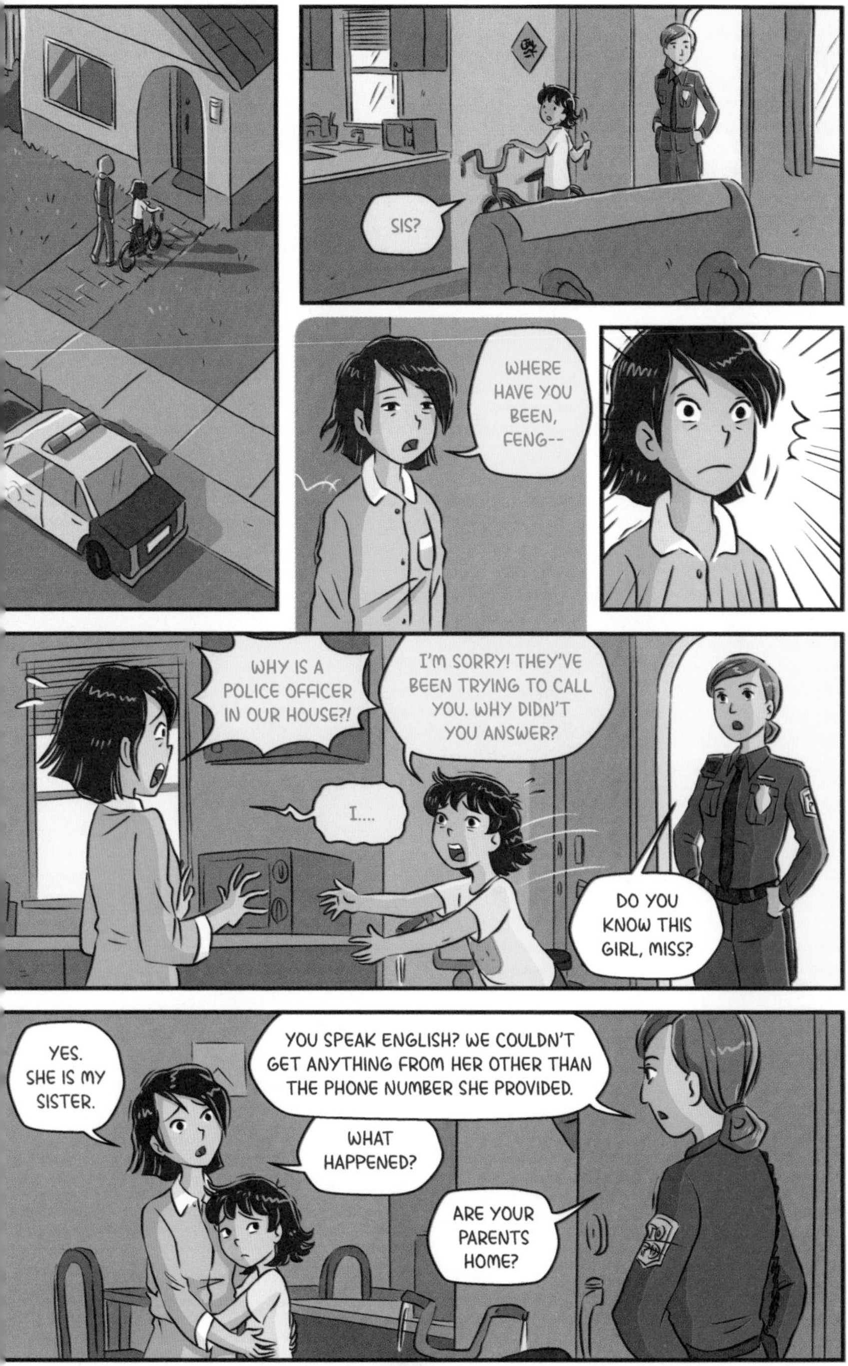
SIS?
WHERE HAVE YOU BEEN, FENG--
WHY IS A POLICE OFFICER IN OUR HOUSE?!
I'M SORRY! THEY'VE BEEN TRYING TO CALL YOU. WHY DIDN'T YOU ANSWER?
I....
DO YOU KNOW THIS GIRL, MISS?
YES. SHE IS MY SISTER.
YOU SPEAK ENGLISH? WE COULDN'T GET ANYTHING FROM HER OTHER THAN THE PHONE NUMBER SHE PROVIDED.
WHAT HAPPENED?
ARE YOUR PARENTS HOME?

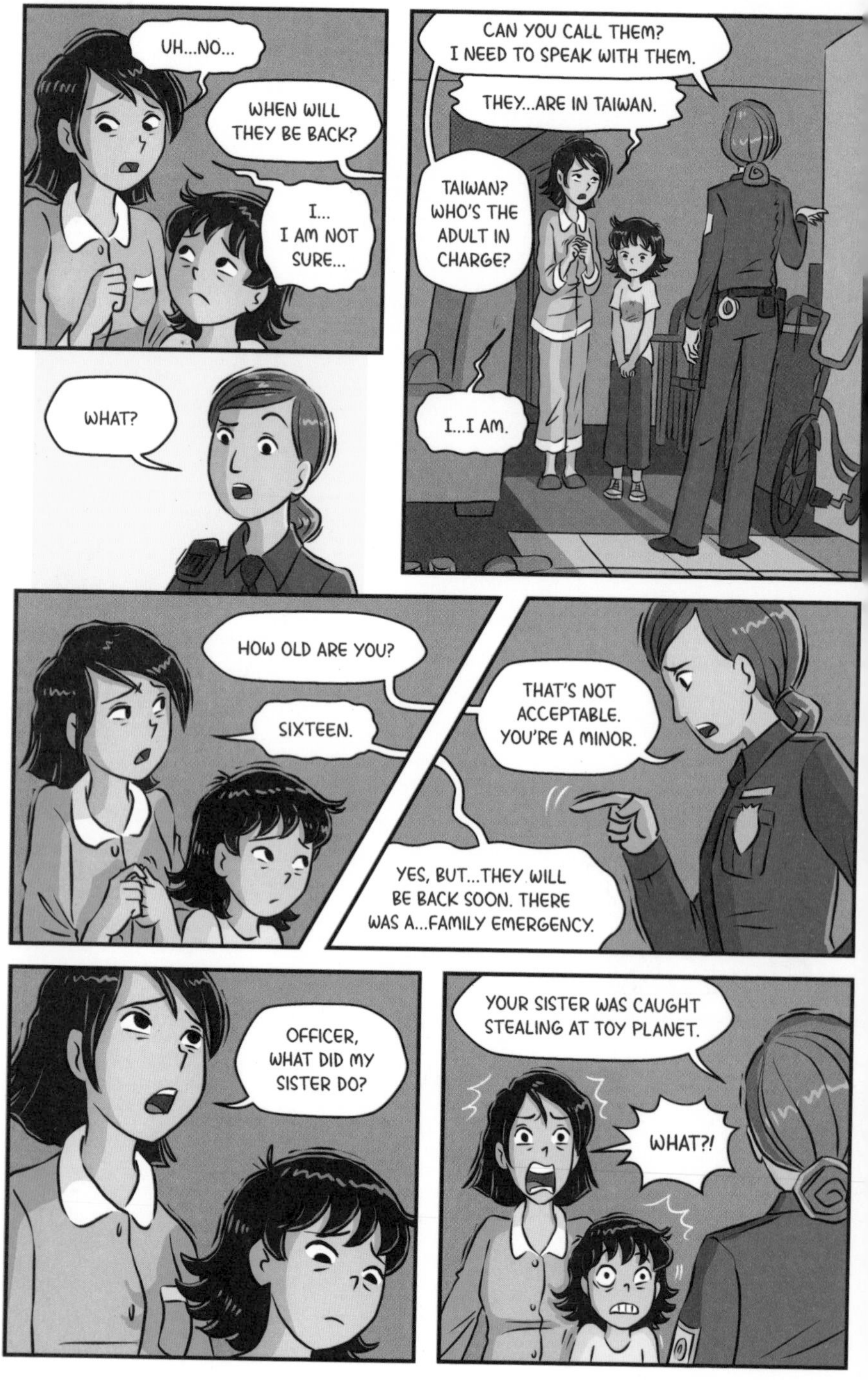
UH...NO...
WHEN WILL THEY BE BACK?
I... I AM NOT SURE...
CAN YOU CALL THEM? I NEED TO SPEAK WITH THEM.
THEY...ARE IN TAIWAN.
TAIWAN? WHO'S THE ADULT IN CHARGE?
I...I AM.
WHAT?
HOW OLD ARE YOU?
SIXTEEN.
THAT'S NOT ACCEPTABLE. YOU'RE A MINOR.
YES, BUT...THEY WILL BE BACK SOON. THERE WAS A...FAMILY EMERGENCY.
OFFICER, WHAT DID MY SISTER DO?
YOUR SISTER WAS CAUGHT STEALING AT TOY PLANET.
WHAT?!

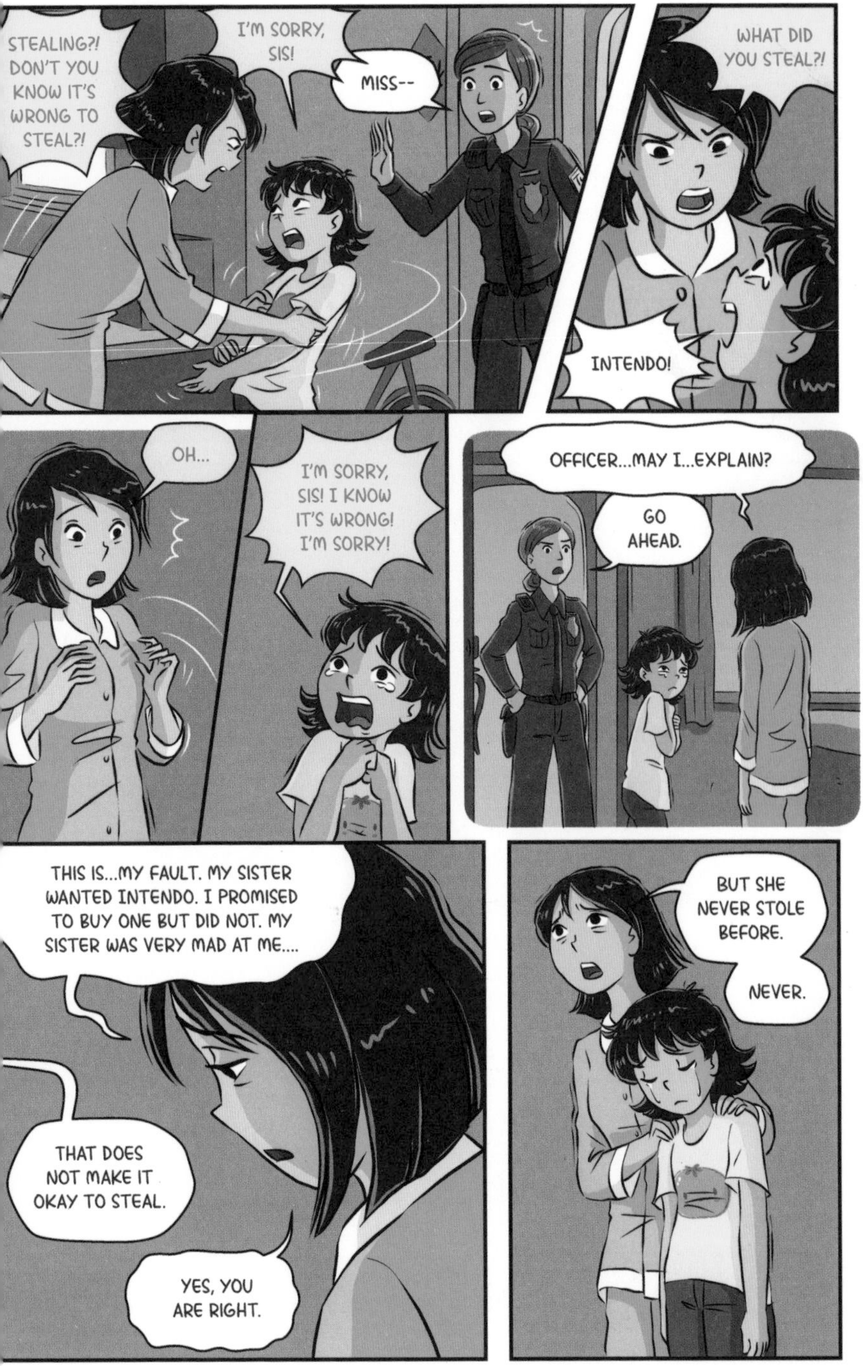

STEALING?! DON'T YOU KNOW IT'S WRONG TO STEAL?!
I'M SORRY, SIS!
MISS--
WHAT DID YOU STEAL?!
INTENDO!
OH...
I'M SORRY, SIS! I KNOW IT'S WRONG! I'M SORRY!
OFFICER...MAY I...EXPLAIN?
GO AHEAD.
THIS IS...MY FAULT. MY SISTER WANTED INTENDO. I PROMISED TO BUY ONE BUT DID NOT. MY SISTER WAS VERY MAD AT ME....
THAT DOES NOT MAKE IT OKAY TO STEAL.
YES, YOU ARE RIGHT.
BUT SHE NEVER STOLE BEFORE.
NEVER.

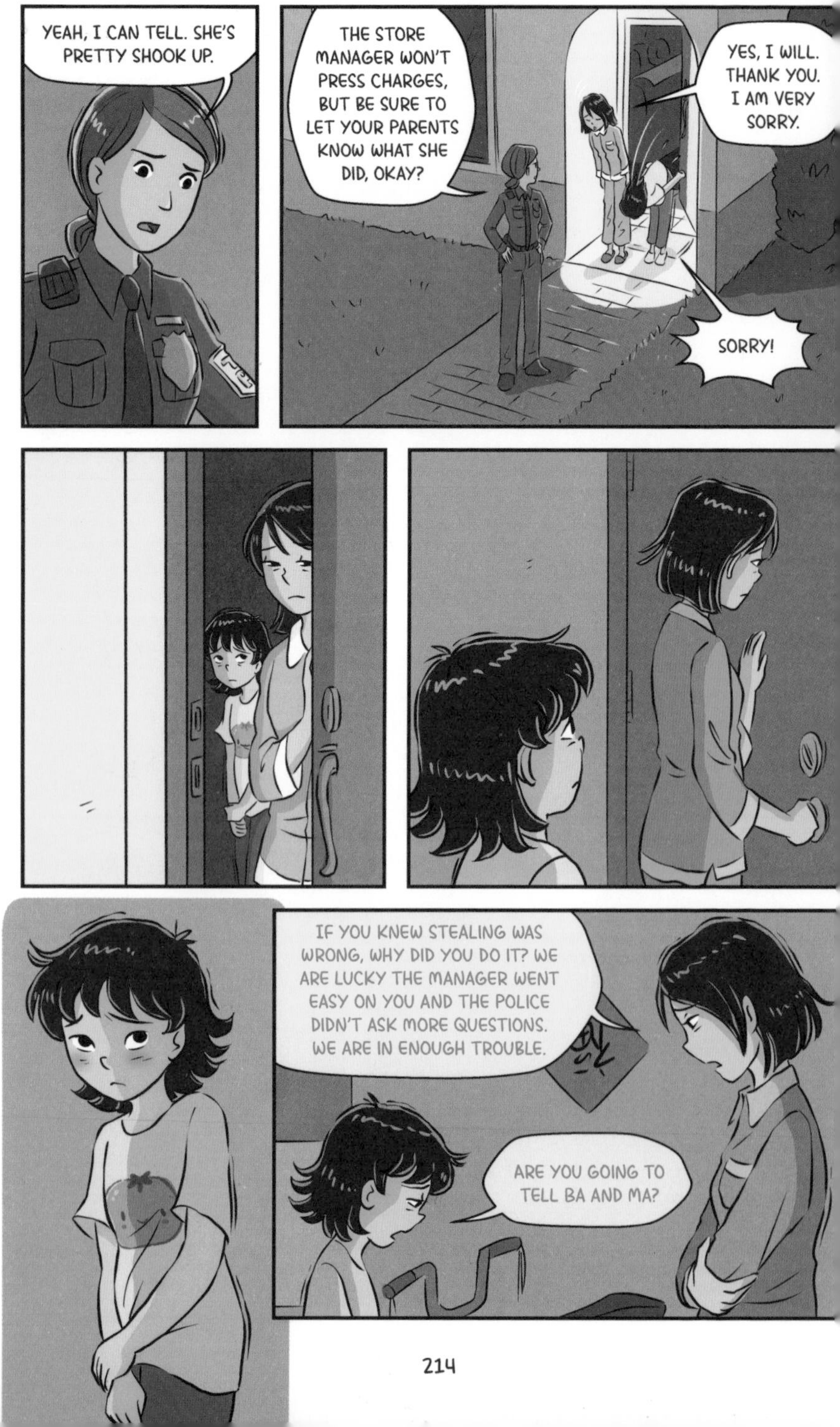
YEAH, I CAN TELL. SHE'S PRETTY SHOOK UP.
THE STORE MANAGER WON'T PRESS CHARGES, BUT BE SURE TO LET YOUR PARENTS KNOW WHAT SHE DID, OKAY?
YES, I WILL. THANK YOU. I AM VERY SORRY.
SORRY!
IF YOU KNEW STEALING WAS WRONG, WHY DID YOU DO IT? WE ARE LUCKY THE MANAGER WENT EASY ON YOU AND THE POLICE DIDN'T ASK MORE QUESTIONS. WE ARE IN ENOUGH TROUBLE.
ARE YOU GOING TO TELL BA AND MA?

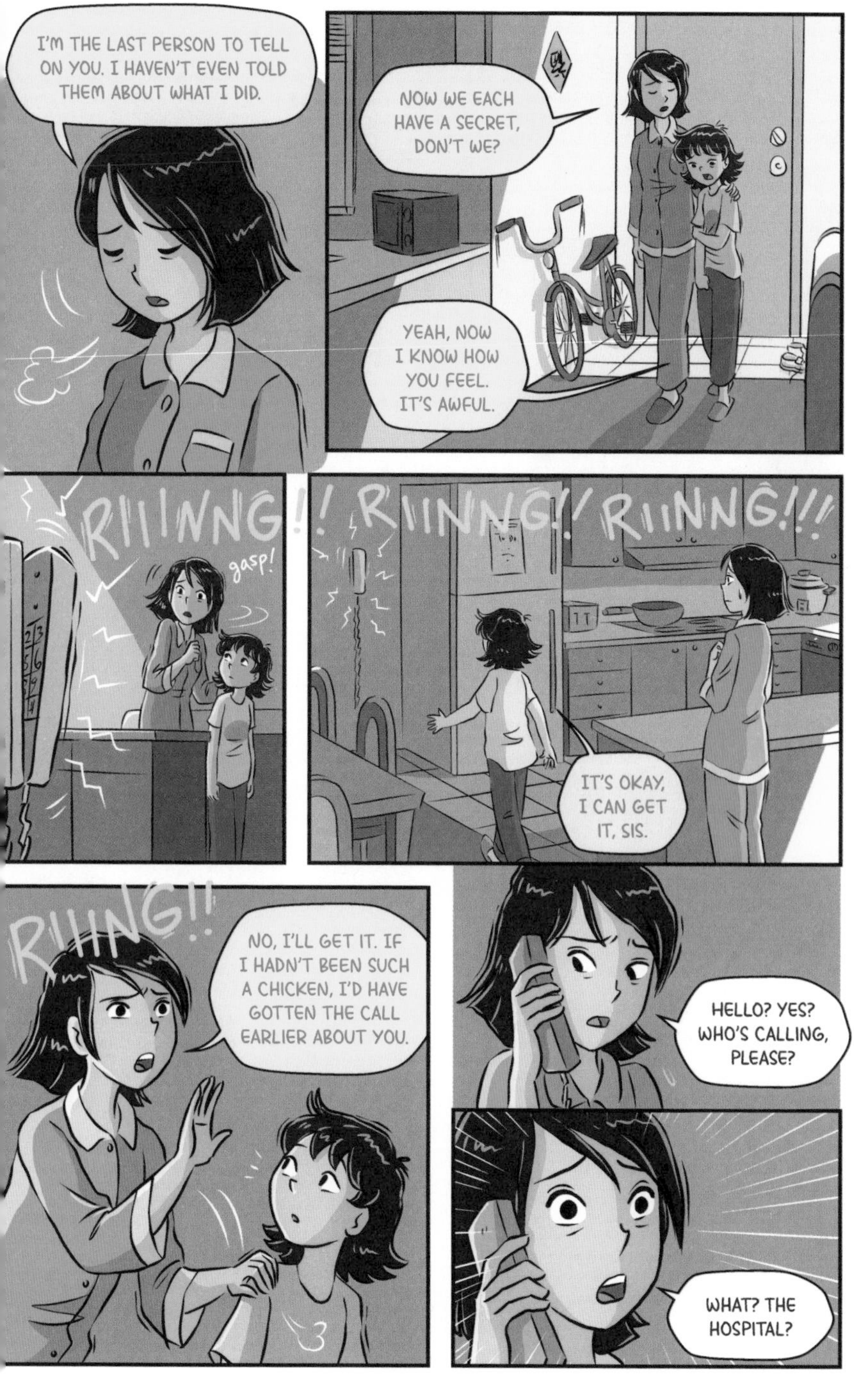
I'M THE LAST PERSON TO TELL ON YOU. I HAVEN'T EVEN TOLD THEM ABOUT WHAT I DID.
NOW WE EACH HAVE A SECRET, DON'T WE?
YEAH, NOW I KNOW HOW YOU FEEL. IT'S AWFUL.
RIIINNG!!
gasp!
RIINNG!!
RIINNG!!!
IT'S OKAY, I CAN GET IT, SIS.
RIIING!!
NO, I'LL GET IT. IF I HADN'T BEEN SUCH A CHICKEN, I'D HAVE GOTTEN THE CALL EARLIER ABOUT YOU.
HELLO? YES? WHO'S CALLING, PLEASE?
WHAT? THE HOSPITAL?

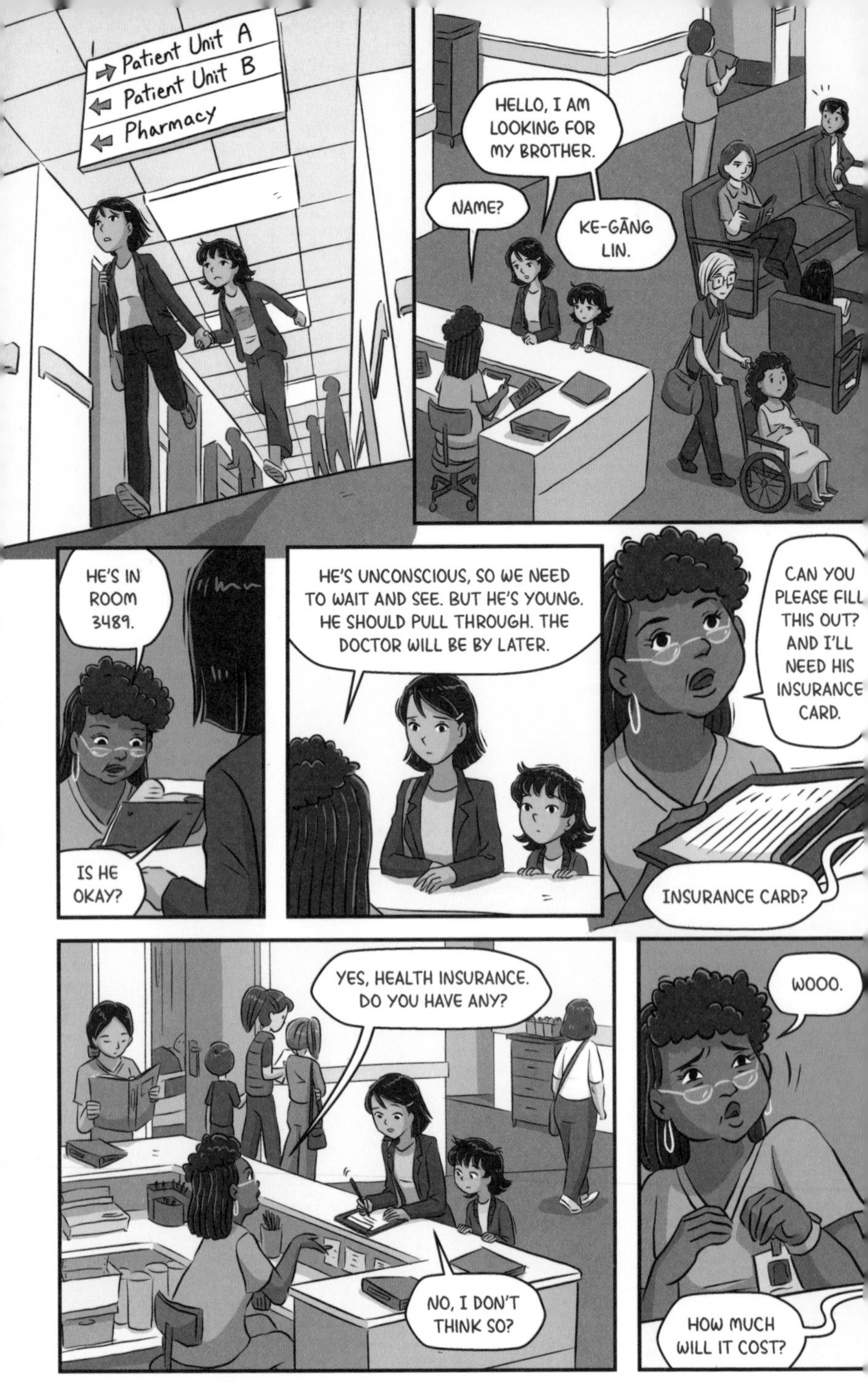
Patient Unit A
Patient Unit B
Pharmacy
HELLO, I AM LOOKING FOR MY BROTHER.
NAME?
KE-GĀNG LIN.
HE'S IN ROOM 3489.
IS HE OKAY?
HE'S UNCONSCIOUS, SO WE NEED TO WAIT AND SEE. BUT HE'S YOUNG. HE SHOULD PULL THROUGH. THE DOCTOR WILL BE BY LATER.
CAN YOU PLEASE FILL THIS OUT? AND I'LL NEED HIS INSURANCE CARD.
INSURANCE CARD?
YES, HEALTH INSURANCE. DO YOU HAVE ANY?
NO, I DON'T THINK SO?
WOOO.
HOW MUCH WILL IT COST?

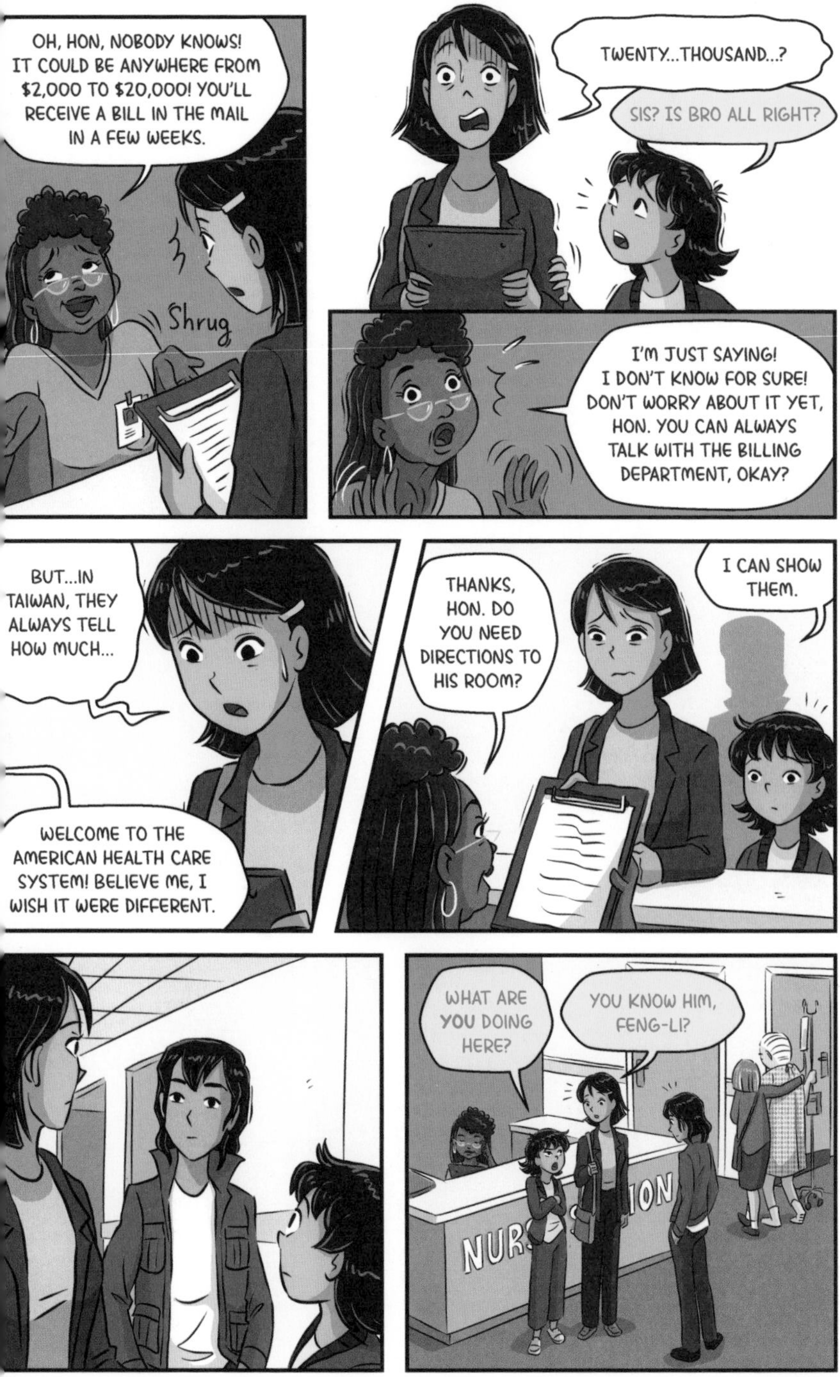
OH, HON, NOBODY KNOWS! IT COULD BE ANYWHERE FROM $2,000 TO $20,000! YOU'LL RECEIVE A BILL IN THE MAIL IN A FEW WEEKS.
Shrug
TWENTY...THOUSAND...?
SIS? IS BRO ALL RIGHT?
I'M JUST SAYING! I DON'T KNOW FOR SURE! DON'T WORRY ABOUT IT YET, HON. YOU CAN ALWAYS TALK WITH THE BILLING DEPARTMENT, OKAY?
BUT...IN TAIWAN, THEY ALWAYS TELL HOW MUCH...
WELCOME TO THE AMERICAN HEALTH CARE SYSTEM! BELIEVE ME, I WISH IT WERE DIFFERENT.
THANKS, HON. DO YOU NEED DIRECTIONS TO HIS ROOM?
I CAN SHOW THEM.
WHAT ARE YOU DOING HERE?
YOU KNOW HIM, FENG-LI?

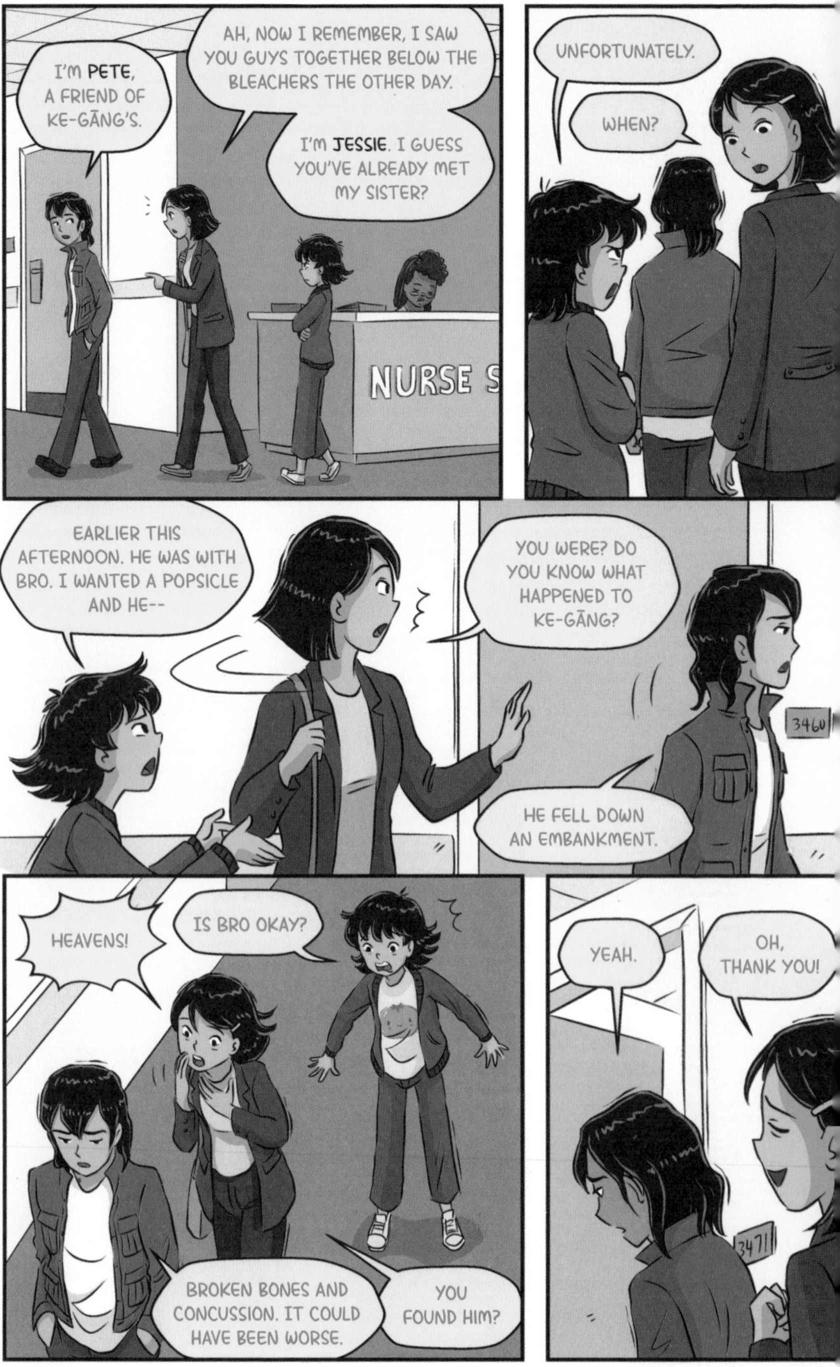
I'M PETE, A FRIEND OF KE-GĀNG'S.
AH, NOW I REMEMBER, I SAW YOU GUYS TOGETHER BELOW THE BLEACHERS THE OTHER DAY.
I'M JESSIE. I GUESS YOU'VE ALREADY MET MY SISTER?
NURSE S
UNFORTUNATELY.
WHEN?
EARLIER THIS AFTERNOON. HE WAS WITH BRO. I WANTED A POPSICLE AND HE--
YOU WERE? DO YOU KNOW WHAT HAPPENED TO KE-GĀNG?
HE FELL DOWN AN EMBANKMENT.
3460
HEAVENS!
IS BRO OKAY?
BROKEN BONES AND CONCUSSION. IT COULD HAVE BEEN WORSE.
YOU FOUND HIM?
YEAH.
OH, THANK YOU!
3471

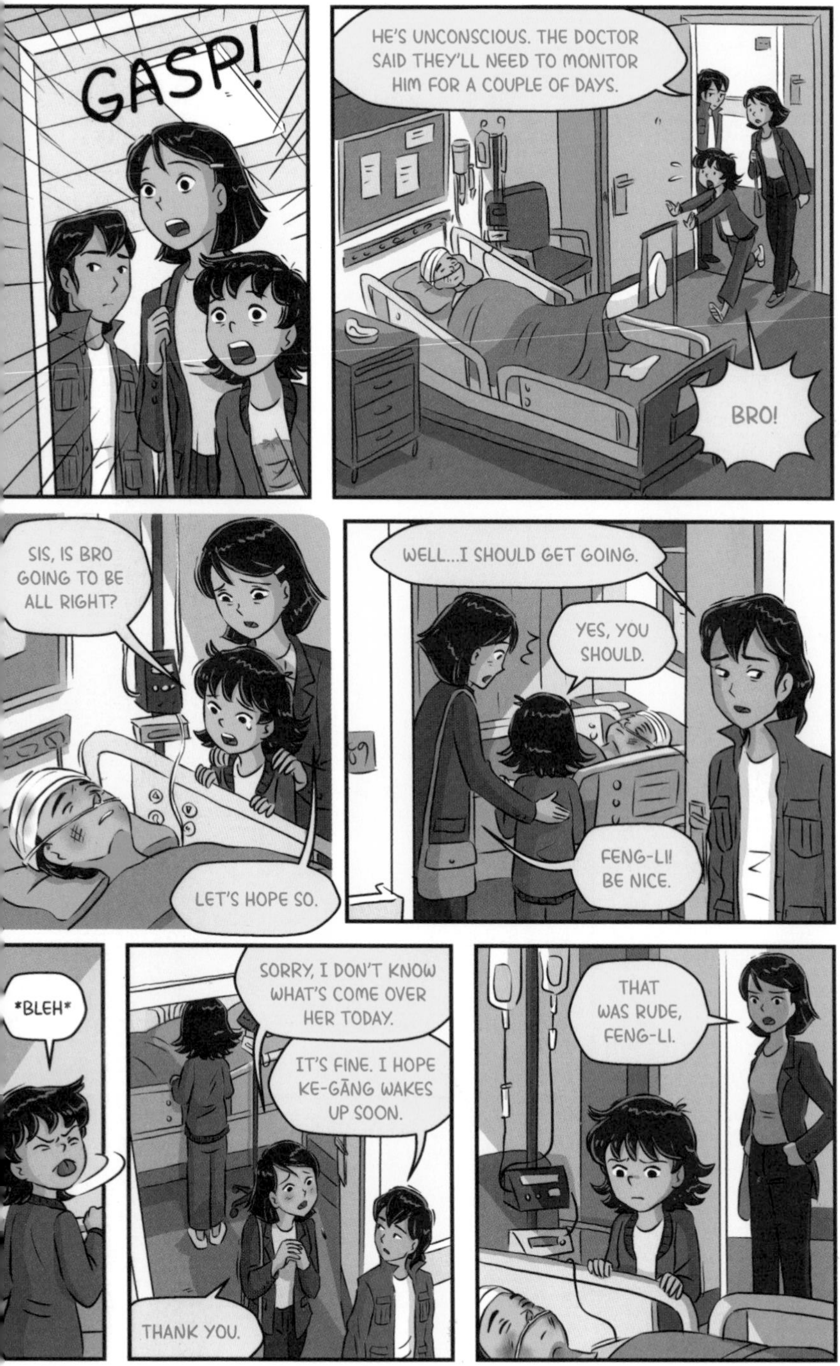
GASP!
HE'S UNCONSCIOUS. THE DOCTOR SAID THEY'LL NEED TO MONITOR HIM FOR A COUPLE OF DAYS.
BRO!
SIS, IS BRO GOING TO BE ALL RIGHT?
LET'S HOPE SO.
WELL...I SHOULD GET GOING.
YES, YOU SHOULD.
FENG-LI! BE NICE.
BLEH
SORRY, I DON'T KNOW WHAT'S COME OVER HER TODAY.
IT'S FINE. I HOPE KE-GĀNG WAKES UP SOON.
THANK YOU.
THAT WAS RUDE, FENG-LI.

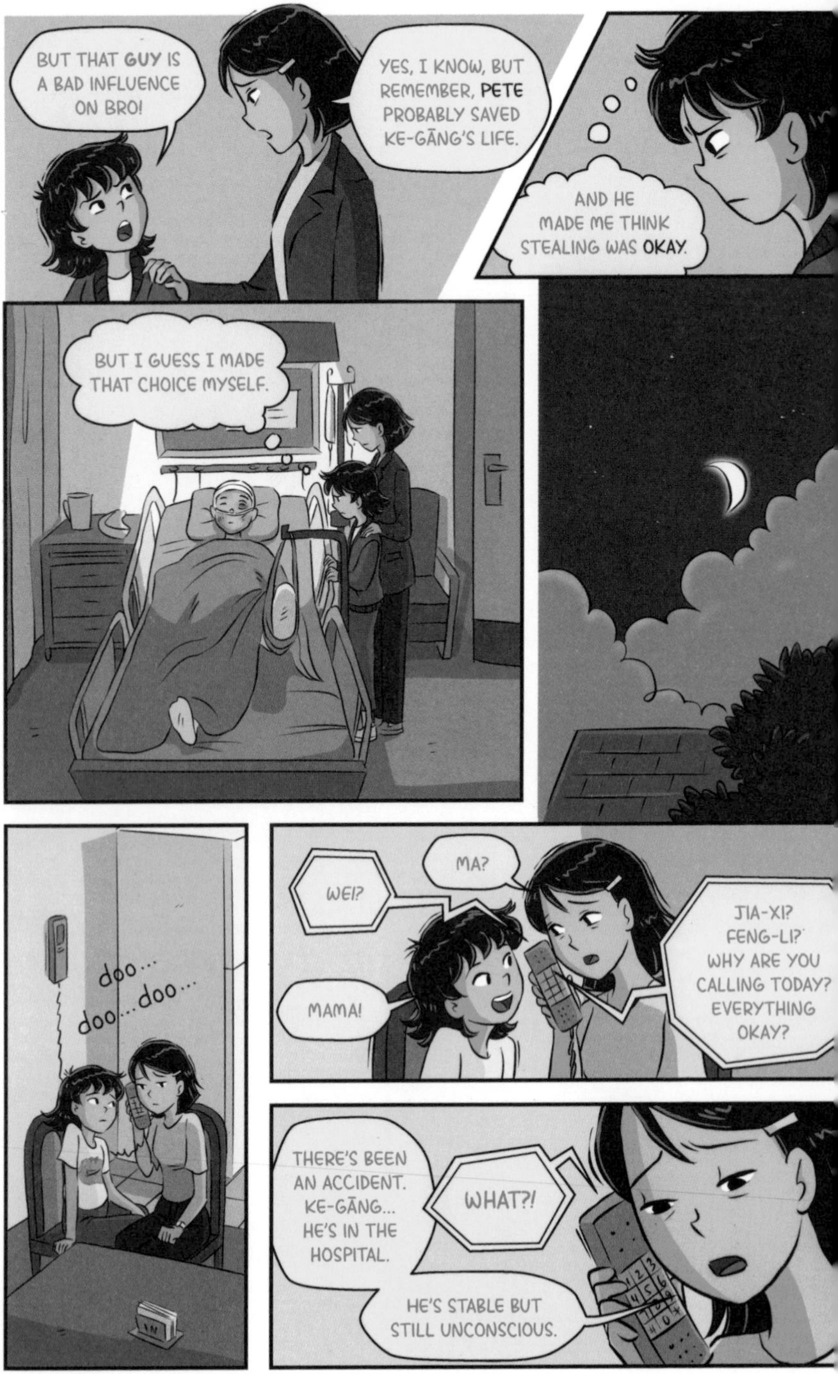
BUT THAT GUY IS A BAD INFLUENCE ON BRO!
YES, I KNOW, BUT REMEMBER, PETE PROBABLY SAVED KE-GĀNG'S LIFE.
AND HE MADE ME THINK STEALING WAS OKAY.
BUT I GUESS I MADE THAT CHOICE MYSELF.
doo... doo... doo...
WEI?
MA?
MAMA!
JIA-XI? FENG-LI? WHY ARE YOU CALLING TODAY? EVERYTHING OKAY?
THERE'S BEEN AN ACCIDENT. KE-GĀNG... HE'S IN THE HOSPITAL.
WHAT?!
HE'S STABLE BUT STILL UNCONSCIOUS.

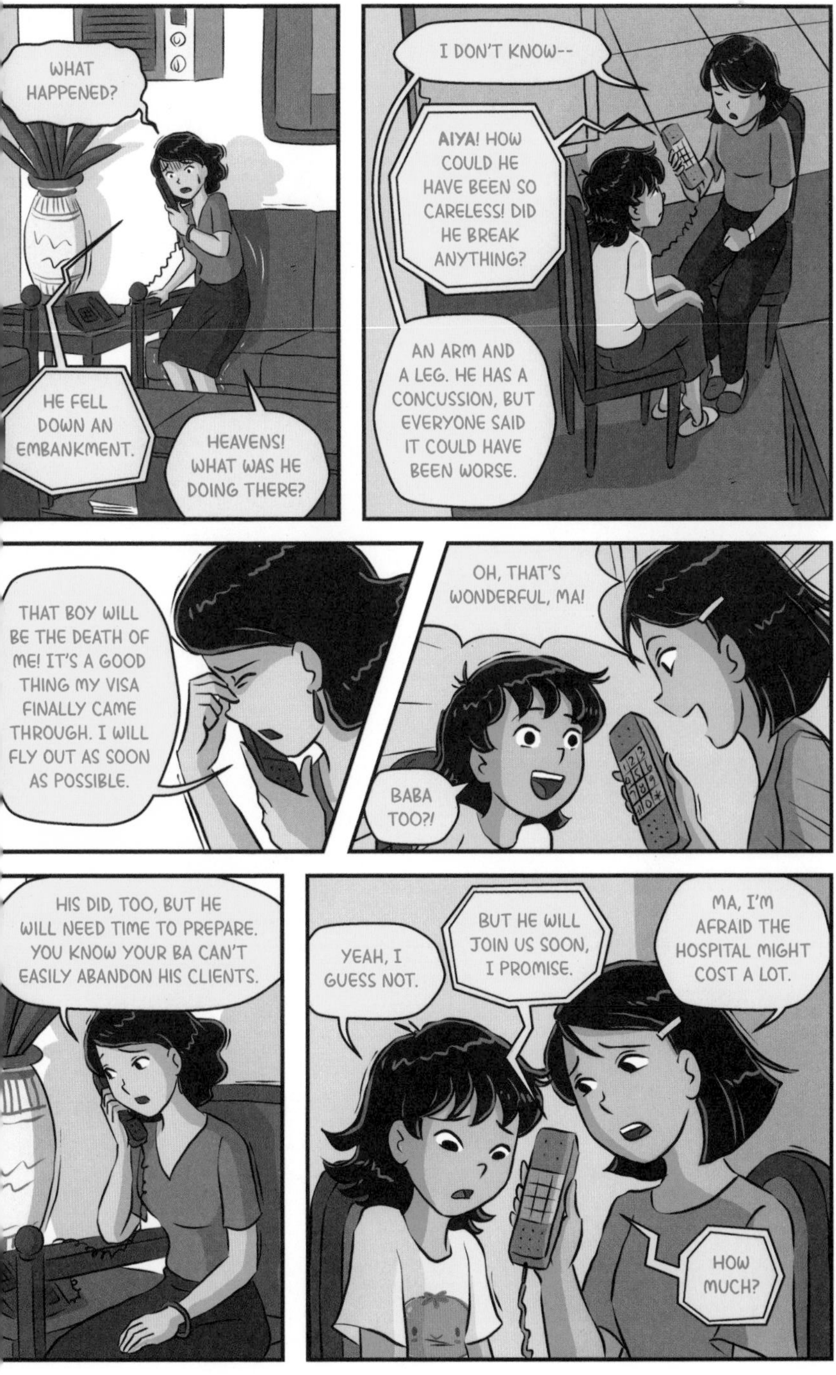
WHAT HAPPENED?
HE FELL DOWN AN EMBANKMENT.
HEAVENS! WHAT WAS HE DOING THERE?
I DON'T KNOW--
AIYA! HOW COULD HE HAVE BEEN SO CARELESS! DID HE BREAK ANYTHING?
AN ARM AND A LEG. HE HAS A CONCUSSION, BUT EVERYONE SAID IT COULD HAVE BEEN WORSE.
THAT BOY WILL BE THE DEATH OF ME! IT'S A GOOD THING MY VISA FINALLY CAME THROUGH. I WILL FLY OUT AS SOON AS POSSIBLE.
OH, THAT'S WONDERFUL, MA!
BABA TOO?!
HIS DID, TOO, BUT HE WILL NEED TIME TO PREPARE. YOU KNOW YOUR BA CAN'T EASILY ABANDON HIS CLIENTS.
YEAH, I GUESS NOT.
BUT HE WILL JOIN US SOON, I PROMISE.
MA, I'M AFRAID THE HOSPITAL MIGHT COST A LOT.
HOW MUCH?

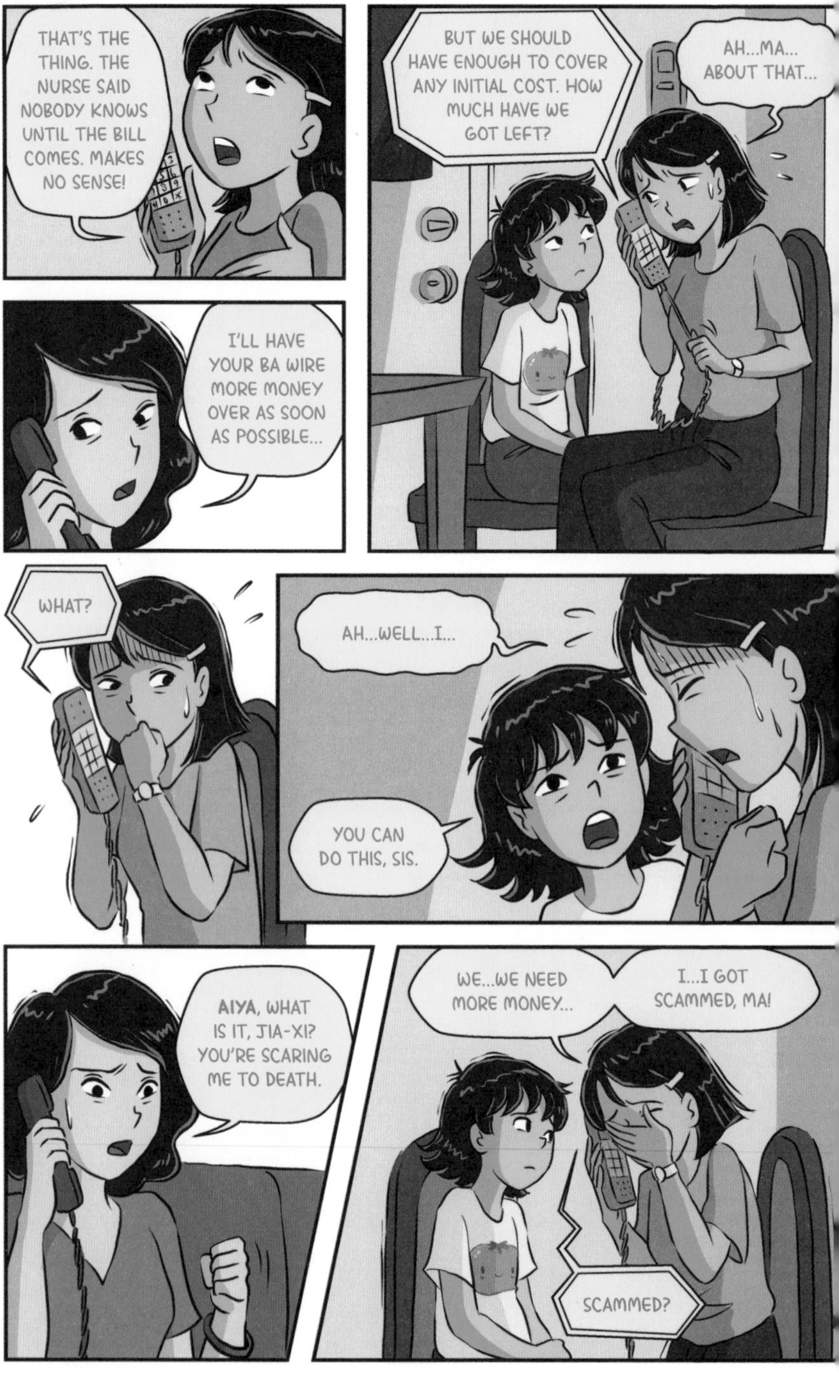
THAT'S THE THING. THE NURSE SAID NOBODY KNOWS UNTIL THE BILL COMES. MAKES NO SENSE!
BUT WE SHOULD HAVE ENOUGH TO COVER ANY INITIAL COST. HOW MUCH HAVE WE GOT LEFT?
AH...MA... ABOUT THAT...
I'LL HAVE YOUR BA WIRE MORE MONEY OVER AS SOON AS POSSIBLE...
WHAT?
AH...WELL...I...
YOU CAN DO THIS, SIS.
AIYA, WHAT IS IT, JIA-XI? YOU'RE SCARING ME TO DEATH.
I...I GOT SCAMMED, MA!
WE...WE NEED MORE MONEY...
SCAMMED?

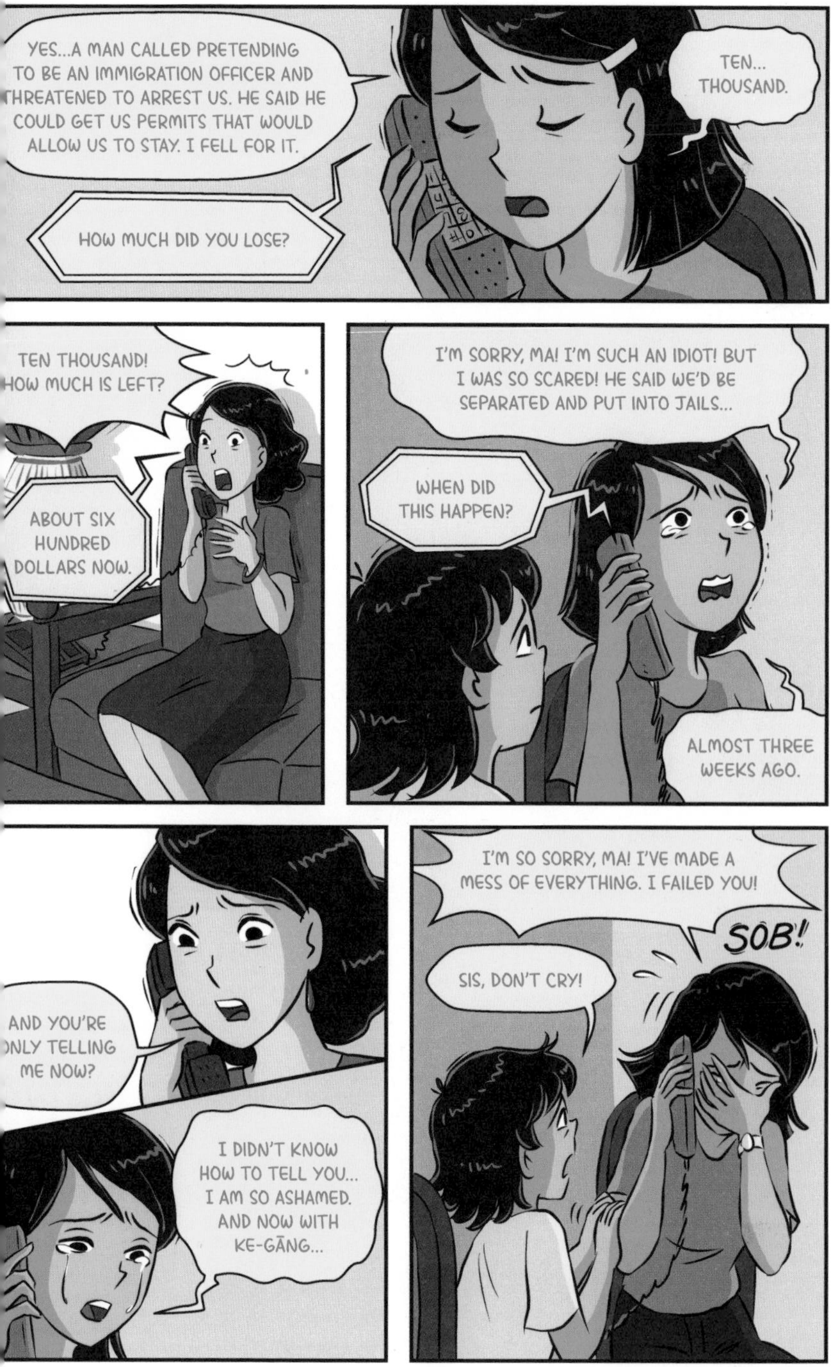
YES...A MAN CALLED PRETENDING TO BE AN IMMIGRATION OFFICER AND THREATENED TO ARREST US. HE SAID HE COULD GET US PERMITS THAT WOULD ALLOW US TO STAY. I FELL FOR IT.
HOW MUCH DID YOU LOSE?
TEN... THOUSAND.
TEN THOUSAND! HOW MUCH IS LEFT?
ABOUT SIX HUNDRED DOLLARS NOW.
I'M SORRY, MA! I'M SUCH AN IDIOT! BUT I WAS SO SCARED! HE SAID WE'D BE SEPARATED AND PUT INTO JAILS...
WHEN DID THIS HAPPEN?
ALMOST THREE WEEKS AGO.
AND YOU'RE ONLY TELLING ME NOW?
I DIDN'T KNOW HOW TO TELL YOU... I AM SO ASHAMED. AND NOW WITH KE-GĀNG...
I'M SO SORRY, MA! I'VE MADE A MESS OF EVERYTHING. I FAILED YOU!
SOB!
SIS, DON'T CRY!

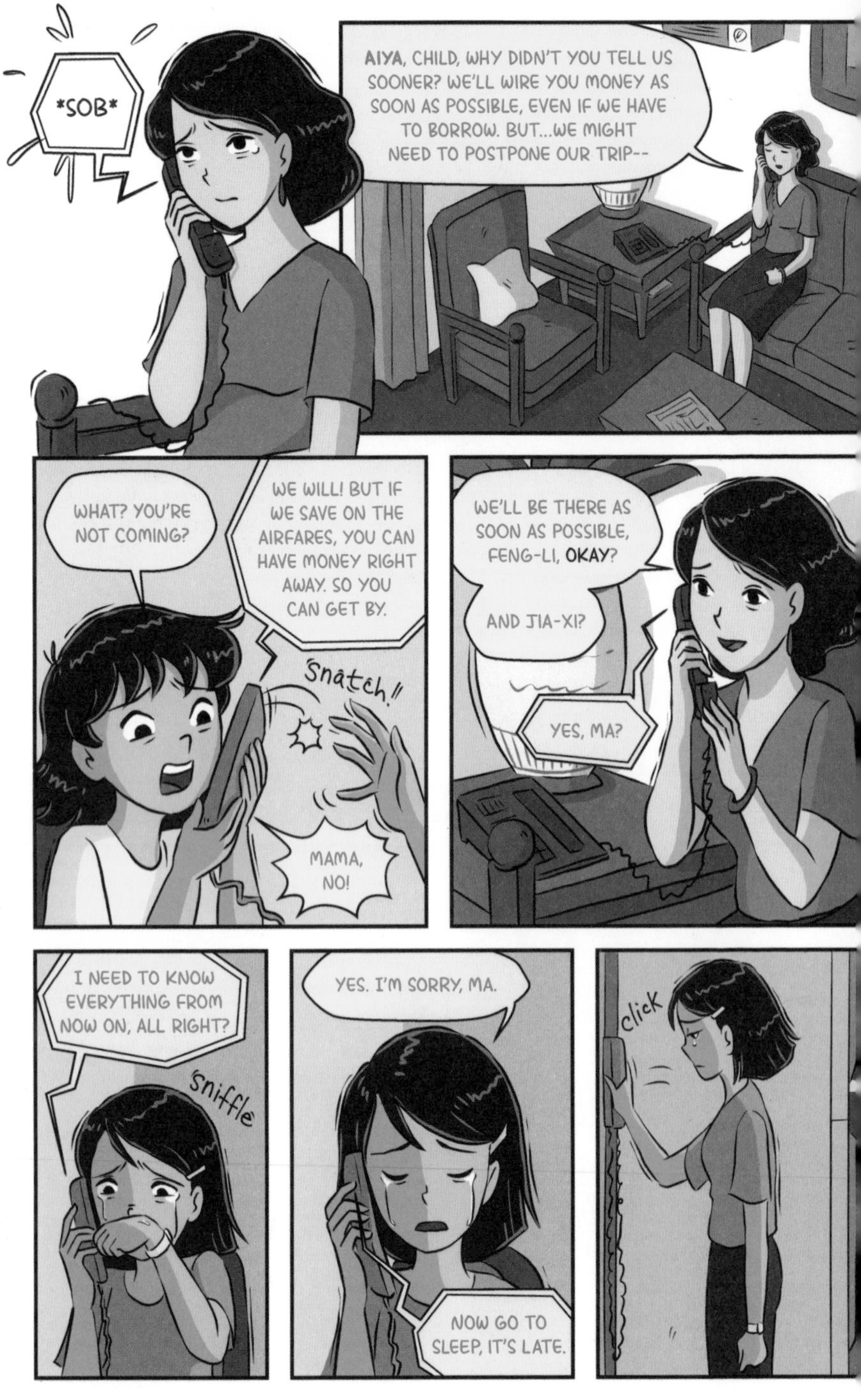
SOB
AIYA, CHILD, WHY DIDN'T YOU TELL US SOONER? WE'LL WIRE YOU MONEY AS SOON AS POSSIBLE, EVEN IF WE HAVE TO BORROW. BUT...WE MIGHT NEED TO POSTPONE OUR TRIP--
WHAT? YOU'RE NOT COMING?
WE WILL! BUT IF WE SAVE ON THE AIRFARES, YOU CAN HAVE MONEY RIGHT AWAY. SO YOU CAN GET BY.
Snatch!!
MAMA, NO!
WE'LL BE THERE AS SOON AS POSSIBLE, FENG-LI, OKAY?
AND JIA-XI?
YES, MA?
I NEED TO KNOW EVERYTHING FROM NOW ON, ALL RIGHT?
sniffle
YES. I'M SORRY, MA.
NOW GO TO SLEEP, IT'S LATE.
click

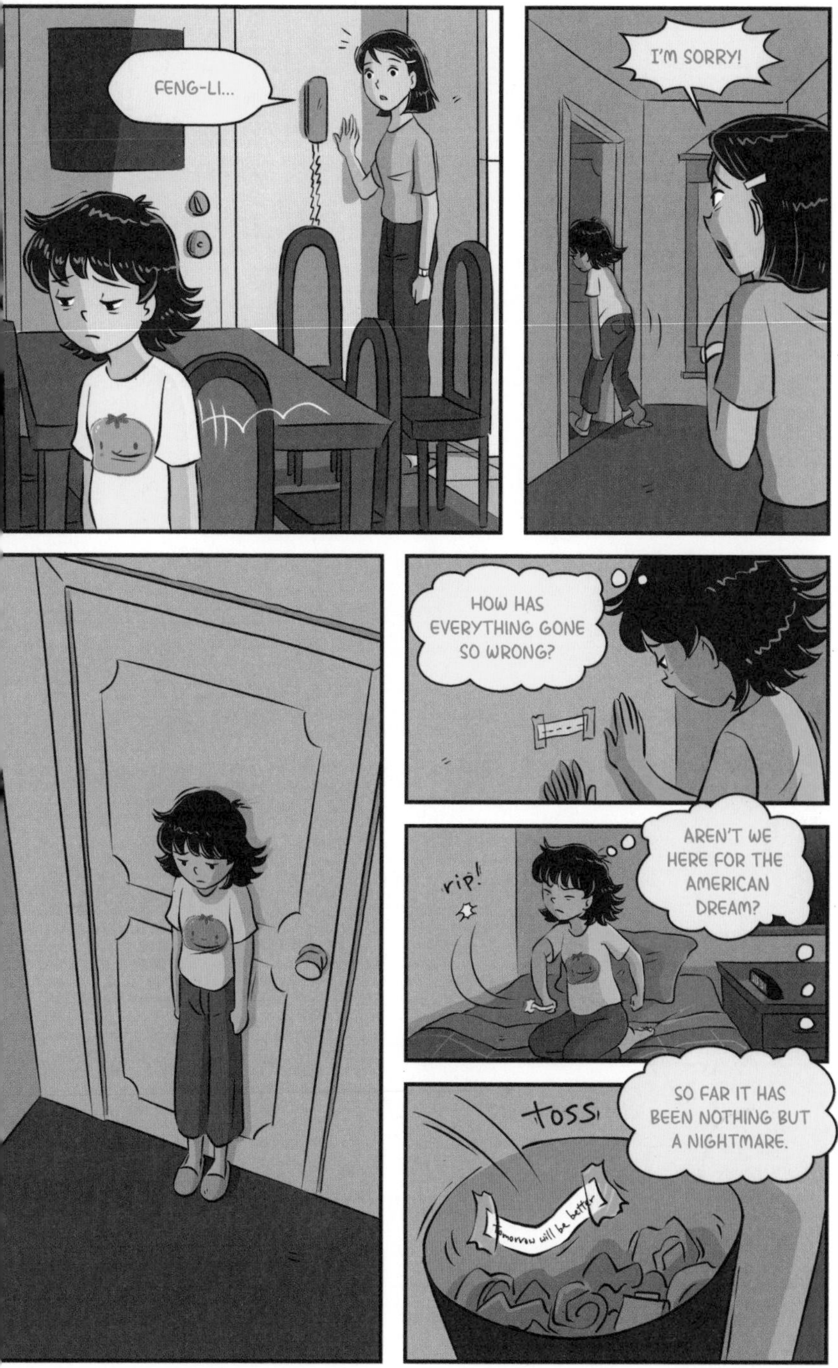
FENG-LI...
I'M SORRY!
HOW HAS EVERYTHING GONE SO WRONG?
rip!
AREN'T WE HERE FOR THE AMERICAN DREAM?
toss
SO FAR IT HAS BEEN NOTHING BUT A NIGHTMARE.
Tomorrow will be better

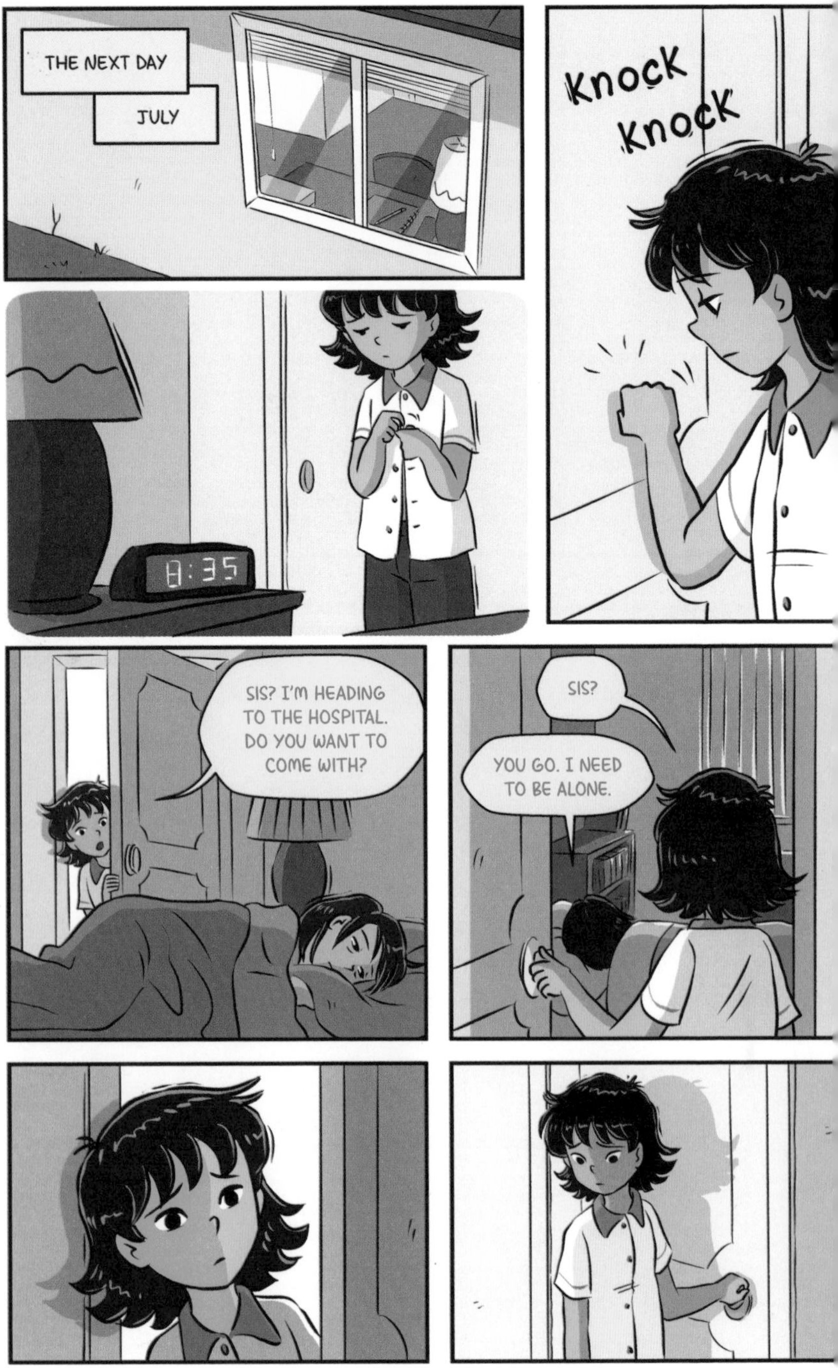
THE NEXT DAY
JULY
KNOCK KNOCK
SIS? I'M HEADING TO THE HOSPITAL. DO YOU WANT TO COME WITH?
SIS?
YOU GO. I NEED TO BE ALONE.

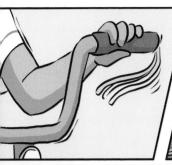

I CAN'T STOP THINKING ABOUT MY OWN BIG MISTAKE.

I FEEL SO GUILTY AND EMBARRASSED...

I WISH THERE WAS SOMETHING I COULD DO.

OUCH!

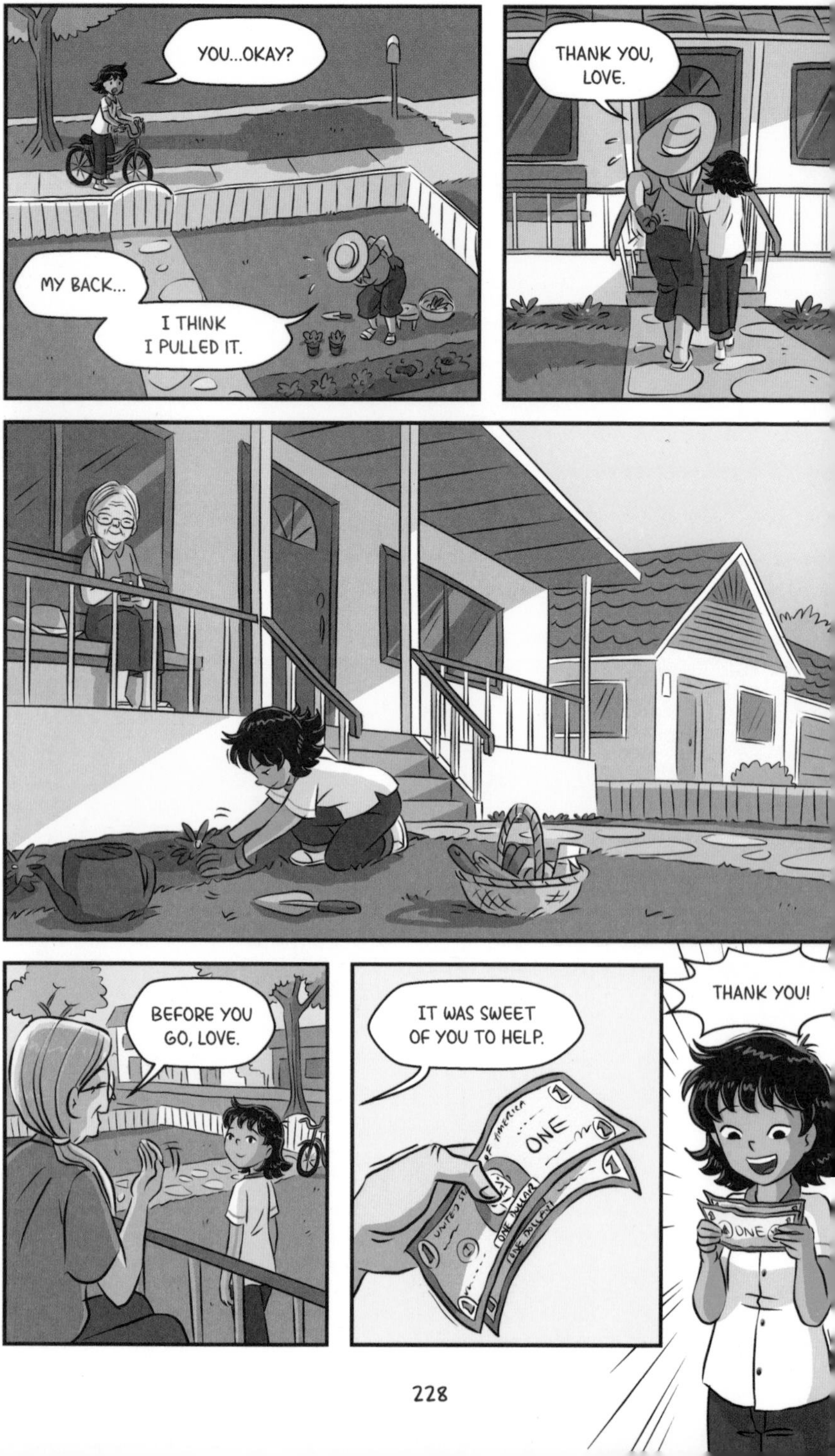
YOU...OKAY?
MY BACK...
I THINK I PULLED IT.
THANK YOU, LOVE.
BEFORE YOU GO, LOVE.
IT WAS SWEET OF YOU TO HELP.
THANK YOU!

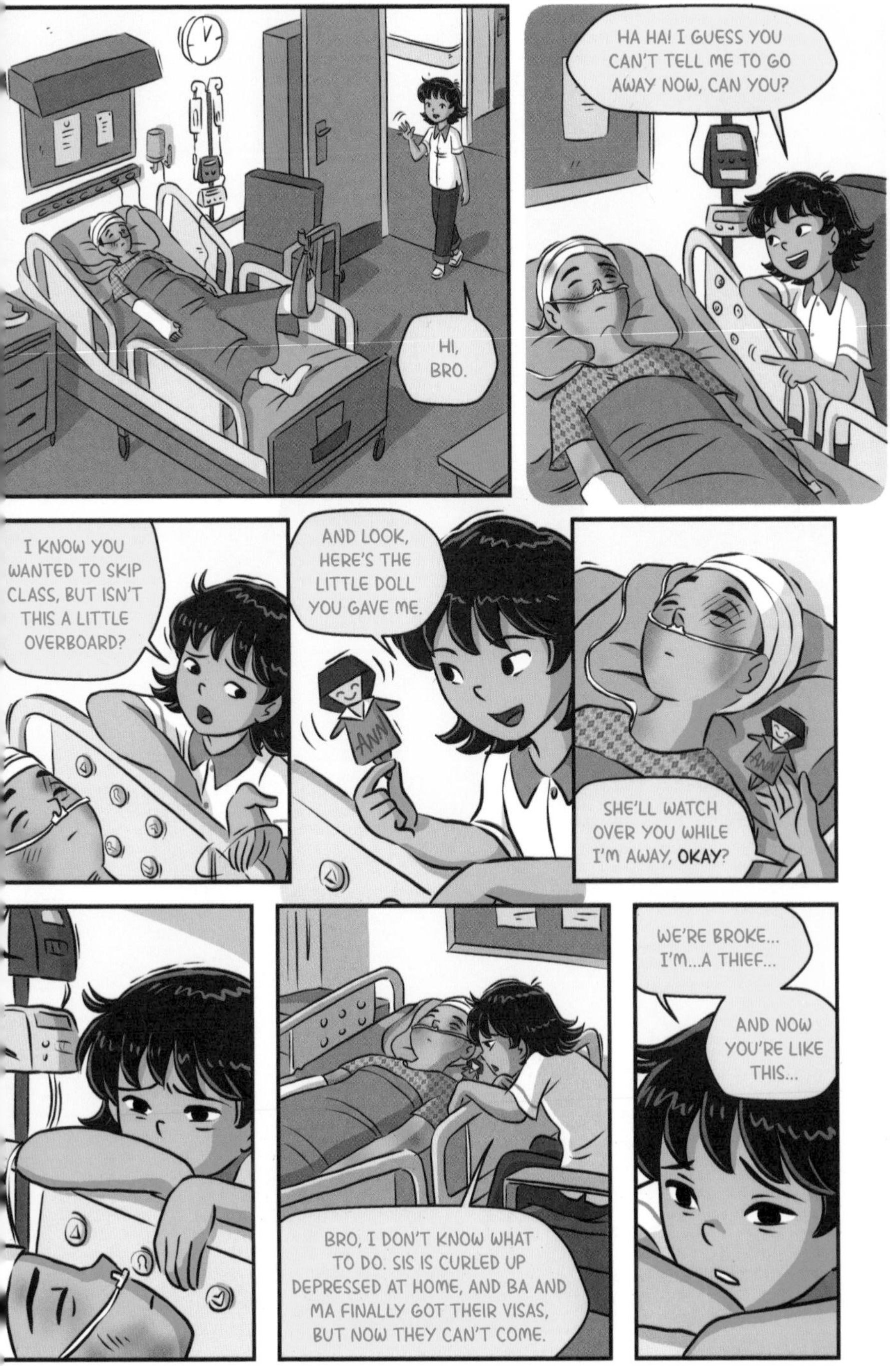
HI, BRO.
HA HA! I GUESS YOU CAN'T TELL ME TO GO AWAY NOW, CAN YOU?
I KNOW YOU WANTED TO SKIP CLASS, BUT ISN'T THIS A LITTLE OVERBOARD?
AND LOOK, HERE'S THE LITTLE DOLL YOU GAVE ME.
ANN
SHE'LL WATCH OVER YOU WHILE I'M AWAY, **OKAY**?
BRO, I DON'T KNOW WHAT TO DO. SIS IS CURLED UP DEPRESSED AT HOME, AND BA AND MA FINALLY GOT THEIR VISAS, BUT NOW THEY CAN'T COME.
WE'RE BROKE... I'M...A THIEF...
AND NOW YOU'RE LIKE THIS...

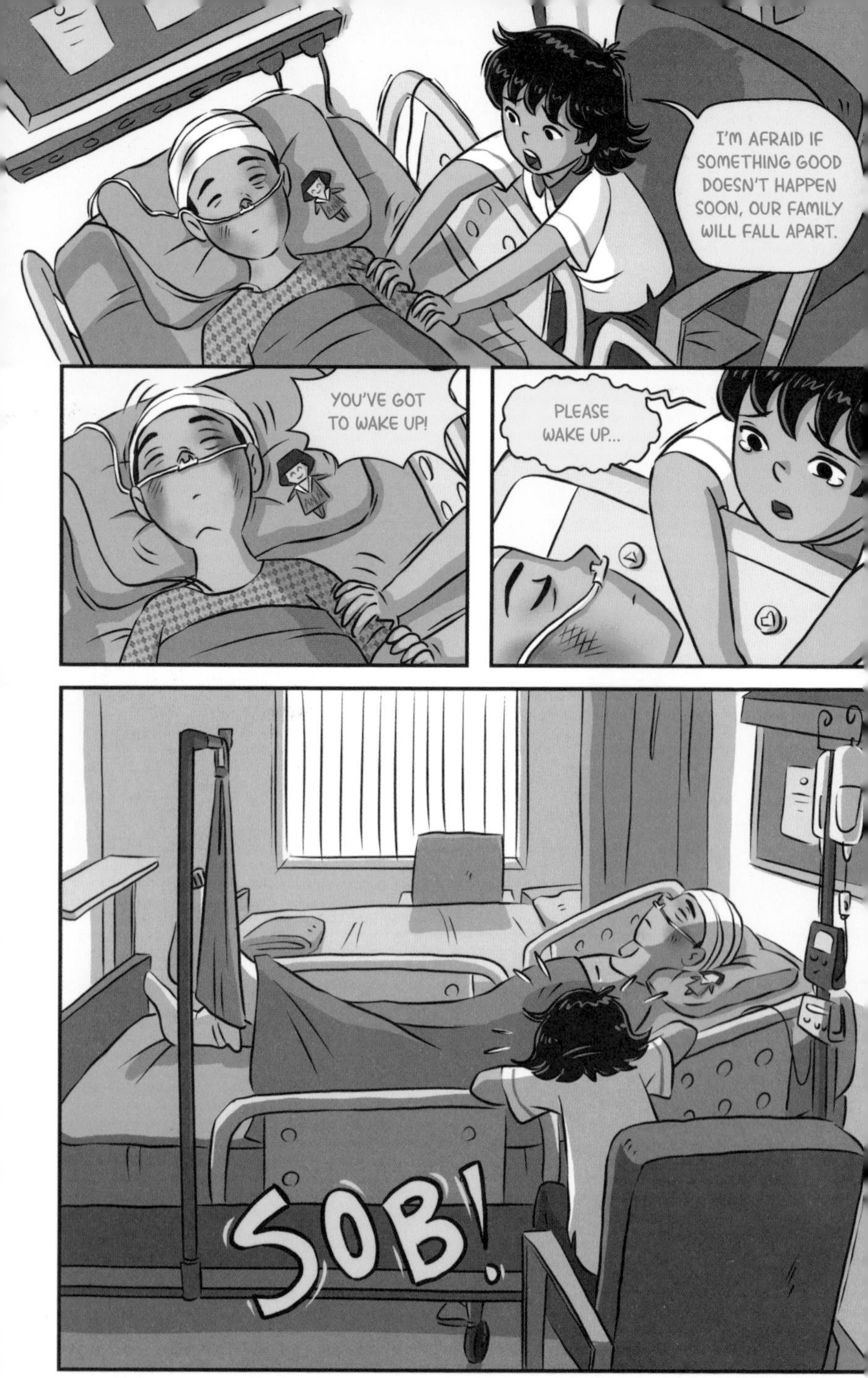
I'M AFRAID IF SOMETHING GOOD DOESN'T HAPPEN SOON, OUR FAMILY WILL FALL APART.
YOU'VE GOT TO WAKE UP!
PLEASE WAKE UP...
SOB!

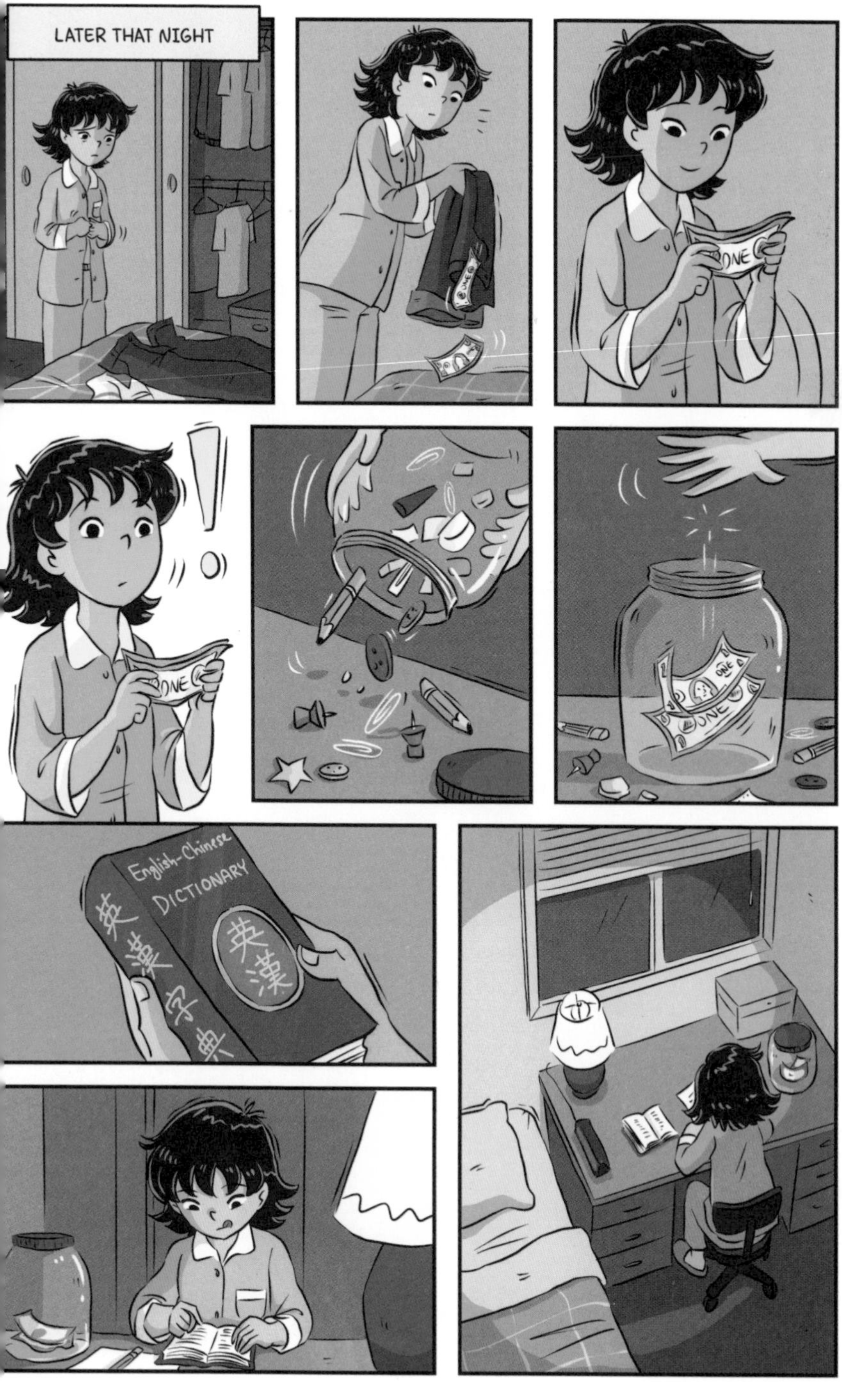
LATER THAT NIGHT
ONE
ONE
!
ONE
ONE
ONE
English-Chinese
DICTIONARY
英漢字典
英漢

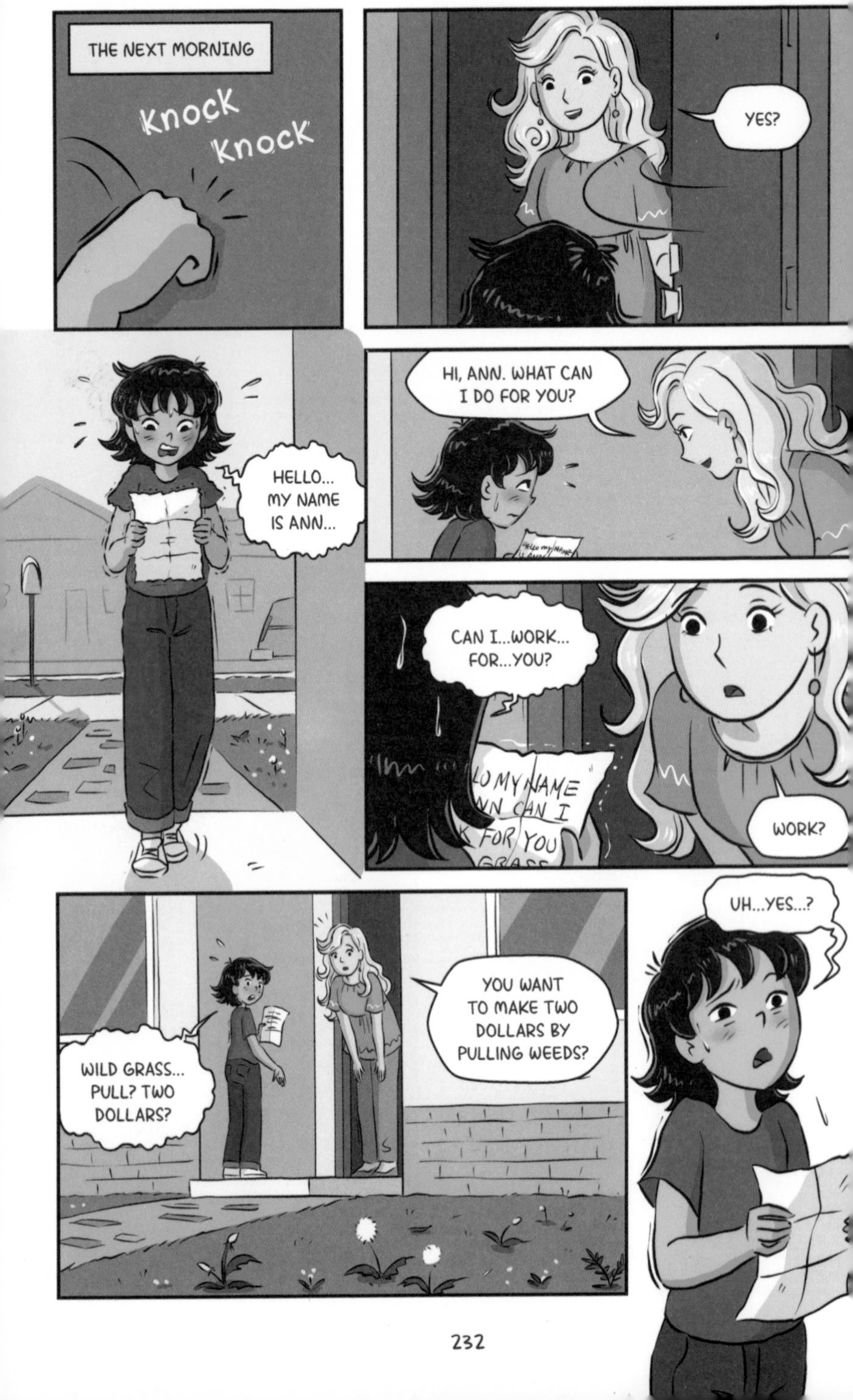

THE NEXT MORNING
Knock
Knock
YES?
HELLO...
MY NAME
IS ANN...
HI, ANN. WHAT CAN I DO FOR YOU?
CAN I...WORK... FOR...YOU?
LO MY NAME
NN CAN I
K FOR YOU
WORK?
WILD GRASS... PULL? TWO DOLLARS?
YOU WANT TO MAKE TWO DOLLARS BY PULLING WEEDS?
UH...YES...?

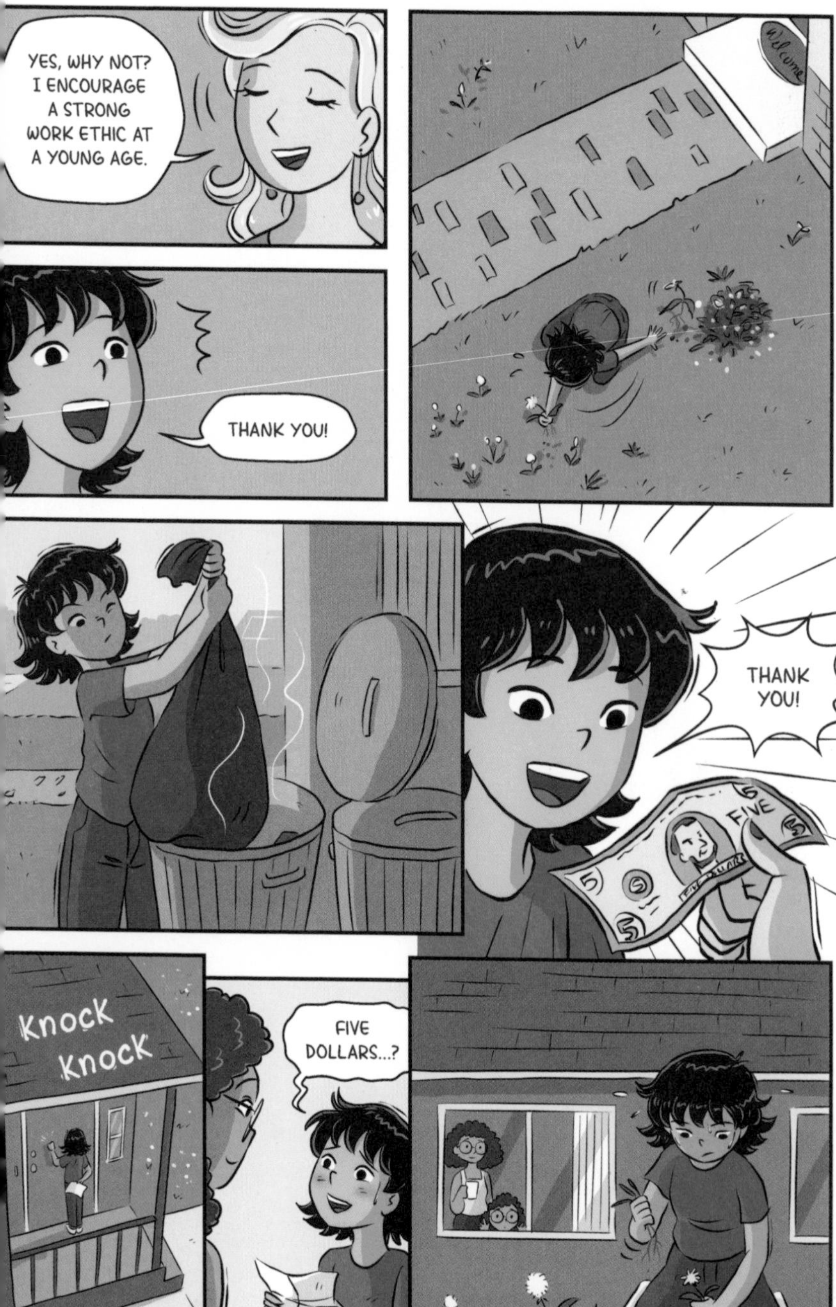
YES, WHY NOT? I ENCOURAGE A STRONG WORK ETHIC AT A YOUNG AGE.
Welcome
THANK YOU!
THANK YOU!
FIVE
Knock Knock
FIVE DOLLARS...?

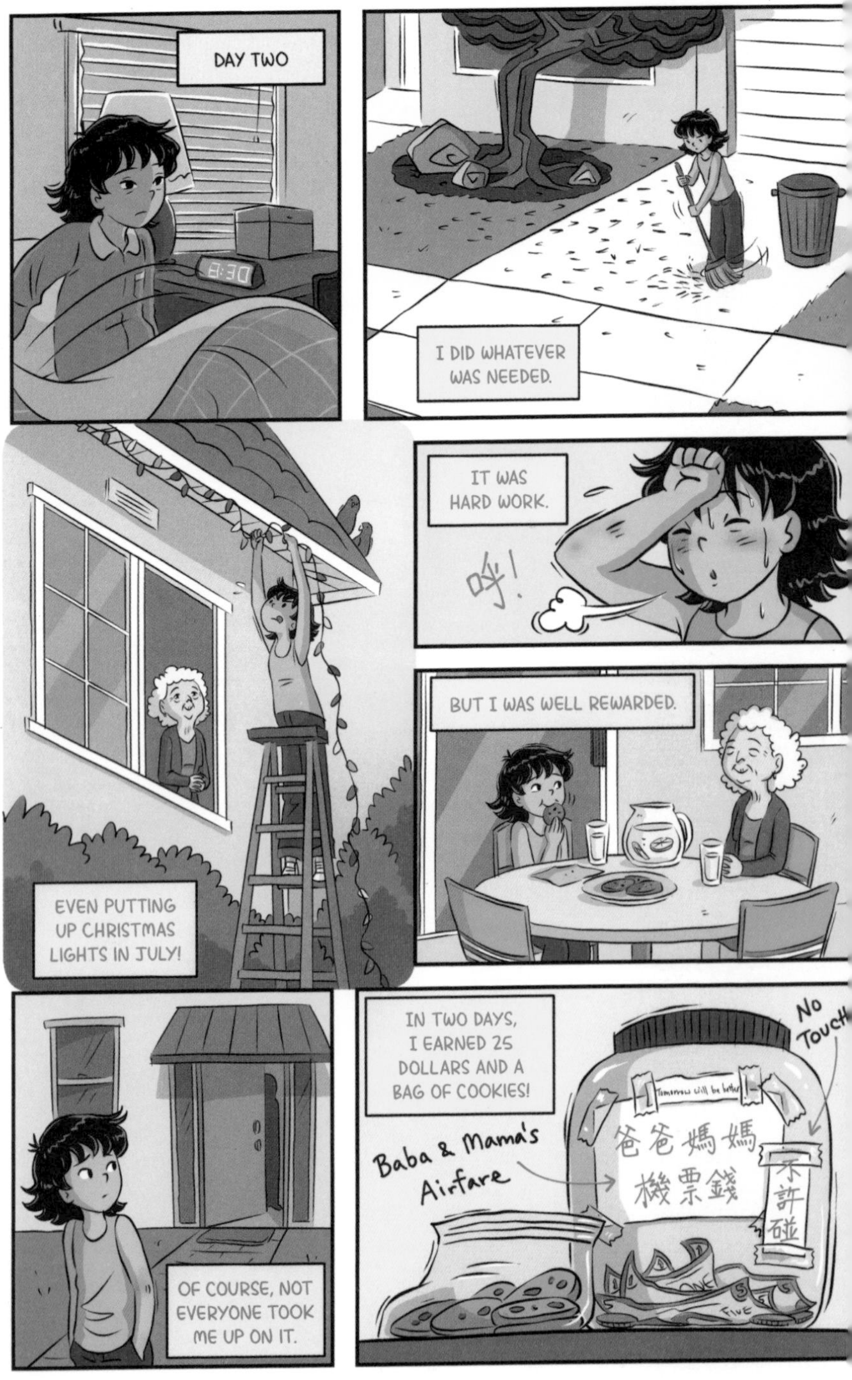
DAY TWO
I DID WHATEVER WAS NEEDED.
EVEN PUTTING UP CHRISTMAS LIGHTS IN JULY!
IT WAS HARD WORK.
呼!
BUT I WAS WELL REWARDED.
OF COURSE, NOT EVERYONE TOOK ME UP ON IT.
IN TWO DAYS, I EARNED 25 DOLLARS AND A BAG OF COOKIES!
Tomorrow will be better
Baba & Mama's Airfare
爸爸媽媽
機票錢
No Touch
不許碰
ONE
FIVE

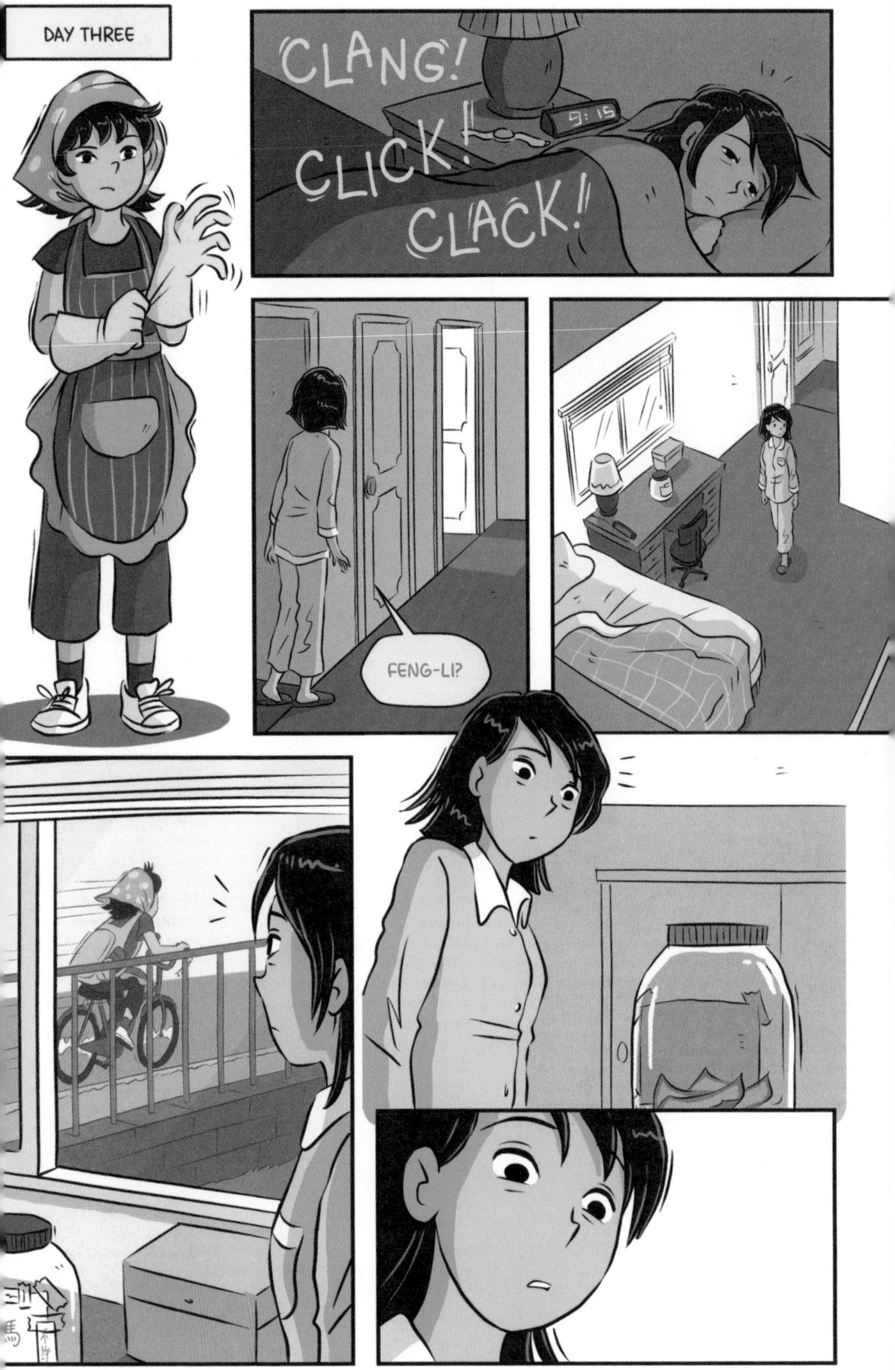
DAY THREE
CLANG!
CLICK!
CLACK!
9:15
FENG-LI?

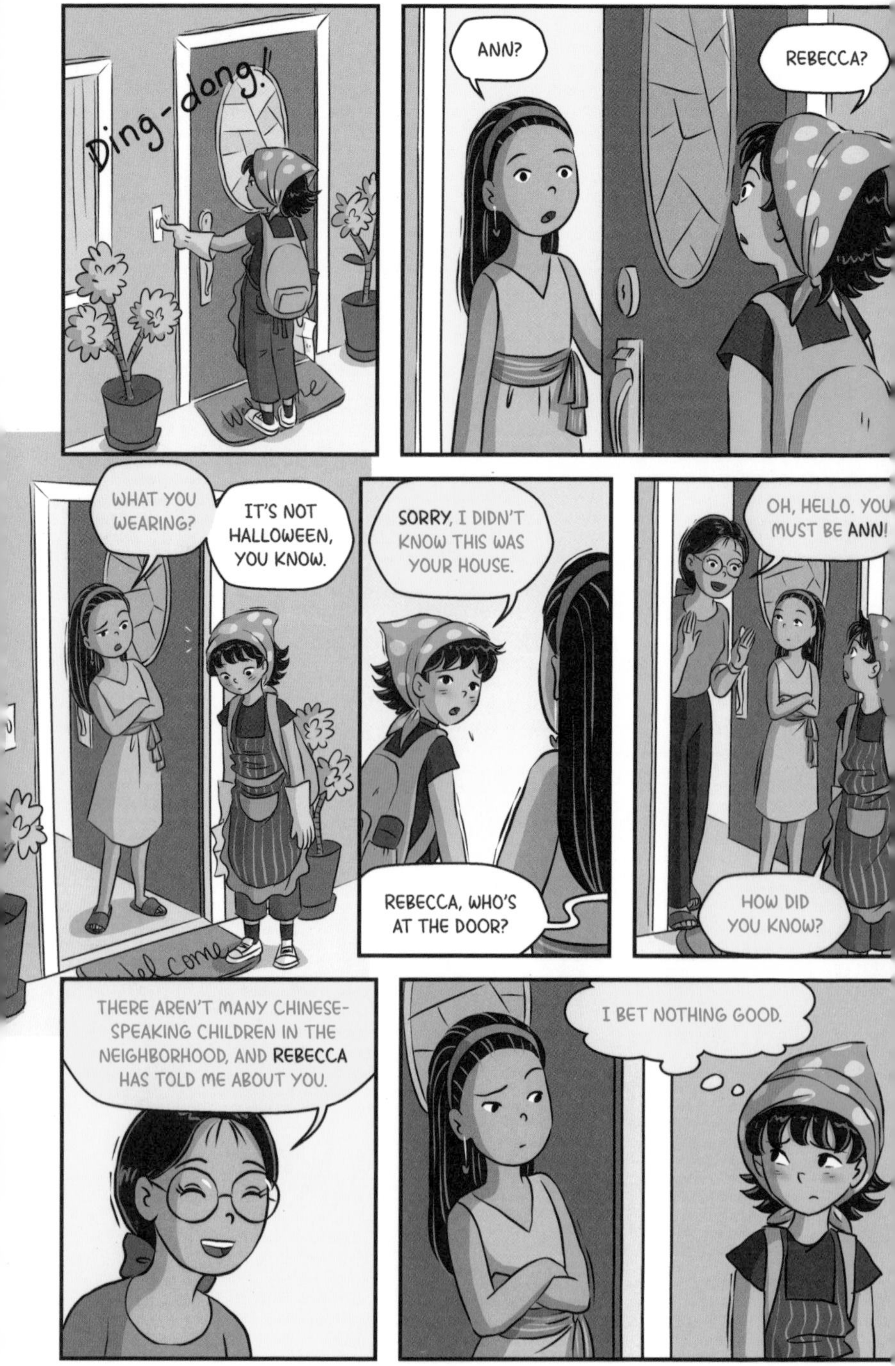
Ding-dong!!
Welcome
ANN?
REBECCA?
WHAT YOU WEARING?
IT'S NOT HALLOWEEN, YOU KNOW.
Welcome
SORRY, I DIDN'T KNOW THIS WAS YOUR HOUSE.
REBECCA, WHO'S AT THE DOOR?
OH, HELLO. YOU MUST BE ANN!
HOW DID YOU KNOW?
THERE AREN'T MANY CHINESE-SPEAKING CHILDREN IN THE NEIGHBORHOOD, AND REBECCA HAS TOLD ME ABOUT YOU.
I BET NOTHING GOOD.

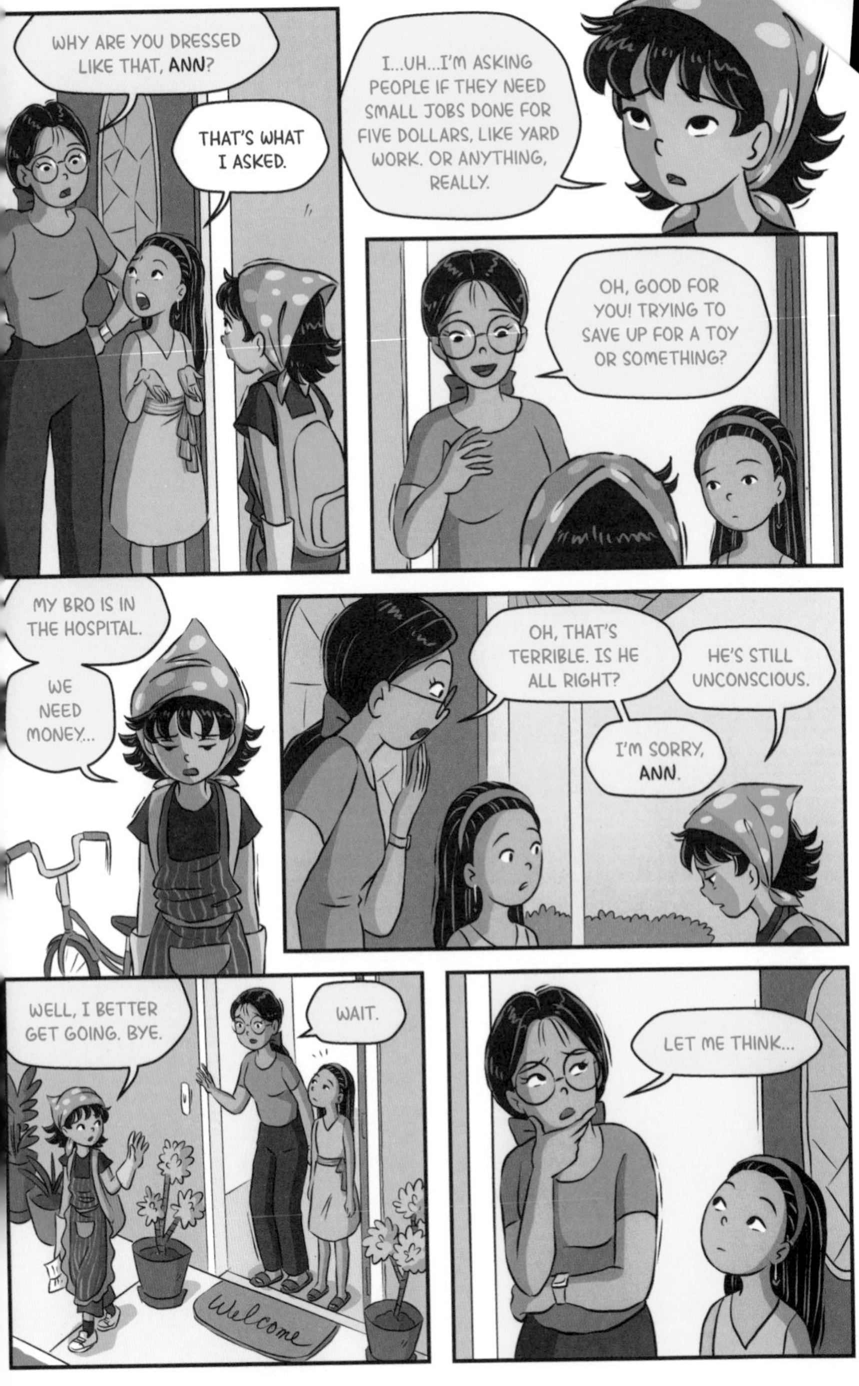
WHY ARE YOU DRESSED LIKE THAT, ANN?
THAT'S WHAT I ASKED.
I...UH...I'M ASKING PEOPLE IF THEY NEED SMALL JOBS DONE FOR FIVE DOLLARS, LIKE YARD WORK. OR ANYTHING, REALLY.
OH, GOOD FOR YOU! TRYING TO SAVE UP FOR A TOY OR SOMETHING?
MY BRO IS IN THE HOSPITAL.
WE NEED MONEY...
OH, THAT'S TERRIBLE. IS HE ALL RIGHT?
HE'S STILL UNCONSCIOUS.
I'M SORRY, ANN.
WELL, I BETTER GET GOING. BYE.
WAIT.
Welcome
LET ME THINK...

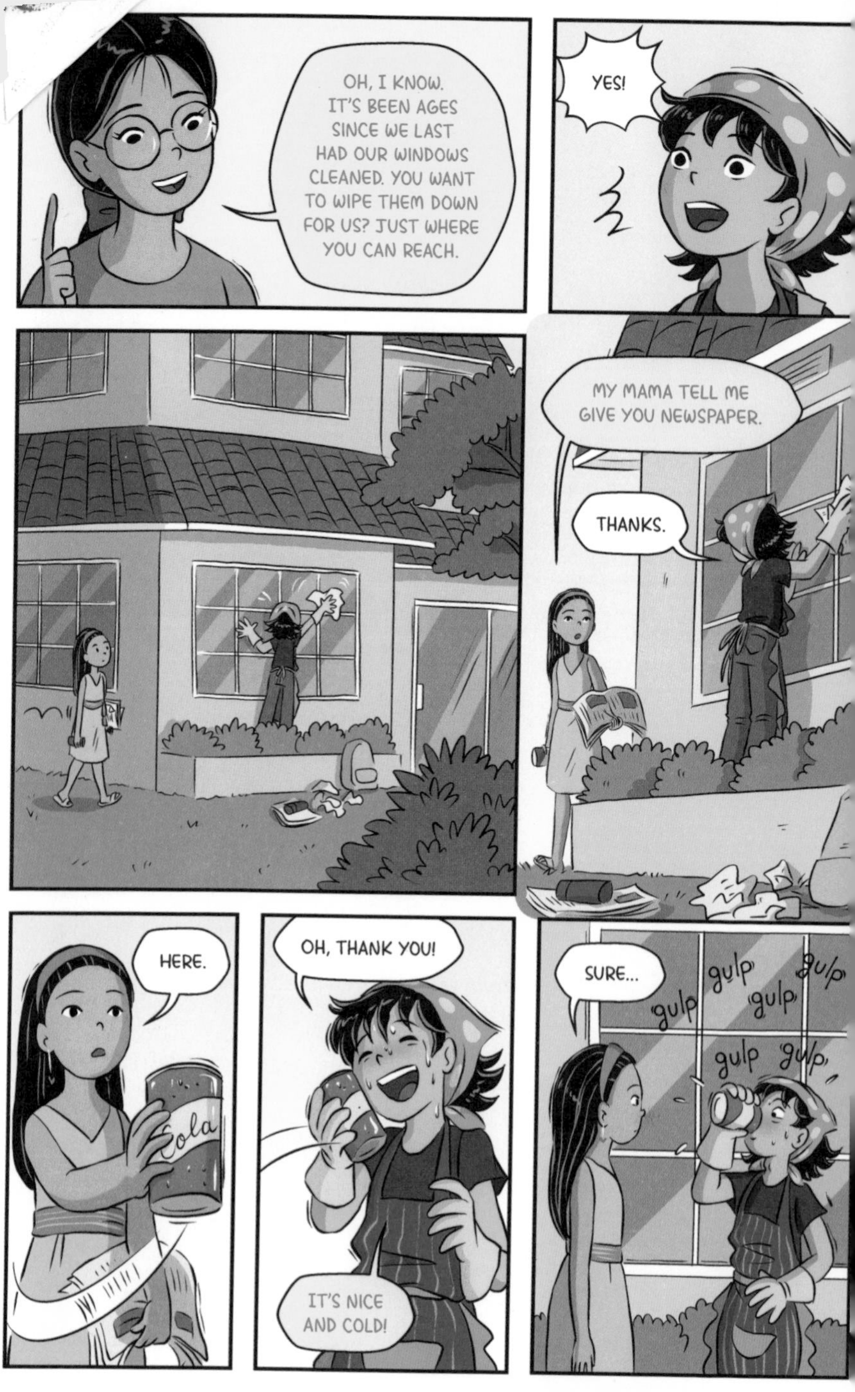
OH, I KNOW. IT'S BEEN AGES SINCE WE LAST HAD OUR WINDOWS CLEANED. YOU WANT TO WIPE THEM DOWN FOR US? JUST WHERE YOU CAN REACH.
YES!
MY MAMA TELL ME GIVE YOU NEWSPAPER.
THANKS.
HERE.
Cola
OH, THANK YOU!
IT'S NICE AND COLD!
SURE...
gulp gulp gulp gulp gulp gulp

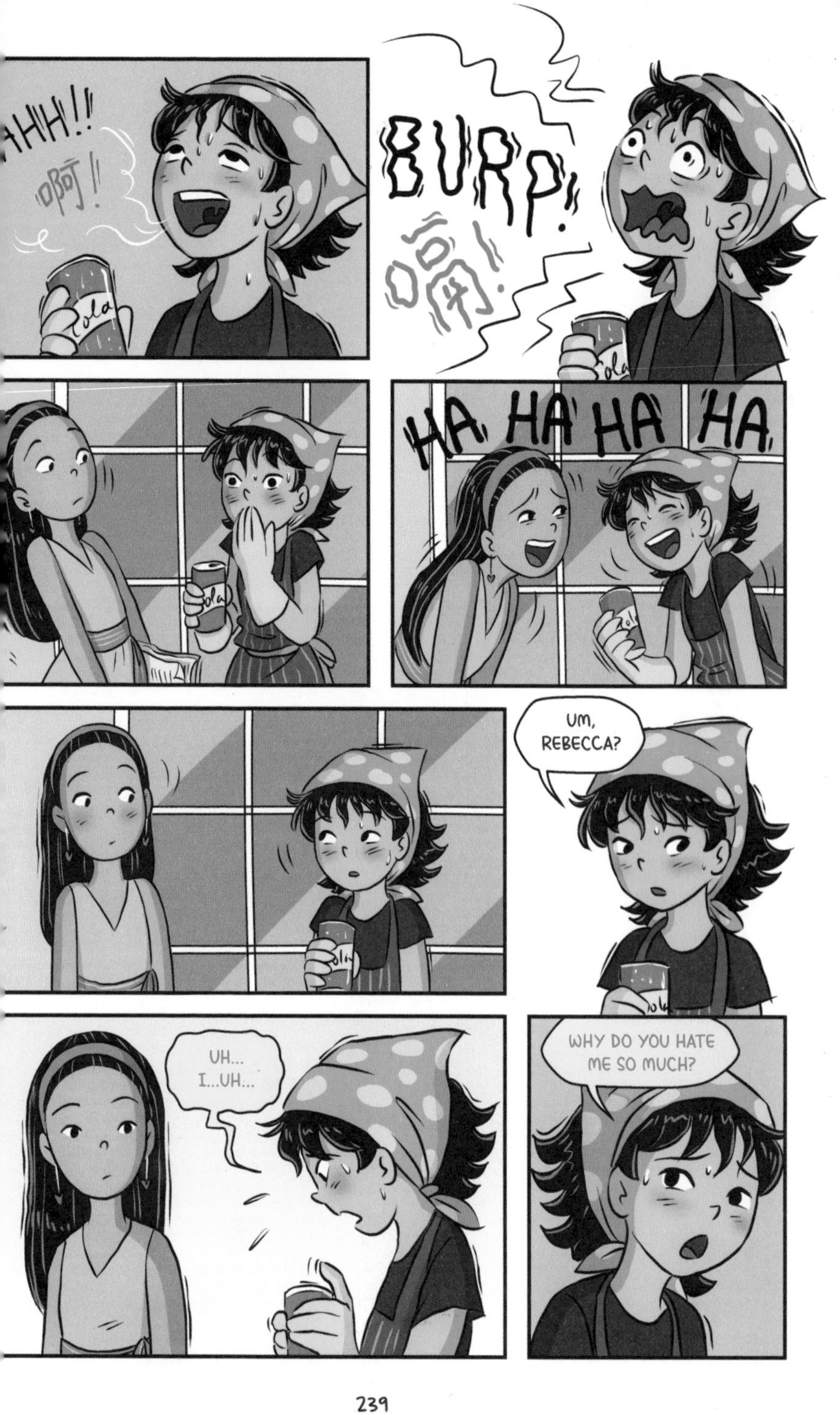

HH!!
啊!!
BURP!
嗝!
HA HA HA HA
UM, REBECCA?
UH... I...UH...
WHY DO YOU HATE ME SO MUCH?

HATE YOU? I NO HATE YOU.

BECAUSE... MY CHINESE... VERY BAD.

YOU COME, OTHER KIDS SEE ME DIFFERENT.

TO THEM, I NO MORE AMERICAN. I, CHINESE.

SO I NO TALK TO YOU...

BUT YOU NEVER WANT TO TALK TO ME. WHY?

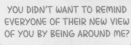

YOU DIDN'T WANT TO REMIND EVERYONE OF THEIR NEW VIEW OF YOU BY BEING AROUND ME?

YEAH.

SORRY...IF YOU FEEL BAD.

I DO. NOBODY LIKES TO BE TREATED DIFFERENTLY. BUT I GET WHY NOW.

OH, HEY, I WAS REALLY IMPRESSED BY THE WAY YOU SCARED OFF THOSE BOYS BACK AT SCHOOL.

GARY AND FRANK?

YEAH, THEY ANNOYING SOMETIMES.

YOU KNOW, BOYS!

HA HA, YEAH. THEY'RE THE SAME HERE AND IN TAIWAN! BUT IT WAS COOL HOW YOU STOOD UP FOR YOURSELF LIKE THAT.

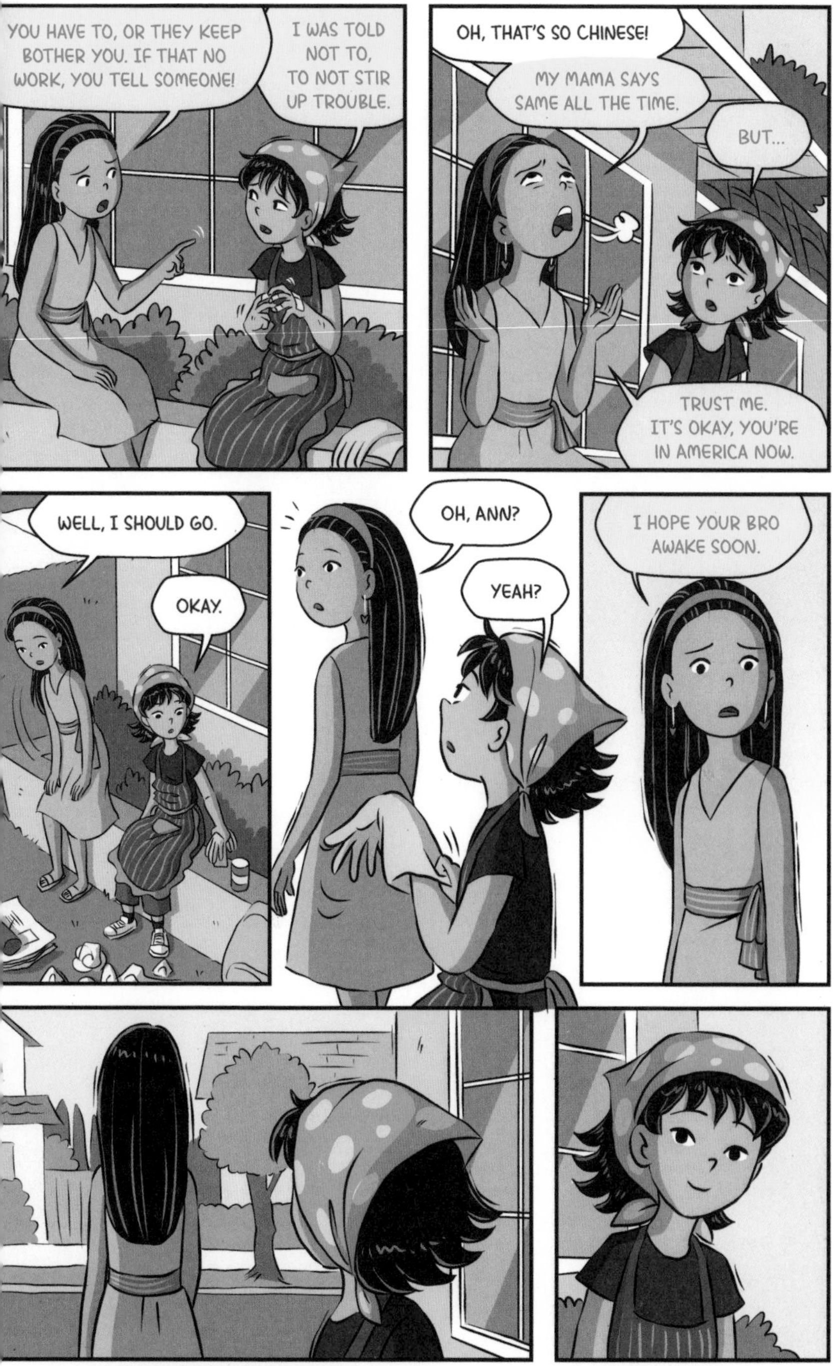
YOU HAVE TO, OR THEY KEEP BOTHER YOU. IF THAT NO WORK, YOU TELL SOMEONE!
I WAS TOLD NOT TO, TO NOT STIR UP TROUBLE.
OH, THAT'S SO CHINESE!
MY MAMA SAYS SAME ALL THE TIME.
BUT...
TRUST ME. IT'S OKAY, YOU'RE IN AMERICA NOW.
WELL, I SHOULD GO.
OKAY.
OH, ANN?
YEAH?
I HOPE YOUR BRO AWAKE SOON.

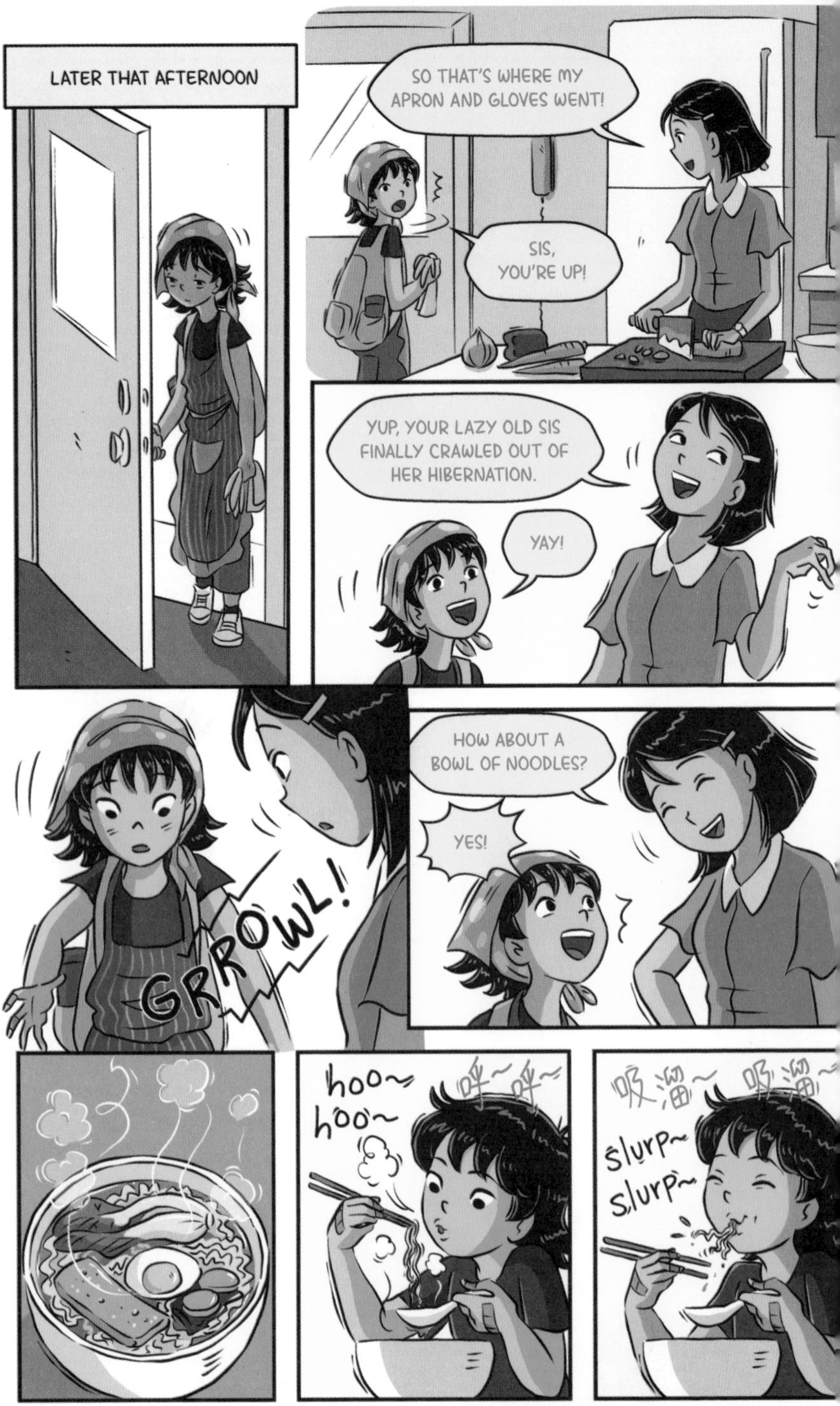
LATER THAT AFTERNOON
SO THAT'S WHERE MY APRON AND GLOVES WENT!
SIS, YOU'RE UP!
YUP, YOUR LAZY OLD SIS FINALLY CRAWLED OUT OF HER HIBERNATION.
YAY!
GRROWL!
HOW ABOUT A BOWL OF NOODLES?
YES!
hoo~ hoo~
呼~呼~
吸溜~ 吸溜~
slurp~ slurp~

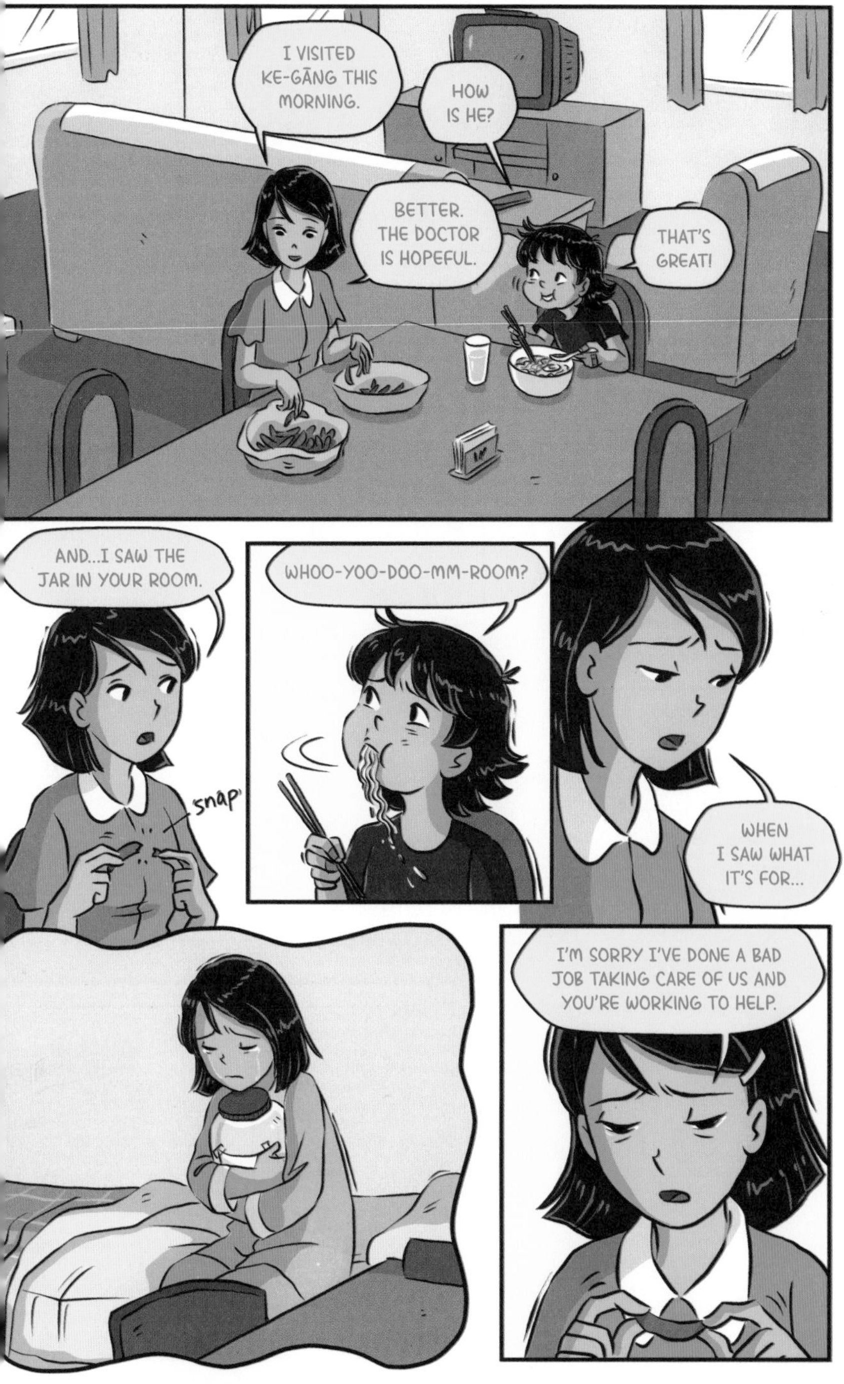
I VISITED KE-GĀNG THIS MORNING.
HOW IS HE?
BETTER. THE DOCTOR IS HOPEFUL.
THAT'S GREAT!
AND...I SAW THE JAR IN YOUR ROOM.
snap
WHOO-YOO-DOO-MM-ROOM?
WHEN I SAW WHAT IT'S FOR...
I'M SORRY I'VE DONE A BAD JOB TAKING CARE OF US AND YOU'RE WORKING TO HELP.

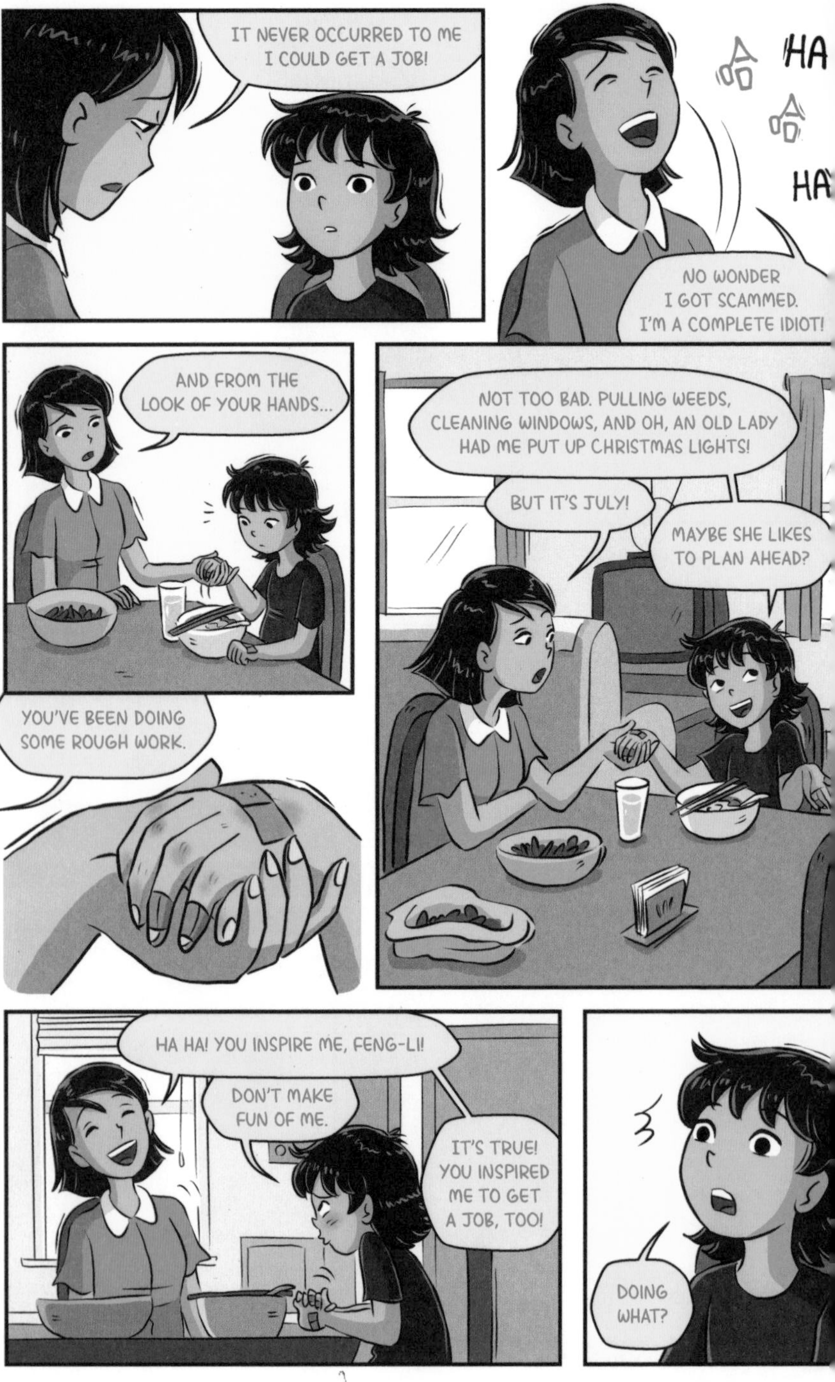
IT NEVER OCCURRED TO ME I COULD GET A JOB!
HA HA
NO WONDER I GOT SCAMMED. I'M A COMPLETE IDIOT!
AND FROM THE LOOK OF YOUR HANDS...
YOU'VE BEEN DOING SOME ROUGH WORK.
NOT TOO BAD. PULLING WEEDS, CLEANING WINDOWS, AND OH, AN OLD LADY HAD ME PUT UP CHRISTMAS LIGHTS!
BUT IT'S JULY!
MAYBE SHE LIKES TO PLAN AHEAD?
HA HA! YOU INSPIRE ME, FENG-LI!
DON'T MAKE FUN OF ME.
IT'S TRUE! YOU INSPIRED ME TO GET A JOB, TOO!
DOING WHAT?

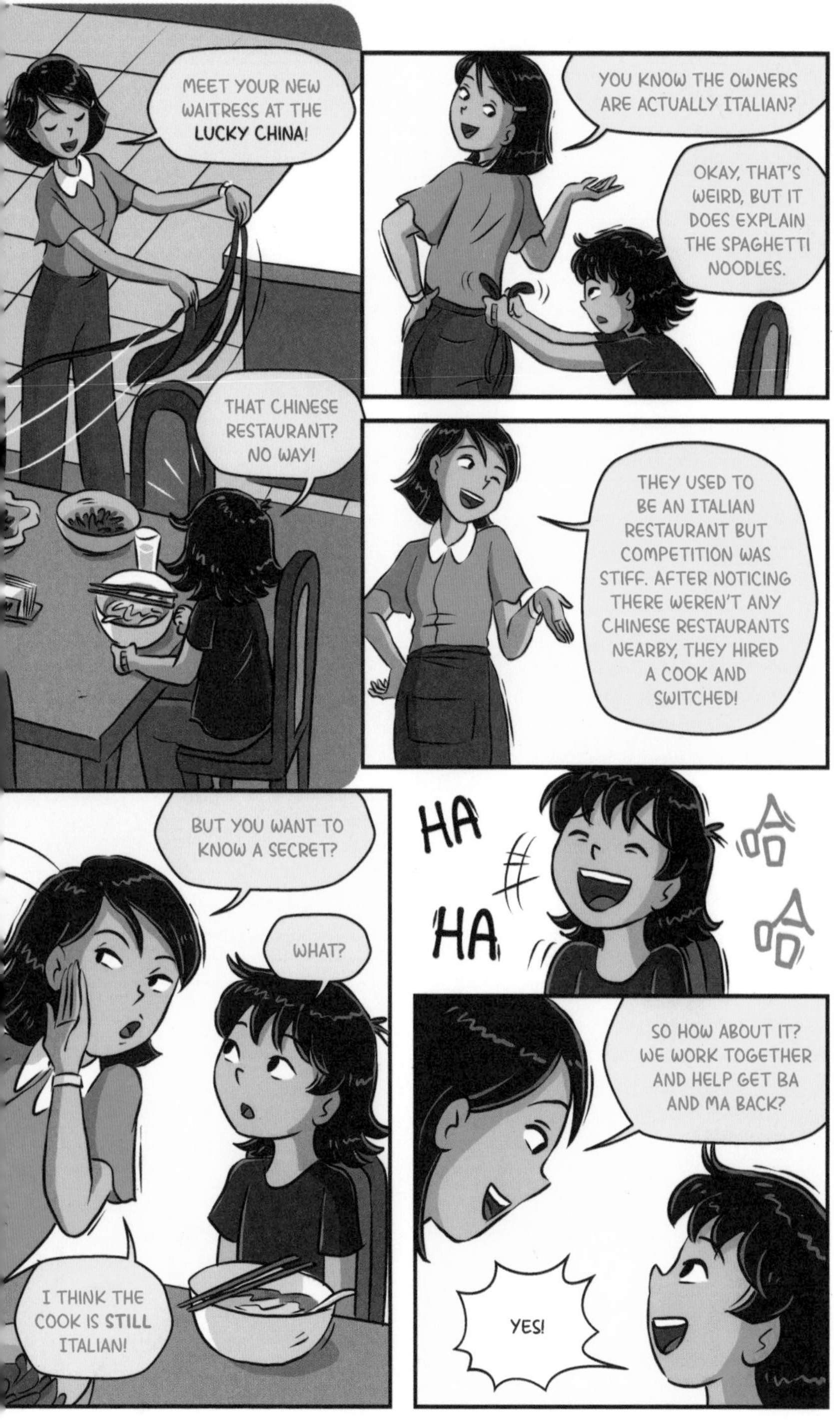
MEET YOUR NEW WAITRESS AT THE LUCKY CHINA!
YOU KNOW THE OWNERS ARE ACTUALLY ITALIAN?
OKAY, THAT'S WEIRD, BUT IT DOES EXPLAIN THE SPAGHETTI NOODLES.
THAT CHINESE RESTAURANT? NO WAY!
THEY USED TO BE AN ITALIAN RESTAURANT BUT COMPETITION WAS STIFF. AFTER NOTICING THERE WEREN'T ANY CHINESE RESTAURANTS NEARBY, THEY HIRED A COOK AND SWITCHED!
BUT YOU WANT TO KNOW A SECRET?
WHAT?
I THINK THE COOK IS STILL ITALIAN!
HA
HA
SO HOW ABOUT IT? WE WORK TOGETHER AND HELP GET BA AND MA BACK?
YES!

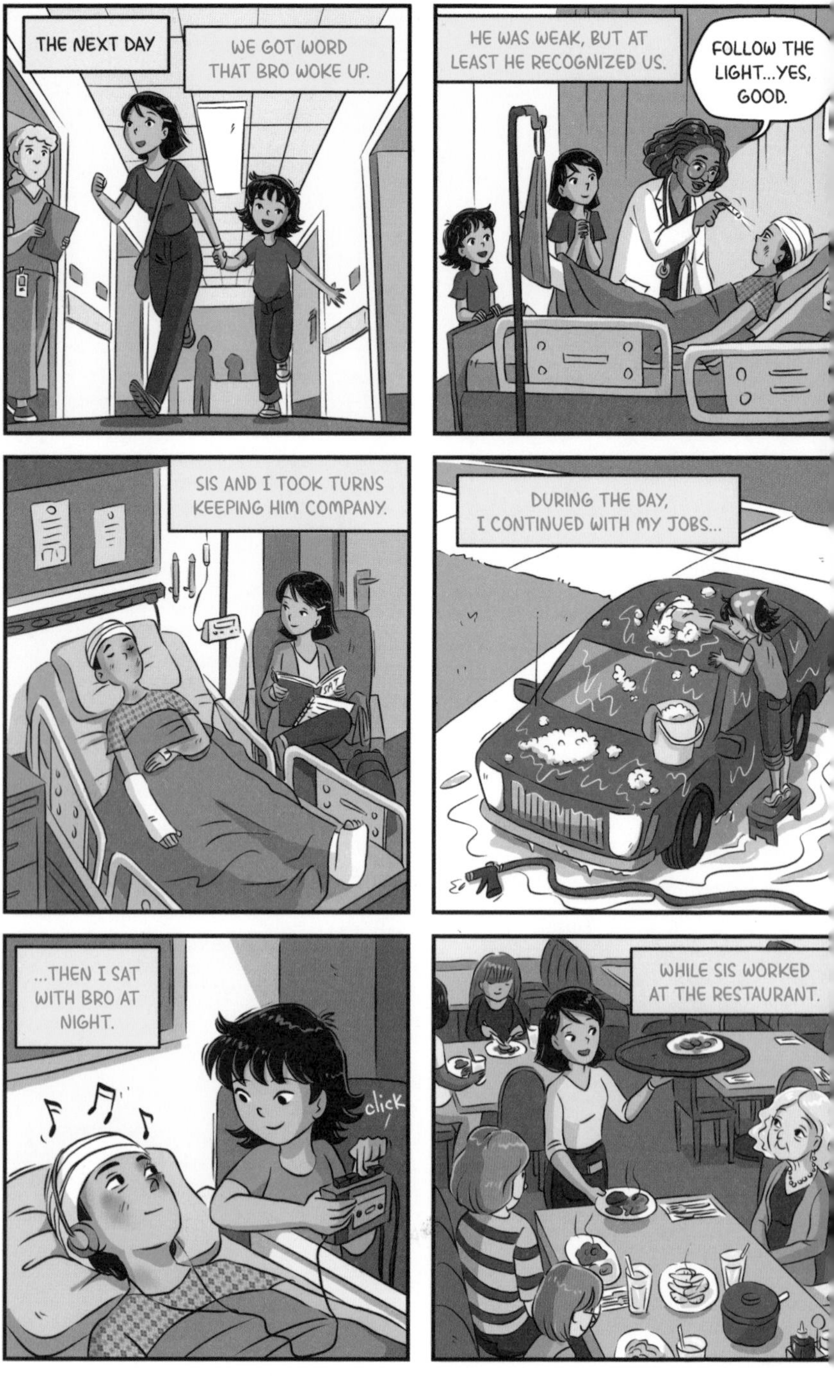
THE NEXT DAY
WE GOT WORD THAT BRO WOKE UP.
HE WAS WEAK, BUT AT LEAST HE RECOGNIZED US.
FOLLOW THE LIGHT...YES, GOOD.
SIS AND I TOOK TURNS KEEPING HIM COMPANY.
SAT
DURING THE DAY, I CONTINUED WITH MY JOBS...
...THEN I SAT WITH BRO AT NIGHT.
click
WHILE SIS WORKED AT THE RESTAURANT.

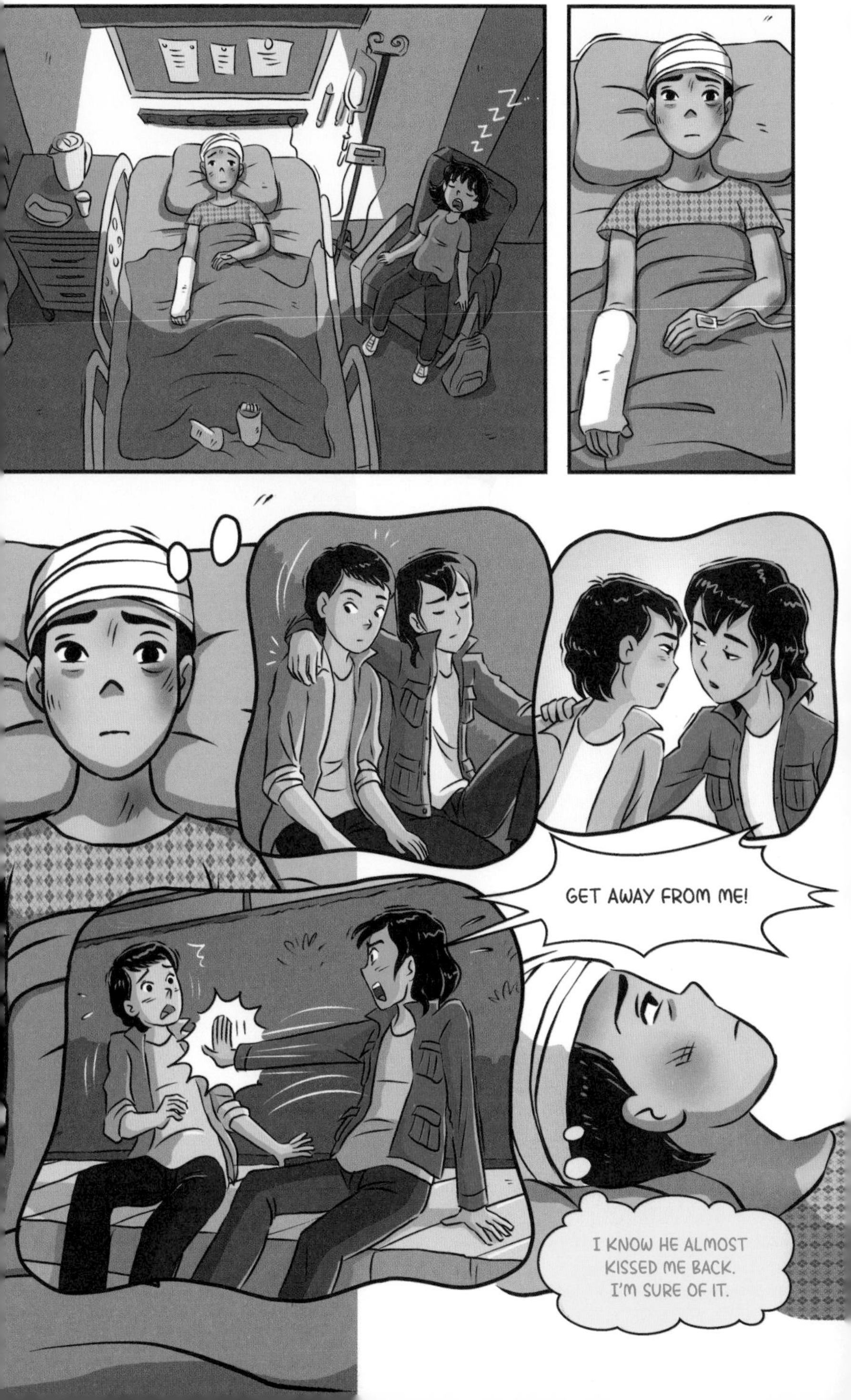
GET AWAY FROM ME!
I KNOW HE ALMOST KISSED ME BACK. I'M SURE OF IT.

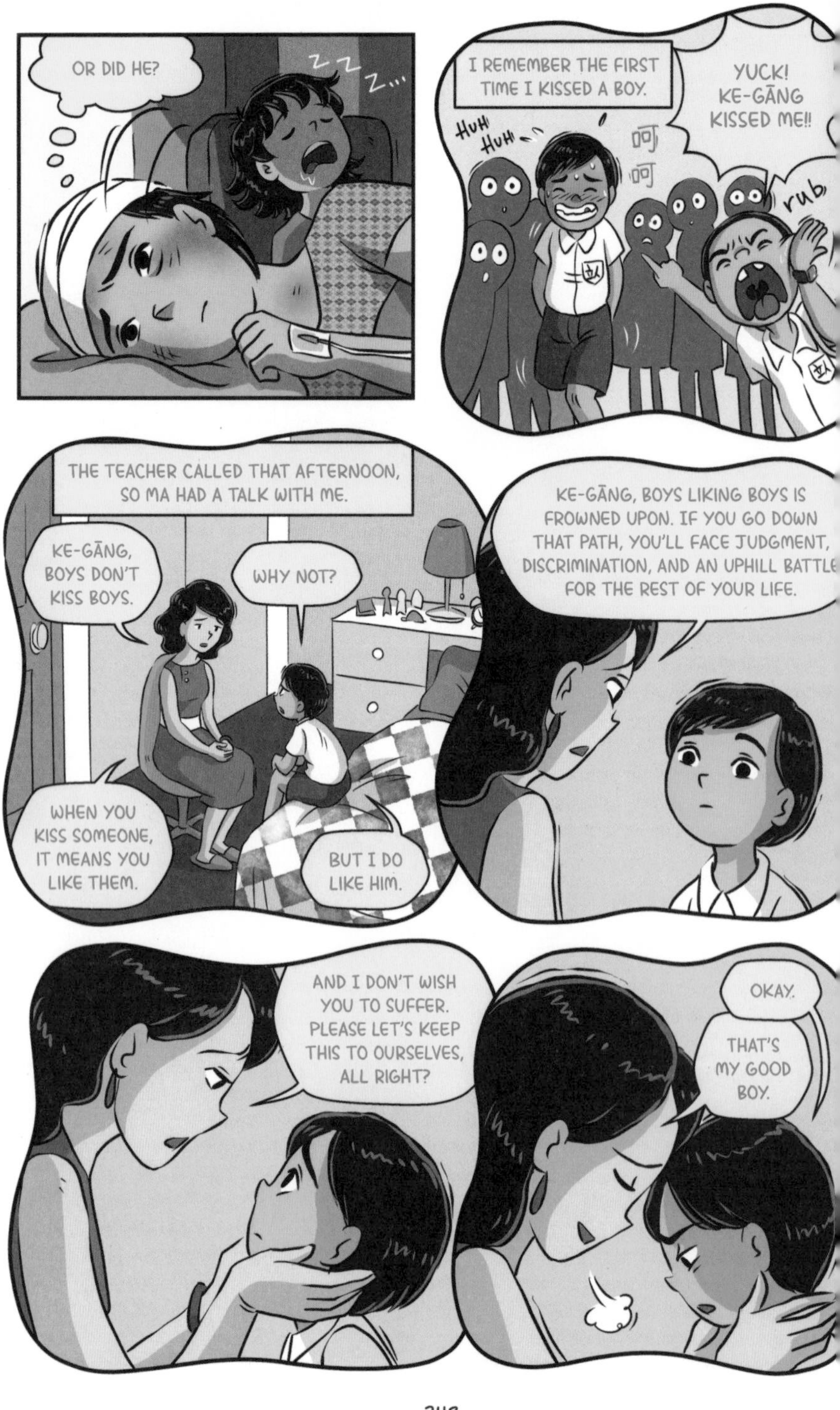
OR DID HE?
Z Z Z...
I REMEMBER THE FIRST TIME I KISSED A BOY.
HUH HUH
呵
呵
YUCK! KE-GĀNG KISSED ME!!
rub
THE TEACHER CALLED THAT AFTERNOON, SO MA HAD A TALK WITH ME.
KE-GĀNG, BOYS DON'T KISS BOYS.
WHY NOT?
WHEN YOU KISS SOMEONE, IT MEANS YOU LIKE THEM.
BUT I DO LIKE HIM.
KE-GĀNG, BOYS LIKING BOYS IS FROWNED UPON. IF YOU GO DOWN THAT PATH, YOU'LL FACE JUDGMENT, DISCRIMINATION, AND AN UPHILL BATTLE FOR THE REST OF YOUR LIFE.
AND I DON'T WISH YOU TO SUFFER. PLEASE LET'S KEEP THIS TO OURSELVES, ALL RIGHT?
OKAY.
THAT'S MY GOOD BOY.

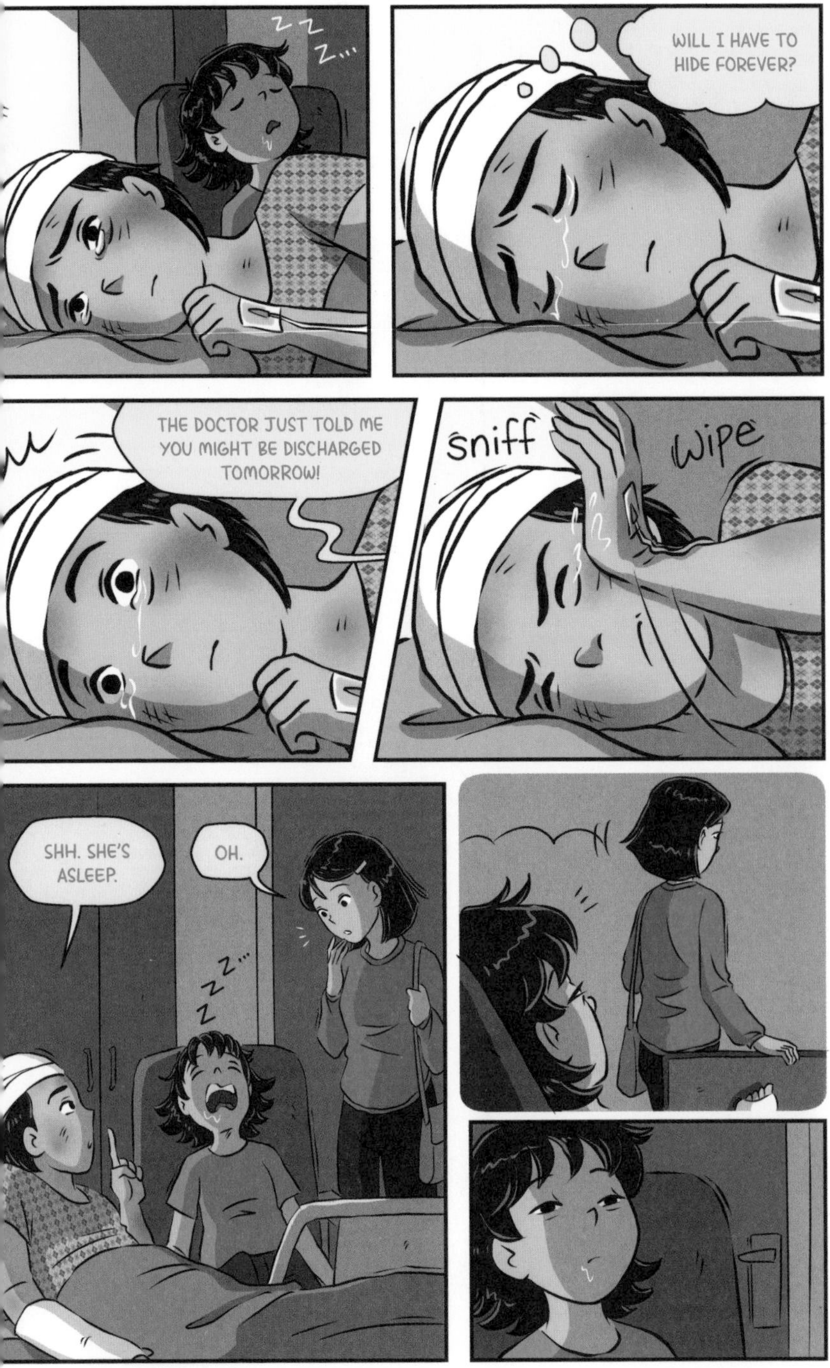
Z Z Z...
WILL I HAVE TO HIDE FOREVER?
THE DOCTOR JUST TOLD ME YOU MIGHT BE DISCHARGED TOMORROW!
sniff
wipe
SHH. SHE'S ASLEEP.
OH.
Z Z Z...

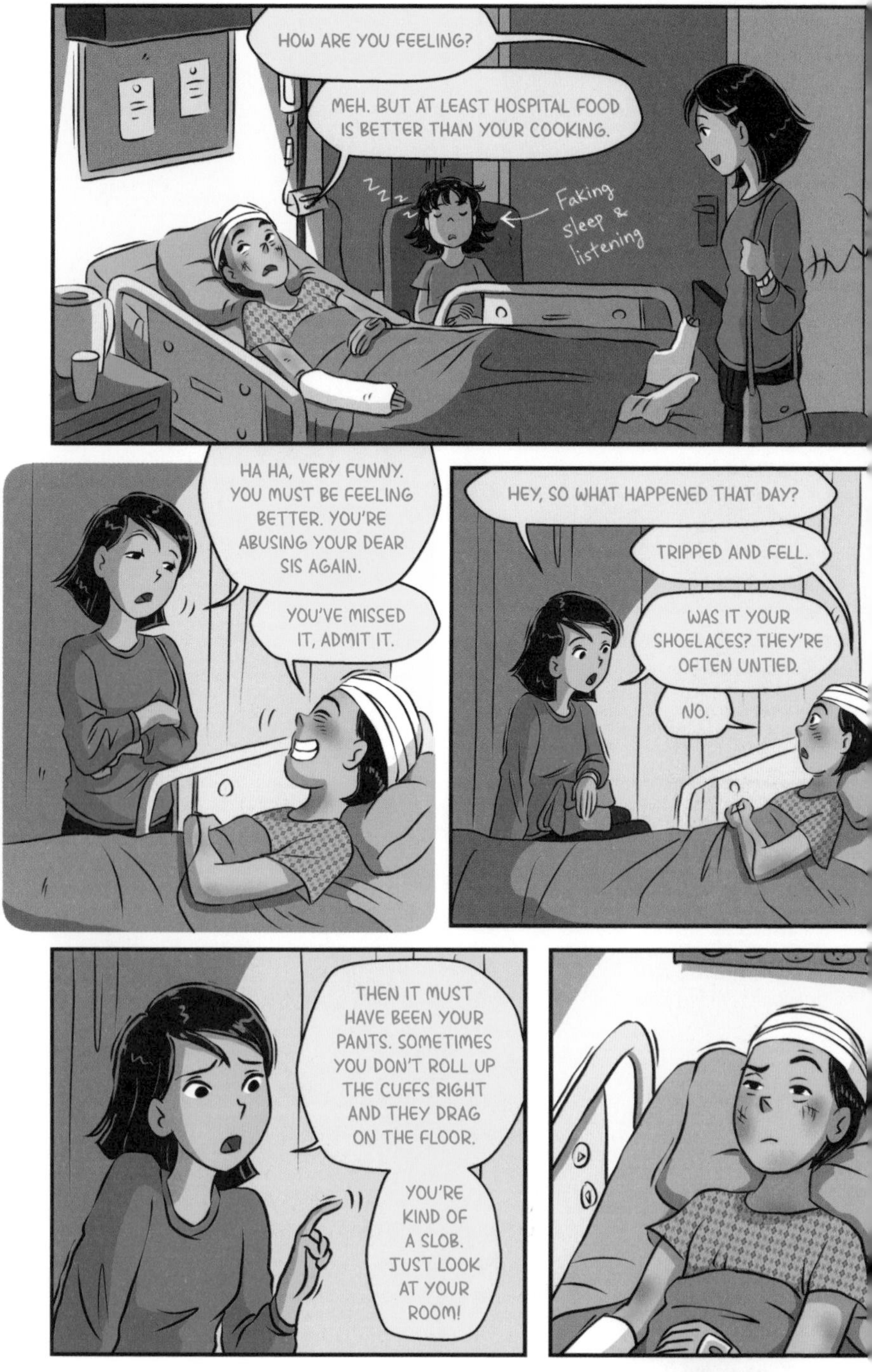
HOW ARE YOU FEELING?
MEH. BUT AT LEAST HOSPITAL FOOD IS BETTER THAN YOUR COOKING.
Z Z Z
Faking sleep & listening
HA HA, VERY FUNNY. YOU MUST BE FEELING BETTER. YOU'RE ABUSING YOUR DEAR SIS AGAIN.
YOU'VE MISSED IT, ADMIT IT.
HEY, SO WHAT HAPPENED THAT DAY?
TRIPPED AND FELL.
WAS IT YOUR SHOELACES? THEY'RE OFTEN UNTIED.
NO.
THEN IT MUST HAVE BEEN YOUR PANTS. SOMETIMES YOU DON'T ROLL UP THE CUFFS RIGHT AND THEY DRAG ON THE FLOOR.
YOU'RE KIND OF A SLOB. JUST LOOK AT YOUR ROOM!

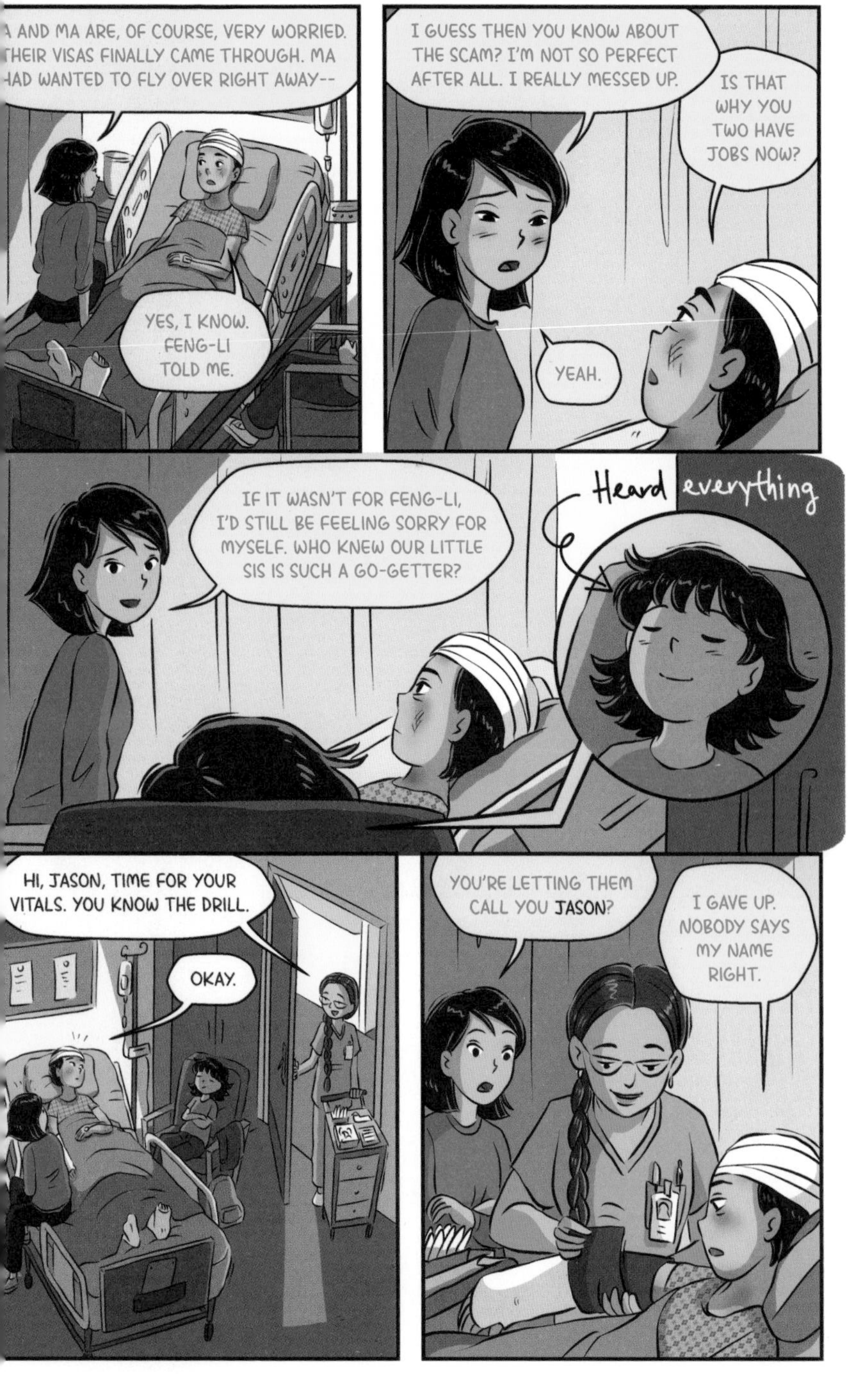
A AND MA ARE, OF COURSE, VERY WORRIED. THEIR VISAS FINALLY CAME THROUGH. MA HAD WANTED TO FLY OVER RIGHT AWAY--
YES, I KNOW. FENG-LI TOLD ME.
I GUESS THEN YOU KNOW ABOUT THE SCAM? I'M NOT SO PERFECT AFTER ALL. I REALLY MESSED UP.
IS THAT WHY YOU TWO HAVE JOBS NOW?
YEAH.
IF IT WASN'T FOR FENG-LI, I'D STILL BE FEELING SORRY FOR MYSELF. WHO KNEW OUR LITTLE SIS IS SUCH A GO-GETTER?
Heard everything
HI, JASON, TIME FOR YOUR VITALS. YOU KNOW THE DRILL.
OKAY.
YOU'RE LETTING THEM CALL YOU JASON?
I GAVE UP. NOBODY SAYS MY NAME RIGHT.

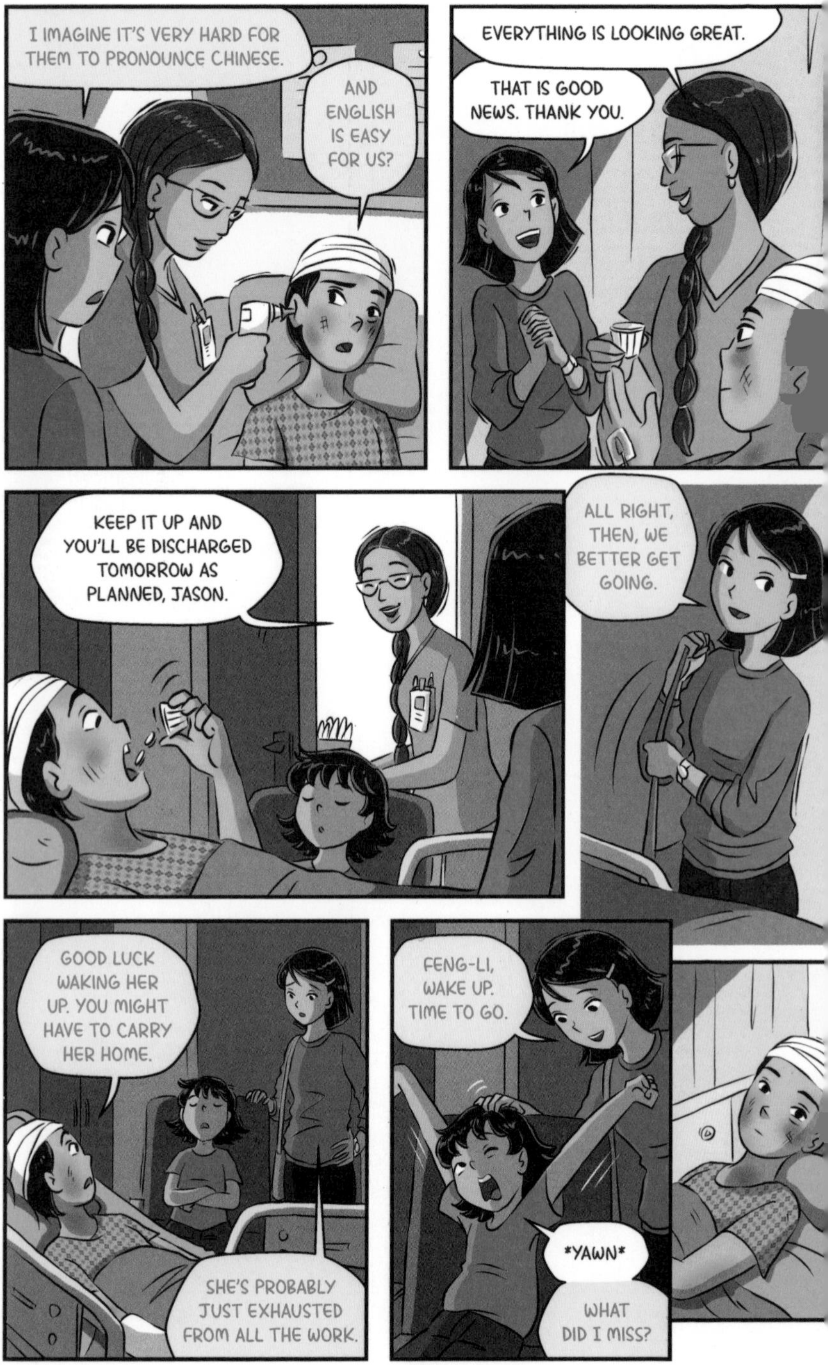
I IMAGINE IT'S VERY HARD FOR THEM TO PRONOUNCE CHINESE.
AND ENGLISH IS EASY FOR US?
EVERYTHING IS LOOKING GREAT.
THAT IS GOOD NEWS. THANK YOU.
KEEP IT UP AND YOU'LL BE DISCHARGED TOMORROW AS PLANNED, JASON.
ALL RIGHT, THEN, WE BETTER GET GOING.
GOOD LUCK WAKING HER UP. YOU MIGHT HAVE TO CARRY HER HOME.
SHE'S PROBABLY JUST EXHAUSTED FROM ALL THE WORK.
FENG-LI, WAKE UP. TIME TO GO.
YAWN
WHAT DID I MISS?

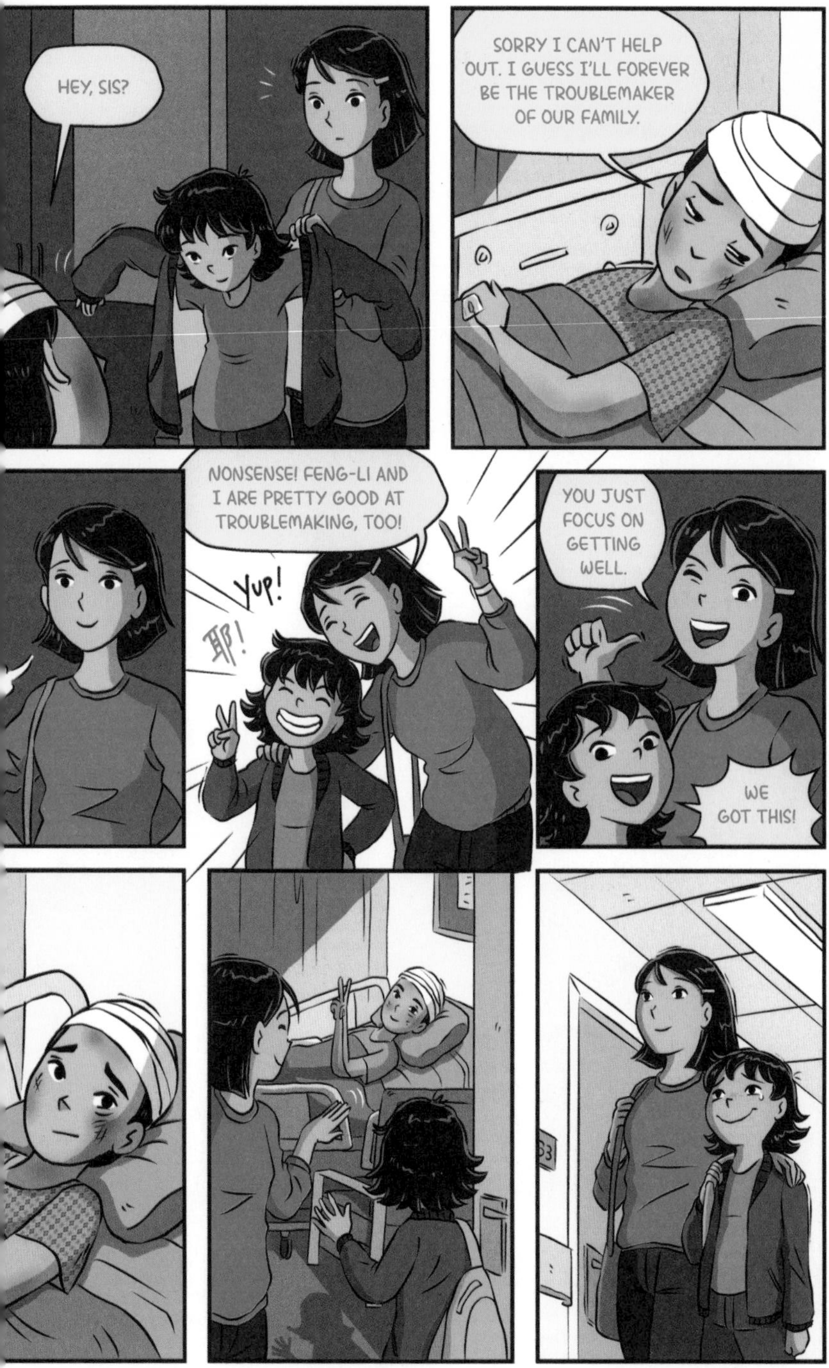
HEY, SIS?
SORRY I CAN'T HELP OUT. I GUESS I'LL FOREVER BE THE TROUBLEMAKER OF OUR FAMILY.
NONSENSE! FENG-LI AND I ARE PRETTY GOOD AT TROUBLEMAKING, TOO!
YUP!
耶!
YOU JUST FOCUS ON GETTING WELL.
WE GOT THIS!

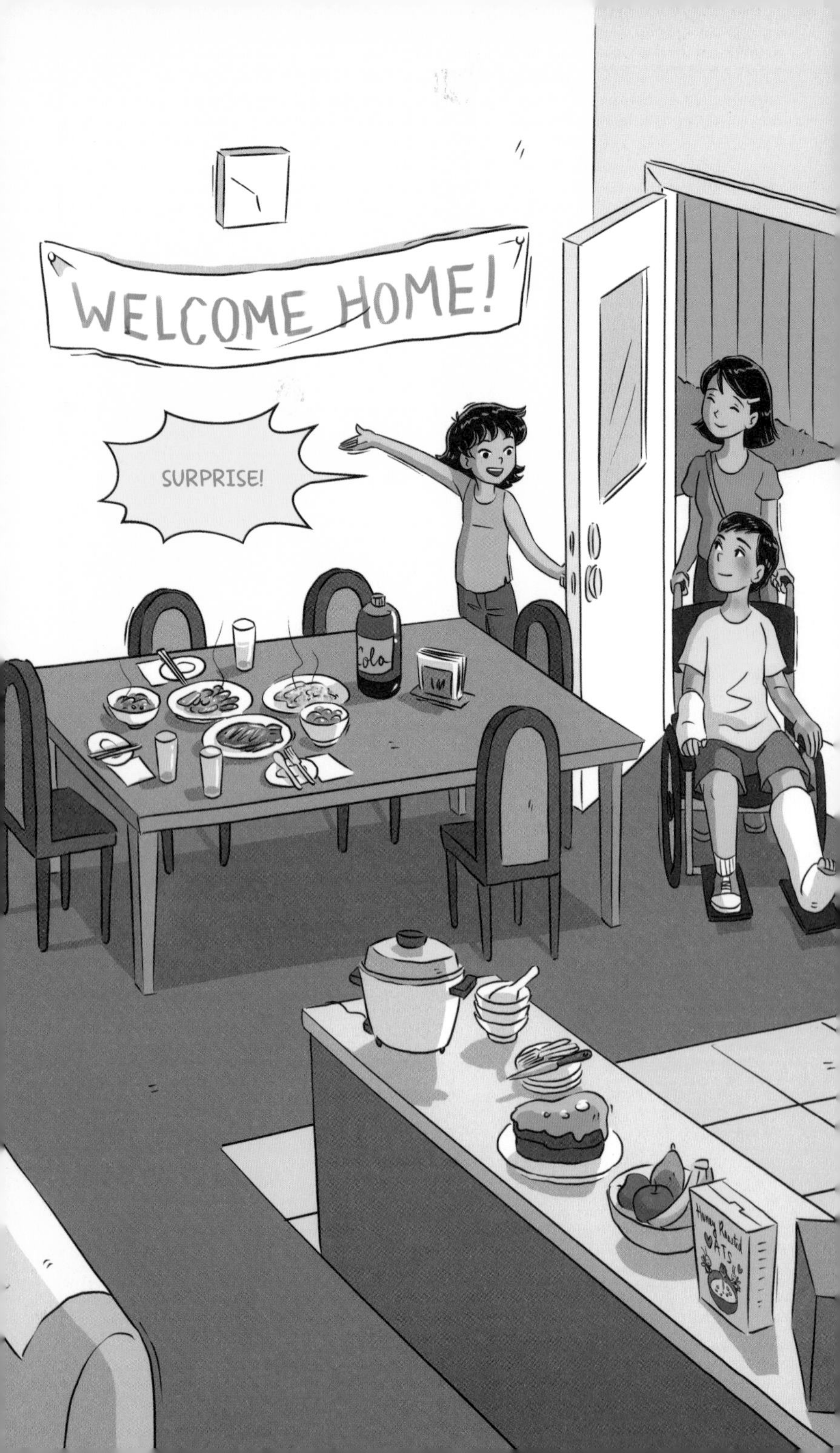
WELCOME HOME!
SURPRISE!
Cola
Honey Roasted OATS

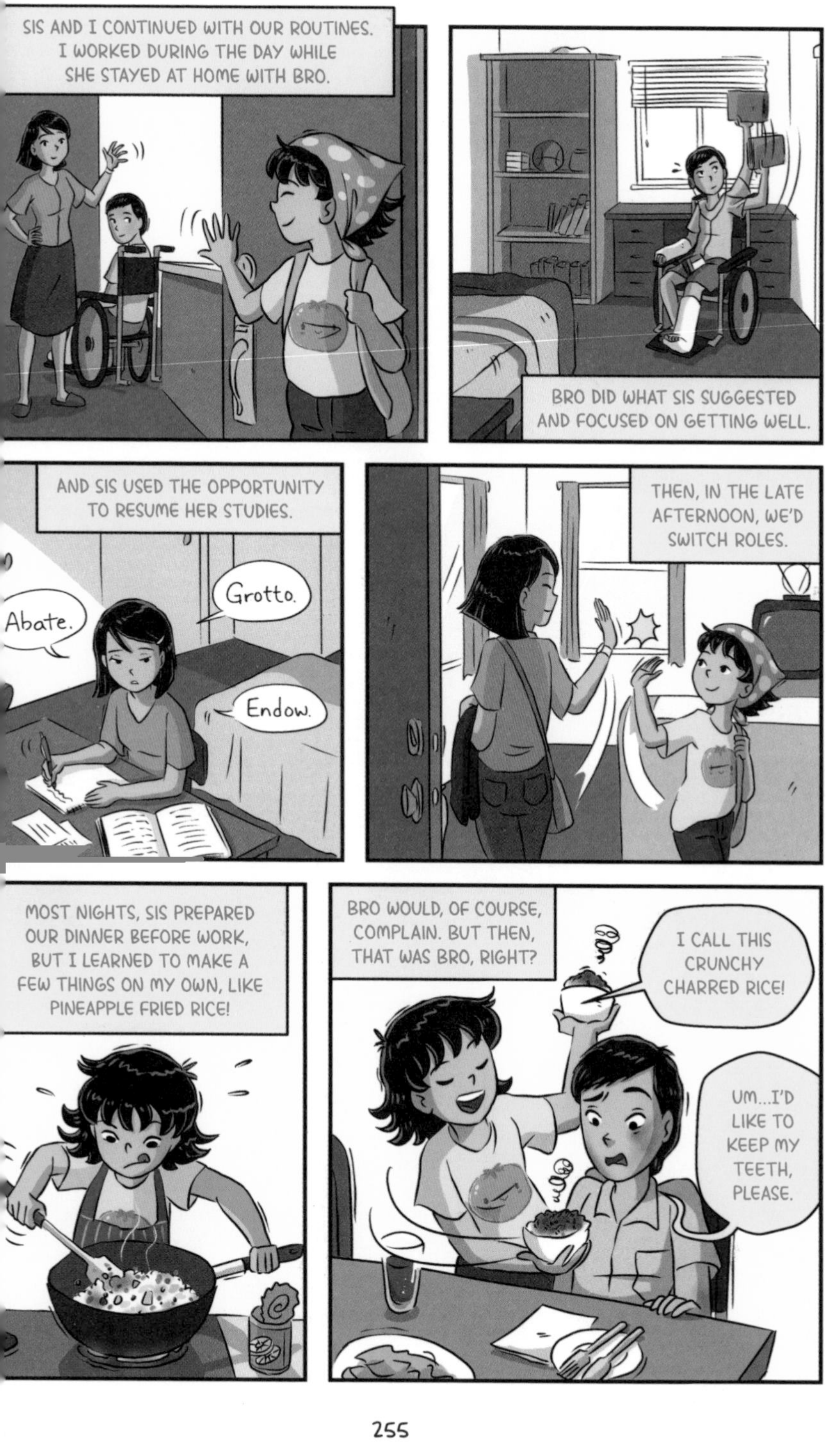
SIS AND I CONTINUED WITH OUR ROUTINES. I WORKED DURING THE DAY WHILE SHE STAYED AT HOME WITH BRO.
BRO DID WHAT SIS SUGGESTED AND FOCUSED ON GETTING WELL.
AND SIS USED THE OPPORTUNITY TO RESUME HER STUDIES.
Abate.
Grotto.
Endow.
THEN, IN THE LATE AFTERNOON, WE'D SWITCH ROLES.
MOST NIGHTS, SIS PREPARED OUR DINNER BEFORE WORK, BUT I LEARNED TO MAKE A FEW THINGS ON MY OWN, LIKE PINEAPPLE FRIED RICE!
BRO WOULD, OF COURSE, COMPLAIN. BUT THEN, THAT WAS BRO, RIGHT?
I CALL THIS CRUNCHY CHARRED RICE!
UM...I'D LIKE TO KEEP MY TEETH, PLEASE.

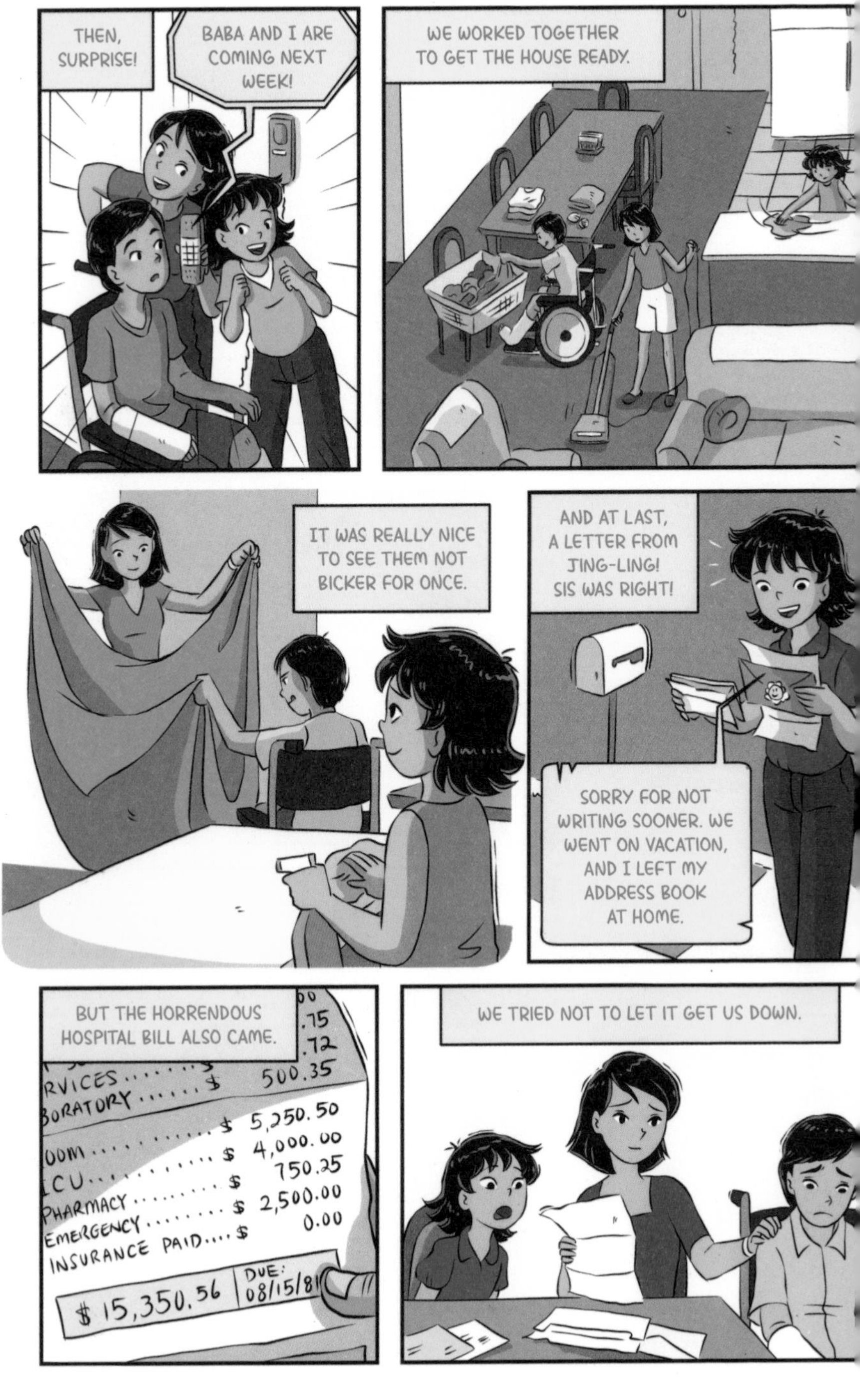
THEN, SURPRISE!
BABA AND I ARE COMING NEXT WEEK!
WE WORKED TOGETHER TO GET THE HOUSE READY.
IT WAS REALLY NICE TO SEE THEM NOT BICKER FOR ONCE.
AND AT LAST, A LETTER FROM JING-LING! SIS WAS RIGHT!
SORRY FOR NOT WRITING SOONER. WE WENT ON VACATION, AND I LEFT MY ADDRESS BOOK AT HOME.
BUT THE HORRENDOUS HOSPITAL BILL ALSO CAME.
.75
.72
RVICES........$ 500.35
BORATORY......$
5,250.50
OOM............$ 4,000.00
ICU............$ 750.25
PHARMACY.........$ 2,500.00
EMERGENCY.........$ 0.00
INSURANCE PAID.....$
$ 15,350.56
DUE: 08/15/81
WE TRIED NOT TO LET IT GET US DOWN.

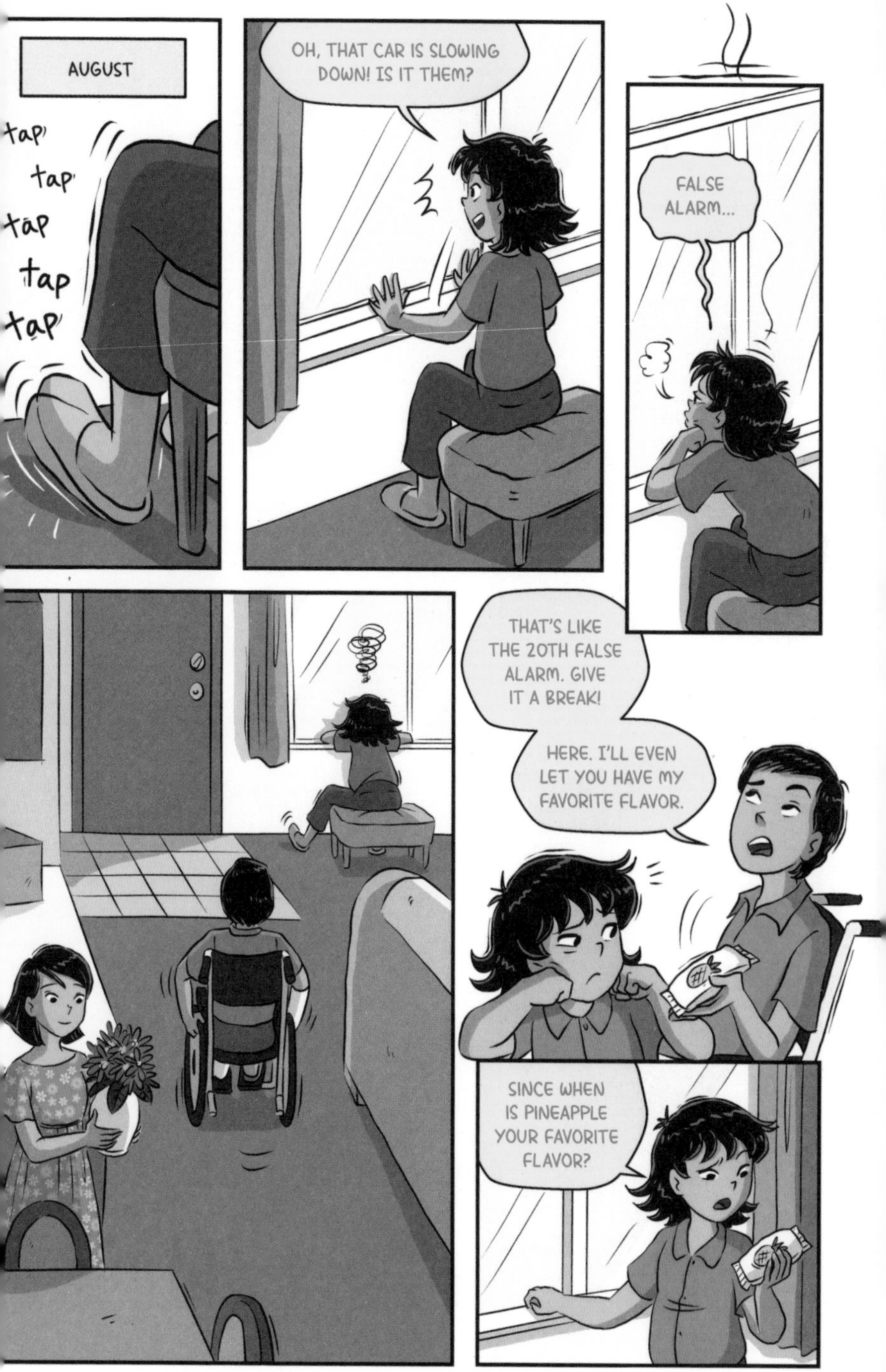
AUGUST
tap
tap
tap
tap
tap
OH, THAT CAR IS SLOWING DOWN! IS IT THEM?
FALSE ALARM...
THAT'S LIKE THE 20TH FALSE ALARM. GIVE IT A BREAK!
HERE. I'LL EVEN LET YOU HAVE MY FAVORITE FLAVOR.
SINCE WHEN IS PINEAPPLE YOUR FAVORITE FLAVOR?

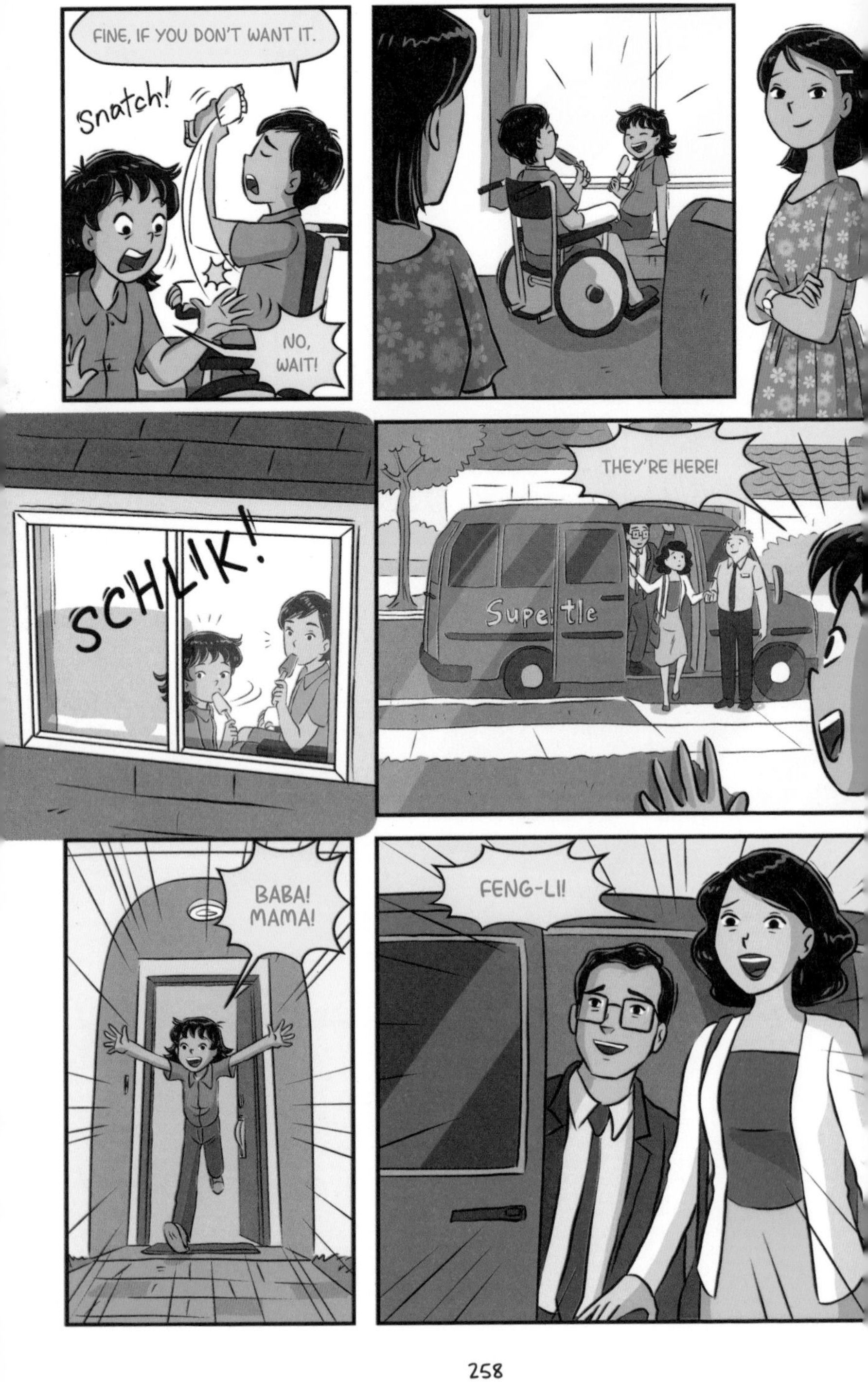
FINE, IF YOU DON'T WANT IT.
Snatch!
NO, WAIT!
SCHLIK!
THEY'RE HERE!
Super tle
BABA! MAMA!
FENG-LI!

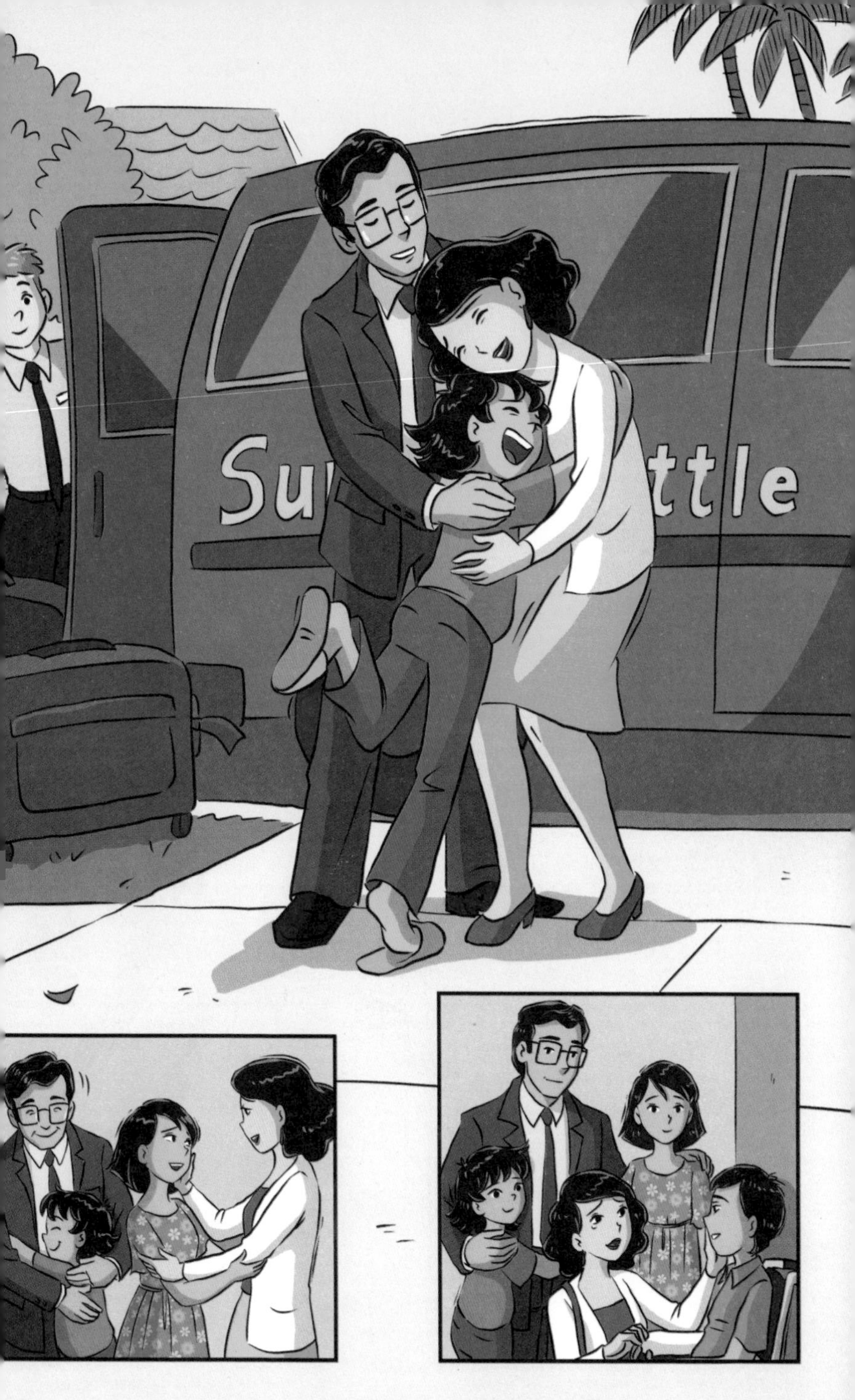

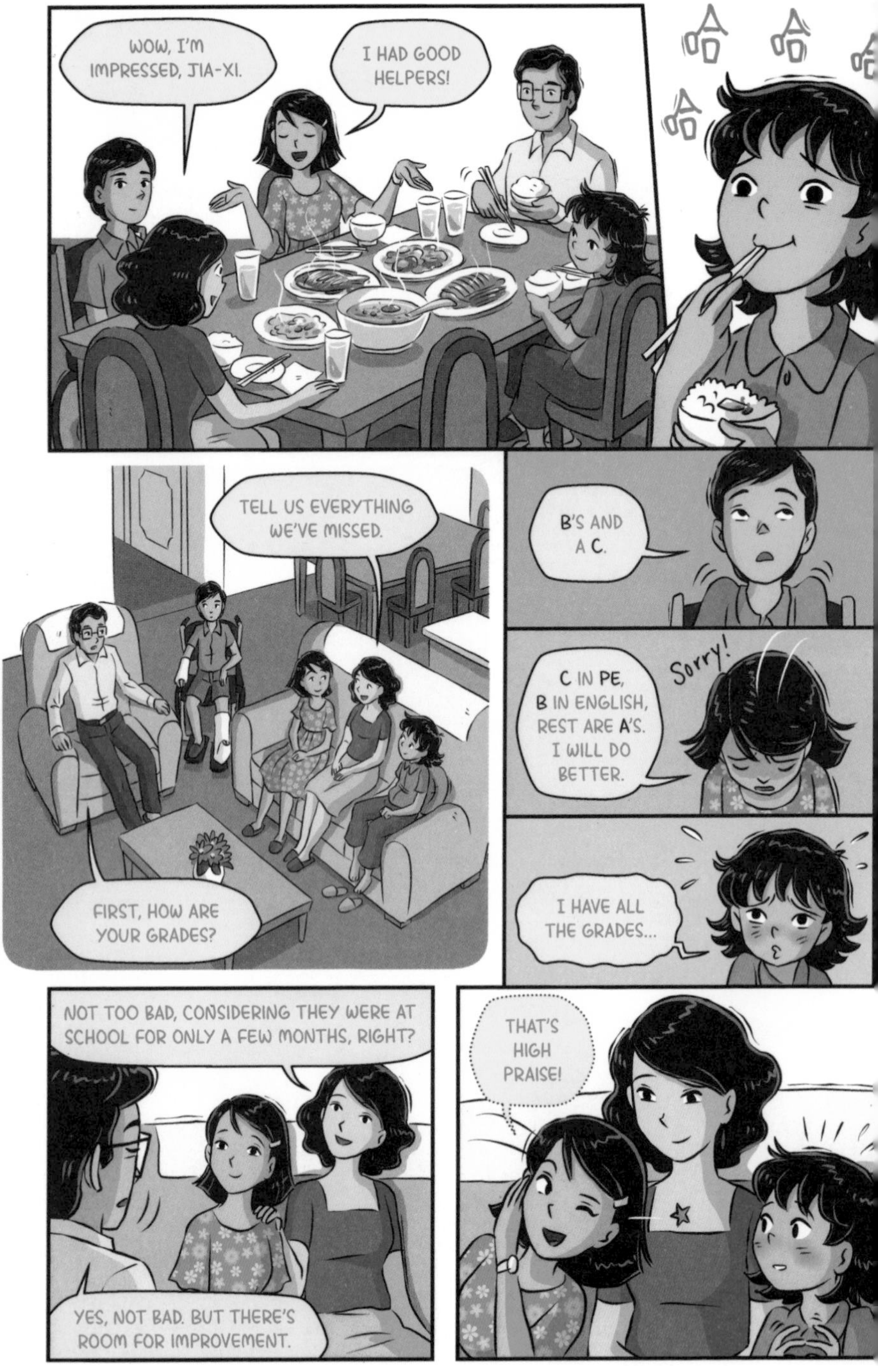
WOW, I'M IMPRESSED, JIA-XI.
I HAD GOOD HELPERS!
TELL US EVERYTHING WE'VE MISSED.
FIRST, HOW ARE YOUR GRADES?
B'S AND A C.
C IN PE, B IN ENGLISH, REST ARE A'S. I WILL DO BETTER.
Sorry!
I HAVE ALL THE GRADES...
NOT TOO BAD, CONSIDERING THEY WERE AT SCHOOL FOR ONLY A FEW MONTHS, RIGHT?
YES, NOT BAD. BUT THERE'S ROOM FOR IMPROVEMENT.
THAT'S HIGH PRAISE!

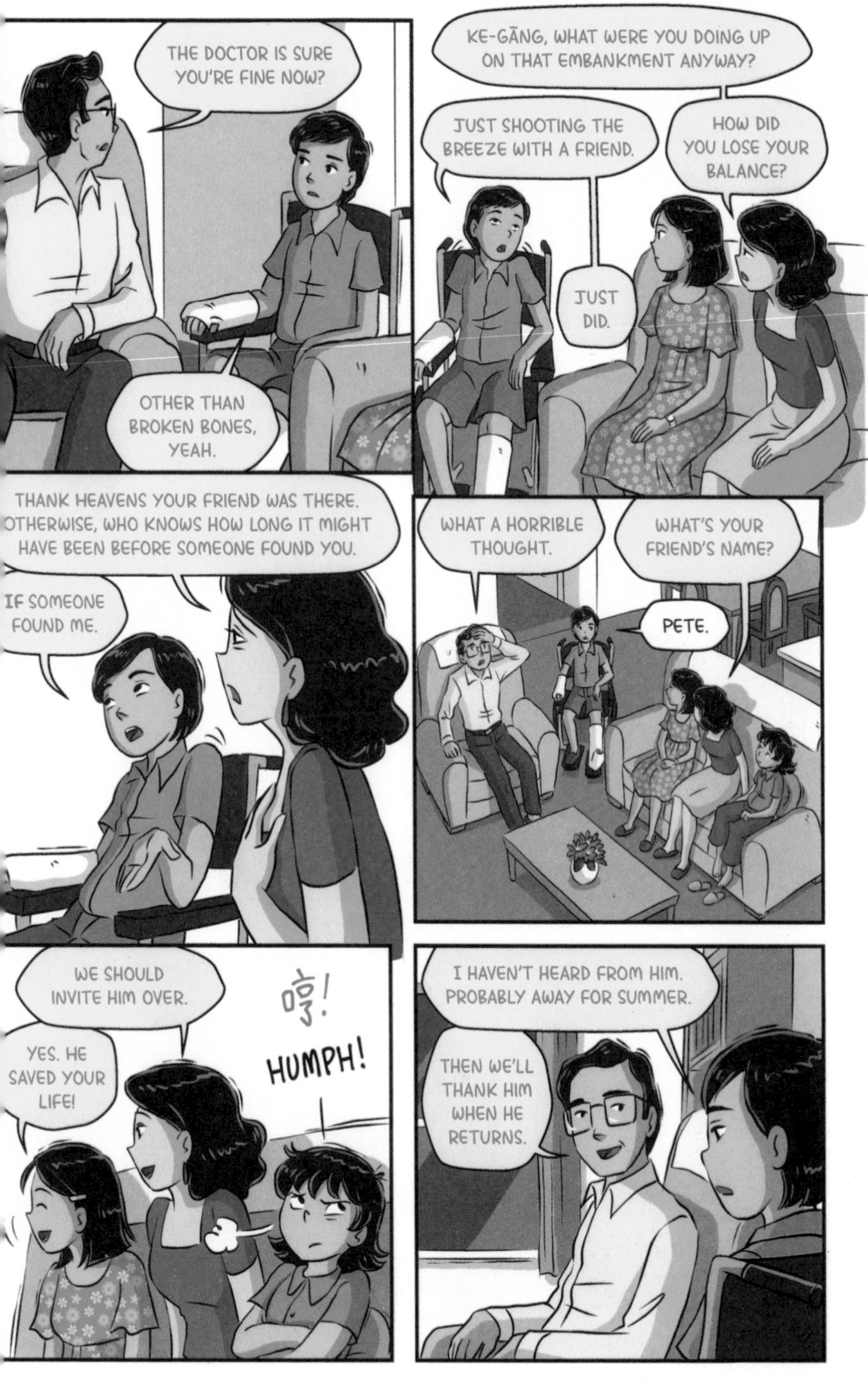

THE DOCTOR IS SURE YOU'RE FINE NOW?
OTHER THAN BROKEN BONES, YEAH.
KE-GĀNG, WHAT WERE YOU DOING UP ON THAT EMBANKMENT ANYWAY?
JUST SHOOTING THE BREEZE WITH A FRIEND.
HOW DID YOU LOSE YOUR BALANCE?
JUST DID.
THANK HEAVENS YOUR FRIEND WAS THERE. OTHERWISE, WHO KNOWS HOW LONG IT MIGHT HAVE BEEN BEFORE SOMEONE FOUND YOU.
IF SOMEONE FOUND ME.
WHAT A HORRIBLE THOUGHT.
WHAT'S YOUR FRIEND'S NAME?
PETE.
WE SHOULD INVITE HIM OVER.
YES. HE SAVED YOUR LIFE!
哼!
HUMPH!
I HAVEN'T HEARD FROM HIM. PROBABLY AWAY FOR SUMMER.
THEN WE'LL THANK HIM WHEN HE RETURNS.

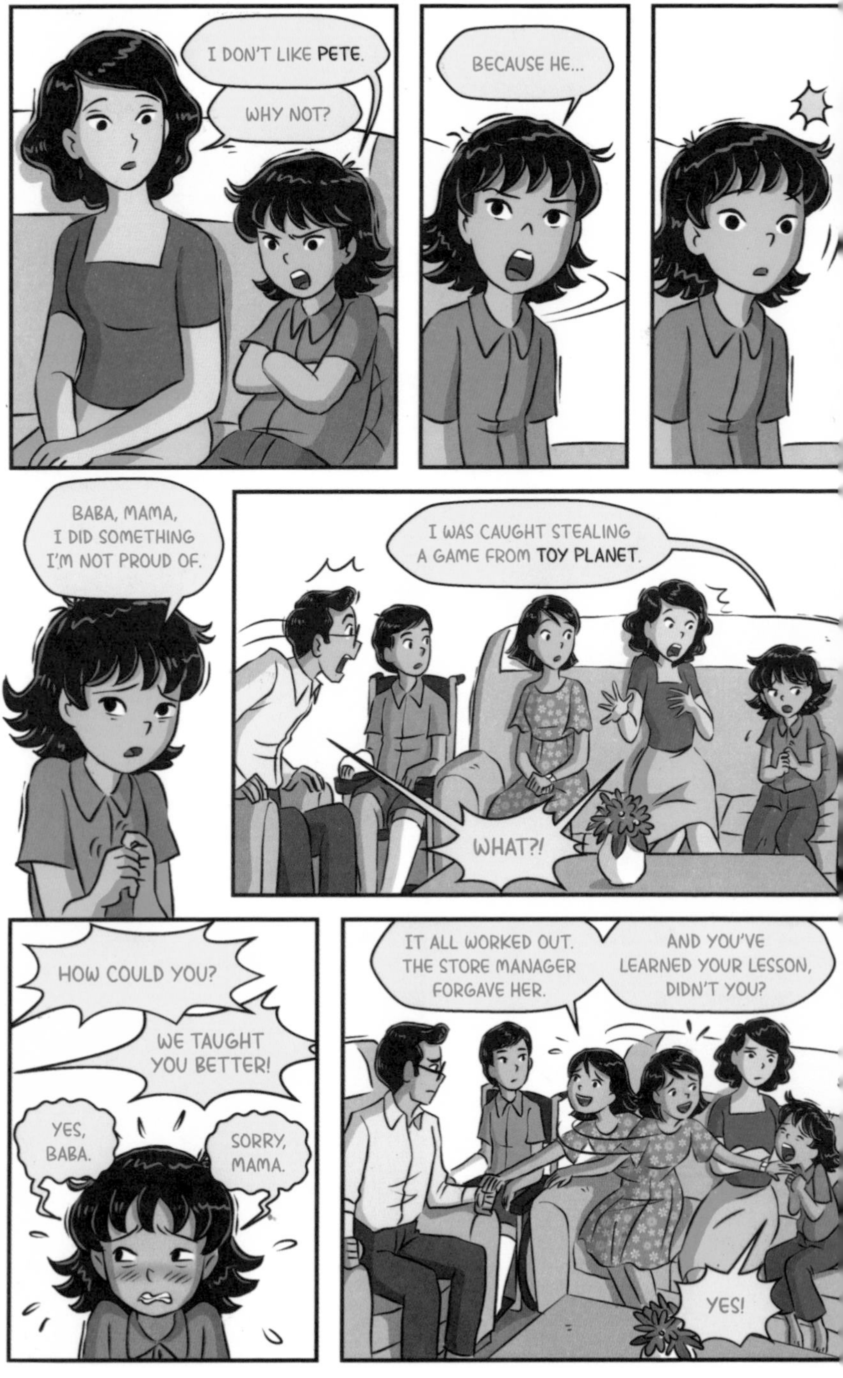
I DON'T LIKE PETE.
WHY NOT?
BECAUSE HE...
BABA, MAMA, I DID SOMETHING I'M NOT PROUD OF.
I WAS CAUGHT STEALING A GAME FROM TOY PLANET.
WHAT?!
HOW COULD YOU?
WE TAUGHT YOU BETTER!
YES, BABA.
SORRY, MAMA.
IT ALL WORKED OUT. THE STORE MANAGER FORGAVE HER.
AND YOU'VE LEARNED YOUR LESSON, DIDN'T YOU?
YES!

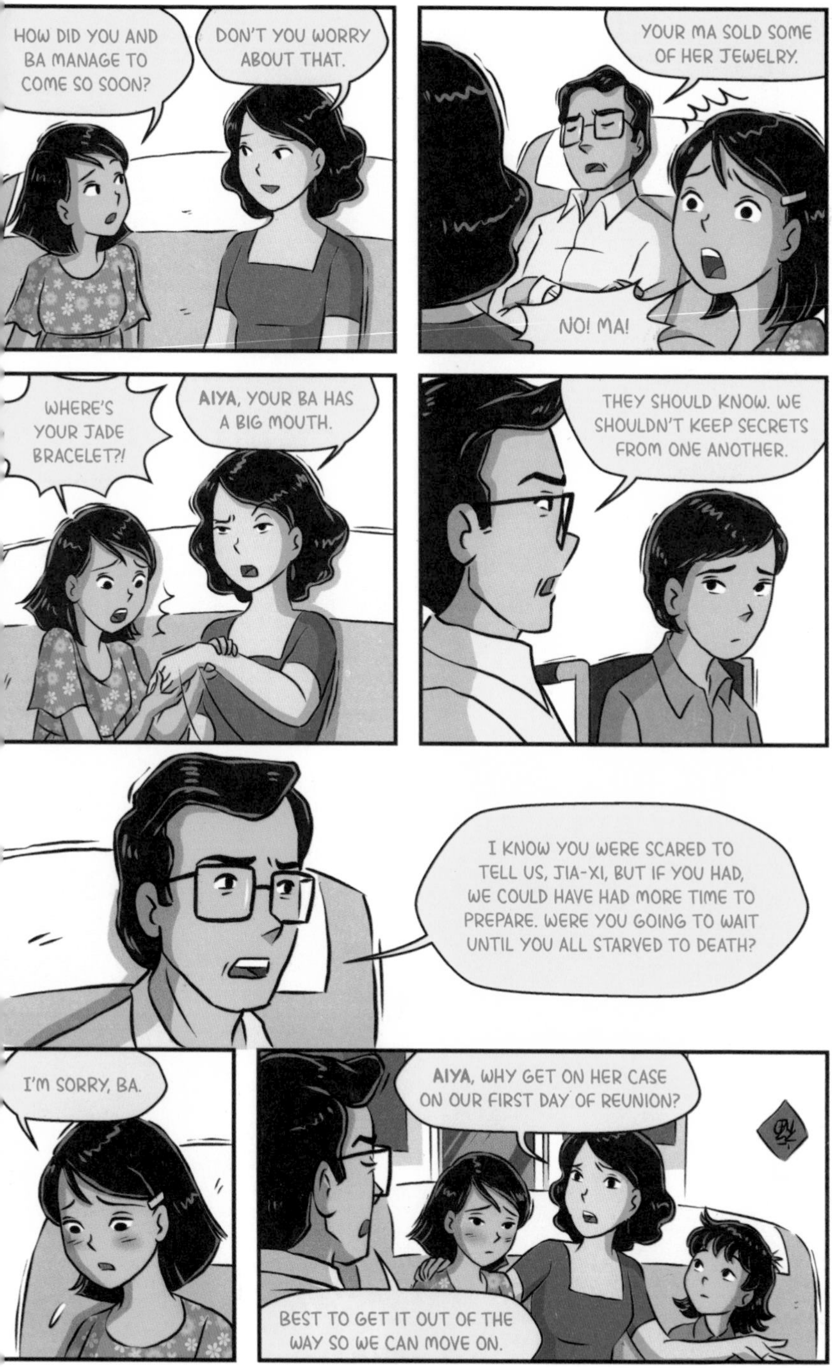
HOW DID YOU AND BA MANAGE TO COME SO SOON?
DON'T YOU WORRY ABOUT THAT.
YOUR MA SOLD SOME OF HER JEWELRY.
NO! MA!
WHERE'S YOUR JADE BRACELET?!
AIYA, YOUR BA HAS A BIG MOUTH.
THEY SHOULD KNOW. WE SHOULDN'T KEEP SECRETS FROM ONE ANOTHER.
I KNOW YOU WERE SCARED TO TELL US, JIA-XI, BUT IF YOU HAD, WE COULD HAVE HAD MORE TIME TO PREPARE. WERE YOU GOING TO WAIT UNTIL YOU ALL STARVED TO DEATH?
I'M SORRY, BA.
AIYA, WHY GET ON HER CASE ON OUR FIRST DAY OF REUNION?
BEST TO GET IT OUT OF THE WAY SO WE CAN MOVE ON.

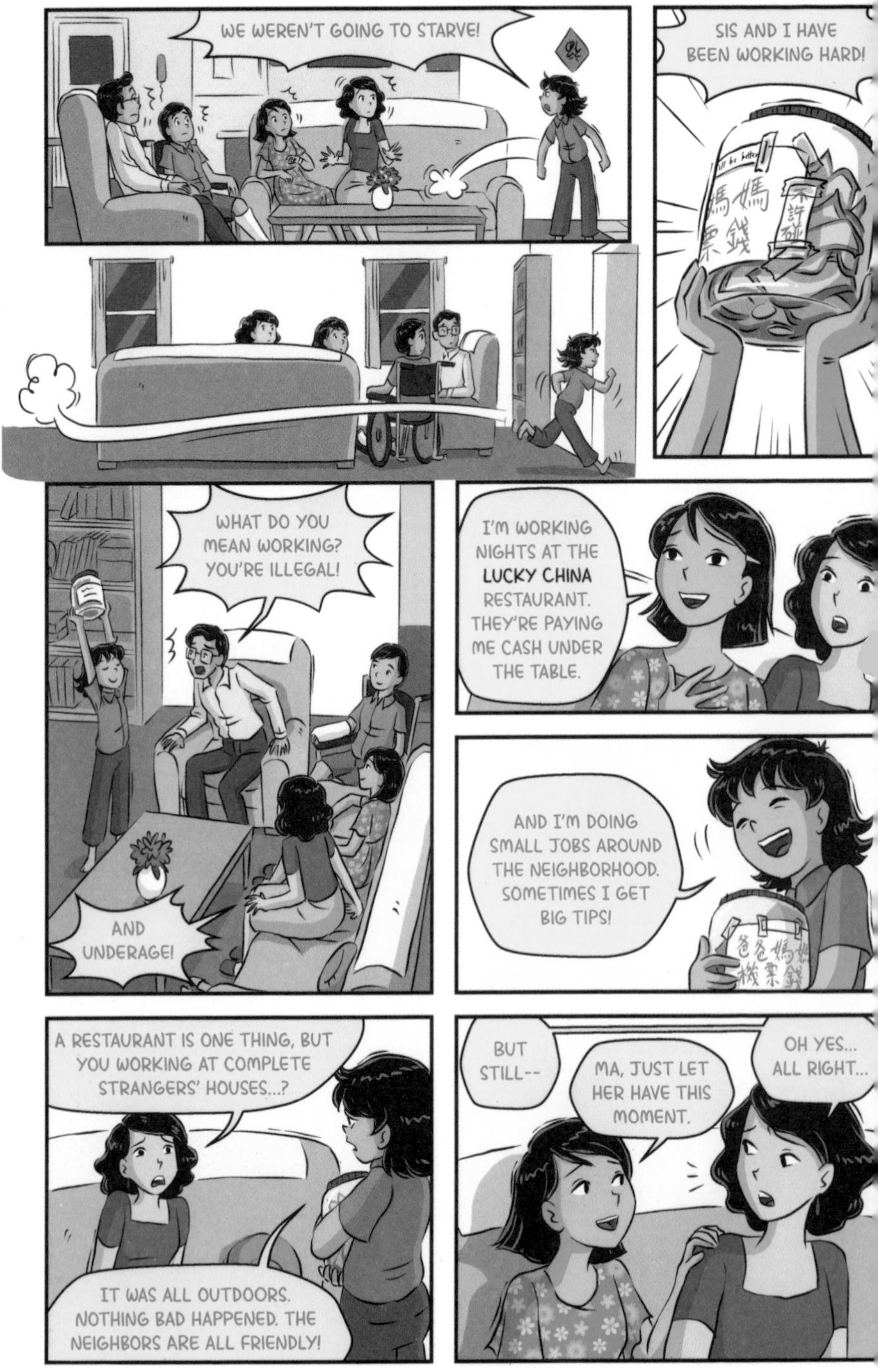
WE WEREN'T GOING TO STARVE!
SIS AND I HAVE BEEN WORKING HARD!
WHAT DO YOU MEAN WORKING? YOU'RE ILLEGAL!
AND UNDERAGE!
I'M WORKING NIGHTS AT THE **LUCKY CHINA** RESTAURANT. THEY'RE PAYING ME CASH UNDER THE TABLE.
AND I'M DOING SMALL JOBS AROUND THE NEIGHBORHOOD. SOMETIMES I GET BIG TIPS!
A RESTAURANT IS ONE THING, BUT YOU WORKING AT COMPLETE STRANGERS' HOUSES...?
IT WAS ALL OUTDOORS. NOTHING BAD HAPPENED. THE NEIGHBORS ARE ALL FRIENDLY!
BUT STILL--
MA, JUST LET HER HAVE THIS MOMENT.
OH YES... ALL RIGHT...

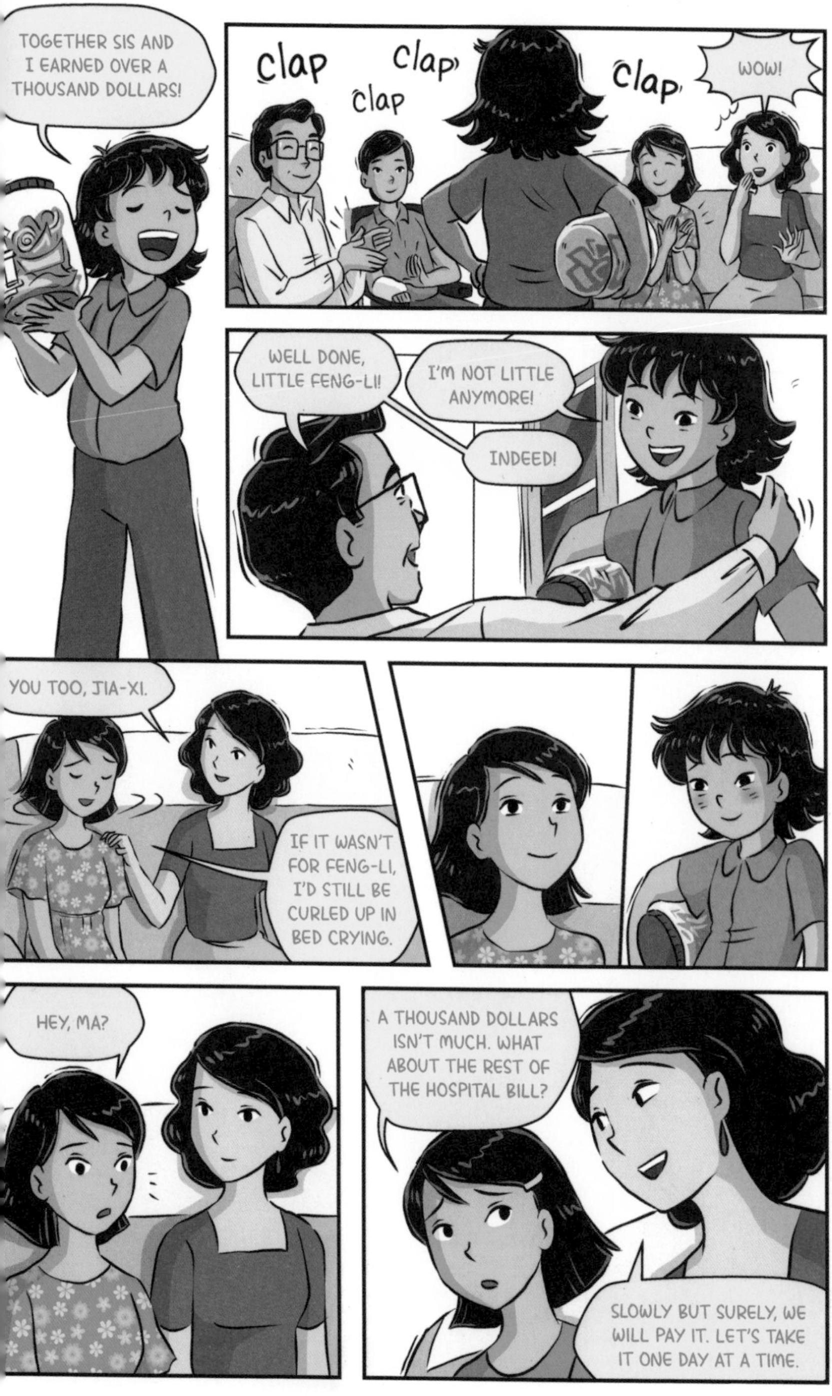
TOGETHER SIS AND I EARNED OVER A THOUSAND DOLLARS!
CLAP
CLAP
CLAP
CLAP
WOW!
WELL DONE, LITTLE FENG-LI!
I'M NOT LITTLE ANYMORE!
INDEED!
YOU TOO, JIA-XI.
IF IT WASN'T FOR FENG-LI, I'D STILL BE CURLED UP IN BED CRYING.
HEY, MA?
A THOUSAND DOLLARS ISN'T MUCH. WHAT ABOUT THE REST OF THE HOSPITAL BILL?
SLOWLY BUT SURELY, WE WILL PAY IT. LET'S TAKE IT ONE DAY AT A TIME.

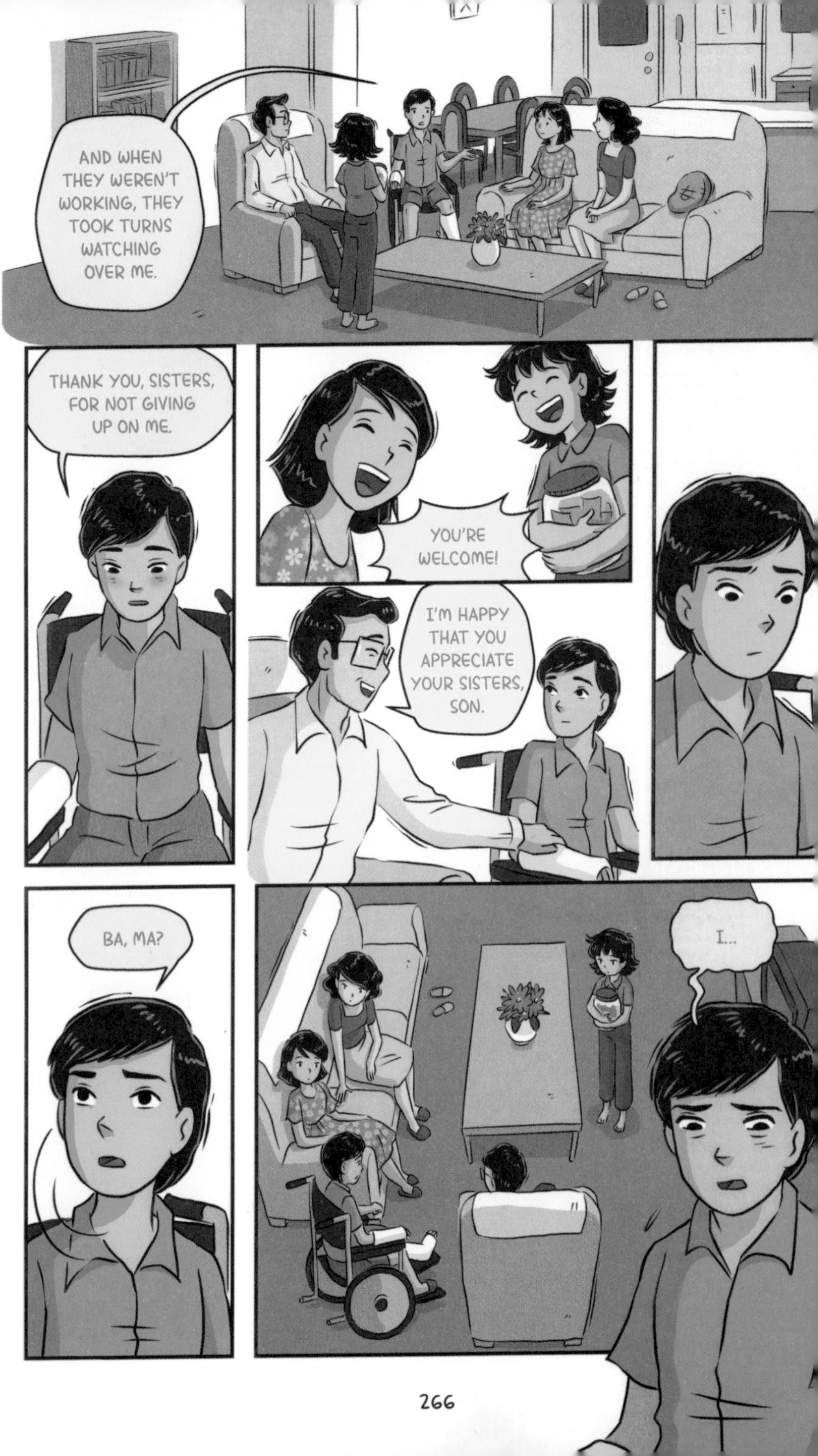
AND WHEN THEY WEREN'T WORKING, THEY TOOK TURNS WATCHING OVER ME.
THANK YOU, SISTERS, FOR NOT GIVING UP ON ME.
YOU'RE WELCOME!
I'M HAPPY THAT YOU APPRECIATE YOUR SISTERS, SON.
BA, MA?
I...

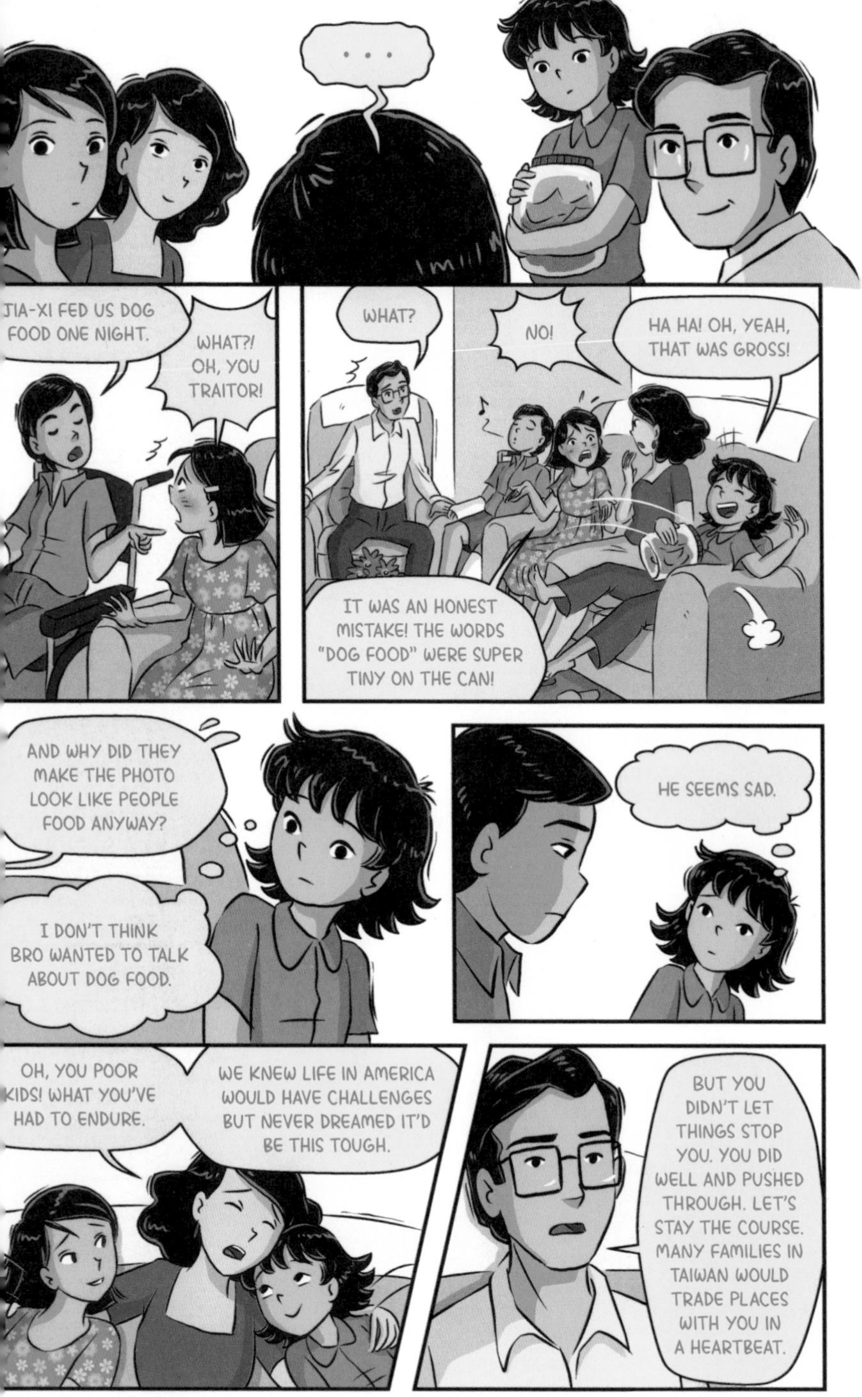
. . .
JIA-XI FED US DOG FOOD ONE NIGHT.
WHAT?! OH, YOU TRAITOR!
WHAT?
NO!
HA HA! OH, YEAH, THAT WAS GROSS!
IT WAS AN HONEST MISTAKE! THE WORDS "DOG FOOD" WERE SUPER TINY ON THE CAN!
AND WHY DID THEY MAKE THE PHOTO LOOK LIKE PEOPLE FOOD ANYWAY?
I DON'T THINK BRO WANTED TO TALK ABOUT DOG FOOD.
HE SEEMS SAD.
OH, YOU POOR KIDS! WHAT YOU'VE HAD TO ENDURE.
WE KNEW LIFE IN AMERICA WOULD HAVE CHALLENGES BUT NEVER DREAMED IT'D BE THIS TOUGH.
BUT YOU DIDN'T LET THINGS STOP YOU. YOU DID WELL AND PUSHED THROUGH. LET'S STAY THE COURSE. MANY FAMILIES IN TAIWAN WOULD TRADE PLACES WITH YOU IN A HEARTBEAT.

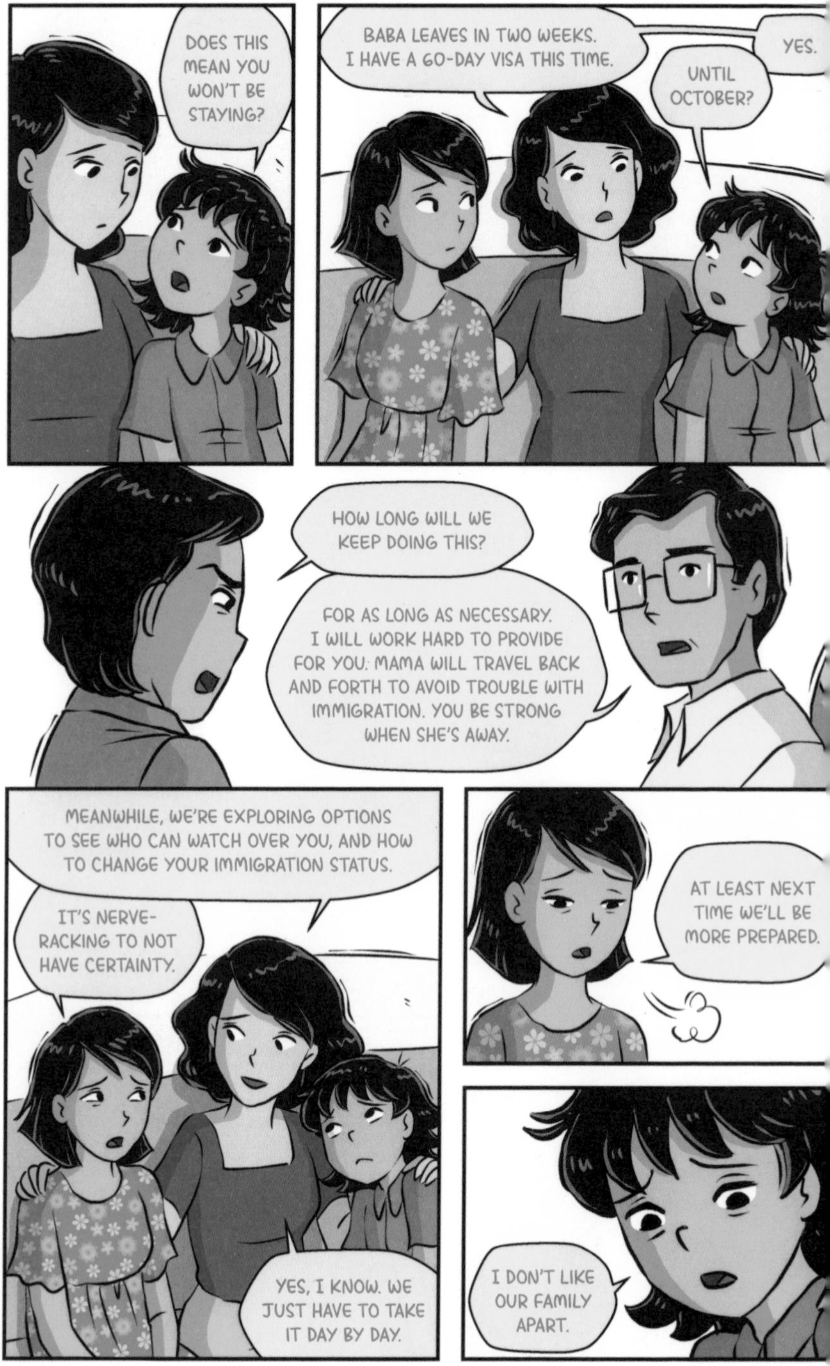
DOES THIS MEAN YOU WON'T BE STAYING?
BABA LEAVES IN TWO WEEKS. I HAVE A 60-DAY VISA THIS TIME.
UNTIL OCTOBER?
YES.
HOW LONG WILL WE KEEP DOING THIS?
FOR AS LONG AS NECESSARY. I WILL WORK HARD TO PROVIDE FOR YOU. MAMA WILL TRAVEL BACK AND FORTH TO AVOID TROUBLE WITH IMMIGRATION. YOU BE STRONG WHEN SHE'S AWAY.
MEANWHILE, WE'RE EXPLORING OPTIONS TO SEE WHO CAN WATCH OVER YOU, AND HOW TO CHANGE YOUR IMMIGRATION STATUS.
IT'S NERVE-RACKING TO NOT HAVE CERTAINTY.
YES, I KNOW. WE JUST HAVE TO TAKE IT DAY BY DAY.
AT LEAST NEXT TIME WE'LL BE MORE PREPARED.
I DON'T LIKE OUR FAMILY APART.

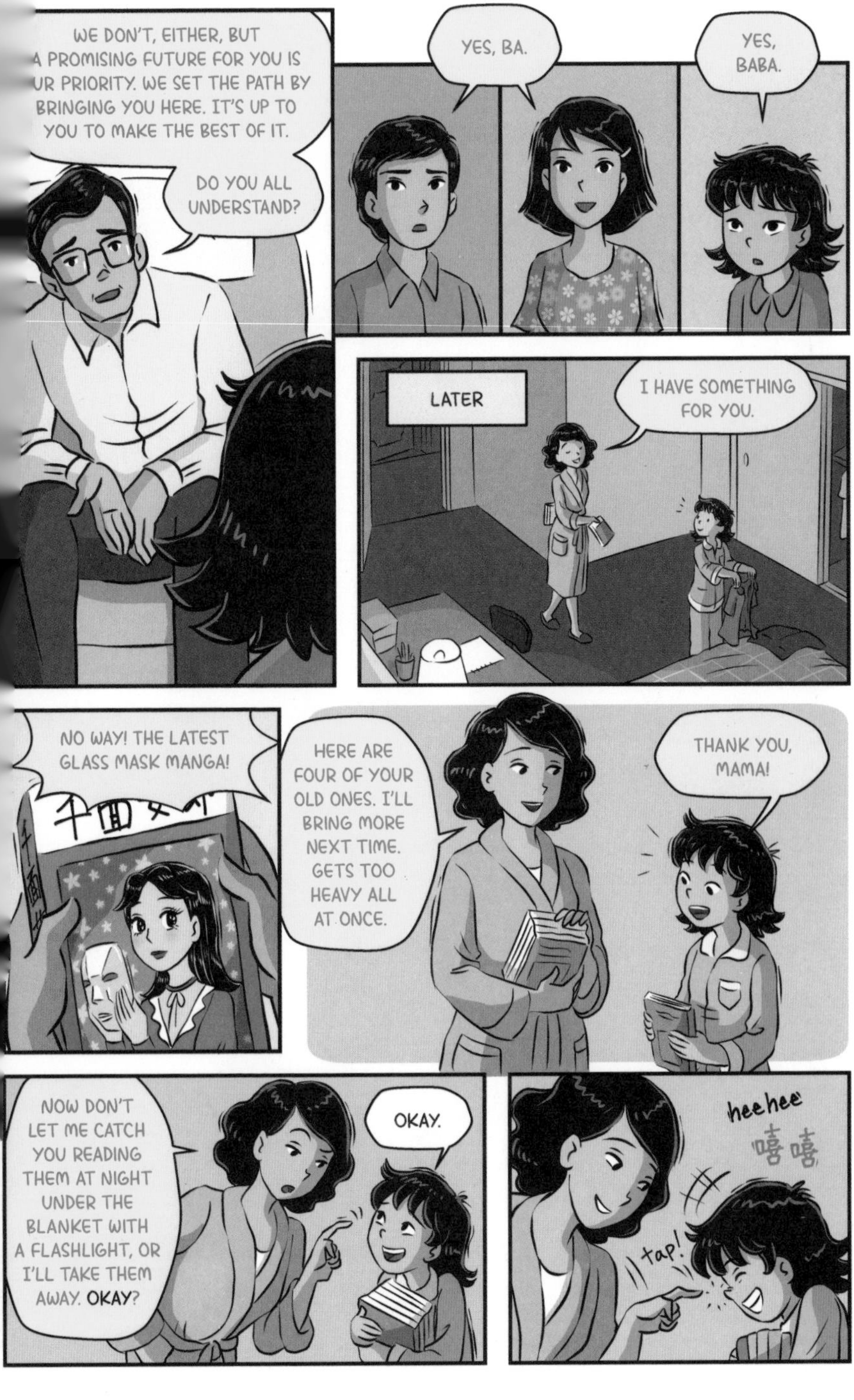
WE DON'T, EITHER, BUT A PROMISING FUTURE FOR YOU IS UR PRIORITY. WE SET THE PATH BY BRINGING YOU HERE. IT'S UP TO YOU TO MAKE THE BEST OF IT.
DO YOU ALL UNDERSTAND?
YES, BA.
YES, BABA.
LATER
I HAVE SOMETHING FOR YOU.
NO WAY! THE LATEST GLASS MASK MANGA!
HERE ARE FOUR OF YOUR OLD ONES. I'LL BRING MORE NEXT TIME. GETS TOO HEAVY ALL AT ONCE.
THANK YOU, MAMA!
NOW DON'T LET ME CATCH YOU READING THEM AT NIGHT UNDER THE BLANKET WITH A FLASHLIGHT, OR I'LL TAKE THEM AWAY. OKAY?
OKAY.
heehee
嘻嘻
tap!

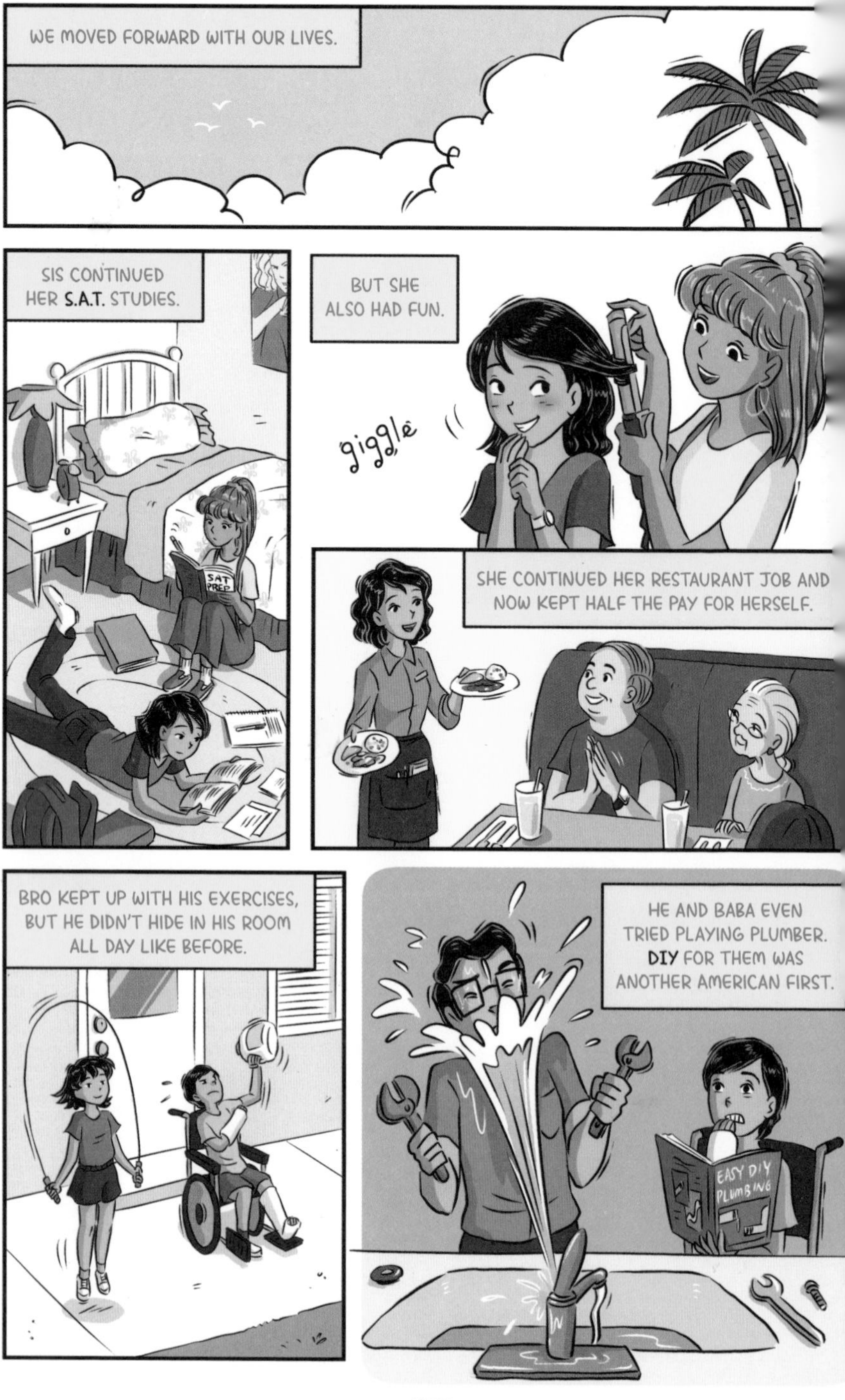
WE MOVED FORWARD WITH OUR LIVES.
SIS CONTINUED HER S.A.T. STUDIES.
SAT PREP
BUT SHE ALSO HAD FUN.
giggle
SHE CONTINUED HER RESTAURANT JOB AND NOW KEPT HALF THE PAY FOR HERSELF.
BRO KEPT UP WITH HIS EXERCISES, BUT HE DIDN'T HIDE IN HIS ROOM ALL DAY LIKE BEFORE.
HE AND BABA EVEN TRIED PLAYING PLUMBER. DIY FOR THEM WAS ANOTHER AMERICAN FIRST.
EASY DIY PLUMBING

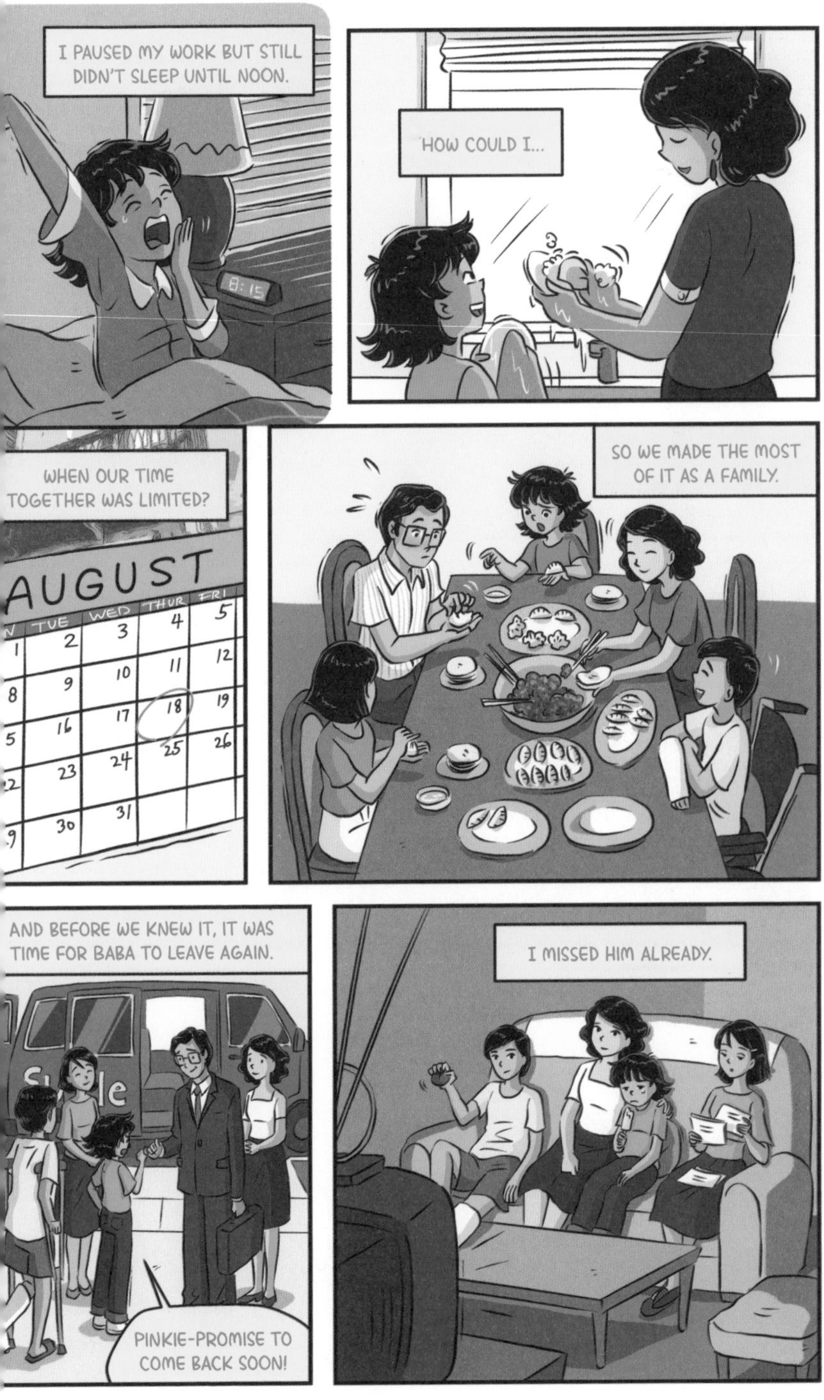
I PAUSED MY WORK BUT STILL DIDN'T SLEEP UNTIL NOON.
8:15
HOW COULD I...
WHEN OUR TIME TOGETHER WAS LIMITED?
AUGUST
TUE WED THUR FRI
SO WE MADE THE MOST OF IT AS A FAMILY.
AND BEFORE WE KNEW IT, IT WAS TIME FOR BABA TO LEAVE AGAIN.
PINKIE-PROMISE TO COME BACK SOON!
I MISSED HIM ALREADY.

THEN SUMMER ENDED, AND SCHOOL STARTED FOR BRO AND SIS.

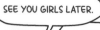

SEE YOU GIRLS LATER.

LATER, ALLIGATOR!

WHY IS MY BROTHER AN ALLIGATOR?

HA HA! IT'S JUST SOMETHING WE SAY!

HEY, GUYS--

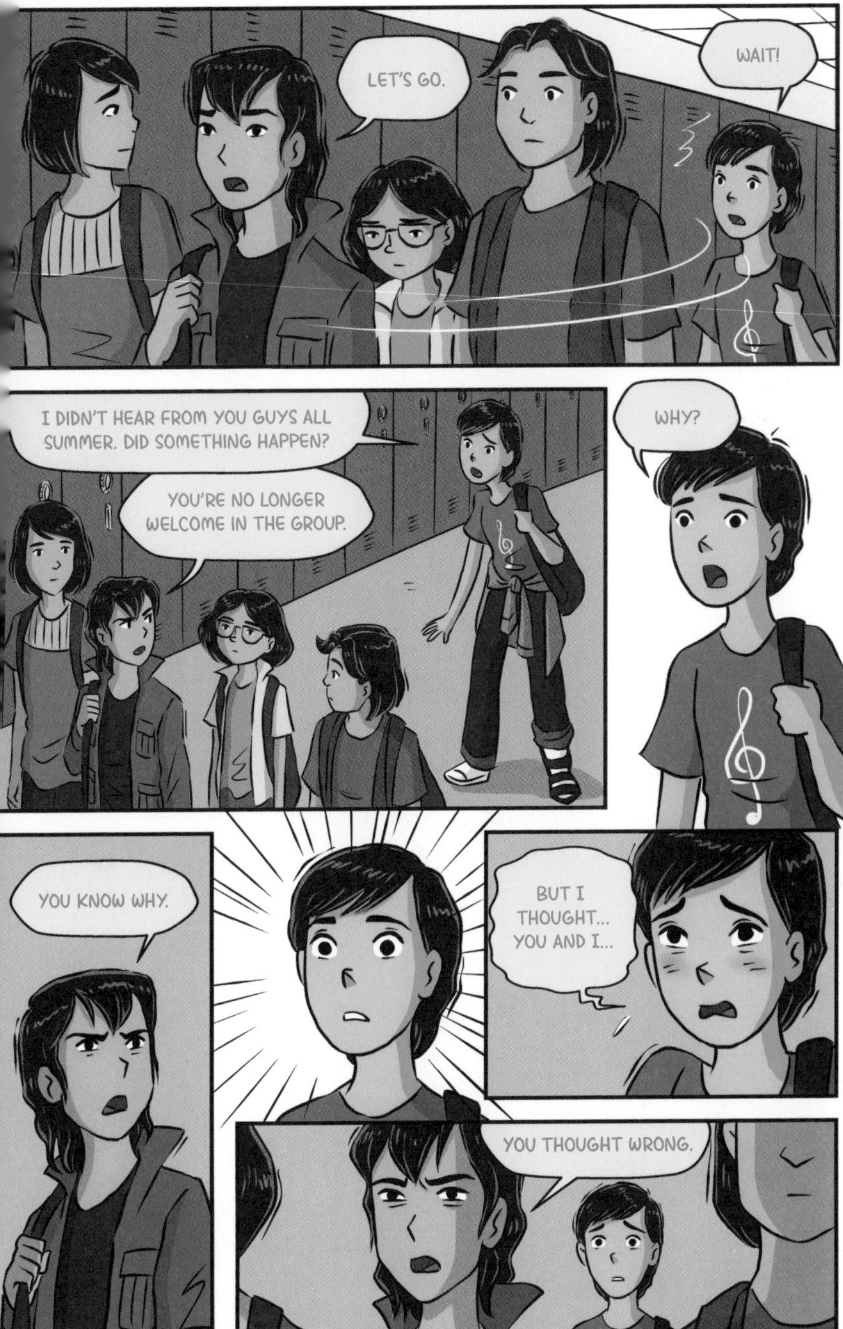
LET'S GO.
WAIT!
I DIDN'T HEAR FROM YOU GUYS ALL SUMMER. DID SOMETHING HAPPEN?
YOU'RE NO LONGER WELCOME IN THE GROUP.
WHY?
YOU KNOW WHY.
BUT I THOUGHT... YOU AND I...
YOU THOUGHT WRONG.

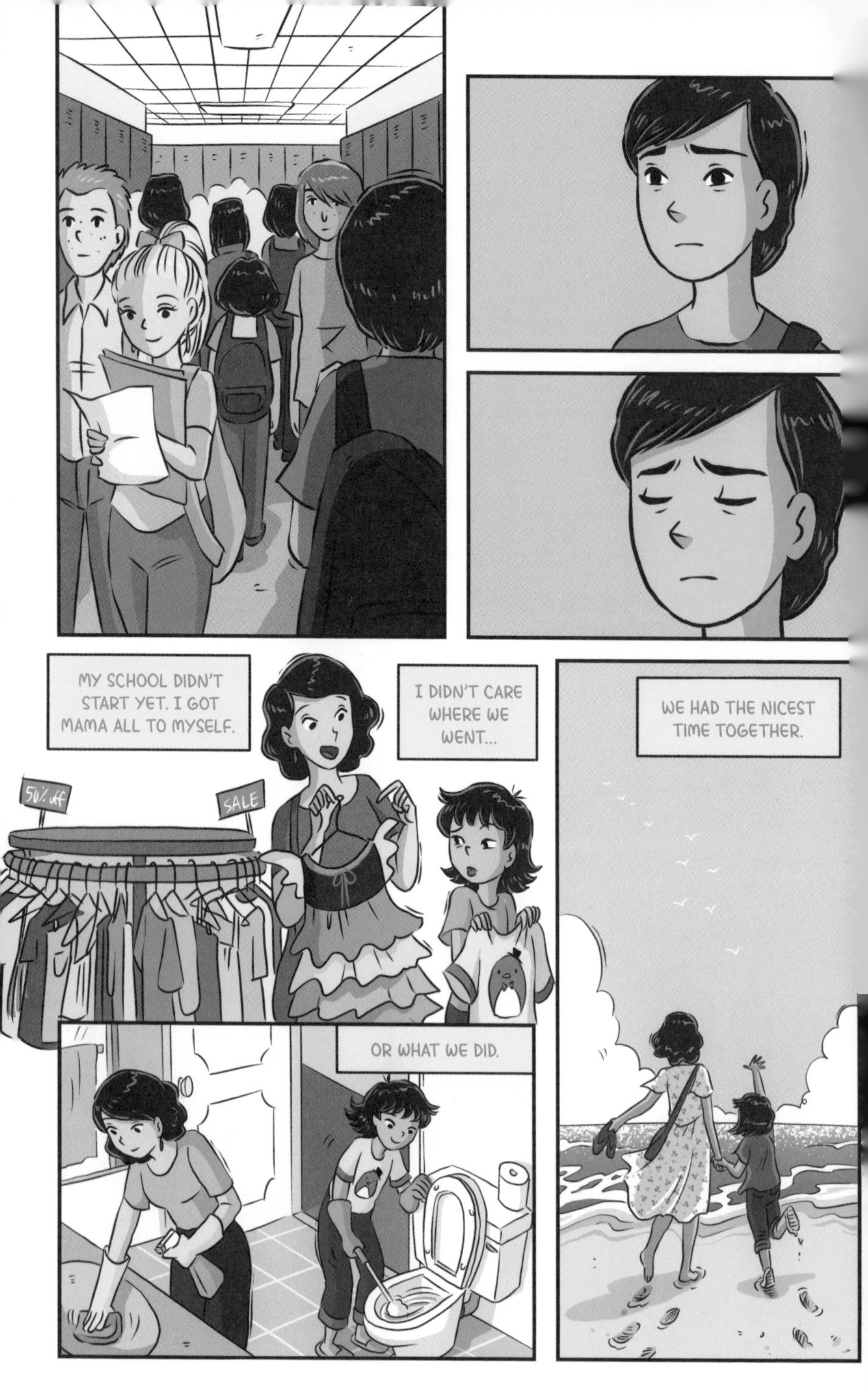
MY SCHOOL DIDN'T START YET. I GOT MAMA ALL TO MYSELF.
I DIDN'T CARE WHERE WE WENT...
50% off
SALE
OR WHAT WE DID.
WE HAD THE NICEST TIME TOGETHER.

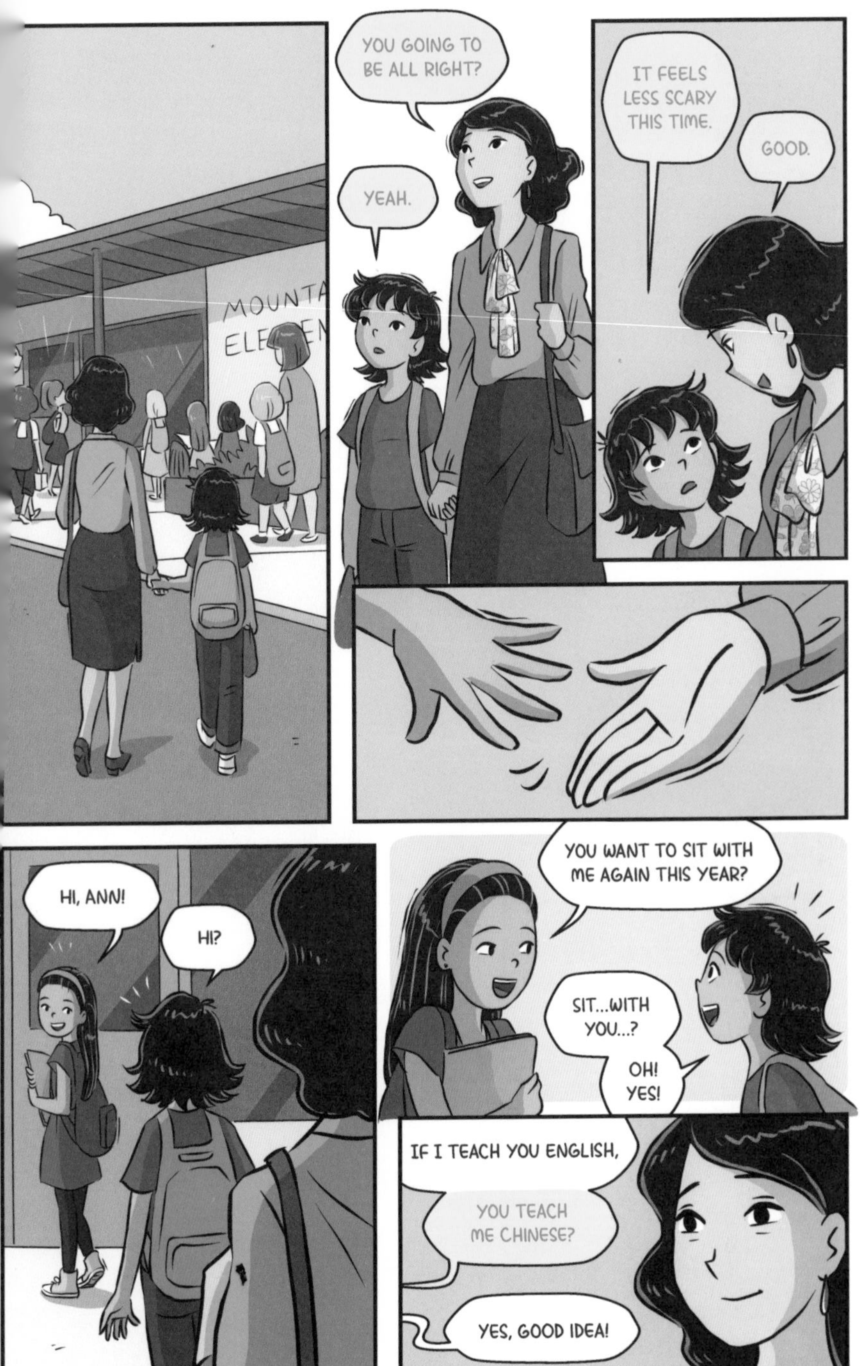
MOUNTA
ELE
YOU GOING TO BE ALL RIGHT?
YEAH.
IT FEELS LESS SCARY THIS TIME.
GOOD.
HI, ANN!
HI?
YOU WANT TO SIT WITH ME AGAIN THIS YEAR?
SIT...WITH YOU...?
OH! YES!
IF I TEACH YOU ENGLISH,
YOU TEACH ME CHINESE?
YES, GOOD IDEA!

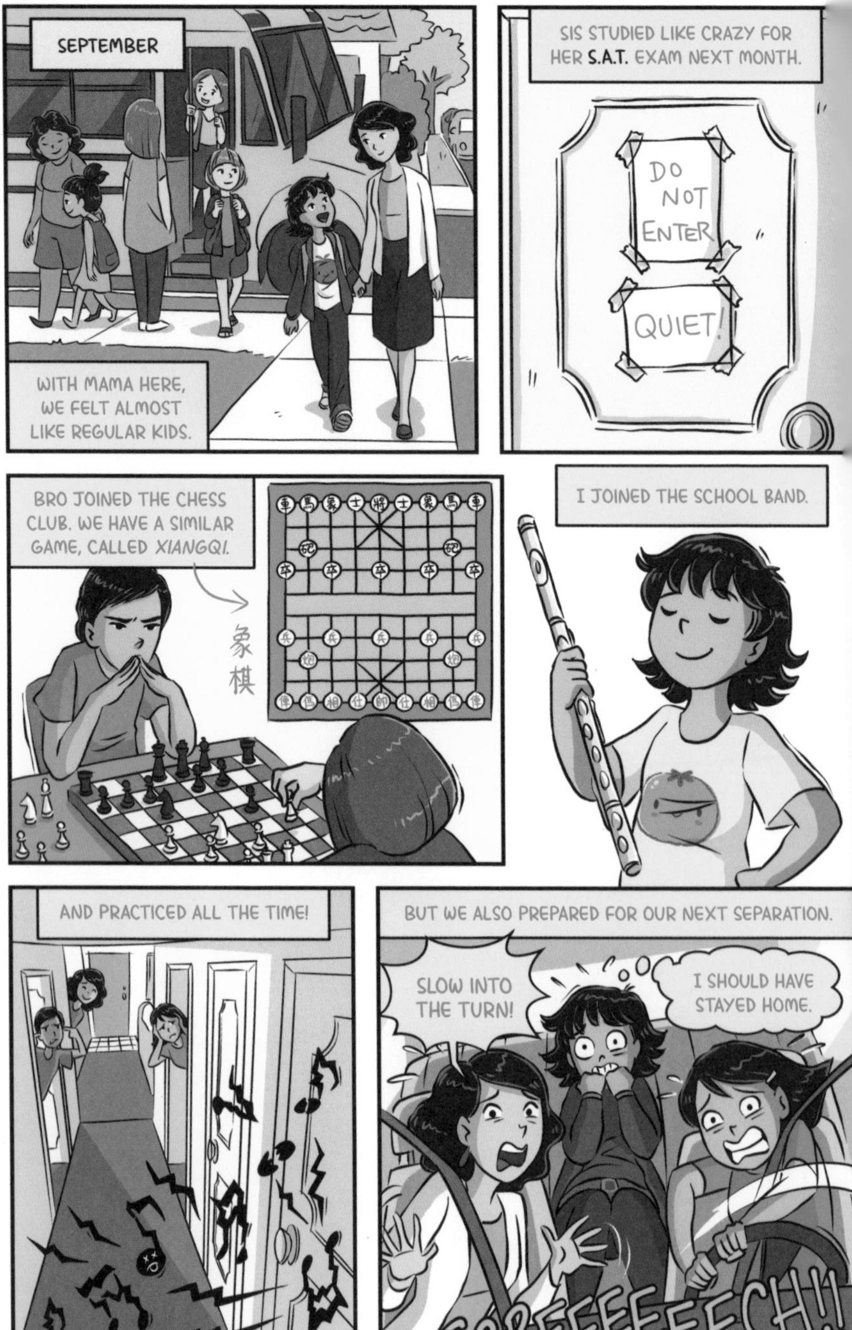
SEPTEMBER
WITH MAMA HERE, WE FELT ALMOST LIKE REGULAR KIDS.
SIS STUDIED LIKE CRAZY FOR HER S.A.T. EXAM NEXT MONTH.
DO NOT ENTER
QUIET!
BRO JOINED THE CHESS CLUB. WE HAVE A SIMILAR GAME, CALLED XIANGQI.
象棋
I JOINED THE SCHOOL BAND.
AND PRACTICED ALL THE TIME!
BUT WE ALSO PREPARED FOR OUR NEXT SEPARATION.
SLOW INTO THE TURN!
I SHOULD HAVE STAYED HOME.
SCREEEEEEECH!!

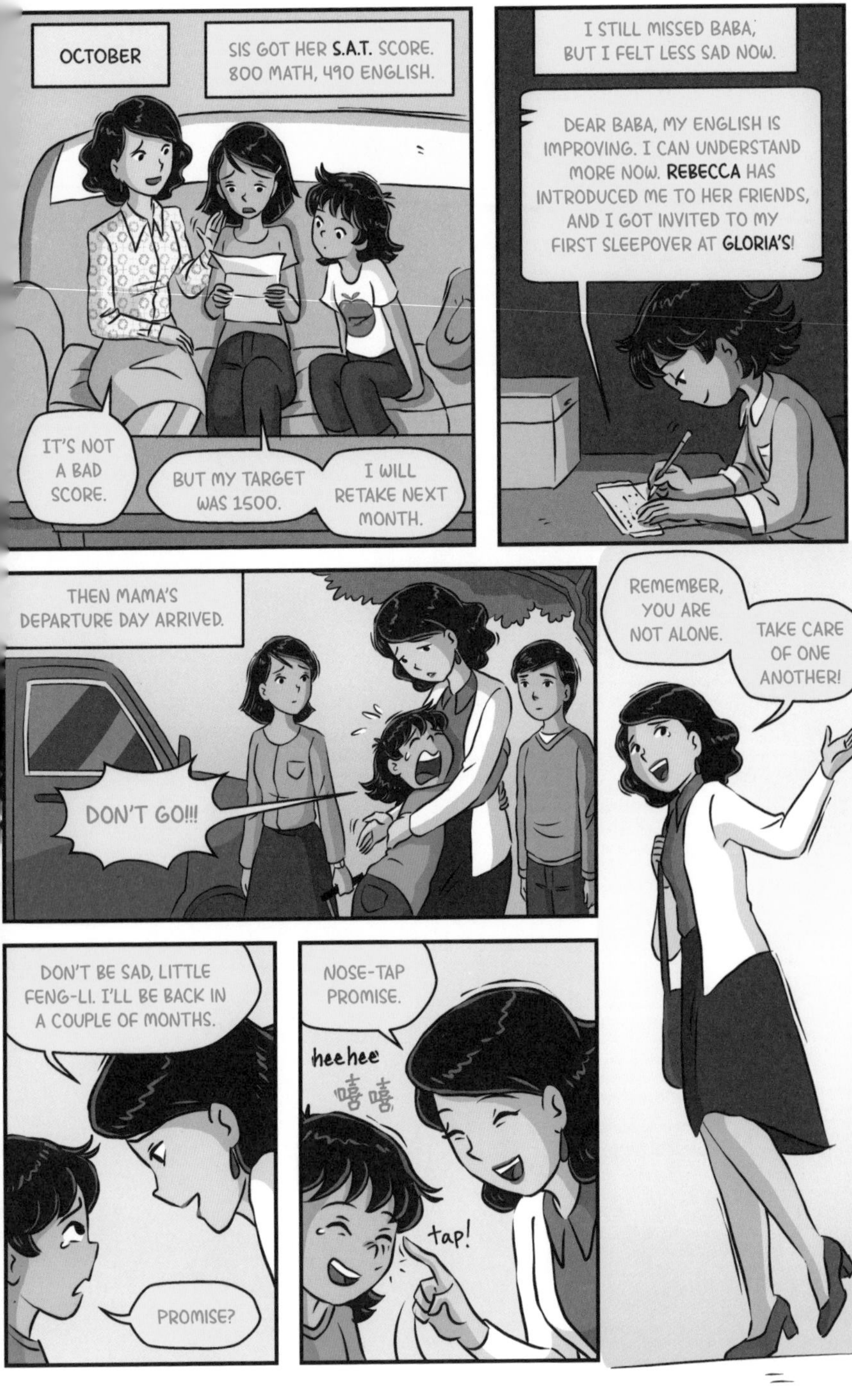
OCTOBER
SIS GOT HER S.A.T. SCORE. 800 MATH, 490 ENGLISH.
IT'S NOT A BAD SCORE.
BUT MY TARGET WAS 1500.
I WILL RETAKE NEXT MONTH.
I STILL MISSED BABA, BUT I FELT LESS SAD NOW.
DEAR BABA, MY ENGLISH IS IMPROVING. I CAN UNDERSTAND MORE NOW. REBECCA HAS INTRODUCED ME TO HER FRIENDS, AND I GOT INVITED TO MY FIRST SLEEPOVER AT GLORIA'S!
THEN MAMA'S DEPARTURE DAY ARRIVED.
DON'T GO!!!
REMEMBER, YOU ARE NOT ALONE.
TAKE CARE OF ONE ANOTHER!
DON'T BE SAD, LITTLE FENG-LI. I'LL BE BACK IN A COUPLE OF MONTHS.
PROMISE?
NOSE-TAP PROMISE.
heehee
嘻嘻
tap!

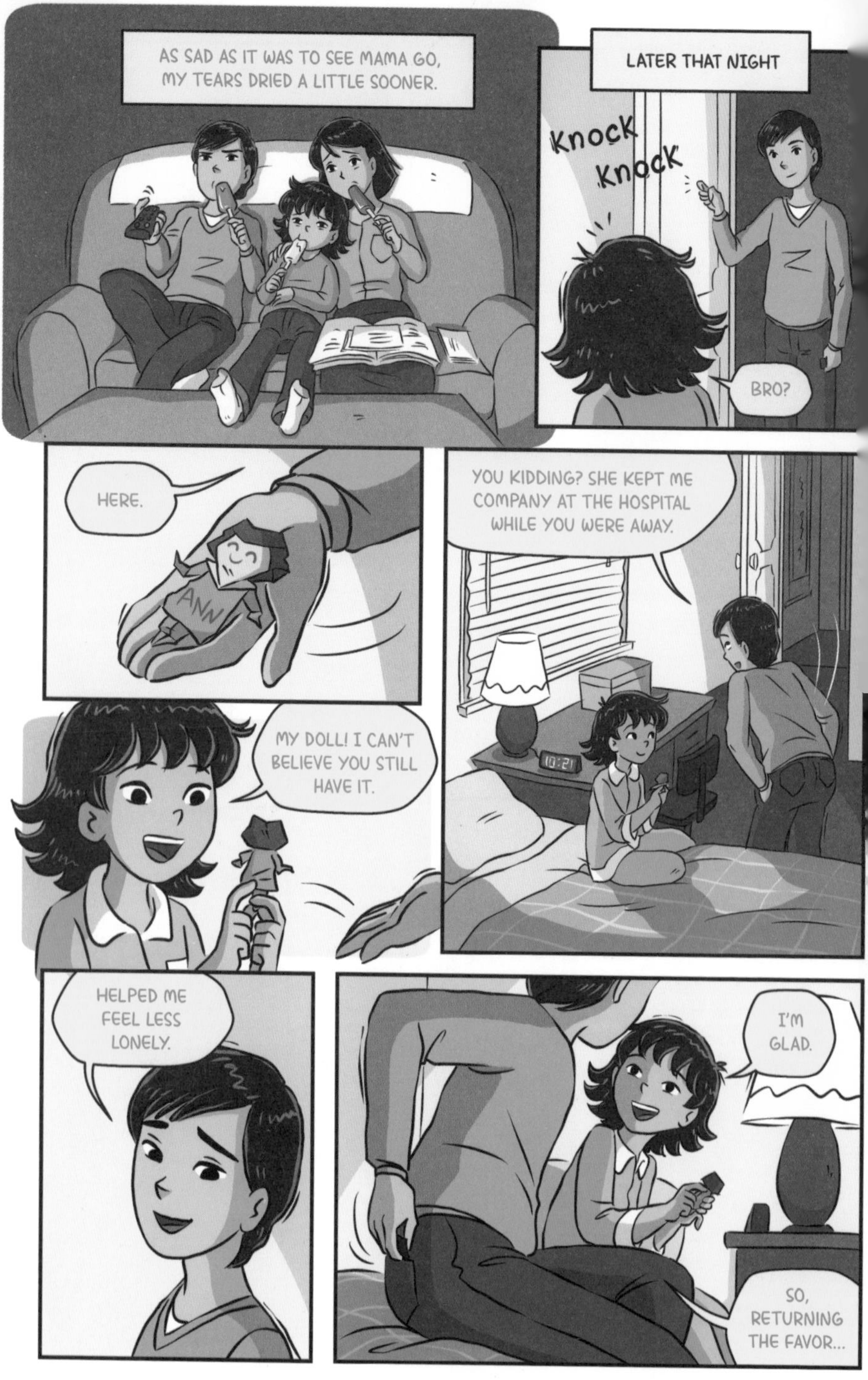
AS SAD AS IT WAS TO SEE MAMA GO, MY TEARS DRIED A LITTLE SOONER.
LATER THAT NIGHT
Knock
Knock
BRO?
HERE.
ANN
YOU KIDDING? SHE KEPT ME COMPANY AT THE HOSPITAL WHILE YOU WERE AWAY.
MY DOLL! I CAN'T BELIEVE YOU STILL HAVE IT.
10:21
HELPED ME FEEL LESS LONELY.
I'M GLAD.
SO, RETURNING THE FAVOR...

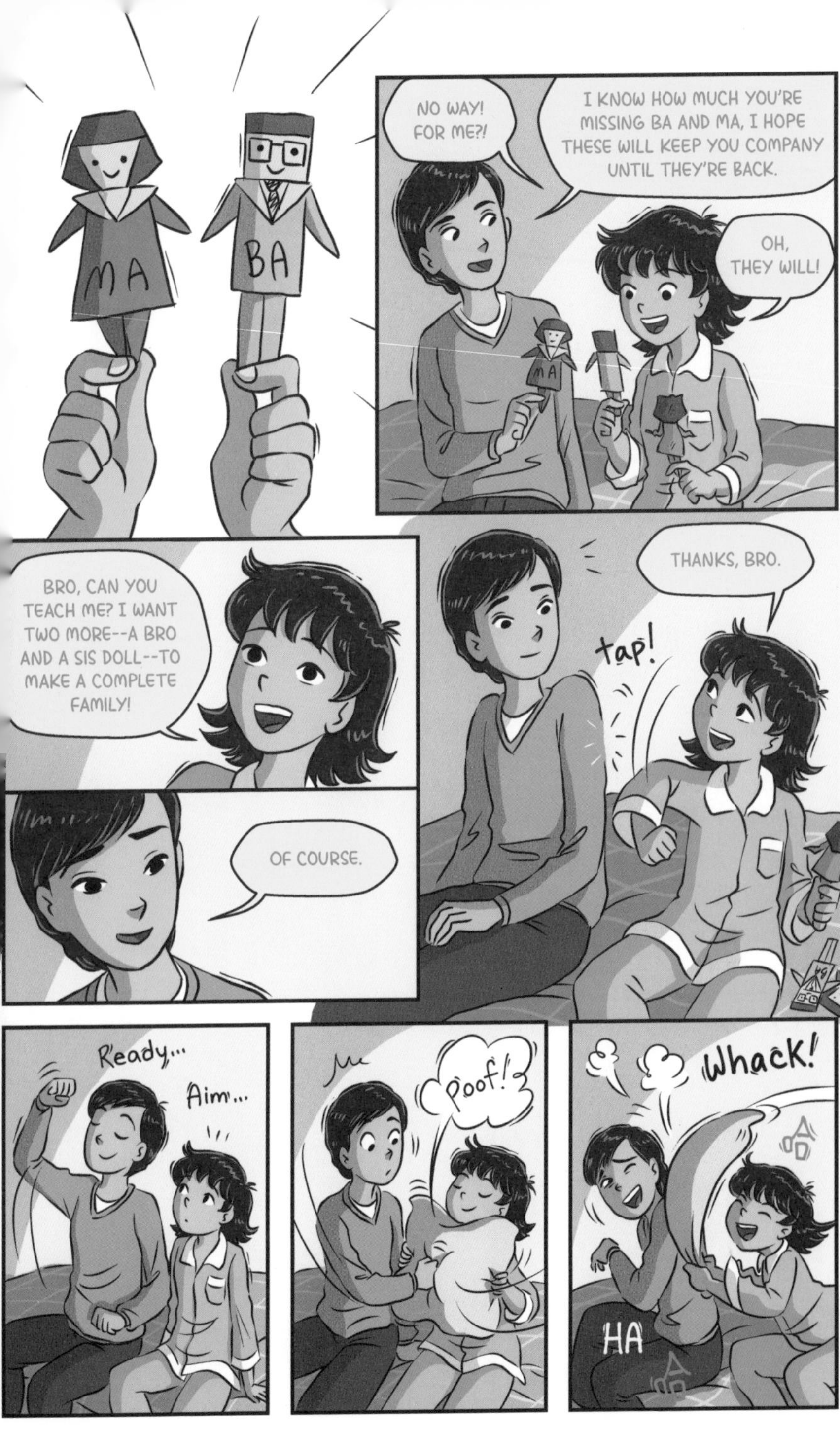
MA
BA
NO WAY! FOR ME?!
I KNOW HOW MUCH YOU'RE MISSING BA AND MA, I HOPE THESE WILL KEEP YOU COMPANY UNTIL THEY'RE BACK.
OH, THEY WILL!
BRO, CAN YOU TEACH ME? I WANT TWO MORE--A BRO AND A SIS DOLL--TO MAKE A COMPLETE FAMILY!
OF COURSE.
THANKS, BRO.
tap!
Ready...
Aim...
Poof!
Whack!
HA

LIKE LAST TIME, WE CARRIED ON AS BEST AS WE COULD.

MORNING, SLEEPYHEADS!

BUT THIS TIME, WE WORKED TOGETHER MORE.

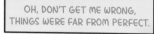

OH, DON'T GET ME WRONG, THINGS WERE FAR FROM PERFECT.

BUT NOW THEY PATCHED THINGS UP SOONER.

COME, COME, LET'S ALL GO FOR A RIDE.

UGH, DO I HAVE TO?

YES! WE'RE ALL BECOMING STINKY TOFUS!

HEE HEE!

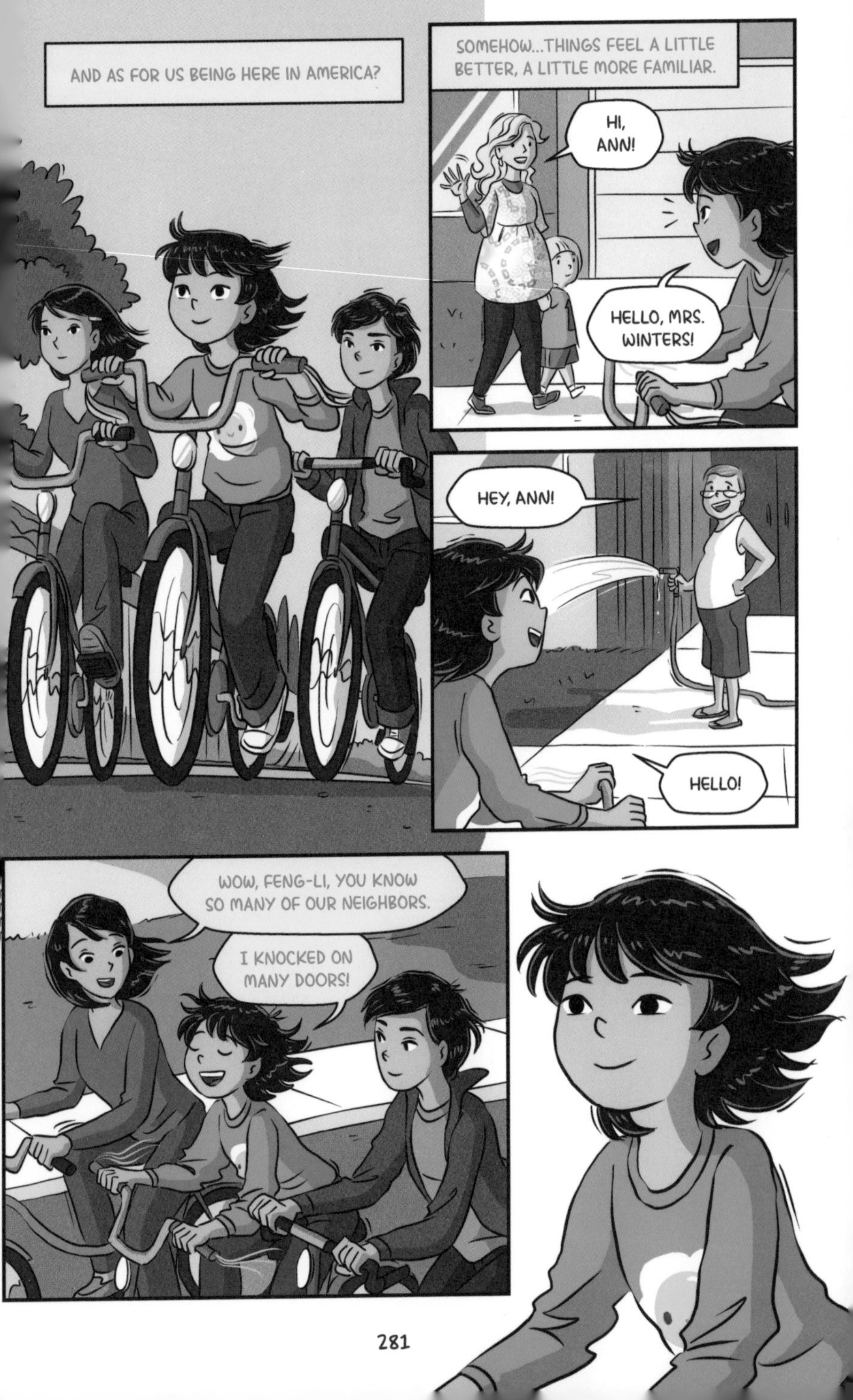
AND AS FOR US BEING HERE IN AMERICA?
SOMEHOW...THINGS FEEL A LITTLE BETTER, A LITTLE MORE FAMILIAR.
HI, ANN!
HELLO, MRS. WINTERS!
HEY, ANN!
HELLO!
WOW, FENG-LI, YOU KNOW SO MANY OF OUR NEIGHBORS.
I KNOCKED ON MANY DOORS!

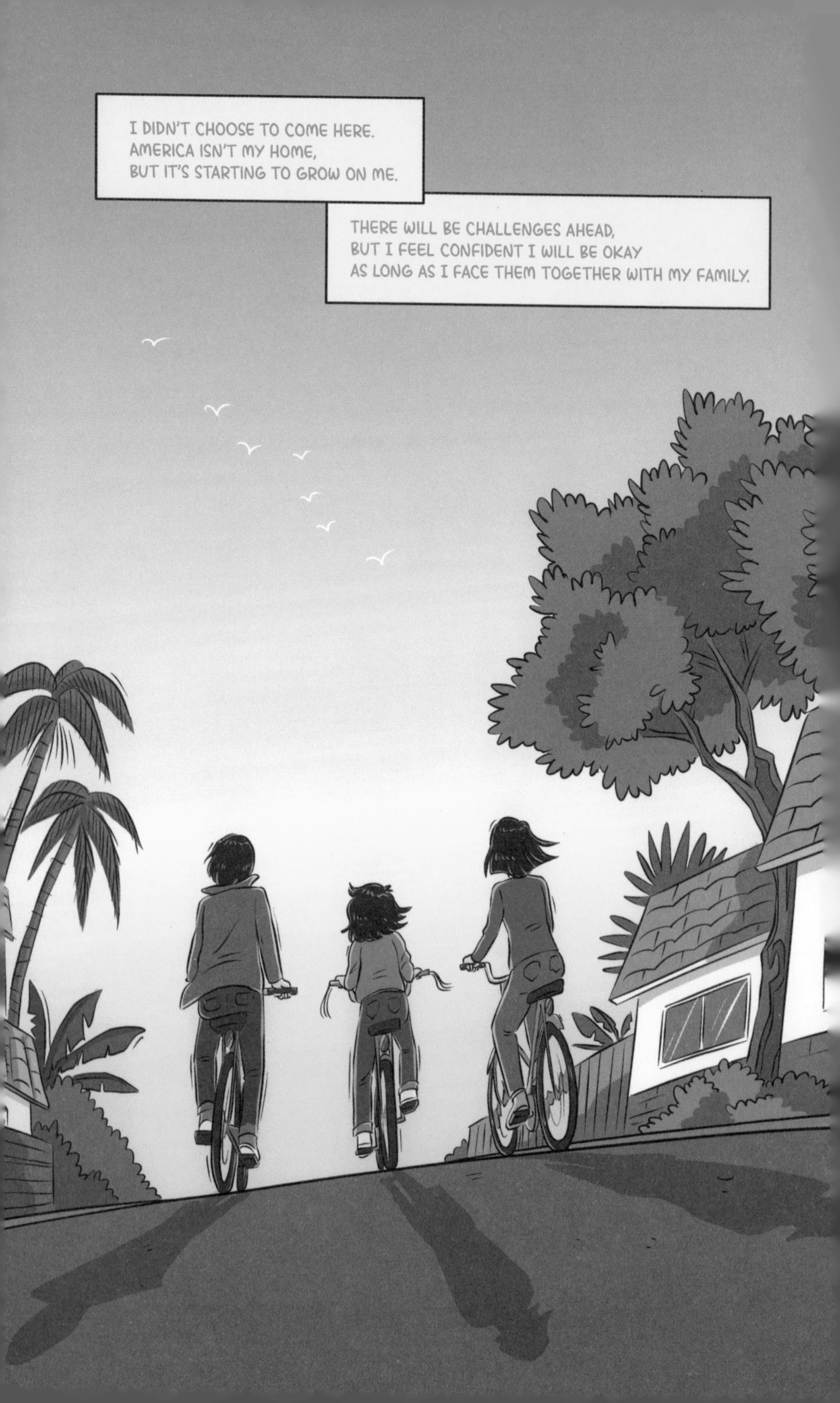
I DIDN'T CHOOSE TO COME HERE. AMERICA ISN'T MY HOME, BUT IT'S STARTING TO GROW ON ME.
THERE WILL BE CHALLENGES AHEAD, BUT I FEEL CONFIDENT I WILL BE OKAY AS LONG AS I FACE THEM TOGETHER WITH MY FAMILY.

To all the parachute kids out there:
When the going gets tough,
remember, you can get through this.
You are never alone. This book is for you.

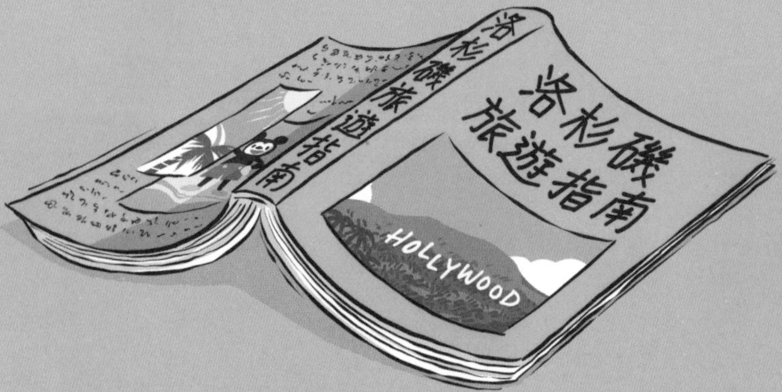
洛杉磯旅遊指南
洛杉磯旅遊指南
HOLLYWOOD

AUTHOR'S NOTE

The term *parachute kids* refers to children from Asia who have been "dropped off" with friends or relatives in foreign countries while their parents stayed behind. This practice has been ongoing for decades and continues today. Parachute kids face the challenges of a new country, culture, and language without their parents. My siblings and I were among these children.

In 1979, when the United States changed its diplomatic recognition of Taiwan to China, my parents—fearing war—made the decision to send us to the United States, while my dad stayed in Taiwan to earn money to support us and my mom visited us whenever she could. Like Feng-Li, I was an excited ten-year-old upon arrival, but soon found myself lonely and friendless. My siblings were around, but they had their own issues and were in no mood to hear about mine. I became unforgiving toward my parents, once even accusing my mother of abandoning me, which caused her much grief. Then, slowly, my English improved, which made all the difference in the world, as I could finally communicate and make friends. Eventually, the foreign turned familiar, and America became my new home. Now I fully appreciate the sacrifice my parents made to give us a more promising future. It could not have been an easy decision, for what parents would willingly break up the family and live apart from their children?

Parachute Kids is not a memoir, but a mixture of fiction, my family's first experiences in America, and anecdotes of immigrant friends I met along the way. I felt compelled to write it because I think it is important for more people to know about these children and their parents.

Asians in general are not very vocal. We are taught to work hard, mind our own business, and as the Chinese saying goes, "eat bitterness." So, to outsiders, it might appear that our achievements were easily attained, that we all come from money,